Praise for Joe Abercrombie

'*The Heroes* is an indictment of war and the duplicity that corrupts men striving for total power: bloody and violent, but never gratuitously so, it's imbued with cutting humour, acute characterisation and world-weary wisdom about the weaknesses of the human race. Brilliant'
The Guardian

'The futility of settling arguments by violence is the clear message of *The Heroes*, making it an anti-war war story – which I suppose all the best war stories are, really – but it's also a very strong continuation of his excellent previous books. Highly recommended both for fantasy readers and lovers of Cornwell and Iggulden' *Bookgeeks*

'[*The Heroes* is a] blood-drenched, thought-provoking dissection of a three-day battle is set in the same world as Abercrombie's *First Law Trilogy* but stands very well alone . . . Abercrombie never glosses over a moment of the madness, passion, and horror of war, nor the tribulations that turn ordinary people into the titular heroes' *Publishers Weekly*

'Joe Abercrombie's *Best Served Cold* is a bloody and relentless epic of vengeance and obsession in the grand tradition, a kind of splatterpunk sword 'n sorcery *Count of Monte Cristo*, Dumas by way of Moorcock. His cast features tyrants and torturers, a pair of poisoners, a serial killer, a treacherous drunk, a red-handed warrior and a blood-soaked mercenary captain. And those are the good guys . . . The battles are vivid and visceral, the action brutal, the pace headlong, and Abercrombie piles the betrayals, reversals, and plot twists one atop another to keep us guessing how it will all come out. This is his best book yet'
George R. R. Martin

'Abercrombie writes dark, adult fantasy, by which I mean there's a lot of stabbing in it, and after people stab each other they sometimes have sex with each other. His tone is morbid and funny and hard-boiled,

RED
COUNTRY

By Joe Abercrombie

RED COUNTRY

JOE ABERCROMBIE

www.orbitbooks.net

Orbit
Hachette Book Group
237 Park Avenue, New York, NY 10017
www.HachetteBookGroup.com

First U.S. Edition: October 2012
First published in Great Britain in 2012 by Gollancz

An imprint of the Orion Publishing Group
Orion House, 5 Upper St Martin's Lane, London wc2h 9ea An Hachette UK Company

Orbit is an imprint of Hachette Book Group, Inc. The Orbit name and logo are trademarks of Little, Brown Book Group Limited.

The Hachette Speakers Bureau provides a wide range of authors for speaking events. To find out more, go to www.hachettespeakersbureau.com or call (866) 376-6591.

The publisher is not responsible for websites (or their content) that are not owned by the publisher.

ISBN: 9780316187213

10 9 8 7 6 5 4 3 2 1

RRD-C

Printed in the United States of America

For Teddy

And Clint Eastwood

But since Clint probably ain't that bothered

Mostly Teddy

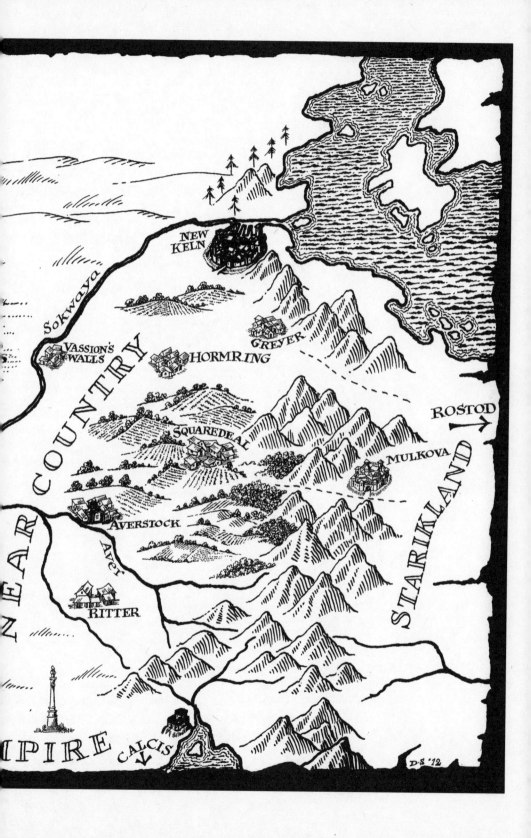

I
TROUBLE

'You, that judge men by the handle
and the sheath,
how can I make you know a good blade?'
Jedediah M. Grant

Some Kind of Coward

'**G**old.' Wist made the word sound like a mystery there was no solving. 'Makes men mad.'

Shy nodded. 'Those that ain't mad already.'

They sat in front of Stupfer's Meat House, which might've sounded like a brothel but was actually the worst place to eat within fifty miles, and that with some fierce competition. Shy perched on the sacks in her wagon and Wist on the fence, where he always seemed to be, like he'd such a splinter in his arse he'd got stuck there. They watched the crowd.

'I came here to get away from people,' said Wist.

Shy nodded. 'Now look.'

Last summer you could've spent all day in town and not seen two people you didn't know. You could've spent some days in town and not seen two people. A lot can change with a few months and a gold find. Now Squaredeal was bursting at its ragged seams with bold pioneers. One-way traffic, headed west towards imagined riches, some charging through fast as the clutter would allow, some stopping off to add their own share of commerce and chaos. Wagon-wheels clattered, mules nickered and horses neighed, livestock honked and oxen bellowed. Men, women and children of all races and stations did plenty of their own honking and bellowing too, in every language and temper. It might've been quite the colourful spectacle if everywhere the blown dust hadn't leached each tone to that same grey ubiquity of dirt.

Wist sucked a noisy mouthful from his bottle. 'Quite the variety, ain't there?'

Shy nodded. 'All set on getting something for nothing.'

All struck with a madness of hope. Or of greed, depending on the observer's faith in humanity, which in Shy's case stood less than brim-full. All drunk on the chance of reaching into some freezing pool out there in the great empty and plucking up a new life with both hands. Leaving their humdrum selves behind on the bank like a shed skin and taking a short cut to happiness.

'Tempted to join 'em?' asked Wist.

Shy pressed her tongue against her front teeth and spat through the gap between. 'Not me.' If they made it across the Far Country alive, the odds were stacked high they'd spend a winter up to their arses in ice water and dig up naught but dirt. And if lightning did strike the end of your spade, what then? Ain't like rich folk got no trouble.

There'd been a time Shy thought she'd get something for nothing. Shed her skin and step away smiling. Turned out sometimes the short cut don't lead quite where you hoped, and cuts through bloody country, too.

'Just the rumour o' gold turns 'em mad.' Wist took another swallow, the knobble on his scrawny neck bobbing, and watched two would-be prospectors wrestle over the last pickaxe at a stall while the trader struggled vainly to calm them. 'Imagine how these bastards'll act if they ever close hands around a nugget.'

Shy didn't have to imagine. She'd seen it, and didn't prize the memories. 'Men don't need much beckoning on to act like animals.'

'Nor women neither,' added Wist.

Shy narrowed her eyes at him. 'Why look at me?'

'You're foremost in my mind.'

'Not sure I like being that close to your face.'

Wist showed her his tombstone teeth as he laughed, and handed her the bottle. 'Why don't you got a man, Shy?'

'Don't like men much, I guess.'

'You don't like anyone much.'

'They started it.'

'All of 'em?'

'Enough of 'em.' She gave the mouth of the bottle a good wipe and made sure she took only a sip. She knew how easy she could turn a sip into a swallow, and the swallow into a bottle, and the bottle into waking up smelling of piss with one leg in the creek. There were folk counting on her, and she'd had her fill of being a disappointment.

The wrestlers had been dragged apart and were spitting insults each in their own tongue, neither quite catching the details but both getting the gist. Looked like the pick had vanished in the commotion, more'n likely spirited away by a cannier adventurer while eyes were elsewhere.

'Gold surely can turn men mad,' muttered Wist, all wistful as his name implied. 'Still, if the ground opened and offered me the good stuff I don't suppose I'd be turning down a nugget.'

Shy thought of the farm, and all the tasks to do, and all the time she hadn't got for the doing of 'em, and rubbed her roughed-up thumbs against her chewed-up fingers. For the quickest moment a trek into the hills didn't sound such a mad notion after all. What if there really was gold up there? Scattered on some stream bed in priceless abundance, longing for the kiss of her itchy fingertips? Shy South, luckiest woman in the Near Country . . .

'Hah.' She slapped the thought away like a bothersome fly. High hopes were luxuries she couldn't stretch to. 'In my experience, the ground ain't giving aught away. No more'n the rest of us misers.'

'Got a lot, do you?'

'Eh?'

'Experience.'

She winked as she handed his bottle back. 'More'n you can imagine, old man.' A damn stretch more'n most of the pioneers, that was sure. Shy shook her head as she watched the latest crowd coming through – a set of Union worthies, by their looks, dressed for a picnic rather than a slog across a few hundred miles of lawless empty. Folk who should've been satisfied with the comfortable lives they had, suddenly deciding they'd take any chance at grabbing more. Shy wondered how long it'd be before they were limping back the other way, broken and broke. If they made it back.

'Where's Gully at?' asked Wist.

'Back on the farm, looking to my brother and sister.'

'Haven't seen him in a while.'

'He ain't been here in a while. Hurts him to ride, he says.'

'Getting old. Happens to us all. When you see him, tell him I miss him.'

'If he was here he'd have drunk your bottle dry in one swallow and you'd be cursing his name.'

'I daresay.' Wist sighed. 'That's how it is with things missed.'

By then, Lamb was fording the people-flooded street, shag of grey hair showing above the heads around him for all his stoop, an even sorrier set to his heavy shoulders than usual.

'What did you get?' she asked, hopping down from the wagon.

Lamb winced, like he knew what was coming. 'Twenty-seven?' His rumble of a voice tweaked high at the end to make a question of it, but what he was really asking was, *How bad did I fuck up?*

Shy shook her head, tongue wedged in her cheek, letting him know he'd fucked up middling to bad. 'You're some kind of a bloody coward, Lamb.' She thumped at the sacks and sent up a puff of grain dust. 'I didn't spend two days dragging this up here to give it away.'

He winced a bit more, grey-bearded face creasing around the old scars and laughter lines, all weather-worn and dirt-grained. 'I'm no good with the bartering, Shy, you know that.'

'Remind me what it is y'are good with?' she tossed over her shoulder as she strode for Clay's Exchange, letting a set of piebald goats bleat past then slipping through the traffic sideways-on. 'Except hauling the sacks?'

'That's something, ain't it?' he muttered.

The store was busier even than the street, smelling of sawn wood and spices and hard-working bodies packed tight. She had to shove between a clerk and some blacker'n black Southerner trying to make himself understood in no language she'd ever heard before, then around a washboard hung from the low rafters and set swinging by a careless elbow, then past a frowning Ghost, his red hair all bound up with twigs, leaves still on and everything. All these folk scrambling west meant money to be made, and woe to the merchant tried to put himself between Shy and her share.

'Clay?' she bellowed, nothing to be gained by whispering. 'Clay!'

The trader frowned up, caught in the midst of weighing flour out on his man-high scales. 'Shy South in Squaredeal. Ain't this my lucky day.'

'Looks that way. You got a whole town full o' saps to *swindle!*' She gave the last word a bit of air, made a few heads turn and Clay plant his big fists on his hips.

'No one's swindling no one,' he said.

'Not while I've got an eye on business.'

'Me and your father agreed on twenty-seven, Shy.'

'You know he ain't my father. And you know you ain't agreed shit 'til I've agreed it.'

Clay cocked an eyebrow at Lamb and the Northman looked straight to the ground, shifting sideways like he was trying and wholly failing to vanish. For all Lamb's bulk he'd a weak eye, slapped down by any glance that held it. He could be a loving man, and a hard worker, and he'd been a fair stand-in for a father to Ro and Pit and Shy too, far as she'd given him the chance. A good enough man, but by the dead he was some kind of coward.

Shy felt ashamed for him, and ashamed of him, and that nettled her.

She stabbed her finger in Clay's face like it was a drawn dagger she'd no qualms about using. 'Squaredeal's a strange sort o' name for a town where you'd claw out a business! You paid twenty-eight last season, and you didn't have a quarter of the customers. I'll take thirty-eight.'

'What?' Clay's voice squeaking even higher than she'd predicted. 'Golden grain, is it?'

'That's right. Top quality. Threshed with my own blistered bloody hands.'

'And mine,' muttered Lamb.

'Shush,' said Shy. 'I'll take thirty-eight and refuse to be moved.'

'Don't do me no favours!' raged Clay, fat face filling with angry creases. 'Because I loved your mother I'll offer twenty nine.'

'You never loved a thing but your purse. Anything short of thirty-eight and I'd sooner set up next to your store and offer all this through-traffic just a little less than what you're offering.'

He knew she'd do it, even if it cost her. Never make a threat you aren't at least halfway sure you'll carry through on. 'Thirty-one,' he grated out.

'Thirty-five.'

'You're holding up all these good folk, you selfish bitch!' Or rather she was giving the good folk notice of the profits he was chiselling and sooner or later they'd catch on.

'They're scum to a man, and I'll hold 'em up 'til Juvens gets back from the land of the dead if it means thirty-five.'

'Thirty-two.'

'Thirty-five.'

'Thirty-three and you might as well burn my store down on the way out!'

'Don't tempt me, fat man. Thirty-three and you can toss in a pair o' those new shovels and some feed for my oxen. They eat almost as much as you.' She spat in her palm and held it out.

Clay bitterly worked his mouth, but he spat all the same, and they shook. 'Your mother was no better.'

'Couldn't stand the woman.' Shy elbowed her way back towards the door, leaving Clay to vent his upset on his next customer. 'Not that hard, is it?' she tossed over her shoulder at Lamb.

The big old Northman fussed with the notch out of his ear. 'Think I'd rather have settled for the twenty-seven.'

'That's 'cause you're some kind of a bloody coward. Better to do it than live with the fear of it. Ain't that what you always used to tell me?'

'Time's shown me the downside o' that advice,' muttered Lamb, but Shy was too busy congratulating herself.

Thirty-three was a good price. She'd worked over the sums, and thirty-three would leave something towards Ro's books once they'd fixed the barn's leaking roof and got a breeding pair of pigs to replace the ones they'd butchered in winter. Maybe they could stretch to some seed too, try and nurse the cabbage patch back to health. She was grinning, thinking on what she could put right with that money, what she could build.

You don't need a big dream, her mother used to tell her when she was in a rare good mood, *a little one will do it.*

'Let's get them sacks shifted,' she said.

He might've been getting on in years, might've been slow as an old favourite cow, but Lamb was strong as ever. No weight would bend the man. All Shy had to do was stand on the wagon and heft the sacks one by one onto his shoulders while he stood, complaining less than the wagon had at the load. Then he'd stroll them across, four at a time, and stack them in Clay's yard easy as sacks of feathers. Shy might've been half his weight, but had the easier task and twenty-five years advantage and still, soon enough, she was leaking water faster than a fresh-dug well, vest plastered to her back and hair to her face, arms pink-chafed by canvas and white-powdered with grain dust, tongue wedged in the gap between her teeth while she cursed up a storm.

Lamb stood there, two sacks over one shoulder and one over the other, hardly even breathing hard, those deep laugh lines striking out from the corners of his eyes. 'Need a rest, Shy?'

She gave him a look. 'A rest from your carping.'

'I could shift some o' those sacks around and make a little cot for you. Might be there's a blanket in the back there. I could sing you to sleep like I did when you were young.'

'I'm still young.'

'Ish. Sometimes I think about that little girl smiling up at me.' Lamb looked off into the distance, shaking his head. 'And I wonder – where did me and your mother go wrong?'

'She died and you're useless?' Shy heaved the last sack up and dropped it on his shoulder from as great a height as she could manage.

Lamb only grinned as he slapped his hand down on top. 'Maybe that's it.' As he turned he nearly barged into another Northman, big as he was and a lot meaner-looking. The man started growling some curse, then stopped in the midst. Lamb kept trudging, head down, how he always did from the least breath of trouble. The Northman frowned up at Shy.

'What?' she said, staring right back.

He frowned after Lamb, then walked off, scratching at his beard.

The shadows were getting long and the clouds pink in the west when Shy dumped the last sack under Clay's grinning face and he held out the money, leather bag dangling from one thick forefinger by the drawstrings. She stretched her back out, wiped her forehead on the back of one glove, then worked the bag open and peered inside.

'All here?'

'I'm not going to rob you.'

'Damn right you're not.' And she set to counting it. *You can always tell a thief,* her mother used to say, *on account of all the care they take with their own money.*

'Maybe I should go through every sack, make sure there's grain in 'em not shit?'

Shy snorted. 'If it was shit would that stop you selling it?'

The merchant sighed. 'Have it your way.'

'I will.'

'She does tend to,' added Lamb.

A pause, with just the clicking of coins and the turning of numbers in her head. 'Heard Glama Golden won another fight in the pit up near Greyer,' said Clay. 'They say he's the toughest bastard in the Near Country and there's some tough bastards about. Take a fool to bet against him now, whatever the odds. Take a fool to fight him.'

'No doubt,' muttered Lamb, always quiet when violence was the subject.

'Heard from a man watched it he beat old Stockling Bear so hard his guts came out of his arse.'

'That's entertainment, is it?' asked Shy.

'Beats shitting your own guts.'

'That ain't much of a review.'

Clay shrugged. 'I've heard worse ones. Did you hear about this battle, up near Rostod?'

'Something about it,' she muttered, trying to keep her count straight.

'Rebels got beat again, I heard. Bad, this time. All on the run now. Those the Inquisition didn't get a hold on.'

'Poor bastards,' said Lamb.

Shy paused her count a moment, then carried on. There were a lot of poor bastards about but they couldn't all be her problem. She'd

9

enough worries with her brother and sister, and Lamb, and Gully, and the farm without crying over others' self-made misfortunes.

'Might be they'll make a stand up at Mulkova, but they won't be standing long.' Clay made the fence creak as he leaned his soft bulk back on it, hands tucked under his armpits with the thumbs sticking up. 'War's all but over, if you can call it a war, and there's plenty of people shook off their land. Shook off or burned out or lost what they had. Passes are opened up, ships coming through. Lots of folk seeing their fortune out west all of a sudden.' He nodded at the dusty chaos in the street, still boiling over even as the sun set. 'This here's just the first trickle. There's a flood coming.'

Lamb sniffed. 'Like as not they'll find the mountains ain't one great piece of gold and soon come flooding back the other way.'

'Some will. Some'll put down roots. The Union'll be coming along after. However much land the Union get, they always want more, and what with that find out west they'll smell money. That vicious old bastard Sarmis is sitting on the border and rattling his sword for the Empire, but his sword's always rattling. Won't stop the tide, I reckon.' Clay took a step closer to Shy and spoke soft, like he had secrets to share. 'I heard tell there's already been Union agents in Hormring, talking annexation.'

'They're buying folk out?'

'They'll have a coin in one hand, sure, but they'll have a blade in the other. They always do. We should be thinking about how we'll play it, if they come to Squaredeal. We should stand together, those of us been here a while.'

'I ain't interested in politics.' Shy wasn't interested in anything might bring trouble.

'Most of us aren't,' said Clay, 'but sometimes politics takes an interest in us all the same. The Union'll be coming, and they'll bring law with 'em.'

'Law don't seem such a bad thing,' Shy lied.

'Maybe not. But taxes follow law quick as the cart behind the donkey.'

'Can't say I'm an enthusiast for taxes.'

'Just a fancier way to rob a body, ain't it? I'd rather be thieved honest with mask and dagger than have some bloodless bastard come at me with pen and paper.'

'Don't know about that,' muttered Shy. None of those she'd robbed had looked too delighted with the experience, and some a lot less than others. She let the coins slide back into the bag and drew the string tight.

'How's the count?' asked Clay. 'Anything missing?'

'Not this time. But I reckon I'll keep watching just the same.'

The merchant grinned. 'I'd expect no less.'

She picked out a few things they needed – salt, vinegar, some sugar since it only came in time to time, a wedge of dried beef, half a bag of nails which brought the predictable joke from Clay that she was half a bag of nails herself, which brought the predictable joke from her that she'd nail his fruits to his leg, which brought the predictable joke from Lamb that Clay's fruits were so small she might not get a nail through. They had a bit of a chuckle over each other's quick wits.

She almost got carried away and bought a new shirt for Pit which was more'n they could afford, good price or other price, but Lamb patted her arm with his gloved hand, and she bought needles and thread instead so she could make him a shirt from one of Lamb's old ones. She probably could've made five shirts for Pit from one of Lamb's, the boy was that skinny. The needles were a new kind, Clay said were stamped out of a machine in Adua, hundreds at a press, and Shy smiled as she thought what Gully would say to that, shaking his white head at them and saying, needles from a machine, what'll be thought of next, while Ro turned them over and over in her quick fingers, frowning down as she worked out how it was done.

Shy paused in front of the spirits to lick her lips a moment, glass gleaming amber in the darkness, then forced herself on without, haggled harder than ever with Clay over his prices, and they were finished.

'Never come to this store again, you mad bitch!' The trader hurled at her as she climbed up onto the wagon's seat alongside Lamb. 'You've damn near ruined me!'

'Next season?'

He waved a fat hand as he turned back to his customers. 'Aye, see you then.'

She reached to take the brake off and almost put her hand in the beard of the Northman Lamb knocked into earlier. He was standing right beside the wagon, brow all ploughed up like he was trying to bring some foggy memory to mind, thumbs tucked into a sword-belt – big, simple hilt close to hand. A rough style of character, a scar born near one eye and jagged through his scraggy beard. Shy kept a pleasant look on her face as she eased her knife out, spinning the blade about so it was hidden behind her arm. Better to have steel to hand and find no trouble than find yourself in trouble with no steel to hand.

The Northman said something in his own tongue. Lamb hunched a little lower in his seat, not even turning to look. The Northman spoke again. Lamb grunted something back, then snapped the reins and the wagon rolled off, Shy swaying with the jolting wheels. She snatched a glance over her shoulder when they'd gone a few strides down the rutted street. The Northman was still standing in their dust, frowning after them.

'What'd he want?'

'Nothing.'

She slid her knife into its sheath, stuck one boot on the rail and sat back, settling her hat brim low so the setting sun wasn't in her eyes. 'The world's brimming over with strange people, all right. You spend time worrying what they're thinking, you'll be worrying all your life.'

Lamb was hunched lower than ever, like he was trying to vanish into his own chest.

Shy snorted. 'You're such a bloody coward.'

He gave her a sideways look, then away. 'There's worse a man can be.'

They were laughing when they clattered over the rise and the shallow little valley opened out in front of them. Something Lamb had said. He'd perked up when they left town, as usual. Never at his best in a crowd.

It gave Shy's spirits a lift besides, coming up that track that was hardly more than two faded lines through the long grass. She'd been through black times in her younger years, midnight black times, when she thought she'd be killed out under the sky and left to rot, or caught and hanged and tossed out unburied for the dogs to rip at. More than once, in the midst of nights sweated through with fear, she'd sworn to be grateful every moment of her life if fate gave her the chance to tread this unremarkable path again. Eternal gratitude hadn't quite come about, but that's promises for you. She still felt that bit lighter as the wagon rolled home.

Then they saw the farm, and the laughter choked in her throat and they sat silent while the wind fumbled through the grass around them. Shy couldn't breathe, couldn't speak, couldn't think, all her veins flushed with ice-water. Then she was down from the wagon and running.

'Shy!' Lamb roared at her back, but she hardly heard, head full of her own rattling breath, pounding down the slope, land and sky jolting around her. Through the stubble of the field they'd harvested not a week before. Over the trampled-down fence and the chicken feathers crushed into the mud.

She made it to the yard – what had been the yard – and stood helpless. The house was all dead charred timbers and rubbish and nothing left standing but the tottering chimney-stack. No smoke. The rain must've put out the fires a day or two before. But everything was burned out. She ran around the side of the blacked wreck of the barn, whimpering a little now with each breath.

Gully was hanged from the big tree out back. They'd hanged him over her mother's grave and kicked down the headstone. He was shot through with arrows. Might've been a dozen, might've been more.

Shy felt like she was kicked in the guts and she bent over, arms hugged around herself, and groaned, and the tree groaned with her as the wind shook its leaves and set Gully's corpse gently swinging. Poor old harmless bastard. He'd called to her as they'd rattled off on the wagon. Said she didn't need to worry 'cause he'd look to the children, and she'd laughed at him and said she didn't need to worry 'cause the children would look to him, and she couldn't see nothing for the aching in her eyes and the wind stinging at them, and she clamped her arms tighter, feeling suddenly so cold nothing could warm her.

She heard Lamb's boots thumping up, then slowing, then coming steady until he stood beside her.

'Where are the children?'

They dug the house over, and the barn. Slow, and steady, and numb to begin with. Lamb dragged the scorched timbers clear while Shy scraped through the ashes, sure she'd scrape up Pit and Ro's bones. But they weren't in the house. Nor in the barn. Nor in the yard. Wilder now, trying to smother her fear, and more frantic, trying to smother her hope, casting through the grass, and clawing at the rubbish, but the closest Shy came to her brother and sister was a charred toy horse Lamb had whittled for Pit years past and the scorched pages of some of Ro's books she let blow through her fingers.

The children were vanished.

She stood there, staring into the wind, back of one raw hand against her mouth and her chest going hard. Only one thing she could think of.

'They're stolen,' she croaked.

Lamb just nodded, his grey hair and his grey beard all streaked with soot.

'Why?'

'I don't know.'

She wiped her blackened hands on the front of her shirt and made fists of them. 'We've got to get after.'

'Aye.'

She squatted down over the chewed-up sod around the tree. Wiped her nose and her eyes. Followed the tracks bent over to another battered patch of ground. She found an empty bottle trampled into the mud, tossed it away. They'd made no effort at hiding their sign. Horse-prints all around, circling the shells of the buildings. 'I'm guessing at about twenty. Might've been forty horses, though. They left the spare mounts over here.'

'To carry the children, maybe?'

'Carry 'em where?'

Lamb just shook his head.

She went on, keen to say anything that might fill the space. Keen to set to work at something so she didn't have to think. 'My way of looking at it, they came in from the west and left going south. Left in a hurry.'

'I'll get the shovels. We'll bury Gully.'

They did it quick. She shinned up the tree, knowing every foot- and handhold. She used to climb it long ago, before Lamb came, while her mother watched and Gully clapped, and now her mother was buried under it and Gully was hanged from it, and she knew somehow she'd made it happen. You can't bury a past like hers and think you'll walk away laughing.

She cut him down, and broke the arrows off, and smoothed his bloody hair while Lamb dug out a hole next to her mother. She closed his popping eyes and put her hand on his cheek and it was cold. He looked so small now, and so thin, she wanted to put a coat on him but there was none to hand. Lamb lowered him in a clumsy hug, and they filled the hole together, and they dragged her mother's stone up straight again and tramped the thrashing grass around it, ash blowing on the cold wind in specks of black and grey, whipping across the land and off to nowhere.

'Should we say something?' asked Shy.

'I've nothing to say.' Lamb swung himself up onto the wagon's seat. Might still have been an hour of light left.

'We ain't taking that,' said Shy. 'I can run faster'n those bloody oxen.'

'Not longer, though, and not with gear, and we'll do no good rushing at this. They've got what? Two, three days' start on us? And they'll be riding hard. Twenty men, you said? We have to be realistic, Shy.'

'Realistic?' she whispered at him, hardly able to believe it.

'If we chase after on foot, and don't starve or get washed away in a storm, and if we catch 'em, what then? We're not armed, even. Not with more'n your knife. No. We'll follow on fast as Scale and Calder can take us.' Nodding at the oxen, grazing a little while they had the chance. 'See if we can pare a couple off the herd. Work out what they're about.'

'Clear enough what they're about!' she said, pointing at Gully's grave. 'And what happens to Ro and Pit while we're fucking *following on*?' She ended up screaming it at him, voice splitting the silence and a couple of hopeful crows taking flight from the tree's branches.

The corner of Lamb's mouth twitched but he didn't look at her. 'We'll follow.' Like it was a fact agreed on. 'Might be we can talk this out. Buy 'em back.'

'Buy 'em? They burn your farm, and they hang your friend, and they steal your children and you want to *pay 'em* for the privilege? You're such a fucking coward!'

Still he didn't look at her. 'Sometimes a coward's what you need.' His voice was rough. Clicking in his throat. 'No shed blood's going to unburn this farm now, nor unhang Gully neither. That's done. Best we can do is get back the little ones, any way we can. Get 'em back safe.' This time the twitch started at his mouth and scurried all the way up his scarred cheek to the corner of his eye. 'Then we'll see.'

Shy took a last look as they lurched away towards the setting sun. Her home. Her hopes. How a day can change things about. Naught left but a few scorched timbers poking at the pinking sky. You don't need a big dream. She felt about as low as she ever had in all her life, and she'd been in some bad, dark, low-down places. Hardly had the strength all of a sudden to hold her head up.

'Why'd they have to burn it all?' she whispered.

'Some men just like to burn,' said Lamb.

Shy looked around at him, the outline of his battered frown showing below his battered hat, the dying sun glimmering in one eye, and thought how strange it was, that he could be so calm. A man who hadn't the guts to argue over prices, thinking death and kidnap through. Being realistic about the end of all they'd worked for.

'How can you sit so level?' she whispered at him. 'Like . . . like you knew it was coming.'

Still he didn't look at her. 'It's always coming.'

The Easy Way

'I have suffered many disappointments.' Nicomo Cosca, captain general of the Company of the Gracious Hand, leaned back stiffly upon one elbow as he spoke. 'I suppose every great man faces them. Abandons dreams wrecked by betrayal and finds new ones to pursue.' He frowned towards Mulkova, columns of smoke drifting from the burning city and up into the blue heavens. 'I have abandoned very many dreams.'

'That must have taken tremendous courage,' said Sworbreck, eye-glasses briefly twinkling as he looked up from his notes.

'Indeed! I lose count of the number of times my death has been prematurely declared by one optimistic enemy or another. Forty years of trials, struggles, challenges, betrayals. Live long enough . . . you see everything ruined.' Cosca shook himself from his reverie. 'But it hasn't been boring, at least! What adventures along the way, eh, Temple?'

Temple winced. He had borne personal witness to five years of occasional fear, frequent tedium, intermittent diarrhoea, failure to avoid the plague, and avoiding fighting as if it was the plague. But he was not paid for the truth. Far from it.

'Heroic,' he said.

'Temple is my notary. He prepares the contracts and sees them honoured. One of the cleverest bastards I ever met. How many languages do you speak, Temple?'

'Fluently, no more than six.'

'Most important man in the whole damn Company! Apart from me, of course.' A breeze washed across the hillside and stirred the wispy white hairs about Cosca's liver-spotted pate. 'I so look forward to telling you my stories, Sworbreck!' Temple restrained another grimace of distaste. 'The Siege of Dagoska!' Which ended in utter disaster. 'The Battle of Afieri!' Shameful debacle. 'The Years of Blood!' Sides

17

changed like shirts. 'The Kadiri Campaign!' Drunken fiasco. 'I even kept a goat for several years. A stubborn beast, but loyal, you'd have to give her that . . .'

Sworbreck achieved the not-inconsiderable feat of performing an obsequious bow while sitting cross-legged against a slab of fallen masonry. 'I have no doubt my readers will thrill to your exploits.'

'Enough to fill twenty volumes!'

'Three will be more than adequate—'

'I was once Grand Duke of Visserine, you know.' Cosca waved down attempts at abasement which had, in fact, not happened. 'Don't worry, you need not call me Excellency – we are all informal here in the Company of the Gracious Hand, are we not, Temple?'

Temple took a long breath. 'We are all informal.' Most of them were liars, all of them were thieves, some of them were killers. Informality was not surprising.

'Sergeant Friendly has been with me even longer than Temple, ever since we deposed Grand Duke Orso and placed Monzcarro Murcatto on the throne of Talins.'

Sworbreck looked up. 'You know the Grand Duchess?'

'Intimately. I consider it no exaggeration to say I was her close friend and mentor. I saved her life at the siege of Muris, and she mine! The story of her rise to power is one I must relate to you at some stage, a noble business. There are precious few persons of quality I have not fought for or against at one time or another. Sergeant Friendly?'

The neckless sergeant looked up, face a blank slab.

'What have you made of your time with me?'

'I preferred prison.' And he returned to rolling his dice, an activity which could fully occupy him for hours at a time.

'He is such a wag, that one!' Cosca waved a bony finger at him, though there was no evidence of a joke. In five years Temple had never heard Sergeant Friendly make a joke. 'Sworbreck, you will find the Company alive with joshing good fun!'

Not to mention simmering feuds, punishing laziness, violence, disease, looting, treachery, drunkenness and debauchery fit to make a devil blush.

'These five years,' said Temple, 'I've hardly stopped laughing.'

There was a time he had found the Old Man's stories hilarious, enchanting, stirring. A magical glimpse of what it was to be without fear. Now they made him feel sick. Whether Temple had learned the truth or Cosca had forgotten it, it was hard to say. Perhaps a little of both.

'Yes, it's been quite a career. Many proud moments. Many triumphs. But defeats, too. Every great man has them. Regrets are the cost of the business, Sazine always used to say. People have often accused me of inconsistency but I feel that I have always, at any given junction, done the same thing. Exactly what I pleased.' The aged mercenary's fickle attention having wandered back to his imagined glorious past, Temple began to ease away, slipping around a broken column. 'I had a happy childhood but a wild youth, filled with ugly incidents, and at seventeen I left my birthplace to seek my fortune with only my wits, my courage, and my trusty blade . . .'

The sounds of boasting mercifully faded as Temple retreated down the hillside, stepping from the shadow of the ancient ruin and into the sun. Whatever Cosca might say, there was little joshing good fun going on down here.

Temple had seen wretchedness. He had lived through more than his share. But he had rarely seen people so miserable as the Company's latest batch of prisoners: a dozen of the fearsome rebels of Starikland chained naked, bloody, filthy and dead-eyed to a stake in the ground. It was hard to imagine them a threat to the greatest nation in the Circle of the World. It was hard to imagine them as humans. Only the tattoos on their forearms showed some last futile defiance.

Fuck the Union. Fuck the King. Read the nearest, a line of bold script from elbow to wrist. A sentiment with which Temple had increasing sympathy. He was developing a sneaking feeling he had found his way onto the wrong side. Again. But it's not always easy to tell when you're picking. Perhaps, as Kahdia once told him, you are on the wrong side as soon as you pick one. But it had been Temple's observation that it was those caught in the middle that always get the worst of it. And he was done with getting the worst.

Sufeen stood by the prisoners, an empty canteen in one hand.

'What are you about?' asked Temple.

'He is wasting water,' said Bermi, lounging in the sun nearby and scratching at his blond beard.

'On the contrary,' said Sufeen. 'I am trying to administer God's mercy to our prisoners.'

One had a terrible wound in his side, undressed. His eyes flickered, his lips mouthed meaningless orders or meaningless prayers. Once you could smell a wound there was little hope. But the outlook for the others was no better. 'If there is a God, He is a smarmy swindler and never to be trusted with anything of importance,' muttered Temple. 'Mercy would be to kill them.'

Bermi concurred. 'I've been saying so.'

'But that would take courage.' Sufeen lifted his scabbard, offering up the hilt of his sword. 'Have you courage, Temple?'

Temple snorted.

Sufeen let the weapon drop. 'Nor I. And so I give them water, and have not enough even of that. What is happening at the top of the hill?'

'We await our employers. And the Old Man is feeding his vanity.'

'That's a hell of an appetite to satisfy,' said Bermi, picking daisies and flicking them away.

'Bigger every day. It rivals Sufeen's guilt.'

'This is not guilt,' said Sufeen, frowning towards the prisoners. 'This is righteousness. Did the priests not teach you that?'

'Nothing like a religious education to cure a man of righteousness,' muttered Temple. He thought of Haddish Kahdia speaking the lessons in the plain white room, and his younger self scoffing at them. Charity, mercy, selflessness. How conscience is that piece of Himself that God puts in every man. A splinter of the divine. One that Temple had spent long years struggling to prise out. He caught the eye of one of the rebels. A woman, hair tangled across her face. She reached out as far as the chains would allow. For the water or the sword, he could not say. *Grasp your future!* called the words inked into her skin. He pulled out his own canteen, frowned as he weighed it in his hand.

'Some guilt of your own?' asked Sufeen.

It might have been a while since he wore them, but Temple had not forgotten what chains felt like. 'How long have you been a scout?' he snapped.

'Eighteen years.'

'You should know by now that conscience is a shitty navigator.'

'It certainly doesn't know the country out here,' added Bermi.

Sufeen spread wide his hands. 'Who then shall show us the way?'

'Temple!' Cosca's cracked howl, floating from above.

'Your guide calls,' said Sufeen. 'You will have to give them water later.'

Temple tossed him the canteen as he headed back up the hillside. 'You do it. Later, the Inquisition will have them.'

'Always the easy way, eh, Temple?' called Sufeen after him.

'Always,' muttered Temple. He made no apology for it.

'Welcome, gentlemen, welcome!' Cosca swept off his outrageous hat as their illustrious employers approached, riding in tight formation around a great fortified wagon. Even though the Old Man had, thank God, quit spirits yet again a few months before, he still seemed always slightly drunk. There was a floppy flourish to his knobbly hands, a lazy drooping of his withered eyelids, a rambling music to his speech. That and you could never be entirely sure what he would do or say next. There had been a time Temple had found that constant uncertainty thrilling, like watching the lucky wheel spin and wondering if his number would come up. Now it felt more like cowering beneath a storm-cloud and waiting for the lightning.

'General Cosca.' Superior Pike, head of his August Majesty's Inquisition in Starikland and the most powerful man within five hundred miles, was the first to dismount. His face was burned beyond recognition, eyes darkly shadowed in a mask of mottled pink, the corner of his mouth curled up in what was either a smile or a trick of the ravages of fire. A dozen of his hulking Practicals, dressed and masked in black and bristling with weaponry, arranged themselves watchfully about the ruin.

Cosca grinned across the valley towards the smouldering city, unintimidated. 'Mulkova burns, I see.'

'Better that it burn in Union hands than prosper under the rebels,' said Inquisitor Lorsen as he got down: tall and gaunt, his eyes bright with zeal. Temple envied him that. To feel certain in the right no matter what wrongs you took part in.

'Quite so,' said Cosca. 'A sentiment with which her citizens no doubt all agree! Sergeant Friendly you know, and this is Master Temple, notary to my company.'

General Brint dismounted last, the operation rendered considerably more difficult since he had lost most of an arm at the Battle of Osrung along with his entire sense of humour, and wore the left sleeve of his crimson uniform folded and pinned to his shoulder. 'You are prepared for legal disagreements, then,' he said, adjusting his sword-belt and eyeing Temple as if he was the morning plague cart.

'The second thing a mercenary needs is a good weapon.' Cosca clapped a fatherly hand on Temple's shoulder. 'The first is good legal advice.'

'And where does an utter lack of moral scruple feature?'

'Number five,' said Temple. 'Just behind a short memory and a ready wit.'

Superior Pike was considering Sworbreck, still scribbling notes. 'And on what does this man advise you?'

'That is Spillion Sworbreck, my biographer.'

'No more than a humble teller of tales!' Sworbreck gave the Superior a flamboyant bow. 'Though I freely confess that my prose has caused grown men to weep.'

'In a good way?' asked Temple.

If he heard, the author was too busy praising himself to respond. 'I compose stories of heroism and adventure to inspire the Union's citizens! Widely distributed now, via the wonders of the new Rimaldi printing press. You have heard, perhaps, of my *Tales of Harod the Great* in five volumes?' Silence. 'In which I mine the mythic splendour of the origin of the Union itself?' Silence. 'Or the eight-volume sequel, *The Life of Casamir, Hero of Angland*?' Silence. 'In which I hold up the mirror of past glories to expose the moral collapse of the present day?'

'No.' Pike's melted face betrayed no emotion.

'I will have copies sent to you, Superior!'

'You could use readings from them to force confessions from your prisoners,' murmured Temple, under his breath.

'Do not trouble yourself,' said Pike.

'No trouble! General Cosca has permitted me to accompany him on his latest campaign while he relates the details of his fascinating career as a soldier of fortune! I mean to make him the subject of my most celebrated work to date!'

The echoes of Sworbreck's words faded into a crushing silence.

'Remove this man from my presence,' said Pike. 'His manner of expression offends me.'

Sworbreck backed down the hillside with an almost reckless speed, shepherded by two Practicals. Cosca continued without the slightest hint of embarrassment.

'General Brint!' and he seized the general's remaining hand in both of his. 'I understand you have some concerns about our participation in the assault—'

'It was the lack of it that bothered me!' snapped Brint, twisting his fingers free.

Cosca pushed out his lips with an air of injured innocence. 'You feel we fell short of our contractual obligations?'

'You've fallen short of honour, decency, professionalism—'

'I recall no reference to them in the contract,' said Temple.

'You were ordered to attack! Your failure to do so cost the lives of several of my men, one a personal friend!'

Cosca waved a lazy hand, as though personal friends were ephemera that could hardly be expected to bear on an adult discussion. 'We were engaged here, General Brint, quite hotly.'

'In a bloodless exchange of arrows!'

'You speak as though a bloody exchange would be preferable.' Temple held out his hand to Friendly. The sergeant produced the contract from an inside pocket. 'Clause eight, I believe.' He swiftly found the place and presented it for inspection. 'Technically, any exchange of projectiles constitutes engagement. Each member of the Company is, in fact, due a bonus as a result.'

Brint looked pale. 'A bonus, too? Despite the fact that not one man was wounded.'

Cosca cleared his throat. 'We do have a case of dysentery.'

'Is that a joke?'

'Not to anyone who has suffered the ravages of dysentery, I assure you!'

'Clause nineteen . . .' Paper crackled as Temple thumbed through the densely written document. ' "Any man rendered inactive by illness during the discharge of his contractual obligations is to be considered a loss to the Company." A further payment is therefore due for the replacement of losses. Not to mention those for prisoners taken and delivered—'

'It all comes down to money, doesn't it?'

Cosca shrugged so high his gilt epaulettes tickled his earlobes. 'What else would it come down to? We are mercenaries. Better motives we leave to better men.'

Brint gazed at Temple, positively livid. 'You must be delighted with your wriggling, you Gurkish worm.'

'You were happy to put your name to the terms, General.' Temple flipped over the back page to display Brint's overwrought signature. 'My delight or otherwise does not enter the case. Nor does my wriggling. And I am generally agreed to be half-Dagoskan, half-Styrian, since you bring my parentage into—'

'You're a brown bastard son of a whore.'

Temple only smiled. 'My mother was never ashamed of her profession – why should I be?'

The general stared at Superior Pike, who had taken a seat on a lichen-splattered block of masonry, produced a haunch of bread and was trying to entice birds down from the crumbling ruin with faint kissing sounds. 'Am I to understand that you approve of this licensed banditry, Superior? This contractual cowardice, this outrageous—'

'General Brint.' Pike's voice was gentle, but somewhere in it had a screeching edge which, like the movement of rusty hinges, enforced wincing silence. 'We all appreciate the diligence you and your men have displayed. But the war is over. We won.' He tossed some crumbs into the grass and watched a tiny bird flit down and begin to peck. 'It is not fitting that we quibble over who did what. You signed the contract. We will honour it. We are not barbarians.'

'*We* are not.' Brint gave Temple, then Cosca, then Friendly a furious glare. They were all, each in his way, unmoved. 'I must get some air. There is a sickening *stench* here!' And with some effort the general hauled himself back into his saddle, turned his horse and thundered away, pursued by several aides-de-camp.

'I find the air quite pleasant,' said Temple brightly, somewhat relieved that confrontation at least was over.

'Pray forgive the general,' said Pike 'He is very much committed to his work.'

'I try always to be forgiving of other men's foibles,' said Cosca. 'I have enough of my own, after all.'

Pike did not attempt to deny it. 'I have further work for you even so. Inquisitor Lorsen, could you explain?' And he turned back to his birds, as though his meeting was with them and the rest a troublesome distraction.

Lorsen stepped forward, evidently relishing his moment. 'The rebellion is at an end. The Inquisition is weeding out all those disloyal to the crown. Some few rebels have escaped, however, scattering through the passes and into the uncivilised west where, no doubt, they will foment new discord.'

'Cowardly bastards!' Cosca slapped at his thigh. 'Could they not stand and be slaughtered like decent men? I'm all for fermentation but fomentation is a damned imposition!'

Lorsen narrowed his eyes as though at a contrary wind, and ploughed on. 'For political reasons, his Majesty's armies are unable to pursue them.'

'Political reasons . . .' offered Temple, 'such as a border?'

'Precisely,' said Lorsen.

Cosca examined his ridged and yellowed fingernails. 'Oh, I've never taken those very seriously.'

'Precisely,' said Pike.

'We want the Company of the Gracious Hand to cross the mountains and pacify the Near Country as far west as the Sokwaya River.

This rot of rebellion must be excised once and for all.' Lorsen cut at imaginary filth with the edge of his hand, voice rising as he warmed to his subject. 'We must clean out this sink of depravity which has too long been allowed to fester on our border! This . . . overflowing latrine! This backed-up sewer, endlessly disgorging its ordure of chaos into the Union!'

Temple reflected that, for a man who professed himself opposed to ordure, Inquisitor Lorsen certainly relished a shit-based metaphor.

'Well, no one enjoys a backed-up sewer,' conceded Cosca. 'Except the sewer-men themselves, I suppose, who scratch out their wretched livings in the sludge. Unblocking the drains is a speciality of ours, isn't it, Sergeant Friendly?'

The big man looked up from his dice long enough to shrug.

'Temple is the linguist but perhaps I might in this case interpret?' The Old Man twisted the waxed tips of his grey moustaches between finger and thumb. 'You wish us to visit a plague upon the settlers of the Near Country. You wish us to make stern examples of every rebel sheltered and every person who gives them shelter. You wish us to make them understand that their only future is with the grace and favour of his August Majesty. You wish us to force them into the welcoming arms of the Union. Do I come close to the mark?'

'Close enough,' murmured Superior Pike.

Temple found that he was sweating. When he wiped his forehead his hand trembled. But what could he do?

'The Paper of Engagement is already prepared.' Lorsen produced his own sheaf of crackling documents, a heavy seal of red wax upon its bottom corner.

Cosca waved it away. 'My notary will look it over. All the legal fiddle-faddle quite swims before my eyes. I am a simple soldier.'

'Admirable,' said Pike, his hairless brows raised by the slightest fraction.

Temple's ink-spotted forefinger traced through the blocks of calligraphy, eyes flickering from one point of interest to another. He realised he was picking nervously at the corners of the pages and made himself stop.

'I will accompany you on the expedition,' said Lorsen. 'I have a list of settlements suspected of harbouring rebels. Or rebellious sentiment.'

Cosca grinned. 'Nothing more dangerous than sentiment!'

'In particular, his Eminence the Arch Lector offers a bonus of fifty thousand marks for the capture, alive, of the chief instigator of the insurrection, the one the rebels call Conthus. He goes also under the name of Symok. The Ghosts call him Black Grass. At the massacre in Rostod he used the alias—'

'No further aliases, I beg you!' Cosca massaged the sides of his skull as if they pained him. 'Since suffering a head-wound at the Battle of Afieri I have been cursed with an appalling memory for names. It is a source of constant embarrassment. But Sergeant Friendly has all the details. If your man Conshus—'

'Conthus.'

'What did I say?'

'Conshus.'

'There you go! If he's in the Near Country, he'll be yours.'

'Alive,' snapped Lorsen. 'He must answer for his crimes. He must be made a lesson of. He must be put on display!'

'And he'll make a most educational show, I'm sure!'

Pike flicked another pinch of crumbs to his gathering flock. 'The methods we leave to you, captain general. We would only ask that there be something left in the ashes to annexe.'

'As long as you realise a Company of mercenaries is more club than scalpel.'

'His Eminence has chosen the method and understands its limitations.'

'An inspirational man, the Arch Lector. We are close friends, you know.'

'His one firm stipulation, clear in the contract, as you see, is that you avoid any Imperial entanglements. Any and all, am I understood?' That grating note entered Pike's voice again. 'Legate Sarmis still haunts the border like an angry phantom. I do not suppose he will cross it but even so he is a man decidedly not to be trifled with, a most bloody-minded and bloody-handed adversary. His Eminence desires no further wars at present.'

'Do not concern yourself, I avoid fighting wherever possible.' Cosca slapped happily at the hilt of his blade. 'A sword is for rattling, not for drawing, eh?'

'We have a gift for you, also.' Superior Pike indicated the fortified wagon, an oaken monster bound in riveted iron and hauled by a team of eight muscular horses. It was halfway between conveyance and castle, with slitted windows and a crenelated parapet about the top, from which defenders might presumably shoot at circling enemies. Far from the most practical of gifts, but then Cosca had never been interested in practicalities.

'For me?' The Old Man pressed his withered hands to his gilded breastplate. 'It shall be my home from home out in the wilderness!'

'There is a . . . *secret* within,' said Lorsen. 'Something his Eminence would very much like to see tested.'

'I love surprises! Ones that don't involve armed men behind me, anyway. You may tell his Eminence it will be my honour.' Cosca stood, wincing as his aged knees audibly clicked. 'How does the Paper of Engagement appear?'

Temple looked up from the penultimate page. 'Er . . .' The contract was closely based on the one he had drawn up for their previous engagement, was watertight in every particular, was even more generous in several. 'Some issues with supply,' he stammered, fumbling for objections. 'Food and weaponry are covered but the clause really should include—'

'Details. No cause for delay. Let's get the papers signed and the men ready to move. The longer they sit idle, the harder to get them off their arses. No force of nature so dangerous to life and commerce as mercenaries without employment.' Except, perhaps, mercenaries with employment.

'It would be prudent to allow me a little longer to—'

Cosca came close, setting his hand on Temple's shoulder again. 'Have you a legal objection?'

Temple paused, clutching for some words which might carry weight with a man with whom nothing carried any weight. 'Not a legal objection, no.'

'A financial objection?' offered Cosca.

'No, General.'

'Then . . . ?'

'Do you remember when we first met?'

Cosca suddenly flashed that luminous smile of which only he was capable, good humour and good intentions radiating from his deep-lined face. 'Of course. I wore that blue uniform, you the brown rags.'

'You said . . .' It hardly felt possible, now. 'You said we would do good together.'

'And haven't we, in the main? Legally *and* financially?' As though the entire spectrum of goodness ranged between those twin poles.

'And . . . morally?'

The Old Man's forehead furrowed as though it was a word in a foreign tongue. 'Morally?'

'General, please.' Temple fixed Cosca with his most earnest

expression. And Temple knew he could be earnest, when he truly believed. Or had a great deal to lose. 'I beg you. Do not sign this paper. This will not be war, it will be murder.'

Cosca's brows went up. 'A fine distinction, to the buried.'

'We are not judges! What happens to the people of these towns once the men get among them, hungry for plunder? Women and children, General, who had no part in any rebellion. We are better than this.'

'We are? You did not say so in Kadir. You persuaded me to sign that contract, if I recall.'

'Well—'

'And in Styria, was it not you who encouraged me to take back what was mine?'

'You had a valid claim—'

'Before we took ship to the North, you helped me persuade the men. You can be damned persuasive when you have a mind.'

'Then let me persuade you now. Please, General Cosca. Do not sign.'

There was a long pause. Cosca heaved in a breath, his forehead creasing yet more deeply. 'A *conscientious* objection, then.'

'Conscience is,' muttered Temple hopefully, 'a splinter of the divine?' Not to mention a shitty navigator, and it had led him into some dangerous waters now. He realised he was picking nervously at the hem of his shirt as Cosca gazed upon him. 'I simply have a feeling this job . . .' He struggled for words that might turn the tide of inevitability. 'Will go bad,' he finished, lamely.

'Good jobs rarely require the services of mercenaries.' Cosca's hand squeezed a little tighter at his shoulder and Temple felt Friendly's looming presence behind him. Still, and silent, and yet very much *there*. 'Men of conscience and conviction might find themselves better suited to other lines of work. His Majesty's Inquisition offers a righteous cause, I understand?'

Temple swallowed as he looked across at Superior Pike, who had now attracted a twittering avian crowd. 'I'm not sure I care for their brand of righteousness.'

'Well, that's the thing about righteousness,' murmured Cosca, 'everyone has their own brand. Gold, on the other hand, is universal. In my considerable experience, a man is better off worrying about what is good for his purse than what is simply . . . good.'

'I just—'

Cosca squeezed still more firmly. 'Without wishing to be harsh,

Temple, it isn't all about *you*. I have the welfare of the whole company to think of. Five hundred men.'

'Five hundred and twelve,' said Friendly.

'Plus one with dysentery. I cannot inconvenience them for the sake of your *feelings*. That would be . . . *immoral*. I need you, Temple. But if you wish to leave . . .' Cosca issued a weighty sigh. 'In spite of all your promises, in spite of my generosity, in spite of everything we have been through together, well . . .' He held out an arm towards burning Mulkova and raised his brows. 'I suppose the door is always open.'

Temple swallowed. He could have left. He could have said he wanted no part of this. Enough is enough, damn it! But that would have taken courage. That would have left him with no armed men at his back. Alone, and weak, and a victim once again. That would have been hard to do. And Temple always took the easy way. Even when he knew it was the wrong way. Especially then, in fact, since easy and wrong make such good company. Even when he had a damn good notion it would end up being the hard way, even then. Why think about tomorrow when today is such a thorny business?

Perhaps Kahdia would have found some way to stop this. Something involving supreme self-sacrifice, most likely. Temple, it hardly needed to be said, was not Kahdia. He wiped away a fresh sheen of sweat, forced a queasy smile onto his face and bowed. 'I remain always honoured to serve.'

'Excellent!' And Cosca plucked the contract from Temple's limp hand and spread it out to sign upon a sheered-off column.

Superior Pike stood, brushing crumbs from his shapeless black coat and sending birds scattering. 'Do you know what's out there, in the west?'

He let the question hang a moment. Below them the faint jingling, groaning, snapping could be heard of his Practicals dragging the prisoners away. Then he answered himself.

'The future. And the future does not belong to the Old Empire – their time is a thousand years past. Nor does it belong to the Ghosts, savages that they are. Nor does it belong to the fugitives, adventurers and opportunist scum who have put the first grasping roots into its virgin soil. No. The future belongs to the Union. We must seize it.'

'We must not be afraid to do what is necessary to seize it,' added Lorsen.

'Never fear, gentlemen.' Cosca grinned as he scratched out the part-ing swirl of his signature. 'We will seize the future together.'

29

Just Men

The rain had stopped. Shy peered through trees alive with the tap-tap of falling water, past a felled trunk abandoned on its trestles, part-stripped, the drawknife left wedged under a curl of bark, and towards the blackened bones of the house.

'Not hard bastards to follow,' muttered Lamb. 'Leave burned-out buildings wherever they go.'

Probably they thought they'd killed anyone cared enough to follow. What might happen once they noticed Lamb and Shy toddling after in their rickety wagon, she was trying not to think about.

Time was she'd thought out everything, every moment of every day – hers, Lamb's, Gully's, Pit and Ro's, too – all parcelled into its proper place with its proper purpose. Always looking forwards, the future better than the now, its shape clear to her as a house already built. Hard to believe since that time it was just five nights spent under the flapping canvas in the back of the cart. Five mornings waking stiff and sore to a dawn like a pit yawning under her feet. Five days following the sign across the empty grassland and into the woods, one eye on her black past, wondering what part of it had crept from the cold earth's clutches and stolen her life while she was grinning at tomorrow.

Her fingertips rubbed nervously against her palm. 'Shall we take a look?' Truth was she was scared what she might find. Scared of looking and scared of not looking. Worn out and scared of everything with a hollow space where her hopes used to be.

'I'll go round the back.' Lamb brushed his knees off with his hat and started circling the clearing, twigs crunching under his boots, a set of startled pigeons yammering into the white sky, giving anyone about fair notice of their arrival. Not that there was anyone about. Leastways, no one living.

There was an overgrown vegetable patch out back, stubborn soil scraped away to make a trench no more than ankle-deep. Next to it a soaked blanket was stretched over something lumpy. From the bottom stuck a pair of boots and a pair of bony bare feet with dirt under the bluish nails.

Lamb squatted down, took one corner and peeled it back. A man's face and a woman's, grey and slack, both with throats cut deep. The woman's head lolled, the wound in her neck yawning wet and purple.

'Ah.' Shy pressed her tongue into the gap between her front teeth and stared at the ground. Would've taken quite the optimist to expect anything else, and she by no means qualified, but those faces still tore at something in her. Worry for Pit and Ro, or worry for herself, or just a sick memory of a sick time when bodies weren't such strange things for her to see.

'Leave 'em be, you bastards!'

First thing Shy took in was the gleam on the arrowhead. Next was the hand that held the drawn bow, knuckles white on dark wood. Last was the face behind – a boy maybe sixteen, a mop of sandy hair stuck to pale skin with the wet.

'I'll kill you! I'll do it!' He eased from the bushes, feet fishing for firm earth to tread on, shadows sliding across his tight face and his hand trembling on the bow.

Shy made herself stay still, some trick to manage with her first two burning instincts to get at him or get away. Her every muscle was itching to do one or the other, and there'd been a time Shy had chased off wherever her instincts led. But since they'd usually led her by an unpleasant route right into the shit, she let the bastards run off without her this time and just stood, looking this boy steady in the eyes. Scared eyes, which was no surprise, open wide and shining in the corners. She kept her voice soft, like they'd met at a harvest dance and had no burned-out buildings, dead folk or drawn bows between them.

'What's your name?'

His tongue darted over his lips, point of the arrow wobbling and making her chest horrible itchy about where it was aimed.

'I'm Shy. This is Lamb.'

The boy's eyes flicked across, and his bow too. Lamb didn't flinch, just put the blanket back how he'd found it and slowly stood. Seeing him with the boy's fresh eyes, he looked anything but harmless. Even with that tangle of grey beard you could tell a man would have to be real careless with his razor to pick up scars like Lamb's by accident.

Shy had always guessed he'd got them in some war up North, but if he'd been a fighter once there was no fight in him now. Some kind of coward like she'd always said. But this boy wasn't to know.

'We been following some men.' Shy kept her voice soft, soft, coaxing the boy's eyes and his arrow's point back to her. 'They burned our farm, up near Squaredeal. They burned it, and they killed a man worked for us, and they took my sister and my little brother . . .' Her voice cracked and she had to swallow and press it out smooth again. 'We been following on.'

'Reckon they been here, too,' said Lamb.

'We been tracking 'em. Maybe twenty men, moving quick.' The arrow-point started to drift down. 'They stopped off at a couple more farms on the way. Same thing. Then we followed 'em into the woods. And here.'

'I'd been hunting,' said the boy quietly.

Shy nodded. 'We were in town. Selling our crop.'

'I came back, and . . .' That point made it right down to the ground, much to Shy's relief. 'Nothing I could've done.'

'No.'

'They took my brother.'

'What was his name?'

'Evin. He was nine years old.'

Silence, with just the trees still dripping and the gentle creak as the boy let his bowstring go slack.

'You know who they were?' asked Lamb.

'I didn't see 'em.'

'You know why they took your brother?'

'I said I wasn't here, didn't I? I wasn't here.'

'All right,' said Shy, calming. 'I know.'

'You following after 'em?' asked the boy.

'We're just about keeping up,' said Lamb.

'Going to get your sister and your brother back?'

'Count on it,' said Shy, as if sounding certain made it certain.

'Can you get mine, too?'

Shy looked at Lamb, and he looked back, and he didn't say nothing. 'We can try,' she said.

'Reckon I'll be coming along with you, then.'

Another silence. 'You sure?' asked Lamb.

'I can do what needs doing, y'old bastard!' screamed the boy, veins popping from his neck.

Lamb didn't twitch a muscle. 'We don't know what'll need doing yet.'

'There's room in the wagon, though, if you want to take your part.' Shy held her hand out to the boy, and he looked at it for a moment, then stepped forward and shook it. He squeezed it too hard, that way men do when they're trying to prove they're tougher than they are.

'My name's Leef.'

Shy nodded towards the two bodies. 'These your folks?'

The boy blinked down at them. 'I been trying to do the burying, but the ground's hard, and I got nothing to dig with.' He rubbed at his broken fingernails with his thumb. 'I been trying.'

'Need some help?' she asked.

His face crushed up, and he hung his head, and he nodded, wet hair dangling.

'We all need some help, time to time,' said Lamb. 'I'll get them shovels down.'

Shy reached out, checked a moment, then gently put her hand on the boy's shoulder. She felt him tense, thought he'd shake it off, but he didn't and she was glad. Maybe she needed it there more than he did.

On they went, gone from two to three but otherwise not much changed. Same wind, same sky, same tracks to be followed, same worried silence between them. The wagon was wearing out on the battered tracks, lurching more with each mile rattled behind those patient oxen. One of the wheels had near shook itself to pieces inside its iron tyre. Shy felt some sympathy, behind her frown she was all shook to pieces herself. They loaded out the gear and let the oxen loose to crop grass, and Lamb lifted one side of the wagon with a grunt and a shrug while Shy did the best she could with the tools she had and her half-sack of nails, Leef eager to do his part but that no more than passing her the hammer when she asked.

The tracks led to a river and forded at a shallow spot. Calder and Scale weren't too keen on the crossing but in the end Shy goaded them over to a tall mill-house, stone-built on three stories. Those they were chasing hadn't bothered to try and burn this one and its wheel still slapped around merrily in the chattering water. Two men and a woman were hanged together in a bunch from the attic window. One had a broken neck stretched out way too long, another feet burned raw, dangling a stride above the mud.

Leef stared up big-eyed. 'What kind o' men do a thing like this?'

'Just men,' said Shy. 'Thing like this don't take no one special.' Though at times it felt to her that they were following something else. Some mad storm blowing mindless through this abandoned country, churning up the dirt and leaving bottles and shit and burned buildings and hanged folk scattered in its wake. A storm that snatched away all the children to who knew where and to what purpose? 'You care to go up there, Leef, and cut these folks down?'

He looked like he didn't much care to, but he drew his knife and went inside to do it anyway.

'Feels like we're doing a lot of burying lately,' she muttered.

'Good thing you got Clay to throw them shovels in,' said Lamb.

She laughed at that, then realised what she was laughing at and turned it into an ugly cough. Leef's head showed at the window and he leaned out, started cutting at the ropes, making the bodies tremble. 'Seems wrong, us having to clean up after these bastards.'

'Someone has to.' Lamb held one of the shovels out to her. 'Or do you want to leave these folks swinging?'

Towards evening, the low sun setting the edges of the clouds to burn and the wind making the trees dance and sweeping patterns in the grass, they came upon a campsite. A big fire had smouldered out under the eaves of a wood, a circle of charred branches and sodden ash three strides across. Shy hopped from the wagon while Lamb was still cooing Scale and Calder to a snorting halt, and she drew her knife and gave the fire a poke, turned up some embers still aglow.

'They were here overnight,' she called.

'We're catching 'em, then?' asked Leef as he jumped down, nocking an arrow loose to his bow.

'I reckon.' Though Shy couldn't help wondering if that was a good thing. She dragged a length of frayed rope from the grass, found a cobweb torn between bushes at the treeline, then a shred of cloth left on a bramble.

'Someone come this way?' asked Leef.

'More'n one. And fast.' Shy slipped through after, keeping low, crept down a muddy slope, slick dirt and fallen leaves treacherous under her boots, trying to keep her balance and peer into the dimness—

She saw Pit, face down by a fallen tree, looking so small there among the knotted roots. She wanted to scream but had no voice, no breath even. She ran, slid on her side in a shower of dead leaves and ran again. She squatted by him, back of his head a clotted mass, hand trembling as she reached out, not wanting to see his face, having to see it. She held her breath as she wrestled him over, his body small but stiff as a board, brushed away the leaves stuck to his face with fumbling fingers.

'Is it your brother?' muttered Leef.

'No.' She was almost sick with relief. Then with guilt that she was relieved, when this boy was dead. 'Is it yours?'

'No,' said Leef.

Shy slid her hands under the dead child and picked him up, struggled up the slope, Leef behind her. Lamb stood staring between the trees at the top, a black shape stamped from the glow of sunset.

'Is it him?' came his cracking voice. 'Is it Pit?'

'No.' Shy laid him on the flattened grass, arms stuck out wide, head tipped back rigid.

'By the dead.' Lamb had his fingers shoved into his grey hair, gripping at his head like it might burst.

'Might be he tried to get away. They made a lesson of him.' She hoped Ro didn't try it. Hoped she was too clever to. Hoped she was cleverer than Shy had been at her age. She leaned on the wagon with her back to the others, squeezed her eyes shut and wiped the tears away. Dug the bastard shovels out and brought them back.

'More fucking digging,' spat Leef, hacking at the ground like it was the one stole his brother.

'Better off digging than getting buried,' said Lamb.

Shy left them to the graves and the oxen to their grazing and spread out in circles, keeping low, fingers combing at the cold grass, trying to read the signs in the fading light. Trying to feel out what they'd done, what they'd do next.

'Lamb.'

He grunted as he squatted beside her, slapping the dirt from his gloves. 'What is it?'

'Looks like three of 'em peeled off here, heading south and east. The rest struck on due west. What do you think?'

'I try not to. You're the tracker. Though when you got so damn good at it, I've no notion.'

'Just a question of thinking it through.' Shy didn't want to admit that chasing men and being chased are sides to one coin, and at being chased she'd two years of the harshest practice.

'They split up?' asked Leef.

Lamb fussed at that notch out of his ear as he looked off south. 'Some style of a disagreement?'

'Could be. Or maybe they sent 'em to circle around, check if anyone was following.'

Leef fumbled for an arrow, eyes darting about the horizon.

Lamb waved him down. 'If they'd a mind to check, they'd have seen us by now.' He kept looking south, off along the treeline towards a low ridge, the way Shy thought those three had gone. 'No. I reckon they had enough. Maybe it all went too far for 'em. Maybe they started thinking they might be the next left hanging. Either way we'll follow. Hope to catch 'em before the wheels come off this cart for good. Or off me either,' he added as he dragged himself up wincing into the wagon's seat.

'The children ain't with those three,' said Leef, turning sullen.

'No.' Lamb settled his hat back on. 'But they might point us the right way. We need to get this wagon fixed up proper, find some new oxen or get ourselves some horses. We need food. Might be those three—'

'You fucking old coward.'

There was a pause. Then Lamb nodded over at Shy. 'Me and her spent years chewing over that topic and you got naught worth adding to the conversation.' Shy looked at them, the boy stood on the ground glowering up, the big old man looking down calm and even from his seat.

Leef curled his lip. 'We need to keep after the children or—'

'Get up on the wagon, boy, or you'll be keeping after the children alone.'

Leef opened his mouth again but Shy caught him by the arm first. 'I want to catch 'em just as much as you, but Lamb's right – there's twenty men out there, bad men, and armed, and willing. There's nothing we could do.'

'We got to catch 'em sooner or later, don't we?' snapped Leef, breathing hard. 'Might as well be now while my brother and yours are still alive!'

Shy had to admit he'd a point but there was no help for it. She held his eye and said it to his face, calm but with no give. 'Get on the wagon, Leef.'

This time he did as he was told, and clambered up among their gear and sat there silent with his back to them.

Shy perched her bruised arse next to Lamb as he snapped the reins and got Scale and Calder reluctantly on the move. 'What do we do if we catch these three?' she muttered, keeping her voice down so Leef

36

wouldn't hear it. 'Chances are they're going to be armed and willing, too. Better armed than us, that's sure.'

'Reckon we'll have to be more willing, then.'

Her brows went up at that. This big, gentle Northman who used to run laughing through the wheat with Pit on one shoulder and Ro on the other, used to sit out at sunset with Gully, passing a bottle between 'em in silence for hours at a time, who'd never once laid a hand on her growing up in spite of some sore provocations, talking about getting red to the elbows like it was nothing.

Shy knew it wasn't nothing.

She closed her eyes and remembered Jeg's face after she stabbed him, bloody hat brim jammed down over his eyes, pitching in the street, still muttering, *Smoke, Smoke.* That clerk in the store, staring at her as his shirt turned black. The look Dodd had as he gawped down at her arrow in his chest. *What did you do that for?*

She rubbed her face hard with one hand, sweating of a sudden, heart banging in her ears hard as it had then, and she twisted inside her greasy clothes like she could twist free of the past. But it had good and caught her up. For Pit and Ro's sake she had to get her hands red again. She curled her fingers around the grip of her knife, took a hard breath and set her jaw. No choice then. No choice now. And for men the likes of the ones they followed no tears needed shedding.

'When we find 'em,' her voice sounding tiny in the gathering darkness, 'can you follow my lead?'

'No,' said Lamb.

'Eh?' He'd been following her lead so long she'd never thought he might find some other path.

When she looked at him, his old, scarred face was twisted like he was in pain. 'I made a promise to your mother. 'Fore she died. Made a promise to look to her children. Pit and Ro . . . and I reckon it covers you too, don't it?'

'I guess,' she muttered, far from reassured.

'I broke a lot of promises in my life. Let 'em wash away like leaves on the water.' He rubbed at his eyes with the back of one gloved hand. 'I mean to keep that one. So when we find 'em . . . you'll be following my lead. This time.'

'All right.' She could say so, if it helped him.

Then she could do what needed doing.

The Best Man

'I believe this is Squaredeal,' said Inquisitor Lorsen, frowning at his map.

'And is Squaredeal on the Superior's list?' asked Cosca.

'It is.' Lorsen made sure there was nothing in his voice that could be interpreted as uncertainty. He was the only man within a hundred miles in possession of anything resembling a cause. He could entertain no doubts.

Superior Pike had said the future was out here in the west, but the town of Squaredeal did not look like the future through Inquisitor Lorsen's eyeglass. It did not look like a present anyone with the choice would want a part in. The people scratching a living out of the Near Country were even poorer than he had expected. Fugitives and outcasts, misfits and failures. Poor enough that supporting a rebellion against the world's most powerful nation was unlikely to be their first priority. But Lorsen could not concern himself with likelihoods. Allowances, explanations and compromises were likewise unaffordable luxuries. He had learned over many painful years managing a prison camp in Angland that people had to be sorted onto the right side or the wrong, and those on the wrong could be given no mercy. He took no pleasure in it, but a better world comes at a price.

He folded his map, scored the sharp crease with the back of his thumbnail and thrust it inside his coat. 'Get your men ready to attack, General.'

'Mmmm.' Lorsen was surprised to see, on glancing sideways, that Cosca was in the midst of sipping from a metal flask.

'Isn't it a little early for spirits?' he forced through clenched teeth. It was, after all, but an hour or two after dawn.

Cosca shrugged. 'A good thing at teatime is surely a good thing at breakfast, too.'

'Likewise a bad thing,' grated Lorsen.

Heedless, Cosca took another taste and noisily smacked his lips. 'Though it might be best if you didn't mention this to Temple. He worries, bless him. He thinks of me almost as a father. He was in some extremity when I came upon him, you know—'

'Fascinating,' snapped Lorsen. 'Get your men *ready*.'

'Right away, Inquisitor.' The venerable mercenary screwed the cap back on – tightly, as if he was resolved never again to unscrew it – then began, with much stiffness and little dignity, to slither down the hillside.

He gave every impression of being a loathsome man, and one who the rude hand of time had in no way improved: inexpressibly vain, trustworthy as a scorpion and an utter stranger to morality. But after a few days with the Company of the Gracious Hand, Inquisitor Lorsen had regretfully concluded that Cosca, or the Old Man as he was fondly known, might be the best among them. His direct underlings offered no counter-arguments. Captain Brachio was a vile Styrian with an eye made always weepy by an old wound. He was a fine rider but fat as a house, and had turned self-serving indolence into a religion. Captain Jubair, a hulking, tar-black Kantic, had done the opposite and turned religion into self-serving madness. Rumour had it he was an ex-slave who had once fought in a pit. Though now far removed, Lorsen suspected some part of the pit remained within him. Captain Dimbik was at least a Union man, but a reject from the army for incompetence and a weak-chinned, petulant one at that who felt the need to affect a threadbare sash as a reminder of past glories. Though balding he had grown his hair long and, rather than merely bald, he now looked both bald and a fool.

As far as Lorsen could tell, none of them truly believed in anything but their own profit. Notwithstanding Cosca's affection, the lawyer, Temple, was the worst of the crew, celebrating selfishness, greed and underhanded manipulation as virtues, a man so slimy he could have found employment as axle grease. Lorsen shuddered as he looked across the other faces swarming about Superior Pike's huge fortified wagon: wretched leavings of every race and mongrel combination, variously scarred, diseased, besmirched, all leering in anticipation of plunder and violence.

But filthy tools can be put to righteous purposes, can they not, and achieve noble ends? He hoped it would prove so. The rebel Conthus was hiding somewhere in this forsaken land, skulking and plotting more sedition and massacre. He had to be rooted out, whatever the costs. He had to be made an example of, so that Lorsen could reap the glory of his capture. He took one last look through his eyeglass towards Squaredeal – all still quiet – before snapping it closed and working his way down the slope.

Temple was talking softly to Cosca at the bottom, a whining note in his voice which Lorsen found especially aggravating. 'Couldn't we, maybe . . . talk to the townspeople?'

'We will,' said Cosca. 'As soon as we've secured forage.'

'Robbed them, you mean.'

Cosca slapped Temple on the arm. 'You lawyers! You see straight to the heart of things!'

'There must be a better way—'

'I have spent my life searching for one and the search has led me here. We signed a contract, Temple, as you well know, and Inquisitor Lorsen means to see us keep our end of the bargain, eh, Inquisitor?'

'I will insist upon it,' grated Lorsen, treating Temple to a poisonous glare.

'If you wanted to avoid bloodshed,' said Cosca, 'you really should have spoken up beforehand.'

The lawyer blinked. 'I did.'

The Old Man raised helpless palms to indicate the mercenaries arming, mounting, drinking and otherwise preparing themselves for violence. 'Not eloquently enough, evidently. How many men have we fit to fight?'

'Four hundred and thirty-two,' said Friendly, instantly. The neckless sergeant appeared to Lorsen to have two uncanny specialities: silent menace and numbers. 'Aside from the sixty-four who chose not to join the expedition, there have been eleven deserters since we left Mulkova, and five taken ill.'

Cosca shrugged them away. 'Some wastage is inevitable. The fewer our numbers, the greater each share of glory, eh, Sworbreck?'

The writer, a ludicrous indulgence on this expedition, looked anything but convinced. 'I . . . suppose?'

'Glory is hard to count,' said Friendly.

'So true,' lamented Cosca. 'Like honour and virtue and all those other desirable intangibles. But the fewer our numbers, the greater each share of the profits too.'

'Profits can be counted.'

'And weighed, and felt, and held up to the light,' said Captain Brachio, rubbing gently at his capacious belly.

'The logical extension of the argument,' Cosca twisted the waxed points of his moustaches sharp, 'would be that all the high ideals in existence are not worth as much as a single bit.'

Lorsen shivered with the most profound disgust. 'That is a world I could not bear to live in.'

The Old Man grinned. 'And yet here you are. Is Jubair in position?'

'Soon,' grunted Brachio. 'We're waiting for his signal.'

Lorsen took a breath through gritted teeth. A crowd of madmen, awaiting the signal of the maddest.

'It is not too late.' Sufeen spoke softly so the others could not hear. 'We could stop this.'

'Why should we?' Jubair drew his sword, and saw the fear in Sufeen's eyes, and felt a pity and a contempt for him. Fear was born of arrogance. Of a belief that everything was not the will of God, and could be changed. But nothing could be changed. Jubair had accepted that many years ago. Since then, he and fear had been entire strangers to each other. 'This is what God wants,' he said.

Most men refused to see the truth. Sufeen stared at him as though he was mad. 'Why would it be God's desire to punish the innocent?'

'Innocence is not for you to judge. Nor is it given to man to understand God's design. If He desires someone saved, He need only turn my sword aside.'

Sufeen slowly shook his head. 'If that is your God, I do not believe in Him.'

'What kind of God would He be if your belief could make the slightest difference? Or mine, or anyone's?' Jubair lifted the blade, patchy sunlight shining down the long, straight edge, glinting in the many nicks and notches. 'Disbelieve this sword, it will still cut you. He is God. We all walk His path regardless.'

Sufeen shook his little head again, as though that might change the way of things. 'What priest taught you this?'

'I have seen how the world is and judged for myself how it must be.' He glanced over his shoulder, his men gathering in the wood, armour and weapons prepared for the work, faces eager. 'Are we ready to attack?'

'I've been down there.' Sufeen pointed through the brush towards Squaredeal. 'They have three constables, and two are idiots. I am not sure anything so vigorous as an attack is really necessary, are you?'

It was true there were few defences. A fence of rough-cut logs had

41

once ringed the town but had been partly torn down to allow for growth. The roof of the wooden watchtower was crusted with moss and someone had secured their washing line to one of its supports. The Ghosts had long ago been driven out of this country and the townsfolk evidently expected no other threat. They would soon discover their error.

Jubair's eyes slid back to Sufeen. 'I tire of your carping. Give the signal.'

The scout had reluctance in his eyes, and bitterness, but he obeyed, taking out the mirror and crawling to the edge of the treeline to signal Cosca and the others. That was well for him. If he had not obeyed, Jubair would most likely have killed him, and he would have been right so to do.

He tipped his head back and smiled at the blue sky through the black branches, the black leaves. He could do anything and it would be right, for he had made himself a willing puppet of God's purpose and in so doing freed himself. He alone free, surrounded by slaves. He was the best man in the Near Country. The best man in the Circle of the World. He had no fear, for God was with him.

God was everywhere, always.

How could it be otherwise?

Checking he wasn't observed, Brachio tugged the locket from his shirt and snapped it open. The two tiny portraits were blistered and faded 'til anyone else would've seen little more than smudges, but Brachio knew them. He touched those faces with a gentle fingertip and in his mind they were as they'd been when he left – soft, perfect and smiling, too long ago.

'Don't worry, my babies,' he cooed to them. 'I'll be back soon.'

A man has to choose what matters and leave everything else to the dogs. Worry about all of it and you'll do no good at all. He was the only man in the Company with any sense. Dimbik was a preening mope. Jubair and sanity were entire strangers to each other. For all his craft and cunning, Cosca was a dreamer – this shit with the biographer was proof enough of that.

Brachio was the best of them because he knew what he was. No high ideals, no grand delusions. He was a sensible man with sensible ambitions, doing what he had to, and he was content. His daughters were all that mattered. New dresses, and good food, and good dowries, and good lives. Better lives than the hell he'd lived—

'Captain Brachio!' Cosca's braying voice, loud as ever, snatched him back to the now. 'There is the signal!'

Brachio snapped the locket closed, wiped his damp eyes on the back of his fist, and straightened the bandolier that held his knives. Cosca had wedged a boot in one stirrup and now bounced once, twice, three times before dragging on his gilt saddle horn. His bulging eyes came level with it before he froze. 'Could somebody—'

Sergeant Friendly slipped a hand under Cosca's arse and twitched him effortlessly into the saddle. Once there, the Old Man spent a moment getting his wind back, then, with some effort, drew his blade and hefted it high. 'Unsheathe your swords!' He considered that. 'Or cheaper weapons! Let us . . . do some *good*!'

Brachio pointed towards the crest of the hill and bellowed, 'Ride!' With a rousing cheer the front rank spurred their horses and thundered off in a shower of dirt and dry grass. Cosca, Lorsen, Brachio and the rest, as befitted commanders, trotted after.

'That's it?' Brachio heard Sworbreck muttering as the shabby valley, and its patchy fields, and the dusty little settlement came into view below. Maybe he'd been expecting a mile-high fortress with domes of gold and walls of adamant. Maybe it would've become one by the time he'd finished writing the scene. 'It looks . . .'

'Doesn't it?' snapped Temple.

Brachio's Styrians were already streaming across the fields towards the town at a greedy gallop while Jubair's Kantics swarmed at it from the other direction, their horses black dots against a rising storm of dust.

'Look at them go!' Cosca swept off his hat and gave it a wave. 'The brave boys, eh? There's vim and brio for you! How I wish I could still charge in there with the rest of them!'

'Really?' Brachio remembered leading a charge and it had been tough, sore, dangerous work, with vim and brio both conspicuous by their absence.

Cosca thought about it for a moment, then jammed his hat back on his balding head and fumbled his sword back into its sheath. 'No. Not really.'

They made their way down at a walk.

If there had been any resistance, by the time they reached Squaredeal it was over.

A man sat in the dust by the road, bloody hands pressed to his face, blinking at Sworbreck as he rode past. A sheep pen had been

43

broken open and the sheep all needlessly slaughtered, a dog already busy among the fluffy corpses. A wagon had been tipped on its side, one wheel still creaking hopelessly around in the air while a Kantic and a Styrian mercenary argued savagely in terms neither could understand over the scattered contents. Two other Styrians were trying to kick the door of a forge from its hinges. Another had climbed onto the roof and was digging clumsily at it, using his axe like a shovel. Jubair sat on his huge horse in the centre of the street, pointing with his outsize sword and booming orders, along with some incomprehensible utterances about the will of God.

Sworbreck's pencil hovered, his fingertips worrying at its string binding, but he could think of nothing to write. In the end he scratched out, absurdly, *No heroism apparent.*

'What are those idiots up to?' murmured Temple. Several Kantics had roped a team of mules to one of the struts of the town's moss-crusted watchtower and were whipping them into a lather in an attempt to pull it down. So far they had failed.

Sworbreck had observed that many of the men found it enjoyable simply to break things. The greater the effort required in putting them back together, the greater the pleasure. As if to illustrate this rule, four of Brachio's men had knocked someone to the ground and were administering a leisurely beating while a fat man in an apron tried without success to calm them.

Sworbreck had rarely observed violence of even the mildest sort. A dispute over narrative structure between two authors of his acquaintance had turned quite ugly, but that scarcely seemed to qualify now. Finding himself suddenly dropped into the midst of battle, as it were, Sworbreck felt both cold and hot at once. Both terribly fearful and terribly excited. He shied away from the spectacle, yet longed to see more. Was that not what he had come for, after all? To witness blood and ordure and savagery at its most intense? To smell the guts drying and hear the wails of the brutalised? So he could say that he had seen it. So he could bring conviction and authenticity to his work. So he could sit in the fashionable salons of Adua and airily declaim on the dark truths of warfare. Perhaps those were not the highest of motives, but certainly not the lowest on show. He made no claim to be the best man in the Circle of the World, after all.

Merely the best writer.

Cosca swung from his saddle, grunted as he twisted the life into his venerable hips, then, somewhat stiffly, advanced on the would-be peacemaker in the apron. 'Good afternoon! I am Nicomo Cosca, captain general of the Company of the Gracious Hand.' He indicated the four Styrians, elbows and sticks rising and falling as they continued their beating. 'I see you have already met some of my brave companions.'

'Name's Clay,' said the fat man, jowls trembling with fear. 'I own the store here—'

'A store? Excellent! May we browse?' Brachio's men were already carrying supplies out by the armload under the watchful eye of Sergeant Friendly. No doubt ensuring any thieving from the Company remained within acceptable limits. Thieving outside the Company was, it appeared, entirely to be encouraged. Sworbreck shuffled his pencil around. A further note about the lack of heroism seemed superfluous.

'Take whatever you need,' said Clay, showing his flour-dusted palms. 'There's no call for violence.' A pause, broken by the crashing of glass and wood and the whimpering of the man on the ground as he was occasionally and unenthusiastically kicked. 'Might I ask why you're here?'

Lorsen stepped forward. 'We are here to root out disloyalty, Master Clay. We are here to stamp out rebellion.'

'You're . . . from the Inquisition?'

Lorsen said nothing, but his silence spoke volumes.

Clay swallowed. 'There's no rebellion here, I assure you.' Though Sworbreck sensed a falseness in his voice. Something more than understandable nervousness. 'We're not interested in politics—'

'Really?' Lorsen's profession evidently required a keen eye for deception also. 'Roll up your sleeves!'

'What?' The merchant attempted to smile, hoping to defuse the situation with soft movements of his fleshy hands, perhaps, but Lorsen would not be defused. He jerked one hard finger and two of his Practicals hastened forward: burly men, masked and hooded.

'Strip him.'

Clay tried to twist away. 'Wait—'

Sworbreck flinched as one of them punched the merchant soundlessly in his gut and doubled him up. The other ripped his sleeve off and wrenched his bare arm around. Bold script was tattooed from his wrist to his elbow, written in the Old Tongue. Somewhat faded with age, but still legible.

Lorsen turned his head slightly sideways so he could read. '*Freedom and justice*. Noble ideals, with which we could all agree. How do they

45

sit with those innocent citizens of the Union massacred by the rebels at Rostod, do you suppose?'

The merchant was only just reclaiming his breath. 'I never killed anyone in my life, I swear!' His face was beaded with sweat. 'The tattoo was a folly in my youth! Did it to impress a woman! I haven't spoken to a rebel for twenty years!'

'And you supposed you could escape your crimes here, beyond the borders of the Union?' Sworbreck had not seen Lorsen smile before, and he rather hoped he never did again. 'His Majesty's Inquisition has a longer reach than you imagine. And a longer memory. Who else in this miserable collection of hovels has sympathies with the rebels?'

'I daresay if they didn't when we arrived,' Sworbreck heard Temple mutter, 'they'll all have them by the time we leave . . .'

'No one.' Clay shook his head. 'No one means any harm, me least of—'

'Where in the Near Country are the rebels to be found?'

'How would I know? I'd tell you if I knew!'

'Where is the rebel leader Conthus?'

'Who?' The merchant could only stare. 'I don't know.'

'We will see what you know. Take him inside. Fetch my instruments. Freedom I cannot promise you, but there will be some justice here today, at least.'

The two Practicals dragged the unfortunate merchant towards his own store, now entirely plundered of anything of value. Lorsen stalked after, every bit as eager to begin his work as the mercenaries had been to begin theirs. The last of the Practicals brought up the rear, the polished wooden case containing the instruments in one hand. With the other he swung the door quietly shut. Sworbreck swallowed, and considered putting his notebook away. He was not sure he would have anything to write today.

'Why do these rebels tattoo themselves?' he muttered. 'Makes them damned easy to identify.'

Cosca was squinting up at the sky and fanning himself with his hat, making his sparse hairs flutter. 'Ensures their commitment, though. Ensures there can be no turning back. They take pride in them. The more they fight, the more tattoos they add. I saw a man hanged up near Rostod with a whole armful.' The Old Man sighed. 'But then men do all manner of things in the heat of the moment that turn out, on sober reflection, to be not especially sensible.'

Sworbreck raised his brows, licked his pencil and copied that down

46

in his notebook. A faint cry echoed from behind the closed door, then another. It made it very difficult to concentrate. Undoubtedly the man was guilty, but Sworbreck could not help placing himself in the merchant's position, and he did not at all enjoy being there. He blinked around at the banal robbery, the careless vandalism, the casual violence, looked for somewhere to wipe his sweaty palms, and ended up wiping them on his shirt. All manner of his standards were rapidly lapsing, it seemed.

'I was expecting it all to be a little more . . .'

'Glorious?' asked Temple. The lawyer had an expression of the most profound distaste on his face as he frowned towards the store.

'Glory in war is rare as gold in the ground, my friend!' said Cosca. 'Or constancy in womenfolk, for that matter! You may use that.'

Sworbreck fingered his pencil. 'Er—'

'But you should have been at the Siege of Dagoska with me! There was glory enough for a thousand tales!' Cosca took him by the shoulder and swept his other arm out as if there were a gilded legion approaching, rather than a set of ruffians dragging furniture from a house. 'The numberless Gurkish marching upon our works! We dauntless few ranged at the battlements of the towering land-walls, hurling our defiance! Then, at the order—'

'General Cosca!' Bermi hurried across the street, lurched back as a pair of horses thundered past, dragging a torn-off door bouncing after them, then came on again, wafting their dust away with his hat. 'We've a problem. Some Northern bastard grabbed Dimbik, put a—'

'Wait.' Cosca frowned. 'Some Northern bastard?'

'That's right.'

'*One* . . . bastard?'

The Styrian scrubbed at his scruffy golden locks and perched the hat on top. 'A big one.'

'How many men has Dimbik?'

Friendly answered while Bermi was thinking about it. 'One hundred and eighteen men in Dimbik's contingent.'

Bermi spread his palms, absolving himself of all responsibility. 'We do anything he'll kill the captain. He said to bring whoever's in charge.'

Cosca pressed the wrinkled bridge of his nose between finger and thumb. 'Where is this mountainous kidnapper? Let us hope he can be reasoned with before he destroys the entire Company.'

'In there.'

The Old Man examined the weathered sign above the doorway. 'Stupfer's Meat House. An unappetising name for a brothel.'

Bermi squinted up. 'I believe it's an inn.'

'Still less appetising.' With a sharp intake of breath, the Old Man stepped over the threshold, gilt spurs clinking.

It took Sworbreck's eyes a moment to adjust. Brightness glimmered through the gaps in the plank walls. Two chairs and a table had been overturned. Several mercenaries stood about, weapons including two spears, two swords, an axe and two flatbows pointed inwards towards the hostage taker, who sat at a table in the centre of the room.

He was the one man who showed no sign of nervousness. A big Northman indeed, hair hanging about his face and mingling with a patchy fur across his shoulders. He sniffed, and calmly chewed, a plate of meat and eggs before him, a fork held clumsily in his left fist in a strangely childlike manner. His right fist held a knife in a much more practised style. It was pressed against the throat of Captain Dimbik, whose bulge-eyed face was squashed helpless into the tabletop.

Sworbreck snatched a breath. Here, if not heroism, was certainly fearlessness. He had himself published controversial material on occasion, and that took admirable strength of will, but he could scarcely understand how a man could so coolly face such odds as these. To be brave among friends was nothing. To have the world against you and pick your path regardless – there is courage. He licked his pencil to scribble out a note to that effect. The Northman looked over at him and Sworbreck noticed something gleam through the lank hair. He felt a freezing shock. The man's left eye was made of metal, glimmering in the gloom of the benighted eatery, his face disfigured by a giant scar. The other eye held only a terrible willingness. As though he could hardly stop himself from cutting Dimbik's throat just to find out what would happen.

'Well, I never did!' Cosca threw up his arms. 'Sergeant Friendly, it's our old companion-in-arms!'

'Caul Shivers,' said Friendly quietly, never taking his eyes from the Northman. Sworbreck was reasonably sure that looks cannot kill, but even so he was very glad he was not standing between them.

Without taking the blade from Dimbik's throat, Shivers clumsily forked up some eggs, chewed as though none of those present had anything better to do, and swallowed. 'Fucker tried to take my eggs,' he said in a grinding whisper.

'You unmannerly brute, Dimbik!' Cosca righted one of the chairs and dropped into it opposite Shivers, wagging a finger in the captain's flushed face. 'I hope this is a lesson to you. Never take eggs from a metal-eyed man.'

Sworbreck wrote that down, although it struck him as an aphorism of limited application. Dimbik tried to speak, perhaps to make that exact point, and Shivers pressed knuckles and knife a little harder into his throat, cutting him off in a gurgle.

'This a friend of yours?' grunted the Northman, frowning down at his hostage.

Cosca gave a flamboyant shrug. 'Dimbik? He's not without his uses, but I'd hardly say he's the best man in the Company.'

It was difficult for Captain Dimbik to make his disagreement known with the Northman's fist pressed so firmly into his throat he could scarcely breathe, but he did disagree, and most profoundly. He was the only man in the Company with the slightest care for discipline, or dignity, or proper behaviour, and look where it had landed him. Throttled by a barbarian in a wilderness slop-house.

To make matters worse, or at any rate no better, his commanding officer appeared perfectly willing to trade carefree smalltalk with his assailant. 'Whatever are the chances?' Cosca was asking. 'Running into each other after all these years, so many hundreds of miles from where we first met. How many miles, would you say, Friendly?'

Friendly shrugged. 'Wouldn't like to guess.'

'I thought you went back to the North?'

'I went back. I came here.' Evidently Shivers was not a man to embroider the facts.

'Came for what?'

'Looking for a nine-fingered man.'

Cosca shrugged. 'You could cut one off Dimbik and save yourself a search.'

Dimbik spluttered and twisted, tangled with his own sash, and Shivers ground the point of the knife into his neck and forced helplessly back against the tabletop.

'It's one particular nine-fingered man I'm after,' came his gravelly voice, without the least hint of excitement at the situation. 'Heard a rumour he might be out here. Black Calder's got a score to settle with him. And so have I.'

'You didn't see enough scores settled back in Styria? Revenge is bad for business. And for the soul, eh, Temple?'

'So I hear,' said the lawyer, just visible out of the corner of Dimbik's eye. How Dimbik hated that man. Always agreeing, always confirming, always looking like he knew better, but never saying how.

'I'll leave the souls to the priests,' came Shivers' voice, 'and the business to the merchants. Scores I understand. Fuck!' Dimbik whimpered, expecting the end. Then there was a clatter as the Northman's fumbled fork fell on the table, egg spattering the floor.

'You might find that easier with both hands.' Cosca waved at the mercenaries around the walls. 'Gentlemen, stand down. Shivers is an old friend and not to be harmed.' The various bows, blades and cudgels drifted gradually from readiness. 'Do you suppose you could release Captain Dimbik now? One dies and all the others get restless. Like ducklings.'

'Ducklings got more fight in 'em than this crowd,' said Shivers.

'They're mercenaries. Fighting is the last thing on their minds. Why don't you fall in with us? It would be just like old times. The camaraderie, the laughter, the excitement!'

'The poison, the treachery, the greed? I've found I work better alone.' The pressure on Dimbik's neck was suddenly released. He was taking a whooping breath when he was lifted by the collar and flung reeling across the room. His legs kicked helplessly as he crashed into one of his fellows, the two of them going down tangled with a table.

'I'll let you know if I run into any nine-fingered men,' said Cosca, pressing hands to knees, baring his yellowed teeth and levering himself to his feet.

'Do that.' Shivers calmly turned the knife that had been at the point of ending Dimbik's life to cutting his meat. 'And shut the door on your way out.'

Dimbik slowly stood, breathing hard, one hand to the sore graze left on his throat, glaring at Shivers. He would have greatly liked to kill this animal. Or at any rate to order him killed. But Cosca had said he was not to be harmed and Cosca, for better or worse, though mostly worse, was his commanding officer. Unlike the rest of this chaff, Dimbik was a soldier. He took such things as respect, and obedience, and procedure seriously. Even if no one else did. It was especially important that he take them seriously because no one else did. He wriggled his rumpled sash back into position, noting with disgust that the worn silk was now sullied with egg. What a fine sash it had been once. One would never know. How he missed the army. The real army, not this twisted mockery of the military life.

He was the best man in the Company, and he was treated with scorn. Given the smallest command, the worst jobs, the meanest share of the plunder. He jerked his threadbare uniform smooth, produced his comb and rearranged his hair, then strode from the scene of his shame and out into the street with the stiffest bearing he could manage.

In the lunatic asylum, he supposed, the one sane man looks mad.

Sufeen could smell burning on the air. It put him in mind of other battles, long ago. Battles that had needed fighting. Or so it seemed, now. He had gone from fighting for his country, to fighting for his friends, to fighting for his life, to fighting for a living, to . . . whatever this was. The men who had been trying to demolish the watchtower had abandoned the project and were sitting around it with bad grace, passing a bottle. Inquisitor Lorsen stood near them, with grace even poorer.

'Your business with the merchant is concluded?' asked Cosca as he came down the steps of the inn.

'It has,' snapped Lorsen.

'And what discoveries?'

'He died.'

A pause. 'Life is a sea of sorrows.'

'Some men cannot endure stern questioning.'

'Weak hearts caused by moral decay, I daresay.'

'The outcome is the same,' said the Inquisitor. 'We have the Superior's list of settlements. Next comes Lobbery, then Averstock. Gather the Company, General.'

Cosca's brow furrowed. It was the most concern Sufeen had seen him display that day. 'Can we not let the men stay overnight, at least? Some time to rest, enjoy the hospitality of the locals—'

'News of our arrival must not reach the rebels. The righteous cannot delay.' Lorsen managed to say it without a trace of irony.

Cosca puffed out his cheeks. 'The righteous work hard, don't they?'

Sufeen felt a withering helplessness. He could hardly lift his arms, he was suddenly so tired. If only there had been righteous men to hand, but he was the nearest thing to one. The best man in the Company. He took no pride in that. Best maggot in the midden would have made a better boast. He was the only man there with the slightest shred of conscience. Except Temple, perhaps, and Temple spent his every waking moment trying to convince himself and everyone else that he had no conscience at all. Sufeen watched him, standing slightly behind

51

Cosca, a little stooped as if he was hiding, fingers fussing, trying to twist the buttons off his shirt. A man who could have been anything, struggling to be nothing. But in the midst of this folly and destruction, the waste of one man's potential hardly seemed worth commenting on. Could Jubair be right? Was God a vengeful killer, delighting in destruction? It was hard at that moment to argue otherwise.

The big Northman stood on the stoop in front of Stupfer's Meat House and watched them mount up, great fists clenched on the rail, afternoon sun glinting on that dead metal ball of an eye.

'How are you going to write this up?' Temple was asking.

Sworbreck frowned down at his notebook, pencil hovering, then carefully closed it. 'I may gloss over this episode.'

Sufeen snorted. 'I hope you brought a great deal of gloss.'

Though it had to be conceded, the Company of the Gracious Hand had conducted itself with unusual restraint that day. They put Squaredeal behind them with only mild complaints about the poor quality of plunder, leaving the merchant's body hanging naked from the watchtower, a sign about his neck proclaiming his fate a lesson to the rebels of the Near Country. Whether the rebels would hear the lesson, and if they did what they would learn from it, Sufeen could not say. Two other men hung beside the trader.

'Who were they?' asked Temple, frowning back.

'The young one was shot running away, I think. I'm not sure about the other.'

Temple grimaced, and twitched, and fidgeted with a frayed sleeve. 'What can we do, though?'

'Only follow our consciences.'

Temple rounded on him angrily. 'For a mercenary you talk a lot about conscience!'

'Why concern yourself unless yours bothers you?'

'As far as I can tell, you're still taking Cosca's money!'

'If I stopped, would you?'

Temple opened his mouth, then soundlessly shut it and scowled off at the horizon, picking at his sleeve, and picking, and picking.

Sufeen sighed. 'God knows, I never claimed to be a good man.' A couple of the outlying houses had been set ablaze, and he watched the columns of smoke drift up into the blue. 'Merely the best in the Company.'

All Got a Past

The rain came hard. It had filled the wagon ruts and the deep-sucked prints of boot and hoof until they were one morass and the main street lacked only for a current to be declared a river. It drew a grey curtain across the town, the odd lamp dimmed as through a mist, orange rumours dancing ghostly in the hundred thousand puddles. It fell in mud-spattering streams from the backed-up gutters on the roofs, and the roofs with no gutters at all, and from the brim of Lamb's hat as he hunched silent and soggy on the wagon's seat. It ran in miserable beads down the sign hung from an arch of crooked timbers that proclaimed this leavings of a town to be Averstock. It soaked into the dirt-speckled hides of the oxen, Calder proper lurching lame now in a back leg and Scale not much better off. It fell on the horses tethered to the rail before the shack that excused itself for a tavern. Three unhappy horses, their coats turned dark by the wet.

'That them?' asked Leef. 'Those their horses?'

'That's them,' said Shy, cold and clammy in her leaking coat as a woman buried.

'What we going to do?' Leef was trying to hide the tense note in his voice and falling well short.

Lamb didn't answer him. Not right away. Instead he leaned close to Shy, speaking soft. 'Say you're caught between two promises, and you can't keep one without breaking the other. What do you do?'

To Shy's mind that verged on the whimsical, considering the task in hand. She shrugged, shoulders chafing in her wet shirt. 'Keep the one most needs keeping, I guess.'

'Aye,' he muttered, staring across that mire of a street. 'Just leaves on the water, eh? Never any choices.' They sat a moment longer, no one doing a thing but getting wetter, then Lamb turned in his seat. 'I'll go in first. Get the oxen settled then the two of you follow, keeping

53

easy.' He swung from the wagon, boots splashing into the mud. 'Unless you've a mind to stay here. Might be best all round.'

'I'll do my part,' snapped Leef.

'You know what your part might be? You ever kill a man?'

'Have you?'

'Just don't get in my way.' Lamb was different somehow. Not hunched any more. Bigger. Huge. Rain pattering on the shoulders of his coat, hint of light down one side of his rigid frown, the other all in darkness. 'Stay out of my way. You got to promise me that.'

'All right,' said Leef, giving Shy a funny look.

'All right,' said Shy.

An odd thing for Lamb to say. You could find meaner lambs than him at every lambing season. But men can be strange that way, with their pride. Shy had never had much use for pride herself. So she guessed she could let him talk his talk, and try and work up to it, and go in first. Worked all right when they had crops to sell, after all. Let him draw the eyes while she slipped up behind. She slid her knife into her sleeve, watching the old Northman struggling to make it across the boggy street with both boots still on, arms wide for balance.

When Lamb faltered, she could do what needed doing. Done it before, hadn't she, with lighter reasons and to men less deserving? She checked her knife would slip clear of her wet sleeve all right, heart thumping in her skull. She could do it again. Had to do it again.

The tavern looked a broke-down hovel from outside and a step indoors revealed no grand deception. The place made Shy come over nostalgic for Stupfer's Meat House – a state of mind she'd never thought to entertain. A sorry tongue of fire squirmed in a hearth blackened past the point of rescue, a sour fragrance of woodsmoke and damp and rank bodies unknown to soap. The counter was a slab of old wood full of splits, polished by years of elbows and warped up in the middle. The Tavern-Keep, or maybe in this place the Hovel-Keep, stood over it wiping out cups.

Narrow and low, the place was still far from full, which on a night foul as this was a poor showing. A set of five with two women in the group Shy took for traders, and not prosperous ones, hunched about some stew at the table furthest from her. A bony man sat alone with only a cup and a wore-out look for company. She recognised that from the black-spotted mirror she used to have and figured him for a farmer. Next table a fellow slumped in a fur coat so big it near drowned him, a shock of grey hair above, a hat with a couple of greasy feathers in the band and a half-empty bottle on the wood in front of him. Opposite, upright as a judge at trial, sat an old Ghost woman with a broken sideways nose, grey hair all bound up with what looked like the tatters of an old Imperial flag, and a face so deep-lined you could've used it for a plate rack. If your plates hadn't all been burned up along with your mirror and everything else you owned, that is.

Shy's eyes crawled to the last members of the merry company like she wanted to pretend they weren't there at all. But they were. Three men, huddled to themselves. They looked like Union men, far as you could tell where anyone was born once they were worn down by a few seasons in the dirt and weather of the Near Country. Two were young, one with a mess of red hair and a twitchy way like he'd a fly down his back. The other had a handsome shape to his face, far as Shy could tell standing to his side, a sheepskin coat cinched in with a fancy metal-studded belt. The third was older, bearded and with a tall hat, weather-stained, cocked to the side like he thought a lot of himself. Which most men do, of course, in proportion inverse to their value.

He had a sword – Shy saw the battered brass tip of the sheath poking out the slit in his coat. Handsome had an axe and a heavy knife tucked in his belt along with a coil of rope. Red Hair's back was to her so she couldn't tell for certain, but no doubt he was entertaining a blade or two as well.

She could hardly believe how ordinary they were. How everyday and dirty humdrum and like a thousand other drifters she'd seen floating through Squaredeal. She watched Handsome slide his hand back and tuck the thumb in that fancy belt so his fingers dangled. Just like anyone might, leaning against a counter after a long ride. Except his ride had led right through her burned-out farm, right through her smashed-up hopes, and carried her brother and sister off into who knew what darkness.

She set her jaw hard and eased into the room, sticking to the shadows, not hiding exactly but making no spectacle of herself neither. Wasn't hard, because Lamb was doing the opposite, much against his usual grain. He'd strolled up to the other end of the counter and was leaning over it with his big fists bunched on the split wood.

'Nice night you've laid on for us,' he was saying to the Tavern-Keep, shedding his hat and making a fuss of flapping the water off it so anyone with a mind to look up was watching him. Only the old Ghost's deep-set eyes followed Shy as she slunk around the walls, and she'd nothing to say about it.

'Little on the rainy side, no?' said the Keep.

'Comes down any harder you could have a sideline in a ferry across the street.'

The Keep eyed his guests with scant delight. 'I could do with some sort o' business turns a profit. Hear tell there's crowds coming through the Near Country but they ain't crowding through here. You looking for a drink?'

Lamb pulled his gloves off and tossed them careless on the counter. 'I'll take a beer.'

The tender reached for a metal cup polished bright by his wiping.

'Not that one.' Lamb pointed at a great pottery mug, old-fashioned and dusty on a high shelf. 'I like something I can feel the heft on.'

'We talking about cups or women now?' asked the Keep as he stretched up to fetch it.

'Why not both?' Lamb was grinning. How could he smile, now? Shy's eyes flickered to the three men down the other end of the counter, bent quiet over their drinks.

'Where you in from?' asked the Keep.

'East.' Lamb shrugged his sodden coat off. 'North and east, near Squaredeal.'

One of the three men, the one with the red hair, looked over at Lamb, and sniffed, and looked away.

'That's a distance. Might be a hundred mile.'

'Might be more, the route I've took, and on a bloody ox-cart, too. My old arse is ground to sausage-meat.'

'Well, if you're thinking of heading further west I'd think again. Lots of folks going that way, gold-hungry. I hear they've got the Ghosts all stirred up.'

'That a fact?'

'A certainty, friend,' threw out the man in the fur coat, sticking his head up like a tortoise from its shell. He'd about the deepest, most gravel-throated voice Shy ever heard, and she'd given ear to some worn-down tones in her time. 'They's stirred up all across the Far Country like you trod on an ant's nest. Riled up and banded up and out looking for ears, just like the old days. I heard Sangeed's even got his sword drawed again.'

'Sangeed?' The Keep wriggled his head around like his collar was too tight.

'The Emperor of the Plains his self.' Shy got the sense the old bastard was quite enjoying his scaremongering. 'His Ghosts massacred a whole fellowship o' prospectors out on the dusty not two weeks ago. Thirty men, maybe. Took their ears and their noses and I shouldn't wonder got their cocks besides.'

'What the hell do they *do* with them?' asked the farmer, staring at the old Ghost woman and giving a shudder. She didn't comment. Didn't even move.

'If you're fixed on going west I'd take plenty of company, and make sure that company has a little good humour and a lot o' good steel, so I would.' And the old-timer sank back into his fur coat.

'Good advice.' Lamb lifted that big mug and took a slow swallow. Shy swallowed with him, suddenly desperate for a beer of her own. Hell, but she wanted to get out of there. Get out or get on with it. But somehow Lamb was just as patient now as when he did the ploughing. 'I ain't sure yet exactly where I'm headed, though.'

'What brought you this far?' asked the Keep.

Lamb had started rolling up his damp shirtsleeves, thick muscles in his grey-haired forearms squirming. 'Followed some men out here.'

Red Hair looked over again, a flurry of twitches slinking through his shoulder and up his face, and this time he kept looking. Shy let the knife slide from her sleeve, out of sight behind her arm, fingers hot and tacky round the grip.

'Why'd you do that?' asked the Keep.

'They burned my farm. Stole my children. Hanged my friend.' Lamb spoke like it wasn't much to comment on, then raised his mug.

The place had fallen so silent of a sudden you could hear him swallow. One of the traders had turned to look over, brow all crinkled up with worry. Tall Hat reached for his cup and Shy saw the tendons start from the back of his hand, he was gripping on so tight. Leef picked out that moment to ease through the door and hover on the threshold, wet and pale and not knowing what to do with himself. But everyone was too fixed on Lamb to pay him any mind.

'Bad men, these, with no scruple,' he went on. 'They been stealing children all across the Near Country and leaving folk hanging in their wake. Might be a dozen I've buried the last few days.'

'How many of the bastards?'

'About twenty.'

'Do we need to get a band up and seek 'em out?' Though the Keep looked like he'd far rather stay and wipe his cups some more, and who could blame him?

Lamb shook his head. 'No point. They'll be long gone.'

57

'Right. Well. Reckon justice'll be catching up with 'em, sooner or later. Justice is always following, they say.'

'Justice can have what's left when I'm done.' Lamb finally had his sleeves rolled how he wanted and turned sideways, leaning easy against the counter, looking straight at those three men at its far end. Shy hadn't known what to expect, but not this, not Lamb just grinning and chatting like he'd never known a worry. 'When I said they've gone that ain't quite all the truth. Three broke off from the rest.'

'That a fact?' Tall Hat spoke up, snatching the conversation from the Keep like a thief snatching a purse.

Lamb caught his eye and held it. 'A certainty.'

'Three men, you say?' Handsome's fussing hand crept round his belt towards his axe. The mood of the place had shifted fast, the weight of coming violence hanging heavy as a storm cloud in that little room.

'Now look,' said the Keep, 'I don't want no trouble in my—'

'I didn't want no trouble,' said Lamb. 'It blew in anyway. Trouble's got a habit that way.' He pushed his wet hair out of his face, and his eyes were wide open and bright, bright, mouth open too, breathing fast, and he was smiling. Not like a man working his way up to a hard task. Like a man enjoying getting to a pleasant one, taking his time about it like you might over a fine meal, and of a sudden Shy saw all those scars anew, and felt this coldness creeping up her arms and down her back and every hair on her standing.

'I tracked those three,' said Lamb. 'Picked up their trail and two days I've followed it.'

Another breathless pause, and the Keep took a step back, cup and cloth still limp in his hands, the ghost of a smile still clinging to his face but the rest all doubt. The three had turned to face Lamb, spreading out a little, backs to Shy, and she found herself easing forwards like she was wading through honey, out of the shadows towards them, tingling fingers shifting around the knife's handle. Every moment was a drawn-out age, breath scratching, catching in every throat.

'Where'd the trail lead?' asked Tall Hat, voice cracking at the end and tailing off.

Lamb's smile spread wider. The smile of a man got exactly what he wanted on his birthday. 'The ends o' your fucking legs.'

Tall Hat twitched his coat back, cloth flapping as he went for his sword.

Lamb flung the big mug at him underhand. It bounced off his head and sent him tumbling in a shower of beer.

A chair screeched as the farmer tried to stumble up and ended tripping over it.

The red-haired lad took a step back, making room or just from shock and Shy slipped her knife around his neck and pressed the flat into it, folding him tight with the other arm.

Someone shouted.

Lamb crossed the room in one spring. He caught Handsome's wrist just as he pulled his axe free, wrenched it up and with the other hand snatched the knife from his fancy belt and rammed it in his groin, dragging up the blade, ripping him wide open, blood spraying the pair of them. He gave a gurgling scream appalling loud in that narrow space and dropped to his knees, eyes goggling as he tried to hold his guts in. Lamb smashed him across the back of the head with the pommel of the knife, cut his scream off and laid him out flat.

One of the trader women jumped up, hands over her mouth.

The red-haired one Shy had a hold of squirmed and she squeezed him tighter and whispered, 'Shush,' grinding the point of her knife into his neck.

Tall Hat floundered up, hat forgotten, blood streaming from the gash the mug had made across his forehead. Lamb caught him around the neck, lifting him easily as if he was made of rags, and smashed his face into the counter, again with a crunch like a breaking pot, again head flopping like a doll's, and blood spotted the Keep's apron, and the wall behind him, and the ceiling, too. Lamb lifted the knife high, flash of his face still stretched wide in that crazy grin, then the blade was a metal blur, through the man's back and with an almighty crack left a split down the length of the bar, splinters flying. Lamb left him nailed there, knees just clear of the floor and his boots scraping at the boards, blood tip-tapping around them like a spilled drink.

All took no longer than Shy would've needed to take three good breaths, if she hadn't been holding hers the while. She was hot now, and dizzy, and the world was too bright. She was blinking. Couldn't quite get a hold on what had happened. She hadn't moved. She didn't move. No one did. Only Lamb, walking forward, eyes gleaming with tears and one side of his face black-dashed and speckled and his bared teeth glistening in his mad smile and each breath a soft growl in his throat like a lover's.

Red Hair whimpered, 'Fuck, fuck,' and Shy pushed the flat of the knife harder into his neck and shushed him up again. He'd a big blade halfway to a sword tucked in his belt and with her free hand she slid that out. Then Lamb was looming over the shrinking pair of them, his head near brushing the low rafters, and he twisted a fistful of the lad's shirt and jerked him out of Shy's limp grip.

'Talk to me.' And he hit the lad across the face, open-handed but hard enough to knock him down if he hadn't been held up.

'I . . .' muttered the lad.

Lamb slapped him again, the sound loud as a clap, the traders up the far end flinching at it but not a one moving. 'Talk.'

'What d'you—'

'Who was in charge?'

'Cantliss. That's his name.' The lad started blathering, words tumbling over each other all slobbery like he couldn't say them fast enough. 'Grega Cantliss. Didn't know how bad a crew they was, just wanted to get from here to there and make a bit of money. I was in the ferrying business back east and one day the rain come up and the ferry got swep' away and—' Slap. 'We didn't want it, you got to believe—' Slap. 'There's some evil ones in with 'em. A Northman called Blackpoint, he shot an old man with arrows. They laughed at it.'

'See me laughing?' said Lamb, cuffing him again.

The red-haired lad held up one useless, shaking hand. 'I didn't laugh none! We didn't want no part of all them killings so we split off! Supposed to be just some robbing, Cantliss told us, but turned out it was children we was stealing, and—'

Lamb cut him off with a slap. 'Why'd he take the children?' And he set him talking with another, the lad's freckled face cut and swelling down one side, blood smearing his nose.

'Said he had a buyer for 'em, and we'd all be rich men if we got 'em there. Said they weren't to be hurt, not a hair on their heads. Wanted 'em perfect for the journey.'

Lamb slapped him again, opening another cut. 'Journey where?'

'To Crease, he said, to begin with.'

'That's up at the head of the Sokwaya,' said Shy. 'Right the way across the Far Country.'

'Cantliss got a boat waiting. Take him upriver . . . upriver . . .'

'To Crease and then where?'

The red-haired lad had slumped in half a faint, lids fluttering. Lamb slapped him again, both sides, shook him by his shirt. 'To Crease and then where?'

'Didn't say. Not to me. Maybe to Taverner.' Looking towards the

60

man nailed to the counter with the knife handle sticking out his back. Shy didn't reckon he'd be telling any tales now.

'Who's buying children?' asked Lamb.

Red Hair drunkenly shook his swollen head. Lamb slapped him again, again, again. One of the trader women hid her face. The other stared, standing rigid. The man beside her dragged her back down into her chair.

'Who's buying?'

'Don't know,' words mangled and bloody drool dangling from his split lip.

'Stay there.' Lamb let the lad go and crossed to Tall Hat, his boots in a bloody puddle, reached around and unbuckled his sword, took a knife from his coat. Then he rolled Handsome over with his foot, left him staring wonky-eyed at the ceiling, a deal less handsome with his insides on the outside. Lamb took the bloody rope from his belt, walked to the red-haired lad and started tying one end around his neck while Shy just watched, numb and weak all over. Weren't clever knots he tied, but good enough, and he jerked the lad towards the door, following along without complaint like a beaten dog.

Then they stopped. The Keep had come around the counter and was standing in the doorway. Just goes to show you never can quite figure what a man will do, or when. He was holding tight to his wiping cloth like it might be a shield against evil. Shy didn't reckon it'd be a very effective one, but she'd some high respect for his guts. Just hoped Lamb didn't end up adding them to Handsome's, scattered bloody on the boards.

'This ain't right,' said the Keep.

'How's you being dead going to make it any righter?' Lamb's voice flat and quiet like it was no kind of threat, just a question. He didn't have to scream it. Those two dead men were doing it for him.

The Keep's eyes darted around but no heroes leaped to his side. All looked scared as if Lamb was death himself come calling. Except the old Ghost woman, sat tall in her chair just watching, and her companion in the fur coat, who still had his boots crossed and, without any quick movements, was pouring himself another drink.

'Ain't right.' But the Keep's voice was weak as watered beer.

'It's right as it's getting,' said Lamb.

'We should put a panel together and judge him proper, ask some—'

Lamb loomed forward. 'All you got to ask is do you want to be in my way.' The Keep shrank back and Lamb dragged the lad past.

Shy hurried after, suddenly unfroze, passing Leef loose-jawed in the doorway.

Outside the rain had slacked to a steady drizzle. Lamb was hauling Red Hair across the mired street towards the arch of crooked timbers the sign hung from. High enough for a mounted man to pass under. Or for one on foot to dangle from.

'Lamb!' Shy hopped down from the tavern's porch, boots sinking to the ankles. 'Lamb!' He weighed the rope then tossed it over the crossbar. 'Lamb!' She struggled across the street, mud sucking at her feet. He caught the loose end of the rope and jerked the slack out, the red-haired lad stumbling as the noose went tight under his chin, bloated face showing dumb like he hadn't worked out yet where he was headed.

'Ain't we seen enough folk hanged?' called Shy as she slopped up. Lamb didn't answer, didn't look at her, just wound the free end of the rope about one forearm.

'It ain't right,' she said. Lamb took a sniff and set himself to haul the lad into the air. Shy snatched hold of the rope by the lad's neck and started sawing at it with the short-sword. It was sharp. Didn't take a moment to cut it through.

'Get running.'

The lad blinked at her.

'Run, you fucking idiot!' She kicked the seat of his trousers and he sloshed a few steps and went over on his face, struggled up and floundered away into the darkness, still with his rope collar.

Shy turned back to Lamb. He was staring at her, stolen sword in one hand, loose length of rope in the other. But like he was hardly seeing her. Like he was hardly him, even. How could this be the man who'd bent over Ro when she had the fever, and sung to her? Sung badly, but sung still, face all wrinkled with care? Now she looked in those black eyes and suddenly this dread crept on her like she was looking into the void. Standing on the edge of nothing and it took every grain of courage she had not to run.

'Bring them three horses over!' she snapped at Leef, who'd wandered out onto the porch with Lamb's coat and hat in his hands. 'Bring 'em now!' And he hopped off to do it. Lamb just stood, staring after the red-haired lad, the rain starting to wash the blood off his face. He took hold of the saddle bow when Leef led the biggest horse over, started to swing himself up and the horse shied, and kicked out, and Lamb gave a grunt as he lost his grip and went over backwards, stirrup flapping as he caught it with a clutching hand, splashing down hard in the mud on his side. Shy knelt by him as he struggled to his hands and knees.

'You hurt?'

He looked up at her and there were tears in his eyes, and he whispered, 'By the dead, Shy. By the dead.' She did her best to drag him up, a bastard of a task since he was a corpse-weight of a sudden. When they finally got him standing he pulled her close by her coat. 'Promise me,' he whispered. 'Promise me you won't get in my way again.'

'No.' She laid a hand on his scarred cheek. 'I'll hold your bridle for you, though.' And she did, and the horse's face, too, and whispered calm words to it and wished there was someone to do the same to her while Lamb dragged himself up into the saddle, slow and weary, teeth gritted like it was an effort. When he got up he sat hunched, right hand on the reins, left hand holding his coat closed at his neck. He looked an old man again. Older than ever. An old man with a terrible weight and worry across his hunched shoulders.

'He all right?' Leef's voice not much above a whisper, like he was scared of being overheard.

'I don't know,' said Shy. Lamb didn't seem like he could hear even, wincing off to the black horizon, almost one with the black sky now.

'You all right?' Leef whispered to her.

'Don't know that either.' She felt the world was all broken up and washed away and she was drifting on strange seas, cut loose from land. 'You?'

Leef just shook his head, and looked down at the mud with eyes all round.

'Best get what we need from the wagon and mount up, eh?'

'What about Scale and Calder?'

'They're blown and we've got to move. Leave 'em.'

The wind dashed rain in her face and she pulled her hat-brim down and set her jaw hard. Her brother and her sister, that's what she'd fix on. They were the stars she'd set her course by, two points of light in the black. They were all that mattered.

So she heeled her new horse and led the three of them out into the gathering night. They hadn't gone far when Shy heard noises beyond the wind and slowed to a walk. Lamb brought his horse about and drew the sword. An old cavalry sword, long and heavy, sharpened on one side.

'Someone's following!' said Leef, fumbling with his bow.

'Put that away! You'll more likely shoot yourself in this light. Or worse yet, me.' Shy heard hooves on the track behind them, and a wagon, too, a glimmer of torchlight through tree-trunks. Folk come out from Averstock to chase them? The Keep firmer set on justice than he'd seemed? She slid the short-sword out by its horn handle, metal glinting with the last red touch of twilight. Shy had no notion what to expect any more. If Juvens himself had trotted from the dark and bid them a good evening she'd have shrugged and asked which way he was headed.

'Hold up!' came a voice as deep and rough as Shy ever heard. Not Juvens himself. The man in the fur coat. He came into sight now, riding with a torch in his hand. 'I'm a friend!' he said, slowing to a walk.

'You're no friend o' mine,' she said back.

'Let's put that right as a first step, then.' He delved into a saddlebag and tossed a half-full bottle across to Shy. A wagon trundled up with a pair of horses pulling. The old Ghost woman had the reins, creased face as empty as it had been at the inn, a singed old chagga pipe gripped between her teeth, not smoking it, just chewing it.

They all sat a moment, in the dark, then Lamb said, 'What do you want?'

The stranger reached up slow and tipped his hat back. 'No need to spill more blood tonight, big man, we're no enemies o' yours. And if I was I reckon I'd be reconsidering that position about now. Just want to talk, is all. Make a proposal that might benefit the crowd of us.'

'Speak your piece, then,' said Shy, pulling the cork from the bottle with her teeth but keeping the sword handy.

'Then I will. My name's Dab Sweet.'

'What?' said Leef 'Like that scout they tell all the stories of?'

'Exactly like. I'm him.'

Shy paused in her drinking. 'You're Dab Sweet? Who was first to lay eyes on the Black Mountains?' She passed the bottle across to Lamb, who passed it straight to Leef, who took a swig, and coughed.

Sweet gave a dry chuckle. 'The mountains saw me first, I reckon, but the Ghosts been there a few hundred years before, and the Imperials before that, maybe, and who knows who back when before the Old Time? Who's to say who's first to anything out in this country?'

'But you killed that great red bear up at the head of the Sokwaya with no more than your hands?' asked Leef, passing the bottle back to Shy.

'I been to the head of the Sokwaya times enough, that's true, but I

64

take some offence at that particular tale.' Sweet grinned, friendly lines spreading out across his weathered face. 'Fighting even a little bear with your hands don't sound too clever to me. My preferred approach to bears – alongside most dangers – is to be where they ain't. But there's all kind of strange water flowed by down the years, and my memory ain't all it was, I'll confess that, too.'

'Maybe you misremembered your name,' said Shy, and took another swig. She had a hell of a thirst on her.

'Woman, I'd accept that for a strong possibility if I didn't have it stamped into my old saddle here.' And he gave the battered leather a friendly pat. 'Dab Sweet.'

'Felt sure from what I've heard you'd be bigger.'

'From what I've heard I should be half a mile high. Folk like to talk. And when they do, ain't really up to me what size I grow to, is it?'

'What's this old Ghost to you?' asked Shy.

So slow and solemn it might've been the eulogy at a funeral, the Ghost said, 'He's my wife.'

Sweet gave his grinding laugh again. 'Sometimes it do feel that way, I'll concede. That there Ghost is Crying Rock. We been up and down every speck o' the Far Country and the Near Country and plenty o' country don't got no names. Right now we're signed on as scouts, hunters and pilots to take a Fellowship of prospectors across the plains to Crease.'

Shy narrowed her eyes. 'That so?'

'From what I heard back there, you'll be headed the same way. You'll be finding no keelboat of your own, not one stopping off to pick you up leastways, and that means out on the lone and level by hoof or wheel or boot. With the Ghosts on the rampage you'll be needing company.'

'Meaning yours.'

'I may not be throttling any bears on the way, but I know the Far Country. Few better. Anyone's going to get you to Crease with your ears still on your head, it's me.'

Crying Rock cleared her throat, shifting her dead pipe from one side of her mouth to the other with her tongue.

'It's me and Crying Rock.'

'And what'd possess you to do us such a favour?' asked Shy. Specially after what they'd just seen.

Sweet scratched at his stubbly beard. 'This expedition got put together before the trouble started on the plains and we've got all

65

sorts along. A few with iron in 'em, but not enough experience and too much cargo.' He was looking over at Lamb with an estimating expression. The way Clay might've sized up a haul of grain. 'Now there's trouble in the Far Country we could use another man don't get sickly at the sight o' blood.' His eyes moved over to Shy. 'And I've a sense you can hold a blade steady too when it's called for.'

She weighed the sword. 'I can just about keep myself from dropping one. What's your offer?'

'Normally folk bring a skill to the company or pay their way. Then everyone shares supplies, helps each other out where they can. The big man—'

'Lamb.'

Sweet raised a brow. 'Really?'

'One name's good as another,' said Lamb.

'I won't deny it, and you go free. I've stood witness to your usefulness. You can pay a half-share, woman, and a full share for the lad, that comes to . . .' Sweet crunched his face up, working the sums.

Shy might've seen two men killed and saved another that night, her stomach still sick and her head still spinning from it, but she wasn't going to let a deal go wandering past.

'We'll all be going free.'

'What?'

'Leef here's the best damn shot with a bow you ever saw. He's an asset.'

Sweet looked less than convinced. 'He is?'

'I am?' muttered Leef.

'We'll all be going free.' Shy took another swig and tossed the bottle back. 'It's that way or no way.'

Sweet narrowed his eyes as he took his own long, slow drink, then he looked over at Lamb again, sat still in the darkness, just the glimmer of the torch in the corners of his eyes, and sighed. 'You like to drive a bargain, don't you?'

'My preferred approach to bad deals is to be where they ain't.'

Sweet gave another chuckle, and he nosed his horse forward, and he stuck the bottle in the crook of his arm, pulled off his glove with his teeth and slapped his hand into hers. 'Deal. Reckon I'm going to like you, girl. What's your name?'

'Shy South.'

Sweet raised that brow again. 'Shy?'

'It's a name, old man, not a description. Now hand me back that bottle.'

And so they headed off into the night, Dab Sweet telling tales in his grinding bass, talking a lot and saying nothing and laughing a fair bit too just as though they hadn't left two men murdered not an hour before, passing the bottle about 'til it was done and Shy tossed it away into the night with a warmth in her belly. When Averstock was just a few lights behind she reined her horse back to a walk and dropped in beside the closest thing she'd ever had to a father.

'Your name hasn't always been Lamb, has it?'

He looked at her, and then away. Hunching down further. Pulling his coat tighter. Thumb slipping out between his fingers over and over, rubbing at the stump of the middle one. The missing one. 'We all got a past,' he said.

Too true, that.

The Stolen

The children were left in a silent huddle each time Cantliss went to round up more. Rounding 'em up, that's what he called it, like they was just unclaimed cattle and no killing was needed. No doing what they'd done at the farm. No laughing about it after when they brought more staring little ones. Blackpoint was always laughing, a lopsided laugh with two of the front teeth missing. Like he'd never heard a joke so funny as murder.

At first Ro tried to guess at where they were. Maybe even leave some sign for those who must be coming after. But the woods and the fields gave way to just a scrubby emptiness in which a bush was quite the landmark. They were headed west, she gathered that much, but no more. She had Pit to think about and the other children too and she tried to keep them fed and cleaned and quiet the best she could.

The children were all kinds, none older than ten. There'd been twenty-one 'til that boy Care had tried to run and Blackpoint came back from chasing him all bloody. So they were down to twenty and no one tried to run after that.

There was a woman with them called Bee who was all right even if she did have scars on her arms from surviving the pox. She held the children sometimes. Not Ro, 'cause she didn't need holding, and not Pit, 'cause he had Ro to hold, but some of the younger ones, and she whispered at them to hush when they cried 'cause she was scared as piss of Cantliss. He'd hit her time to time, and after when she was wiping the blood from her nose she'd make excuses for him. She'd say how he'd had a hard life and been abandoned by his folks and beaten as a child and other such. That sounded to Ro like it should make you slower rather'n quicker to beat others, but she guessed everyone's got their excuses. Even if they're feeble ones.

The way Ro saw it, Cantliss had nothing in him worth a damn.

He rode up front in his fancy tailored clothes like he was some big man with important doings to be about, 'stead of a child-thief and murderer and lowest of the low, aiming to make himself look special by gathering even lower scum about him for a backdrop. At night he'd get a great big fire built 'cause he loved to watch things burn, and he'd drink, and once he'd set to drinking his mouth would get a bitter twist and he'd complain. About how life weren't fair and how he'd been tricked out of an inheritance by a banker and how things never seemed to go his way.

They stopped for a day beside wide water flowing and Ro asked him, 'Where are you taking us?' and he just said, 'Upstream.' A keelboat had tied off at the bank and upstream they'd gone, poled and roped and rowed by a set of men all sinew while the flat land slid by, and way, way off north through the haze three blue peaks showed against the sky.

Ro thought at first it would be a mercy, not to have to ride no more, but now all they could do was sit. Sit under a canopy up front and watch the water and the land drift past and feel their old lives dwindle further and further off, the faces of the folks they'd known harder to bring to mind, until the past all felt like a dream and the future an unknown nightmare.

Blackpoint would get off now and again with his bow, a couple of the others with him, and they'd come back later with meat they'd hunted up. Rest of the time he sat smoking, and watched the children, and grinned for hours at a spell. When Ro saw the missing teeth in that grin she thought about him shooting Gully and leaving him swinging there on the tree full of arrows. When she thought about that she wanted to cry, but she knew she couldn't because she was one of the oldest and the little ones were looking to her to be strong and that's what she meant to be. She reckoned if she didn't cry that was her way of beating them. A little victory, maybe, but Shy always said a win's a win.

Few days on the boat and they saw something burning far off across the grass, plumes of smoke trickling up and fading in that vastness of above and the black dots of birds circling, circling. The chief boatman said they should turn back and he was worried about Ghosts and Cantliss just laughed, and shifted the knife in his belt, and said there was things closer at hand for a man to worry on and that was all the conversation.

That evening one of the men had shaken her wakeful and started talking about how she reminded him of someone, smiling though there was something wrong in his eye and his breath sour with spirits, and he'd caught hold of her arm and Pit had hit him hard as he could which wasn't that hard. Bee woke and screamed and Cantliss came and dragged the man away and Blackpoint kicked him 'til he stopped moving and tossed him in the river. Cantliss shouted at the others to leave the goods well alone and just use their fucking hands, 'cause no bastard would be costing him money, you could bet on that.

She knew she should never have said nothing about it but she couldn't help herself then and she'd burst out, 'My sister's following, you can bet on that if you want to bet! She'll find you out!'

She'd thought Cantliss might hit her then but all he'd done was look at her like she was the latest of many afflictions fate had forced upon him and said, 'Little one, the past is gone, like to that water flowing by. The sooner you put it from your pinprick of a mind the happier you'll be. You got no sister now. No one's following.' And he went off to stand on the prow, tutting as he tried to rub the spotted blood out of his fancy clothes with a damp rag.

'Is it true?' Pit asked her. 'Is no one following?'

'Shy's following.' Ro never doubted it because, you'd best believe, Shy was not a person to be told how things would be. But what Ro didn't say was that she half-hoped Shy wasn't following, because she didn't want to see her sister shot through with arrows, and didn't really know what she could do about all this, 'cause even with the three that left, and the two that took most of the horses off to sell when they got on the boat, and the one that Blackpoint killed, Cantliss still had thirteen men. She didn't see what anyone could do about it.

She wished Lamb was with them, though, because he could've smiled and said, 'It's all right. Don't worry none,' like he did when there was a storm and she couldn't sleep. That would've been fine.

II
FELLOWSHIP

'What a wild life, and what a fresh kind
of existence!
But, ah, the discomforts!'
Henry Wadsworth Longfellow

Conscience and the Cock-Rot

'**P**raying?'

Sufeen sighed. 'No, I am kneeling here with my eyes closed cooking porridge. Yes, I am praying.' He opened one eye a crack and aimed it at Temple. 'Care to join me?'

'I don't believe in God, remember?' Temple realised he was picking at the hem of his shirt again and stopped himself. 'Can you honestly say He ever raised a finger to help you?'

'You don't have to *like* God to believe. Besides, I know I am past help.'

'What do you pray for, then?'

Sufeen dabbed his face with his prayer cloth, eyeing Temple over the fringe. 'I pray for you, brother. You look as if you need it.'

'I've been feeling . . . a little jumpy.' Temple realised he was worrying at his sleeve now, and tore his hand away. For God's sake, would his fingers not be happy until they had unravelled every shirt he possessed? 'Do you ever feel as if there is a dreadful weight hanging over you . . .'

'Often.'

'. . . and that it might fall at any moment . . .'

'All the time.'

'. . . and you just don't know how to get out from under it?'

'But you *do* know.' There was a pause while they watched each other. 'No,' said Temple, taking a step away. 'No, no.'

'The Old Man listens to you.'

'No!'

'You could talk to him, get him to stop this—'

'I tried, he didn't want to hear!'

'Perhaps you didn't try hard enough.' Temple clapped his hands over his ears and Sufeen dragged them away. 'The easy way leads nowhere!'

'You talk to him, then!'

'I'm just a scout!'

'I'm just a lawyer! I never claimed to be a righteous man.'

'No righteous man does.'

Temple tore himself free and strode off through the trees. 'If God wants this stopped, let Him stop it! Isn't He all-powerful?'

'Never leave to God what you can do yourself!' he heard Sufeen call, and hunched his shoulders as though the words were sling-stones. The man was starting to sound like Kahdia. Temple only hoped things didn't end the same way.

Certainly no one else in the Company appeared keen to avoid violence. The woods were alive with eager fighting men, tightening worn-out straps, sharpening weapons, stringing bows. A pair of Northmen were slapping each other to pink-faced heights of excitement. A pair of Kantics were at prayers of their own, kneeling before a blessing stone they had placed with great care on a tree-stump, the wrong way up. Every man takes God for his ally, regardless of which way he faces.

The towering wagon had been drawn up in a clearing, its hardworking horses at their nosebags. Cosca was draped against one of its wheels, outlining his vision for the attack on Averstock to an assembly of the Company's foremost members, switching smoothly between Styrian and common and with expressive gestures of hand and hat for the benefit of those who spoke neither. Sworbreck crouched over a boulder beside him with pencil poised to record the great man at work.

'. . . so that Captain Dimbik's Union contingent can sweep in from the west, alongside the river!'

'Yes, sir,' pronounced Dimbik, sweeping a few well-greased hairs back into position with a licked little finger.

'Brachio will simultaneously bring his men charging in from the east!'

'Simulta what now?' grunted the Styrian, tonguing at a rotten tooth.

'At the same time,' said Friendly.

'Ah.'

'And Jubair will thrust downhill from the trees, completing the encirclement!' The feather on Cosca's hat thrashed as it achieved a metaphorical total victory over the forces of darkness.

'Let no one escape,' ground out Lorsen. 'Everyone must be examined.'

'Of course.' Cosca pushed out his lower jaw and scratched thoughtfully at his neck, where a faint speckling of pink rash was appearing.

'And all plunder declared, assessed and properly noted so that it may be divided according to the Rule of Quarters. Any questions?'

'How many men will Inquisitor Lorsen torture to death today?' demanded Sufeen in ringing tones. Temple stared at him open-mouthed, and he was not alone.

Cosca went on scratching. 'I was thinking of questions relating to our tactics—'

'As many as is necessary,' interrupted the Inquisitor. 'You think I revel in this? The world is a grey place. A place of half-truths. Of half-wrongs and half-rights. Yet there are things worth fighting for, and they must be pursued with all our vigour and commitment. Half-measures achieve nothing.'

'What if there are no rebels down there?' Sufeen shook off Temple's frantic tugging at his sleeve. 'What if you are wrong?'

'Sometimes I will be,' said Lorsen simply. 'Courage lies in bearing the costs. We all have our regrets, but not all of us can afford to be crippled by them. Sometimes it takes small crimes to prevent bigger ones. Sometimes the lesser evil is the greater good. A man of principle must make hard choices and suffer the consequences. Or you could sit and cry over how unfair it all is.'

'Works for me,' said Temple with a laugh of choking falseness.

'It will not work for me.' Sufeen wore a strange expression, as if he was looking through the gathering to something in the far distance, and Temple felt an awful foreboding. Even more awful than usual. 'General Cosca, I want to go down into Averstock.'

'So do we all! Did you not hear my address?'

'Before the attack.'

'Why?' demanded Lorsen.

'To talk to the townsfolk,' said Sufeen. 'To give them a chance to surrender any rebels.' Temple winced. God, it sounded ridiculous. Noble, righteous, courageous and ridiculous. 'To avoid what happened in Squaredeal—'

Cosca was taken aback. 'I thought we were remarkably well behaved in Squaredeal. A company of kittens could have been no gentler! Would you not say so, Sworbreck?'

The writer adjusted his eyeglasses and stammered out, 'Admirable restraint.'

'This is a poor town.' Sufeen pointed into the trees with a faintly shaking finger. 'They have nothing worth taking.'

Dimbik frowned as he scraped at a stain on his sash with a fingernail. 'You can't know that until you look.'

'Just give me a chance. I'm begging you.' Sufeen clasped his hands and looked Cosca in his eye. 'I'm praying.'

'Prayer is arrogance,' intoned Jubair. 'The hope of man to change the will of God. But God's plan is set and His words already spoken.'

'Fuck Him, then!' snapped Sufeen.

Jubair mildly raised one brow. 'Oh, you will find it is God who does the fucking.'

There was a pause, the metallic notes of martial preparations drifting between the tree-trunks along with the morning birdsong.

The Old Man sighed and rubbed at the bridge of his nose. 'You sound determined.'

Sufeen echoed Lorsen's words. 'A man of principle must make hard choices and suffer the consequences.'

'And if I agree to this, what then? Will your conscience continue to prick at our arses all the way across the Near Country and back? Because that could become decidedly tiresome. Conscience can be painful but so can the cock-rot. A grown-up should suffer his afflictions privately and not allow them to become an inconvenience for friends and colleagues.'

'Conscience and the cock-rot are hardly equivalent,' snapped Lorsen.

'Indeed,' said Cosca, significantly. 'The cock-rot is rarely fatal.'

The Inquisitor's face had turned even more livid than usual. 'Am I to understand you are considering this folly?'

'You are, and I am. The town is surrounded, after all, no one is going anywhere. Perhaps this can make all our lives a little easier. What do you think, Temple?'

Temple blinked. 'Me?'

'I am looking at you and using your name.'

'Yes, but . . . me?' There was a good reason why he had stopped making hard choices. He always made the wrong ones. Thirty years of scraping through the poverty and fear between disasters to end up in this fix was proof enough of that. He looked from Sufeen, to Cosca, to Lorsen, and back. Where was the greatest profit? Where the least danger? Who was actually . . . right? It was damned difficult to pick the easy way from this tangle. 'Well . . .'

Cosca puffed out his cheeks. 'The man of conscience and the man of doubts. God help us indeed. You have one hour.'

'I must protest!' barked Lorsen.

'If you must, you must, but I won't be able to hear you with all this noise.'

'What noise?'

Cosca stuck his fingers in his ears. 'Blah-lee-lah-lee-lah-lee-lah-lee-lah . . . !'

He was still doing it as Temple hurried away through the towering trees after Sufeen, their boots crunching on fallen sticks, rotten cones, browned pine needles, the sound of the men fading to leave only the rustling of the branches high above, the twitter and warble of birds.

'Have you gone mad?' hissed Temple, struggling to keep up.

'I have gone sane.'

'What will you do?'

'Talk to them.'

'To who?'

'Whoever will listen.'

'You won't put the world right with talk!'

'What will you use, then? Fire and sword? Papers of Engagement?'

They passed the last group of puzzled sentries, Bermi giving a questioning look from among them and Temple offering only a helpless shrug in return, then they were out into the open, sunlight suddenly bright on their faces. The few dozen houses of Averstock clung to a curve in the river below. 'Houses' was being generous to most of them. They were little better than shacks, with dirt between. They were no better than shacks, with shit between, and Sufeen was already striding purposefully downhill in their direction.

'What the hell is he up to?' hissed Bermi from the shadowy safety of the trees.

'I think he's following his conscience,' said Temple.

The Styrian looked unconvinced. 'Conscience is a shitty navigator.'

'I've often told him so.' Yet Sufeen showed no sign of slowing in his pursuit of it. 'Oh God,' muttered Temple, wincing up at the blue heavens. 'Oh God, oh God.' And he bounded after, grass thrashing about his calves, patched with little white flowers the name of which he did not know.

'Self-sacrifice is not a noble thing!' he called as he caught up. 'I have seen it, and it's an ugly, pointless thing, and nobody thanks you for it!'

'Perhaps God will.'

'If there is a God, He has bigger things to worry about than the likes of us!'

Sufeen pressed on, looking neither left or right. 'Go back, Temple. This is not the easy way.'

'That I fucking realise!' He caught a fistful of Sufeen's sleeve. 'Let's both go back!'

Sufeen shook him off and carried on. 'No.'

'Then I'm coming!'

'Good.'

'Fuck!' Temple hurried to catch up again, the town getting steadily closer and looking less and less like a thing he wished to risk his life for. 'What's your plan? There is a plan, yes?'

'There is . . . part of one.'

'That's not very reassuring.'

'Reassuring you was not my aim.'

'Then you have *fucking* succeeded, my friend.' They passed under the arch of rough-trimmed timbers that served for a gate, a sign creaking beneath it that read *Averstock*. They skirted around the boggiest parts of the boggy main street, between the slumping little buildings, most of warped pine, all on one storey and some barely that.

'God, this is a poor place,' muttered Sufeen.

'It puts me in mind of home,' whispered Temple. Which was far from a good thing. The sun-baked lower city of Dagoska, the seething slums of Styria, the hard-scrabble villages of the Near Country. Every nation was rich in its own way, but poor in the same.

A woman skinned a fly-blown carcass that might have been rabbit or cat and Temple got the feeling she was not bothered which. A pair of half-naked children mindlessly banged wooden swords together in the street. A long-haired ancient whittled a stick on the stoop of one of the few stone-built houses, a sword that was definitely not a toy leaning against the wall behind him. They all watched Temple and Sufeen with sulky suspicion. Some shutters clattered closed and Temple's heart started to pound. Then a dog barked and he nearly shat, sweat standing cold on his brow as a stinking breeze swept past. He wondered if this was the stupidest thing he had ever done in a life littered with idiocy. High on the list, he decided, and still with ample time to bully its way to the top.

Averstock's glittering heart was a shed with a tankard painted on a board above the entrance and a luckless clientele. A pair who looked like a farmer and his son, both red-haired and bony, the boy with a satchel over his shoulder, sat at one table eating bread and cheese far from the freshest. A tragic fellow decked in fraying ribbons was bent over a cup. Temple took him for a travelling bard, and hoped he specialised in sad songs because the sight of him was enough to bring on tears. A woman was cooking over a fire in the blackened hearth, and spared Temple one sour look as he entered.

The counter was a warped slab with a fresh split down its length and a large stain worked into the grain that looked unpleasantly like blood. Behind it the Tavern-Keep was carefully wiping cups with a rag.

'It's not too late,' whispered Temple. 'We could just choke down a cup of whatever piss they sell here, walk straight on through and no harm done.'

'Until the rest of the Company get here.'

'I meant no harm to *us* . . .' But Sufeen was already approaching the counter leaving Temple to curse silently in the doorway for a moment before following with the greatest reluctance.

'What can I get you?' asked the Keep.

'There are some four hundred mercenaries surrounding your town, with every intention of attacking,' said Sufeen, and Temple's hopes of avoiding catastrophe were dealt a shattering blow.

There was a pregnant pause. Heavily pregnant.

'This hasn't been my best week,' grunted the Keep. 'I'm in no mood for jokes.'

'If we were set on laughter I think we could come up with better,' muttered Temple.

Sufeen spoke over him. 'They are the Company of the Gracious Hand, led by the infamous mercenary Nicomo Cosca, and they have been employed by his Majesty's Inquisition to root out rebels in the Near Country. Unless they receive your fullest cooperation, your bad week will get a great deal worse.'

They had the Keep's attention now. They had the attention of every person in the tavern and were not likely to lose it. Whether that was a good thing remained very much to be seen, but Temple was not optimistic. He could not remember the last time he had been.

'And if there is rebels in town?' The farmer leaned against the counter beside them, pointedly rolling up his sleeve. There was a tattoo on his sinewy forearm. *Freedom, liberty, justice.* Here, then, was the scourge of the mighty Union, Lorsen's insidious enemy, the terrifying rebel in the flesh. Temple looked into his eyes. If this was the face of evil, it was a haggard one.

Sufeen chose his words carefully. 'Then they have less than an hour to surrender, and spare the people of this town bloodshed.'

The bony man gave a smile missing several of the teeth and all of the joy. 'I can take you to Sheel. He can choose what to believe.' Clearly he did not believe any of it. Or perhaps even entirely comprehend.

'Take us to Sheel, then,' said Sufeen. 'Good.'

'Is it?' muttered Temple. The feeling of impending disaster was almost choking him now. Or perhaps that was the rebel's breath. He certainly had the breath of evil, if nothing else.

'You'll have to give up your weapons,' he said.

'With the greatest respect,' said Temple, 'I'm not convinced—'

'Hand 'em over.' Temple was surprised to see the woman at the fire had produced a loaded flatbow and was pointing it unwavering at him.

'I am convinced,' he croaked, pulling his knife from his belt between finger and thumb. 'It's only a very small one.'

'Ain't the size,' said the bony man as he plucked it from Temple's hand, 'so much as where you stick it.' Sufeen unbuckled his sword-belt and he took that, too. 'Let's go. And it'd be an idea not to make no sudden moves.'

Temple raised his palms. 'I try always to avoid them.'

'You made one when you followed me down here, as I recall,' said Sufeen.

'And how I regret it now.'

'Shut up.' The bony rebel herded them towards the door, the woman following at a cautious distance, bow levelled. Temple caught the blue of a tattoo on the inside of her wrist. The boy lurched along at the back, one of his legs in a brace and his satchel clutched tight to his chest. It might have been a laughable procession without the threat of death. Temple had always found the threat of death to be a sure antidote to comedy.

Sheel turned out to be the old man who had watched them walk into town a few moments before. What happy times those seemed now. He stiffly stood, waving away a fly, then, almost as an afterthought, even more stiffly bent for his sword before stepping from his porch.

'What's to do, Danard?' he asked in a voice croaky with phlegm.

'Caught these two in the inn,' said the bony man.

'Caught?' asked Temple. 'We walked in and asked for you.'

'Shut up,' said Danard.

'You shut up,' said Sufeen.

Sheel did something between vomiting and clearing his throat, then effortfully swallowed the results. 'Let's all see if we can split the difference between talking too much and not at all. I'm Sheel. I speak for the rebels hereabouts.'

'All four of them?' asked Temple.

'There were more.' He looked sad rather than angry. He looked all squeezed out and, one could only hope, ready to give up.

'My name is Sufeen, and I have come to warn you—'

'We're surrounded, apparently,' sneered Danard. 'Surrender to the Inquisition and Averstock stands another day.'

Sheel turned his watered-down grey eyes on Temple. 'You'd have to agree it's a far-fetched story.'

Easy, hard, it mattered not what crooked path they'd followed here, there was only one way through this now, and that was to convince this man of what they said. Temple fixed him with his most earnest expression. The one with which he had convinced Kahdia he would not steal again, with which he had convinced his wife that everything would be well, with which he had told Cosca he could be trusted. Had they not all believed him?

'My friend is telling you the truth.' He spoke slowly, carefully, as if there were only the two of them there. 'Come with us and we can save lives.'

'He's lying.' The bony man poked Temple in the side with the pommel of Sufeen's sword. 'There ain't no one up there.'

'Why would we come here just to lie?' Temple ignored the prodding and kept his eyes fixed on the old man's wasted face. 'What would we gain?'

'Why do it at all?' asked Sheel.

Temple paused for a moment, his mouth half-open. Why not the truth? At least it was novel. 'We got sick of not doing it.'

'Huh.' That appeared to touch something. The old man's hand drifted from his sword-hilt. Not surrender. A long way from surrender, but something. 'If you're telling the truth and we give up, what then?'

Too much truth is always a mistake. Temple stuck to earnest. 'The people of Averstock will be spared, that I promise you.'

The old man cleared his throat again. God, his lungs sounded bad. Could it be that he was starting to believe? Could it be that this might actually work? Might they not only live out the day, but save lives into the bargain? Might he do something that Kahdia would have been proud of? The thought made Temple proud, just for a moment. He ventured a smile. When did he last feel proud? Had he ever?

81

Sheel opened his mouth to speak, to concede, to surrender . . . then paused, frowning off over Temple's shoulder.

A sound carried on the wind ever so faintly. Hooves. Horses' hooves. Temple followed the old rebel's gaze and saw, up on the grassy side of the valley, a rider coming down at a full gallop. Sheel saw him, too, and his forehead furrowed with puzzlement. More riders appeared behind the first, pouring down the slope, now a dozen, now more.

'No,' muttered Temple.

'Temple!' hissed Sufeen.

Sheel's eyes widened. 'You bastards!'

Temple held up his hand. 'No!'

He heard grunting in his ear, and when Temple turned to tell Sufeen this was hardly the time saw his friend and Danard lurching about in a snarling embrace. He stared at them, open mouthed.

They should have had an hour.

Sheel clumsily drew his sword, metal scraping, and Temple caught his hand before he could swing it and butted him in the face.

There was no thought, it just happened.

The world jolted, Sheel's crackly breath warm on his cheek. They tussled and tore and a fist hit the side of Temple's face and made his ears ring. He butted again, felt nose-bone pop against his forehead and suddenly Sheel was stumbling back and Sufeen was standing beside Temple with the sword in his hands, and looking very surprised that he had it.

Temple stood a moment, trying to work out how they had got here. Then what they should do now.

He heard a flatbow string, the whisper of a bolt passing, maybe.

Then he saw Danard struggling up. 'You fucking—' And his head came apart.

Temple blinked, blood across his face. Saw Sheel reaching for a knife. Sufeen stabbed at him and the old man gave a croaking cough as the metal slid into his side, clutched at himself, face twisted, blood leaking between his fingers.

He muttered something Temple couldn't understand, and tried to draw his knife again, and the sword caught him just above the eye. 'Oh,' he said, blood washing out of the big slit in his forehead and down his face. 'Oh.' Drops sprinkled the mud as he staggered sideways, bounced off his own porch and fell, rolling over, back arching, one hand flapping.

Sufeen stared down at him. 'We were going to save people,' he muttered. There was blood on his lips. He dropped to his knees and the sword bounced out of his limp hand.

Temple grabbed at him. 'What . . .' The knife he had handed over to Danard was buried in Sufeen's ribs to the grip, his shirt quickly turning black. A very small knife, by most standards. But more than big enough.

That dog was still barking. Sufeen toppled forward onto his face. The woman with the flatbow had gone. Was she reloading somewhere, would she pop up ready to shoot again? Temple should probably have taken cover.

He didn't move.

The sound of hooves grew louder. Blood spread out in a muddy puddle around Sheel's split head. The boy slowly backed away, broke into a waddling trot, dragging his crippled leg after. Temple watched him go.

Then Jubair rounded the side of the inn, mud flicking from the hooves of his great horse, sword raised high. The boy tried to turn again, lurched one more desperate step before the blade caught him in the shoulder and spun him across the street. Jubair tore past, shouting something. More horsemen followed. People were running. Screaming. Faint over the rumble of hooves.

They should have had an hour.

Temple knelt beside Sufeen, reached out to turn him over, check his wounds, tear off a bandage, do those things Kahdia had taught him, long ago. But as soon as he saw Sufeen's face he knew he was dead.

Mercenaries charged through the town, howling like a pack of dogs, waving weapons as though they were the winning cards in a game. He could smell smoke.

Temple picked up Sheel's sword, notched blade red-speckled now, stood and walked over to the lame boy. He was crawling towards the inn, one arm useless. He saw Temple and whimpered, clutching handfuls of muck with his good hand. His satchel had come open and coins were spilling out. Silver scattered in the mud.

'Help me,' whispered the boy. 'Help me!'

'No.'

'They'll kill me! They'll—'

'Shut your fucking mouth!' Temple poked the boy in the back with the sword and he gulped, and cowered, and the more he cowered the more Temple wanted to stick the sword through him. It was surprisingly light. It would have been so easy to do. The boy saw it in his face and whined and cringed more, and Temple poked him again.

'Shut your mouth, fucker! Shut your mouth!'

'Temple! Are you all right?' Cosca loomed over him on his tall grey. 'You're bleeding.'

Temple looked down and saw his shirtsleeve was ripped, blood trickling down the back of his hand. He was not sure how that had happened. 'Sufeen is dead,' he mumbled.

'Why do the Fates always take the best of us . . . ?' But Cosca's attention had been hooked by the glint of money in the mud. He held out a hand to Friendly and the sergeant helped him down from his gilt saddle. The Old Man stooped, fishing one of the coins up between two fingers, eagerly rubbing the muck away, and he produced that luminous smile of which only he was capable, good humour and good intentions radiating from his deep-lined face.

'Yes,' Temple heard him whisper.

Friendly tore the satchel from the boy's back and jerked it open. A faint jingle spoke of more coins inside.

Thump, thump, thump, as a group of mercenaries kicked at the door of the inn. One hopped away cursing, pulling his filthy boot off to nurse his toes. Cosca squatted down. 'Where did this money come from?'

'We went on a raid,' muttered the boy. 'All went wrong.' There was a crash as the inn's door gave, a volley of cheering as men poured through the open doorway.

'All went wrong?'

'Only four of us made it back. So we had two dozen horses to trade. Man called Grega Cantliss bought 'em off us, up in Greyer.'

'Cantliss?' Shutters shattered as a chair was flung through the window of the inn and tumbled across the street beside them. Friendly frowned towards the hole it left but Cosca did not so much as twitch. As though there was nothing in the world but him, and the boy, and the coins. 'What sort of man was this Cantliss? A rebel?'

'No. He had nice clothes. Some crazy-eyed Northman with him. He took the horses and he paid with those coins.'

'Where did he get them?'

'Didn't say.'

Cosca peeled up the sleeve on the boy's limp arm to show his tattoo. 'But he definitely wasn't one of you rebels?'

The boy only shook his head.

'That answer will not make Inquisitor Lorsen happy.' Cosca gave a nod so gentle it was almost imperceptible. Friendly put his hands around the boy's neck. That dog was still barking somewhere. Bark, bark, bark. Temple wished someone would shut it up. Across the street three Kantics were savagely beating a man while a pair of children watched.

'We should stop them,' muttered Temple, but all he did was sit down in the road.

'How?' Cosca had more of the coins in his hand, was carefully sorting through them. 'I'm a general, not a God. Many generals get mixed up on that point, but I was cured of the misapprehension long ago, believe me.' A woman was dragged screaming from a nearby house by her hair. 'The men are upset. Like a flood, it's safer to wash with the current than try to dam it up. If they don't have a channel for their anger, why, it could flow anywhere. Even over me.' He grunted as Friendly helped him up to standing. 'And it's not as though any of this was my fault, is it?'

Temple's head was throbbing. He felt so tired he could hardly move. 'It was mine?'

'I know you meant well.' Flames were already hungrily licking at the eaves of the inn's roof. 'But that's how it is with good intentions. Hopefully we've all learned a lesson here today.' Cosca produced a flask and started thoughtfully unscrewing the cap. 'I, about indulging you. You, about indulging yourself.' And he upended it and steadily swallowed.

'You're drinking again?' muttered Temple.

'You fuss too much. A nip never hurt anyone.' Cosca sucked the last drops out and tossed the empty flask to Friendly for a refill. 'Inquisitor Lorsen! So glad you could join us!'

'I hold you responsible for this debacle!' snapped Lorsen as he reined his horse up savagely in the street.

'It's far from my first,' said the Old Man. 'I shall have to live with the shame.'

'This hardly seems a moment for jokes!'

Cosca chuckled. 'My old commander Sazine once told me you should laugh every moment you live, for you'll find it decidedly difficult afterward. These things happen in war. I've a feeling there was some confusion with the signals. However carefully you plan, there are always surprises.' As if to illustrate the point, a Gurkish mercenary capered across the street wearing the bard's beribboned jacket. 'But this boy was able to tell us something before he died.' Silver glinted in Cosca's gloved palm. 'Imperial coins. Given to these rebels by a man called . . .'

'Grega Cantliss,' put in Friendly.

'That was it, in the town of Greyer.'

Lorsen frowned hard. 'Are you saying the rebels have Imperial funding? Superior Pike was very clear that we avoid any entanglements with the Empire.'

Cosca held a coin up to the light. 'You see this face? Emperor Ostus the Second. He died some fourteen hundred years ago.'

'I did not know you were such a keen devotee of history,' said Lorsen.

'I am a keen devotee of money. These are ancient coins. Perhaps the rebels stumbled upon a tomb. The great men of old were sometimes buried with their riches.'

'The great men of old do not concern us,' said Lorsen. 'It's today's rebels we're after.'

A pair of Union mercenaries were screaming at a man on his knees. Asking him where the money was. One of them hit him with a length of wood torn from his own shattered door and when he got groggily up there was blood running down his face. They asked him again. They hit him again, slap, slap, slap.

Sworbreck, the biographer, watched them with one hand over his mouth. 'Dear me,' he muttered between his fingers.

'Like everything else,' Cosca was explaining, 'rebellion costs money. Food, clothes, weapons, shelter. Fanatics still need what the rest of us need. A little less of it, since they have their high ideals to nourish them, but the point stands. Follow the money, find the leaders. Greyer appears on Superior Pike's list anyway, does it not? And perhaps this Cantliss can lead us to this . . . Contus of yours.'

Lorsen perked up at that. 'Conthus.'

'Besides.' Cosca gestured at the rebels' corpses with a loose waft of his sword that nearly took Sworbreck's nose off. 'I doubt we'll be getting any further clues from these three. Life rarely turns out the way we expect. We must bend with the circumstances.'

Lorsen gave a disgusted grunt. 'Very well. For now we follow the money.' He turned his horse about and shouted to one of his Practicals. 'Search the corpses for tattoos, damn it, find me any rebels still alive!'

Three doors down, a man had climbed onto the roof of a house and was stuffing bedding down the chimney while others clustered about the door. Cosca, meanwhile, was holding forth to Sworbreck. 'I share your distaste for this, believe me. I have been closely involved in the burning of some of the world's most ancient and beautiful cities. You should have seen Oprile in flames, it lit the sky for miles! This is scarcely a career highlight.'

Jubair had dragged some corpses into a line and was expressionlessly cutting their heads off. Thud, thud, thud, went his heavy sword. Two of his men had torn apart the arch over the road and were whittling the ends of the timbers to points. One was already rammed into the ground and had Sheel's head on it, mouth strangely pouting.

'Dear me,' muttered Sworbreck again.

'Severed heads,' Cosca was explaining, 'never go out of fashion. Used sparingly and with artistic sensibility, they can make a point a great deal more eloquently than those still attached. Make a note of that. Why aren't you writing?'

An old woman had crawled from the burning house, face stained with soot, and now some of the men had formed a circle and were shoving her tottering back and forth.

'What a waste,' Lorsen was bitterly complaining to one of his Practicals. 'How fine this land could be with the proper management. With firm governance, and the latest techniques of agriculture and forestry. They have a threshing machine now in Midderland which can do in a day with one operator what used to take a dozen peasants a week.'

'What do the other eleven do?' asked Temple, his mouth seeming to move by itself.

'Find other employment,' snarled the Practical.

Behind him another head went up on its stick, long hair stirring. Temple did not recognise the face. The smoked-out house was burning merrily now, flames whipping, air shimmering, the men backing off with hands up against the heat, letting the old woman crawl away.

'Find other employment,' muttered Temple to himself.

Cosca had Brachio by the elbow and was shouting in his ear over the noise. 'You need to round up your men! We must head north and east towards Greyer and seek out news of this Grega Cantliss.'

'It might take a while to calm 'em.'

'One hour, then I ask Sergeant Friendly to bring in the stragglers, in pieces if necessary. Discipline, Sworbreck, is vital to a body of fighting men!'

Temple closed his eyes. God, it stank. Smoke, and blood, and fury, and smoke. He needed water. He turned to ask Sufeen for some and saw his corpse in the mud a few strides away. A man of principle must make hard choices and suffer the consequences.

'We brought your horse down,' said Cosca, as though that should make up for at least some of the day's reverses. 'If you want my advice, keep busy. Put this place at your back as swiftly as possible.'

'How do I forget this?'

'Oh, that's too much to ask. The trick is in learning to just . . .' Cosca stepped carefully back as one of the Styrians rode whooping past, a man's corpse bouncing after his horse. 'Not care.'

'I have to bury Sufeen.'

'Yes, I suppose so. But quickly. We have daylight and not a moment to waste. Jubair! Put that down!' And the Old Man started across the street, waving his sword. 'Burn anything that still needs burning and mount up! We're moving east!'

When Temple turned, Friendly was wordlessly offering him a shovel. The dog had finally stopped barking. A big Northman, a tattooed brute from past the Crinna, had spiked its head on a spear beside the heads of the rebels and was pointing up at it, chuckling.

Temple took Sufeen by the wrists and hauled him onto his shoulder, then up and over the saddle of his scared horse. Not an easy task, but easier than he had expected. Living, Sufeen had been big with talk and movement and laughter. Dead he was hardly any weight at all.

'Are you all right?' Bermi, touching him on the arm.

His concern made Temple want to cry. 'I'm not hurt. But Sufeen is dead.' There was justice.

Two of the Northmen had smashed open a chest of drawers and were fighting over the clothes inside, leaving torn cloth scattered across the muddy street. The tattooed man had tied a stick below the dog's head and was carefully arranging a best shirt with a frilly front upon it, face fixed with artist's concentration.

'You sure you're all right?' Bermi called after him from the midst of the rubbish-strewn street.

'Never better.'

Temple led the horse out of town, then off the track, or the two strips of rutted mud that passed for one, the sounds of barked orders, and burning, and the men reluctantly making ready to leave fading behind him to be replaced by chattering water. He followed the river upstream until he found a pleasant enough spot between two trees, their hanging boughs trailing in the water. He slid Sufeen's body down and rolled it over onto its back.

'I'm sorry,' he said, and tossed the shovel into the river. Then he pulled himself up into his saddle.

Sufeen would not have cared where he was laid out, or how. If there was a God, he was with Him now, probably demanding to know why He had so conspicuously failed as yet to put the world to rights. North and east, Cosca had said. Temple turned his horse towards the west, and gave it his heels, and galloped off, away from the greasy pall of smoke rising from the ruins of Averstock.

Away from the Company of the Gracious Hand. Away from Dimbik, and Brachio, and Jubair. Away from Inquisitor Lorsen and his righteous mission.

He had no destination in mind. Anywhere but with Nicomo Cosca.

New Lives

'And there's the Fellowship,' said Sweet, reining in with fore-arms on saddle horn and fingers dangling.

The wagons were strung out for a mile or so along the bottom of the valley. Thirty or more, some covered with stained canvas, some painted bright colours, dots of orange and purple and twinkling gilt jumping from the dusty brown landscape. Specks of walkers along-side them, riders up ahead. At the back came the beasts – horses, spare oxen, a good-sized herd of cattle – and following hard after a swelling cloud of dust, tugged by the breeze and up into the blue to announce the Fellowship's coming to the world.

'Will you look at that!' Leef kicked his horse forward, standing in his stirrups with a grin all the way across his face. 'D'you see *that*?' Shy hadn't seen him smile before and it made him look young. More boy than man, which he probably was. Made her smile herself.

'I see it,' she said.

'A whole town on the move!'

'True, it's a fair cross section through society,' said Sweet, shifting his old arse in his saddle. 'Some honest, some sharp, some rich, some poor, some clever, some not so much. Lot of prospectors. Some herders and some farmers. Few merchants. All set on a new life out there beyond the horizon. We even got the First of the Magi down there.'

Lamb's head jerked around. 'What?'

'A famous actor. Iosiv Lestek. His Bayaz mesmerised the crowds in Adua, apparently.' Sweet gave his gravelly chuckle. 'About a hundred bloody years ago. He's hoping to bring theatre to the Far Country, I hear, but between you, me and half the population of the Union, his powers are well on the wane.'

'Don't convince as Bayaz any more, eh?' asked Shy.

'He scarcely convinces me as Iosiv Lestek.' Sweet shrugged. 'But what do I know about acting?'

'Even your Dab Sweet's no better'n passable.'

'Let's go down there!' said Leef. 'Get us a better look!'

There was a less romantic feel to the business at close quarters. Isn't there to every business? That number of warm bodies, man and beast, produced a quantity of waste hardly to be credited and certainly not to be smelled without good cause. The smaller and less glamorous animals – dogs and flies, chiefly, though undoubtedly lice, too – didn't stand out from a distance but made double the impression once you were in the midst. Shy was forced to wonder whether the Fellowship might, in fact, be a brave but foolhardy effort to export the worst evils of city-living into the middle of the unspoiled wilderness.

Not blind to this, some of the senior Fellows had removed themselves a good fifty strides from the main body in order to consider the course, meaning argue over it and grab a drink, and were now scratching their heads over a big map.

'Step away from that map 'fore you hurt yourselves!' called Sweet as they rode up. 'I'm back and you're three valleys south o' the course.'

'Only three? Better than I dared hope.' A tall, sinewy Kantic with a fine-shaped skull bald as an egg stepped up, giving Shy and Lamb and Leef a careful look-over on the way. 'You have friends along.'

'This here is Lamb and his daughter Shy.' She didn't bother to correct him on the technicality. 'This lad's name, I must confess, has for the time being slipped from my clutches—'

'Leef.'

'That was it! This here is my . . . *employer*.' Sweet said the word like even admitting its existence was too much cramping of his freedoms 'An unrepentant criminal by the name of Abram Majud.'

'A pleasure to make your acquaintances.' Majud displayed much good humour and a golden front tooth as he bowed to each of them. 'And I assure you I have been repenting ever since I formed this Fellowship.' His dark eyes took on a faraway look, as though he was gazing back across the long miles travelled. 'Back in Keln along with my partner, Curnsbick. A hard man, but a clever one. He has invented a portable forge, among other things. I am taking it to Crease, with the intention of founding a metalwork business. We might also look into staking some mining claims in the mountains.'

'Gold?' asked Shy.

'Iron and copper.' Majud leaned in to speak softly. 'In my most humble opinion, only fools think there is gold in gold. Are the three of you minded to join up with our Fellowship?'

'That we are,' said Shy. 'We've business of our own in Crease.'

'All are welcome! The rate for buying in—'

'Lamb here is a serious fighting man,' cut in Sweet.

Majud paused, lips pressed into an appraising line. 'Without offence, he looks a little . . . *old.*'

'No one'll be arguing on that score,' said Lamb

'I lack the freshest bloom myself,' added Sweet. 'You're no toddler if it comes to that. If it's youth you want, the lad with him is well supplied.'

Majud looked still less impressed by Leef. 'I seek a happy medium.'

Sweet snorted. 'Well you won't find many o' them out here. We don't got enough fighters. With the Ghosts fixed on blood it's no time to be cutting costs. Believe me, old Sangeed won't stop to argue prices with you. Lamb's in or I'm out and you can scout your way around in circles 'til your wagons fall apart.'

Majud looked up at Lamb, and Lamb looked back, still and steady. Seemed he'd left his weak eye back in Squaredeal. A few moments to consider, and Majud had seen what he needed to. 'Then Master Lamb goes free. Two paid shares comes to—'

Sweet scratched wincing at the back of his neck. 'I made a deal with Shy they'd all three come free.'

Majud's eyes shifted to her with what might have been grudging respect. 'It would appear she got the better of that particular negotiation.'

'I'm a scout, not a trader.'

'Perhaps you should be leaving the trading to those of us who are.'

'I traded a damn sight better than you've scouted, by all appearances.'

Majud shook his fine-shaped head. 'I have no notion of how I will explain this to my partner Curnsbick.' He walked off, wagging one long finger. 'Curnsbick is not a man to be trifled with on expenses!'

'By the dead,' grumbled Sweet, 'did you ever hear such carping? Anyone would think we'd set out with a company o' women.'

'Looks like you have,' said Shy. One of the brightest of the wagons – scarlet with gilt fixtures – was rattling past with two women in its seat. One was in full whore's get-up, hat clasped on with one hand and a smile gripped no less precariously to her painted face. Presumably advertising her availability for commerce in spite of the ongoing trek.

The other was more soberly dressed for travel, handling the reins calmly as a coachman. A man sat between them in a jacket that matched the wagon, bearded and hard-eyed. Shy took him for the pimp. He had a pimpy look about him, sure enough. She leaned over and spat through the gap in her teeth.

The idea of getting to business in a lurching wagon, half-full of rattling pans and the other of someone else getting to business hardly stoked the fires of passion in Shy. But then those particular embers had been burning so low for so long she'd a notion they'd smouldered out all together. Working a farm with two children and two old men surely can wither the romance in you.

Sweet gave the ladies a wave, and pushed his hat brim up with a knobby knuckle, and under his breath said, 'Bloody hell but nothing's how it used to be. Women, and dandified tailoring, and ploughs and portable forges and who knows what horrors'll be next. Time was there was naught out here but earth and sky and beasts and Ghosts, and far wild spaces you could breathe in. Why, I've spent twelve months at a time with only a horse for company.'

Shy spat again. 'I never in my life felt so sorry for a horse. Reckon I'll take a ride round and greet the Fellowship. See if anyone's heard a whisper of the children.'

'Or Grega Cantliss.' And Lamb frowned hard as he said the name.

'All right,' said Sweet. 'You watch out, though, you hear?'

'I can look after myself,' said Shy.

The old scout's weathered face creased up as he smiled. 'It's everyone else I'm worried for.'

The nearest wagon belonged to a man called Gentili, an ancient Styrian with four cousins along he called the boys, though they weren't much younger than he was and hadn't a word of common between them. He was set stubborn on digging a new life out of the mountains and must've been quite the optimist, since he could scarcely stand up in the dry, let alone to his waist in a freezing torrent. He'd heard of no stolen children. She wasn't even sure he heard the question. As a parting shot he asked Shy if she fancied sharing his new life with him as his fifth wife. She politely declined.

Lord Ingelstad had suffered misfortunes, apparently. When he used the word, Lady Ingelstad – a woman not born to hardships but determined to stomp them all to pieces even so – scowled at him as though she felt she'd suffered all his misfortunes plus one extra, and that her choice of husband. To Shy his misfortunes smelled like dice and debts, but since her own course through life had hardly been the straightest she thought she'd hold off on criticism and let misfortunes stand. Of child-stealing bandits, among many other things, he was entirely ignorant. As his parting shot he invited her and Lamb to a hand of cards that night. Stakes would be small, he promised, though in Shy's experience they always begin that way and don't have to rise far to land everyone in trouble. She politely declined that, too, and suggested a man who'd suffered so much misfortune might take pains not to court any more. He took the point with ruddy-faced good humour and called the same offer to Gentili and the boys. Lady Ingelstad looked like she'd be killing the lot of them with her teeth before she saw a hand dealt.

The next wagon might have been the biggest in the Fellowship, with glass windows and *The Famous Iosiv Lestek* written along the side in already peeling purple paint. Seemed to Shy that if a man was that famous he wouldn't have to paint his name on a wagon, but since her own brush with fame had been through bills widely posted for her arrest she hardly considered herself an expert.

A scratty-haired boy was driving and the great man sat swaying beside him, old and gaunt and leached of all colour, swaddled in a threadbare Ghost blanket. He perked up at the opportunity to boast as Shy and Lamb trotted over.

'I . . . am Iosiv Lestek.' It was a shock to hear the voice of a king boom from that withered head, rich and deep and fruity as plum sauce. 'I daresay the name is familiar.'

'Sorry to say we don't get often to the theatre,' said Lamb.

'What brings you to the Far Country?' asked Shy.

'I was forced to abandon a role at Adua's House of Drama due to illness. The ensemble was crushed to lose me, of course, quite *crushed*, but I am fully recovered.'

'Good news.' She dreaded to picture him before his recovery. He seemed a corpse raised by sorcery now.

'I am in transit to Crease to take a leading part in a cultural extravaganza!'

'Culture?' Shy eased up her hat brim to survey the empty country ahead, grey grass and ill scrub and parched slopes of baked brown boulder, no sign of life but for a couple of hopeful hawks circling on high. 'Out there?'

'Even the meanest hearts hunger for a glimpse of the sublime,' he informed them.

'I'll take your word on that,' said Lamb.

Lestek was busy smiling out at the reddening horizon, a hand so pale as almost to be see-through clutched against his chest. She got the feeling he was one of those men didn't really see the need for two sides to a conversation. 'My greatest performance is yet ahead of me, that much I know.'

'Something to look forward to,' muttered Shy, turning her horse.

A group of a dozen or so Suljuks watched the exchange, clustered to themselves around a rotten-looking wagon. They spoke no common, and Shy could barely recognise a word of Suljuk let alone understand one, so she just nodded to them as she rode by and they nodded back, pleasantly inscrutable to each other.

Ashjid was a Gurkish priest, fixed on being the first to spread the word of the Prophet west to Crease. Or actually the second, since a man called Oktaadi had given up after three months there and been skinned by the Ghosts on the return trip. Ashjid was having a good stab at spreading the word to the Fellowship in the meantime through daily blessings, though so far his only convert was a curious retard responsible for collecting drinking water. He had no information for them beyond the revelation of the scripture, but he asked God to smile upon their search and Shy thanked him for that. Seemed better to her to have blessings than curses, for all time's plough would more'n likely turn up what it turned regardless.

The priest pointed out a stern-looking type on a neatly kept wagon as Savian, a man not to be fiddled with. He'd a long sword at his side looked like it had seen plenty of action and a grey-stubbled face looked like it had seen plenty more, eyes narrowed to slits in the shadow of his low hat-brim.

'My name's Shy South, this is Lamb.' Savian just nodded, like he accepted that was a possibility but had no set opinion on it. 'I'm looking for my brother and sister. Six years and ten.' He didn't even nod to that. A tight-mouthed bastard, and no mistake. 'They were stole by a man named Grega Cantliss.'

'Can't help you.' A trace of an Imperial accent, and all the while Savian looked at her long and level, like he'd got just her measure and wasn't moved by it. Then his eyes shifted to Lamb, and took his measure, too, and wasn't moved by that either. He put a fist over his mouth and gave a long, gravelly cough.

'That cough sounds bad,' she said.

'When's a cough good?'

Shy noticed a flatbow hooked to the seat beside him. Not loaded, but full-drawn and with a wedge in the trigger. Exactly as ready as it needed to be. 'You along to fight?'

'Hoping I won't have to.' Though the whole set of him said his hopes hadn't always washed out in that regard.

'What kind of a fool hopes for a fight, eh?'

'Sad to say there's always one or two about.'

Lamb snorted. 'There's the sorry truth.'

'What's your business in the Far Country?' asked Shy, trying to chisel something more from that hardwood block of a face.

'My business.' And he coughed again. Even when he did that his mouth hardly moved. Made her wonder if he'd any muscles in his head.

'Thought we might try our hand at prospecting.' A woman had poked her face out from the wagon. Lean and strong, hair cut short and with these blue, blue eyes looked like they saw a long way. 'I'm Corlin.'

'My niece,' added Savian, though there was something odd about the way they looked at each other. Shy couldn't quite get it pegged.

'Prospecting?' she asked, pushing her hat back. 'Don't see a lot of women at that business.'

'Are you saying there's a limit on what a woman can do?' asked Corlin.

Shy raised her brows. 'Might be one on what she's dumb enough to try.'

'It seems neither sex has a monopoly on hubris.'

'Seems not,' said Shy, adding, under her breath, 'whatever the fuck that means.' She gave the two of them a nod and pulled her horse about. 'Be seeing you on the trail.'

Neither Corlin nor her uncle answered, just gave each other some deadly competition at who could stare after her the hardest.

'Something odd about them two,' she muttered to Lamb as they rode off. 'Didn't see no mining gear.'

'Maybe they mean to buy it in Crease.'

'And pay five times the going rate? You look in their eyes? Don't reckon they're a pair used to making fool deals.'

'You don't miss a trick, do you?'

'I try to be aware of 'em, at least, in case they end up being played on me. You think they're trouble?'

Lamb shrugged. 'I think you're best off treating folk the way you'd want to be treated and leaving their choices to them. We're all of us trouble o' one kind or another. Half this whole crowd probably got a sad story to tell. Why else would they be plodding across the long and level nowhere with the likes of us for company?'

All Raynault Buckhorm had to tell about was hopes, though he did it with something of a stutter. He owned half the cattle with the Fellowship, employed a good few of the men to drive 'em, and was making his fifth trip to Crease where he said there was always call for meat, this time bringing his wife and children and planning to stay. The exact number of children was hard to reckon but the impression was of many. Buckhorm asked Lamb if he'd seen the grass out there in the Far Country. Best damn grass in the Circle of the World, he thought. Best water, too. Worth facing the weather and the Ghosts and the murderous distance for that grass and that water. When Shy told him about Grega Cantliss and his band he shook his head and said he could still be surprised by how low men could sink. Buckhorm's wife Luline – possessed of a giant smile but a tiny body you could hardly believe had produced such a brood – shook her head too, and said it was the most awful thing she'd ever heard, and she wished there was something she could do, and probably would've hugged her if they hadn't had the height of a horse between them. Then she gave Shy a little pie and asked if she'd spoken to Hedges.

Hedges was a shifty sort with a wore-out mule, not enough gear and a charmless habit of talking to her from the neck down. He'd never heard of Grega Cantliss but he did point out his ruined leg, which he said he'd got leading a charge at the battle of Osrung. Shy had her doubts about that story. Still, her mother used to say, *you're best off looking for the best in people*, and it was good advice even if the woman never had taken it herself. So Shy offered Hedges Luline Buckhorm's pie and he looked her in the eye finally and said, 'You're all right.'

'Don't let a pie fool you.' But when she rode off he was still looking down at it in his dirty hand, like it meant so much he couldn't bring himself to eat it.

Shy went on around them 'til her voice was sore from sharing her troubles and her ears from lending them to others' dreams. A Fellowship was a good name for it, she reckoned, 'cause they were a good-humoured and a giving company, in the main. Raw and strange and foolish, some of them, but all fixed on finding a better tomorrow. Even Shy felt it, time and trouble-toughened, work and weather-worn, weighed down with worries about Pit and Ro's future and Lamb's past. The new wind on her face and the new hopes ringing in her ears and she found a dopey smile creeping under her nose as she threaded between the wagons, nodding to folks she didn't know, slapping the backs of those she'd only just met. Soon as she'd remember why she was there and wipe that smile away she'd find it was back, like pigeons shouted off a new-sown field.

Soon enough she stopped trying. Pigeons'll ruin your crop, but what harm will smiles do, really?

So she let it sit there. Felt good on her.

'Lots of sympathy,' she said, once they'd talked to most everyone, and the sun had sunk to a gilt sliver ahead of them, the first torches lit so the Fellowship could slog another mile before making camp. 'Lots of sympathy but not much help.'

'I guess sympathy's something,' said Lamb. She waited for more but he just sat hunched, nodding along to the slow walk of his horse.

'They seem all right, though, mostly.' Gabbing just to fill the hole, and feeling annoyed that she had to. 'Don't know how they'll fare if the Ghosts come and things get ugly, but they're all right.'

'Guess you never know how folk'll fare if things get ugly.'

She looked across at him. 'You're damn right there.'

He caught her eye for a moment, then guiltily looked away. She opened her mouth but before she could say more, Sweet's deep voice echoed through the dusk, calling halt for the day.

The Rugged Outdoorsman

Temple wrenched himself around in his saddle, heart suddenly bursting—

And saw nothing but moonlight on shifting branches. It was so dark he could scarcely see that. He might have heard a twig torn loose by the wind, or a rabbit about its harmless nocturnal business in the brush, or a murderous Ghost savage daubed with the blood of slaughtered innocents, fixed on skinning him alive and wearing his face as a hat.

He hunched his shoulders as another chilly gust whipped up, shook the pines and chilled him to his marrow. The Company of the Gracious Hand had enveloped him in its foul embrace for so long he had come to take the physical safety it provided entirely for granted. Now he keenly felt its loss. There were many things in life one did not fully appreciate until one had cavalierly tossed them aside. Like a good coat. Or a very small knife. Or a few-score hardened killers and an affable geriatric villain.

The first day he had ridden hard and worried only that they would catch him. Then, when the second morning dawned chill and vastly empty, that they wouldn't. By the third morning he was feeling deeply aggrieved at the thought that they might not even have tried. Fleeing the Company, directionless and unequipped, into the unmapped wasteland, was looking less and less like the easy way to anything.

Temple had played many parts during his thirty ill-starred years alive. Beggar, thief, unwilling trainee priest, ineffective surgeon, disgusted butcher, sore-handed carpenter, briefly a loving husband and even more briefly a doting father followed closely by a wretched mourner and bitter drunk, overconfident confidence trickster, prisoner of the Inquisition then informant for them, translator, accountant and lawyer, collaborator with a whole range of different wrong sides, accomplice to mass murder, of course, and, most recently and disastrously, man of conscience. But rugged outdoorsman made no appearance on the list.

Temple did not even have the equipment to make a fire. Or, had he had it, known how to use it. He had nothing to cook anyway. And now he was lost in every sense of the word. The barbs of hunger, cold and fear had quickly come to bother him vastly more than the feeble prodding of his conscience ever had. He should probably have thought more carefully before fleeing, but flight and careful thought are like oil and water, ever reluctant to mix. He blamed Cosca. He blamed Lorsen. He blamed Jubair, and Sheel, and Sufeen. He blamed every fucker available excepting, of course, the one who was actually to blame, the one sitting in his saddle and getting colder, hungrier, and more lost with every unpleasant moment.

'Shit!' he roared at nothing.

His horse checked, ears swivelling, then plodded on. It was becoming resignedly immune to his outbursts. Temple peered up through the crooked branches, the moon casting a glow through the fast-moving streaks of cloud.

'God?' he muttered, too desperate to feel a fool. 'Can you hear me?' No answer, of course. God does not answer, especially not the likes of him. 'I know I haven't been the best man. Or even a particularly good one . . .' He winced. Once you accept He's up there, and all-knowing and all-seeing and so on, you probably have to accept that there's no point gilding the truth for Him. 'All right, I'm a pretty poor one, but . . . far from the worst about?' A proud boast, that. What a headstone it would make. Except, of course, there would be no one to carve it when he died out here alone and rotted in the open. 'I am sure I could improve, though, if you could just see your way to giving me . . . one more chance?' Wheedling, wheedling. 'Just . . . *one* more?'

No reply but another chill gust filling the trees with whispers. If there was a God, He was a tight-mouthed bastard, and no—

Temple caught the faintest glimmer of flickering orange through the trees.

A fire! Jubilation sprang to life in his breast!

Then caution smothered it.

Whose fire? Ear-collecting barbarians, but a step above wild animals?

He caught a whiff of cooking meat and his stomach gave a long, squelching growl, so loud he worried it might give him away. Temple had spent a great deal of his early life hungry and become quite adept at it, but, as with so many things, to do it well one has to stay in practice.

He gently reined in his horse, slid as quietly as he could from the saddle and looped the reins around a branch. Keeping low, he eased through the brush, tree-limbs casting clawing shadows towards him, breathing curses as he caught his clothes, his boots, his face on snatching twigs.

The fire had been built in the middle of a narrow clearing, a small animal neatly skinned and spitted on sticks above it. Temple suppressed a powerful impulse to dive at it teeth first. A single blanket was spread out between the fire and a worn saddle. A round shield leaned against a tree, metal rim and wooden front marked with the scars of hard use. Next to it was an axe with a heavy bearded head. It took no expert in the use of weapons to see this was a tool not for chopping wood but people.

The gear of one man, but clearly a man it would be a bad idea to be caught stealing the dinner of.

Temple's eyes crawled from meat to axe and back, and his mouth watered with an intensity almost painful. Possible death by axe loomed large at any time, but at that moment certain death from hunger loomed larger yet. He slowly straightened, preparing to—

'Nice night for it.' Northern words in a throaty whisper of a voice, just behind Temple's ear.

He froze, small hairs tingling up his neck. 'Bit windy,' he managed to croak.

'I've seen worse.' A cold and terrible point pricked at the small of Temple's back. 'Let's see your weapons, slow as snails in winter.'

'I am . . . unarmed.'

A pause. 'You're what?'

'I had a knife, but . . .' He had given it to a bony farmer who killed his best friend with it. 'I lost it.'

'Out in the big empty without a blade?' As though it was strange as to be without a nose. Temple gave a girlish squeak as a big hand slipped under his arm and started to pat him down. 'Nor have you, 'less you're hiding one up your arse.' An unpleasing notion. 'I ain't looking there.' That was some relief. 'You a madman?'

'I am a lawyer.'

'Can't a man be both?'

Self-evidently. 'I . . . suppose.'

Another pause. 'Cosca's lawyer?'

'I was.'

'Huh.' The point slipped away, its absence leaving a prickling spot in Temple's back. Even unpleasant things can be sorely missed, apparently, if you have lived with them long enough.

A man stepped past Temple. A great, black, shaggy shape, knife-blade glinting in one hand. He dragged a long sword from his belt and tossed it on the blanket, then lowered himself cross-legged, firelight twinkling red and yellow in the mirror of his metal eye.

'Life takes you down some strange paths, don't it?' he said.

'Caul Shivers,' muttered Temple, not at all sure whether to feel better or worse.

Shivers reached out and turned the spit between finger and thumb, fat dripping into the flames. 'Hungry?'

Temple licked his lips. 'Is that just a question . . . or an invitation?'

'I've got more'n I can eat. You'd best bring that horse up before it shakes loose. Watch your step, though.' The Northman jerked his head back into the trees. 'There's a gorge that way might be twenty strides deep, and with some angry water at the bottom.'

Temple brought the horse up and hobbled it, stripped its saddle and the damp blanket beneath, abandoned it to nuzzle at whatever grass it could find. A sad fact, but the hungrier a man is the less he tends to care about the hunger of others. Shivers had carved the carcass down to the bones and was eating from a tin plate with the point of his knife. More meat lay gleaming on some torn-off bark on the other side of the fire. Temple sank to his knees before it as though it were a most hallowed altar.

'My very great thanks.' He closed his eyes as he began to eat, sucking the juice from every morsel. 'I was starting to think I'd die out here.'

'Who says you won't?'

A shred of meat caught in Temple's throat and he gave an awkward cough. 'Are you alone?' he managed to gasp out – anything but more of the crushing silence.

'I've learned I make poor company.'

'You aren't worried about the Ghosts?'

The Northman shook his head.

'I hear they've killed a lot of people in the Far Country.'

'Once they've killed me I'll worry.' Shivers tossed down his plate and leaned back on one elbow, his ruined face shifting further into the darkness. 'A man can spend the time he's given crapping his arse out over what might be, but where does it get you?'

Where indeed? 'Still hunting for your nine-fingered man?'

'He killed my brother.'

Temple paused with another piece of meat halfway to his mouth. 'I'm sorry.'

'You're sorrier'n me, then. My brother was a shit. But family is family.'

'I wouldn't know.' Temple's relatives had rarely stayed long in his life. A dead mother, a dead wife, a dead daughter. 'Closest thing I have to family is . . .' He realised he had been about to say Sufeen, and now he was dead as well. 'Nicomo Cosca.'

Shivers grunted. Almost a chuckle. 'In my experience, he ain't the safest man to have at your back.'

'What is your experience?'

'We were both hired to kill some men. In Styria, ten years ago or so. Friendly, too. Some others. A poisoner. A torturer.'

'Sounds quite the merry company.'

'I ain't the wag I seem. Things got . . .' Shivers scratched ever so gently at the great scar under his metal eye. 'A bit unpleasant.'

'Things tend to get unpleasant when Cosca's involved.'

'They can get plenty unpleasant without him.'

'More so with,' muttered Temple, looking into the fire. 'He never cared much, but he used to care a little. He's got worse.'

'That's what men do.'

'Not all of them.'

'Ah.' Shivers showed his teeth. 'You're one of them optimists I've heard about.'

'No, no, not me,' said Temple. 'I always take the easy way.'

'Very wise. I find hoping for a thing tends to bring on the opposite.' The Northman slowly turned the ring on his little finger round and around, the stone glittering the colour of blood. 'I had my dreams of being a better man, once upon a time.'

'What happened?'

Shivers stretched out beside the fire, boots up on his saddle, and started to shake a blanket over himself. 'I woke up.'

Temple woke to that first washed out, grey-blue touch of dawn, and found himself smiling. The ground was cold and hard, the blanket was far too small and smelled powerfully of horse, the evening meal had been inadequate, and yet it was a long time since he had slept so soundly. Birds twittered, wind whispered and through the trees he could hear the faint rushing of water.

Fleeing the Company suddenly seemed a masterful plan, boldly executed. He wriggled over under his blanket. If there was a God, it turned out He was the forgiving fellow Kahdia had always—

Shivers' sword and shield had gone and another man squatted on his blanket.

He was stripped to the waist, his pale body a twisted mass of sinew. Over his bottom half he wore a filthy woman's dress, slit up the middle then stitched with twine to make loose trousers. One side of his head was shaved, the orange hair on the other scraped up into stiff spikes with some kind of fat. In one dangling hand he held a hatchet, in the other a bright knife.

A Ghost, then.

He stared unblinking across the dead fire at Temple with piercing blue eyes and Temple stared back, considerably less piercingly, and found he had gently pulled his horse-stinking blanket up under his chin in both fists.

Two more men slipped silently from the trees. One wore as a kind of helmet, though presumably not for protection against any earthly weapon, an open box of sticks joined at the corners with feathers and secured to a collar made from an old belt. The other's cheeks were striped with self-inflicted scars. In different circumstances – on stage, perhaps, at a Styrian carnival – they might have raised quite the laugh. Here, in the untracked depths of the Far Country and with Temple their only audience, merriment was notable by its absence.

'Noy.' A fourth Ghost had appeared as if from nowhere, between man and boy with yellow hair about his pale face and a line of dried-out brown paint under his eyes. Temple hoped it was paint. The bones of some small animal, stitched to the front of a shirt made from a sack, rattled as he danced from one foot to the other, smiling radiantly all the while. He beckoned Temple up.

'Noy.'

Temple very slowly got to his feet, smiling back at the boy, and then at the others. Keep smiling, keep smiling, everything on a friendly footing. 'Noy?' he ventured.

The boy hit him across the side of the head.

It was the shock more than the force that put Temple down. So he told himself. The shock, and some kind of primitive understanding that there was nothing to be gained by staying up. The world swayed as he lay there. His hair was tickly. He touched his scalp and there was blood on his fingers.

Then he saw the boy had a rock in his hand. A rock painted with blue rings. And now with just a few spots of Temple's red blood.

'Noy!' called the boy, beckoning again.

Temple was in no particular rush to rise. 'Look,' he said, trying common first. The boy slapped him with his empty hand. 'Look!' Giving Styrian a go. The boy slapped him a second time. He tried Kantic. 'I do not have any—' The boy hit him with the rock again, caught him across the cheek and put him on his side.

Temple shook his head. Groggy. Couldn't hear that well.

He grabbed at the nearest thing. The boy's leg, maybe.

He clambered up as far as his knees. His knees or the boy's knees. Someone's knees.

His mouth tasted of blood. His face was throbbing. Not hurting exactly. Numb.

The boy was saying something to the others, raising his arms as if asking for approval.

The one with the spikes of hair nodded gravely and opened his mouth to speak, and his head flew off.

The one beside him turned, slightly impeded by his stick helmet. Shivers' sword cut his arm off above the elbow and thudded deep into his chest, blood flooding from the wound. He stumbled wordlessly back, the blade lodged in his ribs.

The one with the scarred face flew at Shivers, stabbing at him, clawing at his shield, the two of them lurching about the clearing, feet kicking sparks from the embers of the fire.

All this in a disbelieving, wobbly breath or two, then the boy hit Temple over the head again. That seemed ridiculously unfair. As if Temple was the main threat. He dragged himself up the leg with a surge of outraged innocence. Shivers had forced the scarred Ghost onto his knees now and was smashing his head apart with the rim of his shield. The boy hit Temple again but he clung on, caught a fistful of bone-stitched shirt as his knees buckled.

They went down, scratching, punching, gouging. Temple was on the bottom, teeth bared, and he forced his thumb up the Ghost's nose and wrestled him over and all the while he could not help thinking how amazingly silly and wasteful this all was, and then that effective fighters probably leave the philosophising until after the fight.

The Ghost kneed at him, screaming in his own language, and

they were rolling between the trees, sliding downhill, and Temple was punching at the Ghost's bloody face with his bloody knuckles, screeching as the Ghost caught his forearm and bit it, and then there were no trees, only loose earth under them, then the sound of the river grew very loud, and there was no earth at all, and they were falling.

He vaguely remembered Shivers saying something about a gorge.

Wind rushed, and turning weightlessness, and rock and leaf and white water. Temple let go of the Ghost, both of them falling without a sound. It all felt so unlikely. Dreamlike. Would he wake soon with a jolt, back with the Company of the—

The jolt came when he hit the water.

Feet-first, by blind luck, and then he was under, gripped by cold, crushed by the surging weight of it, ripped five ways at once in a current so strong it felt as though it would tear his arms from their sockets. Over and over, a leaf in the torrent, helpless.

His head left the flood and he heaved in a shuddering breath, spray in his face, roar of the furious water. Dragged under again and something thumped hard at his shoulder and twisted him over, showed him the sky for just a moment. Limbs so heavy now, a sore temptation to stop fighting. Temple had never been much of a fighter.

He caught a glimpse of driftwood, dried-out and bleached bone-white by sun and water. He snatched at it, lungs bursting, clawed at it as he came right-side-up. It was part of a tree. A whole tree trunk with leafless branches still attached. He managed to heave his chest over it, coughing, spitting, face scraping against rotten wood.

He breathed. A few breaths. An hour. A hundred years.

Water lapped at him, tickled him. He raised his head so he could see the sky. A mighty effort. Clouds shifted across the deep and careless blue.

'Is this your idea of a fucking joke?' he croaked, before a wave slapped him in the face and made him swallow water. No joke, then. He lay still. Too tired and hurting for anything else. The water had calmed now, at least. The river wider, slower, the banks lower, long grass shelving down to the shingle.

He let it all slide by. He trusted to God, since there was no one else. He hoped for heaven.

But he fully expected the alternative.

Driftwood

'Whoa!' called Shy. 'Whoa!'

Maybe it was the noise of the river, or maybe they somehow sensed she'd done some low-down things in her life, but, as usual, the oxen didn't take a shred of notice and kept on veering for the deeper water. Dumb stubborn bloody animals. Once they'd an idea in mind they'd keep towards it regardless of all urgings to the contrary. Nature giving her a taste of her own cooking, maybe. Nature was prone to grudges that way.

'Whoa, I said, you bastards!' She gripped at her soaked saddle with her soaked legs, wound the rope a couple of times around her right forearm and gave a good haul. The other end was tight-knotted to the lead yoke and the line snapped taught and sprayed water. Same time Leef nudged his pony up from the downstream side and snapped out a neat little flick with his goad. He'd turned out to have quite a knack as a drover. One of the front pair gave an outraged snort but its blunt nose shifted left, back to the chosen course, towards the stretch of wheel-scarred shingle on the far bank where the half of the Fellowship already across was gathered.

Ashjid the priest was one of them, arms thrust up to heaven like his was the most important job around, chanting a prayer to calm the waters. Shy had observed no becalming. Not of the waters, and for damn sure not of her.

'Keep 'em straight!' growled Sweet, who'd reined his dripping horse up on a sandbar and was taking his ease — something he took an aggravating amount of.

'Keep them straight!' echoed Majud from behind, gripping so hard to the seat of his wagon it was a wonder he didn't rip it off. He wasn't comfortable with water, apparently, which was quite an inconvenience in a frontiersman.

'What d'you think I'm aiming to do, you idle old fucks?' hissed Shy, digging her horse out left and giving the rope another heave. 'See us all flushed out to sea?'

It didn't look unlikely. They'd doubled up the oxen, teams of six or eight or even a dozen hitched to the heaviest loads, but still it was far from easy going. If the wagons weren't hitting deep water and threatening to float away, they were doing the opposite and getting bogged in the shallows.

One of Buckhorm's wagons was stranded now and Lamb was in the river to his waist, straining at the back axle while Savian leaned from his horse to smack at the lead oxen's rump. He hit it that hard Shy was worried he'd break the beast's back, but in the end he got it floundering on and Lamb sloshed back wearily to his horse. Unless your name was Dab Sweet, it was hard work all round.

But then work had never scared Shy. She'd learned early that once you were stuck with a task you were best off giving it your all. The hours passed quicker then, and you were less likely to get a belting, too. So she'd worked hard at errands soon as she could run, at farming when a woman grown, and between the two at robbing folk and been damn good at it, though that was probably better not dwelt on. Her work now was finding her brother and sister, but since fate had allotted her oxen to drive through a river in the meantime, she reckoned she'd try her hardest at that in spite of the smell and the strain on her sore arms and the freezing water washing at her arse-crack.

They finally floundered out onto the sandbar, animals streaming and blowing, cartwheels crunching in the shingle, Shy's horse trembling under her and that the second one she'd blowed out that day.

'Call this a damn ford?' she shouted at Sweet over the noise of the water.

He grinned back at her, leathery face creased up with good humour. 'What'd you call it?'

'A stretch of river 'bout the same as any other, and just as apt to be drowned in.'

'You should've told me if you couldn't swim.'

'I can, but this wagon's no fucking salmon, I can tell you that.'

Sweet turned his horse about with the slightest twist of his heel. 'You disappoint me, girl. I had you marked for an adventurer!'

'Never by choice. You ready?' she called out to Leef. The lad nodded. 'How about you?'

Majud waved a weak hand. 'I fear I will never be ready. Go. Go.'

So Shy wound the rope tight again, heaved in a good breath, gave herself a thought of Ro's face and Pit's, and set off after Sweet. Cold gripped her calves, then her thighs, oxen peering nervous towards the far bank, her horse snorting and tossing its head, none of them any keener on another dip than she was, Leef working the goad and calling out, 'Easy, easy.'

The last stretch was the deepest, water surging around the oxen and making white bow-waves on their upstream flanks. Shy hauled at the rope, making them strain into the current at a diagonal just to end up with a straight course, while the wagon jolted over the broken stream-bed, wheels half-under, then squealing axles under, then the whole thing halfway to floating and a damn poor shape for a boat.

She saw one of the oxen was swimming, neck stretched as it struggled to keep its flaring nostrils above the water, then two, scared eyes rolling towards her, then three, and Shy felt the rope tugging hard, and she wound it tighter about her forearm and put all her weight into it, hemp gripping at her leather glove, biting at the skin above it.

'Leef!' she growled through her gritted teeth, 'Get it over to—'

One of the leaders slipped, craggy shoulder-blades poking up hard as it struggled for a footing, and then it veered off to the right and took its neighbour's legs away too and the pair of them were torn sideways by the river. The rope jerked Shy's right arm straight like it would rip her muscles joint from joint, dragging her half-out of the saddle before she knew a thing about it.

Now the front two oxen were thrashing, sending up spray, dragging the next yoke out of true while Leef screeched and lashed at them. Might as well have been lashing at the river, which he mostly was. Shy dragged with all her strength. Might as well have been dragging at a dozen dead oxen. Which she soon would be.

'Fuck!' she gasped, rope slipping suddenly through her right hand and zipping around her forearm, just managing to hold on, blood in the hemp and mixing with the beaded water, spray in her face and wet hair and the terrified lowing of the animals and the terrified wailing of Majud.

The wagon was skidding, grinding, near to floating, near to tipping. The first animal had found ground again somehow and Savian was smacking at it and snarling, Shy with neck stretched back and dragging, dragging, rope ripping at her arm and her horse shuddering under her. Glimpse of the far bank, people waving, their shouts and her breath and the thrashing of the beasts making just one echoing throb in her skull.

'Shy.' Lamb's voice. And there was a strong arm around her and she knew she could let go.

Like when she fell off the barn roof and Lamb had lifted her up. 'All right, now. Quiet, now.' Sun flickering through her lids and her mouth tasting like blood, but not scared any more. Later, years later, him bandaging the burns on her back. 'It'll pass. It'll pass.' And her walking up to the farm after that black time gone, not knowing what she'd find there, or who, and seeing him sat by the door with that same smile as always. 'Good to have you back,' like she'd only left a moment before, hugging her tight and feeling that prickle of tears under her closed lids . . .

'Shy?'

'Uh.' Lamb was setting her down on the bank, blurred faces flickering into focus around her.

'You all right, Shy?' Leef was calling. 'She all right?'

'Give her some room.'

'Let her breathe, now.'

'I'm breathing,' she grunted, waving their pawing hands away, fighting up to sitting though she wasn't sure what'd happen when she got there.

'Hadn't you better stay still a while?' asked Lamb. 'You have to be—'

'I'm fine,' she snapped, swallowing the need to puke. 'Grazed my pride a little, but that'll scab over.' It had scars enough on it already, after all. 'Gave my arm a scrape.' She winced as she pulled her glove off with her teeth, every joint in her right arm throbbing, grunted as she worked the trembling fingers. The raw rope-burn coiled bloody around her forearm like a snake up a branch.

'Scraped it bad.' Leef slapped at his forehead. 'My fault! If I'd just—'

'No one's fault but my own. Should've let go the damn rope.'

'I for one am grateful you did not.' Majud must've finally prised his fingers free of his wagon-seat. Now he draped a blanket over Shy's shoulders. 'I am far from a strong swimmer.'

Shy squinted at him and that brought the burning to the back of her throat again, so she looked to the wet shingle between her knees instead. 'You ever think a journey over twenty unbridged rivers might've been a mistake?'

'Every time we cross one, but what can a merchant do when he smells opportunity at the other side? Much as I detest hardship, I love profit more.'

'Just what we need out here.' Sweet twisted his hat back firm onto his head as he stood. 'More greed. All right! Drama's done, everyone, she yet lives! Let's get these teams unhitched and back across, the rest of them wagons ain't going to fly over!'

Corlin shoved between Lamb and Leef with a bag in one hand and knelt next to Shy, taking her arm and frowning down at it. She'd such a manner of knowing exactly what she was about made you hardly even think to ask whether she did.

'You going to be all right?' asked Leef.

Shy waved him away. 'You can go on. You all can.' She'd known some folks couldn't get enough pity, but it'd always made her feel uncomfortable right into her arse.

'You're sure?' asked Lamb, looking down at her from what seemed a great height.

'I daresay you've got better places to be than in my way,' snapped Corlin, already cleaning the cuts.

They drifted off, back towards the ford, Lamb with one last worried look over his shoulder, leaving Corlin to bind Shy's arm with quick, deft hands, wasting no time and making no mistakes.

'Thought they'd never leave.' And she slipped a little bottle out of her bag and into Shy's free hand.

'Now that's good doctoring.' Shy took a sneaky swig and curled her lips back at the burning.

'Why do a thing badly?'

'I'm always amazed how some folk can't help themselves.'

'True enough.' Corlin glanced up from her work towards the ford, where they were manhandling Gentili's rickety wagon to the far bank, one of the ancient prospectors waving his spindly arms as a wheel caught in the shallows. 'There's a few like that along on this trip.'

'I guess most of 'em mean well.'

'Someday you can build a boat from meaning well and see how it floats.'

'Tried that. Sank with me on it.'

The corner of Corlin's mouth twitched up. 'I think I might have been on that voyage. Icy water, wasn't it?' Lamb had dropped in beside Savian, the two old men straining at the stuck wheel, the whole wagon rocking with their efforts. 'You see a lot of strong men out here in the wilderness. Trappers and hunters hardly spent a night of their lives under a roof. Men made of wood and leather. Not sure I ever saw one stronger than your father, though.'

'He ain't my father,' muttered Shy, taking another swig from the bottle. 'And your uncle's no weakling neither.'

Corlin cut a bandage from the roll with a flick of a bright little knife. 'Maybe we should give up on oxen and get those two old bastards to haul the wagons.'

'Expect we'd get there faster.'

'You reckon you could get Lamb into a yoke?'

'Easily, but I don't know how Savian might respond to a whipping.'

'You'd probably break your whip on him.'

The wagon finally ground free and lurched on, Gentili's old cousin flailing about in the seat. Behind in the water, Savian gave Lamb an approving thump on the shoulder.

'They've struck up quite the friendship,' said Shy. 'For two men never say a word.'

'Ah, the unspoken camaraderie of veterans.'

'What makes you think Lamb's a veteran?'

'Everything.' And Corlin slid a pin neatly through the bandage to hold it closed. 'You're done.' She glanced towards the river, the men calling out as they splashed around in the water, and suddenly she sprang up and shouted, 'Uncle, your shirt!'

Seemed like mad over-modesty to panic about a torn sleeve when half the men in the Fellowship were stripped to the waist and a couple all the way to their bare arses. Then, as Savian twisted to look, Shy caught a glimpse of his bare forearm. It was blue-black with tattooed letters.

No need to ask what he was a veteran of. He was a rebel. More than likely he'd been fighting in Starikland and was on the run, for all Shy knew hotly pursued by his Majesty's Inquisition.

She looked up, and Corlin looked down, and neither one of them quite managed to hide what they were thinking.

'Just a torn shirt. Nothing to worry about.' But Corlin's blue, blue eyes were narrowed and Shy realised she still had that bright little knife in her hand and of a sudden felt the need to pick her words with care.

'I daresay we've all got a rip or two behind us.' Shy handed the bottle back to Corlin and slowly stood. 'Ain't none of my affair to go picking at other folks' stitches. Their business is their business.'

Corlin took a swig of her own, looking at Shy all the while over the bottle. 'That's a fine policy.'

'And this a fine bandage.' Shy grinned as she worked her fingers. 'Can't say I've ever had a better.'

'You had a lot?'

'Been cut enough, but mostly I just had to let 'em bleed. No one interested in doing the bandaging, I guess.'

'Sad story.'

'Oh, I can tell 'em all day long . . .' She frowned towards the river. 'What's that?'

A dead tree was washing slowly towards them, snagging in the shallows then drifting on, tangles of foamy grass caught up in its branches. There was something draped over the trunk. Someone, limbs trailing. Shy threw her blanket off and hurried to the bank, slid into the water, cold gripping her legs again and making her shiver.

She waded out and caught hold of a branch, winced as pain shot through all the joints of her right arm and into her ribs, had to flounder around to use her left instead.

The passenger was a man, head turned so she couldn't see his face, only a mass of black hair, wet shirt rucked up to show a patch of brown midriff.

'That's a funny-looking fish,' said Corlin, looking down from the bank with hands on hips.

'You want to leave the jokes 'til you've helped me land him?'

'Who is he?'

'He's the Emperor of fucking Gurkhul! How should I know who he is?'

'That's exactly my point.'

'Maybe we can ask once we've dragged him out?'

'That might be too late.'

'Once he's washed out to sea it surely will be!'

Corlin sucked sourly at her teeth, then stomped down the bank and into the river without breaking stride. 'On your head be it if he turns out a murderer.'

'No doubt it will be.' Together they heaved the tree and its human cargo grinding onto the bank, broken branches leaving grooves through the gravel, and stood looking down, soaked through, Shy's stomach sticking unpleasantly to her wet shirt with each shivering in-breath.

'All right, then.' Corlin reached down to take the man under his arms. 'Keep your knife handy, though.'

'My knife's always handy,' said Shy.

With a grunt and a heave, Corlin twisted him over and onto his back, one leg flopping after. 'Any idea what the Emperor of Gurkhul looks like?'

'Better fed,' muttered Shy. He had a lean look to him, fibres in his stretched-out neck, sharp cheekbones, one with an ugly cut down it.

'Better dressed,' said Corlin. He had nothing but the torn clothes he was tangled with, and one boot. 'Older, too.' He couldn't have been much over thirty, short black beard on his cheeks, grey scattered in his hair.

'Less . . . earnest,' said Shy. It was the best word she could think of for that face. He looked almost peaceful in spite of the cut. Like he'd just closed his eyes to philosophise a moment.

'It's the earnest-looking bastards need the most watching.' Corlin tipped his face one way, then the other. 'But he is pretty. For flotsam.' She leaned further to put her ear over his mouth, then rocked back on her haunches, considering.

'He alive?' asked Shy.

'One way to find out.' Corlin slapped him across the face, and none too gently.

When Temple opened his eyes he saw only a blinding brightness.

Heaven!

But should heaven hurt so much?

Hell, then.

But surely hell would be hot?

And he felt very cold.

He tried to lift his head and decided it was far too much effort. Tried to move his tongue and decided that was no better. A wraith-like figure floated into view, surrounded by a nimbus of sparkling light, painful to look upon.

'God?' Temple croaked.

The slap made a hollow boom in his head, brought fire to the side of his face and snapped everything into focus.

Not God.

Or not the way He was usually portrayed.

This was a woman, and a pale-skinned one. Not old in years, but Temple got the feeling those years had been testing. A long, pointed face, made to look longer by the red-brown hair hanging about it, stuck to pale cheeks with wet, wedged under a ragged hat salt-stained about the band. Her mouth was set in a suspicious frown, with faint lines at the corners that suggested it often was. She looked used to hard work and hard choices, but there was a soft dusting of freckles across the narrow bridge of her nose.

Another woman's face hovered behind. Older and squarer with short hair stirred by the wind and blue eyes that looked as if they were stirred by nothing.

Both women were wet. So was Temple. So was the shingle under him. He could hear the washing of a river and, fainter in the background, the calls of men and beasts. There was only one explanation, reached gradually and by a process of ponderous elimination.

He was still alive.

These two women could scarcely have seen as weak, watery and unconvincing a smile as he mustered at that moment. 'Hello,' he croaked.

'I'm Shy,' said the younger.

'You needn't be,' said Temple. 'I feel we know each other quite well already.'

Under the circumstances he thought it a solid effort, but she did not smile. People rarely find jokes based on their own name amusing. They, after all, have heard them a thousand times.

'My name is Temple.' He tried to rise again, and this time made it as far as his elbows before giving up.

'Not the Emperor of Gurkhul, then,' muttered the older woman, for some reason.

'I am . . .' Trying to make up his mind exactly what he was now. 'A lawyer.'

'So much for earnest.'

'Don't know that I ever been this close to a lawyer before,' said Shy.

'Is it all you hoped for?' asked the other woman.

'So far it's middling.'

'You're not catching me at my best.' With a little help from the two women he dragged himself to sitting, noting with a pang of nervousness that Shy kept one hand on the grip of a knife. Not a shy knife, judging by the sheath, and that hard set to her mouth made him think she would not be shy about using it.

He was careful to make no sudden moves. Not that it was difficult. Painstaking ones were enough of a challenge.

'How does a lawyer get into a river?' asked the older woman. 'Give bad advice?'

'It's good advice usually lands you in trouble.' He tried another smile, somewhat closer to his usual winning formula. 'You did not tell me your name.'

It won nothing from her. 'No. You weren't pushed, then?'

'Me and another man sort of . . . pushed each other.'

'What happened to him?'

Temple gave a helpless shrug. 'For all I know he'll float by presently.'

'You armed?'

'He ain't even shod,' said Shy.

Temple peered down at his bare foot, tendons standing stark from the skin as he wriggled the toes. 'I used to have a very small knife but . . . that didn't turn out too well. I think it's fair to say . . . I've had a bad week.'

'Some days work out.' Shy started to help him up. 'Some don't.'

'You sure about this?' asked her companion.

'What's the choice, throw him back in the water?'

'I've heard worse ideas.'

'You can stay here, then.' And Shy dragged Temple's arm around her neck and hauled him to his feet.

God, he was hurting. His head felt like a melon someone had taken a hammer to. God, he was cold. He could hardly have been colder if he had died in the river. God, he was weak. His knees trembled so badly he could hear them flapping at the insides of his wet trousers. Just as well he had Shy to lean on. She did not feel like she would collapse any time soon. Her shoulder was firm as wood under his hand.

'Thank you,' he said, and meant it, too. 'Thank you so much.' He had always been at his best with someone strong to lean on. Like a flowering creeper adorning a deep-rooted tree. Or a songbird perched on a bull's horn. Or a leech on a horse's arse.

They struggled up the bank, his booted foot and his bare foot scraping at the mud. Behind them, cattle were being driven across the river, riders leaning from saddles to wave their hats or their ropes, yipping and calling, the beasts swarming, swimming, clambering one over another, thrashing up clouds of spray.

'Welcome to our little Fellowship,' said Shy.

A mass of wagons, animals and people were gathered in the lee of a wind-bent copse just beyond the river. Some worked timber for repairs. Some struggled to get stubborn oxen into yokes. Some were busy changing clothes soaked in the crossing, sharp tan-lines on bare limbs. A pair of women were heating soup over a fire, Temple's stomach giving a painful grumble at the smell of it. Two children laughed as they chased a three-legged dog around and around.

He did his best to smile, and nod, and ingratiate himself as Shy helped him through their midst with her strong hand under his armpit, but a few curious frowns were his whole harvest. Mostly these people were fixed on their work, all of them aimed squarely at grinding a profit out of this unforgiving new land with one kind of hard labour or another. Temple winced, and not just from the pain and the cold. When he'd signed up with Nicomo Cosca, it had been on the understanding that he'd never come this close to hard work again.

'Where is the Fellowship heading?' he asked. It would be just his luck to hear Squaredeal or Averstock, settlements whose remaining citizens he rather hoped never to be reacquainted with.

'West,' said Shy. 'Right across the Far Country to Crease. That suit?'

Temple had never heard of Crease. Which was the highest recommendation for the place. 'Anywhere but where I came from suits well enough. West will be wonderful. If you'll have me.'

'Ain't me you got to convince. It's these old bastards.'

There were five of them, standing in a loose group at the head of the column. Temple was slightly unnerved to see the nearest was a Ghost woman, long and lean with a face worn tough as saddle-leather, bright eyes looking straight through Temple and off to the far horizon. Next to her, swaddled in a huge fur coat and with a pair of knives and a gilt-sheathed hunting sword at his belt, a smallish man with a shag of grey hair and beard and a curl to his mouth as if Temple was a joke he didn't find funny but was too polite to frown at.

'This here is the famous scout Dab Sweet and his associate Crying Rock. And this the leader of our merry Fellowship, Abram Majud.' A bald, sinewy Kantic, face composed of unforgiving angles with two careful, slanted eyes in the midst. 'This is Savian.' A tall man, with iron grey stubble and a stare like a hammer. 'And this is . . .' Shy paused, as though trying to think up the right word. 'Lamb.'

Lamb was a huge old Northman, slightly hunched as if he was trying to look smaller than he was, a piece missing from his ear and a face that, through a tangle of hair and beard, looked as if it had seen long use as a millstone. Temple wanted to wince just looking at that collection of breaks, nicks and scars, but he grinned through it like the professional he was, and smiled at each of these geriatric adventurers as though he never saw in one place such a collection of the beautiful and promising.

'Gentlemen, and . . .' He glanced at Crying Rock, realised the word hardly seemed to fit but had entirely backed himself into a corner. 'Lady . . . it is my honour to meet you. My name is Temple.'

'Speaks nice, don't he?' rumbled Sweet, as though that was a black mark against him already.

'Where did you find him?' growled Savian. Temple had not failed at as many professions as he had without learning to recognise a dangerous man, and he feared this one straight away.

'Fished him out of the river,' said Shy.

'You got a reason not to throw him back?'

'Didn't want to kill him, I guess.'

Savian looked straight at Temple, flint-eyed, and shrugged. 'Wouldn't be killing him. Just letting him drown.'

There was a moment of silence for Temple to consider that, while the wind blew chill through his soaked trousers and the five old worthies treated him each to their own style of appraisal, suspicion or scorn.

It was Majud who spoke first. 'And where did you float in from, Master Temple? You do not appear to be native to these parts.'

'No more than you, sir. I was born in Dagoska.'

'An excellent city for commerce in its day, rather less so since the demise of the Guild of Spicers. And how does a Dagoskan come to be out here?'

Here is the perennial trouble with burying your past. Others are forever trying to dig it up. 'I must confess . . . I had fallen in with some bad company.'

Majud indicated his companions with a graceful gesture. 'It happens to the best of us.'

'Bandits?' asked Savian.

All that and worse. 'Soldiers,' said Temple, putting it in the best light possible short of an outright lie. 'I left them and struck out on my own. I was set upon by Ghosts, and in the struggle rolled down a slope and . . . into a gorge.' He pressed gently at his battered face, remembering that sickening moment when he ran out of ground. 'Followed by a long fall into water.'

'I been there,' murmured Lamb, with a faraway look.

Sweet puffed up his chest and adjusted his sword-belt. 'Whereabouts did you run across these Ghosts?'

Temple could only shrug. 'Upriver?'

'How far and how many?'

'I saw four. It happened at dawn and I've been floating since.'

'Might be no more'n twenty miles south.' Sweet and Crying Rock exchanged a long glance, grizzled concern on his part, stony blankness on hers. 'We'd best ride out and take a look that way.'

'Hmm,' murmured the old Ghost.

'Do you expect trouble?' asked Majud.

'Always. That way you'll only be pleasantly surprised.' Sweet walked between Lamb and Savian, giving each of them a slap on the shoulder as he passed. 'Good work at the river. Hope I'm as useful when I reach your age.' He slapped Shy, too. 'And you, girl. Might want to let go the rope next time, though, eh?' It was only then that Temple noticed the bloody bandage around her limp arm. He had never been particularly sensitive to the hurts of others.

Majud showed off a gold front tooth as he smiled. 'I imagine you would be grateful to travel with our Fellowship?'

Temple sagged with relief. 'Beyond grateful.'

'Every member has either paid for their passage or contributes their skills.'

Temple unsagged. 'Ah.'

'Do you have a profession?'

'I have had several.' He thought quickly through the list for those that were least likely to land him immediately back in the river. 'Trainee priest, amateur surgeon—'

'We've got a surgeon,' said Savian.

'And a priest, more's the pity,' added Shy.

'Butcher—'

'We have hunters,' said Majud.

'—carpenter—'

'A wagon-man?'

Temple winced. 'House-builder.'

'We need no houses out here. Your most recent work?'

Mercenary usually won few friends. 'I was a lawyer,' he said, before realising that often won still fewer.

Savian was certainly not one of them. 'There's no law out here but what a man brings with him.'

'Have you ever driven oxen?' asked Majud.

'I am afraid not.'

'Herded cattle?'

'Sadly, no.'

'Handled horses?'

'One at a time?'

119

'Experience in combat?' grated Savian.

'Very little, and that far more than I'd like.' He feared this interview was not showing him in his best light, if there was such a thing. 'But . . . I am determined to start fresh, to earn my place, to work as hard as any man – or woman – here and . . . keen to learn,' he finished, wondering if so many exaggerations had ever been worked into one sentence.

'I wish you every success with your education,' said Majud, 'but passengers pay one hundred and fifty marks.'

A brief silence as they all, particularly Temple, considered the likelihood of his producing such a sum. Then he patted at his wet trouser-pockets. 'I find myself a little short.'

'How short?'

'One hundred and fifty marks-ish?'

'You let us join for nothing and I reckon you're getting your money's worth,' said Shy.

'Sweet made that deal.' Majud ran an appraising eye over Temple and he found himself trying to hide his bare foot behind the other. Without success. 'And you at least brought two boots apiece. This one will need clothes, and footwear, and a mount. We simply cannot afford to take in every stray that happens across our path.'

Temple blinked, not entirely sure where this left him.

'Where does that leave him?' asked Shy.

'Waiting at the ford for a Fellowship with different requirements.'

'Or another set of Ghosts, I guess?'

Majud spread his hands. 'If it were up to me I would not hesitate before helping you, but I have the feelings of my partner Curnsbick to consider, and he has a heart of iron where business is concerned. I am sorry.' He did look a little sorry. But he did not look like he would be changing his mind.

Shy glanced sideways at Temple. All he could do was stare back as earnestly as possible.

'Shit.' She planted her hands on her hips and shook her head at the sky for a moment, then curled back her top lip to show a noticeable gap between her front teeth and neatly spat through it. 'I'll buy him in, then.'

'Really?' asked Majud, brows going up.

'Really?' asked Temple, no less shocked.

'That's right,' she snapped. 'You want the money now?'

'Oh, don't trouble yourself.' Majud had the trace of a smile about his lips. 'I know your touch with figures.'

'I don't like this.' Savian propped the heel of his hand on the grip of one of his knives. 'This bastard could be anyone.'

'So could you,' said Shy. 'I've no notion what you were doing last month, or what you'll get to next, and for a fact it's none o' my business. I'm paying, he's staying. You don't like it, you can float off downriver, how's that?' She glared right into Savian's stony face all the while and Temple found he was liking her more and more.

Savian pursed his thin lips a fraction. 'Got anything to say about this, Lamb?'

The old Northman looked slowly from Temple to Shy and back. It appeared he did nothing quickly. 'I reckon everyone should get a chance,' he said.

'Even those don't deserve it?'

'Especially them, maybe.'

'You can trust me,' said Temple, treating the old men to his most earnest look. 'I won't let you down, I promise.' He had left a trail of broken promises across half the Circle of the World, after all. One extra would hardly keep him out of heaven.

'You saying so don't necessarily make it so, does it?' Savian leaned forward, narrowing his eyes even further, a feat that might have been considered impossible but a moment before. 'I'm watching you, boy.'

'That is . . . a tremendous comfort,' squeaked Temple as he backed slowly away. Shy had already turned on her heel and he hurried to catch her up.

'Thank you,' he said. 'Truly. I'm not sure what I can do to repay you.'

'Repay me.'

He cleared his throat. 'Yes. Of course.'

'With one-quarter interest. I ain't no charity.'

Now he was liking her less. 'I begin to see that. Principal plus a quarter. Far more than fair. I always pay my debts.' Except, perhaps, the financial ones.

'Is it true you're keen to learn?'

He was keener to forget. 'I am.'

'And to work as hard as any man here?'

Judging by the dustiness, sweatiness, sunburn and generally ruined appearance of most of the men, that claim seemed now rather rash. 'Yes?'

'Good, 'cause I'll work you, don't worry on that score.'

He was worrying on several scores, but the lack of hard labour had not been among them. 'I can . . . hardly wait to start.' He was getting the distinct sensation that he had whisked his neck from one noose only to have another whipped tight around it. Looked at with the benefit of hindsight, his life, which at the time had felt like a series of ingenious escapes, resembled rather more closely a succession of nooses, most of them self-tied. The self-tied ones will still hang you, though.

Shy was busy kneading at her injured arm and planning strategy. 'Might be Hedges has some clothes'll fit. Gentili's got an old saddle will serve and Buckhorm's got a mule I believe he'd sell.'

'A mule?'

'If that's too fucking lowly you can always walk to Crease.'

Temple thought it unlikely he would make it as far as the mule on foot, so he smiled through the pain and consoled himself with the thought that he would repay her. For the indignity, if not the money.

'I shall feel grateful for every moment spent astride the noble beast,' he forced out.

'You should feel grateful,' she snapped.

'I will,' he snapped back.

'Good,' she said.

'Good.'

A pause. 'Good.'

Reasons

'Some country, ain't it?'

'Looks like quite a bloody lot of country to me,' said Leef. Sweet spread his arms and pulled in such a breath you'd have thought he could suck the whole world through his nose. 'It's the Far Country, true enough! Far 'cause it's so damn far from anywhere a civilised man would care to go. And Far 'cause it's so damn far from here to anywhere else he'd want to go.'

'Far 'cause it's so damn far to anything at all,' said Shy, staring out across that blank expanse of grass, gently shifting with the wind. A long, long way off, so pale they might've been no more'n wishes, the grey outline of hills.

'But damn civilised men, eh, Lamb?'

Lamb raised a mild eyebrow. 'We can't just let 'em be?'

'Maybe even borrow some hot water off 'em once in a while,' muttered Shy, scratching at her armpit. She'd a fair few passengers along for the ride now, not to mention dust crusted to every bit of her and her teeth tasting of salt dirt and dry death.

'Damn 'em, say I, and hot water, too! You can strike off south to the Empire and ask old Legate Sarmis for a bath if that's your style. Or trek back east to the Union and ask the Inquisition.'

'Their water might be too hot for comfort,' she muttered.

'Just tell me where a body can feel as free as this!'

'Can't think of nowhere,' she admitted, though to her mind there was something savage in all that endless empty. You could come to feel squashed by all that room.

But not Dab Sweet. He filled his lungs to bursting one more time. 'She's easy to fall in love with, the Far Country, but she's a cruel mistress. Always leading you on. That's how it's been with me, ever since I was younger'n Leef here. The best grass is always just past the horizon.

The sweetest water's in the next river. The bluest sky over some other mountain.' He gave a long sigh. 'Afore you know it, your joints snap of a morning and you can't sleep two hours together without needing to piss and of a sudden you realise your best country's all behind you, never even appreciated as you passed it by, eyes fixed ahead.'

'Summers past love company,' mused Lamb, scratching at the star-shaped scar on his stubbled cheek. 'Seems every time you turn around there's more o' the bastards at your back.'

'Comes to be everything reminds you of something past. Somewhere past. Someone. Yourself, maybe, how you were. The now gets fainter and the past more and more real. The future worn down to but a stub.'

Lamb had a little smile at his mouth's corner as he stared into the distance. 'The happy valleys o' the past,' he murmured.

'I love old-bastard talk, don't you?' Shy cocked a brow at Leef. 'Makes me feel healthy.'

'You young shrimps think tomorrow can be put off for ever,' grumbled Sweet. 'More time got like money from a bank. You'll learn.'

'If the Ghosts don't kill us all first,' said Leef.

'Thanks for raising that happy possibility,' said Sweet. 'If philosophy don't suit, I do have other occupation for you.'

'Which is?'

The old scout nodded down. Scattered across the grass, flat and white and dry, were a bumper harvest of cow-leavings, fond mementoes of some wild herd roving the grassland. 'Collecting bullshit.'

Shy snorted. 'Ain't he collected bullshit enough listening to you and Lamb sing the glories o' yesteryear?'

'You can't burn fond remembrances, more's the pity, or I'd be toasty warm every night.' Sweet stuck an arm out to the level sameness in every direction, the endless expanse of earth and sky and sky and earth away to nowhere. 'Ain't a stick of timber for a hundred miles. We'll be burning cow flats 'til after we cross the bridge at Sictus.'

'And cooking over 'em, too?'

'Might improve the flavour o' what we been eating,' said Lamb.

'All part o' the charm,' said Sweet. 'Either way, all the young 'uns are gathering fuel.'

Leef's eyes flickered to Shy. 'I ain't that young.' And as though to prove it he fingered his chin where he'd started to lovingly cultivate a meagre harvest of blond hairs.

Shy wasn't sure she couldn't have fielded more beard and Sweet was unmoved. 'You're young enough to get shitty-handed in service of the Fellowship, lad!' And he slapped Leef on the back, much to the lad's hunch-shouldered upset. 'Why, brown palms are a mark of high courage and distinction! The medal of the plains!'

'You want the lawyer to lend you a hand?' asked Shy. 'For three bits he's yours for the afternoon.'

Sweet narrowed his eyes. 'I'll give you two for him.'

'Done,' she said. It was hardly worth haggling when the prices were so small.

'Reckon he'll enjoy that, the lawyer,' said Lamb, as Leef and Sweet headed back towards the Fellowship, the scout holding forth again on how fine things used to be.

'He ain't along for his amusement.'

'I guess none of us are.'

They rode in silence for a moment, just the two of them and the sky, so big and deep it seemed any moment there might be nothing holding you to the ground any more and you'd just fall into it and never stop. Shy worked her right arm a little, shoulder and elbow still weak and sore, grumbles up into her neck and down into her ribs but getting looser each day. For sure she'd lived through worse.

'I'm sorry,' said Lamb, out of nowhere.

Shy looked over at him, hunched and sagging like he'd an anchor chained around his neck. 'I've always thought so.'

'I mean it, Shy. I'm sorry. For what happened back there in Averstock. For what I did. And what I didn't do.' He spoke slower and slower until Shy got the feeling each word was a battle to fight. 'Sorry that I never told you what I was . . . before I came to your mother's farm . . .' She watched him all the while, mouth dry, but he just frowned down at his left hand, thumb rubbing at that stump of a finger over and over. 'All I wanted was to leave the past buried. Be nothing and nobody. Can you understand that?'

Shy swallowed. She'd a few memories at her back she wouldn't have minded sinking in a bog. 'I reckon.'

'But the seeds of the past bear fruit in the present, my father used to say. I'm that much of a fool I got to teach myself the same lesson over and over, always pissing into the wind. The past never stays buried. Not one like mine, leastways. Blood'll always find you out.'

'What were you?' Her voice sounded a tiny croak in all that space. 'A soldier?'

That frown of his got harder still. 'A killer. Let's call it what it is.'

'You fought in the wars? Up in the North?'

'In wars, in skirmishes, in duels, in anything offered, and when I ran out of fights I made my own, and when I ran out of enemies I turned my friends into more.'

She'd thought any answers would be better than none. Now she wasn't so sure. 'I guess you had your reasons,' she muttered, so weak it turned into a wheedling question.

'Good ones, at first. Then poor ones. Then I found you could still shed blood without 'em and gave up on the bastards altogether.'

'You got a reason now, though.'

'Aye. I've a reason now.' He took a breath and drew himself up straighter. 'Those children . . . they're all the good I done in my life. Ro and Pit. And you.'

Shy snorted. 'If you're counting me in your good works you got to be desperate.'

'I am.' He looked across at her, so fixed and searching she'd trouble meeting his eye. 'But as it happens you're about the best person I know.'

She looked away, working that stiff shoulder again. She'd always found soft words a lot tougher to swallow than hard. A question of what you're used to, maybe. 'You got a damn limited circle of friends.'

'Enemies always came more natural to me. But even so. I don't know where you got it, but you've a good heart, Shy.'

She thought of him carrying her from that tree, singing to the children, putting the bandages on her back. 'So have you.'

'Oh, I can fool folk. The dead know I can fool myself.' He looked back to the flat horizon. 'But no, Shy, I don't have a good heart. Where we're going, there'll be trouble. If we're lucky, just a little, but luck ain't exactly stuck to me down the years. So listen. When I next tell you to stay out of my way, you stay out, you hear?'

'Why? Would you kill me?' She meant it half as a joke, but his cold voice struck her laughter dead.

'There's no telling what I'll do.'

The wind gusted into the silence and swept the long grass in waves and Shy thought she heard shouting sifting on it. An unmistakable note of panic.

'You hear that?'

Lamb turned his horse towards the Fellowship. 'What did I say about luck?'

They were in quite the spin, all bunched up and shouting over or riding into each other, wagons tangled and dogs darting under the wheels and children crying and a mood of terror like Glustrod had risen from the grave up ahead and was fixed on their destruction.

'Ghosts!' Shy heard someone wail. 'They'll have our ears!'

'Calm down!' Sweet was shouting. 'It ain't bloody Ghosts and they don't want your ears! Travellers like us, is all!'

Peering off to the north Shy saw a line of slow-moving riders, wriggling little specks between the vast black earth and the vast white sky.

'How can you be sure?' shrieked Lord Ingelstad, clutching a few prized possessions to his chest as if he was about to make a dash for it, though where he'd dash to was anyone's guess.

''Cause Ghosts fixed on blood don't just trot across the horizon! You lot sit tight here and try not to injure yourselves. Me and Crying Rock'll go parley.'

'Might be these travellers know something about the children,' said Lamb, and he spurred his horse after the two scouts, Shy following.

She'd thought their own Fellowship worn down and dirty, but they were a crowd of royalty beside the threadbare column of beggars they came upon, broken-down and feverish in the eyes, their horses lean round the rib and yellow at the tooth, a handful of wagons lurching after and a few flyblown cattle dragging at the rear. A Fellowship of the damned and no mistake.

'How do,' said Sweet.

'How do?' Their leader reined in, a big bastard in a tattered Union soldier's coat, gold braid around the sleeves all torn and dangling. 'How do?' He leaned from his horse and spat. 'A year older'n when we come the other way and not a fucking hour richer, that's how we do. Enough of the Far Country for these boys. We're heading back to Starikland. You want our advice, you'll do the same.'

'No gold up there?' asked Shy.

'Maybe there's some, girl, but I ain't dying for it.'

'No one's ever giving aught away,' said Sweet. 'There's always risks.'

The man snorted. 'I was laughing at the risks when I came out last year. You see me laughing now?' Shy didn't, much. 'Crease is at bloody war, killings every night and new folk piling in every day. They hardly even bother to bury the bodies any more.'

'They were always keener there on digging than filling in, as I recall,' said Sweet.

'Well, they got worse. We pushed on up to Beacon, into the hills, to find us a claim to work. Place was crawling with men hoping for the same.'

'Beacon was?' Sweet snorted. 'It weren't more'n three tents last time I was there.'

'Well, it's a whole town now. Or was, at least.'

'Was?'

'We stopped there a night or two then off into the wilds. Come back to town after we'd checked a few creeks and found naught but cold mud . . .' He ran out of words, just staring at nothing. One of his fellows took his hat off, the brim half-torn away, and looked into it. Strange to see in that hammered-out face, but there were tears in his eyes.

'And?' asked Sweet.

'Everyone gone. Two hundred people in that camp, or more. Just gone, you understand?'

'Gone where?'

'To fucking hell was our guess, and we ain't planning on joining 'em. The place empty, mark you. Meals still on the table and washing still hung out and all. And in the square we find the Dragon Circle painted ten strides across.' The man shivered. 'Fuck that, is what I'm saying.'

'Fuck it to hell,' agreed his neighbour, jamming his ruined hat back on.

'Ain't been no Dragon People seen in years,' said Sweet, but looking a little worried. He never looked worried.

'Dragon People?' asked Shy. 'What are they? A kind of Ghosts?'

'A kind,' grunted Crying Rock.

'They live way up north,' said Sweet. 'High in the mountains. They ain't to be dabbled with.'

'I'd sooner dabble with Glustrod his self,' said the man in the Union coat. 'I fought Northmen in the war and I fought Ghosts on the plains and I fought Papa Ring's men in Crease and I gave not a stride to any of 'em.' He shook his head. 'But I ain't fighting those Dragon bastards. Not if the mountains was made of gold. Sorcerers, that's what they are. Wizards and devils and I'll have none of it.'

'We appreciate the warning,' said Sweet, 'but we've come this far and I reckon we'll go on.'

'May you all get rich as Valint and Balk combined, but you'll be doing it without me.' He waved on his slumping companions. 'Let's go!'

Lamb caught him by the arm as he was turning back. 'You heard of Grega Cantliss?'

The man tugged his sleeve free. 'He works for Papa Ring, and you won't find a blacker bastard in the Far Country. A Fellowship of thirty got killed and robbed up in the hills near Crease last summer, ears cut off and skinned and interfered with, and Papa Ring said it must be Ghosts and no one proved it otherwise. But I heard a whisper it was Cantliss did it.'

'Him and us got business,' said Shy.

The man turned his sunken eyes on her. 'Then I'm sorry for you, but I ain't seen him in months and I don't plan to lay eyes on the bastard ever again. Not him, not Crease, not any part of this blasted country.' And he clicked his tongue and rode away, heading eastwards.

They sat there a moment and watched the defeated shamble back the long way to civilisation. Not a sight to make anyone too optimistic about the destination, even if they'd been prone to optimism, which Shy wasn't.

'Thought you knew everyone in the Far Country?' she said to Sweet.

The old scout shrugged. 'Those who been about a while.'

'Not this Grega Cantliss, though?'

His shrug rose higher. 'Crease is crawling with killers like a tree-stump with woodlice. I ain't out there often enough to tell one from another. We both get there alive, I can make you an introduction to the Mayor. Then you can get some answers.'

'The Mayor?'

'The Mayor runs things in Crease. Well, the Mayor and Papa Ring run things, and it's been that way ever since there was two planks nailed together in that place, and all that time neither one's been too friendly with the other. Sounds like they're getting no friendlier.'

'The Mayor can help us find Cantliss?' asked Lamb.

Sweet's shrug went higher yet. Any further and it'd knock his hat off. 'The Mayor can always help you. If you can help the Mayor.' And he gave his horse his heels and trotted back towards the Fellowship.

Oh God, the Dust

'**W**ake up.'

'No.' Temple strove to pull his miserable scrap of blanket over his face. 'Please, God, no.'

'You owe me one hundred and fifty-three marks,' said Shy, looking down. Every morning the same. If you could even call it morning. In the Company of the Gracious Hand, unless there was booty in the offing, few would stir until the sun was well up, and the notary stirred last of all. In the Fellowship they did things differently. Above Shy the brighter stars still twinkled, the sky about them only a shade lighter than pitch.

'Where did the debt begin?' he croaked, trying to clear yesterday's dust from his throat.

'One hundred and fifty-six.'

'What?' Nine days of back-breaking, lung-shredding, buttock-skinning labour and he had shaved a mere three marks from the bill. Say what you will about Nicomo Cosca, the old bastard had been a handsome payer.

'Buckhorm docked you three for that cow you lost yesterday.'

'I am no better than a slave,' Temple murmured bitterly.

'You're worse. A slave I could sell.' Shy poked him with her foot and he struggled grumbling up, pulled his oversized boots onto feet dewy from sticking out beyond the bottom of his undersized blanket, shrugged his fourth-hand coat over his one sweat-stiffened shirt and limped for the cook's wagon, clutching at his saddle-bludgeoned backside. He badly wanted to weep but refused to give Shy the satisfaction. Not that anything satisfied her.

He stood, sore and miserable, choking down cold water and half-raw meat that had been buried under the fire the previous night. Around him men readied themselves for the day's labours and spoke in hushed tones, words smoking on the dawn chill, of the gold that awaited them at trail's end, eyes wide with wonder as if, instead of yellow metal, it was the secret of existence they hoped to find written in the rocks of those unmapped places.

'You're riding drag again,' said Shy.

Many of Temple's previous professions had involved dirty, danger-ous, desperate work but none had approached, for its excruciating mixture of tedium, discomfort, and minute wages, the task of riding drag behind a Fellowship.

'Again?' His shoulders slumped as if he had been told he would be spending the morning in hell. Which he more or less had been.

'No, I'm joking. Your legal skills are in high demand. Hedges wants you to petition the King of the Union on his behalf, Lestek's decided to form a new country and needs advice on the constitution and Crying Rock's asked for another codicil to her will.'

They stood there in the almost-darkness, the wind cutting across the emptiness and finding out the hole near his armpit.

'I'm riding drag.'

'Yes.'

Temple was tempted to beg, but this time his pride held out. Perhaps at lunch he would beg. Instead he took up the mass of decayed leather that served him for saddle and pillow both and limped for his mule. It watched him approach, eyes inflamed with hatred.

He had made every effort to cast the mule as a partner in this unfortunate business but the beast could not be persuaded to see it that way. He was its arch-enemy and it took every opportunity to bite or buck him, and had on one occasion most memorably pissed on his ill-fitting boots while he was trying to mount. By the time he had finally saddled and turned the stubborn animal towards the back of the column, the lead wagons were already rolling, their grinding wheels already sending up dust.

Oh God, the dust.

Concerned about Ghosts after Temple's encounter, Dab Sweet had led the Fellowship into a dry expanse of parched grass and sun-bleached bramble, where you only had to look at the desiccated ground to stir up dust. The further back in the column you were, the closer compan-ions you and dust became, and Temple had spent six days at the very back. Much of the time it blotted out the sun and entombed him in a perpetual soupy gloom, landscape expunged, wagons vanished, often the cattle just ahead made insubstantial phantoms. Every part of him was dried out by wind and impregnated by dirt. And if the dust did not choke you the stink of the animals would finish the job.

He could have achieved the same effect by rubbing his arse with wire wool for fourteen hours while eating a mixture of sand and cow-shit.

No doubt he should have been revelling in his luck and thanking God that he was alive, yet he found it hard to be grateful for this purgatory of dust. Gratitude and resentment are brothers eternal, after all. Time and again he considered how he might escape, slip from beneath his smothering debt and be free, but there was no way out, let alone an easy one. Surrounded by hundreds of miles of open country and he was imprisoned as surely as if he had been in a cage. He complained bitterly to everyone who would listen, which was no one. Leef was the nearest rider, and the boy was self-evidently in the throes of an adolescent infatuation with Shy, had cast her somewhere between lover and mother, and exhibited almost comical extremes of jealousy whenever she talked or laughed with another man, which, alas for him, was often. Still, he need not have worried. Temple had no romantic designs in that direction on the ringleader of his tormentors.

Though he had to concede there was something oddly interesting about that swift, strong, certain way she had, always on the move, first to work and last to rest, standing when others sat, fiddling with her hat, or her belt, or her knife, or the buttons on her shirt. He did occasionally catch himself wondering whether she was as hard all over as her shoulder had been under his hand. As her side had been pressed up against his. Would she kiss as hard as she haggled . . . ?

When Sweet finally brought them to a miserable trickle of a stream, it was the best they could do to stop a stampede from cattle and people both. The animals wedged in and clambered over each other, churning the bitter water brown. Buckhorm's children frolicked and splashed. Ashjid thanked God for His bounty while his idiot nodded and chuckled and filled the drinking barrels. Iosiv Lestek dabbed his pale face and quoted pastoral poetry at length. Temple found a spot upstream and flopped down on his back in the mossy grass, smiling wide as the damp soaked gently through his clothes. His standard for a pleasurable sensation had decidedly lowered over the past few weeks. In fact he was greatly enjoying the sun's warmth on his face, until it was suddenly blotted out.

'My daughter getting her money's worth out of you?' Lamb stood over him. Luline Buckhorm had cut her childrens' hair that morning and the Northman had reluctantly allowed himself to be put at the back of the queue. He looked bigger, and harder, and even more scarred with his grey hair and beard clipped short.

'I daresay she'll turn a profit if she has to sell me for meat.'

'I wouldn't put it past her,' said Lamb, offering a canteen.

'She's a hard woman,' said Temple as he took it.

'Not all through. Saved you, didn't she?'

'She did,' he was forced to admit, though he wondered whether death would have been kinder.

'Reckon she's just soft enough, then, don't you?'

Temple swilled water around his mouth. 'She certainly seems angry about something.'

'She's been often disappointed.'

'Sad to say I doubt I'll be reversing that trend. I've always been a deeply disappointing man.'

'I know that feeling.' Lamb scratched slowly at his shortened beard. 'But there's always tomorrow. Doing better next time. That's what life is.'

'Is that why you two are out here?' asked Temple, handing back the canteen. 'For a fresh beginning?'

Lamb's eyes twitched towards him. 'Didn't Shy tell you?'

'When she talks to me it's mostly about our debt and how slowly I'm clearing it.'

'I hear that ain't moving too quick.'

'Every mark feels like a year off my life.'

Lamb squatted beside the stream. 'Shy has a brother and a sister. They were . . . taken.' He held the canteen under the water, bubbles popping. 'Bandits stole 'em, and burned our farm, and killed a friend of ours. They stole maybe twenty children all told and took them up the river towards Crease. We're following on.'

'What happens when you find them?'

He pushed the cork back into the canteen, hard enough that the scarred knuckles of his big right hand turned white. 'Whatever needs to. I made a promise to their mother to keep those children safe. I broken a lot of promises in my time. This one I mean to keep.' He took a long breath. 'And what brought you floating down the river? I've always been a poor judge of men, but you don't look the type to carve a new life from the wilderness.'

'I was running away. One way and another I've made quite a habit of it.'

'Done a fair bit myself. I find the trouble is, though, wherever you run to . . . there y'are.' He offered out his hand to pull Temple up, and Temple reached to take it, and stopped.

'You have nine fingers.'

Suddenly Lamb was frowning at him, and he didn't look like such a slow and friendly old fellow any more. 'You a missing-finger enthusiast?'

'No, but . . . I may have met one. He said he'd been sent to the Far Country to find a nine-fingered man.'

'I probably ain't the only man in the Far Country missing a finger.'

Temple felt the need to pick his words carefully. 'I have a feeling you're the sort of man that sort of man might be looking for. He had a metal eye.'

No flash of recognition. 'A man with a missing eye after a man with a missing finger. There's a song in there somewhere, I reckon. He give a name?'

'Caul Shivers.'

Lamb's scarred face twisted as though he'd bitten into something sour. 'By the dead. The past just won't stay where you put it.'

'You do know him, then?'

'I did. Long time back. But you know what they say – old milk turns sour but old scores just get sweeter.'

'Talking of scores.' A second shadow fell across him and Temple squinted around. Shy stood over him again, hands on her hips. 'One hundred and fifty-two marks. And eight bits.'

'Oh God! Why didn't you just leave me in the river?'

'It's a question I ask myself every morning.' That pointed boot of hers poked at his back. 'Now up you get. Majud wants a Bill of Ownership drawn up on a set of horses.'

'Really?' he asked, hope flickering in his breast.

'No.'

'I'm riding drag again.'

Shy only grinned, and turned, and walked way.

'Just soft enough, did you say?' Temple muttered.

Lamb stood, wiping his hands dry on the seat of his trousers. 'There's always tomorrow.'

Sweet's Crossing

'Did I exaggerate?' asked Sweet.

'For once,' said Corlin, 'no.'

'It surely is a big one,' muttered Lamb.

'No doubt,' added Shy. She wasn't a woman easily impressed, but the Imperial bridge at Sictus was some sight, specially for those who'd scarcely seen a thing you could call a building in weeks. It crossed the wide, slow river in five soaring spans, so high above the water you could hardly fathom the monstrous scale of it. The sculptures on its pitted pedestals were wind-worn to melted lumps, its stonework sprouted with pink-flowered weeds and ivy and even whole spreading trees, and all along its length and in clusters at both ends it was infested with itinerant humanity. Even so diminished by time it was a thing of majesty and awe, more like some wonder of the landscape than a structure man's ambition could ever have contemplated, let alone his hands assembled.

'Been standing more'n a thousand years,' said Sweet.

Shy snorted. 'Almost as long as you been sitting that saddle.'

'And in all that time I've changed my trousers but twice.'

Lamb shook his head. 'Ain't something I can endorse.'

'Changing 'em so rarely?' asked Shy.

'Changing 'em at all.'

'This'll be our last chance to trade before Crease,' said Sweet. 'Less we have the good luck to run into a friendly party.'

'Good luck's never a thing to count on,' said Lamb.

'Specially not in the Far Country. So make sure and buy what you need, and make sure you don't buy what you don't.' Sweet nodded at a polished chest of drawers left abandoned beside the way, fine joints all sprung open from the rain, in which a colony of huge ants appeared to have taken up residence. They'd been passing all kinds of weighty possessions over the past few miles, scattered like driftwood after a flood. Things folk had thought they couldn't live without when they and civilisation parted. Fine furniture looked a deal less appealing when you had to carry it. 'Never own a thing you couldn't swim a river with, old Corley Ball used to tell me.'

'What happened to him?' asked Shy.

'Drowned, as I understand.'

'Men rarely live by their own lessons,' murmured Lamb, hand resting on the hilt of his sword.

'No, they don't,' snapped Shy, giving him a look. 'Let's get on down there, hope to make a start on the other side before nightfall.' And she turned and waved the signal to the Fellowship to move on.

'Ain't long before she takes charge, is it?' she heard Sweet mutter.

'Not if you're lucky,' said Lamb.

Folk had swarmed to the bridge like flies to a midden, sucked in from across the wild and windy country to trade and drink, fight and fuck, laugh and cry and do whatever else folk did when they found themselves with company after weeks or months or even years without. There were trappers and hunters and adventurers, all with their own wild clothes and hair but the same wild smell and that quite ripe. There were peaceable Ghosts set on selling furs or begging up scraps or tottering about drunk as shit on their profits. There were hopeful folk on their way to the gold-fields seeking to strike it rich and bitter folk on the way back looking to forget their failures, and merchants and gamblers and whores aiming to build their fortunes on the backs of both sets and each other. All as boisterous as if the world was ending tomorrow, crowded at smoky fires among the furs staked out to dry and the furs being pressed for the long trip back where they'd make some rich fool in Adua a hat to burn their neighbours up with jealousy.

'Dab Sweet!' growled a fellow with a beard like a carpet.

'Dab Sweet!' called a tiny woman skinning a carcass five times her size.

'Dab Sweet!' shrieked a half-naked old man building a fire out of smashed picture-frames, and the old scout nodded back and gave a how-do to each, by all appearances known intimately to half the plains.

Enterprising traders had draped wagons with gaudy cloth for stalls, lining the buckled flags of the Imperial road leading up to the bridge and making a bazaar of it, ringing with shouted prices and the complaints of livestock and the rattle of goods and coinage of every stamp. A woman with eyeglasses sat behind a table made from an old door with a set of dried-out, stitched up heads laid out on it. Above a sign read *Ghost Skulls Bought and Sold.* Food, weapons, clothing, horses, spare wagon parts and anything else that might keep a man alive out in the Far Country was going for five times its value. Treasured possessions from cutlery to windowpanes, abandoned by naïve colonists, were hawked off by cannier opportunists for next to nothing.

'Reckon there'd be quite a profit in bringing swords out here and hauling furniture back,' muttered Shy.

'You've always got your eye open for a deal,' said Corlin, grinning sideways at her. You couldn't find a calmer head in a crisis but the woman had a sticky habit the rest of the time of always seeming to know better.

'They won't seek you out.' Shy dodged back in her saddle as a streak of bird shit spattered the road beside her horse. There were crowds of birds everywhere, from the huge to the tiny, squawking and twittering, circling high above, sitting in beady-eyed rows, pecking at each other over the flyblown rubbish heaps, waddling up to thieve every crumb not currently held on to and a few that were, leaving bridge, and tents, and even a fair few of the people all streaked and crusted with grey droppings.

'You'll be needing one o' these!' a merchant screamed at them, thrusting a disgruntled tomcat at Shy by the scruff of the neck while all around him from tottering towers of cages other mangy specimens stared out with the haunted look of the long-imprisoned. 'Crease is crawling with rats the size o' horses!'

'Then you'd best get some bigger cats!' Corlin shouted back, and then to Shy, 'Where's your slave got to?'

'Helping Buckhorm drive his cattle through this shambles, I daresay. And he ain't a slave,' she added, further niggled. She seemed to be forever calling upon herself to defend from others a man she'd sooner have been attacking herself.

'All right, your man-whore.'

'Ain't that either, far as I'm aware.' Shy frowned at one example of the type, peering from a greasy tent-flap with his shirt open to his belly. 'Though he does often say he's had a lot of professions . . .'

'He might want to think about going back to that one. It's about the only way I can see him clearing that debt of yours out here.'

'We'll see,' said Shy. Though she was starting to think Temple wasn't much of an investment. He'd be paying that debt 'til doomsday if he didn't die first – which looked likely – or find some other fool to stick to and slip away into the night – which looked even more likely. All those times she'd called Lamb a coward. He'd never been scared of work, at least. Never once complained, that she could recall. Temple could hardly open his mouth without bitching on the dust or the weather or the debt or his sore arse.

'I'll give him a sore arse,' she muttered, 'useless bastard . . .'

Maybe you're best off looking for the best in people but if Temple had one he was keeping it well hid. Still. What can you expect when you fish men out of the river? Heroes?

Two towers had once stood watch at each end of the bridge. At the near side they were broken off a few strides up and the fallen stone scattered and overgrown. A makeshift gate had been rigged between them – as shoddy a piece of joinery as Shy ever saw and she'd done some injuries to wood herself – bits of old wagon, crate and cask bristling with scavenged nails and even a wheel lashed to the front. A boy was perched on a sheared-off column to one side, menacing the crowds with about the most warlike expression Shy ever saw.

'Customers, Pa!' he called as Lamb and Sweet and Shy approached, the wagons of the Fellowship spread out in the crush and jolting after.

'I see 'em, son. Good work.' The one who spoke was a hulking man, bigger'n Lamb even and with a riot of ginger beard. For company he had a stringy type with the knobbliest cheeks you ever saw and a helmet looked like it had been made for a man with cheeks of only average knobbliness. It fit him like a teacup on a mace end. Another worthy made himself known on top of one of the towers, bow in hand. Red Beard stepped in front of the gate, his spear not quite pointed at them, but surely not pointed away.

'This here's our bridge,' he said.

'It's quite something.' Lamb pulled off his hat and wiped his forehead. 'Wouldn't have pegged you boys for masonry on this scale.'

Ginger Beard frowned, not sure whether he was being insulted. 'We didn't build it.'

'But it's ours!' shouted Knobbly, as though it was the shouting of it made it true.

'You big idiot!' added the boy from his pillar.

'Who says it's yours?' asked Sweet.

'Who says it isn't?' snapped Knobbly. 'Possession is most o' the law.'

Shy glanced over her shoulder but Temple was still back with the herd. 'Huh. When you actually want a bloody lawyer there's never one to hand . . .'

'You want to cross, there's a toll. A mark a body, two marks a beast, three marks a wagon.'

'Aye!' snarled the boy.

'Some doings.' Sweet shook his head as if at the decay of all things worthy. 'Charging a man just to roll where he pleases.'

'Some people will turn a profit from anything.' Temple had finally arrived astride his mule. He'd pulled the rag from his dark face and the dusty yellow stripe around his eyes lent him a clownish look. He offered up a watery smile, like it was a gift Shy should feel grateful for.

'One hundred and forty-four marks,' she said. His smile slipped and that made her feel a little better.

'Guess we'd better have a word with Majud,' said Sweet. 'See about a whip-around for the toll.'

'Hold up there,' said Shy, waving him down. 'That gate don't look up to much. Even I could kick that in.'

Red Beard planted the butt of his spear on the ground and frowned up at her. 'You want to try it, woman?'

'Try it, bitch!' shouted the boy, his voice starting somewhat to grate at Shy's nerves.

She held up her palms. 'We've no violent intentions at all, but the Ghosts ain't so peaceful lately, I hear . . .' She took a breath, and let the silence do her work for her. 'Sangeed's got his sword drawn again.'

Red Beard shifted nervously. 'Sangeed?'

'The very same.' Temple hopped aboard the plan with some nimbleness of mind. 'The Terror of the Far Country! A Fellowship of fifty was massacred not a day's ride from here.' He opened his eyes very wide and drew his fingers down his ears. 'Not an ear left between them.'

'Saw it ourselves,' threw in Sweet. 'They done outrages upon those corpses it pains me to remember.'

'Outrages,' said Lamb. 'I was sick.'

'Him,' said Shy, 'sick. Things as they are I'd want a decent gate to hide behind. The one at the other end bad as this?'

'We don't got a gate at the other end,' said the boy, before Red Beard shut him up with a dirty look.

The damage was done, though. Shy took a sharper breath. 'Well, that's up to you, I reckon. It is your bridge. But . . .'

'What?' snapped Knobbly.

'It so happens we got a man along by the name of Abram Majud. A wonder of a smith, among other things.'

Red Beard snorted. 'And he brought his forge with him, did he?'

139

'Why, that he did,' said Shy. 'His Curnsbick patent portable forge.'
'His what?'

'As wondrous a creation of the modern age as your bridge is one of the ancient,' said Temple, earnest as you like.

'Half a day,' said Shy, 'and he'll have you a set of bands, bolts and hinges both ends of this bridge it'd take an army to get through.'

Red Beard licked his lips, and looked at Knobbly, and he licked his lips, too. 'All right, I tell you what, then. Half price if you fix up our gates—'

'We go free or not at all.'

'Half-price,' growled Red Beard.

'Bitch!' added his son.'

Shy narrowed her eyes at him. 'What do you reckon, Sweet?'

'I reckon I've been robbed before and at least they didn't dress it up any, the—'

'Sweet?' Red Beard's tone switched from bullying to wheedling. 'You're Dab Sweet, the scout?'

'The one killed that there red bear?' asked Knobbly.

Sweet drew himself up in his saddle. 'Twisted that furry fucker's head off with these very fingers.'

'Him?' called the boy. 'He's a bloody midget!'

His father shut him up with a wave. 'No one cares how big he is. Tell you what, could we use your name on the bridge?' He swept one hand through the air, like he could see the sign already. 'We'll call it Sweet's Crossing.'

The celebrated frontiersman was all bafflement. 'It's been here a thousand years, friend. Ain't no one going to believe I built it.'

'They'll believe you use it, though. Every time you cross this river you come this way.'

'I come whatever way makes best sense on that occasion. Reckon I'd be a piss-poor pilot were it any other how, now, wouldn't I?'

'But we'll say you come this way!'

Sweet sighed. 'Sounds a damn fool notion to me but I guess it's just a name.'

'He usually charges five hundred marks for the usage of it,' put in Shy.

'What?' said Red Beard.

'What?' said Sweet.

'Why,' said Temple, nimble with this notion, too, 'there is a manufacturer of biscuits in Adua who pays him a thousand marks a year just to put his face on the box.'

'What?' said Knobbly.

'What?' said Sweet.

'But,' went on Shy, 'seeing as we're using your bridge ourselves—'

'And it is a wonder of the ancient age,' put in Temple.

'—we can do you a cut-price deal. One hundred and fifty only, our Fellowship cross free and you can put his name to the bridge. How's that? You've made three hundred and fifty marks today and you didn't even move!'

Knobbly looked delighted with his profit. Red Beard yet doubted. 'We pay you that, what's to stop you selling his name to every other bridge, ford and ferry across the Far Country?'

'We'll draw up a contract, good and proper, and all make our marks to it.'

'A con . . . tract?' He could hardly speak the word, it was that unfamiliar. 'Where the hell you going to find a lawyer out here?'

Some days don't work out. Some days do. Shy slapped a hand down on Temple's shoulder, and he grinned at her, and she grinned back. 'We've got the good fortune to be travelling with the best damn lawyer west of Starikland!'

'He looks like a fucking beggar to me,' sneered the boy.

'Looks can lie,' said Lamb.

'So can lawyers,' said Sweet. 'It's halfway a habit with those bastards.'

'He can draw up the papers,' said Shy. 'Just twenty-five marks.' She spat in her free hand and offered it down.

'All right, then.' Red Beard smiled, or at least it looked like he might've in the midst of all that beard, and he spat, and they shook.

'In what language shall I draft the papers?' asked Temple.

Red Beard looked at Knobbly and shrugged. 'Don't matter. None of us can read.' And they turned away to see about getting the gate open.

'One hundred and nineteen marks,' muttered Temple in her ear, and while no one was looking nudged his mule forward, stood in his stirrups and shoved the boy off his perch, sending him sprawling in the mud next to the gate. 'My humble apologies,' he said. 'I did not see you there.'

He probably shouldn't have, just for that, but Shy found afterwards he'd moved up quite considerably in her estimation.

Dreams

Hedges hated this Fellowship. That stinking brown bastard Majud and that stuttering fuck Buckhorn and that old fake Sweet and their little-minded rules. Rules about when to eat and when to stop and what to drink and where to shit and what size of dog you could have along. It was worse'n being in the bloody army. Strange thing about the army – when he was in it he couldn't wait to get out, but soon as he was out he missed it.

He winced as he rubbed at his leg, trying to knead out the aches, but they was always there, laughing at him. Damn, but he was sick of being laughed at. If he'd known the wound would go bad he never would've stabbed himself. Thinking he was the clever one as he watched the rest of the battalion charge off after that arsehole Tunny. Little stab in the leg was a whole lot better than the big one through the heart, wasn't it? Except the enemy had left the wall the night before and they hadn't even had to fight. The battle over and him the only casualty, kicked out of the army with one good leg and no prospects. Misfortunes. He'd always been dogged by 'em.

The Fellowship weren't all bad, though. He turned in his battered saddle and picked out Shy South, riding back there near the cattle. She wasn't what you'd call a beauty but there was something to her, not caring about nothing, shirt dark with sweat so you could get a notion of her shape – and there was nothing wrong with it, far as he could tell. He'd always liked a strong woman. She weren't lazy either, always busy at something. No notion why she was laughing with that spice-eating arsehole Temple, worthless brown fuck if ever there was, she should've come over to him, he'd have given her something to smile at.

Hedges rubbed at his leg again, and shifted in his saddle, and spat. She was all right, but most of 'em were bastards. His eyes found Savian, swaying on his wagon-seat next to that sneering bitch of his, sharp chin up like she was better'n everyone else and Hedges in particular. He spat again. Spit was free so he might as well use plenty.

People spoke over him, looked through him, and when they passed a bottle round it never got to him, but he had eyes, and he had ears, and he'd seen that Savian in Rostod, after the massacre, dishing out orders like he was the big man, that hard-faced bitch of a niece loitering, too, maybe, and he'd heard the name *Conthus*. Heard it spoken soft and the rebels scraping the bloodstained ground with their noses like he was great Euz his self. He'd seen what he'd seen and he'd heard what he'd heard and that old bastard weren't just some other wanderer with dreams of gold. His dreams were bloodier. The worst of rebels, and no notion anyone knew it. Look at him sitting there like the last word in the argument, but Hedges would be the one had the last word. He'd had his misfortunes but he could smell an opportunity, all right. Just a case of finding out the moment to turn his secret into gold.

In the meantime, wait, and smile, and think about how much he hated that stuttering fuck Buckhorm.

He knew it was a waste of strength he didn't have, but sometimes Raynault Buckhorm hated his horse. He hated his horse, and he hated his saddle, and his canteen and his boots and his hat and his face-rag. But he knew his life depended on them sure as a climber's on his rope. There were plenty of spectacular ways to die out in the Far Country, skinned by a Ghost or struck by lightning or swept away in a flood. But most deaths out here would make a dull story. A mean horse in your string could kill you. A broken saddle-girth could kill you. A snake under your bare foot could kill you. He'd known this would be hard. Everyone had said so, shaking their heads and clucking like he was mad to go. But hearing it's one thing, and living it another. The work, the sheer graft of it, and the weather always wrong. You were burned by the sun or chafed by the rain and forever torn at by the wind, ripping across the plains to nowhere.

Sometimes he'd look out at the punishing emptiness ahead and wonder – has anyone else ever stood here? The thought would make him dizzy. How far had they come? How far still to go? What happened if Sweet didn't come back from one of his three-day scouts? Could they find their way through this ocean of grass without him?

He had to appear fixed, though, had to stay cheerful, had to be strong. Like Lamb. He took a look sideways at the big Northman, who'd got down to roll Lord Ingelstad's wagon out of a rut. Buckhorm didn't think him and all his sons could've managed it, but Lamb just shrugged it free without a word. Ten years Buckhorm's senior at the least, but might as well have been carved out of rock still, never tiring, never complaining. Folk were looking to Buckhorm for an example, and if he weakened everyone might, and then what? Turn back? He glanced over his shoulder, and though every direction looked about the same, saw failure that way.

He saw his wife, too, plodding away from the column with some of the other women to make water. He'd a sense she wasn't happy, which was a heavy burden and a sore confusion to him. Wasn't as if all this was for his benefit, was it? He'd been happy enough in Hormring, but a man should work to give his wife and children the things they haven't got, grab them a better future, and out there in the west was where he'd seen it. He didn't know what to do to make her happy. Did his husband's duties every night, didn't he, sore or not, tired or not?

Sometimes he felt like asking her – what do you want? The question sitting on his clumsy tongue but his bloody stutter would come on hard then and he never could spit it free. He'd have liked to get down and walk with her a spell, talk like they used to, but then who'd keep the cattle moving? Temple? He barked a joyless laugh at that, turned his eyes on the drifter. There was one of those fellows thought the world owed him an easy ride. One of those men floats from one disaster to another pretty as a butterfly leaving others to clean up his spillings. He wasn't even minding the task he was being paid for, just toddling along on his mule clowning with Shy South. Buckhorm shook his head at that odd couple. Out of the two of them, no doubt she was the better man.

Luline Buckhorm took her place in the circle, studiously looking outwards.

Her wagon was at a halt, as it always was unless she was on hand to shift it by force of will, three of her older children fighting over the reins, their mindless bickering floating out over the grass.

Sometimes she hated her children, with their whining and their sore spots and their endless, gripping, crushing needs. When do we stop? When do we eat? When do we get to Crease? Their impatience all the harder to bear because of her own. All desperate for anything to break up the endless plodding sameness of the trek. Must have been well into autumn now, but except for the wind having an even chillier slap to it, how could you even tell the time of year out here? So flat, so endlessly flat, and yet she still felt they were toiling always uphill, the incline greater with every day trudged by.

She heard Lady Ingelstad dropping her skirts and felt her push into place beside. It was a great equaliser, the Far Country. A woman who wouldn't have deigned to look at her back in civilisation, whose husband had sat on the Open Council of the Union, fool though he was, and here they were making piss together. Sisbet Peg took up her place in the middle of the circle, squatting over the bucket, safe from prying eyes, no more than sixteen and just married, still fresh in love and talking like her husband was the answer to every question, bless her. She'd learn.

Luline caught that slime Hedges peering over as he swayed past on his mangy mule, and she gave him a stern frown back and closed up tight to Lady Ingelstad's shoulder, planted hands on hips and made herself big, or as big as she got at least, making sure he'd catch sight of nothing but disapproval. Then Raynault trotted up and put himself between Hedges and the women, striking up some halting conversation.

'A good man, your husband,' said Lady Ingelstad approvingly. 'You can always rely on him to do the decent thing.'

'That you can,' said Luline, making sure she sounded proud as any wife could be.

Sometimes she hated her husband, with his grinding ignorance of her struggles, and his chafing assumptions of what was woman's work and what was man's. Like knocking in a fence-post then getting drunk was real labour, but minding a crowd of children all day and night was fun to feel grateful for. She looked up and saw white birds high in the sky, flying in a great arrow to who knew where, and wished she could join them. How many steps had she trudged beside that wagon, now?

She'd liked it in Hormring, good friends and a house she'd spent years getting just so. But no one ever asked what her dream was, oh no, she was just expected to sell her good chair and the good fire it had stood beside and chase off after his. She watched him trot up to the head of the column, pointing something out to Majud. The big men, with the big dreams to discuss.

Did it never occur to him that she might want to ride, and feel the fresh wind, and smile at the wide-open country, and rope cattle, and consider the route, and speak up in the meetings while he trudged beside the squealing wagon, and changed the shitty wrappings on their youngest, and shouted at the next three in line to stop shouting, and had his nipples chewed raw every hour or two while still being

145

expected to have a good dinner ready and do the wifely duties every bloody night, sore or not, tired or not?

A fool question. It never did occur to him. And when it occurred to her, which was plenty, there was always something stopped her tongue sure as if she had the stutter, and made her just shrug and be sulky silent.

'Will you look at that?' murmured Lady Ingelstad. Shy South had swung down from her saddle not a dozen strides from the column and was squatting in the long grass in the shadow of her horse making a spatter, reins in her teeth and trousers around ankles, the side of her pale arse plain to see.

'Incredible,' someone muttered.

She pulled her trousers up, gave a friendly wave, then closed her belt, spat the reins into her hand and was straight back in the saddle. The whole business had taken no time at all, and been done exactly when and how she wanted. Luline Buckhorm frowned around at the outward-facing circle of women, changing over so that one of the whores could take her turn above the bucket. 'There a reason we can't do the same?' she muttered.

Lady Ingelstad turned an iron frown upon her. 'There most certainly is!' They watched Shy South ride off, shouting something to Sweet about closing the wagons up. 'Although, at present, I must confess it eludes me.'

A sharp cry from the column that sounded like her eldest daughter and Luline's heart near leaped from her chest. She took a lurching step, wild with panic, then saw the children were just fighting on the wagon's seat again, shrieking and laughing.

'Don't you worry,' said Lady Ingelstad, patting her hand as she stepped back into place in the circle. 'All's well.'

'Just so many dangers out here.' Luline took a breath and tried to calm her beating heart. 'So much could go wrong.' Sometimes she hated her family, and sometimes her love for them was like a pain in her. Probably it was a puzzle there was no solving.

'Your turn,' said Lady Ingelstad.

'Right.' Luline started hitching up her skirts as the circle closed around her. Damn, had there ever been so much trouble taken over making piss?

The famous Iosiv Lestek grunted, and squeezed, and finally spattered a few more drops into the can. 'Yes . . . yes . . .' But then the wagon

146

jolted, pans and chests all rattling, he released his prick to grab the rail, and when he steadied himself the tap of joy was turned firmly off.

'Why is man cursed with such a thing as age?' he murmured, quoting the last line of *The Beggar's Demise*. Oh, the silence into which he had murmured those words at the peak of his powers! Oh, the applause that had flooded after! Tremendous acclaim. And now? He had supposed himself in the wilderness when his company had toured the provinces of Midderland, never guessing what real wilderness might look like. He peered out of the window at the endless grass. A great ruin hove into view, some forgotten fragment of the Empire, countless years abandoned. Toppled columns, grass-seeded walls. There were many of them scattered across this part of the Far Country, their glories faded, their stories unknown, their remains scarcely arousing interest. Relics of an age long past. Just as he was.

He remembered, with powerful nostalgia, a time in his life when he had pissed bucket-loads. Sprayed like a handpump without even considering it, then whisked onstage to bask in the glow of the sweet-smelling whale-oil lamps, to coax the sighs from the audience, to wallow in the fevered applause. That ugly pair of little trolls, playwright and manager, entreating him to stay on another season, and begging, and grovelling, and offering more while he refused to dignify them with a reply, busy with his powder. He had been invited to the Agriont to tread the stage of the palace itself before his August Majesty and the entire Closed Council! He had played the First of the Magi before the First of the Magi – how many actors could say the same? He had pranced upon a pavement of abject critics, of ruined competitors, of adoring enthusiasts and scarcely even noticed them beneath his feet. Failure was for other men to consider.

And then his knees failed him, then his guts, then his bladder, then the audiences. The playwright smirking as he suggested a younger man for the lead – but still a worthy part in support for him, of course, just while he gathered his strength. Lurching on stage, stuttering his lines, sweating in the glare of the stinking lamps. Then the manager smirking as he suggested they part ways. Such a wonderful collaboration for them both, how many years had it been, such reviews, such audiences, but time for them both to seek new successes, to follow new dreams . . .

'Oh, treachery, thy noisome visage shown—'

The wagon lurched and the miserable dribblings he had laboured the last hour for slopped from the can and over his hand. He scarcely even noticed. He rubbed at his sweaty jaw. He needed to shave.

Some standards had to be maintained. He was bringing culture to the wasteland, was he not? He picked up Camling's letter and scanned it once again, mouthing the words to himself. He was possessed of an excessively ornamented style, this Camling, but was pleasingly abject in his praise and appreciation, in his promises of fine treatment, in his plans for an epoch-making event to be staged within the ancient Imperial amphitheatre of Crease. A show for the ages, as he put it. A cultural extravaganza!

Iosiv Lestek was not finished yet. Not he! Redemption can come in the most unlooked-for places. And it was some while since his last hallucinatory episode. Definitely on the mend! Lestek set down the letter and boldly took up prick once again, gazing through the window at the slowly passing ruins.

'My best performance is ahead of me . . .' he grunted, gritting his teeth as he squeezed a few more drops into the can.

'Wonder what it's like,' said Sallit, staring wistfully at that bright-coloured wagon, *The Famous Iosiv Lestek* written along the side in purple letters. Not that she could read it. But that was what Luline Buckhorm had told her it said.

'What what's like?' asked Goldy, twitching the reins.

'Being an actor. Up on stage in front of an audience and all.' She'd seen some players once. Her mother and father took her. Before they died. Of course before that. Not big-city actors, but even so. She'd clapped until her hands hurt.

Goldy scraped a loose lock of hair back under her battered hat. 'Don't you play a role every time you get a customer?'

'Not quite the same, is it?'

'Smaller audience, but otherwise not much different.' They could hear Najis seeing to one of Gentili's old cousins in the back of the wagon, moaning away. 'Seem to like it, might be a tip in it.' At least there was the chance it would finish quicker. That had to be a good thing.

'Never been that good at pretending,' Sallit muttered. Not pretending to like it, anyway. Got in the way of pretending not to be there at all.

'Ain't always about the fucking. Not always. Not just the fucking, anyway.' Goldy had been around. She was hellish practical. Sallit wished she could be practical. Maybe she'd get there. 'Just treat 'em like they're somebody. That's all anyone wants, ain't it?'

'I suppose.' Sallit would've liked to be treated like somebody, instead of a thing. Folk looked at her, they just saw a whore. She wondered if anyone in the Fellowship knew her name. Less feeling than for cattle, and less value placed on you, too. What would her parents have made of this, their girl a whore? But they lost their say when they died, and it seemed Sallit had lost her say as well. She guessed there was worse.

'Just a living. That's the way to look at it. You're young, love. You've got time to work.' A heated bitch was trotting along beside the column and a crowd of a dozen or more dogs of every shape and size were loping hopefully after. 'Way o' the world,' said Goldy, watching them pass. 'Put the work in, you can come out rich. Rich enough to retire comfortable, anyway. That's the dream.'

'Is it?' Sounded like a pretty poor kind of dream to Sallit. To not have the worst.

'Not much action now, that's true, but we get to Crease, you'll see the money come in. Lanklan knows what he's about, don't you worry on that score.'

Everyone wanted to get to Crease. They'd wake up talking of the route, begging Sweet to know how many miles they'd gone, how many still to go, counting them off like days of a hard sentence. But Sallit dreaded the place. Sometimes Lanklan would talk about how many lonely men were out there, eyes aglitter, and how they'd have fifty clients a day like that was something to look forward to. Sounded like hell to Sallit. Sometimes she didn't much like Lanklan, but Goldy said as pimps went he was a keeper.

Najis' squealing was building to a peak now, impossible to ignore.

'How far is it still to go?' asked Sallit, trying to cover over it with talk.

Goldy frowned out towards the horizon. 'Lot of ground and a lot of rivers.'

'That's what you said weeks back.'

'It was true then and it's true now. Don't worry, love. Dab Sweet'll get us there.'

Sallit hoped he didn't. She hoped the old scout led 'em round in a great circle and all the way back to New Keln and her mother and father smiling in the doorway of the old house. That was all she wanted. But they were dead of the shudders, and out here in the great empty was no place for dreams. She took a hard breath, rubbed the pain out of her nose, making sure not to cry. That wasn't fair on the rest. Didn't help her when they cried, did it?

'Good old Dab Sweet.' Goldy snapped the reins and clucked at the oxen. 'Never been lost in his life, I hear.'

'Not lost, then,' said Crying Rock.

Sweet took his eyes off the coming rider to squint up at her, perched on top of one of the broken walls with the sinking sun behind, swinging a loose leg, that old flag unwrapped from her head for once and her hair shook out long, silver with a few streaks of gold still in it. 'When have you ever known me to be lost?'

'When I'm not there to point the way?'

He gave a sorry grin at that. Only a couple of times on this trip he'd needed to slip off in the darkness on a clear night to fiddle at his astrolabe and take a proper bearing. He'd won it off a retired sea-captain in a card game and it had proved damned useful down the years. It was like being at sea, sometimes, the plains. Naught but the sky and the horizon and the moaning bloody cargo. A man needed a trick or two to keep pace with his legend.

That red bear? It was a spear he'd killed it with, not his bare hands, and it had been old, and slow, and not that big. But it had been a bear, and he'd killed it, all right. Why couldn't folk be satisfied with that? Dab Sweet killed a bear! But no, they had to paint a taller picture with every telling – bare hands, then saving a woman, then there were three bears – until he himself could only disappoint beside it. He leaned back against a broken pillar, arms folded, and watched that horseman coming at a gallop, no saddle, Ghost fashion, with a sour, sour feeling in his gut.

'Who made me fucking admirable?' he muttered. 'Not me, that's sure.'

'Huh,' said Crying Rock.

'I never had an elevated motive in my life.'

'Uh.'

There was a time he'd heard tales of Dab Sweet and he'd stuck thumbs in his belt and chin to the sky and tricked himself that was how his life had been. But the years scraped by hard as ever and he got less and the stories more 'til they were tales of a man he'd never met succeeding at what he'd never have dreamed of attempting. Sometimes they'd stir some splinter of remembrance of mad and desperate fights or tedious slogs to nowhere or withering passages of cold and hunger and he'd shake his head and wonder by what fucking alchemy these episodes of rank necessity were made noble adventures.

'What do they get?' he asked. 'A parcel o' stories to nod their heads to. What do I got? Naught to retire on, that's sure. Just a worn-out saddle and a sack full of other men's lies to carry.'

'Uh,' said Crying Rock, like that was just the way of things.

'Ain't fair. Just ain't fair.'

'Why would it be fair?'

He grunted his agreement to that. He wasn't getting old no more. He *was* old. His legs ached when he woke and his chest ached when he lay down and the cold got in him deep and he looked at the days behind and saw how heavily they outnumbered those ahead. He'd set to wondering how many more nights he could sleep under the pitiless sky, yet still men looked at him awestruck like he was great Juvens, and if they landed in a real fix he'd sing a storm to sleep or shoot down Ghosts with lightning from his arse. He had no lightning, not he, and sometimes after he'd talked to Majud and played that role of knows-it-all-and-never-shirks better than Iosiv Lestek himself could have managed, he'd mount his horse and his hands would be all atremble and his eye dim and he'd say to Crying Rock, 'I've lost my nerve,' and she'd just nod like that was the way of things.

'I was something once, wasn't I?' he muttered.

'You're still something,' said Crying Rock.

'What, though?'

The rider reined in a few strides distant, frowning at Sweet, and at Crying Rock, and at the ruins they were waiting in, suspicious as a spooked stag. After a moment he swung a leg over and slid down.

'Dab Sweet,' said the Ghost.

'Locway,' said Sweet. It'd have to be him. He was one of the new type, sulky-like, just saw the bad in everything. 'Why ain't Sangeed here?'

'You can speak to me.'

'I can, but why should I?'

Locway bristled up, all chafe and pout like the young ones always were. Most likely Sweet had been no different in his youth. Most likely he'd been worse, but damn if all the posturing didn't make him tired these days. He waved the Ghost down. 'All right, all right, we'll talk.' He took a breath, that sour feeling getting no sweeter. He'd been planning this a long time, argued every side of it and picked his path, but taking the last step was still proving an effort.

'Talk, then,' said Locway.

'I'm bringing a Fellowship, might be a day's quick ride south of us. They've got money.'

'Then we will take it,' said Locway.

'You'll do as you're fucking told is what you'll do,' snapped Sweet. 'Tell Sangeed to be at the place we agreed on. They're jumpy as all hell as it is. Just show yourselves in fighting style, do some riding round, shout a lot and shoot an arrow or two and they'll be keen to pay you off. Keep things easy, you understand?'

'I understand,' said Locway, but Sweet had his doubts that he knew what easy looked like.

He went close to the Ghost, their faces level since he was fortunately standing upslope, and put his thumbs in his sword-belt and jutted his jaw out. 'No killing, you hear? Nice and simple and everyone gets paid. Half for you, half for me. You tell Sangeed that.'

'I will,' said Locway, staring back, challenging him. Sweet had a sore temptation to stab him and damn the whole business. But better sense prevailed. 'What do you say to this?' Locway called to Crying Rock.

She looked down at him, hair shifting with the breeze, and kept swinging that loose leg. Just as if he hadn't spoke at all. Sweet had himself a bit of a chuckle.

'Are you laughing at me, little man?' snapped Locway.

'I'm laughing and you're here,' said Sweet. 'Draw your own fucking conclusions. Now off and tell Sangeed what I said.'

He frowned after Locway for a long time, watching him and his horse dwindle to a black spot in the sunset and thinking how this particular episode weren't likely to show up in the legend of Dab Sweet. That sour feeling was worse'n ever. But what could he do? Couldn't be guiding Fellowships for ever, could he?

'Got to have something to retire on,' he muttered. 'Ain't too greedy a dream, is it?'

He squinted up at Crying Rock, binding her hair back into that twisted flag again. Most men would've seen nothing, maybe. But he who'd known her so many years caught the disappointment in her face. Or maybe just his own, reflected back like in a still pool.

'I never been no fucking hero,' he snapped. 'Whatever they say.'

She just nodded, like that was the way of things.

The Folk were camped among the ruins, Sangeed's tall dwelling built in the angle of the fallen arm of a great statue. No one knew now who the statue had been. An old God, died and fallen away into the past, and it seemed to Locway that the Folk would soon join him.

The camp was quiet and the dwellings few, the young men ranging far to hunt. On the racks only lean shreds of meat drying. The shuttles of the blanket weavers clacked and rattled, chopping the time up into ugly moments. Brought to this, they who had ruled the plains. Weaving for a pittance, and stealing money so they could buy from their destroyers the things that should have been theirs already.

The black spots had come in the winter and carried away half the children, moaning and sweating. They had burned their dwellings and drawn the sacred circles in the earth and said the proper words but it made no difference. The world was changing, and the old rituals held no power. The children had still died, the women had still dug, the men had still wept, and Locway had wept most bitterly of all.

Sangeed had put his hand upon his shoulder and said, 'I fear not for myself. I had my time. I fear for you and the young ones, who must walk after me, and will see the end of things.' Locway feared, too. Sometimes he felt that all his life was fear. What way was that for a warrior?

He left his horse and picked his way through the camp. Sangeed was brought from his lodge, his arms across the shoulders of his two strong daughters. His spirit was being taken piece by piece. Each morning there was less of him, that mighty frame before which the world had trembled withered to a shell.

'What did Sweet say?' he whispered.

'That a Fellowship is coming, and will pay. I do not trust him.'

'He has been a friend to the Folk.' One of Sangeed's daughters wiped the spit from the corner of his slack mouth. 'We will meet him.' And already he was starting to sleep.

'We will meet him,' said Locway, but he feared what might happen.

He feared for his baby son, who only three nights before had given his first laugh and so become one of the Folk. It should have been a moment for rejoicing, but Locway had only fear in him. What world was this to be born into? In his youth the Folk's flocks and herds had been strong and numerous, and now they were stolen by the newcomers, and the good grazing cropped away by the passing Fellowships, and the beasts hunted to nothing, and the Folk scattered and taken to shameful ways. Before, the future had always looked like the past. Now he knew the past was a better place, and the future full of fear and death.

But the Folk would not fade without a fight. And so Locway sat beside his wife and son as the stars were opened, and dreamed of a better tomorrow he knew would never come.

The Wrath of God

'Don't much care for the look o' that cloud!' called Leef, pushing hair out of his face that the wind straight away snatched back into it.

'If hell has clouds,' muttered Temple, 'they look like that one.' It was a grey-black mountain on the horizon, a dark tower boiling into the very heavens, making of the sun a feeble smudge and staining the sky about it strange, warlike colours. Every time Temple checked it was closer. All the endless, shelterless Far Country to cast into shadow and where else would it go but directly over his head? Truly, he exerted an uncanny magnetism on anything dangerous.

'Let's get these fires lit and back to the wagons!' he called, as though some planks and canvas would be sure protection against the impending fury of the skies. The wind was not helping with the task. Nor did the drizzle, when it began to fall a moment later. Nor did the rain that came soon after that, whipping from everywhere at once, cutting through Temple's threadbare coat as if he was wearing nothing. He bent cursing over his little heap of cow-leavings, dissolving rapidly in his wet hands into their original, more fragrant state while he fumbled with a smouldering stick of wood.

'Ain't much fun trying to set fire to wet shit, is it?' shouted Leef.

'I've had better jobs!' Though the same sense of distasteful futility had applied to most of them, now Temple considered it.

He heard hooves and saw Shy swing from her saddle, hat clasped to her head. She had to come close and shout over the rising wind and Temple found himself momentarily distracted by her shirt, which had stuck tight to her with wet and come open a button, showing a small tanned triangle of skin below her throat and a paler one around it, sharp lines of her collarbones faintly glistening, perhaps just the suggestion of—

154

'I said, where's the herd?' she bellowed in his face.

'Er . . .' Temple jerked a thumb over his shoulder. 'Might be a mile behind us!'

'Storm was making 'em restless.' Leef's eyes were narrowed against the wind, or possibly at Temple, it was hard to say which.

'Buckhorm was worried they might scatter. He sent us to light some fires around the camp.' Temple pointed out the crescent of nine or ten they had managed to set a flame to before the rain came. 'Maybe steer the herd away if they panic!' Though their smouldering efforts did not look capable of diverting a herd of lambs. The wind was blowing up hard, ripping the smoke from the fires and off across the plain, making the long grass thrash, dragging the dancing seed heads out in waves and spirals. 'Where's Sweet?'

'No telling. We'll have to work this one out ourselves.' She dragged him up by his wet coat. 'You'll get no more fires lit in this! We need to get back to the wagons!'

The three of them struggled through what was now lashing rain, stung and buffeted by gusts, Shy tugging her nervous horse by the bridle. A strange gloom had settled over the plain and they scarcely saw the wagons until they stumbled upon them in a mass, folk tugging desperately at oxen, trying to hobble panicked horses and tether snapping livestock or wrestling with their own coats or oilskins, turned into thrashing adversaries by the wind.

Ashjid stood in the midst, eyes bulging with fervour, sinewy arms stretched up to the pouring heavens, the Fellowship's idiot kneeling at his feet, the whole like a sculpture of some martyred Prophet. 'There is no running from the sky!' he was shrieking, finger outstretched. 'There is no hiding from God! God is always watching!'

It seemed to Temple he was that most dangerous kind of priest – one who really believes. 'Have you ever noticed that God is wonderful at watching,' he called, 'but quite poor when it comes to helping out?'

'We got bigger worries than that fool and his idiot,' snapped Shy. 'Got to get the wagons closed up – if the herd charges through here there's no telling what'll happen!'

The rain was coming in sheets now, Temple was as wet as if he had been dunked in the bath. His first in several weeks, come to think of it. He saw Corlin, teeth gritted and her hair plastered to her skull, struggling with ropes as she tried to get some snapping canvas lashed. Lamb was near her, heavy shoulder set to a wagon and straining as if he might move it on his own. He even was, a little. Then a couple of bedraggled Suljuks jumped in beside him and between them got it rolling. Luline Buckhorm was lifting her children up into a wagon and Temple went to help them, scraping the hair from his eyes.

'Repent!' shrieked Ashjid. 'This is no storm, this is the wrath of God!'

Savian dragged him close by his torn robe. 'This is a storm. Keep talking and I'll show you the wrath of God!' And he flung the old man on the ground.

'We need to get . . .' Shy's mouth went on but the wind stole her words. She tugged at Temple and he staggered after, no more than a few steps but they might as well have been miles. It was black as night, water coursing down his face, and he was shivering with cold and fear, hands helplessly dangling. He turned, bearings suddenly fled and panic gripping him.

Which way were the wagons? Where was Shy?

One of his fires still smouldered nearby, sparks showering out into the dark, and he tottered towards it. The wind came up like a door slamming on him and he pushed and struggled, grappling at it like one drunkard with another. Then, suddenly, a sharper trickster than he, it came at him the other way and bowled him over, left him thrashing in the grass, Ashjid's mad shrieking echoing in his ears, calling on God to smite the unbeliever.

Seemed harsh. You can't just choose to believe, can you?

He crawled on hands and knees, hardly daring to stand in case he was whisked into the sky and dashed down in some distant place, bones left to bleach on earth that had never known men's footsteps. A flash split the darkness, raindrops frozen streaks and the wagons edged with white, figures caught straining as if in some mad tableau then all sunk again in rain-lashed darkness.

A moment later thunder ripped and rattled, turning Temple's knees to jelly and seeming shake the very earth. But thunder should end and this only drummed louder and louder, the ground trembling now for certain, and Temple realised it was not thunder but hooves. Hundreds of hooves battering the earth, the cattle driven mad by the storm, so many dozen tons of meat hurtling at him where he knelt helpless. Another flash and he saw them, rendered devilish by the darkness, one heaving animal with hundreds of goring horns, a furious mass boiling across the plain towards him.

'Oh God,' he whispered, sure that, slippery as he was, death's icy grip was on him at last. 'Oh God.'

'Come on, you fucking idiot!'

Someone tugged at him and another flash showed Shy's face, hatless with hair flattened and her lips curled back, all dogged determination, and he had never been so glad to be insulted in his life. He stumbled with her, the pair of them jerked and buffeted by the wind like corks in a flood, the rain become a scriptural downpour, like to the fabled flood with which God punished the arrogance of old Sippot, the thunder of hooves merged with the thunder of the angry sky to make one terrifying din.

A double blink of lightning lit the back of a wagon, canvas awning madly jerking, and below it Leef's face, wide-eyed, shouting encouragements drowned in the wind, one arm stretched starkly out.

And suddenly that hand closed around Temple's and he was dragged inside. Another flash showed him Luline Buckhorm and some of her children, huddled together amongst the sacks and barrels along with two of the whores and one of Gentili's cousins, all wet as swimmers. Shy slithered into the wagon beside him, Leef dragging her under the arms, while outside he could hear a veritable river flowing around the wheels. Together they wrestled the flapping canvas down.

Temple fell back, in the pitch darkness, and someone sagged against him. He could hear their breath. It might have been Shy, or it might have been Leef, or it might have been Gentili's cousin, and he hardly cared which.

'God's teeth,' he muttered, 'but you get some weather out here.'

No one answered. Nothing to say, or too drained to say it, or perhaps they could not hear him for the hammering of the passing cattle and the hail battering the waxed canvas just above their heads.

The path the herd had taken wasn't hard to follow – a stretch of muddied, trampled earth veering around the camp and spreading out beyond as the cattle had scattered, here or there the corpse of a dead cow huddled, all gleaming and glistening in the bright wet morning.

'The good people of Crease may have to wait a little longer for the word of God,' said Corlin.

'Seems so.' Shy had taken it at first for a heap of wet rags. But crouching beside it she'd seen a corner of black cloth flapping with some white embroidery, and recognised Ashjid's robe. She took off her hat. Felt like the respectful thing to do. 'Ain't much left of him.'

'I suppose that's what happens when a few hundred cattle trample a man.'

'Remind me not to try it.' Shy stood and jammed her hat back on. 'Guess we'd best tell the others.'

It was all activity in the camp, folk putting right what the storm spoiled, gathering what the storm scattered. Some of the livestock might've wandered miles, Leef and a few others off rounding them up. Lamb, Savian, Majud and Temple were busy mending a wagon that the wind had dragged over and into a ditch. Well, Lamb and Savian were doing the lifting while Majud was tending to the axle with grip and hammer. Temple was holding the nails.

'Everything all right?' he asked as they walked up.

'Ashjid's dead,' said Shy.

'Dead?' grunted Lamb, setting the wagon down and slapping his hands together.

'Pretty sure,' said Corlin. 'The herd went over him.'

'Told him to stay put,' growled Savian. That man was all sentiment.

'Who's going to pray for us now?' Majud even looked worried about it.

'You need praying for?' asked Shy. 'Didn't pick you for piety.'

The merchant stroked at his pointed chin. 'Heaven is at the bottom of a full purse, but . . . I have become used to a morning prayer.'

'And me,' said Buckhorm, who'd drifted over to join the conversation with a couple of his several sons.

'What do you know,' muttered Temple. 'He made some converts after all.'

'Say, lawyer!' Shy called at him. 'Wasn't priest among your past professions?'

Temple winced and leaned in to speak quietly. 'Yes, but of all the many shameful episodes in my past, that is perhaps the one that shames me most.'

Shy shrugged. 'There's always a place for you behind the herd if that suits you better.'

Temple thought a moment, then turned to Majud. 'I was given personal instruction over the course of several years by Kahdia, High Haddish of the Great Temple in Dagoska and world-renowned orator and theologian.'

'So . . .' Buckhorm pushed his hat back with a long finger. 'Cuh . . . can you say a prayer or can't you?'

Temple sighed. 'Yes. Yes, I can.' He added in a mutter to Shy. 'A prayer from an unbelieving preacher to an unbelieving congregation from a score of nations where they all disbelieve in different things.'

Shy shrugged. 'We're in the Far Country now. Guess folk need something new to doubt.' Then, to the rest, 'He'll say the best damn prayer you ever heard! His name's Temple, ain't it? How religious can you get?'

Majud and Buckhorm traded sceptical glances. 'If a Prophet can fall from the sky, I suppose one can wash from a river, too.'

'Ain't exactly raining . . . other options.'

'It's rained everything else,' said Lamb, peering up at the heavens.

'And what shall be my fee?' asked Temple.

Majud frowned. 'We did not pay Ashjid.'

'Ashjid's only care was for God. I have myself to consider also.'

'Not to mention your debts,' added Shy.

'Not to mention those.' Temple gave Majud an admonishing glance. 'And, after all, your support for charity was clearly demonstrated when you refused to offer help to a drowning man.'

'I assure you I am as charitable as anyone, but I have the feelings of my partner Curnsbick to consider and Curnsbick has an eye on every bit.'

'So you often tell us.'

'And you were not drowning at the time, only wet.'

'One can still be charitable to the wet.'

'You weren't,' added Shy.

Majud shook his head. 'You two would sell eyeglasses to a blind man.'

'No less use than prayers to a villain,' put in Temple, with a pious fluttering of his lashes.

The merchant rubbed at his bald scalp. 'Very well. But I buy nothing without a sample. A prayer now, and if the words convince me I will pay a fair price this morning and every morning. I will hope to write it off to sundry expenses.'

'Sundry it is.' Shy leaned close to Temple. 'You wanted a break from riding drag, this could be a steady earner. Give it some belief, lawyer.'

'All right,' Temple muttered back. 'But if I'm the new priest, I want the old one's boots.' He clambered up onto one of the wagons, makeshift congregation shuffling into an awkward crescent. To Shy's surprise it was nearly half the Fellowship. Nothing moves people to prayer like death, she guessed, and last night's demonstration of God's wrath didn't hurt attendance either. All the Suljuks were there. Lady Ingelstad tall and curious. Gentili with his ancient family. Buckhorm with his young one. Most of the whores and their pimp, too, though

Shy had a suspicion he was keeping an eye on his goods rather than moved by love of the Almighty.

There was a silence, punctuated only by the scraping of Hedges' knife as he salvaged the dead cattle for meat, and the scraping of Savian's shovel as he put the remains of the Fellowship's previous spiritual advisor to rest. Without his boots. Temple held one hand in the other and humbly turned his face towards the heavens. Deep and clear now, with no trace of last night's fury.

'God—'

'Close, but no!' And at that moment old Dab Sweet came riding up, reins dangling between two fingers. 'Morning, my brave companions!'

'Where the hell have you been?' called Majud.

'Scouting. It's what you pay me for, ain't it?'

'That and help in storms.'

'I can't hold your hand across every mile o' the Far Country. We been out north,' jerking his thumb over his shoulder.

'Out north,' echoed Crying Rock, who had somehow managed to ride into the encampment from the opposite direction in total silence.

'Following some Ghost signs, trying to guide you clear of any nasty surprises.'

'Ghost signs?' asked Temple, looking a little sick.

Sweet held up a calming hand. 'No need for anyone to shit their britches yet. This is the Far Country, there's always Ghosts around. Question is which ones and how many. We was worried those tracks might belong to some o' Sangeed's people.'

'And?' asked Corlin.

''Fore we could get a sight of 'em, that storm blew in. Best thing we could do was find a rock to shelter by and let it blow along.'

'Hah huh,' grunted Crying Rock, presumably in agreement.

'You should have been here,' grumbled Lord Ingelstad.

'Even I can't be everywhere, your Lordship. But keep complaining, by all means. Scorn is the scout's portion. Everyone's got a better way of doing things 'til they're called on to actually tell you what it might be. It was our surmise that among the whole Fellowship you'd enough stout hearts and level heads to see it through – not that I'd count your Lordship with either party – and what do you know?' Sweet stuck out his bottom lip and nodded around at the dripping camp and its bedraggled occupants. 'Few head of cattle lost but that was quite a storm last night. Could've been plenty worse.'

'Shall I get down?' asked Temple.

'Not on my account. What you doing up there, anyhow?'

'He was about to say the morning prayer,' said Shy.

'He was? What happened to the other God-tickler? What's his name?'

'Herd ran over him in the night,' said Corlin, without emotion wasted on the fact.

'I guess that'll do it.' Sweet reached into his saddlebag and eased out a half-full bottle. 'Well, then, have at it, lawyer.' And he treated himself to a long swig.

Temple sighed, and looked at Shy. She shrugged, and mouthed, 'Drag,' at him. He sighed again and turned his eyes skywards.

'God,' he began for a second time. 'For reasons best known to yourself, you have chosen to put a lot of bad people in the world. People who would rather steal a thing than make it. Who would rather break a thing than grow it. People who will set fire to a thing just to watch it burn. I know. I've run across a few of them. I've ridden with them.' Temple looked down for a moment. 'I suppose I've been one of them.'

'Oh, he's good,' muttered Sweet, handing the bottle to Shy. She took a taste, making sure it wasn't too deep.

'Perhaps they seem like monsters, these people.' Temple's voice rose high and fell low, hands stroking and plucking and pointing in a fashion Shy had to concede was quite arresting. 'But the truth is, it takes no sorcery to make a man do bad things. Bad company. Bad choices. Bad luck. A no more than average level of cowardice.' Shy offered the bottle to Lamb but he was fixed so tight to the sermon he didn't notice. Corlin took it instead.

'But gathered here today, humbly seeking your blessing, you see a different kind of people.' Quite a few of them, in fact, as the flock was steadily swelling. 'Not perfect, surely. Each with their faults. Some uncharitable.' And Temple gave Majud a stern look. 'Some prone to drink.' Corlin paused with the bottle halfway to her mouth. 'Some just a little on the grasping side.' His eye fell on Shy, and damn it if she didn't even feel a little shamed for a moment, and that took some heavy doing.

'But every one of these people came out here to make something!' A ripple of agreement went through the Fellowship, heads bobbing as they nodded along. 'Every one of them chose to take the hard way! The right way!' He really was good. Shy could hardly believe it was the same man who moaned ten times a day about dust, pouring out his heart like he'd God's words in him after all. 'To brave the perils of the wilderness so they could build new lives with their hands and their sweat and their righteous effort!' Temple spread his own hands wide to encompass the gathering. 'These are the good people, God! Your children, ranged before you, hopeful and persevering! Shield them from the storm! Guide them through the trials of this day, and every day!'

'Hurrah!' cried the idiot, leaping up and punching the air, faith switched smoothly to a new Prophet, whooping and capering and shouting, 'Good people! Good people!' until Corlin caught hold of him and managed to shut him up.

'Good words,' said Lamb as Temple hopped down from the wagon. 'By the dead, those were some good words.'

'Mostly another man's, if I'm honest.'

'Well, you surely say 'em like you believe 'em,' said Shy.

'A few days riding drag and you'll believe in anything,' he muttered. The congregation was drifting apart, heading to their morning tasks, a couple of them thanking Temple as they moved off to get underway. Majud was left, lips appraisingly pressed together.

'Convinced?' asked Shy.

The merchant reached into his purse – which wasn't far from a miracle in itself – and pulled out what looked like a two mark piece. 'You should have stuck to prayers,' he said to Temple. 'They're in greater demand than laws out here.' And he flicked the coin spinning into the air, flashing with the morning sun.

Temple grinned, reaching out to catch it.

Shy snatched it from the air first.

'One hundred and twelve,' she said.

The Practical Thinkers

'You owe me—'

'One hundred and two marks,' said Temple, turning over. He was already awake. He had started waking before dawn, lately, ready the moment his eyes came open.

'That's right. Get up. You're wanted.'

'I've always had that effect on women. It's a curse.'

'For them, no doubt.'

Temple sighed as he started to roll up his blanket. He was a little sore, but it would wear off. He was getting hard from the work. Tough in places that had been soft a long time. He had been obliged to tighten his belt by a couple of notches. Well, not notches exactly, but he had twice shifted the bent nail that served for a buckle in the old saddle-girth that served for a belt.

'Don't tell me,' he said. 'I'm riding drag.'

'No. Once you've led the Fellowship in prayer, Lamb's lending you his horse. You're coming hunting with me and Sweet today.'

'Do you have to taunt me like this every morning?' he asked as he pulled his boots on. 'What happened to make you this way?'

She stood looking at him, hands on hips. 'Sweet found a stretch of timber over yonder and reckons there might be game. If you'd rather ride drag, you can ride drag. Thought you might appreciate the break is all, but have it your way.' And she turned and started to walk off.

'Wait, you're serious?' Trying to hurry after her and pull on his other boot at the same time.

'Would I toy with your feelings?'

'I'm going hunting?' Sufeen had asked him to go hunting a hundred times and he had always said he could not imagine anything more boring. After a few weeks with the dust, had he been the quarry he would have dashed off laughing across the plains.

'Calm down,' said Shy. 'No one's fool enough to give you a bow. Me and Sweet'll do the shooting while Crying Rock scares up the game. You and Leef can follow on and skin, butcher and cart. Wouldn't be a bad idea to grab some wood for a shitless fire or two either.'

'Skinning, butchering and shitless fires! Yes, my Queen!' He remembered those few months butchering cattle in the sweltering meat district of Dagoska, the stink and the flies, the back-breaking effort and horrible clamour. He had thought it like hell. Now he dropped to his knees, and grabbed her hand, and kissed it in thanks for the chance.

She jerked it free. 'Stop embarrassing yourself.' It was still too dark to see her face, but he thought he could hear a smile in her voice. She slid her sheathed knife from her belt. 'You'll need this.'

'A knife of my own! And quite a large one!' He stayed on his knees and thrust his fists into the sky. 'I'm going hunting!'

One of Gentili's venerable cousins, on his way shambling past to empty his bladder, shook his head and grumbled, 'Who gives a fuck?'

As the first signs of dawn streaked the sky and the wheels of the Fellowship began to turn, the five of them rode off across the scrubby grass, Leef on an empty wagon for carrying the carcasses, Temple trying to persuade Lamb's horse that they were on the same side. They crested the edge of what passed for a valley out here but would barely have qualified as a ditch anywhere else, some ill-looking trees huddling in its base, browned and broken. Sweet sat slumped in his saddle, scanning those unpromising woods. God only knew what for.

'Look about right?' he grunted to Crying Rock.

'About.' The Ghost gave her old grey a tap with her heels and they were off down the long slope.

The lean deer that came bouncing from the trees and straight into Sweet's bolts and Shy's arrows were a different prospect from the big, soft oxen that had swung from the hooks in Dagoska's stinking warehouses, but the principles came back quickly enough. Soon Temple was making a few swift slits with the blade then peeling the skins off whole while Leef held the front hooves. He even took a sprinkling of pride in the way he got the guts sliding out in one mass, steaming in the chill morning. He showed Leef the trick of it and soon they were bloody to their elbows, and laughing, and flicking bits of gut at each other like a pair of boys.

Soon enough they had five tough little carcases stretched out and glistening in the back of the wagon and the last skinned and headed, the offal in a flyblown heap and the hides in a red and brown tangle like clothes discarded by a set of eager swimmers.

Temple wiped Shy's knife on one of them and nodded off up the rise. 'I'd best see what's keeping those two.'

'I'll get this last one gutted.' Leef grinned up at him as he dragged himself onto Lamb's horse. 'Thanks for the pointers.'

'Teaching is the noblest of callings, Haddish Kahdia used to tell me.'

'Who's he?'

Temple thought about that. 'A good, dead man, who gave his life for mine.'

'Sounds like a shitty trade,' said Leef.

Temple snorted. 'Even I think so. I'll be back before you know it.' He pushed up the valley, following the treeline, enjoying the turn of speed he got from Lamb's horse and congratulating himself that he was finally making some progress with that boy. A hundred strides further on and he saw Sweet and Shy watching the trees from horseback.

'Can't you sluggards kill any faster?' he called at them.

'You finish that lot already?' asked Shy.

'Skinned, gutted and eager for the pot.'

'I'll be damned,' grunted Sweet, ivory-stocked flatbow propped on his thigh. 'Reckon someone who knows the difference better check up on the lawyer's handiwork. Make sure he hasn't skinned Leef by mistake.'

Shy brought her horse around and they rode back towards the wagon. 'Not bad,' she said, giving him an approving nod. It might well have been the first he had received from her, and he found he quite liked having one. 'Reckon we might make a plainsman o' you yet.'

'That or I'll make snivelling townsfolk of the lot of you.'

'Take stronger stuff than you're made of to get that done.'

'I'm made of pretty weak stuff, all in all.'

'I don't know.' She was looking sideways at him, one appraising brow up. 'I'm starting to think there might be some metal under all that paper.'

He tapped his chest with a fist. 'Tin, maybe.'

'Well, you wouldn't forge a sword from it, but tin'll make a decent bucket.'

'Or a bath.'

She closed her eyes. 'By the dead, a bath.'

'Or a roof.'

'By the dead, a roof,' as they crested the rise and looked down towards the trees, 'can you remember what a roof—'

The wagon came into view below, and the heap of skins, and next to them Leef lying on the ground. Temple knew it was him because of his boots. He couldn't see the rest, because two figures knelt over him. His first thought was that the lad must have had a fall and the other two were helping him up.

Then one turned towards them, and he was dressed in a dozen different skins all patchwork-stitched and carried a red knife. He gave a hellish shriek, tongue sticking stiff from his yawning mouth, high and heedless as a wolf at the moon, and started to bound up the slope towards them.

Temple could only sit and gawp as the Ghost rushed closer, until he could see the eyes bulging in his red-painted face. Then Shy's bowstring hummed just by his ear, and the arrow flickered across the few strides between them and into the Ghost's bare chest, stopped him cold like a slap in the face.

Temple's eyes darted to the other Ghost, standing now in a cloak of grass and bones, slipping his own bow off his back and reaching for an arrow from a skin quiver tied to his bare leg. Shy rode down the hill, giving a scream hardly more human than the Ghost's had been, tugging out that short-sword she wore.

The Ghost got his arrow free, then spun around and sat down. Temple looked over to see Sweet lowering his flatbow. 'There'll be more!' he shouted, hooking the stirrup on the end of his bow over one boot and hauling the string back with one hand, turning his horse with a twitch of the other and scanning the treeline.

The Ghost tried to lift his arrow and fumbled it, tried to reach for another, couldn't straighten his arm because of the bolt in it. He screamed something at Shy as she rode up, and she hit him across the face with her sword and sent him tumbling.

Temple spurred down the slope after her and slid from his saddle near Leef. One of the boy's legs kicked as if he was trying to get up. Shy leaned over him and he touched her hand and opened his mouth but only blood came. Blood from his mouth and from his nose and from the jagged leavings where his ear used to be and the knife-cuts in his arms and the arrow wound in his chest. Temple stared down, hands twitching in dumb helplessness.

'Get him on your horse!' snarled Shy, and Temple came alive of a sudden and seized Leef under his arms. Crying Rock had come from somewhere and was beating the Ghost Shy had shot with a club. Temple could hear the crunching of it as he started dragging Leef towards his horse, stumbled and fell, struggled up and on again.

'Leave him!' shouted Sweet. 'He's all done, a fool can see it!'

Temple ignored him, teeth gritted, trying to haul Leef up onto the horse by belt and bloody shirt. For a skinny lad he was quite the weight. 'Not leaving him,' hissed Temple. 'Not leaving him . . . not leaving him . . .'

The world was just him and Leef and the horse, just his aching muscles and the boy's dead weight and his mindless, bubbling groan. He heard the hooves of Sweet's horse thumping away. Heard shouting in no language he knew, voices hardly human. Leef lolled, and slipped, and the horse shifted, then Shy was there next to him, growling in her throat, effort and fear and anger, and together they hauled Leef up over the saddle-horn, broken arrow-shaft sticking black into the air.

Temple's hands were covered in blood. He stood looking at them for a moment.

'Go!' shrieked Shy. 'Go you fucking idiot!'

He scrambled into the saddle, fumbling for the reins with sticky fingers, hammering with his heels, almost falling off as his horse – Lamb's horse – leaped into life, and he was riding, riding, wind whipping in his face, whipping the garbled shouting from his mouth, whipping the tears from his eyes. The flat horizon bounced and shuddered and Leef jolted over the saddle horn, Sweet and Crying Rock two wriggling specks against the sky. Shy up ahead, bent low over the saddle, tail of her horse streaming, and she snatched a look behind, and he saw the fear in her face, didn't want to look, had to look.

There they were at his heels like messengers from hell. Painted faces, painted horses, childishly daubed and stuck with skins, feathers, bones, teeth and one with a human hand dried and shrunken bouncing around his neck and one with a headdress made of bulls' horns and one wearing a great copper dish as a breastplate, shining and flashing with the afternoon sun, a mess of flying red and yellow hair and brandished weapons hooked and beaked and jagged-edged all screaming furiously and fixed on his most horrible murder and Temple went freezing cold right into his arse.

'Oh God oh God oh fuck oh God . . .'

His brainless swearing drumming away like the hooves of his horse – Lamb's horse – and an arrow flickered past and into the grass. Shy screamed at him over her shoulder but the words were gone in the wind. He clung to the reins, clung to the back of Leef's shirt, his breath whooping and his shoulders itching and knowing for sure that he was a dead man and worse than dead and all he could think was that he should have ridden drag after all. Should have stayed on the hill above Averstock. Should have stepped forward when the Gurkish came for Kahdia instead of standing in that silent, helpless line of shame with all the others.

Then he saw movement up ahead and realised it was the Fellowship, shapes of wagons and cattle on the flat horizon, riders coming out to meet them. He glanced over his shoulder and saw the Ghosts were dropping back, peeling away, could hear their whooping calls, one of them sending an arrow looping towards him and falling well short and he sobbed with relief, had just the presence of mind left to rein in as he came close, his horse – Lamb's horse – quivering almost as much as he was.

Chaos among the wagons, panic spreading as if there had been six hundred Ghosts instead of six, Luline Buckhorm screaming for a missing child, Gentili all tangled up with a rust-stained breastplate even older than he was, a couple of cattle loose and charging through the midst and Majud standing on his wagon's seat and yelling demands for calm no one could hear.

'What happened?' growled Lamb, steady as ever, and Temple could only shake his head. No words in him. Had to force his aching hand open to let go of Leef's shirt as Lamb slid him from the horse and lowered him to the ground.

'Where's Corlin?' Shy was shouting, and Temple slithered from the saddle, legs numb as two dry sticks. Lamb was cutting Leef's shirt, fabric ripping under the blade, and Temple leaned down, wiping the blood away from the arrow shaft, wiping the blood but as soon as he wiped it there was more, Leef's body all slick with it.

'Give me the knife,' snapping his fingers, and Lamb pushed it into his hand and he stared at that arrow, what to do, what to do, pull it out, or cut it out, or push it through, and trying to remember what Kahdia had told him about arrow-wounds, something about what the best chance was, the best chance, but he couldn't fix on anything, and Leef's eyes were crossed, his mouth hanging open and his hair all matted with blood.

Shy scrambled down next to him and said, 'Leef? Leef?' And Lamb gently laid him flat, and Temple stuck the knife in the earth and rocked back on his heels. They came to him then in a strange rush, all the things he knew about the boy. That he'd been in love with Shy, and that Temple had been starting to win him round, that he'd lost his parents, that he'd been trying to find his brother stolen by bandits, that he'd been a good man with oxen and a hard worker . . . but all that now was hacked off in the midst and would never be resolved, all his dreams and hopes and fears ended here on the trampled grass and cut out from the world forever.

Hell of a thing.

Savian was roaring, and coughing, and pointing everywhere with his flatbow, trying to get the wagons dragged into some kind of fort with barrels and clothes-chests and rope coils stacked up to hide behind, the cattle corralled inside and the women and children to the safest place, though Shy had no notion where that might be. Folk were scrambling about like the idea of Ghosts had never been discussed before, running to do what they were told or exactly what they hadn't been, to tug at stubborn animals or find stowed weapons or save their gear or their children or just to stare and clutch at themselves like they were stabbed and their ears off already.

Iosiv Lestek's big wagon had run into a ditch and a couple of men were struggling to rock it free. 'Leave it!' shouted Savian. 'We ain't going to act our way out o' this!' And they left it colourfully advertising the world's finest theatrical entertainment to the empty plains.

Shy shouldered her way through the madness and up onto Majud's wagon. Away to the south, across the waving, shifting grass, three Ghosts rode around in circles, one shaking a horned lance at the sky, and Shy thought she could hear them singing, high and joyful. Sweet watched, his loaded flatbow propped on one knee, rubbing at his bearded jaw, and it felt like there was a small piece of calm around him she gratefully squatted in.

'How's the boy?'

'Dead,' said Shy, and it made her sick that was all she had to say.

'Ah, damn it.' Sweet gave a bitter grimace, and closed his eyes and pressed them with finger and thumb. 'Damn it.' Then he trained them on the mounted Ghosts on the horizon, shaking his head. 'Best fix ourselves on making sure the rest of us don't go the same way.'

Savian's cracked voice shouted on and all around folk were clambering onto the wagons with bows in unpractised hands, new ones never drawn with purpose and antiques long out of service.

'What are they singing of?' asked Shy, pulling an arrow from her quiver and slowly turning it round and round, feeling the roughness against her fingertips like wood was a new thing never felt before.

Sweet snorted. 'Our violent demise. They reckon it's near at hand.'

'Is it?' she couldn't help asking.

'Depends.' Sweet's jaw muscles worked under his beard, then he slowly, calmly spat. 'On whether those three are some of Sangeed's main warband or he's split it up into smaller parties.'

'And which is it?'

'Guess we can count 'em when they arrive, and if there's a few dozen we'll know we've a chance, and if there's a few hundred we'll have our profound fucking doubts.'

Buckhorm had clambered up on the wagon, a mail shirt flapping at his thighs that suited him even worse than it fitted him. 'Why are we just waiting?' he hissed, the Ghosts chased his stutter away for now. 'Why don't we move?'

Sweet turned his slow grey eyes on him. 'Move where? Ain't no castles nearby.' He looked back to the plains, empty in every direction, and the three Ghosts circling at the edge of that shallow valley, faint singing keening across the empty grass. 'One patch of nowhere's as good to die on as another.'

'Our time's better spent getting ready for what's coming than running from it.' Lamb stood tall on the next wagon. He'd built up quite the collection of knives the last few weeks and now he was checking them one by one, calm as if he was getting ready to plough a field back on the farm instead of fight for his life in wild and lawless country. More than calm, now Shy thought about it. Like it was a field he'd long dreamed of ploughing but was only now getting the chance at.

'Who are you?' she said.

He looked up from his blades for a moment. 'You know me.'

'I know a big, soft Northman scared to whip a mule. I know a beggar turned up to our farm in the night to work for crusts. I know a man used to hold my brother and sing when he had the fever. You ain't that man.'

'I am.' He stepped across the gap between the wagons, and he put his arms around her crushing tight, and she heard him whisper in her ear. 'But that's not all I am. Stay out of my way, Shy.' Then he hopped down from the wagon. 'You'd better keep her safe!' he called to Sweet.

'You joking?' The old scout was busy sighting down his bow. 'I'm counting on her to save me!'

Just then Crying Rock gave a high shout and pointed off to the south, and over the crest they boiled as if from some nightmare, relics of a savage age long past, toothed with a hundred jagged stolen blades and chipped-stone axes and sharp arrows glinting and a lifetime of laughed-at stories of massacre came boiling with them and stole Shy's breath.

'We're all going to lose our ears!' someone whimpered.

'Ain't like you use 'em now, is it? Sweet levelled his flatbow with a grim smile. 'Looks like a few dozen to me.'

Shy knelt there trying to count them but some horses had other horses painted on their sides and some had no riders and some had two or carried scarecrow figures made to look like men and others flapping canvas stretched on sticks to make them giants bloated like bodies drowned, all swimming and blurring before her leaking eyes, mindless and deadly and unknowable as a plague.

Shy thought she could hear Temple praying. She wished she knew how.

'Easy!' Savian was shouting. 'Easy!' Shy hardly knew what he meant. One Ghost wore a hood crusted with fragments of broken glass that sparkled like jewels, mouth yawning in a spit-stringed scream. 'Stand and live! Run and die!' She'd always had a knack for running and no stomach for standing, and if there'd ever been a time to run, her whole body was telling her that time was now. 'Under that fucking paint they're just men!' A Ghost stood in his or her or its stirrups and shook a feathered lance, naked but for paint and a necklace of ears bouncing and swinging around its neck.

'Stand together or die alone!' roared Savian, and one of the whores whose name Shy had forgotten stood with a bow in her hand and her yellow hair stirred by the wind, and she nodded to Shy and Shy nodded back. Goldy, that was it. Stand together. That's why they call it a Fellowship, ain't it?

The first bowstring went, panicky and pointless, arrow falling well short, then more and Shy shot her own, barely picking out one target there were so many. Arrows flickered down and fell among the waving grass and the heaving flesh and here or there a shape tumbled from a saddle or a horse veered. The Ghost with the hood slumped back, Savian's bolt through its painted chest, but the rest swarmed up to the feeble ring of wagons and swallowed it whole, whirling and rearing and sending up a murk of dust until they and their painted horses were phantoms indeed, their screams and shrieks and animal howls disembodied and treacherous as the voices a madman hears.

Arrows dropped around Shy, zip and clatter as one tumbled from a crate, another lodged in a sack just beside her, a third left trembling in the wagon's seat. She nocked a shaft and shot again, and again, and again, shot at nothing, at anything, crying with fear and anger and her teeth crushed together and her ears full of joyous wailing and her own spat curses. Lestek's mired wagon was a red hump with shapes crawling over it, hacking it with axes, stabbing it with spears like hunters that had brought down some great beast.

A pony stuck with arrows tottered sideways past, biting at its neighbour and, while Shy stared at it, a ragged shape came hurtling over the side of the wagon. She saw just a bulging eye in a face red-painted like an eye and she grabbed at it, her finger in a mouth and ripping at a cheek and together they tumbled off the wagon, rolling in the dust. There were strong hands around her head, lifting it and twisting it while she snarled and tried to find her knife and suddenly her head burst with light and the world was quiet and strange all shuffling feet and choking dust and she felt a burning, ripping pain under her ear and she screamed and thrashed and bit at nothing but couldn't get free.

Then the weight was off and she saw Temple wrestling with the Ghost, both gripping a red knife and she clambered up, slow as corn growing, fumbled her sword free and took a step through the rocking world and stabbed the Ghost, realised it was Temple she'd stabbed they were so tangled. She caught the Ghost around the throat and clutched him close and pushed the sword into his back, dragged at it and shoved at it, scraping on bone until she had it all the way into him, hand slippery hot.

Arrows fluttered down, gentle as butterflies, and fell among the cattle and they snorted their upset, some feathered and bloodied. They jostled unhappily at each other and one of Gentili's old cousins knelt on the ground with two arrows in his side, one dangling broken.

'There! There!' And she saw something slithering in under a wagon, a clawing hand, and she stomped on it with her boot and nearly fell, and one of the miners was beside her hacking with a shovel and some of the whores stabbing at something with spears, screaming and stabbing like they were chasing a rat.

Shy caught sight of a gap between the wagons and beyond the Ghosts flooding up on foot in a gibbering crowd, and she heard Temple breathe something in some tongue of his own and a woman near her moan — or was it her voice? The heart went out of her and she took a cringing step back, as though an extra stride of mud would be a shield, all thoughts of standing far in a vanished past as the first Ghost loomed up, an antique greatsword brown with rust clutched in painted fists and a man's skull worn over its face as a mask.

Then with a roar that was half a laugh Lamb was in their midst, twisted face a grinning mockery of the man she knew, more horrible to her than any mask a Ghost might wear. His swung sword was a blur and the skull-face burst in a spray of black, body sagging like an empty sack. Savian was stabbing from a wagon with a spear, stabbing into the shrieking mass and Crying Rock beating with her club and others cutting at them and mouthing curses in every language in the Circle of the World, driving them back, driving them out. Lamb swung again and folded a ragged shape in half, kicked the corpse away, opened a great wound in a back, white splinters in red, hacking and chopping and he lifted a wriggling Ghost and dashed its head against the rim of a barrel. Shy knew she should help but instead she sat down on a wagon-wheel and was sick while Temple watched her, lying on his side, clutching at his rump where she'd stabbed him.

She saw Corlin stitching up a cut in Majud's leg, thread in her teeth, cool as ever though with sleeves red speckled to the elbow from the wounds she'd tended. Savian was already shouting out, voice gravelly hoarse, to close up the wagons, plug that gap, toss the bodies out, show 'em they were ready for more. Shy didn't reckon she was ready for more. She sat with hands braced against her knees to stop everything from shaking, blood tickling at the side of her face, sticky in her hair, staring at the corpse of the Ghost she'd killed.

They were just men, like Savian said. Now she got a proper look, she saw this one was a boy no older than Leef. No older than Leef had been. Five of the Fellowship were killed. Gentili's cousin shot with arrows, and two of Buckhorm's children found under a wagon with their ears cut off, and one of the whores had been dragged away and no one knew how or when.

There weren't many who didn't have some cuts or scrapes and none who wouldn't start when they heard a wolf howl for all their days. Shy couldn't make her hands stop trembling, ear burning where the Ghost had made a start at claiming it for a prize. She wasn't sure whether it was just a nick or if her ear was hanging by a flap and hardly dared find out.

But she had to get up. She thought of Pit and Ro out in the far wilderness, scared as she was, and that put the heat into her and got her teeth gritted and her legs moving and she growled as she dragged herself up onto Majud's wagon.

She'd half-expected the Ghosts would have vanished, drifted away like smoke on the wind, but they were there, still of this world and this time even if Shy could hardly believe it, milling in chaos or rage away across the grass, singing and wailing to each other, steel still winking.

'Kept your ears, then?' asked Sweet, and frowned as he pressed his thumb against the cut and made her wince. 'Just about.'

'They'll be coming again,' she muttered, forcing herself to look at those nightmare shapes.

'Maybe, maybe not. They're just testing us. Figuring whether they want to give us a proper try.'

Savian clambered up beside him, face set even harder and eyes even narrower than usual. 'If I was them I wouldn't stop until we were all dead.'

Sweet kept staring out across the plain. Seemed he was a man made for that purpose. 'Luckily for us, you ain't them. Might look a savage but he's a practical thinker, your average Ghost. They get angry quick but they hold no grudges. We prove hard to kill, more'n likely they'll try to talk. Get what they can by way of meat and money and move on to easier pickings.'

'We can buy our way out of this?' asked Shy.

'Ain't much God's made can't be bought out of if you've got the coin,' said Sweet, and added in a mutter, 'I hope.'

'And once we've paid,' growled Savian, 'what's to stop them following on and killing us when it suits?'

Sweet shrugged. 'You wanted predictable, you should've stayed in Starikland. This here is the Far Country.'

And at that moment the axe-scarred door of Lestek's wagon banged open and the noted actor himself struggled out, in his nightshirt, rheumy eyes wild and sparse white hair in disarray. 'Bloody critics!' he boomed, shaking an empty can at the distant Ghosts.

'It will be all right,' Temple said to Buckhorm's son. His second son, he thought. Not one of the dead ones. Of course not one of them, because it would not be all right for them, they already had lost everything. That thought was unlikely to comfort their brother, though, so Temple said, 'It will be all right,' again, and tried to make it earnest, though the painful pounding of his heart, not to mention of his wounded buttock, made his voice wobble. It sounds funny, a wounded buttock. It is not.

'It *will* be all right,' he said, as if the emphasis made it a cast-iron fact. He remembered Kahdia saying the same to him when the siege had begun, and the fires burned all across Dagoska, and it was painfully clear that nothing would be all right. It had helped, to know that someone had the strength to tell the lie. So Temple squeezed the shoulder of Buckhorm's second son and said, 'It . . . will be . . . all right,' his voice surer this time, and the boy nodded, and Temple felt stronger himself, that he could give strength to someone else. He wondered how long that strength would last when the Ghosts came again.

Buckhorm thrust his shovel into the dirt beside the graves. He still wore his old chain-mail shirt, still with the buckles done up wrong so it was twisted at the front, and he wiped his sweaty forehead with the back of his hand and left a smear of dirt across it.

'It'd mean a lot to us if you'd suh . . . say something.'

Temple blinked at him. 'Would it?' But perhaps worthwhile words could come from worthless mouths, after all.

The great majority of the Fellowship were busy strengthening the defences, such as they were, or staring at the horizon while they chewed their fingernails bloody, or too busy panicking about the great likelihood of their own deaths to concern themselves with anyone else's. In attendance about the five mounds of earth were Buckhorm, his stunned and blinking wife and their remaining brood of eight, who ranged from sorrow to terror to uncomprehending good humour; two of the whores and their pimp, who had been nowhere to be seen during the attack but had at least emerged in time to help with the digging; Gentili and two of his cousins; and Shy, frowning down at the heaped earth over Leef's grave, shovel gripped white-knuckle hard in her fists. She had small hands, Temple noticed suddenly, and felt a strange welling of sympathy for her. Or perhaps that was just self-pity. More than likely the latter.

'God,' he croaked, and had to clear his throat. 'It seems . . . sometimes . . . that you are not out here.' It had mostly seemed to Temple, with all the blood and waste that he had seen, that He was not anywhere. 'But I know you are,' he lied. He was not paid for the truth. 'You are everywhere. Around us, and in us, and watching over us.' Not doing much about it, mind you, but that was God for you. 'I ask you . . . I beg you, watch over these boys, buried in strange earth, under strange skies. These men and women, too. You know they had their shortcomings. But they set out to make something in the wilderness.' Temple felt the sting of tears himself, had to bite his lip for a moment, look to the sky and blink them back. 'Take them to your arms, and give them peace. There are none more deserving.'

They stood in silence for a while, the wind tugging at the ragged hem of Temple's coat and snatching Shy's hair across her face, then Buckhorm held out his palm, coins glinting there. 'Thank you.'

Temple closed the drover's calloused hand with both of his. 'My honour to do it.' Words did nothing. The children were still dead. He would not take money for that, whatever his debts.

The light was starting to fade when Sweet swung down from Majud's wagon, the sky pinking in the west and streaks of black cloud spread across it like breakers on a calm sea. 'They want to talk!' he shouted. 'They've lit a fire halfway to their camp and they're waiting for word!' He looked pretty damn pleased about it. Probably Temple should have been pleased, but he was sitting near Leef's grave, weight uncomfortably shifted off his throbbing buttock, feeling as if nothing would ever please him again.

'*Now* they want to talk,' said Luline Buckhorm, bitterly. 'Now my two boys are dead.'

Sweet winced. 'Better'n when all your boys are. I'd best go out there.'

'I'll be coming,' said Lamb, dry blood still speckled on the side of his face.

'And me,' said Savian. 'Make sure those bastards don't try anything.'

Sweet combed at his beard with his fingers. 'Fair enough. Can't hurt to show 'em we've got iron in us.'

'I will be going, too.' Majud limped up, grimacing badly so that gold tooth glinted, trouser-leg flapping where Corlin had cut it free of his wound. 'I swore never to let you negotiate in my name again.'

'You bloody won't be going,' said Sweet. 'Things tend sour we might have to run, and you're running nowhere.'

Majud ventured some weight on his injured leg, grimaced again, then nodded over at Shy. 'She goes in my place, then.'

'Me?' she muttered, looking over. 'Talk to those fuckers?'

'There is no one else I trust to bargain. My partner Curnsbick would insist on the best price.'

'I could get to dislike Curnsbick without ever having met the man.'

Sweet was shaking his head. 'Sangeed won't take much to a woman being there.'

It looked to Temple as though that made up Shy's mind. 'If he's a practical thinker he'll get over it. Let's go.'

They sat in a crescent about their crackling fire, maybe a hundred strides from the Fellowship's makeshift fort, the flickering lights of their own camp dim in the distance. The Ghosts. The terrible scourge of the plains. The fabled savages of the Far Country.

Shy tried her best to stoke up a towering hatred for them, but when she thought of Leef cold under the dirt, all she felt was sick at the waste of it, and worried for his brother and hers who were still lost as ever, and worn through and chewed up and hollowed out. That and, now she saw them sitting tame with no death cries or shook weapons, she'd rarely seen so wretched-looking a set of men, and she'd spent a good stretch of her life in desperate straits and most of the rest bone-poor.

They wore half-cured hides, and ragged skins, and threadbare fragments of a dozen different scavenged costumes, the bare skin showing stretched pale and hungry-tight over the bone. One was smiling, maybe at the thought of the riches they were soon to win, and he'd but one rotten tooth in his head. Another frowned solemnly under a helmet made from a beaten-out copper kettle, spout sticking from his forehead. Shy took the old Ghost in the centre for the great Sangeed. He wore a cloak of feathers over a tarnished breastplate looked like it had made some general of the Empire proud a thousand years ago. He had three necklaces of human ears, proof she supposed of his great prowess, but he was long past his best. She could hear his breathing, wet and crackly, and one half of his leathery face sagged, the drooping corner of his mouth glistening with stray spit.

Could these ridiculous little men and the monsters that had come screaming for them on the plain be the same flesh? A lesson she should've remembered from her own time as a fearsome bandit – between the horrible and pitiful there's never much of a divide, and most of that is in how you look at it.

If anything, it was the old men on her side of the fire that scared her more now – deep-lined faces made devilish strangers by the shifting flames, eyes gleaming in chill-shadowed sockets, the head of the bolt in Savian's loaded flatbow coldly glistening, Lamb's face bent and twisted like a weather-worn tree, etched with old scars, no clue to his thoughts, not even to her who'd known him all these years. Especially not to her, maybe.

Sweet bowed his head and said a few words in the Ghosts' tongue, making big gestures with his arms. Sangeed said a few back, slow and grinding, coughed, and managed a few more.

'Just exchanging pleasantries,' Sweet explained.

'Ain't nothing pleasant about this,' snapped Shy. 'Let's get done and get back.'

'We can talk in your words,' said one of the Ghosts in a strange sort of common like he had a mouthful of gravel. He was a young one, sitting closest to Sangeed and frowning across the fire. His son, maybe. 'My name is Locway.'

'All right.' Sweet cleared his throat. 'Here's a right fucking fuck up, then, ain't it, Locway? There was no call for no one to die here. Now look. Corpses on both sides just to get to where we could've started if you'd just said how do.'

'Every man takes his life in his hands who trespasses upon our lands,' said Locway. Looked like he took himself mighty seriously, which was quite the achievement for someone wearing a ripped-up pair of old Union cavalry trousers with a beaver pelt over the crotch.

Sweet snorted. 'I was riding these plains long before you was sucking tit, lad. And now you're going to tell me where I can ride?' He curled his tongue and spat into the fire.

'Who gives a shit who rides where?' snapped Shy. 'Ain't like it's land any sane man would want.'

The young Ghost frowned at her. 'She has a sour tongue.'

'Fuck yourself.'

'Enough,' growled Savian. 'If we're going to deal, let's deal and go.'

Locway gave Shy a hard look, then leaned to speak to Sangeed, and the so-called Emperor of the Plains mulled his words over for a moment, then croaked a few of his own.

'Five thousands of your silver marks,' said Locway, 'and twenty of cattle, and twenty of horses, and you leave with your ears. That is the word of dread Sangeed.' And the old Ghost lifted his chin and grunted.

'You can have two thousand,' said Shy.

'Three thousand, then, and the animals.' His haggling was almost as piss-weak as his clothes.

'My people agreed to two. That's what you're getting. Far as cattle go, you can have the dozen you were fool enough to make meat of with your arrows, that's all. The horses, no.'

'Then perhaps we will come and take them,' said Locway.

'You can come and fucking try.'

His face twisted and he opened his mouth to speak but Sangeed touched his shoulder and mumbled a few words, looking all the time

178

at Sweet. The old scout nodded to him, and the young Ghost sourly worked his mouth. 'Great Sangeed accepts your offering.'

Sweet rubbed his hands on his crossed legs and smiled. 'All right, then. Good.'

'Uh.' Sangeed broke out in a lopsided grin.

'We are agreed,' said Locway, no smile of his own.

'All right,' said Shy, though she took no pleasure in it. She was worn down to a nub, just wanted to sleep. The Ghosts stirred, relaxing a little, the one with the rotten tooth grinning wider'n ever.

Lamb slowly stood, the sunset at his back, a towering piece of black with the sky all bloodstained about him.

'I've a better offer,' he said.

Sparks whirled about his flicking heels as he jumped the fire. There was a flash of orange steel and Sangeed clutched his neck, toppling backwards. Savian's bowstring went and the Ghost with the kettle fell, bolt through his mouth. Another leaped up but Lamb buried his knife in the top of his head with a crack like a log splitting.

Locway scrambled to his feet just as Shy was doing the same, but Savian dived and caught him around the neck, rolling over onto his back and bringing the Ghost with him, thrashing and twitching, a hatchet in his hand but pinned helpless, snarling at the sky.

'What you doing?' called Sweet, but there wasn't much doubt by then. Lamb was holding up the last of the Ghosts with one fist and punching him with the other, knocking out the last couple of teeth, punching him so fast Shy could hardly tell how many times, whipping sound of his arm inside his sleeve and his big fist crunching, crunching and the black outline of the Ghost's face losing all shape, and Lamb tossed his body fizzling in the fire.

Sweet took a step back from the shower of sparks. 'Fuck!' His hands tangled in his grey hair like he couldn't believe what he was seeing. Shy could hardly believe it either, cold all over and sitting frozen, each breath whooping a little in her throat, Locway snarling and struggling still but caught tight in Savian's grip as a fly in honey.

Sangeed tottered up, one hand clutching at his chopped-open throat, clawing fingers shining with blood. He had a knife but Lamb stood waiting for it, and caught his wrist as though it was a thing ordained, and twisted it, and forced Sangeed down on his knees, drooling blood into the grass. Lamb planted one boot in the old Ghost's armpit and drew his sword with a faint ringing of steel, paused a moment to stretch his neck one way and the other, then lifted the blade and

179

brought it down with a thud. Then another. Then another, and Lamb let go of Sangeed's limp arm, reached down and took his head by the hair, a misshapen thing now, split open down one cheek where one of Lamb's blows had gone wide of the mark.

'This is for you,' he said, and tossed it in the young Ghost's lap.

Locway stared at it, chest heaving against Savian's arm, a strip of tattoo showing below the old man's rucked-up sleeve. The Ghost's eyes moved from the head to Lamb's face, and he bared his teeth and hissed out, 'We will be coming for you! Before dawn, in the darkness, we will be coming for you!'

'No.' Lamb smiled, his teeth and his eyes and the blood streaked down his face all shining with the firelight. 'Before dawn . . .' He squatted in front of Locway, still held helpless. 'In the darkness . . .' He gently stroked the Ghost's face, the three fingers of his left hand leaving three black smears down pale cheek. 'I'll be coming for you.'

They heard sounds, out there in the night. Talking at first, muffled by the wind. People demanded to know what was being said and others hissed at them to be still. Then Temple heard a cry and clutched at Corlin's shoulder. She brushed him off.

'What's happening?' demanded Lestek.

'How can we know?' snapped Majud back.

They saw shadows shifting around the fire and a kind of gasp went through the Fellowship.

'It's a trap!' shouted Lady Ingelstad, and one of the Suljuks started yammering in words not even Temple could make sense of. A spark of panic, and there was a general shrinking back in which Temple was ashamed to say he took a willing part.

'They should never have gone out there!' croaked Hedges, as though he had been against it from the start.

'Everyone be calm.' Corlin's voice was hard and level and did no shrinking whatsoever.

'There's someone coming!' Majud pointed out into the darkness. Another spark of panic, another shrinking back in which, again, Temple was a leading participant.

'No one shoot!' Sweet's gravel bass echoed from the darkness. 'That's all I need to crown my fucking day!' And the old scout stepped into the torchlight, hands up, Shy behind him.

The Fellowship breathed a collective sigh of relief, in which Temple was among the loudest, and rolled away two barrels to let the negotiators into their makeshift fort.

'What happened?'

'Did they talk?'

'Are we safe?'

Sweet just stood there, hands on hips, slowly shaking his head. Shy frowned off at nothing. Savian came behind, narrowed eyes giving away as little as ever.

'Well?' asked Majud. 'Do we have a deal?'

'They're thinking it over,' said Lamb, bringing up the rear.

'What did you offer? What happened, damn it?'

'He killed them,' muttered Shy.

There was a moment of confused silence. 'Who killed who?' squeaked Lord Ingelstad.

'Lamb killed the Ghosts.'

'Don't overstate it,' said Sweet. 'He let one go.' And he pushed back his hat and sagged against a wagon tyre.

'Sangeed?' grunted Crying Rock. Sweet shook his head. 'Oh,' said the Ghost.

'You . . . killed them?' asked Temple.

Lamb shrugged. 'Out here when a man tries to murder you, maybe you pay him for the favour. Where I come from we got a different way of doing things.'

'He killed them?' asked Buckhorm, eyes wide with horror.

'Good!' shouted his wife, shaking one small fist. 'Good someone had the bones to do it! They got what they had coming! For my two dead boys!'

'We've got eight still living to think about!' said her husband.

'Not to mention every other person in this Fellowship!' added Lord Ingelstad.

'He was right to do it,' growled Savian. 'For those that died and those that live. You trust those fucking animals out there? Pay a man to hurt you, all you do is teach him to do it again. Better they learn to fear us.'

'So *you* say!' snapped Hedges.

'That I do,' said Savian, flat and cold. 'Look on the upside – we might've saved a great deal of money here.'

'Scant comfort if it cuh . . . if it costs us all our lives!' snapped Buckhorm.

The financial argument looked to have gone a long way towards bringing Majud around, though. 'We should have made the choice together,' he said.

'A choice between killing and dying ain't no choice at all.' And Lamb brushed through the gathering as though they were not there and to an empty patch of grass beside the nearest fire.

'Hell of a fucking gamble, ain't it?'

'A gamble with our lives!'

'A chance worth taking.'

'You are the expert,' said Majud to Sweet. 'What do you say to this?'

The old scout rubbed at the back of his neck. 'What's to be said? It's done. Ain't no undoing it. Less your niece is so good a healer she can stitch Sangeed's head back on?'

Savian did not answer.

'Didn't think so.' And Sweet climbed back up onto Majud's wagon and perched in his place behind his arrow-prickled crate, staring out across the black plain, distinguishable from the black sky now only by its lack of stars.

Temple had suffered some long and sleepless nights during his life. The night the Gurkish had finally broken through the walls and the Eaters had come for Kahdia. The night the Inquisition had swept the slums of Dagoska for treason. The night his daughter died, and the night not long after when his wife followed. But he had lived through none longer than this.

People strained their eyes into the inky nothing, occasionally raising breathless alarms at some imagined movement, the bubbling cries of one of the prospectors who had an arrow-wound in his stomach, and who Corlin did not expect to last until dawn, as the backdrop. On Savian's order, since he had stopped making suggestions and taken unquestioned command, the Fellowship lit torches and threw them out into the grass beyond the wagons. Their flickering light was almost worse than darkness because, at its edges, death always lurked.

Temple and Shy sat together in silence, with a palpable emptiness where Leef's place used to be, Lamb's contented snoring stretching out the endless time. In the end Shy nodded sideways, and leaned against him, and slept. He toyed with the idea of shouldering her off into the fire, but decided against. It could well have been his last chance to feel the touch of another person, after all. Unless he counted the Ghost who would kill him tomorrow.

As soon as there was grey light enough to see by, Sweet, Crying Rock and Savian mounted up and edged towards the trees, the rest of the

Fellowship gathered breathless on the wagons to watch, hollow-eyed from fear and lack of sleep, clutching at their weapons or at each other. The three riders came back into view not long after, calling out that in the lee of the timber there were fires still smoking on which the Ghosts had burned their dead.

But they were gone. It turned out they were practical thinkers after all.

Now the enthusiasm for Lamb's courage and swift action was unanimous. Luline Buckhorm and her husband were both tearful with gratitude on behalf of their dead sons. Gentili would have done just the same in his youth, apparently. Hedges would have done it if it weren't for his leg, injured in the line of duty at the Battle of Osrung. Two of the whores offered a reward in kind, which Lamb looked minded to accept until Shy declined on his behalf. Then Lestek clambered on a wagon and suggested in quavering tones that Lamb be rewarded with four hundred marks from the money saved, which he looked minded to refuse until Shy accepted on his behalf.

Lord Ingelstad slapped Lamb on the back, and offered him a swig from his best bottle of brandy, aged for two hundred years in the family cellars in faraway Keln which were now, alas, the property of a creditor.

'My friend,' said the nobleman, 'you're a bloody hero!'

Lamb looked at him sideways as he raised the bottle. 'I'm bloody, all right.'

The Fair Price

I t was cold as hell up in them hills. The children all cold, and scared, huddling together at night close to the fires with cheeks pinched and pinked and their breath smoking in each other's faces. Ro took Pit's hands and rubbed them between hers and breathed on them and tried to wrap the bald furs tighter against the dark.

Not long after they got off the boat, a man had come and said Papa Ring needed everyone and Cantliss had cursed, which never took much, and sent seven of his men off. That left just six with that bastard Blackpoint but no one spoke of running now. No one spoke much at all, as if with each mile poled or rode or trod the spirit went out of them, then the thought, and they became just meat on the hoof, trailing slack and wretched to whatever slaughterhouse Cantliss had in mind.

The woman called Bee had been sent off, too, and she'd cried and asked Cantliss, 'Where you taking the children?' And he'd sneered, 'Get back to Crease and mind your business, damn you.' So it was up to Ro and the boy Evin and a couple of the other older ones to see to the blisters and fears of the rest.

High they went into the hills, and higher, twisting by scarce-trodden ways cut by the water of long ago. They camped among great rocks that had the feel of buildings fallen, buildings ancient as the mountains. The trees grew taller and taller until they were pillars of wood that seemed to pierce the sky, their lowest branches high above, creaking in the silent forest bare of brush, without animals, without insects.

'Where you taking us?' Ro asked Cantliss for the hundredth time, and for the hundredth time he said, 'On,' jerking his unshaved face towards the grey outlines of the peaks beyond, his fancy clothes worn out to rags.

They passed through some town, all wood-built and not built well,

184

and a lean dog barked at them but there were no people, not a one. Blackpoint frowned up at the empty windows and licked at the gap in his teeth and said, 'Where did they all go to?' He spoke in Northern but Lamb had taught Ro enough to understand. 'I don't like it.'

Cantliss just snorted. 'You ain't meant to.'

Up, and on, and the trees withered to brown and stunted pine then twisted twig then there were no trees. It turned from icy cold to strangely warm, the soft breeze across the mountainside like breath, and then too hot, too hot, the children toiling on, pink faces sweat-beaded, up bare slopes of rock yellow with crusted sulphur, the ground warm to touch as flesh, the very land alive. Steam popped and hissed from cracks like mouths and in cupped stones lay salt-crusted pools, the water bubbling with stinking gas, frothing with multicoloured oils and Cantliss warned them not to drink for it was poison.

'This place is wrong,' said Pit.

'It's just a place.' But Ro saw the fear in the eyes of the other children, and in the eyes of Cantliss' men, and felt it, too. It was a dead place.

'Is Shy still following?'

'Course she is.' But Ro didn't think she could be, not so far as this, so far it seemed they weren't in the world any more. She could hardly remember what Shy looked like, or Lamb, or the farm as it had been. She was starting to think all that was gone, a dream, a whisper, and this was all there was.

The way grew too steep for horses, then for mules, so one man was left waiting with the animals. They climbed a deep, bare valley where the cliffs were riddled with holes too square for nature to have made, heaped mounds of broken rock beside the way that put Ro in mind of the spoil of mines. But what ancient miners had delved here and for what excavated in this blasted place she could not guess.

After a day breathing its ugly fume, noses and throats raw from the stink, they came upon a great needle of rock set on its end, pitted and stained by weather and time but bare of moss or lichen or plant of any kind. As they came close in a group all tattered reluctance, Ro saw it was covered with letters, and though she couldn't read them knew it for a warning. In the rocky walls above, the blue sky so far away, were more holes, many more, and towering, creaking scaffolds of old wood held platforms, ropes and buckets and evidence of fresh diggings.

Cantliss held up his open hand. 'Stop here.'

'What now?' asked Blackpoint, fingering the hilt of his sword.

'Now we wait.'

'How long?'

'Not long, brother.' A man leaned against a rock, quite at his ease. How Ro had missed him there she could not tell because he was by no means small. Very tall, and dark-skinned, head shaved to the faintest silver stubble, and he wore a simple robe of undyed cloth. In the crook of one heavy-muscled arm he had a staff as tall as he was, in the other hand a small and wrinkled apple. Now he bit into it and said, 'Greetings,' with his mouth half-full, and he smiled at Cantliss, and at Blackpoint and the other men, his face alive with friendly creases unfitting to these grim surroundings, and he smiled at the children, and at Ro in particular, she thought. 'Greetings, children.'

'I want my money,' said Cantliss.

The smile did not leave the old man's face. 'Of course. Because you have a hole in you and you believe gold will fill it.'

'Because I got a debt, and if I don't pay I'm a dead man.'

'We are all dead men, brother, in due course. It is how we get there that counts. But you will have your fair price.' His eyes moved over the children. 'I count but twenty.'

'Long journey,' said Blackpoint, one hand resting on his sword. 'Bound to be some wastage.'

'Nothing is bound to be, brother. What is so is so because of the choices we make.'

'I ain't the one buys children.'

'I buy them. I do not kill them. Is it the hurting of weak things that fills the hole in you?'

'I ain't got no hole in me,' said Blackpoint.

The old man took a last bite from his apple. 'No?' And he tossed the core to Blackpoint. The Northman reached for it on an instinct, then grunted. The old man had covered the ground between them in two lightning steps and struck him in the chest with the end of his staff.

Blackpoint shuddered, letting fall the core and fumbling for his sword but he had no strength left to draw it, and Ro saw it was not a staff but a spear, the long blade sticking bloody from Blackpoint's back. The old man lowered him to the ground, put a gentle hand on his face and closed his eyes.

'It is a hard thing to say, but I feel the world is better without him.'

Ro looked at the Northman's corpse, clothes already dark with blood, and found that she was glad, and did not know what that meant.

'By the dead,' breathed one of Cantliss' men, and looking up Ro

186

saw many figures had come silent from the mines and out onto the scaffolds, looking down. Men and women of all races and ages, but all wearing the same brown cloth and all with heads shaved bald.

'A few friends,' said the old man, standing.

Cantliss' voice quavered, thin and wheedling. 'We did our best.'

'It saddens me, that this might be your best.'

'All I want is the money.'

'It saddens me, that money might be all a man wants.'

'We had a deal.'

'That also saddens me, but so we did. Your money is there.' And the old man pointed out a wooden box sitting on a rock they had passed on the way. 'I wish you joy of it.'

Cantliss snatched up the box and Ro saw the glitter of gold inside. He smiled, dirty face warm with the reflected glow. 'Let's go.' And he and his men backed off.

One of the little children started snivelling then, because little children will come to love even the hateful if that is all they have, and Ro put a hand on her shoulder and said, 'Shhh,' and tried to be brave as the old man walked up to stand towering over her.

Pit clenched his little fists and said, 'Don't hurt my sister!'

The man swiftly knelt so that his bald head was level with Ro's, huge-looking so close, and he put one great hand gently upon Ro's shoulder and one upon Pit's and he said, 'Children, my name is Waerdinur, the thirty-ninth Right Hand of the Maker, and I would never harm either one of you, nor allow anyone else so to do. I have sworn it. I have sworn to protect this sacred ground and the people upon it with my last blood and breath and only death will stop me.'

He brought out a fine chain and hung it around Ro's neck, and strung upon it, resting on her chest, was a piece of dull, grey metal in the shape of a teardrop.

'What's this?' she asked.

'It is a dragon's scale.'

'A real one?'

'Yes, a real one. We all have them.' He reached into his robe and pulled out his own to show to her.

'Why do I have one?'

He smiled, eyes glimmering with tears. 'Because you are my daughter now.' And he put his arms around her and held her very tight.

III
CREASE

'The town, with less than one thousand
permanent residents, was filled with so much
vileness that the very atmosphere appeared
impregnated with the odour of abomination;
murder ran riot, drunkenness was the rule,
gambling a universal pastime, fighting
a recreation.'

J. W. Buel

Hell on the Cheap

Crease at night?

Picture hell on the cheap. Then add more whores.

The greatest settlement of the new frontier, that prospector's paradise, the Fellowship's long-anticipated destination, was wedged into a twisting valley, steep sides dotted with the wasted stumps of felled pines. It was a place of wild abandon, wild hope, wild despair, everything at extremes and nothing in moderation, dreams trodden into the muck and new ones sucked from bottles to be vomited up and trodden down in turn. A place where the strange was commonplace and the ordinary bizarre, and death might be along tomorrow so you'd best have all your fun today.

At its muddy margins, the city consisted mostly of wretched tents, scenes better left unwitnessed by mankind assaulting the eye through wind-stirred flaps. Buildings were botched together from split pine and high hopes, held up by the drunks slumped against both sides, women risking their lives to lean from wonky balconies and beckon in the business.

'It's got bigger,' said Corlin, peering through the jam of wet traffic that clogged the main street.

'Lot bigger,' grunted Savian.

'I'd have trouble saying better, though.'

Shy was trying to imagine worse. A parade of crazed expressions reeled at them through the litter-strewn mud. Faces fit for some nightmare stage show. A demented carnival permanently in town. Off-key giggling split the jagged night and moans of pleasure or horror, the calls of pawnbrokers and the snorts of livestock, the groaning of ruined bedsteads and the squeaking of ruined violins. All composing a desperate music together, no two bars alike, spilling into the night through ill-fitting doors and windows, roars of laughter at a joke or a good spin of the gaming wheel hardly to be told from roars of anger at an insult or the bad turn of a card.

'Merciful heaven,' muttered Majud, one sleeve across his face against the ever-shifting stench.

'Enough to make a man believe in God,' said Temple. 'And that He's somewhere else.'

Ruins loomed from the wet night. Columns on inhuman scale towered to either side of the main street, so thick three men couldn't have linked their arms around them. Some were toppled short, some sheared off ten strides up, some still standing so high the tops were lost to the dark above, the shifting torchlight picking out stained carvings, letters, runes in alphabets centuries forgotten, mementoes of ancient happenings, winners and losers a thousand years dust.

'What did this place used to be?' muttered Shy, neck aching from looking up.

'Cleaner, at a guess,' said Lamb.

Shacks had sprouted around those ancient columns like unruly fungi from the trunks of dead trees. Folk had built teetering scaffolds up them, and chiselled bent props into them, and hung ropes from the tops and even slung walkways between, until some were entirely obscured by incompetent carpentry, turned to nightmare ships run thousands of miles aground, decked out in torches and lanterns and garish advertising for every vice imaginable, the whole so precarious you could see the buildings shifting when the breeze got stiff.

The valley opened up as the remnants of the Fellowship threaded its way further and the general mood intensified to something between orgy, riot and an outbreak of fever. Wild-eyed revellers rushed at it all open-mouthed, fixed on ripping through a lifetime of fun before sunup, as if violence and debauch wouldn't be there on the morrow.

Shy had a feeling they would.

'It's like a battle,' grunted Savian.

'But without any sides,' said Corlin.

'Or any victory,' said Lamb.

'Just a million defeats,' muttered Temple.

Men tottered and lurched, limped and spun with gaits grotesque or comical, drunk beyond reason, or crippled in head or body, or half-mad from long months spent digging alone in high extremities where words were a memory. Shy directed her horse around a man making a spatter all down his own bare legs, trousers about ankles in the muck, cock in one wobbling hand while he slobbered at a bottle in the other.

'Where the hell do you start?' Shy heard Goldy asking her pimp. He had no answer.

The competition was humbling, all right. The women came in every shape, colour and age, lolling in the national undress of a score of different nations and displaying flesh by the acre. Gooseflesh, mostly, since the weather was tending chilly. Some cooed and simpered or blew kisses, others shrieked unconvincing promises about the quality of their services at the torchlit dark, still others abandoned even that much subtlety and thrust their hips at the passing Fellowship with the most warlike expressions. One let a pair of pendulous, blue-veined teats dangle over the rail of a balcony and called out, 'What d'you think o' these?'

Shy thought they looked about as appealing as a pair of rotten hams. You never can tell what'll light the fire in some folk, though. A man looked up eagerly with one hand down the front of his trousers noticeably yanking away, others stepping around him like a wank in the street was nothing to remark upon. Shy blew out her cheeks.

'I been to some low-down places and I done some low-down shit when I got there, but I never saw the like o' this.'

'Likewise,' muttered Lamb, frowning about with one hand resting on the hilt of his sword. Seemed to Shy it rested there a lot these days, and had got pretty comfortable too. He weren't the only one with steel to hand, mind you. The air of menace was thick enough to chew, gangs of ugly-faced and ugly-purposed men haunting the porches, armed past their armpits, aiming flinty frowns across at groups no better favoured on the other side of the way.

While they were stopped waiting for the traffic to clear, a thug with too much chin and nowhere near enough forehead stepped up to Majud's wagon and growled, 'Which side o' the street you on?'

Never a man to be rushed, Majud considered a moment before answering. 'I have purchased a plot on which I mean to site a business, but until I see it—'

'He ain't talking about plots, fool,' snorted another tough with hair so greasy he looked like he'd dipped his head in cold stew. 'He means are you on the Mayor's side or Papa Ring's side?'

'I am here to do business.' Majud snapped his reins and his wagon lurched on. 'Not to take sides.'

'Only thing on neither side o' the street is the sewer!' shouted Chinny after him. 'You want to go in the fucking sewer, do you?'

The way grew wider and busier still, a crawling sea of muck, the columns even higher above it, the ruin of an ancient theatre cut from the hillside where the valley split in two ahead of them. Sweet was waiting near a sprawling heap of building like a hundred shacks piled on top of each other. Looked as if some optimist had taken a stab at it with whitewash but given up halfway and left the rest to slowly peel, like a giant lizard in the midst of moulting.

'This here is Papa Ring's Emporium of Romance, Song and Dry Goods, known locally as the Whitehouse,' Sweet informed Shy as she hitched her horse. 'Over yonder,' and the old scout nodded across the stream that split the street in two, serving at once for drinking water and sewer and crossed by a muddle of stepping stones, wet planks and improvised bridges, 'is the Mayor's Church of Dice.'

The Mayor had occupied the ruins of some old temple – a set of pillars with half a moss-caked pediment on top – and filled in the gaps with a riot of planks to consecrate a place of worship for some very different idols.

'Though, being honest,' continued Sweet, 'they both offer fucking, drink and gambling so the distinction is largely in the signage. Come on, the Mayor's keen to meet you.' He stepped back to let a wagon clatter past, showering mud from its back wheels over all and sundry, then set off across the street.

'What shall I do?' called Temple, still on his mule with a faceful of panic.

'Take in the sights. Reckon there's a lifetime of material for a preacher. But if you're tempted by a sample, don't forget you got debts!' Shy forded the road after Lamb, trying to pick the firmest patches as the slop threatened to suck her boots right off, around a monstrous boulder she realised was the head of a fallen statue, half its face mud-sunk while the other still wore a pitted frown of majesty, then up the steps of the Mayor's Church of Dice, between two groups of frowning thugs and into the light.

The heat was a slap, such a reek of sweltering bodies that Shy – no stranger to the unwashed – felt for a moment like she might drown in it. Fires were stoked high and the air was hazy with their smoke, and chagga smoke, and the smoke from cheap lamps burning cheap oil with a fizz and sputter, and her eyes set right away to watering. Stained walls half green wood and half moss-crusted stone trickled with the wet of desperate breath. Mounted in alcoves above the swarming humanity were a dozen sets of dusty Imperial armour that must've belonged to some general of antiquity and his guards, the proud past staring down in faceless disapproval at the sorry now.

'It gets worse?' muttered Lamb.

'What gets better?' asked Sweet.

The air rang with the rattle of thrown dice and bellowed odds, thrown insults and bellowed warnings. There was a band banging away like their lives were at stake and some drunken prospectors were singing along but didn't know even a quarter of the words and were making up the balance with swears at random. A man reeled past clutching at a broken nose and blundered into the counter – gleaming wood and more'n likely the only thing in the place that came near clean – stretching what looked like half a mile and every inch crammed with clients clamouring for drink. Stepping back, Shy nearly tripped over a card-game. One of the players had a woman astride him, sucking at his face like he'd a gold nugget down his gullet and with just a bit more effort she'd get her tongue around it.

'Dab Sweet?' called a man with a beard seemed to go right up to his eyes, slapping the scout on the arm. 'Look, Sweet's back!'

'Aye, and brought a Fellowship with me.'

'No trouble with old Sangeed on the way?'

'There was,' said Sweet. 'As a result of which he's dead.'

'Dead?'

'No doubt o' that.' He jerked his thumb at Lamb. 'It was this lad did—'

But the man with all the beard was already clambering up on the nearest table sending glasses, cards and counters clattering. 'Listen up, all o' you! Dab Sweet killed that fucker Sangeed! That old Ghost bastard's dead!'

'A cheer for Dab Sweet!' someone roared, a surge of approval battered the mildewed rafters and the band struck up an even wilder tune than before.

'Hold on,' said Sweet, 'Wasn't me killed him—'

Lamb steered him on. 'Silence is the warrior's best armour, the saying goes. Just show us to the Mayor.'

They threaded through the heaving crowd, past a cage where a pair of clerks weighed out gold dust and coins in a hundred currencies and transformed it through the alchemy of the abacus to gambling chips and back. A few of the men Lamb brushed out of the way didn't much care for it, turned with a harsh word in mind, but soon reconsidered when they saw his face. Same face that, slack and sorry, boys used to laugh at back in Squaredeal. He was a man much changed since those days, all right. Or maybe just a man revealed.

A couple of nail-eyed thugs blocked the bottom of the stairs but Sweet called, 'These two are here to see the Mayor!' and bundled them up with a deal of back-slappery, along a balcony overlooking the swarming hall and to a heavy door flanked by two more hard faces.

'Here we go,' said Sweet, and knocked.

It was a woman who answered. 'Welcome to Crease,' she said.

She wore a black dress with a shine to the fabric, long-sleeved and buttoned all the way to her throat. Late in her forties was Shy's guess, hair streaked with grey. She must've been quite the beauty in her day, though, and her day weren't entirely past either. She took Shy's hand in one of hers and clasped it with the other one besides and said, 'You must be Shy. And Lamb.' She gave Lamb's weathered paw the same treatment, and he thanked her too late in a creaky voice and took his battered hat off as an afterthought, sparse hair overdue for a cut left flapping at all angles.

But the woman smiled like she'd never been treated to so gallant a gesture. She shut the door and with its solid click into the frame the madness outside was shut away and all was calm and reasonable. 'Do sit. Master Sweet has told me of your troubles. Your stolen children. A terrible thing.' And she had such pain in her face you'd have thought it was her babies had vanished.

'Aye,' muttered Shy, not sure what to do with that much sympathy.

'Would either of you care for a drink?' She poured four healthy measures of spirit without need for an answer. 'Please forgive this place, it's a struggle to get good furniture out here, as you can imagine.'

'Guess we'll manage,' said Shy, even though it was about the most comfortable chair she'd ever sat in and about the nicest room besides, Kantic hangings at the windows, candles in lamps of coloured glass, a great desk with a black leather top just a little stained with bottle rings.

She'd real fine manners, Shy thought, this woman, as she handed out the drinks. Not that haughty, down-the-nose kind that idiots thought lifted you above the crowd. The kind that made you feel you were worth something even if you were dog-tired and dog-filthy and had near worn the arse out of your trousers and not even you could tell how many hundred miles of dusty plain you'd covered since your last bath.

Shy took a sip, noted the drink was just as far out of her class as everything else, cleared her throat and said, 'We were hoping to see the Mayor.'

The woman perched herself against the edge of the desk – Shy had a feeling she'd have looked comfortable sitting on an open razor – and said, 'You are.'

'Hoping?'

'Seeing her.'

Lamb shifted awkwardly in his chair, like it was too comfortable for him to be comfortable in.

'You're a woman?' asked Shy, head somewhat scrambled from the hell outside and the clean calm in here.

The Mayor only smiled. She did that a lot but somehow you never tired of it. 'They have other words for what I am on the other side of the street, but, yes.' She tossed down her drink in a way that suggested it wasn't her first, wouldn't be her last and wouldn't make much difference either. 'Sweet tells me you're looking for someone.'

'Man by the name of Grega Cantliss,' said Shy.

'I know Cantliss. Preening scum. He robs and murders for Papa Ring.'

'Where can we find him?' asked Lamb.

'I believe he's been out of town. But I expect he'll be back before long.'

'How long are we talking about?' asked Shy.

'Forty-three days.'

That kicked the guts out of her. She'd built herself up to good news, or at least to news. Kept herself going with thoughts of Pit and Ro's smiling faces and happy hugs of reunion. Should've known better but hope's like damp – however much you try to keep it out there's always a little gets in. She knocked back the balance of her drink, not near so sweet now, and hissed, 'Shit.'

'We've come a long way.' Lamb carefully placed his own glass on the desk, and Shy noticed with a hint of worry his knuckles were white with pressure. 'I appreciate your hospitality, no doubt I do, but I ain't in any mood to fuck around. Where's Cantliss?'

'I'm rarely in the mood to fuck around either.' The rough word sounded double harsh in the Mayor's polished voice, and she held Lamb's eye like manners or no she wasn't someone to be pushed around. 'Cantliss will be back in forty-three days.'

Shy had never been one to mope. A moment to tongue at the

gap between her teeth and dwell on all the unfairness the world had inflicted on her undeserving carcass and she was on to the what nexts. 'Where's the magic in forty-three days?'

'That's when things are coming to a head here in Crease.'

Shy nodded towards the window and the sounds of madness drifting through. 'Strikes me they always are.'

'Not like this one.' The Mayor stood and offered out the bottle.

'Why not?' said Shy, and Lamb and Sweet were turning nothing down either. Refusing to drink in Crease seemed wrong-headed as refusing to breathe. Especially when the drink was so fine and the air so shitty.

'Eight years we've been here, Papa Ring and I, staring across the street at each other.' The Mayor drifted to the window and looked out at the babbling carnage below. She had a trick of walking so smooth and graceful it seemed it must done with wheels rather'n legs. 'There was nothing on the map out here but a crease when we arrived. Twenty shacks among the ruins, places where trappers could see out the winter.'

Sweet chuckled. 'You were quite a sight among 'em.'

'They soon got used to me. Eight years, while the town grew up around us. We outlasted the plague, and four raids by the Ghosts, and two more by bandits, and the plague again, and after the big fire came through we rebuilt bigger and better and were ready when they found the gold and the people started coming. Eight years, staring across the street at each other, and snapping at each other, and in the end all but at war.'

'You going to come near a point?' asked Shy.

'Our feud was getting bad for business. We agreed to settle it according to mining law, which is the only kind out here for the moment, and I can assure you people take it very seriously. We treated the town as a plot with two rival claims, winner takes all.'

'Winner of what?' asked Lamb.

'A fight. Not my choice but Papa Ring manoeuvred me into it. A fight, man against man, bare-fisted, in a Circle marked out in the old amphitheatre.'

'A fight in the Circle,' muttered Lamb. 'To the death, I daresay?'

'I understand more often than not that's where these things end up. Master Sweet tells me you may have some experience in that area.'

Lamb looked over at Sweet, then glanced at Shy, then back to the Mayor and grunted, 'Some.'

There was a time, not all that long ago, Shy would've laughed her arse off at the notion of Lamb in a fight to the death. Nothing could've been less funny now.

Sweet was chuckling as he put down his empty glass, though. 'I reckon we can drop the pretence, eh?'

'What pretence?' asked Shy.

'Lamb,' said Sweet. 'That's what. You know what I call a wolf wearing a sheep mask?'

Lamb looked back at him. 'I've a feeling you can't keep it to yourself.'

'A wolf.' The old scout wagged a finger across the room, looking quite decidedly pleased with himself. 'I'd a crazy guess about you the moment I saw a big nine-fingered Northman kill the hell out o' two drifters back in Averstock. When I saw you crush Sangeed like a beetle I was sure. I must admit it did occur when I asked you along that you and the Mayor might be the answer to each other's problems—'

'Ain't you a clever little bastard?' snarled Lamb, eyes burning and the veins suddenly popping from his thick neck. 'Best be careful when you pull that mask off, fucker, you might not like what's under there!'

Sweet twitched, Shy flinched, the comfortable room of a sudden feeling balanced on the brink of a great pit and that an awful dangerous place for a chat. Then the Mayor smiled as if this was all a joke between friends, gently took Lamb's trembling hand and filled his glass, fingers lingering on his just a moment.

'Papa Ring's brought in a man to fight for him,' she carried on, smooth as ever. 'A Northman by the name of Golden.'

'Glama Golden?' Lamb shrank back into his chair like he'd been embarrassed by his own temper.

'I've heard the name,' said Shy. 'Heard it'd be a fool who'd bet against him in a fight.'

'That would depend who he was fighting. None of my men is a match for him, but you . . .' She leaned forwards and the sweet whiff of perfume, rare as gold among the reeks of Crease, even got Shy a little warm under the collar. 'Well, from what Sweet tells me, you're more than a match for anyone.'

There was a time Shy would have laughed her arse off at that, too. Now, she wasn't even near a chuckle.

'Might be my best years are behind me,' muttered Lamb.

'Come, now. I don't think either one of us is over the hill quite yet. I need your help. And I can help you.' The Mayor looked Lamb in the face and he looked back like no one else was even there. Shy got a worried feeling, then. Like she'd somehow been out-bartered by this woman without prices even being mentioned.

'What's to stop us finding the children some other how?' she snapped, her voice sounding harsh as a graveyard crow's.

'Nothing,' said the Mayor simply. 'But if you want Cantliss, Papa Ring will put himself in your way. And I'm the only one who can get him out of it. Would you say that's fair, Dab?'

'I'd say it's true,' said Sweet, still looking a little unnerved. 'Fair I'll leave to better judges.'

'But you needn't decide now. I'll arrange a room for you over at Camling's Hostelry. It's the closest thing to neutral ground we have here. If you can find your children without my help, go with my blessing. If not . . .' And the Mayor gave them one more smile. 'I'll be here.'

''Til Papa Ring kicks you out of town.'

Her eyes flickered to Shy's and there was anger there, hot and sharp. Just for a moment, then she shrugged. 'I'm still hoping to stay.' And she poured another round of drinks.

Plots

'It is a plot,' said Temple.

Majud slowly nodded. 'Undeniably.'

'Beyond that,' said Temple, 'I would not like to venture.'

Majud slowly shook his head. 'Nor I. Even as its owner.'

It appeared the amount of gold in Crease had been drastically over-stated, but no one could deny there had been a mud strike here of epic proportions. There was the treacherous slop that constituted the main street and in which everyone was forced to take their wading, cursing, shuffling chances. There was the speckly filth that showered from every wagon-wheel to inconceivable heights when it was raining, sprinkling every house, column, beast and person. There was an insidious, watery muck that worked its way up from the ground, leaching into wood and canvas and blooming forth with moss and mould, leaving black tidemarks on the hems of every dress in town. There was an endless supply of dung, shit, crap and night soil, found in every colour and configuration and often in the most unlikely places. Finally, of course, there was the all-pervasive moral filth.

Majud's plot was rich in all of these and more.

An indescribably haggard individual stumbled from one of the wretched tents pitched higgledy-piggledy upon it, hawked up at great length and volume, and spat upon the rubbish-strewn mud. Then he turned the most bellicose of expressions towards Majud and Temple, scratched at his infested beard, dragged up his decaying full-body undershirt so it could instantly slump once more, and returned to the unspeakable darkness whence he came.

'The location is good,' said Majud.

'Excellent,' said Temple.

'Right on the main street.' Although Crease was so narrow that it was virtually the only street. Daylight revealed a different side to the thoroughfare: no cleaner, perhaps even less so, but at least the sense of a riot in a madhouse had faded. The flood of intoxicated criminals between the ruined columns had become a more respectable trickle. The whorehouses, gaming pits, husk-shacks and drinking dens were no doubt still taking customers but no longer advertising as if the world would end tomorrow. Premises with less spectacular strategies for fleecing passers-by came to the fore: eateries, money changers, pawnshops, blacksmiths, stables, butchers, combined stables and butchers, ratters and hatters, animal and fur traders, land agents and mineral consultancies, merchants in mining equipment of the most execrable quality, and a postal service whose representative Temple had seen dumping letters in a stream scarcely even out of town. Groups of bleary prospectors slogged miserably back to their claims, probably in hopes of scraping enough gold dust from the freezing stream-beds for another night of madness. Now and again a dishevelled Fellowship came chasing their diverse dreams into town, usually wearing the same expressions of horror and amazement that Majud and Temple had worn when they first arrived.

That was Crease for you. A place where everyone was passing through.

'I have a sign,' said Majud, patting it affectionately. It was painted clean white with gilt lettering and proclaimed:*Majud and Curnsbick Metalwork, Hinges, Nails, Tools, Wagon Fixings, High-Quality Smithing of All Varieties*. Then it said *Metalwork* in five other languages – a sensible precaution in Crease, where it sometimes seemed no two people spoke quite the same tongue, let alone read it. In Northern it had been spelled wrong, but it was still vastly superior to most of the gaudy shingles dangling over the main street. A building across the way sported a red one on which yellow letters had run into drips on the bottom edge. It read, simply, *Fuck Palace*.

'I brought it all the way from Adua,' said Majud.

'It is a noble sign, and embodies your high achievement in coming so far. All you need now is a building to hang it on.'

The merchant cleared his throat, its prominent knobble bobbing. 'I remember house-builder being among your impressive list of previous professions.'

'I remember you being unimpressed,' said Temple. ' "We need no houses out here," were your very words.'

'You have a sharp memory for conversations.'

'Those on which my life depend in particular.'

202

'Must I apologise at the start of our every exchange?'

'I see no pressing reason why not.'

'Then I apologise. I was wrong. You have proved yourself a staunch travelling companion, not to mention a valued leader of prayer.' A stray dog limped across the plot, sniffed at a turd, added one of its own and moved on. 'Speaking as a carpenter—'

'Ex-carpenter.'

'—how would you go about building on this plot?'

'If you held a knife to my throat?' Temple stepped forwards. His boot sank in well beyond the ankle, and it was only with considerable effort he was able to drag it squelching free.

'The ground is not the best,' Majud was forced to concede.

'The ground is always good enough if one goes deep enough. We would begin by driving piles of fresh hardwood.'

'That task would require a sturdy fellow. I will have to see if Master Lamb can spare us a day or two.'

'He is a sturdy fellow.'

'I would not care to be a pile under his hammer.'

'Nor I.' Temple had felt very much like a pile under a hammer ever since he had abandoned the Company of the Gracious Hand, and was hoping to stop. 'A hardwood frame upon the piles, then, jointed and pegged, beams to support a floor of pine plank to keep your customers well clear of the mud. Front of the ground floor for your shop, rear for office and workshop, contract a mason for a chimney-stack and a stone-built addition to house your forge. On the upper floor, quarters for you. A balcony overlooking the street appears to be the local fashion. You may festoon it with semi-naked women, should you so desire.'

'I will probably avoid the local fashion to that degree.'

'A steeply pitched roof would keep off the winter rains and accommodate an attic for storage or employees.' The building took shape in Temple's imagination, his hand sketching out the rough dimensions, the effect only slightly spoiled by a clutch of feral Ghost children frolicking naked in the shit-filled stream beyond.

Majud gave a curt nod of approval. 'You should have said architect rather than carpenter.'

'Would that have made any difference?'

'To me it would.'

'But, don't tell me, not to Curnsbick.'

'His heart is of iron—'

'I got one!' A filth-crusted individual rode squelching down the street into town, pushing his blown nag as fast as it would hobble, one arm raised high as though it held the word of the Almighty. 'I got one!' he roared again. Temple caught the telltale glint of gold in his hand. Men gave limp cheers, called out limp congratulations, gathered around to clap the prospector on the back as he slid from his horse, hoping perhaps his good fortune might rub off.

'One of the lucky ones,' said Majud as they watched him waddle, bow-legged, up the steps into the Mayor's Church of Dice, a dishevelled crowd trailing after, eager at the chance even of seeing a nugget.

'I fully expect he'll be destitute by lunchtime,' said Temple.

'You give him that long?'

One of the tent-flaps was thrust back. A grunt from within and an arc of piss emerged, spattered against the side of one of the other tents, sprinkled the mud, drooped to a dribble and stopped. The flap closed.

Majud gave vent to a heavy sigh. 'In return for your help in constructing the edifice discussed, I would be prepared to pay you the rate of one mark a day.'

Temple snorted. 'Curnsbick has not chased all charity from the Circle of the World, then.'

'The Fellowship may be dissolved but still I feel a certain duty of care towards those I travelled with.'

'That, or you expected to find a carpenter here but now perceive the local workmanship to be . . . inferior.' Temple cocked a brow at the building beside the plot, every door and window-frame at its own wrong angle, leaning sideways even with the support of an ancient stone block half-sunk in the ground. 'Perhaps you would like a place of business that will not wash away in the next shower. Does the weather get harsh here, do you suppose, in winter?'

A brief pause while the wind blew up chill and made the canvas of the tents flap and the wood of the surrounding buildings creak alarmingly. 'What fee would you demand?' asked Majud.

Temple had been giving serious consideration to the idea of slipping away and leaving his debt to Shy South forever stalled at seventy-six marks. But the sad fact was he had nowhere to slip to and no one to slip with, and was even more useless alone than in company. That left him with money to find. 'Three marks a day.' A quarter of what Cosca used to pay him, but ten times his wages riding drag.

Majud clicked his tongue. 'Ridiculous. That is the lawyer in you speaking.'

'He is a close friend of the carpenter.'

'How do I know your work will be worth the price?'

'I challenge you to find anyone less than entirely satisfied with the quality of my joinery.'

'You have built no houses here!'

'Then yours shall be unique. Customers will flock to see it.'

'One and a half marks a day. Any more and Curnsbick will have my head!'

'I would hate to have your death upon my conscience. Two it is, with meals and lodging provided.' And Temple held out his hand.

Majud regarded it without enthusiasm. 'Shy South has set an ugly precedent for negotiation.'

'Her ruthlessness approaches Master Curnsbick's. Perhaps they should go into business together.'

'If two jackals can share a carcass.' They shook. Then they considered the plot again. The intervening time had in no way improved it.

'The first step would be to clear the ground,' said Majud.

'I agree. Its current state is a veritable offence against God. Not to mention public health.' Another occupant had emerged from a structure of mildewed cloth sagging so badly that it must have been virtually touching the mud inside. This one wore nothing but a long grey beard not quite long enough to protect his dignity, or at least everyone else's, and a belt with a large knife sheathed upon it. He sat down in the dirt and started chewing savagely at a bone. 'Master Lamb's help might come in useful there also.'

'Doubtless.' Majud clapped him on the shoulder. 'I shall seek out the Northman while you begin the clearance.'

'Me?'

'Who else?'

'I am a carpenter, not a bailiff!'

'A day ago you were a priest and cattleman and a moment before that a lawyer! A man of your varied talents will, I feel sure, find a way.' And Majud was already hopping briskly off down the street.

Temple rolled his eyes from the earthbound refuse to the clean, blue heavens. 'I'm not saying I don't deserve it, but you surely love to test a man.' Then he hitched up his trouser-legs and stepped gingerly towards the naked beggar with the bone, limping somewhat since the buttock Shy pricked on the plains was still troubling him in the mornings.

'Good day!' he called.

The man squinted up at him, sucking a strip of gristle from his bone. 'I don't fucking think so. You got a drink?'

'I thought it best to stop.'

'Then you need a good fucking reason to bother me, boy.'

'I have a reason. Whether you will consider it a good one I profoundly doubt.'

'You can but try.'

'The fact is,' ventured Temple, 'we will soon be building on this plot.'

'How you going to manage that with me here?'

'I was hoping you could be persuaded to move.'

The beggar checked every part of his bone for further sustenance and, finding none, tossed it at Temple. It bounced off his shirt. 'You ain't going to persuade me o' nothing without a drink.'

'The thing is, this plot belongs to my employer, Abram Majud, and—'

'Who says so?'

'Who . . . says?'

'Do I fucking stutter?' The man took out his knife as if he had some everyday task that required one, but the subtext was plain. It really was a very large blade and, given the prevailing filthiness of everything else within ten strides, impressively clean, edge glittering with the morning sun. 'I asked who says?'

Temple took a wobbly step back. Straight into something very solid. He spun about, expecting to find himself face to face with one of the other tent-dwellers, probably sporting an even bigger knife – God knew there were so many big knives in Crease the distinction between them and swords was a total blur – and was hugely relieved to find Lamb towering over him.

'*I* say,' said Lamb to the beggar. 'You could ignore me. You could wave that knife around a little more. But you might find you're wearing it up your arse.'

The man looked down at his blade, perhaps wishing he had opted for a smaller one after all. Then he put it sheepishly away. 'Reckon I'll just move along.'

Lamb gave that a nod. 'I reckon.'

'Can I get my trousers?'

'You'd fucking better.'

He ducked into his tent and came out buttoning up the most ragged article of clothing Temple ever saw. 'I'll leave the tent, if it's all the same. Ain't that good a one.'

'You don't say,' said Temple.

The man loitered a moment longer. 'Any chance of that drink do you—'

'Get gone,' growled Lamb, and the beggar scampered off like he'd a mean dog at his heels.

'There you are, Master Lamb!' Majud waded over, trouser-legs held up by both hands to display two lean lengths of muddy calf. 'I was hoping to persuade you to work on my behalf and here I find you already hard at it!'

'It's nothing,' said Lamb.

'Still, if you could help us clear the site I'd be happy to pay you—'

'Don't worry about it.'

'Truly?' The watery sun gleamed from Majud's golden tooth. 'If you were to do me this favour I would consider you a friend for life!'

'I should warn you, friend o' mine can be a dangerous position.'

'I feel it is worth the risk.'

'If it'll save a couple of bits,' threw in Temple.

'I got all the money I need,' said Lamb, 'but I always been sadly short on friends.' He frowned over at the vagrant with the underclothes, just poking his head out of his tent and into the light. 'You!' And the man darted back inside like a tortoise into its shell.

Majud raised his brows at Temple. 'If only everyone was so accommodating.'

'Not everyone has been obliged to sell themselves into slavery.'

'You could've said no.' Shy was on the rickety porch of the building next door, leaning on the rail with boots crossed and fingers dangling. For a moment Temple hardly recognised her. She had a new shirt, sleeves rolled up with her tanned forearms showing, one with the old rope burn coiled pink around it, a sheepskin vest on top which was no doubt yellow by any reasonable estimation but looked white as a heavenly visitation in the midst of all that dirt. The same stained hat but tipped back, hair less greasy and more red, stirring in the breeze.

Temple stood and looked at her, and found he quite enjoyed it. 'You look . . .'

'Clean?'

'Something like that.'

'You look . . . surprised.'

'Little bit.'

'Did you think I stunk out of choice?'

'No, I thought you couldn't help yourself.'

She spat daintily through the gap between her front teeth, narrowly missing his boots. 'Then you discover your error. The Mayor was kind enough to lend me her bath.'

'Bathing with the Mayor, eh?'

She winked. 'Moving up in the world.'

Temple plucked at his own shirt, only held together by the more stubborn stains. 'Do you think she'd give me a bath?'

'You could ask. But I reckon there's about a four in five chance she'd have you killed.'

'I like those odds. Lots of people are five in five on my untimely death.'

'Something to do with you being a lawyer?'

'As of today, I will have you know, I am a carpenter and architect.'

'Well, your professions slip on and off easy as a whore's drawers, don't they?'

'A man must follow the opportunities.' He turned to take in the plot with an airy wave. 'I am contracted to build upon this unrivalled site a residence and place of business for the firm of Majud and Curnsbick.'

'My congratulations on leaving the legal profession and becoming a respectable member of the community.'

'Do they have such a thing in Crease?'

'Not yet, but I reckon it's on the way. You stick a bunch of drunken murderers together, ain't long before some turn to thieving, then to lying, then to bad language, and pretty soon to sobriety, raising families and making an honest living.'

'It's a slippery slope, all right.' Temple watched Lamb shepherd a tangle-haired drunkard off the plot, few possessions dragging in the muck behind him. 'Is the Mayor going to help you find your brother and sister?'

Shy gave a long sigh. 'Maybe. But she's got a price.'

'Nothing comes for free.'

'Nothing. How's carpenter's pay?'

Temple winced. 'Barely enough to scrape by on, sadly—'

'Two marks a day, plus benefits!' called Majud as he dismantled the most recently vacated tent. 'I've known bandits kinder to their victims!'

'Two marks from that miser?' Shy gave an approving nod. 'Well done. I'll take a mark a day towards the debt.'

'A mark,' Temple managed to force out. 'Very reasonable.' If there was a God His bounty was only lent, never given.

'I thought the Fellowship dissolved!' Dab Sweet pulled his horse up beside the plot, Crying Rock haunting his shoulder. Neither of them appeared to have ventured within spitting range of a bath, or a change of clothes either. Temple found that strangely reassuring. 'Buckhorm's out of town with his grass and his water, Lestek's dressing the theatre for his grand debut and most of the rest split up to dig gold their own way, but here's the four of you still, inseparable. Warms my heart that I forged such camaraderie out in the wilderness.'

'Don't pretend you got a heart,' said Shy.

'Got to be something pumps the black poison through my veins, don't there?'

'Ah!' shouted Majud. 'If it is not the new Emperor of the Plains, the conqueror of great Sangeed, Dab Sweet!'

The scout gave Lamb a nervous sideways glance. 'I've made no effort to spread that rumour.'

'And yet it has taken to this town like fire to tinder! I have heard half a dozen versions, none particularly close to my own remembrance. Most recently, I was told you shot the Ghost from a mile's distance and with a stiff side wind.'

'I heard you impaled him on the horns of an enraged steer,' said Shy.

'And in the newest version to reach my ear,' said Temple, 'you killed him in a duel over the good name of a woman.'

Sweet snorted. 'Where the hell do they get this rubbish? Everyone knows there's no women o' my acquaintance with a good name. This your plot?'

'It is,' said Majud.

'It is a plot,' said Crying Rock solemnly.

'Majud has contracted me to build a shop upon it,' said Temple.

'More buildings?' Sweet wriggled his shoulders. 'Bloody roofs hanging over you. Walls bearing in on you. How can you take a breath in those things?'

Crying Rock shook her head. 'Buildings.'

'A man can't think of nothing when he's in one but how to get back out. I'm a wanderer and that's a fact. Born to be under the sky.' Sweet watched Lamb drag another wriggling drunk from a tent one-handed and toss him rolling into the street. 'Man has to be what he is, don't he?'

Shy frowned up. 'He can try to be otherwise.'

'But more often than not it don't stick. All that trying, day after day, it wears you right through.' The old scout gave her a wink. 'Lamb taking up the Mayor's offer?'

'We're thinking on it,' she snapped back.

Temple looked from one to the other. 'Am I missing something?'

'Usually,' said Shy, still giving Sweet the eyeball. 'If you're heading on out of town, don't let us hold you up.'

'Wouldn't dream of it.' The old scout pointed down the main street, busier with traffic as the day wore on, weak sun raising a little steam from the wet mud, the wet horses, the wet roofs. 'We're signed up to guide a Fellowship of prospectors into the hills. Always work for guides around Crease. Everyone here wants to be somewhere else.'

'Not I,' said Majud, grinning as Lamb kicked another tent over.

'Oh no.' Sweet gave the plot a final glance, smile lurking at the corner of his mouth. 'You lot are right where you belong.' And he trotted on out of town, Crying Rock at his side.

Words and Graces

Shy didn't much care for pretension, and despite having crawled through more than her share was no high enthusiast for dirt. The dining room of Camling's Hostelry was an unhappy marriage of the two uglier by far than either one alone. The tabletops were buffed to a prissy shine but the floor was caked with boot-mud. The cutlery had bone handles but the walls were spattered hip high with ancient food. There was a gilt-framed painting of a nude who'd found something to smirk about but the plaster behind was blistered with mould from a leak above.

'State o' this place,' muttered Lamb.

'That's Crease for you,' said Shy. 'Everything upside down.'

On the trail she'd heard the stream-beds in the hills were lined with nuggets, just itching for greedy fingers to pluck them free. Some lucky few who'd struck gold in Crease might've dug it from the earth but it looked to Shy like most had found a way to dig it out of other folks. It weren't prospectors crowding the dining room of Camling's and forming a grumpy queue besides, it was pimps and gamblers, racketeers and money lenders, and merchants pedalling the same stuff they might anywhere else at half the quality and four times the price.

'A damn superfluity of shysters,' muttered Shy as she stepped over a pair of dirty boots and dodged a careless elbow. 'This the future of the Far Country?'

'Of every country,' muttered Lamb.

'Please, please, my friends, do sit!' Camling, the proprietor, was a long, oily bastard with a suit wearing through at the elbows and a habit of laying soft hands where they weren't wanted which had already nearly earned him Shy's fist in his face. He was busy flicking crumbs from a table perched on an ancient column top some creative carpenter had laid the floorboards around. 'We try to stay neutral but any friend of the Mayor's is a friend of mine, indeed they are!'

'I'll face the door,' said Lamb, shifting his chair around.

Camling drew out the other for Shy. 'And may I say how positively radiant you are this morning?'

'You can say it, but I doubt anyone'll be taking your word over the evidence o' their senses.' She levered her way to sitting, not easy since the ancient carvings on the column were prone to interfere with her knees.

'On the contrary, you are a positive ornament to my humble dining room.'

Shy frowned up. A slap in the face she could take in good part but all this fawning she didn't trust in the least. 'How about you bring the food and hold on to the blather?'

Camling cleared his throat. 'Of course.' And slipped away into the crowd.

'That Corlin over there?'

She was wedged into a shadowy corner, eyeing the gathering with her mouth pressed into that tight line of hers, like it'd take a couple of big men with pick and crowbar to get a word out.

'If you say so,' said Lamb, squinting across the room. 'My eyes ain't all they were.'

'I say so. And Savian, too. Thought they were meant to be prospecting?'

'Thought you didn't believe they would be?

'Looks like I was right.'

'You usually are.'

'I'd swear she saw me.'

'And?'

'And she ain't given so much as a nod.'

'Maybe she wishes she hadn't seen you.'

'Wishing don't make it so.' Shy slipped from the table, having to make room for a big bald bastard who insisted on waving his fork around when he talked.

'. . . there's still a few coming in but less than we hoped. Can't be sure how many more'll turn up. Sounds like Mulkova was bad . . .' Savian stopped short when he saw Shy coming. There was a stranger wedged even further into the shadows between him and Corlin, under a curtained window.

'Corlin,' said Shy.

'Shy,' said Corlin.

'Savian,' said Shy.

He just nodded.

'I thought you two were out digging?'

'We're putting it off a while.' Corlin held Shy's eye all the time. 'Might leave in a week. Might be later.'

'Lot of other folks coming through with the same idea. You want to claim aught but mud you'd best get into them hills.'

'The hills have been there since great Euz drove the devils from the world,' said the stranger. 'I predict that they will persist into next week.' He was an odd one, with bulging eyes, a long tangle of grey beard and hair and eyebrows hardly shorter. Odder yet, Shy saw now he had a pair of little birds, tame as puppies, pecking seed from his open palm.

'And you are?' asked Shy.

'My name is Zacharus.'

'Like the Magus?'

'Just like.'

Seemed a foolish sort of thing to take the name of a legendary wizard, but then you might have said the same for naming a woman after social awkwardness. 'Shy South.' She reached for his hand and an even smaller bird hopped from his sleeve and snapped at her finger, gave her the hell of a shock and made her jerk it back. 'And, er, that's Lamb over there. We rolled out from the Near Country in a Fellowship with these two. Faced down Ghosts and storms and rivers and an awful lot of boredom. High times, eh?'

'Towering,' said Corlin, eyes narrowed to blue slits. Shy was getting the distinct feeling they wanted her somewhere else and that was making her want to stay. 'And what's your business, Master Zacharus?'

'The turning of ages.' He had a trace of an Imperial accent, but it was strange somehow, crackly as old papers. 'The currents of destiny. The rise and fall of nations.'

'There a good living in that?'

He flashed a faintly crazy smile made of a lot of jagged yellow teeth. 'There is no bad living and no good death.'

'Right y'are. What's with the birds?'

'They bring me news, companionship, songs when I am melancholy and, on occasion, nesting materials.'

'You have a nest?'

'No, but they think I should.'

'Course they do.' The old man was mad as a mushroom, but she doubted folk hard-headed as Corlin and Savian would be wasting time on him if that was the end of the story. There was something off-putting to the way those birds stared, heads on one side, unblinking. Like they'd figured her for a real idiot.

She thought the old man might share their opinion. 'What brings you here, Shy South?'

'Come looking for two children stole from our farm.'

'Any luck?' asked Corlin.

'Six days I been up and down the Mayor's side of the street asking every pair of ears, but children ain't exactly a common sight around here and no one's seen a hair of them. Or if they have they ain't telling me. When I say the name Grega Cantliss they shut up like I cast a spell of silence.'

'Spells of silence are a challenging cloth to weave,' mused Zacharus, frowning up into an empty corner. 'So many variables.' There was a flapping outside and a pigeon stuck its head through the curtains and gave a burbling coo. 'She says they are in the mountains.'

'Who?'

'The children. But pigeons are liars. They only tell you what you want to hear.' And the old man stuck his tongue in the seeds in his palm and started crunching them between his yellow front teeth.

Shy was already minded to beat a retreat when Camling called from behind. 'Your breakfast!'

'What do you reckon those two are about?' asked Shy as she slipped back into her chair and flicked away a couple of crumbs their host had missed.

'Prospecting, I heard,' said Lamb.

'You ain't been listening to me at all, have you?'

'I try to avoid it. If they want our help I daresay they'll ask. 'Til then, it ain't our business.'

'Can you imagine either of them asking for help?'

'No,' said Lamb. 'So I reckon it'll never be our business, will it?'

'Definitely not. That's why I want to know.'

'I used to be curious. Long time ago.'

'What happened?'

Lamb waved his three-fingered hand at his scar-covered face.

Breakfast was cold porridge, runny egg and grey bacon, and the porridge weren't the freshest and the bacon may well not have derived from a pig. All whisked in front of Shy on imported crockery with trees and flowers painted into it in gilt, Camling with an air of smarmy pride like there was no finer meal to be had anywhere in the Circle of the World.

'This from a horse?' she muttered to Lamb, prodding at that meat and half-expecting it to tell her to stop.

'Just be thankful it ain't from the rider.'

'On the trail we ate shit, but at least it was honest shit. What the hell's this?'

'Dishonest shit?'

'That's Crease for you. You can get fine Suljuk plates but only slops to eat off 'em. Everything back to bloody front . . .' She realised the chatter had all faded, the scraping of her fork about the only noise. Hairs prickled on the back of her neck and she slowly turned.

Six men were adding their boot-prints to the mud-caked floor. Five were the kind of thugs you saw a lot of in Crease, spreading out among the tables to find watchful places, each wearing that ready slouch said they were better'n you 'cause there were more of them and they all had blades. The sixth was a different prospect. Short but hugely wide and with a big belly on him, too, a suit of fine clothes bulging at the buttons like the tailor had been awful optimistic with the measurements. He was black-skinned with a fuzz of grey hair, one earlobe stretched out around a thick golden ring, hole in the middle big enough almost for Shy to have got her fist through.

He looked pleased with himself to an untold degree, smiling on everything as though it was all exactly the way he liked it. Shy disliked him right off. Most likely jealousy. Nothing ever seemed to be the way she liked it, after all.

'Don't worry,' he boomed in a voice spilling over with good humour, 'you can all keep on eating! If you want to be shitting water all day!' And he burst out laughing, and slapped one of his men on the back and near knocked him into some fool's breakfast. He made his way between the tables, calling out hellos by name, shaking hands and patting shoulders, a long stick with a bone handle tapping at the boards.

Shy watched him come, easing a little sideways in her chair and slipping the bottom button of her vest open so the grip of her knife poked out nice and perky. Lamb just sat eating with eyes on his food. Not looking up even when the fat man stopped right next to their table and said, 'I'm Papa Ring.'

'I'd made a prediction to that effect,' said Shy.

'You're Shy South.'

'It ain't a secret.'

'And you must be Lamb.'

'If I must, I guess I must.'

'Look for the big fucking Northman with the face like a chopping block, they told me.' Papa Ring swung a free chair away from the next-door table. 'Mind if I sit?'

'What if I said yes?' asked Shy.

He paused halfway down, leaning heavy on his stick. 'Most likely I'd say sorry but sit anyway. Sorry.' And he lowered himself the rest of the way. 'I've got no fucking graces at all, they tell me. Ask anyone. No fucking graces.'

Shy took the quickest glance across the room. Savian hadn't even looked up, but she caught the faintest gleam of a blade ready under the table. That made her feel a little better. He didn't give much to your face, Savian, but he was a reassurance at your back.

Unlike Camling. Their proud host was hurrying over now, rubbing his hands together so hard Shy could hear them hiss. 'Welcome, Papa, you're very welcome.'

'Why wouldn't I be?'

'No reason, no reason at all.' If Camling had rubbed his hands any faster he might've made fire. 'As long as there's no . . . trouble.'

'Who'd want trouble? I'm here to talk.'

'Talk's how it always begins.'

'Talk's how everything begins.'

'My concern is how it will conclude.'

'How's a man to know that 'til he's talked?' asked Lamb, still not looking up.

'Exactly so,' said Papa Ring, smiling like it was the best day of his life.

'All right,' said Camling, reluctantly. 'Will you be taking food?'

Ring snorted. 'Your food is shit, as these two unfortunates are only now discovering. You can lose yourself.'

'Now look, Papa, this is my place—'

'Happy chance.' Of a sudden Ring's smile seemed to have an edge to it. 'You'll know just where to lose yourself.'

Camling swallowed, then scraped away with the sourest of expressions. The chatter gradually came up again, but honed to a nervous point now.

'One of the strongest arguments I ever saw for there being no God is the existence of Lennart Camling,' muttered Ring, as he watched

216

their host depart. The joints of his chair creaked unhappily as he settled back, all good humour again. 'So how are you finding Crease?'

'Filthy in every sense.' Shy poked her bacon away, then tossed her fork down and pushed the plate away, too. There could never be too great a distance between her and that bacon, far as she was concerned. She let her hands flop into her lap where one just happened to rest right on her knife's handle. Imagine that.

'Dirty's how we like it. You meet the Mayor?'

'I don't know,' said Shy, 'did we?'

'I know you did.'

'Why ask, then?'

'Watching my manners, such as they are. Though I don't deceive myself they come close to hers. She's got graces, don't she, our Mayor?' And Ring gently rubbed the polished wood of the table with one palm. 'Smooth as mirror glass. When she talks you feel swaddled in a goose-down blanket, don't you? The worthier folks around here, they tend to move in her orbit. Those manners. That way. The worthy folks lap that stuff up. But let's not pretend you all are two of the worthy ones, eh?'

'Could be we're aspiring to be worthier,' said Shy.

'I'm all for aspiration,' said Ring. 'God knows I came here with nothing. But the Mayor won't help you better yourselves.'

'And you will?'

Ring gave a chuckle, deep and joyful, like you might get from a kindly uncle. 'No, no, no. But at least I'll be honest about it.'

'You'll be honest about your dishonesty?'

'I never claimed to do anything other than sell folk what they want and make no judgements on 'em for their desires. Daresay the Mayor gave you the impression I'm quite the evil bastard.'

'We can get that impression all by ourselves,' said Shy.

Ring grinned at her. 'Quick, aren't you?'

'I'll try not to leave you behind.'

'She do all the talking?'

'The vast majority,' said Lamb, out the side of his mouth.

'Reckon he's waiting for something worth replying to,' said Shy.

Ring kept grinning. 'Well that's a very reasonable policy. You seem like reasonable folks.'

Lamb shrugged. 'You ain't really got to know us yet.'

'That's the very reason I came along. To get to know you better. And maybe just to offer some friendly advice.'

'I'm getting old for advice,' said Lamb. 'Even the friendly kind.'

'You're getting old for brawling, too, but I do hear tell you might be involving yourself in some bare-fist business we got coming to Crease.'

Lamb shrugged again. 'I fought a bout or two in my youth.'

'I see that,' said Ring, with an eye on Lamb's battered face, 'but, keen devotee though I am of the brawling arts, I'd rather this fight didn't happen at all.'

'Worried your man might lose?' asked Shy.

She really couldn't drag Ring's grin loose at all. 'Not really. My man's famous for beating a lot of famous men, and beating 'em bad. But the fact is I'd rather the Mayor packed up nice and quiet. Don't get me wrong, I don't mind seeing a little blood spilled. Shows people you care. But too much is awful bad for business. And I got big plans for this place. Good plans . . . But you don't care about that, do you?'

'Everyone's got plans,' said Shy, 'and everyone thinks theirs are good. It's when one set of good plans gets tangled with another things tend to slide downhill.'

'Just tell me this, then, and if the answer's yes I'll leave you to enjoy your shitty breakfast in peace. Have you given the Mayor a certain yes or can I still make you a better offer?' Ring's eyes moved between them, and neither spoke, and he took that for encouragement, and maybe it was. 'I may not have the graces but I'm always willing to deal. Just tell me what she's promised you.'

Lamb looked up for the first time. 'Grega Cantliss.'

Shy was watching him hard and she saw Ring's smile slip at the name. 'You know him, then?' she asked.

'He works for me. Has worked for me, at times.'

'Was he working for you when he burned my farm, and killed my friend, and stole two children from me?' asked Lamb.

Ring sat back, rubbing at his jaw, a trace of frown showing. 'Quite an accusation. Stealing children. I can tell you now I'd have no part of that.'

'Seems you got one even so,' said Shy.

'Only your word for it. What kind of a man would I be if I gave my people up on your say-so?'

'I don't care one fucking shit what kind of man y'are,' snarled Lamb, knuckles white around his cutlery, and Ring's men stirred unhappily, and Shy saw Savian sitting up, watchful, but Lamb took no notice of any of it. 'Give me Cantliss and we're done. Get in my way, there'll be trouble.' And he frowned as he saw he'd bent his knife at a right angle against the tabletop.

Ring mildly raised his brows. 'You're very confident. Given nobody's heard of you.'

'I been through this before. I got a fair idea how it turns out.'

'My man ain't bent cutlery.'

'He will be.'

'Just tell us where Cantliss is,' said Shy, 'and we'll be on our way and out of yours.'

Papa Ring looked for the first time like he might be running short of patience. 'Girl, do you suppose you could sit back and let me and your father talk this out?'

'Not really. Maybe it's my Ghost blood but I'm cursed with a contrary temperament. Folk warn me off a thing, I just start thinking on how to go about it. Can't help myself.'

Ring took a long breath and forced himself back to reasonable. 'I understand. Someone stole my children, there'd be nowhere in the Circle of the World for those bastards to run to. But don't make me your enemy when I can every bit as easily be your friend. I can't just hand you Cantliss. Maybe that's what the Mayor would do but it ain't my way. I tell you what, though, next time he comes to town we can all sit down and talk this out, get to the truth of it, see if we can't find your young ones. I'll help you every way I can, you got my word.'

'Your word?' And Shy curled back her lip and spat onto her cold bacon. If it was bacon.

'I got no graces but I got my word.' And Ring stabbed at the table with his thick forefinger. 'That's what everything stands on, on my side of the street. Folk are loyal to me 'cause I'm loyal to them. Break that, I got nothing. Break that, I am nothing.' He leaned closer, beckoning like he had the killer offer to make. 'But forget my word and just look at it this way – you want the Mayor's help, you're going to have to fight for it and, believe me, that'll be one hell of a fight. You want my help?' He gave the biggest shrug his big shoulders could manage, like even considering an alternative was madness. 'All you got to do is *not* fight.'

Shy didn't like the feel of this bastard one bit, but she didn't like the feel of the Mayor much more and she had to admit there was something in what he was saying.

Lamb nodded as he straightened out his knife between finger and thumb and tossed it on his plate. Then he stood. 'What if I'd rather fight?' And he strode for the door, the queue for breakfast scurrying to part for him.

Ring blinked, brows drawn in with puzzlement. 'Who'd rather fight?' Shy got up without answering and hurried after, weaving between the tables. 'Just think about it, that's all I'm asking! Be reasonable!'

And they were out into the street. 'Hold up there, Lamb! Lamb!'

She dodged through a bleating mass of little grey sheep, had to lurch back to let a pair of wagons squelch past. She caught sight of Temple, sitting high up astride a big beam, hammer in hand, the strong square frame of Majud's shop already higher than the slumping buildings on either side. He raised one hand in greeting.

'Seventy!' she bellowed at him. She couldn't see his face but the shoulders of his silhouette slumped in a faintly heartening way.

'Will you hold up?' She caught Lamb by the arm just as he was getting close to the Mayor's Church of Dice, the thugs around the door, hardly to be told from the ones who'd come with Papa Ring, watching them hard-eyed. 'What do you think you're doing?'

'Taking the Mayor up on her offer.'

'Just 'cause that fat fool rubbed you the wrong way?'

Lamb came close and suddenly it seemed that he was looming over her from quite the height. 'That and 'cause his man stole your brother and sister.'

'You think I'm happy about that?' she hissed at him, getting angry now. 'But we don't know the ins and outs of it! He seemed reasonable enough, considering'

Lamb frowned back towards Camling's. 'Some men only listen to violence.'

'Some men only talk it. Never took you for one of 'em. Did we come for Pit and Ro or for blood?'

She'd meant to make a point not ask a question but for a moment it looked like he had to consider the answer. 'I'm thinking I might get all three.'

She stared at him for a moment. 'Who the fuck *are* you? There was a time men could rub your face in the dung and you'd just thank 'em and ask for more.'

'And you know what?' He peeled her fingers from his arm with a grip that was almost painful. 'I've remembered I didn't like it much.' And he stomped muddy footprints up the steps of the Mayor's place, leaving Shy behind in the street.

That Simple

Temple tapped a few more shavings from the joint, then nodded to Lamb and together they lowered the beam, tenon sliding snugly into mortise.

'Hah!' Lamb slapped Temple on the back. 'Naught so nice as to see a job done well. You got clever hands, lad. Damn clever for a man washes up out of streams. Sort of hands you can turn to anything.' He looked down at his own big, battered, three-fingered hand and made a fist of it. 'Mine only ever really been good for one thing.' And he thumped at the beam until it came flush.

Temple had expected carpentry to be almost as much of a chore as riding drag, but he had to admit he was enjoying himself, and it was getting harder every day to pretend otherwise. There was something in the smell of fresh-sawn timber – when the mountain breeze slipped into the valley long enough for one to smell anything but shit – that wafted away his suffocating regrets and let him breathe free. His hands had found old skills with hammer and chisel and he had worked out the habits of the local wood, pale and straight and strong. Majud's hirelings silently conceded he knew his business and soon were taking his instructions without a second word, working at scaffold and pulleys with little skill but great enthusiasm, the frame sprouting up twice as fast and twice as fine as Temple had hoped.

'Where's Shy?' he asked, offhand, as though it was no part of a plan to dodge his latest payment. It was getting to be a game between them. One he never seemed to win.

'She's still touring town, asking questions about Pit and Ro. New folk coming in every day to ask. Probably she's trying Papa Ring's side of the street by now.'

'Is that safe?'

'I doubt it.'

'Shouldn't you stop her?'

Lamb snorted as he pushed a peg into Temple's fishing hand. 'Last time I tried to stop Shy she was ten years old and it didn't stick then.'

Temple worked the peg into its hole. 'Once she has a destination in mind, she isn't one to stop halfway.'

'Got to love that about her.' Lamb had a trace of pride in his voice as he passed the mallet. 'She's no coward, that girl.'

'So why are you helping me not her?'

''Cause I reckon I've found a way to Pit and Ro already. I'm just waiting for Shy to come round to the cost.'

'Which is?'

'The Mayor wants a favour.' There was a long pause, measured out by the tapping of Temple's mallet, accompanied by the distant sounds of other hammers on other more slovenly building sites scattered about the town. 'She and Papa Ring bet Crease on a fight.'

Temple looked around. 'They bet Crease?'

'They each own half the town, more or less.' Lamb looked out at it, crammed thoughtlessly into both sides of that winding valley like the place was an almighty gut, people and goods and animals squeezing in one end and shit and beggars and money squirting out the other. 'But the more you get the more you want. And all either one o' them wants is the half they haven't got.'

Temple puffed out his cheeks as he twisted at the next peg. 'I imagine one of them is sure to be disappointed.'

'At least one. The worst enemies are those that live next door, my father used to tell me. These two have been squabbling for years and neither one's come out on top, so they're putting on a fight. Winner takes all.' A group of half-tame Ghosts had spilled from one of the worse whorehouses – the better ones wouldn't let them in the door – and had knives out, taunting each other in common, knowing no words but swearing and the language of violence. That was more than enough to get by on in Crease. 'Two men in a Circle,' murmured Lamb, 'more'n likely with a considerable audience and a fair few side bets. One comes out alive, one comes out otherwise, and everyone else comes out thoroughly entertained.'

'Shit,' breathed Temple.

'Papa Ring's brought in a man called Glama Golden. A Northman. Big name in his day. I hear he's been fighting for money in pits and pens all across the Near Country and done a lot of winning, too. The Mayor, well, she's been searching high and low for someone to stand up for her . . .' He gave Temple a long look and it was easy enough to guess the rest.

'Shit.' It was one thing to fight for your life out there on the plains when the Ghosts were coming at you and offering no alternatives. Another to wait weeks for the moment, choose to step out in front of a crowd and batter, twist and crush the life from a man with your hands. 'Have you had any practice at . . . that sort of thing?'

'As luck would have it – my luck being what it is – more'n a little.'

'Are you sure the Mayor's on the right side of this?' asked Temple, thinking of all the wrong sides he had taken.

Lamb frowned down at the Ghosts, who had evidently resolved their differences without bloodshed and were noisily embracing. 'In my experience there's rarely such a thing as a right side, and when there is I've an uncanny knack of picking out the other. All I know is Grega Cantliss killed my friend and burned my farm and stole two children I swore to protect.' Lamb's voice had a cold edge on it as he shifted his frown to the Whitehouse, cold enough to bring Temple out in gooseflesh all over. 'Papa Ring's standing by him, so he's made himself my enemy. The Mayor's standing against him, and that makes her my friend.'

'Are things ever really that simple?'

'When you step into a Circle with the intention of killing a man, it's best if they are.'

'Temple?' The sun was low and the shadow of one of the great columns had fallen across the street below, so it took a moment to work out who was calling from the swirling traffic. 'Temple?' Another moment before he placed the smiling face tipped towards him, bright-eyed and with a bushy yellow beard. 'That you up there?' Still a third before he connected the world in which he knew that man to the world he lived in now, and recognition washed over him like a bucket of ice-water over a peaceful sleeper.

'Bermi?' he breathed.

'Friend of yours?' asked Lamb.

'We know each other,' Temple managed to whisper.

He slipped down the ladder with shaky hands, all the time tingling with the rabbit's urge to run. But where to? He had been beyond lucky to survive the last time he fled the Company of the Gracious Hand and was far from sure his divine support would stretch to another effort. He picked his way to Bermi with reluctant little steps, picking at the hem of his shirt, like a child that knows he has a slap coming and more than likely deserves it.

'You all right?' asked the Styrian. 'You look ill.'

'Is Cosca with you?' Temple could hardly get the words out he felt that sick. God might have blessed him with clever hands but He'd cursed him with a weak stomach.

Bermi was all smiles, though. 'I'm happy to say he's not, nor any of those other bastards. I daresay he's still floundering about the Near Country bragging to that bloody biographer and searching for ancient gold he'll never find. If he hasn't given up and gone back to Starikland to get drunk.'

Temple closed his eyes and expelled a lungful of the most profound relief. 'Thank heaven.' He put his hand on the Styrian's shoulder and leaned over, bent nearly double, head spinning.

'You sure you're all right?'

'Yes, I am.' He grabbed Bermi around the back and hugged him tight. 'Better than all right!' He was ecstatic! He breathed free once again! He kissed Bermi's bearded cheek with a noisy smack. 'What the hell brings you to the arse of the world?'

'You showed me the way. After that town – what was the name of it?'

'Averstock,' muttered Temple.

Bermi's eyes took on a guilty squint. 'I've done things I'm not proud of, but that? Nothing else but murder. Cosca sent me to find you, afterwards.'

'He did?'

'Said you were the most important man in the whole damn Company. Two days out I ran into a Fellowship coming west to mine for gold. Half of them were from Puranti – from my home town, imagine that! It's as if God has a purpose!'

'Almost as if.'

'I left the Company of the Fucking Finger and off we went.'

'You put Cosca behind you.' Cheating death once again had given Temple a faintly drunken feeling. 'Far, far behind.'

'You a carpenter now?'

'One way to clear my debts.'

'Shit on your debts, brother. We're heading back into the hills. Got a claim up on the Brownwash. Men are just sieving nuggets out of the mud up there!' He slapped Temple on the shoulder. 'You should come with us! Always room for a carpenter with a sense of humour. We've a cabin but it could do with some work.'

Temple swallowed. How often on the trail, choking on the dust of Buckhorm's herd or chafing under the sting of Shy's jibes, had he dreamed of an offer just like this? An easy way, unrolling before his willing feet. 'When do you leave?'

'Five days, maybe six.'

'What would a man need to bring?'

'Just some good clothes and a shovel, we've got the rest.'

Temple looked for the trick in Bermi's face but there was no sign of one. Perhaps there was a God after all. 'Are things ever really that simple?'

Bermi laughed. 'You're the one always loved to make things complicated. This is the new frontier, my friend, the land of opportunities. You got anything keeping you here?'

'I suppose not.' Temple glanced up at Lamb, a big black shape on the frame of Majud's building. 'Nothing but debts.'

Yesterday's News

'I'm looking for a pair of children.'

Blank faces.

'Their names are Ro and Pit.'

Sad shakes of the head.

'They're ten and six. Seven. He'd be seven now.'

Sympathetic mumbles.

'They were stole by a man named Grega Cantliss.'

A glimpse of scared eyes as the door slammed in her face.

Shy had to admit she was getting tired. She'd near worn her boots through tramping up and down the crooked length of main street, which wormed longer and more crooked every day as folk poured in off the plains, throwing up tents or wedging new hovels into some sliver of mud or just leaving their wagons rotting alongside the trail. Her shoulders were bruised from pushing through the bustle, her legs sore from scaling the valley sides to talk to folk in shacks clinging to the incline. Her voice was a croak from asking the same old questions over and over in the gambling halls and husk-dens and drinking sheds until she could hardly tell them apart one from another. There were a good few places they wouldn't let her in, now. Said she put off the customers. Probably she did. Probably Lamb had the right of it just waiting for Cantliss to come to him, but Shy had never been much good at waiting. *That's your Ghost blood*, her mother would've said. But then her mother hadn't been much good at waiting either.

'Look here, it's Shy South.'

'You all right, Hedges?' Though she could tell the answer at a glance. He'd never looked flushed with success but he'd had a spark of hope about him on the trail. It had guttered since and left him greyed out and ragged. Crease was no place to make your hopes healthier. No place to make anything healthier, far as she could tell. 'Thought you were looking for work?'

'Couldn't find none. Not for a man with a leg like this. Wouldn't have thought I led the charge up there at Osrung, would you?' She wouldn't have, but he'd said so already so she kept her silence. 'Still looking for your kin?'

'Will be until I find 'em. You heard anything?'

'You're the first person said more'n five words together to me in a week. Wouldn't think I led a charge, would you? Wouldn't think that.' They stood there awkward, both knowing what was coming next. Didn't stop it coming, though. 'Can you spare a couple o' bits?'

'Aye, a few.' She delved in her pocket and handed him the coins Temple had handed her an hour before, then headed on quick. No one likes to stand that close to failure, do they? Worried it might rub off.

'Ain't you going to tell me not to drink it all?' he called after her.

'I'm no preacher. Reckon folk have the right to pick their own method of destruction.'

'So they do. You're not so bad, Shy South, you're all right!'

'We'll have to differ on that,' she muttered, leaving Hedges to shuffle for the nearest drinking hole, never too many steps away in Crease even for a man whose steps were miserly as his.

'I'm looking for a pair of children.'

'I cannot assist you there, but I have other tidings!' This woman was a strange-looking character, clothes that must've been fine in their time but their time long past and the months since full of mud and stray food. She drew back her sagging coat with a flourish and produced a sheaf of crumpled papers.

'What are they, news-bills?' Shy was already regretting talking to this woman but the path here was a narrow stretch of mud between sewer-stream and rotten porches and her bulging belly wasn't giving space to pass.

'You have a keen eye for quality. You wish to make a purchase?'

'Not really.'

'The faraway happenings of politics and power are of no interest?'

'They never seem to bear much on my doings.'

'Perhaps it is your ignorance of current affairs keeps you down so?'

'I always took it to be the greed, laziness and ill-temper of others plus a fair share of bad luck, but I reckon you'll have it your way.'

'Everyone does.' But the woman didn't move.

Shy sighed. Given her knack for upsetting folk she thought she might give indulgence a try. 'All right, then, deliver me from ignorance.'

The woman displayed the upmost bill and spoke with mighty self-importance. 'Rebels defeated at Mulkova – routed by Union troops under General Brint! How about that?'

'Unless they been defeated there a second time, that happened before I even left the Near Country. Everyone knows it.'

'The lady requires something fresher,' muttered the old woman, rooting through her thumbed-over bundle. 'Styrian conflict ends! Sipani opens gates to the Snake of Talins!'

'That was at least two years before.' Shy was starting to think this woman was touched in the head, if that even meant anything in a place where most were happy-mad, dismal-mad, or some other kind of mad that defied further description.

'A challenge indeed.' The woman licked a dirty finger to leaf through her wares and came up with one that looked a veritable antique. 'Legate Sarmis menaces border of the Near Country? Fears of Imperial incursion?'

'Sarmis has been menacing for decades. He's the most menacing Legate you ever heard of.'

'Then it's true as it ever was!'

'News spoils quick, friend, like milk.'

'I say it gets better if carefully kept, like wine.'

'I'm glad you like the vintage, but I ain't buying yesterday's news.'

The woman cradled her papers like a mother hiding an infant from bird attack, and as she leaned forward Shy saw the top was tore off her tall hat and got a view of the scabbiest scalp imaginable and a smell of rot almost knocked her over. 'No worse than tomorrow's, is it?' And the woman swept her aside and strode on waving her old bills over her head. 'News! I have news!'

Shy took a long, hard breath before she set off. Damn, but she was tired. Crease was no place to get less tired, far as she could tell.

'I'm looking for a pair of children.'

The one in the middle treated her to something you'd have had to call a leer. 'I'll give you children, girl.'

The one on the left burst out laughing. The one on the right grinned, and a bit of chagga juice dribbled out of his mouth and ran down into his beard. From the look of his beard it wasn't his first dribble either. They were an unpromising trio all right, but if Shy had stuck to the promising she'd have been done in Crease her first day there.

'They were stolen from our farm.'

'Probably nothing else there worth stealing.'

'Being honest, I daresay you're right. Man called Grega Cantliss stole 'em.'

The mood shifted right off. The one on the right stood up, frowning. The one on the left spat juice over the railing. Leery leered more'n ever. 'You got some gall asking questions over here, girl. Some fucking gall.'

'You ain't the first to say so. Probably best I just take my gall away on down the street.'

She made to move on but he stepped down from the porch to block her way, pointed a waving finger towards her face. 'You know what, you've got kind of a Ghosty look to you.'

'Half-breed, maybe,' grunted one of his friends.

Shy set her jaw. 'Quarter, as it goes.'

Leery took his leer into realms of facial contortion. 'Well, we don't care for your kind over on this side o' the street.'

'Better quarter-Ghost than all arsehole, surely?'

There was that knack for upsetting folk. His brows drew in and he took a step at her. 'Why, you bloody—'

Without thinking she put her right hand on the grip of her knife and said, 'You'd best stop right there.'

His eyes narrowed. Annoyed. Like he hadn't expected straight-up defiance but couldn't back down with his friends watching. 'You'd best not put your hand on that knife unless you're going to use it, girl.'

'Whether I use it or not depends on whether you stop there or not. My hopes ain't high but maybe you're cleverer than you look.'

'Leave her be.' A big man stood in the doorway. Big hardly did him justice. His fist up on the frame beside him looked about the size of Shy's head.

'You can stay out o' this,' said Leery.

'I could, but I'm not. You say you're looking for Cantliss?' he asked, eyes moving over to Shy.

'That's right.'

'Don't tell her nothing!' snapped Squinty.

The big man's eyes drifted back. 'You can shut up . . .' He had to duck his head to get through the doorway. 'Or I can shut you up.' The other two men backed off to give him room – and he needed a lot. He looked bigger still as he stepped out of the shadows, taller'n Lamb, even, and maybe bigger in the chest and shoulder, too. A real monster, but he spoke soft, accent thick with the North. 'Don't pay these idiots no mind. They've got big bones for fights they're sure of winning but otherwise not enough for a toothpick.' He took the couple of steps down into the street, boards groaning under his great boots, and stood towering over Leery.

'Cantliss is from the same cloth,' he said. 'A puffed-up fool with a lot of vicious in him.' For all his size there was a sad sag to his face. A droop to his blond moustache, a sorry greying to the stubble about it. 'More or less what I used to be, if it comes to that. He owes Papa Ring a lot of money, as I heard it. Ain't been around for a while now, though. Not much more I can tell you.'

'Well, thanks for that much.'

'My pleasure.' The big man turned his washed-out blue eyes on Leery. 'Get out of her way.'

Leery gave Shy a particularly nasty leer, but Shy had been treated to a lot of harsh expressions in her time and after a while they lose their sting. He made to go back up the steps but the big man didn't let him. 'Get out of her way, that way.' And he nodded over at the stream.

'Stand in the sewer?' said Leery.

'Stand in the sewer. Or I'll lay you out in it.'

Leery cursed to himself as he clambered down the slimy rocks and stood up to his knees in shitty water. The big man put one hand on his chest and with the other offered Shy the open way.

'My thanks,' she said as she stepped past. 'Glad I found someone decent this side of the street.'

The man gave a sad snort. 'Don't let a small kindness fool you. Did you say you're looking for children?'

'My brother and sister. Why?'

'Might be I can help.'

Shy had learned to treat offers of help, and for that matter everything else, with a healthy suspicion. 'Why would you?'

'Because I know how it feels to lose your family. Like losing a part of you, ain't it?' She thought about that for a moment, and reckoned he had it right. 'Had to leave mine behind, in the North. I know it was the best thing for 'em. The only thing. But it still cuts at me now. Didn't ever think it would. Can't say I valued 'em much when I had 'em. But it cuts at me.'

He'd such a sorry sag to his great shoulders then that Shy had to take pity on him. 'Well, you're welcome to follow along, I guess. It's been my observation that folk take me more serious when I've a great big bastard looking over my shoulder.'

'That is a sadly universal truth,' he said as he fell into step, two of his near enough to every three of hers. 'You here alone?'

'Came with my father. Kind of my father.'

'How can someone be kind of your father?'

'He's managed it.'

'He father to these other two you're looking for?'

'Kind of to them, too,' said Shy.

'Shouldn't he be helping look?'

'He is, in his way. He's building a house, over on the other side of the street.'

'That new one I've seen going up?'

'Majud and Curnsbick's Metalwork.'

'That's a good building. And that's a rare thing around here. Hard to see how it'll find your young ones, though.'

'He's trusting someone else to help with that.'

'Who?'

Normally she'd have kept her cards close, so to speak, but something in his manner brought her out. 'The Mayor.'

He took a long suck of breath. 'I'd sooner trust a snake with my fruits than that woman with anything.'

'She sure is a bit too smooth.'

'Never trust someone who don't use their proper name, I was always told.'

'You haven't told me your name yet.'

The big man gave a weary sigh. 'I was hoping to avoid it. People tend to look at me different, once they know what it is.'

'One o' those funny ones, is it? Arsehowl, maybe?'

'That'd be a mercy. My name'll make no one laugh, sad to say. You'd never believe how I worked at blowing it up bigger. Years of it. Now there ain't no getting out from under its shadow. I've forged the links of my own chain and no mistake.'

'I reckon we're all prone to do that.'

'More'n likely.' He stopped and offered one huge hand, and she took it, her own seeming little as a child's in its great warm grip. 'My name's—'

'Glama Golden!'

Shy saw the big man flinch a moment, and his shoulders hunch, then he slowly turned. A young man stood in the street behind. A big lad, with a scar through his lips and a tattered coat. He had an unsteady look to him made Shy think he'd been drinking hard. To puff his courage up, maybe, though folk didn't always bother with a reason to drink in Crease. He raised an unsteady finger to point at them, and his other hand hovered around the handle of a big knife at his belt.

'You're the one killed Stockling Bear?' he sneered. 'You're the one won all them fights?' He spat in the mud just near their feet. 'You don't look much!'

'I ain't much,' said the big man, softly.

The lad blinked, not sure what to do with that. 'Well . . . I'm fucking calling you out, you bastard!'

'What if I ain't listening?'

The lad frowned at the people on the porches, all stopped their business to watch. He ran his tongue around the inside of his mouth, not sure of himself. Then he looked over at Shy, and took one more stab at it. 'Who's this bitch? Your fucking—'

'Don't make me kill you, boy.' Golden didn't say it like a threat. Pleading, almost, his eyes sadder'n ever.

The lad flinched a little, and his fingers twitched, and he came over pale. The bottle's a shifty banker – it might lend you courage but it's apt to call the debt in sudden. He took a step back and spat again. 'Ain't fucking worth it,' he snapped.

'No, it ain't.' Golden watched the lad all the way as he backed slowly off, then turned and started walking off fast. A few sighs of relief, a few shrugs, and the talk started building back up.

Shy swallowed, mouth suddenly dried out and sticky-feeling. 'You're Glama Golden?'

He slowly nodded. 'Though I know full well there ain't much golden about me these days.' He rubbed his great hands together as he watched that lad lose himself in the crowd, and Shy saw they were shaking. 'Hell of a thing, being famous. Hell of a thing.'

'You're the one standing for Papa Ring in this fight that's coming?'

'That I am. Though I have to say I'm hopeful it won't happen. I hear the Mayor's got no one to fight for her.' His pale eyes narrowed as he looked back to Shy. 'Why, what've you heard?'

'Nothing,' she said, trying her best to smile and failing at it. 'Nothing at all.'

Blood Coming

It was just before dawn, clear and cold, the mud crusted with frost. The lamps in the windows had mostly been snuffed, the torches lighting the signs had guttered out and the sky was bright with stars. Hundreds upon hundreds of them, sharp as jewels, laid out in swirls and drifts and twinkling constellations. Temple opened his mouth, cold nipping at his cheeks, turning, turning until he was dizzy, taking in the beauty of the heavens. Strange, that he had never noticed them before. Maybe his eyes had been always on the ground.

'You reckon there's an answer up there?' asked Bermi, his breath and his horse's breath smoking on the dawn chill.

'I don't know where the answer is,' said Temple.

'You ready?'

He turned to look at the house. The big beams were up, most of the rafters and the window and door-frames, too, the skeleton of the building standing bold and black against the star-scattered sky. Only that morning Majud had been telling him what a fine job he was doing, how even Curnsbick would have considered his money well spent. He felt a flush of pride, and wondered when he had last felt one. But Temple was a man who abandoned everything half-done. That was a long-established fact.

'You can ride on the packhorse. It's only a day or two into the hills.'

'Why not?' A few hundred miles on a mule and his arse was carved out of wood.

Over towards the amphitheatre the carpenters were already making a desultory start. They were throwing up a new bank of seating at the open side so they could cram in a few score more onlookers, supports and cross-braces just visible against the dark hillside, bent and badly bolted, some of the timbers without the branches even properly trimmed.

'Only a couple of weeks to the big fight.'

'Shame we'll miss it,' said Bermi. 'Better get on, the rest of the lads'll be well ahead by now.'

Temple pushed his new shovel through one of the packhorse's straps, moving slower, and slower, then stopping still. It had been a day or two since he'd seen Shy, but he kept reminding himself of the debt in her absence. He wondered if she was out there somewhere, still doggedly searching. You could only admire someone who stuck at a thing like that, no matter the cost, no matter the odds. Especially if you were a man who could never stick at anything. Not even when he wanted to.

Temple thought about that for a moment, standing motionless up to his ankles in half-frozen mud. Then he walked to Bermi and slapped his hand down on the Styrian's shoulder. 'I won't be going. My bottomless thanks for the offer, but I've a building to finish. That and a debt to pay.'

'Since when do you pay your debts?'

'Since now, I suppose.'

Bermi gave him a puzzled look, as if he was trying to work out where the joke might be. 'Can I change your mind?'

'No.'

'Your mind always shifted with the breeze.'

'Looks like a man can grow.'

'What about your shovel?'

'Consider it a gift.'

Bermi narrowed his eyes. 'There's a woman involved, isn't there?'

'There is, but not in the way you're thinking.'

'What's she thinking?'

Temple snorted. 'Not that.'

'We'll see.' Bermi hauled himself into his saddle. 'I reckon you'll regret it, when we come back through with nuggets big as turds.'

'I'll probably regret it a lot sooner than that. Such is life.'

'You're right there.' The Styrian swept off his hat and raised it high in salute. 'No reasoning with the bastard!' And he was off, mud flicking from the hooves of his horse as he headed out up the main street, scattering a group of reeling-drunk miners on the way.

Temple gave a long sigh. He wasn't sure he didn't regret it already. Then he frowned. One of those stumbling miners looked familiar: an old man with a bottle in one hand and tear-tracks gleaming on his cheeks.

'Iosiv Lestek?' Temple twitched up his trousers to squelch out into the street. 'What happened to you?'

'Disgrace!' croaked the actor, beating at his breast. 'The crowd . . . wretched. My performance . . . abject. The cultural extravaganza . . . a debacle!' He clawed at Temple's shirt. 'I was pelted from the stage. I! Iosiv Lestek! He who ruled the theatres of Midderland as if they were a private fief!' He clawed at his own shirt, stained up the front. 'Pelted with *dung*! Replaced by a trio of girls with bared bubs. To rapturous applause, I might add. Is that all audiences care for these days? Bubs?'

'I suppose they've always been popular—'

'All finished!' howled Lestek at the sky.

'Shut the fuck up!' someone roared from an upstairs window.

Temple took the actor by the arm. 'Let me take you back to Camling's—'

'Camling!' Lestek tore free, waving his bottle. 'That cursed maggot! That treacherous cuckoo! He has ejected me from his Hostelry! I! Me! Lestek! I will be revenged upon him, though!'

'Doubtless.'

'He will see! They will all see! My best performance is yet ahead of me!'

'You will show them, but perhaps in the morning. There are other hostelries—'

'I am penniless! I sold my wagon, I let go my props, I pawned my costumes!' Lestek dropped to his knees in the filth. 'I have nothing but the rags I wear!'

Temple gave a smoking sigh and looked once more towards the star-prickled heavens. Apparently he was set on the hard way. The thought made him oddly pleased. He reached down and helped the old man to his feet. 'I have a tent big enough for two, if you can stand my snoring.'

Lestek stood swaying for a moment. 'I don't deserve such kindness.'

Temple shrugged. 'Neither did I.'

'My boy,' murmured the actor, opening wide his arms, tears gleaming again in his eyes.

Then he was sick down Temple's shirt.

Shy frowned. She'd been certain Temple was about to get on that packhorse and ride out of town, trampling her childish trust under hoof and no doubt the last she'd ever hear of him. But all he'd done was give a man a shovel and wave him off. Then haul some shit-covered old drunk into the shell of Majud's building. People are a mystery there's no solving, all right.

She was awake a lot in the nights, now. Watching the street. Maybe thinking she'd see Cantliss ride in – not that she even had the first clue what he looked like. Maybe thinking she'd catch a glimpse of Pit and Ro, if she even recognised them any more. But mostly just picking at her worries. About her brother and sister, about Lamb, about the fight that was coming. About things and places and faces she'd rather have forgotten.

Jeg with his hat jammed down saying, 'Smoke? Smoke?' and Dodd all surprised she'd shot him and that bank man saying so politely, 'I'm afraid I can't help you,' with that puzzled little smile like she was a lady come for a loan rather'n a thief who'd ended up murdering him for nothing. That girl they'd hanged in her place whose name Shy had never known. Swinging there with a sign around her twisted neck and her dead eyes asking, *why me and not you?* and Shy still no closer to an answer.

In those slow, dark hours her head filled with doubts like a rotten rowboat with bog water, going down, going down for all her frantic bailing, and she'd think of Lamb dead like it was already done and Pit and Ro rotting in the empty somewhere and she'd feel like some kind of traitor for thinking it, but how do you stop a thought once it's in there?

Death was the one sure thing out here. The one fact among the odds and chances and bets and prospects. Leef, and Buckhorm's sons, and how many Ghosts out there on the plain? Men in fights in Crease, and folk hung on tissue-paper evidence or dead of fever or of silly mishaps like that drover kicked in the head by his brother's horse yesterday, or the shoe-merchant they found drowned in the sewer. Death walked among them daily, and presently would come calling on them all.

Hooves in the street and Shy craned to see, a set of torches flickering, folk retreating to their porches from the flying mud of a dozen horsemen. She turned to look at Lamb, a big shape under his blanket, shadow pooled in its folds. At the head-end she could just see his ear, and the big notch out of it. Could just hear his soft, slow breathing.

'You awake?'

He took a longer breath. 'Now I am.'

The men had reined in before the Mayor's Church of Dice, torch-light shifting over their hard-used, hard-bitten faces, and Shy shrank back. Not Pit or Ro and not Cantliss either. 'More thugs arrived for the Mayor.'

'Lots of thugs about,' grunted Lamb. 'Don't take no reader of the runes to see blood coming.'

Hooves thumped on by in the street and a flash of laughter and a woman shouting then quiet, with just the quick tap-tap of a hammer from over near the amphitheatre to remind them that the big show was on its way.

'What happens if Cantliss don't come?' She spoke at the dark. 'How do we find Pit and Ro then?'

Lamb slowly sat up, scrubbing his fingers through his grey hair. 'We'll just have to keep looking.'

'What if . . .' For all the time she'd spent thinking it she hadn't crossed the bridge of actually making the words 'til now. 'What if they're dead?'

'We keep looking 'til we're sure.'

'What if they died out there on the plains and we'll never know for sure? Every month passes there's more chance we'll never know, ain't there? More chance they'll just be lost, no finding 'em.' Her voice was turning shrill but she couldn't stop it rising, wilder and wilder. 'They could be anywhere by now, couldn't they, alive or dead? How do we find two children in all the unmapped empty they got out here? When do we stop, is what I'm asking? When *can* we stop?'

He pushed his blanket back, padded over and winced as he squatted, looking up into her face. 'You can stop whenever you want, Shy. You come this far and that's a long, hard way, and more'n likely there's a long, hard way ahead yet. I made a promise to your mother and I'll keep on. Long as it takes. Ain't like I got better offers knocking my door down. But you're young, still. You got a life to lead. If you stopped, no one could blame you.'

'I could.' She laughed then, and wiped the beginnings of a tear on the back of her hand. 'And it ain't like I got much of a life either, is it?'

'You take after me there,' he said, pulling back the covers on her bed, 'daughter or not.'

'Guess I'm just tired.'

'Who wouldn't be?'

'I just want 'em back,' as she slid under the blankets.

'We'll get 'em back,' as he dropped them over her and laid a weighty hand on her shoulder. She could almost believe him, then. 'Get some sleep now, Shy.'

Apart from the first touch of dawn creeping between the curtains and across Lamb's bedspread in a grey line, the room was dark.

'You really going to fight that man Golden?' she asked, after a while. 'He seemed all right to me.'

Lamb was silent long enough she started to wonder whether he was asleep. Then he said, 'I've killed better men for worse reasons, I'm sorry to say.'

The Sleeping Partner

In general, Temple was forced to concede, he was a man who had failed to live up to his own high standards. Or even to his low ones. He had undertaken a galaxy of projects. Many of those any decent man would have been ashamed of. Of the remainder, due to a mixture of bad luck, impatience and a shiftless obsession with the next thing, he could hardly remember one that had not tailed off into disappointment, failure or outright disaster.

Majud's shop, as it approached completion, was therefore a very pleasant surprise.

One of the Suljuks who had accompanied the Fellowship across the plains turned out to be an artist of a roofer. Lamb had applied his nine digits to the masonry and proved himself more than capable. More recently the Buckhorns had shown up in full numbers to help saw and nail the plank siding. Even Lord Ingelstad took a rare break from losing money to the town's gamblers to give advice on the paint. Bad advice, but still.

Temple took a step back into the street, gazing up at the nearly completed façade, lacking only for balusters to the balcony and glass in the windows, and produced the broadest and most self-satisfied grin he had entertained in quite some time. Then he was nearly pitched on his face by a hearty thump on the shoulder.

He turned, fully expecting to hear Shy grate out the glacial progress of his debt to her, and received a second surprise.

A man stood at his back. Not tall, but broad and possessed of explosive orange sideburns. His thick eyeglasses made his eyes appear minute, his smile immense by comparison. He wore a tailored suit, but his heavy hands were scarred across the backs by hard work.

'I had despaired of finding decent carpentry in this place!' He raised an eyebrow at the new seating haphazardly sprouting skywards around the ancient amphitheatre. 'But what should I find, just at my lowest ebb?' And he seized Temple by the arms and pointed him back towards Majud's shop. 'But this invigorating example of the joiner's craft! Bold in design, diligent in execution and in a heady fusion of styles aptly reflecting the many-cultured character of the adventurers braving this virgin land. And all on my behalf! Sir, I am quite humbled!'

'Your . . . behalf?'

'Indeed!' He pointed towards the sign above the front door. 'I am Honrig Curnsbick, the better half of Majud and Curnsbick!' And he flung his arms around Temple and kissed him on both cheeks, then rooted in his waistcoat pocket and produced a coin. 'A little something extra for your trouble. Generosity repays itself, I have always said!'

Temple blinked down at the coin. It was a silver five-mark piece. 'You have?'

'I have! Not always financially, not always immediately, but in goodwill and friendship which ultimately are beyond price!'

'They are? I mean . . . you think they are?'

'I do! Where is my partner, Majud? Where is that stone-hearted old money-grubber?'

'I do not believe he is expecting your arrival—'

'Nor do I! But how could I stay in Adua while . . . *this*,' and he spread his arms wide to encompass swarming, babbling, fragrant Crease, 'all *this* was happening without me? Besides, I have a fascinating new idea I wish to discuss with him. Steam, now, is the thing.'

'Is it?'

'The engineering community is in an uproar following a demonstration of Scibgard's new coal-fired piston apparatus!'

'Whose what?'

Curnsbick perched eyeglasses on broad forehead to squint at the hills behind the town. 'The results of the first mineral investigations are quite fascinating. I suspect the gold in these mountains is black, my boy! Black as . . .' He trailed off, staring up the steps of the house. 'Not . . . can it be . . .' He fumbled down his eyeglasses and let fall his jaw. 'The famous Iosiv Lestek?'

The actor, swaddled in a blanket and with several days' grey growth upon his grey cheeks, blinked back from the doorway. 'Well, yes—'

'My dear sir!' Curnsbick trotted up the steps, caused one of Buckhorm's sons to fumble his hammer by flicking a mark at him, seized the actor by the hand and pumped it more vigorously than any piston apparatus could have conceived of. 'An honour to make your acquaintance, sir, a perfect honour! I was transported by your Bayaz on one occasion back in Adua. Veritably transported!'

'You do me too much kindness,' murmured Lestek as Majud's ruthlessly pleasant partner steered him into the shop. 'Though I feel sure my best work still lies ahead of me . . .'

Temple blinked after them. Curnsbick was not quite what he had been led to expect. But then what was in life? He stepped back once again, losing himself again in happy contemplation of his building, and was nearly knocked onto his face by another slap on the shoulder. He rounded on Shy, decidedly annoyed this time.

'You'll get your money, you bloodsucking—'

A monstrous fellow with a tiny face perched on an enormous bald head stood at his back. 'The Mayor . . . wants . . . to see you,' he intoned, as though they were lines for a walk-on part badly memorised.

Temple was already running through the many reasons why someone powerful might want him dead. 'You're sure it was me?' The man nodded. Temple swallowed. 'Did she say why?'

'Didn't say. Didn't ask.'

'And if I would rather remain here?'

That minuscule face crinkled smaller still with an almost painful effort of thought. 'Wasn't an option . . . she discussed.'

Temple took a quick glance about but there was no help in easy reach and, in any case, the Mayor was one of those inevitable people. If she wanted to see him, she would see him soon enough. He shrugged, once more whisked helpless as a leaf on the winds of fate, and trusted to God. For reasons best known to Himself, He'd been coming though for Temple lately.

The Mayor gazed across her desk in thoughtful silence for a very long time.

People with elevated opinions of themselves no doubt delight in being looked upon in such a manner, mentally listing the many wonderful characteristics the onlooker must be in dumbstruck admiration of. For Temple it was torture. Reflected in that estimating gaze he saw all his own disappointment in himself, and wriggled in his chair wishing the ordeal would end.

'I am hugely honoured by the kind invitation, your . . . Mayor . . . ness,' he ventured, able to bear it no longer, 'but—'

'Why are we here?'

The old man by the window, whose presence was so far a mystery, gave vent to a crackly chuckle. 'Juvens and his brother Bedesh debated that very question for seven years and the longer they argued, the further away was the answer. I am Zacharus.' He leaned forward, holding out one knobbly-knuckled hand, black crescents of dirt ingrained beneath the fingernails.

'Like the Magus?' asked Temple, tentatively offering his own.

'Exactly like.' The old man seized his hand, twisted it over and probed at the callous on his middle finger, still pronounced even though Temple had not held a pen in weeks. 'A man of letters,' said Zacharus, and a group of pigeons perched on the window sill all at once reared up and flapped their wings at each other.

'I have had . . . several professions.' Temple managed to worm his hand from the old man's surprisingly powerful grip. 'I was trained in history, theology and law in the Great Temple of Dagoska by Haddish Kahdia—' The Mayor looked up sharply at the name. 'You knew him?'

'A lifetime ago. A man I greatly admired. He always preached and practised the same. He did what he thought right, no matter how difficult.'

'My mirror image,' muttered Temple.

'Different tasks need different talents,' observed the Mayor. 'Do you have experience with treaties?'

'As it happens, I negotiated a peace agreement and trimmed a border or two last time I was in Styria.' He had served as a tool in a shameful and entirely illegal land-grab, but honesty was an advantage to carpenters and priests, not to lawyers.

'I want you to prepare a treaty for me,' said the Mayor. 'One that brings Crease, and a slab of the Far Country around it, into the Empire and under its protection.'

'Into the Old Empire? The great majority of the settlers come from the Union. Would that not be the natural—'

'Absolutely not the Union.'

'I see. Not wishing to talk myself into trouble – I do that rather too often – but . . . the only laws people seem to respect out here are the ones with a point on the end.'

'Now, perhaps.' The Mayor swept to the window and looked down into the swarming street. 'But the gold will run out and the prospectors will drift off, and the fur will run out and the trappers will drift off, then the gamblers, then the thugs, then the whores. Who will remain? The likes of your friend Buckhorm, building a house and raising cattle a day's ride out of town. Or your friend Majud, whose

242

very fine shop and forge you have been chafing your hands on these past weeks. People who grow things, sell things, make things.' She gracefully acquired a glass and bottle on the way back. 'And those kinds of people like laws. They don't like lawyers much, but they consider them a necessary evil. And so do I.'

She poured out a measure but Temple declined. 'Drink and I have had some long and painful conversations and found we simply can't agree.'

'Drink and I can't agree either.' She shrugged and tossed it down herself. 'But we keep on having the argument.'

'I have a rough draft . . .' Zacharus rummaged in his coat, producing a faint smell of musty onions and a grubby sheaf of odd-sized papers, scrawled upon with the most illegible handwriting imaginable. 'The principal points covered, as you see. The ideal is the status of a semi-independent enclave under the protection of and paying nominal taxes to the Imperial government. There is precedent. The city of Calcis enjoys similar status. Then there is . . . was . . . what's it called? Thingy. You know.' He screwed up his eyes and slapped at the side of his head as if he could knock the answer free.

'You have some experience with the law,' said Temple as he leafed through the document.

The old man waved a dismissive and gravy-stained hand. 'Imperial law, a long time ago. This treaty must be binding under Union law and mining traditions also.'

'I will do the best I can. It will mean nothing until it is signed, of course, by a representative of the local population and, well, by the Emperor, I suppose.'

'An Imperial Legate speaks for the Emperor.'

'You have one handy?'

Zacharus and the Mayor exchanged a glance. 'The legions of Legate Sarmis are said to be within four weeks' march.'

'I understand Sarmis is . . . not a man anyone would choose to invite. His legions even less so.'

The Mayor gave a resigned shrug. 'Choice does not enter into it. Papa Ring is keen for Crease to be brought into the Union. I understand his negotiations in that direction are well advanced. That *cannot* be allowed to happen.'

'I understand,' said Temple. That their escalating squabble had acquired an international dimension and might well escalate further still. But escalating squabbles are meat and drink to a lawyer. He had to confess some trepidation at the idea of going back to that profession, but it certainly looked like the easy way.

'How long will it take you to prepare the document?' asked the Mayor.

'A few days. I have Majud's shop to finish—'

'Make this a priority. Your fee will be two hundred marks.'

'Two . . . hundred?'

'Is that sufficient?'

Most definitely the easy way. Temple cleared his throat and said in a voice slightly hoarse, 'That will be adequate but . . . I must complete the building first.' He surprised himself with that even more than the Mayor had surprised him with the fee.

Zacharus nodded approvingly. 'You are a man who likes to see things through.'

Temple could only smile. 'The absolute opposite but . . . I've always liked the idea of being one.'

Fun

They were all in attendance, more or less. The whole Fellowship reunited. Well, not Leef, of course, or the others left in the dirt out there on the flat and empty. But the rest. Laughing and backslapping and lying about how well things were going now. Some misting up at rose-tinted remembrances of the way things had been on the trail. Some observing what a fine building the firm of Majud and Curnsbick had to work with. Probably Shy should've been joshing away with the rest. How long since she had some fun, after all? But she'd always found fun was easier talked of and looked forward to than actually had.

Dab Sweet was complaining about the faithlessness of those prospectors he'd guided into the mountains and who'd stiffed him on the payment before he could stiff them. Crying Rock was nodding along and grumbling, 'Mmm,' at all the wrong moments. Iosiv Lestek was trying to impress one of the whores with tales of his heyday on the stage. She was asking whether that was before the amphitheatre got built, which by most estimates was well over a thousand years ago. Savian was swapping grunts with Lamb in one corner, tight as if they'd known each other since boys. Hedges was lurking in another, nursing a bottle. Buckhorm and his wife still had a fair old brood running about folks' legs despite the ones they'd lost in the wilderness.

Shy gave a sigh and drank another silent toast to Leef and the rest who couldn't be there. Probably the company of the dead suited her better right then.

'I used to ride drag behind an outfit like this!'

She turned towards the door and got quite the shock. Temple's more successful twin stood there in a new black suit, all tidy as a princess, his dusty tangle of hair and beard barbered close. He'd come upon a

245

new hat and a new manner besides, swaggering in more like owner than builder.

Wasn't until she felt a sting of disappointment to see him so unfamiliar that she realised how much she'd been looking forward to seeing him the same.

'Temple!' came the merry calls and they crowded round to approve of him.

'Who'd have thought you could fish such a carpenter from a river?' Curnsbick was asking, an arm around Temple's shoulders like he'd known him all his life.

'A lucky find indeed!' said Majud, like he was the one did the fishing and lent the money and Shy hadn't been within a dozen miles at the time.

She worked her tongue around, reflecting that it surely was hard to get even the little credit you deserved, leaned to spit through the gap in her teeth, then saw Luline Buckhorm watching her with a warning eyebrow up and swallowed it instead.

Probably she should've been glad she'd saved a man from drowning and steered him to a better life, her faith justified against all contrary opinion. Let ring the bells! But instead she felt like a secret only she'd enjoyed was suddenly common knowledge, and found she was brooding on how she might go about spoiling it all for him, and then was even more annoyed that she was thinking like a mean child, and turned her back on the room and took another sour pull at her bottle. The bottle never changed unexpectedly, after all. It always left you equally disappointed.

'Shy?'

She made sure she looked properly surprised, like she'd no idea he'd be in the room. 'Well, if it ain't everyone's favourite chunk o' driftwood, the great architect himself.'

'The very same,' said Temple, tipping that new hat.

'Drink?' she asked him, offering the bottle.

'I shouldn't.'

'Too good to drink with me these days?'

'Not good enough. I can never stop halfway.'

'Halfway to where?'

'Face down in the shit was my usual destination.'

'You take a sip, I'll try and catch you if you fall, how's that?'

'I suppose it wouldn't be the first time.' He took the bottle, and a

246

sip, and grimaced like she'd kicked him in the fruits. 'God! What the hell's it made of?'

'I've decided it's one of those questions you're happier without an answer to. Like how much that finery o' yours cost.'

'I haggled hard,' thumping at his chest as he tried to get his voice back. 'You would've been proud.'

Shy snorted. 'Pride ain't common with me. And it still must've cost a fair sum for a man with debts.'

'Debts, you say?'

Here was familiar ground, at least. 'Last we spoke it was—'

'Forty-three marks?' Eyes sparkling with triumph, he held out one finger. A purse dangled from the tip, gently swinging.

She blinked at it, then snatched it from his finger and jerked it open. It held the confusion of different coinage you usually found in Crease, but mostly silver, and at a quick assay there could easily have been sixty marks inside.

'You turned to thievery?'

'Lower yet. To law. I put ten extra in there for the favour. You did save my life, after all.'

She knew she should be smiling but somehow she was doing just the opposite. 'You sure your life's worth that much?'

'Only to me. Did you think I'd never pay?'

'I thought you'd grab your first chance to wriggle out of it and run off in the night. Or maybe die first.'

Temple raised his brows. 'That's about what I thought. Looks like I surprised us both. Pleasantly, though, I hope.'

'Of course,' she lied, pocketing the purse.

'Aren't you going to count it?'

'I trust you.'

'You do?' He looked right surprised about it and so was she, but she realised it was true. True of a lot of folk in that room.

'If it ain't all there I can always track you down and kill you.'

'It's nice to know that's an option.'

They stood side by side, in silence, backs to the wall, watching a room full of their friends chatter. She glanced at him and he slowly looked sideways, like he was checking whether she was looking, and when he got there she pretended she'd been looking past him at Hedges all along. Tense having him next to her of a sudden. As if without that debt between them they were pressed up too close for comfort.

247

'You did a fine job on the building,' was the best she could manage after digging away for something to say.

'Fine jobs and paid debts. I can think of a few acquaintances who wouldn't recognise me.'

'I'm not sure I recognise you.'

'That good or bad?'

'I don't know.' A long pause, and the room was getting hot from all the folk blathering in it, and her face was hot in particular, and she passed Temple the bottle, and he shrugged and took a sip and passed it back. She took a bigger one. 'What do we talk about, now you don't owe me money?'

'The same things as everyone else, I suppose.'

'What do they talk about?'

He frowned at the crowded room. 'The high quality of my crafts-manship appears to be a popular—'

'Your head swells any bigger you won't be able to stand.'

'A lot of people are talking about this fight that's coming—'

'I've heard more'n enough about that.'

'There's always the weather.'

'Muddy, lately, in main street, I've observed.'

'And I hear there's more mud on the way.' He grinned sideways at her and she grinned back, and the distance didn't feel so great after all.

'Will you say a few words before the fun starts?' It was when Curns-bick loomed suddenly out of nowhere Shy realised she was already more'n a bit drunk.

'Words about what?' she asked.

'I apologise, my dear, but I was speaking to this gentleman. You look surprised.'

'Not sure which shocks me more, that I'm a dear or he's a gentle-man.'

'I stand by both appellations,' said the inventor, though Shy wasn't sure what the hell he meant by it. 'And as ex-spiritual advisor to this ex-Fellowship, and architect and chief carpenter of this outstanding edifice, what gentleman better to address our little gathering at its completion?'

Temple raised his palms helplessly as Curnsbick hustled him off and Shy took another swig. The bottle was getting lighter all the time. And she was getting less annoyed.

Probably there was a link between the two.

*

'My old teacher used to say you know a man by his friends!' Temple called at the room. 'Guess I can't be quite the shit I thought I was!'

A few laughs and some shouts of, 'Wrong! Wrong!'

'Not long ago I barely knew one person I could have called decent. Now I can fill a room I built with them. I used to wonder why anyone would come out to this God-forsaken arse of the world who didn't have to. Now I know. They come to be part of something new. To live in new country. To be new people. I nearly died out on the plains, and I can't say I would have been widely mourned. But a Fellowship took me in and gave me another chance I hardly deserved. Not many of them were keen to begin with, I'll admit, but . . . one was, and that was enough. My old teacher used to say you know the righteous by what they give to those who can't give back. I doubt anyone who's had the misfortune to bargain with her would agree, but I will always count Shy South among the righteous.'

A general murmur of agreement, and some raised glasses, and he saw Corlin slapping Shy on the back and her looking sour beyond belief.

'My old teacher used to say there is no better act than the raising of a good building. It gives something to those that live in it, and visit it, and even pass it by every day it stands. I haven't really tried at much in life, but I've tried to make a good building of this. Hopefully it will stand a little longer than some of the others hereabouts. May God smile on it as He has smiled on me since I fell in that river, and bring shelter and prosperity to its occupants.'

'And liquor is free to all!' bellowed Curnsbick. Majud's horrified complaints were drowned out in the stampede towards the table where the bottles stood. 'Especially the master carpenter himself.' And the inventor conjured a glass into Temple's hand and poured a generous measure, smiling so broadly Temple could hardly refuse. He and drink might have had their disagreements, but if the bottle was always willing to forgive, why shouldn't he? Was not forgiveness neighbour to the divine? How drunk could one get him?

Drunk enough for another, as it turned out.

'Good building, lad, I always knew you had hidden talents,' rambled Sweet as he sloshed a third into Temple's glass. 'Well hidden, but what's the point in an obvious hidden talent?'

'What indeed?' agreed Temple, swallowing a fourth. He could not have called it a pleasant taste now, but it was no longer like swallowing red-hot wire wool. How drunk could four get him, anyway?

Buckhorm had produced a fiddle now and was hacking out a tune while Crying Rock did injury to a drum in the background. There was dancing. Or at least well-meaning clomping in the presence of music if not directly related to it. A kind judge would have called it dancing and Temple was feeling like a kind judge then, and with each drink – and he'd lost track of the exact number – he got more kind and less judging, so that when Luline Buckhorm laid small but powerful hands upon him he did not demur and in fact tested the floorboards he had laid only a couple of days before with some enthusiasm.

The room grew hotter and louder and dimmer, sweat-shining faces swimming at him full of laughter and damn it but he was enjoying himself like he couldn't remember when. The night he joined the Company of the Gracious Hand, maybe, and the mercenary life was all a matter of good men facing fair risks together and laughing at the world and nothing to do with theft, rape and murder on an industrial scale. Lestek tried to add his pipe to the music, failed in a coughing fit and had to be escorted out for air. Temple thought he saw the Mayor, talking softly to Lamb under the watchful eyes of a few of her thugs. He was dancing with one of the whores and complimenting her on her clothes, which were repugnantly garish, and she couldn't hear him anyway and kept shouting, 'What?' Then he was dancing with one of Gentili's cousins, and complimenting him on his clothes, which were dirt-streaked from prospecting and smelled like a recently opened tomb, but the man still beamed at the compliment. Corlin came past in stately hold with Crying Rock, both of them looking grave as judges, both trying to lead, and Temple near choked on his tongue at the unlikeliness of the couple. Then suddenly he was dancing with Shy and to his mind they were making a pretty good effort at it, quite an achievement since he still had a half-full glass in one hand and she a half-empty bottle.

'Never thought you'd be a dancer,' he shouted in her ear. 'Too hard for it.'

'Never thought you'd be one,' her breath hot against his cheek. 'Too soft.'

'No doubt you're right. My wife taught me.'

She stiffened then, for a moment. 'You've got a wife?'

'I did have. And a daughter. They died. Long time ago, now. Sometimes it doesn't feel so long.'

She took a drink, looking at him sideways over the neck of the bottle, and there was something to that glance gave him a breathless tingle. He leaned to speak to her and she caught him around the head and kissed him quite fiercely. If he'd had time he would've reasoned she wasn't the type for gentle kisses but he didn't get time to reason, or kiss back, or push her off, or even work out which would be his preference before she twisted his head away and was dancing with Majud, leaving him to be manhandled about the floor by Corlin.

'You think you're getting one from me you've another thing coming,' she growled.

He leaned against the wall, head spinning, face sweating, heart pounding as if he had a dose of the fever. Strange, what sharing a little spit can do. Well, along with a few measures of raw spirits on a man ten years sober. He looked at his glass, thought he'd be best off throwing the contents down the wall, then decided he put more value on the wall than himself and drank them instead.

'You all right?'

'She kissed me,' he muttered.

'Shy?'

Temple nodded, then realised it was Lamb he'd said it to, and shortly thereafter that it might not have been the cleverest thing to say.

But the big Northman only grinned. 'Well, that's about the least surprising thing I ever heard. Everyone in the Fellowship saw it coming. The snapping and arguing and niggling over the debt. Classic case.'

'Why did no one say anything?'

'Several talked of nothing else.'

'I mean to me.'

'In my case, 'cause I had a bet with Savian on when it would happen. We both thought a lot sooner'n this, but I won. He can be a funny bastard, that Savian.'

'He can . . . what?' Temple hardly knew what shocked him more, that Shy kissing him came as no surprise, or that Savian could be funny. 'Sorry to be so predictable.'

'Folk usually prefer the obvious outcome. Takes bones to defy expectation.'

'Meaning I don't have any.'

Lamb only shrugged as though that was a question that hardly needed answering. Then he picked up his battered hat.

'Where are you going?' asked Temple.

'Ain't I got a right to my own fun?' He put a hand on Temple's shoulder. A friendly, fatherly hand, but a frighteningly firm one, too. 'Be careful with her. She ain't as tough as she looks.'

'What about me? I don't even look tough.'

'That's true. But if Shy hurts you I won't break her legs.'

By the time Temple had worked that one out, Lamb was gone. Dab Sweet had commandeered the fiddle and was up on a table, stomping so the plates jumped, sawing away at the strings like they were around his sweetheart's neck and he had moments to save her.

'I thought we were dancing?'

Shy's cheek had colour in it and her eyes were shining deep and dark and for reasons he couldn't be bothered to examine but probably weren't all that complicated anyway she looked dangerously fine to him right then. So, fuck it all, he tossed down his drink with a manly flick of the wrist then realised the glass was empty, threw it away, snatched her bottle while she grabbed his other hand and they dragged each other in amongst the lumbering bodies.

It was a long time since Shy had got herself properly reeling drunk but she found the knack came back pretty quick. Putting one foot in front of the other had become a bit of a challenge but if she kept her eyes wide open on the ground and really thought about it she didn't fall over too much. The hostelry was way too bright and Camling said something about a policy on guests and she laughed in his face and told him there were more whores than guests in this fucking place and Temple laughed as well and snorted snot down his beard. Then he chased her up the stairs with his hand on her arse which was funny to begin with then a bit annoying and she slapped him and near knocked him down the steps he was that surprised, but she caught him by the shirt and dragged him after and said sorry for the slap and he said what slap and started kissing her on the top landing and tasted like spirits. Which wasn't a bad way to taste in her book.

'Isn't Lamb here?'

'Staying at the Mayor's place now.'

Bloody hell things were spinning by then. She was fumbling in her trousers for the key and laughing and then she was fumbling in his trousers and they were up against the wall and kissing again her mouth full of his breath and his tongue and her hair then the door banging open and the two of them tumbling through and across the dim-lit floorboards. She crawled on top of him and they were grunting away, room reeling, and she felt the burn of sick at the back of her throat but swallowed it and didn't much care as it tasted no worse than the first time and Temple seemed to be a long way from complaining or probably even noticing either, he was too busy struggling with the buttons on her shirt and couldn't have been making harder work of it if they'd been the size of pinheads.

She realised the door was open still and kicked out at it but judged the distance all wrong and kicked a hole in the plaster beside the frame instead, started laughing again. Got the door shuddering shut with the next kick and he had her shirt open now and was kissing at her chest which felt all right actually if a bit ticklish, her own body looking all pale and strange to her and she was wondering when was the last time she did anything like this and deciding it was way too long. Then he'd stopped and was staring down in the darkness, eyes just a pair of glimmers.

'Are we doing the right thing?' he asked, so comic serious for a moment she wanted to laugh again.

'How the fuck should I know? Get your trousers off.'

She was trying to wriggle free of her own but still had her boots on and was getting more and more tangled, knew she should've taken the boots off first but it was a bit late now and she grunted and kicked and her belt thrashed about like a snake cut in half, her knife flopping off the end of it and clattering against the wall, until she got one boot off and one trouser-leg and that seemed good enough for the purpose.

They'd made it to the bed somehow and were tangled up with each other more naked than not, warm and pleasantly wriggling, his hand between her legs and her shoving her hips against it, both laughing less and grunting more, slow and throaty, bright dots fizzing on the inside of her closed lids so she had to open her eyes so she didn't feel like she'd fall right off the bed and out the ceiling. Eyes open was worse, the room turning around her loud with her breath and her thudding heartbeat and the warm rubbing of skin on skin and the springs in the old mattress shrieking with complaint but no one giving too much of a shit for their objections.

Something about her brother and sister niggled at her, and Gully swinging, and Lamb and a fight, but she let it all drift past like smoke and spin away with the spinning ceiling.

How long since she had some fun, after all?

'Oh,' groaned Temple. 'Oh no.'

He moaned a piteous moan as of the cursed dead in hell, facing an eternity of suffering and regretting most bitterly their lives wasted in sin.

'God help me.'

But God had the righteous to assist and Temple could not pretend to be in that category. Not after last night's fun.

Everything hurt him. The blanket across his bare legs. A fly buzzing faintly up near the ceiling. The sun sneaking around the edges of the curtains. The sounds of Crease life and Crease death beyond them. He remembered now why he had stopped drinking. What he could not remember was why it had felt like a good idea to start again.

He winced at the hacking, gurgling noise that had woken him, managed to lift his head a few degrees and saw Shy kneeling over the night pot. She was naked except for one boot and her trousers tangled around that ankle, ribs standing stark as she retched. A strip of light from the window cut over one shoulder-blade bright, bright, and found a big scar, a burn like a letter upside down.

She rocked back, turned eyes sunken in dark rings on him and wiped a string of spit from the corner of her mouth. 'Another kiss?'

The sound he made was indescribable. Part laugh, part belch, part groan. He could not have made it again in a year of trying. But why would he have wanted to?

'Got to get some air.' Shy dragged up her trousers but left the belt dangling and they sagged off her arse as she tottered to the window.

'Don't do it,' moaned Temple, but there was no stopping her. Not without moving, and that was inconceivable. She hauled the curtains away and pushed the window wide, while he struggled feebly to shield his eyes from the merciless light.

Shy was cursing as she fished around under the other bed. He could hardly believe it when she came up with a quarter-full bottle, pulled the cork with her teeth and sat there gathering her courage, like a swimmer staring into an icy pool.

'You're not going to—'

She tipped the bottle up and swallowed, clapped the back of her hand to her mouth, stomach muscles fluttering, and burped, and grimaced, and shivered, and offered it to him.

'You?' she asked, voice wet with rush back.

He wanted to be sick just looking. 'God, no.'

'It's the only thing'll help.'

'Is the cure for a stab-wound really another one?'

'Once you set to stabbing yourself it can be hard to stop.'

She shrugged her shirt over that scar, and after doing a couple of buttons realised she had them in the wrong holes and the whole front twisted, gave up and slumped down on the other bed. Temple wasn't sure he'd ever seen anyone look so worn out and defeated, not even in the mirror.

He wondered whether he should put his clothes on. Some of the muddy rags scattered across the boards bore a faint resemblance to part of his new suit, but he could not be sure. Could not be sure of anything. He forced himself to sit, dragging his legs off the bed as if they were made of lead. When he was sure his stomach would not immediately rebel, he looked at Shy and said, 'You'll find them, you know.'

'How do I know?'

'Because no one deserves a good turn of the card more.'

'You don't know what I deserve.' She slumped back on her elbows, head sinking into her bony shoulders. 'You don't know what I've done.'

'Can't be worse than what you did to me last night.'

She didn't laugh. She was looking past him, eyes focused far away. 'When I was seventeen I killed a boy.'

Temple swallowed. 'Well, yes, that is worse.'

'I ran off from the farm. Hated it there. Hated my bitch mother. Hated my bastard stepfather.'

'Lamb?'

'No, the first one. My mother got through 'em. I had some fool notion I'd open a store. Things went wrong right off. Didn't mean to kill that boy, but I got scared and I cut him.' She rubbed absently under her jaw with a fingertip. 'He wouldn't stop bleeding.'

'Did he have it coming?'

'Guess he must've. Got it, didn't he? But he had a family, and they chased me, and I ran, and I got hungry so I started stealing.' She droned it all out in a dead monotone. 'After a while I got to thinking no one gives you a fair chance and taking things is easier than making 'em. I fell in with some low company and dragged 'em lower. More robbing, and more killings, and maybe some had it coming, and maybe some didn't. Who gets what they deserve?'

Temple thought of Kahdia. 'I'll admit God can be a bit of a shit that way.'

'In the end there were bills up over half the Near Country for my arrest. Smoke, they called me, like I was something to be scared of, and put a price on my head. About the only time in my life I was thought worth something.' She curled her lips back from her teeth. 'They caught some woman and hanged her in my place. Didn't even look like me, but she got killed and I got away with it and I don't know why.'

There was a heavy silence, then. She raised the bottle and took a couple of good, long swallows, neck working with the effort, and she came up gasping for air with eyes watering hard. That was an excellent moment for Temple to mumble his excuses and run. A few months ago, the door would have been swinging already. His debts were settled, after all, which was better than he usually managed on his way out. But he found this time he did not want to leave.

'If you want me to share your low opinion of yourself,' he said, 'I'm afraid I can't oblige. Sounds to me like you made some mistakes.'

'You'd call all that mistakes?'

'Some pretty stupid ones, but yes. You never chose to do evil.'

'Who chooses evil?'

'I did. Pass me that bottle.'

'What's this?' she asked as she tossed it across. 'A shitty-past competition?

'Yes, and I win.' He closed his eyes and forced down a swallow, burning and choking all the way. 'After my wife died, I spent a year as the most miserable drunk you ever saw.'

'I've seen some pretty fucking miserable ones.'

'Then picture worse. I thought I couldn't get any lower, so I signed up as lawyer for a mercenary company, and found I could.' He raised the bottle in salute. 'The Company of the Gracious Hand, under Captain General Nicomo Cosca! Oh, noble brotherhood!' He drank again. It felt good in a hideous way, like picking at a scab.

'Sounds fancy.'

'That's what I thought.'

'Wasn't fancy?'

'A worse accumulation of human scum you never saw.'

'I've seen some pretty fucking bad ones.'

'Then picture worse. To begin with I believed there were good reasons for what they did. What *we* did. Then I convinced myself there were good reasons. Then I knew there weren't even good excuses, but did it anyway because I was too coward not too. We were sent to the Near Country to root out rebels. A friend of mine tried to save some people. He was killed. And them. They killed each other. But I squirmed away, as always, and I ran like the coward I am, and I fell in a river and, for reasons best known only to Himself, God sent a good woman to fish my worthless carcass out.'

'As a point of fact, God sent a murdering outlaw.'

'Well, His ways are damned mysterious. I can't say I took to you right away, that's true, but I'm starting to think God sent exactly what I needed.' Temple stood. It wasn't easy, but he managed it. 'I feel like all my life I've been running. Maybe it's time for me to stick. To try it, at least.' He sank down beside her, the creaking of the bedsprings going right through him. 'I don't care what you've done. I owe you. Only my life, now, but still. Let me stick.' He tossed the empty bottle aside, took a deep breath, licked his finger and thumb-tip and smoothed down his beard. 'God help me, but I'll take that kiss now.'

She squinted at him, every colour in her face wrong – skin a little yellow, eyes a little pink, lips a little blue. 'You serious?'

'I may be a fool, but I'm not letting a woman who can fill a sick pot without spilling pass me by. Wipe your mouth and come here.'

He shifted towards her, someone clattering in the corridor outside, and her mouth twitched up in a smile. She leaned towards him, hair tickling his shoulder, and her breath smelled foul and he did not care. The doorknob turned and rattled, and Shy bellowed at the door, so close and broken-voiced it felt like a hatchet blow in Temple's forehead, 'You got the wrong fucking room, idiot!'

Against all expectation, the door lurched open anyway and a man stepped in. A tall man with close-cropped fair hair and sharp clothes. He had a sharp expression too as his eyes wandered unhurried about the place, as if this was his room and he was both annoyed and amused to find someone else had been fucking in it.

'I think I got it right,' he said, and two other men appeared in the doorway, and neither looked like men you'd be happy to see anywhere, let alone uninvited in your hotel room. 'I heard you been looking for me.'

'Who the fuck are you?' growled Shy, eyes flickering to the corner where her knife was lying sheathed on the floor.

The newcomer smiled like a conjurer about to pull off the trick you won't believe. 'Grega Cantliss.'

Then a few things happened at once. Shy flung the bottle at the doorway and dived for her knife. Cantliss dived for her, the other two tangled in the doorway behind him.

And Temple dived for the window.

Statements about sticking notwithstanding, before he knew it he was outside, air whooping in his throat in a terrified squeal as he dropped, then rolling in the cold mud, then floundering up and sprinting naked across the main street, which in most towns would have been considered poor form but in Crease was not especially remarkable. He heard someone bellow and forced himself on, slipping and sliding and his heart pounding so hard he thought he might have to hold his skull together, the Mayor's Church of Dice lurching closer.

When the guards at the door saw him they smiled, then they frowned, then they caught hold of him as he scrambled up the steps.

'The Mayor's got a rule about trousers—'

'Got to see Lamb. Lamb!'

One of them punched him in the mouth, snapped his head back and sent him stumbling against the door-frame. He knew he deserved it more than ever, but somehow a fist in the face always came as a surprise.

'Lamb!' he screeched again, covering his head as best he could. 'La—ooof.' The other's fist sank into his gut and doubled him up, drove his wind right out and dropped him to his knees, blowing bloody bubbles. While he was considering the stones under his face in breathless silence, one of the guards grabbed him by the hair and started dragging him up, raising his fist high.

'Leave him be.' To Temple's great relief, Savian caught that fist before it came down with one knobbly hand. 'He's with me.' He grabbed Temple under the armpit with the other and dragged him through the doorway, shrugging off his coat and throwing it around Temple's shoulders. 'What the hell happened?'

'Cantliss,' croaked Temple, limping into the gaming hall, waving a weak arm towards the hostelry, only able to get enough breath for one wheezing word at a time. 'Shy—'

'What happened?' Lamb was thumping down the steps from the Mayor's room, barefooted himself and with his shirt half-buttoned, and for a moment Temple was wondering why he came that way, and then he saw the drawn sword in Lamb's fist and felt very scared, and then he saw something in Lamb's face that made him feel more scared still.

'Cantliss . . . at Camling's . . .' he managed to splutter.

Lamb stood a moment, eyes wide, then he strode for the door, brushing the guards out of his way, and Savian strode after.

'Everything all right?' The Mayor stood on the balcony outside her rooms in a Gurkish dressing gown, a pale scar showing in the hollow between her collar bones. Temple blinked up, wondering if Lamb had been in there with her, then pulled his borrowed coat around him and hurried after the others without speaking. 'Put some trousers on!' she called after him.

When Temple struggled up the steps of the hostelry, Lamb had Camling by the collar and had dragged him most of the way over his own counter with one hand, sword in the other and the proprietor desperately squealing, 'They just dragged her out! The Whitehouse, maybe, I have no notion, it was none of my doing!'

Lamb shoved Camling tottering away and stood, breath growling in his throat. Then he put the sword carefully on the counter and his palms flat before it, fingers spreading out, the wood gleaming in the space where the middle one should have been. Savian walked around behind the counter, shouldering Camling out of the way, took a glass and bottle from a high shelf, blew out one then pulled the cork from the other.

'You need a hand, you got mine,' he grunted as he poured.

Lamb nodded. 'You should know lending me a hand can be bad for your health.'

Savian coughed as he nudged the glass across. 'My health's a mess.'

'What are you going to do?' asked Temple.

'Have a drink.' And Lamb picked up the glass and drained it, white stubble on his throat shifting. Savian tipped the bottle to fill it again.

'Lamb!' Lord Ingelstad walked in somewhat unsteadily, his face pale and his waistcoat covered in stains. 'He said you'd be here!'

'Who said?'

Ingelstad gave a helpless chuckle as he tossed his hat on the counter, a few wisps of stray hair left standing vertically from his head. 'Strangest thing. After that fun at Majud's place, I was playing cards over at Papa Ring's. Entirely lost track of time and I was somewhat behind financially, I'll admit, and a gentleman came in to tell Papa something, and he told me he'd forget my debt if I brought you a message.'

'What message?' Lamb drank again, and Savian filled his glass again.

Ingelstad squinted at the wall. 'He said he's playing host to a friend of yours . . . and he'd very much like to be a gracious host . . . but you'll have to kiss the mud tomorrow night. He said you'll be dropping anyway, so you might as well drop willingly and you can both walk out of Crease free people. He said you have his word on that. He was very particular about it. You have his word, apparently.'

'Well, ain't I the lucky one,' said Lamb.

Lord Ingelstad squinted over at Temple as though only just noticing his unusual attire. 'It appears some people have had an even heavier night than I.'

'Can you take a message back?' asked Lamb.

'I daresay a few more minutes won't make any difference to Lady Ingelstad's temper at this point. I am *doomed* whatever.'

'Then tell Papa Ring I'll keep his word safe and sound. And I hope he'll do the same for his guest.'

The nobleman yawned as he jammed his hat back on. 'Riddles, riddles. Then off to bed for me!' And he strutted back out into the street.

'What are you going to do?' whispered Temple.

'There was a time I'd have gone charging over there without a thought for the costs and got bloody.' Lamb lifted the glass and looked at it for a moment. 'But my father always said patience is the king of virtues. A man has to be realistic. Has to be.'

'So what are you going to do?'

'Wait. Think. Prepare.' Lamb swallowed the last measure and bared his teeth at the glass. 'Then get bloody.'

High Stakes

'A trim?' asked Faukin, directing his blank, bland, professional smile towards the mirror. 'Or something more radical?'

'Shave it all off, hair and beard, close to the skull as you can get.'

Faukin nodded as though that would have been his choice. The client always knows best, after all. 'A wet shave of the pate, then.'

'Wouldn't want to give the other bastard anything to hold on to. And I reckon it's a little late to damage my looks, don't you?'

Faukin gave his blank, bland, professional chuckle and began, comb struggling with the tangles in Lamb's thick hair, the snipping of the scissors cutting the silence up into neat little fragments. Outside the window the noise of the swelling crowd grew louder, more excited, and the tension in the room swelled with it. The grey cuttings spilled down the sheet, scattered across the boards in those tantalising patterns that looked to hold some meaning one could never quite grasp.

Lamb stirred at them with his foot. 'Where does it all go, eh?'

'Our time or the hair?'

'Either one.'

'In the case of the time, I would ask a philosopher rather than a barber. In the case of the hair, it is swept up and thrown out. Unless on occasion one might have a lady friend who would care to be entrusted with a lock . . .'

Lamb glanced over at the Mayor. She stood at the window, keeping one eye on Lamb's preparations and the other on those in the street, a slender silhouette against the sunset. He dismissed the notion with an explosive snort. 'One moment it's a part of you, the next it's rubbish.'

'We treat whole men like rubbish, why not their hair?'

Lamb sighed. 'I guess you've got the right of it.'

Faukin gave the razor a good slapping on the strap. Clients usually appreciated a flourish, a mirror flash of lamplight on steel, an edge of drama to proceedings.

'Careful,' said the Mayor, evidently in need of no extra drama today. Faukin had to confess to being considerably more scared of her than he was of Lamb. The Northman he knew for a ruthless killer, but suspected him of harbouring principles of a kind. He had no such suspicions about the Mayor. So he gave his blank, bland, professional bow, ceased his sharpening, brushed up a lather and worked it into Lamb's hair and beard, then began to shave with patient, careful, hissing strokes.

'Don't it ever bother you that it always grows back?' asked Lamb. 'There's no beating it, is there?'

'Could not the same be said of every profession? The merchant sells one thing to buy another. The farmer harvests one set of crops to plant another. The blacksmith—'

'Kill a man and he stays dead,' said Lamb, simply.

'But . . . if I might observe without causing offence . . . killers rarely stop at one. Once you begin, there is always someone else that needs killing.'

Lamb's eyes moved to Faukin's in the mirror. 'You're a philosopher after all.'

'On a strictly amateur footing.' Faukin worked the warm towel with a flourish and presented Lamb shorn, as it were, a truly daunting array of scars laid bare. In all his years as a barber, including three in the service of a mercenary company, he had never attended upon a head so battered, dented and otherwise manhandled.

'Huh.' Lamb leaned closer to the mirror, working his lopsided jaw and wrinkling his bent nose as though to convince himself it was indeed his own visage gazing back. 'There's the face of an evil bastard, eh?'

'I would venture to say a face is no more evil than a coat. It is the man beneath, and his actions, that count.'

'No doubt.' Lamb looked up at Faukin for a moment, and then back to himself. 'And there's the face of an evil bastard. You done the best a man could with it, though. Ain't your fault what you're given to work with.'

'I simply try to do the job exactly as I'd want it done to me.'

'Treat folk the way you'd want to be treated and you can't go far wrong, my father used to tell me. Seems our jobs are different after all. Aim o' mine is to do to the other man exactly what I'd least enjoy.'

'Are you ready?' The Mayor had silently drifted closer and was looking at the pair of them in the mirror.

Lamb shrugged. 'Either a man's always ready for a thing like this or he'll never be.'

'Good enough.' She came closer and took hold of Faukin's hand. He felt a strong need to back away, but clung to his blank, bland professionalism a moment longer. 'Any other jobs today?'

Faukin swallowed. 'Just the one.'

'Across the street?'

He nodded.

The Mayor pressed a coin into his palm and leaned close. 'The time is fast approaching when every person in Crease will have to choose one side of the street. I hope you choose wisely.'

Sunset had lent the town a carnival atmosphere. There was a single current to the crowds of drunk and greedy and it flowed to the amphitheatre. As he passed, Faukin could see the Circle marked out on the ancient cobbles at its centre, six strides across, torches on close-set poles to mark the edge and light the action. The ancient banks of stone seating and the new teetering stands of bodged-together carpentry were already boiling with an audience such as that place had not seen in centuries. Gamblers screeched for business and chalked odds on high boards. Hawkers sold bottles and hot gristle for prices outrageous even in this home of outrageous prices.

Faukin gazed at all those people swarming over each other, most of whom could hardly have known what a barber was let alone thought of employing one, reflected for the hundredth time that day, the thousandth time that week, the millionth time since he arrived that he should never have come here, clung tight to his bag and hurried on.

Papa Ring was one of those men who liked to spend money less the more of it he had. His quarters were humble indeed by comparison with the Mayor's, the furniture an improvised and splinter-filled collection, the low ceiling lumpy as an old bedspread. Glama Golden sat before a cracked mirror lit by smoking candles, something faintly absurd in that huge body crammed onto a stool and draped in a threadbare sheet, his head giving the impression of teetering on top like a cherry on a cream cake.

Ring stood at the window just as the Mayor had, his big fists clamped behind his back, and said, 'Shave it all off.'

'Except the moustache.' Golden gathered up the sheet so he could

263

stroke at his top lip with huge thumb and forefinger. 'Had that all my life and it's going nowhere.'

'A most resplendent article of facial hair,' said Faukin, though in truth he could see more than a few grey hairs despite the poor light. 'To remove it would be a deep regret.'

In spite of being the undoubted favourite in the coming contest, Golden's eyes had a strange, haunted dampness as they found Faukin's in the mirror. 'You got regrets?'

Faukin lost his blank, bland, professional smile for a moment. 'Don't we all, sir?' He began to cut. 'But I suppose regrets at least prevent one from repeating the same mistakes.'

Golden frowned at himself in that cracked mirror. 'I find however high I stack the regrets, I still make the same mistakes again and again.'

Faukin had no answer for that, but the barber holds the advantage in such circumstances: he can let the scissors fill the silence. Snip, snip, and the yellow cuttings scattered across the boards in those tantalising patterns that looked to hold some meaning one could never quite grasp.

'Been over there with the Mayor?' called Papa Ring from the window.

'Yes, sir, I have.'

'How'd she seem?'

Faukin thought about the Mayor's demeanour and, more importantly, about what Papa Ring wanted to hear. A good barber never puts truth before the hopes of his clients. 'She seemed very tense.'

Ring stared back out of the window, thick thumb and fingers fussing nervously behind his back. 'I guess she would be.'

'What about the other man?' asked Golden. 'The one I'm fighting?'

Faukin stopped snipping for a moment. 'He seemed thoughtful. Regretful. But fixed on his purpose. In all honesty . . . he seemed very much like you.' Faukin did not mention what had only just occurred.

That he had, in all likelihood, given one of them their last haircut.

Bee was mopping up when he passed by the door. She hardly even had to see him, she knew him by his footsteps. 'Grega?' She dashed out into the hall, heart going so hard it hurt. 'Grega!'

He turned, wincing, like hearing her say his name made him sick. He looked tired, more'n a little drunk, and sore. She could always tell his moods. 'What?'

She'd made up all kinds of little stories about their reunion. One where he swept her into his arms and told her they could get married now. One where he was wounded and she'd to nurse him back to health. One where they argued, one where they laughed, one where he cried and said sorry for how he'd treated her.

But she hadn't spun no stories where she was just ignored.

'That all you got to say to me?'

'What else would there be?' He didn't even look her in the eye. 'I got to go talk to Papa Ring.' And he made off up the hall.

She caught his arm. 'Where are the children?' Her voice all shrill and bled out from her own disappointment.

'Mind your own business.'

'I am. You made me help, didn't you? You made me bring 'em!'

'You could've said no.' She knew it was true. She'd been so keen to please him she'd have jumped in a fire on his say-so. Then he gave a little smile, like he'd thought of something funny. 'But if you must know, I sold 'em.'

She felt cold to her stomach. 'To who?'

'Those Ghosts up in the hills. Those Dragon fuckers.'

Her throat was all closed up, she could hardly talk. 'What'll they do with 'em?'

'I don't know. Fuck 'em? Eat 'em? What do I care? What did you think I was going to do, start up an orphanage?' Her face was burning now, like he'd slapped her. 'You're such a stupid sow. Don't know that I ever met anyone stupider than you. You're stupider than—'

And she was on him and tearing at his face with her nails and she'd probably have bitten him if he hadn't hit her first, just above the eye, and she tumbled into the corner and caught a faceful of floor.

'You mad bitch!' She started to push herself up, all groggy, that familiar pulsing in her face, and he was touching his scratched cheek like he couldn't believe it. 'What did you do that for?' Then he was shaking out his fingers. 'You hurt my fucking hand!' And he took a step towards her as she tried to stand and kicked her in the ribs, folded her gasping around his boot.

'I hate you,' she managed to whisper, once she was done coughing.

'So?' And he looked at her like she was a maggot.

She remembered the day he'd chosen her out of all the room to dance with and nothing had ever felt so fine, and of a sudden it was like she saw the whole thing fresh, and he seemed so ugly, so petty and vain and selfish beyond enduring. He just used people and threw them away and left a trail of ruin behind him. How could she ever have loved him? Just because for a few moments he'd made her feel one step above shit. The rest of the time ten steps below.

'You're so small,' she whispered at him. 'How did I not see it?'

He was pricked in his vanity then and he took another step at her, but she found her knife and whipped it out. He saw the blade, and for a moment he looked surprised, then he looked angry, then he started laughing like she was a hell of a joke.

'As if you've got the bones to use it!' And he sauntered past, giving her plenty of time to stab him if she'd wanted to. But she just knelt there, blood leaking out her nose and tapping down the front of her dress. Her best dress, which she'd worn three days straight 'cause she knew he'd be coming.

Once the dizziness had passed she got up and went to the kitchen. Everything was trembling but she'd taken worse beatings and worse disappointments, too. No one there so much as raised a brow at her bloody nose. The Whitehouse was that kind of place.

'Papa Ring said I need to feed that woman.'

'Soup in the pot,' grunted the cook's boy, perched on a box to look out of a high little window where all he got was a view of boots outside.

So she put a bowl on a tray with a cup of water and carried it down the damp-smelling stair to the cellar, past the big barrels in the darkness and the bottles on the racks gleaming with the torchlight.

The woman in the cage uncrossed her legs and stood, sliding her tight-bound hands up the rail behind her, one eye glinting through the hair tangled across her face as she watched Bee come closer. Warp sat in front at his table, ring of keys on it, pretending to read a book. He loved to pretend, thought it made him look right special, but even Bee, who weren't no wonder with her letters, could tell he had it upside down.

'What d'you want?' And he turned a sneer on her like she was a slug in his breakfast.

'Papa Ring said to feed her.'

She could almost see his brain rattling around in his big fat head. 'Why? Ain't like she'll be here much longer.'

'You think he tells me why?' she snapped. 'But I'll go back and tell Papa you wouldn't let me in if you—'

'All right, get it done, then. But I've got my eye on you.' He leaned close and blasted her with his rotting breath. 'Both eyes.'

He unlocked the gate and swung it squealing open and Bee ducked inside with her tray. The woman watched her. She couldn't move far from the rail, but even so she was backed up tight against it. The cage smelled of sweat and piss and fear, the woman's and all the others' who'd been kept in here before and no bright futures among 'em, that was a fact. No bright futures anywhere in this place.

Bee set the tray down and took the cup of water. The woman sucked at it thirstily, no pride left in her if she'd had any to begin with. Pride don't last long in the Whitehouse, and especially not down here. Bee leaned close and whispered.

'You asked me about Cantliss before. About Cantliss and the children.'

The woman stopped swallowing and her eyes flickered over to Bee's, bright and wild.

'He sold the children to the Dragon People. That's what he said.' Bee looked over her shoulder but Warp was already sitting back at his table and pulling at his jug, not looking in the least. He wouldn't think Bee would do anything worth attending to in her whole life. Right now that worked for her. She stepped closer, slipped out the knife and sawed through the ropes around one of the woman's rubbed-raw wrists.

'Why?' she whispered.

'Because Cantliss needs hurting.' Even then she couldn't bring herself to say killing, but they both knew what she meant. 'I can't do it.' Bee pressed the knife, handle first, into the woman's free hand where it was hidden behind her back. 'Reckon you can, though.'

Papa Ring fidgeted at the ring through his ear, an old habit went right back to his days as a bandit in the Badlands, his nerves rising with the rising noise in a painful lump under his jaw. He'd played a lot of hands, rolled a lot of dice, spun a lot of wheels, and maybe the odds were all stacked on his side, but the stakes had never been higher. He wondered whether she was nervous, the Mayor. No sign of it, standing alone on her balcony bolt upright with the light behind her, that stiff pride of hers showing even at this distance. But she had to be scared. Had to be.

How often had they stood here, after all, glaring across the great divide, planning each other's downfall by every means fair or foul, the number of men they paid to fight for them doubling and doubling again, the stakes swelling ever higher. A hundred murders and stratagems and manoeuvrings and webs of petty alliances broken and re-formed, and it all came down to this.

He slipped into one of his favourite furrows of thought, what to do with the Mayor when he won. Hang her as a warning? Have her stripped naked and beaten through town like a hog? Keep her as his whore? As anyone's? But he knew it was all fancy. He'd given his word she'd be let go and he'd keep it. Maybe folk on the Mayor's side of the street took him for a low bastard and maybe they were right, but all his life he'd kept his word.

It could give you some tough moments, your word. Could force you into places you didn't want to be, could serve you up puzzles where the right path weren't easy to pick. But it wasn't meant to be easy, it was meant to be right. There were too many men always did the easy thing, regardless.

Grega Cantliss, for instance.

Papa Ring looked sourly sideways. Here he was, three days late as always, slumped on Ring's balcony as if he had no bones in him and picking his teeth with a splinter. In spite of a new suit he looked sick and old and had fresh scratches on his face and a stale smell about him. Some men use up fast. But he'd brought what he owed plus a healthy extra for the favour. That was why he was still breathing. Ring had given his word, after all.

The fighters were coming out now with an accompanying rise in the mood of the mob. Golden's big shaved head bobbed above the crowd, a knot of Ring's men around him clearing folks away as they headed for the theatre, old stones lit up orange in the fading light. Ring hadn't mentioned the woman to Golden. He might be a magician with his fists but that man had a bad habit of getting distracted. So Ring had just told him to let the old man live if he got the chance, and considered that a promise kept. A man's got to keep his word but there has to be some give in it or you'll get nothing done.

He saw Lamb now, coming down the steps of the Mayor's place between the ancient columns, his own entourage of thugs about him. Ring fussed with his ear again. He'd a worry the old Northman was one of those bastards you couldn't trust to do the sensible thing. A right wild card, and Papa Ring liked to know what was in the deck. Specially when the stakes were high as this.

'I don't like the looks of that old bastard,' Cantliss said.

Papa Ring frowned at him. 'Do you know what? Neither do I.'

'You sure Golden'll take him?'

'Golden's taken everyone else, hasn't he?'

'I guess. Got a sad sort o' look to him though, for a winner.'

Ring could've done without this fool picking at his worries. 'That's why I had you steal the woman, isn't it? Just in case.'

Cantliss rubbed at his stubbly jaw. 'Still seems a hell of a risk.'

'One I wouldn't have had to take if you hadn't stole that old bastard's children and sold 'em to the savage.'

Cantliss' head jerked around with surprise.

'I can add two and two,' growled Ring, and felt a shiver like he was dirty and couldn't clean it off. 'How much lower can a man stoop? Selling children?'

Cantliss looked deeply wounded. 'That's so *fucking* unfair! You just said get the money by winter or I'd be a dead man. You didn't concern yourself with the source. You want to give me the money back, free yourself of its base origins?'

Ring looked at the old box on the table, and thought about that bright old gold inside, and frowned back out into the street. He hadn't got where he'd got by giving money back.

'Didn't think so.' Cantliss shook his head like stealing children was a fine business scheme for which he deserved the warmest congratulation. 'How was I to know this old bastard would wriggle out the long grass?'

'Because,' said Ring, speaking very slow and cold, 'you should have learned by now there's consequences when you *fucking* do a thing, and a man can't wonder through life thinking no further ahead than the end of his cock!'

Cantliss worked his jaw and muttered, 'So fucking unfair,' and Ring was forced to wonder when was the last time he'd punched a man in the face. He was sorely, sorely tempted. But he knew it would solve nothing. That's why he'd stopped doing it and started paying other people to do it for him.

'Are you a child yourself, to whine about what's fair?' he asked. 'You think it's fair I have to stand up for a man can't tell a good hand of cards from a bad but still has to bet an almighty pile of money he don't have on the outcome? You think it's fair I have to threaten some girl's life to make sure of a fight? How does that reflect on me, eh? How's that for the start of my new era? You think it's fair I got to keep my word to men don't care a damn about theirs? Eh? What's God-fucked fair about all that? Go and get the woman.'

'Me?'

'Your bloody mess I'm aiming to clean up, isn't it? Bring her up here so our friend Lamb can see Papa Ring's a man of his word.'

'I might miss the start,' said Cantliss, like he couldn't believe he'd be inconvenienced to such an extent by a pair of very likely deaths.

'You keep talking you'll be missing the rest of your fucking life, boy. Get the woman.'

Cantliss stomped for the door and Ring thought he heard him mutter, 'Ain't fair.'

He gritted his teeth as he turned back towards the theatre. That bastard made trouble everywhere he went and had a bad end coming, and Ring was starting to hope it'd come sooner rather than later. He straightened his cuffs, and consoled himself with the thought that once the Mayor was beaten the bottom would fall right out of the henchman market and he could afford to hire himself a better class of thug. The crowd was falling silent now, and Ring reached for his ear then stopped himself, stifling another swell of nerves. He'd made sure the odds were all stacked on his side, but the stakes had never been higher.

'Welcome all!' bellowed Camling, greatly relishing the way his voice echoed to the very heavens, 'To this, the historic theatre of Crease! In the many centuries since its construction it can rarely have seen so momentous an event as that which will shortly be played out before your fortunate eyes!'

Could eyes be fortunate independently of their owners? This question gave Camling an instant's pause before he dismissed it. He could not allow himself to be distracted. This was his moment, the torchlit bowl crammed with onlookers, the street beyond heaving with those on tiptoe for a look, the trees on the valley side above even carrying cargoes of intrepid observers in their upper branches, all hanging upon his every word. Noted hotelier he might have been, but he was without doubt a sad loss to the performing arts.

'A fight, my friends and neighbours, and what a fight! A contest of strength and guile between two worthy champions, to be humbly refereed by myself, Lennart Camling, as a respected neutral party and long-established leading citizen of this community!'

He thought he heard someone call, 'Cockling!' but ignored it.

'A contest to settle a dispute between two parties over a claim, according to mining law—'

'Get the fuck on with it!' someone shouted.

There was a scattering of laughs, boos and jeers. Camling gave a long pause, chin raised, and treated the savages to a lesson in cultured gravity. The type of lesson he had been hoping Iosiv Lestek might administer, what a farce *that* had turned out to be. 'Standing for Papa Ring, a man who needs no introduction—'

'Why give him one, then?' More laughter.

'—who has forged a dread name for himself across the fighting pits, cages and Circles of the Near and Far Countries ever since he left his native North. A man undefeated in twenty-two encounters. Glama . . . Golden!'

Golden shouldered his way into the Circle, stripped to the waist, his huge body smeared with grease to frustrate an opponent's grasp, great slabs of muscle glistening white by torchlight and reminding Camling of the giant albino slugs he sometimes saw in his cellar and was irrationally afraid of. With his skull shaved, the Northman's luxuriant moustache looked even more of an absurd affectation, but the volume of the crowd's bellows only increased. A breathless frenzy had descended upon them and they no doubt would have cheered an albino slug if they thought it might bleed for their entertainment.

'And, standing for the Mayor, his opponent . . . Lamb.' Much less enthusiastic cheering as the second fighter stepped into the Circle to a last frantic round of betting. He was likewise shaved and greased, his body so covered with a multitude of scars that, even if he had no fame as a fighter, his familiarity with violence was not to be doubted.

Camling leaned close to whisper, 'Just that for a name?'

'Good as another,' said the old Northman, without removing his steady gaze from his opponent. No doubt everyone considered him the underdog. Certainly Camling had almost discounted him until that very moment: the older, smaller, leaner man, the gambler's odds considerably against him, but Camling noticed something in his eye that gave him pause. An eager look, as though he had an awful hunger and Golden was the meal.

The bigger man's face, by contrast, held a trace of doubt as Camling ushered the two together in the centre of the Circle. 'Do I know you?' he called over the baying of the audience. 'What's your real name?'

Lamb stretched his neck out to one side and then the other. 'Maybe it'll come to you.'

Camling held one hand high. 'May the best man win!' he shrieked.

Over the sudden roar he heard Lamb say, 'It's the worst man wins these.'

*

This would be Golden's last fight. That much he knew.

They circled each other, footwork, footwork, step and shuffle, each feeling out the other, the wild noise of the crowd and their shaken fists and twisted faces pushed off to one side. No doubt they were eager for the fight to start. They didn't realise that oftentimes the fight was won and lost here, in the slow moments before the fighters even touched.

By the dead, though, Golden was tired. Failures and regrets dragging after him like chains on a swimmer, heavier with each day, with each breath. This had to be his last fight. He'd heard the Far Country was a place where men could find their dreams, and come searching for a way to claim back all he'd lost, but this was all he'd found. Glama Golden, mighty War Chief, hero of Ollensand, who'd stood tall in the songs and on the battlefield, admired and feared in equal measure, rolling in the mud for the amusement of morons.

A tilt of the waist and a dip of the shoulder, a couple of lazy ranging swings, getting the other man's measure. He moved well, this Lamb, whatever his age. He was no stranger to this business – there was a snap and steadiness to his movements and he wasted no effort. Golden wondered what his failures had been, what his regrets. What dream had he come chasing after into this Circle?

'Leave him alive if you can,' Ring had said, which only showed how little he understood in spite of his endless bragging about his word. There were no choices in a fight like this, life and death on the Leveller's scales. There was no place for mercy, no place for doubts. He could see in Lamb's eyes that he knew it, too. Once two men step into the Circle, nothing beyond its edge can matter, past or future. Things fall the way they fall.

Golden had seen enough.

He squeezed his teeth together and rushed across the Circle. The old man dodged well but Golden still caught him by the ear and followed with a heavy left in the ribs, felt the thud right up his arm, warming every joint. Lamb struck back but Golden brushed it off and as quickly as they'd come together they were apart, circling again, watching, a gust swirling around the theatre and dragging out the torch flames.

He could take a punch, this old man, still moving calm and steady, showing no pain. Golden might have to break him down piece by piece, use his reach, but that was well enough. He was warming to the task. His breath came faster and he growled along with it, his face finding a fighting snarl, sucking in strength and pushing out doubt, all his shame and disappointment made tinder for his anger.

Golden slapped his palms together hard, feinted right then hissed as he darted in, faster and sharper than before, catching the old man with two more long punches, bloodying his bent nose, staggering him and dancing away before he could think of throwing back, the stone bowl ringing with encouragements and insults and fresh odds in a dozen languages.

Golden settled to the work. He had the reach and the weight and the youth but he took nothing for granted. He would be cautious. He would make sure.

This would be his last fight, after all.

'I'm coming, you bastard, I'm coming!' shouted Pane, hobbling down the hall on his iffy leg.

Bottom of the pile, that's what he was. But he guessed every pile needs someone on the bottom, and probably he didn't deserve to be no higher. The door was jolting in its frame from the blows outside. They should've had a slot to look through. He'd said that before but no one took no notice. Probably they couldn't hear him through that heap of folks on top. So he had to wrestle the bolt back and haul the door open a bit to see who was calling.

There was an old drunk outside. Tall and bony with grey hair plastered to one side of his head and big hands flapping and a tattered coat with what looked like old vomit down one side and fresh down the other. 'I wanna get fucked,' he said in a voice like rotten wood splitting.

'Don't let me stop you.' And Pane swung the door shut.

The old man wedged a boot in it and the door bounced back open. 'I wanna get fucked, I says!'

'We're closed.'

'You're what?' The old man craned close, most likely deaf as well as drunk.

Pane heaved the door open wider so he could shout it. 'There's a fight on, case you didn't notice. We're closed!'

'I did notice and I don't care a shit. I want fucking and I want it now. I got dust and I heard tell the Whitehouse is never closed to business. Not never.'

'Shit,' hissed Pane. That was true. 'Never closed,' Papa Ring was always telling 'em. But then they'd been told to be careful, and triple careful today. 'Be triple careful today,' Papa had told them all. 'I can't stand a man ain't careful.' Which had sounded strange, since no one round here was ever the least bit careful.

'I want a fuck,' grunted the old man, hardly able to stand up straight, he was that drunk. Pane pitied the girl got that job, he stank like all the shit in Crease. Usually there'd be three guards at the door but the others had all snuck off to watch the fight and left him on his own, bottom of the bloody heap that he was.

He gave a strangled groan of upset, turned to shriek for someone just a little higher up the heap, and to his great and far from pleasant surprise an arm slipped tight around his neck and a cold point pressed into his throat and he heard the door swing shut behind.

'Where's the woman you took?' The old man's breath stank like a still but his hands were tight as vices. 'Shy South, skinny thing with a big mouth. Where is she?'

'I don't know nothing about no woman,' Pane managed to splutter, trying to say it loud enough to get someone's attention but half-swallowing his words from the pressure.

'Guess I might as well open you up, then.' And Pane felt the point of the knife dig into his jaw.

'Fuck! All right! She's in the cellar!'

'Lead on.' And the old man started moving him. One step, two, and suddenly it just got to Pane what a damn indignity this was on top of everything else, and without thinking he started twisting and thrashing and elbowing away, struggling like this was his moment to get out from under the bottom of that heap and finally be somebody worthy of at least his own respect.

But the old man was made of iron. That knotty hand clamped Pane's windpipe shut so he couldn't make more'n a gurgle and he felt the knife's point burning across his face, right up under his eye.

'Struggle any more and that eye's coming out,' and there was a terrible coldness in the old man's voice froze all the fight right out. 'You're just the fool who opens the door, so I reckon you don't owe Papa Ring too much. He's finished anyway. Take me to the woman and do nothing stupid, you'll live to be the fool who opens someone else's door. Make sense?'

The hand released enough for him to choke, 'Makes sense.' It did make sense, too. That was about as much fight as Pane had showed in his whole life and where'd it got him? He was just the fool who opened the door.

Bottom of the pile.

Golden had bloodied the old man's face up something fierce. Drizzle was streaking through the light about the torches, cool on his forehead but he was hot inside now, doubts banished. He had Lamb's measure and even the blood in his mouth tasted like victory.

This would be his last fight. Back to the North with Ring's money and win back his lost honour and his lost children, cut his revenge out of Cairm Ironhead and Black Calder, the thought of those hated names and faces bringing up the fury in a sudden blaze.

Golden roared and the crowd roared with him, carried him across the Circle as if on the crest of a wave. The old man pushed away one punch and slipped under another, found a hold on Golden's arm and they slapped and twisted, fingers wriggling for a grip, hands slippery with grease and drizzle, feet shuffling for advantage. Golden strained, and heaved, and finally with a bellow got Lamb off his feet, but the old man hooked his leg as he went down and they crashed together onto the stones, the crowd leaping up in joy as they fell.

Golden was on top. He tried to get a hand around the old man's throat, fumbled with a notch out of his ear, tried to rip at it but it was too slippery, tried to inch his hand up onto Lamb's face so he could get his thumbnail in his eye, the way he had with that big miner back in the spring, and of a sudden his head was dragged down and there was a burning, tugging pain in his mouth. He bellowed and twisted and growled, clawed at Lamb's wrist with his nails and, with a stinging and ripping right through his lip and into his gums he tore himself free and thrashed away.

As Lamb rolled up he saw the old man had yellow hairs caught in one fist and Golden realised he'd torn half his moustache out. There was laughter in the crowd, but all he heard was the laughter years behind him as he trudged from Skarling's Hall and into exile.

The rage came up white-hot and Golden charged in shrieking, no thoughts except the need to smash Lamb apart with his fists. He caught the old man square in the face and sent him staggering right out of the Circle, folk on the front row of stone benches scattering like starlings. Golden came after him, spewing curses, raining blows, fists knocking Lamb left and right like he was made of rags. The old man's hands dropped, face slack, eyes glassy, and Golden knew the moment was come. He stepped in, swinging with all his strength, and landed the father of all punches right on the point of Lamb's jaw.

He watched the old man stumble, fists dangling, waiting for Lamb's knees to buckle so he could spring on top of him and put an end to it.

But Lamb didn't fall. He tottered back a pace or two into the Circle and stood, swaying, blood drooling from his open mouth and his face tipped into shadow. Then Golden caught something over the thunder of the crowd, soft and low but there was no mistaking it.

The old man was laughing.

Golden stood, chest heaving, legs weak, arms heavy from his efforts, and he felt a chill doubt wash over him because he wasn't sure he could hit a man any harder than that.

'Who are you?' he roared, fists aching like he'd been beating a tree.

Lamb gave a smile like an open grave, and stuck out his red tongue, and smeared blood from it across his cheek in long streaks. He held up his left fist and gently uncurled it so he looked at Golden, eyes wide and weeping wet like two black tar-pits, through the gap where his middle finger used to be.

The crowd had fallen eerily quiet, and Golden's doubt turned to a sucking dread because he finally knew the old man's name.

'By the dead,' he whispered, 'it can't be.'

But he knew it was. However fast, however strong, however fearsome you make yourself, there's always someone faster, stronger, more fearsome, and the more you fight the sooner you'll meet him. No one cheats the Great Leveller for ever and now Glama Golden felt the sweat turn cold on him, and the fire inside guttered out and left only ashes.

And he knew this would be his last fight indeed.

'So fucking unfair,' Cantliss muttered to himself.

All that effort spent dragging those mewling brats across the Far Country, all that risk taken bringing 'em to the Dragon People, every bit repaid and interest too and what thanks? Just Papa Ring's endless moaning and another shitty task to get through besides. However hard he worked things never went his way.

'A man just can't get a fair go,' he snapped at nothing, and saying it made his face hurt and he gingerly pressed the scratches and that made his hand hurt and he reflected bitterly on the wrong-headed stupidity of womankind.

'After everything I done for that whore . . .'

That idiot Warp was pretending to read as Cantliss stalked around the corner.

'Get up, idiot!' The woman was still in the cage, still tied and helpless, but she was watching him in a style made him angrier than ever, level and steady like she'd something on her mind other than fear. Like she'd a plan and he was a piece of it. 'What d'you think you're looking at, bitch?' he snapped.

Clear and cold she said, 'A fucking coward.'

He stopped short, blinking, hardly able to believe it at first. Even this skinny thing disrespecting him? Even this, who should have been snivelling for mercy? If you can't get a woman's respect tying her up and beating her, when can you fucking get it? 'What?' he whispered, going cold all over.

She leaned forwards, mocking eyes on him all the way, curled her lips back, pressed her tongue into the gap between her teeth, and with a jerk of her head spat across the cage and through the bars and it spattered against Cantliss' new shirt.

'Coward cunt,' she said.

Taking a telling from Papa Ring was one thing. This was another. 'Get that cage open!' he snarled, near choking on fury.

'Right y'are.' Warp was fumbling with his ring of keys, trying to find the right one. There were only three on there. Cantliss tore it out of his hand, jammed the key in the lock and ripped back the gate, edge clanging against the wall and taking a chunk out of it.

'I'll learn you a fucking lesson!' he screamed, but the woman watched him still, teeth bared and breathing so hard he could see the specks of spit off her lips. He caught a twisted handful of her shirt, half-lifting her, stitches ripping, and he clamped his other hand around her jaw, crushing her mouth between his fingers like he'd crush her face to pulp and—

Agony lanced up his thigh and he gave a whooping shriek. Another jolt and his leg gave so he tottered against the wall.

'What you—' said Warp, and Cantliss heard scuffling and grunting and he twisted around, only just staying on his feet for the pain right up into his groin.

Warp was against the cage, face a picture of stupid surprise, the woman holding him up with one hand and punching him in the gut with the other. With each punch she gave a spitty snort and he gave a cross-eyed gurgle and Cantliss saw she had a knife, strings of blood slopping off it and spattering the floor as she stabbed him. Cantliss realised she'd stabbed him, too, and he gave a whimper of outrage at the hurt and injustice of it, took one hopping step and flung himself at her, caught her around the back and they tumbled through the cage

277

door and crashed together onto the packed-dirt floor outside, the knife bouncing away.

She was slippery as a trout, though, slithered out on top and gave him a couple of hard punches in the mouth, snapping his head against the ground before he knew where he was. She lunged for the knife but he caught her shirt before she got there and dragged her back, ragged thing ripped half-off, the pair of them wriggling across the dirt floor towards the table, grunting and spitting. She punched him again but it only caught the top of his skull and he tangled his hand in her hair and dragged her head sideways. She squealed and thrashed but he had her now and smacked her skull into the leg of the table, and again, and she went limp long enough for him to drag his weight on top of her, groaning as he tried to use his stabbed leg, all wet and warm now from his leaking blood.

He could hear her breath whooping in her throat as they twisted and strained and she kneed at him but his weight was on her and he finally got his forearm across her neck and started pressing on it, shifted his body and reached out, stretching with his fingers, and gathered in the knife, and he chuckled as his hand closed around it because he knew he'd won.

'Now we'll thucking thee,' he hissed, a bit messed-up with his lips split and swollen, and he lifted the blade so she got a good look at it, her face all pinked from lack of air with bloody hair stuck across it, and her bulging eyes followed the point as she strained at his arm, weaker and weaker, and he brought the knife high, did a couple of fake little stabs to taunt her, enjoying the way her face twitched each time. 'Now we'll thee!' He brought it higher still to do the job for real.

And Cantliss' wrist was suddenly twisted right around and he gasped as he was dragged off her, and as he was opening his mouth something smashed into it and sent everything spinning. He shook his head, could hear the woman coughing what sounded like a long way away. He saw the knife on the ground, reached for it.

A big boot came down and smashed his hand into the dirt floor. Another swung past and its toe flicked the blade away. Cantliss groaned and tried to move his hand but couldn't.

'You want me to kill him?' asked an old man, looking down.

'No,' croaked the girl, stooping for the knife. 'I want to kill him.' And she took a step at Cantliss, spitting blood in his face through the gap between her teeth.

'No!' he whimpered, trying to scramble back with his useless leg but still with his useless hand pinned under the old man's boot. 'You need me! You want your children back, right? Right?' He saw her face and knew he had a chink to pick at. 'Ain't easy getting up there! I can show you the ways! You need me! I'll help! I'll put it right! Wasn't my fault, it was Ring. He said he'd kill me! I didn't have no choice! You need me!' And he blathered and wept and begged but felt no shame because when he's got no other choice a sensible man begs like a bastard.

'What a thing is this,' muttered the old-timer, lip curled with contempt.

The girl came back from the cage with the rope she'd been bound with. 'Best keep our options open, though.'

'Take him with us?'

She squatted down and gave Cantliss a red smile. 'We can always kill him later.'

Abram Majud was deeply concerned. Not about the result, for that no longer looked in doubt. About what would come after.

With each exchange Golden grew weaker. His face, as far as could be told through the blood and swelling, was a mask of fear. Lamb's smile, by terrible contrast, split wider with every blow given or received. It had become the demented leer of a drunkard, of a lunatic, of a demon, no trace remaining of the man Majud had laughed with on the plains, an expression so monstrous that observers in the front row scrambled back onto the benches behind whenever Lamb lurched close.

The audience was turning almost as ugly as the show. Majud dreaded to imagine the total value of wagers in the balance, and he had already seen fights break out among the spectators. The sense of collective insanity was starting to remind him strongly of a battle – a place he had very much hoped never to visit again – and in a battle he knew there are always casualties.

Lamb sent Golden reeling with a heavy right hand, caught him before he fell, hooked a finger in his mouth and ripped his cheek wide open, blood spotting the nearest onlookers.

'Oh my,' said Curnsbick, watching the fight through his spread fingers.

'We should go.' But Majud saw no easy way to manage it. Lamb had hold of Golden's arm, was wrapping his own around it, forcing him onto his knees, the pinned hand flopping uselessly. Majud heard Golden's bubbling scream, then the sharp pop as his elbow snapped back the wrong way, skin horribly distended around the joint.

Lamb was on him like a wolf on the kill, giggling as he seized Golden around the throat, arching back and smashing his forehead into his face, and again, and again, the crowd whooping their joy or dismay at the outcome.

Majud heard a wail, saw bodies heaving in the stands, what looked like two men stabbing another. The sky was suddenly lit by a bloom of orange flame, bright enough almost to feel the warmth of. A moment later a thunderous boom shook the arena and terrified onlookers flung themselves down, hands clasped over their heads, screams of bloodlust turned to howls of dismay.

A man staggered into the Circle, clutching at his guts, and fell not far from where Lamb was still intent on smashing Golden's head apart with his hands. Fire leaped and twisted in the drizzle on Papa Ring's side of the street. A fellow not two strides away was hit in the head by a piece of debris as he stood and knocked flying.

'Explosive powder,' muttered Curnsbick, his eyeglasses alive with the reflections of fire.

Majud seized him by the arm and dragged him along the bench. Between the heaving bodies he could see Lamb's hacked-out smile lit by one guttering torch, beating someone's head against one of the pillars with a regular crunch, crunch, the stone smeared black. Majud had a suspicion the victim was Camling. The time for referees was plainly long past.

'Oh my,' muttered Curnsbick. 'Oh my.'

Majud drew his sword. The one General Malzagurt had given him as thanks for saving his life. He hated the damn thing but was glad of it now. Man's ingenuity has still developed no better tool for getting people out of the way than a length of sharpened steel.

Excitement had devolved into panic with the speed of a mudslide. On the other side of the Circle, the new-built stand was starting to rock alarmingly as people boiled down it, trampling each other in their haste to get away. With a tortured creak the whole structure lurched sideways, buckling, spars splintering like matchsticks, twisting, falling, people pitching over the poorly made railings and tumbling through the darkness.

Majud dragged Curnsbick through it all, ignoring the fighting, the injured, a woman propped on her elbows staring at the bone sticking out of her leg. It was every man for himself and perhaps, if they were lucky, those closest to him, no choice but to leave the rest to God.

'Oh my,' burbled Curnsbick.

In the street it was no longer like a battle, it was one. People dashed gibbering through the madness, lit by the spreading flames on Ring's side of the street. Blades glinted, men clashed and fell and rolled, floundered in the stream, the sides impossible to guess. He saw someone toss a burning bottle whirling onto a roof where it shattered, curling lines of fire shooting across the thatch and catching hungrily in spite of the wet.

He glimpsed the Mayor, still staring across the maddened street from her balcony. She pointed at something, spoke to a man beside her, calmly directing. Majud acquired the strong impression that she had never intended to sit back and meekly abide by the result.

Arrows flickered in the darkness. One stuck in the mud near them, burning. Majud's ears rang with words screeched in languages he did not know. There was another thunderous detonation and he cowered as timbers span high, smoke roiling up into the wet sky.

Someone had a woman by the hair, was dragging her kicking through the muck.

'Oh my,' said Curnsbick, over and over.

A hand clutched at Majud's ankle and he struck out with the flat of his sword, tore free and struggled on, not looking back, sticking to the porches of the buildings on the Mayor's side of the street. High above, at the top of the nearest column, three men were silhouetted, two with bows, a third lighting their pitch-soaked arrows so they could calmly shoot them at the houses across the way.

The building with the sign that said *Fuck Palace* was thoroughly ablaze. A woman leaped from the balcony and crumpled in the mud, wailing. Two corpses lay nearby. Four men stood with naked swords, watching. One was smoking a pipe. Majud thought he was a dealer from the Mayor's Church of Dice.

Curnsbick tried to pull his arm free. 'We should—'

'No!' snapped Majud, dragging him on. 'We shouldn't.'

Mercy, along with all the trappings of civilised behaviour, was a luxury they could ill afford. Majud dragged out the key to their shop and thrust it into Curnsbick's trembling hand while he faced the street, sword up.

'Oh my,' the inventor was saying as he struggled with the lock, 'oh my.'

They spilled inside, into the still safety, the darkness of the shop flickering with slashes of orange and yellow and red. Majud shouldered the door shut, gasped with relief as he felt the latch drop, spun about when he felt a hand on his shoulder and nearly took Temple's head off with his flailing sword.

'What the hell's going on?' A strip of light wandered across one half of Temple's stricken face. 'Who won the fight?'

Majud put the point of his sword on the floor and leaned on the pommel, breathing hard. 'Lamb tore Golden apart. Literally.'

'Oh my,' whimpered Curnsbick, sliding down the wall until his arse thumped against the floor.

'What about Shy?' asked Temple.

'I've no idea. I've no idea about anything.' Majud eased the door open a crack to peer out. 'But I suspect the Mayor is cleaning house.'

The flames on Papa Ring's side of the street were lighting the whole town in garish colours. The Whitehouse was ablaze to its top floor, fire shooting into the sky, ravenous, murderous, trees burning on the slopes above, ash and embers fluttering in the rain.

'Shouldn't we help?' whispered Temple.

'A good man of business remains neutral.'

'Surely there's a moment to cease being a good man of business, and try to be merely a good man.'

'Perhaps.' Majud heaved the door shut again. 'But this is not that moment.'

Old Friends

'Well, then!' shouted Papa Ring, and he swallowed, and he blinked into the sun. 'Here we are, I guess!' There was a sheen of sweat across his forehead, but Temple could hardly blame him for that. 'I haven't always done right!' Someone had ripped the ring from his ear and the distorted lobe flopped loose as he turned his head. 'Daresay most of you won't miss me none! But I've always done my best to keep my word, at least! You'd have to say I always kept my—'

Temple heard the Mayor snap her fingers and her man booted Ring in the back and sent him lurching off the scaffold. The noose jerked tight and he kicked and twisted, rope creaking as he did the hanged man's dance, piss running from one of his dirty trouser-legs. Little men and big, brave men and cowards, powerful men and meagre, they all hang very much the same. That made eleven of them dangling. Ring, and nine of his henchmen, and the woman who had been in charge of his whores. A half-hearted cheer went up from the crowd, more habit than enthusiasm. Last night's events had more than satisfied even Crease's appetite for death.

'And that's the end of that,' said the Mayor under her breath.

'It's the end of a lot,' said Temple. One of the ancient pillars the Whitehouse had stood between had toppled in the heat. The other loomed strangely naked, cracked and soot-blackened, the ruins of the present tangled charred about the ruins of the past. A good half of the buildings on Ring's side of the street had met the same fate, yawning gaps burned from the jumble of wooden shack and shanty, scavengers busy among the wreckage.

'We'll rebuild,' said the Mayor. 'That's what we do. Is that treaty ready yet?'

'Very nearly done,' Temple managed to say.

'Good. That piece of paper could save a lot of lives.'

'I see that saving lives is our only concern.' He trudged back up the steps without waiting for a reply. He shed no tears for Papa Ring, but he had no wish to watch him kick any longer.

With a fair proportion of the town's residents dead by violence, fire or hanging, a larger number run off, a still larger number even now preparing to leave, and most of the rest in the street observing the conclusion of the great feud, the Mayor's Church of Dice was eerily empty, Temple's footsteps echoing around the smoke-stained rafters. Dab Sweet, Crying Rock and Corlin sat about one table, playing cards under the vacant gaze of the ancient armour ranged about the walls.

'Not watching the hanging?' asked Temple.

Corlin glanced at him out of the corner of her eye and treated him to a hiss of contempt. More than likely she had heard the story of his naked dash across the street.

'Nearly got hanged myself one time, up near Hope,' said Sweet. 'Turned out a misunderstanding, but even so.' The old scout hooked a finger in his collar and dragged it loose. 'Strangled my enthusiasm for the business.'

'Bad luck,' intoned Crying Rock, seeming to stare straight through her cards, half of which faced in and the other half out. Whether it was the end of Sweet's enthusiasm, or his near-hanging, or hanging in general that was bad luck she didn't clarify. She was not a woman prone to clarification.

'And when there's death outside is the one time a man can get some room in here.' Sweet rocked his chair back on two legs and deposited his dirty boot on the table. 'I reckon this place has turned sour. Soon there'll be more money in taking folk away than bringing 'em in. Just need to round up a few miserable failures desperate to see civilisation again and we're on our way back to the Near Country.'

'Maybe I'll join you,' said Temple. A crowd of failures sounded like ideal company for him.

'Always welcome.' Crying Rock let fall a card and started to rake in the pot, her face just as slack as if she'd lost. Sweet tossed his hand away in disgust. 'Twenty years I been losing to this cheating bloody Ghost and she still pretends she don't know how to play the game!'

Savian and Lamb stood at the counter, warming themselves at a bottle. Shorn of hair and beard the Northman looked younger, even bigger, and a great deal meaner. He also looked as if he had made every effort to fell a tree with his face. It was a misshapen mass of scab and bruise, a ragged cut across one cheekbone roughly stitched and his hands both wrapped in stained bandages.

'All the same,' he was grunting through bloated lips, 'I owe you big.'

'Daresay I'll find a way for you to pay,' answered Savian. 'Where d'you stand on politics?'

'These days, as far away from it as I can . . .'

They shut up tight when they saw Temple. 'Where's Shy?' he asked.

Lamb looked at him, one eye swollen nearly shut and the other infinitely tired. 'Upstairs in the Mayor's rooms.'

'Will she see me?'

'That's up to her.'

Temple nodded. 'You've got my thanks as well,' he said to Savian. 'For what that's worth.'

'We all give what we can.'

Temple wasn't sure whether that was meant to sting. It was one of those moments when everything stung. He left the two old men and made for the stairs. Behind him he heard Savian mutter, 'I'm talking about the rebellion in Starikland.'

'The one just finished?'

'That and the next one . . .'

He lifted his fist outside the door, and paused. There was nothing to stop him letting it drop and riding straight out of town, to Bermi's claim, maybe, or even on to somewhere no one knew what a disappointing cock he was. If there was any such place left in the Circle of the World. Before the impulse to take the easy way could overwhelm him, he made himself knock.

Shy's face looked little better than Lamb's, scratched and swollen, nose cut across the bridge, neck a mass of bruises. It hurt him to see it. Not as much as if he'd taken the beating, of course. But it hurt still. She didn't look upset to see him. She didn't look that interested. She left the door open, limping slightly, and showed her teeth as she sank down on a bench under the window, bare feet looking very white against the floorboards.

'How was the hanging?' she asked.

He stepped inside and gently pushed the door to. 'Very much like they always are.'

'Can't say I've ever understood their appeal.'

'Perhaps it makes people feel like winners, seeing someone else lose so hard.'

'Losing hard I know all about.'

'Are you all right?'

She looked up and he could hardly meet her eye. 'Bit sore.'

'You're angry with me.' He sounded like a sulking child.

'I'm not. I'm just sore.'

'What good would I have done if I'd stayed?'

She licked at her split lip. 'I daresay you'd just have got yourself killed.'

'Exactly. But instead I ran for help.'

'You ran all right, that I can corroborate.'

'I got Savian.'

'And Savian got me. Just in time.'

'That's right.'

'That's right.' She held her side as she slowly fished up one boot and started to pull it on. 'So I guess what we're saying is, I owe you my life. Thanks, Temple, you're a fucking hero. Next time I see a bare arse vanishing out my window I'll know to just lie back and await salvation.'

They looked at each other in silence, while outside in the street the hanging crowd started to drift away. Then he sank into a chair facing her. 'I'm fucking ashamed of myself.'

'That's a great comfort. I'll use your shame as a poultice on my grazes.'

'I've got no excuse.'

'And yet I feel one's coming.'

His turn to grimace. 'I'm a coward, simple as that. I've been running away so long it's come to be a habit. Not easy, changing old habits. However much we might—'

'Don't bother.' She gave a long, pained sigh. 'I got low expectations. To be fair, you already exceeded 'em once when you paid your debt. So you tend to the cowardly. Who doesn't? You ain't the brave knight and I ain't the swooning maiden and this ain't no storybook, that's for sure. You're forgiven. You can go your way.' And she waved him out the door with the scabbed back of her hand.

That was closer to forgiveness than he could have hoped for, but he found he was not moving. 'I don't want to go.'

'I'm not asking you to jump again, you can use the stairs.'

'Let me make it right.'

She looked up at him from under her brows. 'We're heading into the mountains, Temple. That bastard Cantliss'll show us where these Dragon People are, and we're going to try and get my brother and sister back, and I can't promise there'll be anything made right at all. A few promises I can make – it'll be hard and cold and dangerous and there

286

won't even be any windows to jump out of. You'll be about as useful there as a spent match, and let's neither one of us offend honesty by pretending otherwise.'

'Please.' He took a wheedling step towards her, 'Please give me one more—'

'Leave me be,' she said, narrowing her eyes at him. 'I just want to sit and hurt in peace.'

So that was all. Maybe he should have fought harder, but Temple had never been much of a fighter. So he nodded at the floor, and quietly shut the door behind him, and went back down the steps, and over to the counter.

'Get what you wanted?' asked Lamb.

'No,' said Temple, spilling a pocketful of coins across the wood. 'What I deserved.' And he started drinking.

He was vaguely aware of the dull thud of hooves out in the street, shouting and the jingle of harness. Some new Fellowship pulling into town. Some new set of forthcoming disappointments. But he was too busy with his own even to bother to look up. He told the man behind the counter to leave the bottle.

This time there was no one else to blame. Not God, not Cosca, certainly not Shy. Lamb had been right. The trouble with running is wherever you run to, there you are. Temple's problem was Temple, and it always had been. He heard heavy footsteps, spurs jingling, calls for drink and women, but he ignored them, inflicted another burning glassful on his gullet, banged it down, eyes watering, reached for the bottle.

Someone else got there first.

'You'd best leave that be,' growled Temple.

'How would I drink it then?'

At the sound of that voice a terrible chill prickled his spine. His eyes crawled to the hand on the bottle – aged, liver-spotted, dirt beneath the cracked nails, a gaudy ring upon the first finger. His eyes crawled past the grubby lacework on the sleeve, up the mud-spotted material, over the breastplate, gilt peeling, up a scrawny neck speckled with rash, and to the face. That awfully familiar, hollowed visage: the nose sharp, the eyes bright, the greyed moustaches waxed to curling points.

'Oh God,' breathed Temple.

'Close enough,' said Nicomo Cosca, and delivered that luminous smile of which only he was capable, good humour and good intentions radiating from his deep-lined face. 'Look who it is, boys!'

287

At least two dozen well-known and deeply detested figures had made their way in after the Old Man. 'Whatever are the odds?' asked Brachio, showing his yellow teeth. He had a couple fewer knives in his bandolier than when Temple had left the Company, but was otherwise unchanged.

'Rejoice, ye faithful,' rumbled Jubair, quoting scripture in Kantic, 'for the wanderer returns.'

'Scouting, were you?' sneered Dimbik, smoothing his hair down with a licked finger and straightening his sash, which had devolved into a greasy tatter of indeterminate colour. 'Finding us a path to glory?'

'Ah, a drink, a drink, a drink . . .' Cosca took a long and flamboyant swig from Temple's bottle. 'Did I not tell you all? Wait long enough and things have a habit of returning to their proper place. Having lost my Company, I was for some years a penniless wanderer, buffeted by the winds of fate, most *roughly* buffeted, Sworbreck, make a note of that.' The writer, whose hair had grown considerably wilder, clothes shabbier, nostril rims pinker and hands more tremulous since last they met, fumbled for his pencil. 'But here I am, once more in command of a band of noble fighting men! You will scarcely believe it, but Sergeant Friendly was at one time forced into the criminal fraternity.' The neckless sergeant hoisted one brow a fraction. 'But he now stands beside me as the staunch companion he was born to be. And you, Temple? What role could fit your high talents and low character so well as that of my legal advisor?'

Temple hopelessly shrugged. 'None that I can think of.'

'Then let us celebrate our inevitable reunion! One for me.' The Old Man took another hefty swig, then grinned as he poured the smallest dribble of spirit into Temple's glass. 'And one for you. I thought you stopped drinking?'

'It felt like a perfect moment to start again,' croaked Temple. He had been expecting Cosca to order his death but, almost worse, it appeared the Company of the Gracious Hand would simply reabsorb him without breaking stride. If there was a God, He had clearly taken a set dislike to Temple over the past few years. But Temple supposed he could hardly blame Him. He was coming to feel much the same.

'Gentlemen, welcome to Crease!' The Mayor came sweeping through the doorway. 'I must apologise for the mess, but we have—' She saw the Old Man and her face drained of all colour. The first time Temple had seen her even slightly surprised. 'Nicomo Cosca,' she breathed.

'None other. You must be the Mayor.' He stiffly bowed, then looking slyly up added, 'These days. It is a morning of reunions, apparently.'

'You know each other?' asked Temple.

'Well,' muttered the Mayor. 'What . . . astonishing luck.'

'They do say luck is a woman.' The Old Man made Temple grunt by poking him in the ribs with the neck of his own bottle. 'She's drawn to those who least deserve her!'

Out of the corner of his eye, Temple saw Shy limping down the stairs and over towards Lamb who, along with Savian, was watching the new arrivals in careful silence. Cosca, meanwhile, was strutting to the windows, spurs jingling. He took a deep breath, apparently savouring the odour of charred wood, and started to swing his head gently in time to the creaking of the bodies on their scaffold. 'I love what you've done with the place,' he called to the Mayor. 'Very . . . apocalyptic. You make something of a habit of leaving settlements you preside over in smoking ruins.'

Something they had in common, as far as Temple could tell. He realised he was picking at the stitches holding his buttons on and forced himself to stop.

'Are these gentlemen your whole contingent?' asked the Mayor, eyeing the filthy, squinting, scratching, spitting mercenaries slouching about her gaming hall.

'Dear me, no! We lost a few on the way across the Far Country – the inevitable desertions, a round of fever, a little trouble with the Ghosts – but these stalwarts are but a representative sample. I have left the rest beyond the city limits because if I were to bring some three hundred—'

'Two hundred and sixty,' said Friendly. The Mayor looked paler yet at the number.

'Counting Inquisitor Lorsen and his Practicals?'

'Two hundred and sixty-eight.' At the mention of the Inquisition, the Mayor's face had turned positively deathly.

'If I were to bring two hundred and sixty eight travel-sore fighting men into a place like this, there would, frankly, be carnage.'

'And not the good sort,' threw in Brachio, dabbing at his weepy eye.

'There is a good sort?' murmured the Mayor.

Cosca thoughtfully worked the tip of one moustache between thumb and forefinger. 'There are . . . *degrees*, anyway. And here he is!'

His black coat was weather-worn, a patchy yellow-grey beard had sprouted from cheeks more gaunt than ever, but Inquisitor Lorsen's eyes were just as bright with purpose as they had been when the Company left Mulkova. More so, if anything.

'This is Inquisitor Lorsen.' Cosca scratched thoughtfully at his rashy neck. 'My current employer.'

'An honour.' Though Temple detected the slightest strain in the Mayor's voice. 'If I may ask, what business might his Majesty's Inquisition have in Crease?'

'We are hunting escaped rebels!' called Lorsen to the room at large. 'Traitors to the Union!'

'We are far from the Union here.'

The Inquisitor's smile seemed to chill the whole room. 'The reach of his Eminence lengthens yearly. Large rewards are being offered for the capture of certain persons. A list will be posted throughout town, at its head the traitor, murderer and chief fomenter of rebellion, Conthus!'

Savian gave vent to a muffled round of coughing and Lamb slapped him on the back, but Lorsen was too busy frowning down his nose at Temple to notice. 'I see you have been reunited with this slippery liar.'

'Come now.' Cosca gave Temple's shoulder a fatherly squeeze. 'A degree of slipperiness, and indeed of lying, is a positive boon in a notary. Beneath it all there has never been a man of such conscience and moral courage. I'd trust him with my life. Or at least my hat.' And he swept it off and hung it over Temple's glass.

'As long as you trust him with none of my business.' Lorsen waved to his Practicals. 'Come. We have questions to ask.'

'He seems charming,' said the Mayor as she watched him leave.

Cosca scratched at his rash again and held up his fingernails to assess the results. 'The Inquisition makes a point of recruiting only the most well-mannered fanatical torturers.'

'And the most foul-mannered old mercenaries too, it would appear.'

'A job is a job. But I have my own reasons for being here also. I came looking for a man called Grega Cantliss.'

There was a long pause as that name settled upon the room like a chilly snowfall.

'Fuck,' he heard Shy breathe.

Cosca looked about expectantly. 'The name is not unknown, then?'

'He has at times passed through.' The Mayor had the air of choosing her words very carefully. 'If you were to find him, what then?'

'Then I and my notary – not to mention my employer the noble Inquisitor Lorsen – could be very much out of your way. Mercenaries have, I am aware, a poor reputation, but believe me when I say we are not here to cause trouble.' He swilled some spirit lazily around in the bottom of the bottle. 'Why, do you have some notion of Cantliss' whereabouts?'

A pregnant silence ensued while a set of long glances were exchanged. Then Lamb slowly lifted his chin. Shy's face hardened. The Mayor graced them with the tiniest apologetic shrug. 'He is chained up in my cellar.'

'Bitch,' breathed Shy.

'Cantliss is ours.' Lamb pushed himself up from the counter and stood tall, bandaged left hand sitting loose on the hilt of his sword.

Several of the mercenaries variously puffed themselves up and found challenging stances of one kind or another, like tomcats opening hostilities in a moonlit alley. Friendly only watched, dead-eyed, dice clicking in his fist as he worked them gently around each other.

'Yours?' asked Cosca.

'He burned my farm and stole my son and daughter and sold 'em to some savages. We've tracked him all the way from the Near Country. He's going to take us up into the mountains and show us where these Dragon People are.'

The Old Man's body might have stiffened down the years but his eyebrows were still some of the most limber in the world, and they reached new heights now. 'Dragon People, you say? Perhaps we can help each other?'

Lamb glanced about the dirty, scarred and bearded faces. 'Guess you can never have too many allies.'

'Quite so! A man lost in the desert must take such water as he is offered, eh, Temple?'

'Not sure I wouldn't rather go thirsty,' muttered Shy.

'I'm Lamb. That's Shy.' The Northman raised his glass, the stump of his middle finger plainly visible in spite of the bandages.

'A nine-fingered Northman,' mused the captain general. 'I do believe a fellow called Shivers was looking for you in the Near Country.'

'Haven't seen him.'

'Ah.' Cosca waved his bottle at Lamb's injuries. 'I thought perhaps this might be his handiwork.'

'No.'

'You appear to have many enemies, Master Lamb.'

'Sometimes it seems I can't shit without making a couple more.'

'It all depends who you shit on, I suppose? A fearsome fellow, Caul Shivers, and I would not judge the years to have mellowed him. We knew each other back in Styria, he and I. Sometimes I feel I have met everyone in the world and that every new place is peopled with old faces.' His considering gaze came to rest on Savian. 'Although I do not recognise this gentleman.'

'I'm Savian.' And he coughed into his fist.

'And what brings you to the Far Country? Your health?'

Savian paused, mouth a little open, while an awkward silence stretched out, several of the mercenaries still with hands close to weapons, and suddenly Shy said, 'Cantliss took one of his children, too, he's been tracking 'em along with us. Lad called Collem.'

The silence lasted a little longer then Savian added, almost reluctantly, 'My lad, Collem.' He coughed again, and raspingly cleared his throat. 'Hoping Cantliss can lead us to him.'

It was almost a relief to see two of the Mayor's men dragging the bandit across the gaming hall. His wrists were in manacles, his once fine clothes were stained rags and his face as bruised as Lamb's, one hand hanging useless and one leg dragging on the boards behind him.

'The elusive Grega Cantliss!' shouted Cosca as the Mayor's men flung him cringing down. 'Fear not. I am Nicomo Cosca, infamous soldier of fortune, et cetera, et cetera, and I have some questions for you. I advise you to consider your answers carefully as your life may depend upon them, and so forth.'

Cantliss registered Shy, Savian, Lamb and the score or more of mercenaries, and with a coward's instinct Temple well recognised quickly perceived the shift in the balance of power. He eagerly nodded.

'Some months ago you bought some horses in a town called Greyer. You used coins like these.' Cosca produced a tiny gold piece with a magician's flourish. 'Antique Imperial coins, as it happens.'

Cantliss' eyes flickered over Cosca's face as though trying to read a script. 'I did. That's a fact.'

'You bought those horses from rebels, fighting to free Starikland from the Union.'

'I did?'

'You did.'

'I did!'

Cosca leaned close. 'Where did the coins come from?'

'Dragon People paid me with 'em,' said Cantliss. 'Savages in the mountains up beyond Beacon.'

'Paid you for what?'

He licked his scabbed lips. 'For children.'

'An ugly business,' muttered Sworbreck.

'Most business is,' said Cosca, leaning closer and closer towards Cantliss. 'They have more of these coins?'

'All I could ever want, that's what he said.'

'Who said?'

'Waerdinur. He's their leader.'

'All I could ever want.' Cosca's eyes glimmered as brightly as his imagined gold. 'So you are telling me these Dragon People are in league with the rebels?'

'What?'

'That these savages are funding, and perhaps harbouring, the rebel leader Conthus himself?'

There was a silence while Cantliss blinked up. 'Er . . . yes?'

Cosca smiled very wide. 'Yes. And when my employer Inquisitor Lorsen asks you the same question, what will your answer be?'

Now Cantliss smiled, too, sensing that his chances might have drastically improved. 'Yes! They got them that Conthus up there, no doubt in my mind! Hell, he's more'n likely going to use their money to start a new war!'

'I knew it!' Cosca poured a measure of spirit into Lamb's empty glass. 'We must accompany you into the mountains and pull up this very root of insurrection! This wretched man will be our guide and thereby win his freedom.'

'Yes, indeed!' shouted Cantliss, grinning at Shy and Lamb and Savian, then squawking as Brachio hauled him to his feet and man-handled him towards the door, wounded leg dragging.

'Fuckers,' whispered Shy.

'Realistic,' Lamb hissed at her, one hand on her elbow.

'What luck for all of us,' Cosca was expounding, 'that I should arrive as you prepare to leave!'

'Oh, I've always had the luck,' muttered Temple.

'And me,' murmured Shy.

'Realistic,' hissed Lamb.

'A party of four is easily dismissed,' Cosca was telling the room. 'A party of three hundred, so much less easily!'

'Two hundred and seventy-two,' said Friendly.

'If I could have a word?' Dab Sweet was approaching the counter. 'You're planning on heading into the mountains, you'll need a better scout than that half-dead killer. I stand ready and willing to offer my services.'

'So generous,' said Cosca. 'And you are?'

'Dab Sweet.' And the famous scout removed his hat to display his own thinning locks. Evidently he had caught the scent of a more profitable opportunity than shepherding the desperate back to Starikland.

'The noted frontiersman?' asked Sworbreck, looking up from his papers. 'I thought you'd be younger.'

Sweet sighed. 'I used to be.'

'You're aware of him?' asked Cosca.

The biographer pointed his nose towards the ceiling. 'A man by the name of Marin Glanhorm – I refuse to use the term writer in relation to him – has penned some most inferior and far-fetched works based upon his supposed exploits.'

'Those was unauthorised,' said Sweet. 'But I've exploited a thing or two, that's true. I've trodden on every patch of this Far Country big enough to support a boot, and that includes them mountains.' He beckoned Cosca closer, spoke softer. 'Almost as far as Ashranc, where those Dragon People live. Their sacred ground. My partner, Crying Rock, she's been even further, see . . .' He gave a showman's pause. 'She used to be one of 'em.'

'True,' grunted Crying Rock, still occupying her place at the table, though Corlin had vanished leaving only her cards.

'Raised up there,' said Sweet. 'Lived up there.'

'Born up there, eh?' asked Cosca.

Crying Rock solemnly shook her head. 'No one is born in Ashranc.' And she stuck her dead chagga pipe between her teeth as though that was her last word on the business.

'She knows the secret ways up there, though, and you'll need 'em, too, 'cause those Dragon bastards won't be extending no warm welcomes once you're on their ground. It's some strange, sulphurous ground they've got but they're jealous about it as mean bears, that's the truth.'

'Then the two of you would be an invaluable addition to our expedition,' said Cosca. 'What would be your terms?'

'We'd settle for a twentieth share of any valuables recovered.'

'Our aim is to root out rebellion, not valuables.'

Sweet smiled. 'There's a risk of disappointment in any venture.'

'Then welcome aboard! My notary will prepare an agreement!'

'Two hundred and seventy-four,' mused Friendly. His dead eyes drifted to Temple. 'And you.'

Cosca began to slosh out drinks. 'Why are all the really interesting

294

people always advanced in years?' He nudged Temple in the ribs. 'Your generation really isn't producing the goods.'

'We cower in giants' shadows and feel our shortcomings most keenly.'

'Oh, you've been missed, Temple! If I've learned one thing in forty years of warfare, it's that you have to look on the funny side. The tongue on this man! Conversationally, I mean, not sexually, I can't vouch for that. Don't include that, Sworbreck!' The biographer sullenly crossed something out. 'We shall leave as soon as the men are rested and supplies gathered!'

'Might be best to wait 'til winter's past,' said Sweet.

Cosca leaned close. 'Do you have any notion what will happen if I leave my Company quartered here for four months? The state of the place now barely serves as a taster.'

'You got any notion what'll happen if three hundred men get caught in a real winter storm up there?' grunted Sweet, pulling his fingers through his beard.

'None whatsoever,' said Cosca, 'but I can't wait to find out. We must seize the moment! That has always been my motto. Note that down, Sworbreck.'

Sweet raised his brows. 'Might not be long 'til your motto is, "I can't feel my fucking feet." '

But the captain general was, as usual, not listening. 'I have a premonition we will all find what we seek in those mountains!' He threw one arm about Savian's shoulders and the other about Lamb's. 'Lorsen his rebels, I my gold, these worthy folk their missing children. Let us toast our alliance!' And he raised Temple's nearly empty bottle high.

'Shit on this,' breathed Shy through gritted teeth.

Temple could only agree. But that appeared to be all his say in the matter.

Nowhere to Go

Ro pulled off the chain with the dragon's scale and laid it gently on the furs. Shy once told her you can waste your life waiting for the right moment. Now was good as any.

She touched Pit's cheek in the dark and he stirred, the faintest smile on his face. He was happy here. Young enough to forget, maybe. He'd be safe, or safe as he could be. In this world there are no certainties. Ro wished she could say goodbye but she was worried he'd cry. So she gathered her bundle and slipped out into the night.

The air was sharp, snow gently falling but melting as soon as it touched the hot ground and dry a moment later. Light spilled from some of the houses, windows needing neither glass nor shutter cut from the mountain or from walls so old and weathered Ro couldn't tell them from the mountain. She kept to the shadows, rag-wrapped feet silent on the ancient paving, past the great black cooking slab, surface polished to a shine by the years, steam whispering from it as the snow fell.

The Long House door creaked as she passed and she pressed herself against the pitted wall, waiting. Through the window she could hear the voices of the elders at their Gathering. Three months here and she already knew their tongue.

'The Shanka are breeding in the deeper tunnels.' Uto's voice. She always counselled caution.

'Then we must drive them out.' Akosh. She was always bold.

'If we send enough for that there will be few left behind. One day men will come from outside.'

'We put them off in the place they call Beacon.'

'Or we made them curious.'

'Once we wake the Dragon it will not matter.'

'It was given to me to make the choice.' Waerdinur's deep voice. 'The

Maker did not leave our ancestors here to let his works fall into decay. We must be bold. Akosh, you will take three hundred of us north into the deep places and drive out the Shanka, and keep the diggings going over winter. After the thaw you will return.'

'I worry,' said Uto. 'There have been visions.'

'You always worry . . .'

Their words faded into the night as Ro padded past, over the great sheets of dulled bronze where the names were chiselled in tiny characters, thousands upon thousands stretching back into the fog of ages. She knew Icaray was on guard tonight and guessed he would be drunk, as always. He sat in the archway, head nodding, spear against the wall, empty bottle between his feet. The Dragon People were just people, after all, and each had their failings like any other.

Ro looked back once and thought how beautiful it was, the yellow-lit windows in the black cliff-face, the dark carvings on the steep roofs against a sky blazing with stars. But it wasn't her home. She wouldn't let it be. She scurried past Icaray and down the steps, hand brushing the warm rock on her right because on her left, she knew, was a hundred strides of empty drop.

She came to the needle and found the hidden stair, striking steeply down the mountainside. It scarcely looked hidden at all but Waerdinur had told her that it had a magic, and no one could see it until they were shown it. Shy had always told her there were no such things as Magi or demons and it was all stories, but out here in this far, high corner of the world all things had their magic. To deny it felt as foolish as denying the sky.

Down the winding stair, switching back and forth, away from Ashranc, the stones growing colder underfoot. Into the forest, great trees on the bare slopes, roots catching at her toes and tangling at her ankles. She ran beside a sulphurous stream, bubbling through rocks crusted with salt. She stopped when her breath began to smoke, the cold biting in her chest, and she bound her feet more warmly, unrolled the fur and wrapped it around her shoulders, ate and drank, tied her bundle and hurried on. She thought of Lamb plodding endlessly behind his plough and Shy swinging the scythe sweat dripping from her brows and saying through her gritted teeth, *You just keep on. Don't think of stopping. Just keep on*, and Ro kept on.

The snow had settled in slow melting patches here, the branches dripping tap, tap and how she wished she had proper boots. She heard wolves sorrowful in the high distance and ran faster, her feet wet and her legs sore, downhill, downhill, clambering over jagged rock and sliding in scree, checking with the stars the way Gully taught her once, sitting out beside the barn in the dark of night when she couldn't sleep.

The snow had stopped falling but it was drifted deep now, sparkling as dawn came fumbling through the forest, her feet crunching, her face prickling with the cold. Ahead the trees began to thin and she hurried on, hoping perhaps to look out upon fields or flower-filled valleys or a merry township nestled in the hills.

She burst out at the edge of a dizzy cliff and stared far over high and barren country, sharp black forest and bare black rock slashed and stabbed with white snow fading into long grey rumour without a touch of people or colour. No hint of the world she had known, no hope of deliverance, no heat now from the earth beneath and all was cold inside and out and Ro breathed into her trembling hands and wondered if this was the end of the world.

'Well met, daughter.' Waerdinur sat cross-legged behind her, his back against a tree-stump, his staff, or his spear – Ro still was not sure which it was – in the crook of one arm. 'Do you have meat there in your bundle? I was not prepared for a journey and you have led me quite a chase.'

In silence she gave him a strip of meat and sat down beside him and they ate and she found she was very glad he had come.

After a time he said, 'It can be difficult to let go. But you must see the past is done.' And he pulled out the dragon scale that she had left behind and put the chain around her neck and she did not try to stop him.

'Shy'll be coming . . .' But her voice sounded tiny, thinned by the cold, muffled in the snow, lost in the great emptiness.

'It may be so. But do you know how many children have come here in my lifetime?'

Ro said nothing.

'Hundreds. And do you know how many families have come to claim them?'

Ro swallowed, and said nothing.

'None.' Waerdinur put his great arm around her and held her tight and warm. 'You are one of us now. Sometimes people choose to leave us. Sometimes they are made to. My sister was. If you really wish to go, no one will stop you. But it is a long, hard way, and to what? The world out there is a red country, without justice, without meaning.'

Ro nodded. That much she'd seen.

298

'Here life has purpose. Here we need you.' He stood and held out his hand. 'Can I show you a wondrous thing?'

'What thing?'

'The reason why the Maker left us here. The reason we remain.'

She took his hand and he hoisted her up easily onto his shoulders. She put her palm on the smooth stubble of his scalp and said, 'Can we shave my head tomorrow?'

'Whenever you are ready.' And he set off up the hillside the way she had come, retracing her footprints through the snow.

IV
DRAGONS

'There are many humorous things
in the world,
among them the white man's notion that he
is less savage than the other savages.'
Mark Twain

In Threes

'**F**uck, it's cold,' whispered Shy.

They'd found a shred of shelter wedged in a hollow among frozen tree-roots, but when the wind whipped up it was still like a slap in the face, and even with a piece of blanket double-wrapped around her head so just her eyes showed, it left Shy's face red and stinging as a good slapping might've. She lay on her side, needing a piss but hardly daring to drop her trousers in case she ended up with a yellow icicle stuck to her arse to add to her discomforts. She dragged her coat tight around her shoulders, then the frost-crusted wolfskin Sweet had given her tight around that, wriggled her numb toes in her icy boots and pressed her dead fingertips to her mouth so she could make the most of her breath while she still had some.

'Fuck, it's cold.'

'This is nothing,' grunted Sweet. 'Got caught in drifts one time in the mountains near Hightower for two months. So cold the spirits froze in the bottles. We had to crack the glass off and pass the booze around in lumps.'

'Shhh,' murmured Crying Rock, faintest puff of smoke spilling from her blued lips. 'Til that moment Shy had been wondering whether she'd frozen to death hours before with her pipe still clamped in her mouth. She'd scarcely even blinked all morning, staring through the brush they'd arranged the previous night as cover and down towards Beacon.

Not that there was much to see. The camp looked dead. Snow in the one street was drifted up against doors, thick on roofs toothed with glinting icicles, pristine but for the wandering tracks of one curious wolf. No smoke from the chimneys, no light from the frozen flaps of the half-buried tents. The old barrows were just white humps. The broken tower which in some forgotten past must've held the beacon the place was named for held nothing but snow now. Aside from wind sad in the mangy pines and making a shutter somewhere tap, tap, tap, the place was silent as Juvens' grave.

Shy had never been much for waiting, that wasn't news, but lying up here in the brush and watching reminded her too much of her outlaw days. On her belly in the dust with Jeg chewing and chewing and spitting and chewing in her ear and Neary sweating an inhuman quantity of salt water, waiting for travellers way out of luck to pass on the road below. Pretending to be the outlaw, Smoke, half-crazy with meanness, when what she really felt like was a painfully unlucky little girl, half-crazy with constant fear. Fear of those chasing her and fear of those with her and fear of herself most of all. No clue what she'd do next. Like some hateful lunatic might seize her hands and her mouth and use them like a puppet any moment. The thought of it made her want to wriggle out of her own sore skin.

'Be still,' whispered Lamb, motionless as a felled tree.

'Why? There's no one bloody here, place is dead as a——'

Crying Rock raised one gnarled finger, held it in front of Shy's face, then gently tilted it to point towards the treeline on the far side of the camp.

'You see them two big pines?' whispered Sweet. 'And them three rocks like fingers just between? That's where the hide is.'

Shy stared at that colourless tangle of stone and snow and timber until her eyes ached. Then she caught the faintest twitch of movement.

'That's one of them?' she breathed.

Crying Rock held up two fingers.

'They go in pairs,' said Sweet.

'Oh, she's good,' whispered Shy, feeling a proper amateur in this company.

'The best.'

'How do we flush 'em out?'

'They'll flush 'emselves out. Long as that drunk madman Cosca comes through on his end of it.'

'Far from a certainty,' muttered Shy. In spite of Cosca's talk about haste his Company had loitered around Crease like flies around a turd for a whole two weeks to resupply, which meant to cause every kind of unsavoury chaos and steadily desert. They'd taken even longer slogging across the few dozen miles of high plateau between Crease and Beacon as the weather turned steadily colder, a good number of Crease's most ambitious whores, gamblers and merchants straggling after in hopes of wrenching free any money the mercenaries had somehow left unspent. All the while the Old Man smiled upon this tardy shambles like it was exactly the plan discussed, spinning far-fetched yarns about his glorious past for the benefit of his idiot biographer. 'Seems to me talk and action have come properly uncoupled for that bastard—'

'Shhh,' hissed Lamb.

Shy pressed herself against the dirt as a gang of outraged crows took off clattering into the frozen sky below. Shouting drifted deadened on the wind, then the rattle of gear, then horsemen came into view. Twenty or more, floundering up through the snow drifted in the valley and making damned hard work of it, dipping and bobbing, riders slapping at their mounts' steaming flanks to keep them on.

'The drunk madman comes through,' muttered Lamb.

'This time.' Shy had a strong feeling Cosca didn't make a habit of it.

The mercenaries dismounted and spread out through the camp, digging away at doorways and windows, ripping open tents with canvas frozen stiff as wood, raising a whoop and a clamour which in that winter deadness sounded noisy as the battle at the end of time. That these scum were on her side made Shy wonder whether she was on the right side, but she was where she was. Making the best from different kinds of shit was the story of her life.

Lamb touched her arm and she followed his finger to the hide, caught a dark shape flitting through the trees behind it, keeping low, quickly vanished among the tangle of branch and shadow.

'There goes one,' grunted Sweet, not keeping his voice so soft now the mercenaries were raising hell. 'Any luck, that one'll run right up to their hidden places. Right up to Ashranc and tell the Dragon People there's twenty horsemen in Beacon.'

'When strong seem weak,' muttered Lamb, 'when weak seem strong.'

'What about the other one?' asked Shy.

Crying Rock tucked away her pipe and produced her beaked club, as eloquent an answer as was called for, then slipped limber as a snake around the tree she had her back to and into cover.

'To work,' said Sweet, and started to wriggle after her, a long stretch faster than Shy had ever seen him move standing. She watched the two old scouts crawl between the black tree-trunks, through the snow and the fallen pine needles, working their way towards the hide and out of sight.

She was left shivering on the frozen dirt next to Lamb, and waiting some more.

Since Crease he'd stuck to shaving his head and it was like he'd shaved all sentiment off, too, hard lines and hard bones and hard past laid bare. The stitches had been pulled with the point of Savian's knife and the marks of the fight with Glama Golden were fast fading, soon to be lost among all the rest. A lifetime of violence written so plain into that beaten anvil of a face she'd no notion how she never read it there before.

Hard to believe how easy it had been to talk to him once. Or talk at him, at least. Good old cowardly Lamb, he'll never surprise you. Safe and comfortable as talking to herself. Now there was a wider and more dangerous gulf between them each day. So many questions swimming round her head but now she finally got her mouth open, the one that dropped out she hardly cared about the answer to.

'Did you fuck the Mayor, then?'

Lamb left it long enough to speak, she thought he might not bother. 'Every which way and I don't regret a moment.'

'I guess a fuck can still be a wonderful thing between folk who've reached a certain age.'

'No doubt. Specially if they didn't get many beforehand.'

'Didn't stop her knifing you in the back soon as it suited her.'

'Get many promises from Temple 'fore he jumped out your window?'

Shy felt the need for a pause of her own. 'Can't say I did.'

'Huh. I guess fucking a person don't stop them fucking you.'

She gave a long, cold, smoking sigh. 'For some of us it only seems to increase the chances . . .'

Sweet came trudging from the pines near the hide, ungainly in his swollen fur coat, and waved up. Crying Rock followed and bent down, cleaning her club in the snow, leaving the faintest pink smear on the blank white.

'I guess that's it done,' said Lamb, wincing as he clambered up to a squat.

'I guess.' Shy hugged herself tight, too cold to feel much about it but cold. She turned, first time she'd looked at him since they started speaking. 'Can I ask you a question?'

The jaw muscles worked on the side of his head. 'Sometimes ignorance is the sweetest medicine.' He turned this strange, sick, guilty look on her, like a man who's been caught doing murder and knows the game's all up. 'But I don't know how I'd stop you.' And she felt worried to the pit of her stomach and could hardly bring herself to speak, but couldn't stand to stay silent either.

'Who are you?' she whispered. 'I mean . . . who were you? I mean—shit.'

She caught movement – a figure flitting through the trees towards Sweet and Crying Rock.

'Shit!' And she was running, stumbling, blundering, snagged a numb foot at the edge of the hollow and went tumbling through the brush, floundered up and was off across the bare slope, legs so caught up in the virgin snow it felt like she was dragging two giant stone boots after her.

'Sweet!' she wheezed. The figure broke from the trees and over the unspoiled white towards the old scout, hint of a snarling face, glint of a blade. No way Shy could get there in time. Nothing she could do.

'Sweet!' she wailed one more time, and he looked up, smiling, then sideways, eyes suddenly wide, shrinking away as the dark shape sprang for him. It twisted in the air, fell short and went tumbling through the snow. Crying Rock rushed up and hit it over the head with her club. Shy heard the sharp crack a moment after.

Savian pushed some branches out of his way and trudged through the snow towards them, frowning at the trees and calmly cranking his flatbow.

'Nice shot,' called Crying Rock, sliding her club into her belt and jamming that pipe between her teeth.

Sweet pushed back his hat. 'Nice shot, she says! I've damn near shat myself.'

Shy stood with her hands on her hips and tried to catch her smoking breath, chest on fire from the icy coldness of it.

Lamb walked up beside her, sheathing his sword. 'Looks like they sometimes go in threes.'

Among the Barbarians

'They hardly look like demons.' Cosca nudged the Dragon Woman's cheek with his foot and watched her bare-shaved head flop back. 'No scales. No forked tongues. No flaming breath. I feel a touch let down.'

'Simple barbarians,' grunted Jubair.

'Like the ones out on the plains.' Brachio took a gulp of wine and peered discerningly at the glass. 'A step above animals and not a high step.'

Temple cleared his sore throat. 'No barbarian's sword.' He squatted down and turned the blade over in his hands: straight, and perfectly balanced, and meticulously sharpened.

'These ain't no common Ghosts,' said Sweet. 'They ain't really Ghosts at all. They aim to kill and know how. They don't scare at nothing and know each rock o' this country, too. They did for every miner in Beacon without so much as a struggle.'

'But clearly they bleed.' Cosca poked his finger into the hole made by Savian's flatbow bolt and pulled it out, fingertip glistening red. 'And clearly they die.'

Brachio shrugged. 'Everyone bleeds. Everyone dies.'

'Life's one certainty,' rumbled Jubair, rolling his eyes towards the heavens. Or at least the mildewed ceiling.

'What is this metal?' Sworbreck pulled an amulet from the Dragon Woman's collar, a grey leaf dully gleaming in the lamplight. 'It is very thin but . . .' He bared his teeth as he strained at it. 'I cannot bend it. Not at all. The workmanship is remarkable.'

Cosca turned away. 'Steel and gold are the only metals that interest me. Bury the bodies away from the camp. If I've learned one thing in forty years of warfare, Sworbreck, it's that you have to bury the bodies far from camp.' He drew his cloak tight at the icy blast as the door was opened. 'Damn this cold.' Hunched jealously over the fire, he looked like nothing so much as an old witch over her cauldron, thin hair hanging lank, grasping hands like black claws against the flames. 'Reminds me of the North, and that can't be a good thing, eh, Temple?'

'No, General.' Being reminded of any moment in the past ten years was no particularly good thing in Temple's mind – the whole a desert of violence, waste and guilt. Except, perhaps, gazing out over the free plains from his saddle. Or down on Crease from the frame of Majud's shop. Or arguing with Shy over their debt. Dancing, pressed tight against her. Leaning to kiss her, and her smile as she leaned to kiss him back . . . He shook himself. All thoroughly, irredeemably fucked. Truly, you never value what you have until you jump out of its window.

'That cursed retreat.' Cosca was busy wrestling with his own failures. There were enough of them. 'That damned snow. That treacherous bastard Black Calder. So many good men lost, eh, Temple? Like . . . well . . . I forget the names, but my point holds.' He turned to call angrily over his shoulder. 'When you said "fort" I was expecting something more . . . substantial.'

Beacon's chief building was, in fact, a large log cabin on one and a half floors, separated into rooms by hanging animal skins and with a heavy door, narrow windows, access to the broken tower in one corner and a horrifying array of draughts.

Sweet shrugged. 'Standards ain't high in the Far Country, General. Out here you put three sticks together, it's a fort.'

'I suppose we must be glad of the shelter we have. Another night in the open you'd have to wait for spring to thaw me out. How I long for the towers of beautiful Visserine! A balmy summer night beside the river! The city was mine, once, you know, Sworbreck?'

The writer winced. 'I believe you have mentioned it.'

'Nicomo Cosca, Grand Duke of Visserine!' The Old Man paused to take yet another swig from his flask. 'And it shall be mine again. My towers, my palace, and my respect. I have been often disappointed, that's true. My back is a tissue of metaphorical scars. But there is still time, isn't there?'

'Of course.' Sworbreck gave a false chuckle. 'You have many successful years ahead of you, I'm sure!'

'Still a little time to make things right . . .' Cosca was busy staring at the wrinkled back of his hand, wincing as he worked the knobbly fingers. 'I used to be a wonder with a throwing knife, you know, Sworbreck. I could bring down a fly at twenty paces. Now?' He gave vent to an explosive snort. 'I can scarcely see twenty paces on a clear day. That's the most wounding betrayal of all. The one by your own flesh. Live long enough, you see everything ruined . . .'

The next whirlwind heralded Sergeant Friendly's arrival, blunt nose and flattened ears slightly pinked but otherwise showing no sign of discomfort at the cold. Sun, rain or tempest all seemed one to him.

'The last stragglers are into camp along with the Company's baggage,' he intoned.

Brachio poured himself another drink. 'Hangers-on swarm to us like maggots to a corpse.'

'I am not sure I appreciate the image of our noble brotherhood as a suppurating carcass,' said Cosca.

'However accurate it may be,' murmured Temple.

'Who made it all the way here?'

Friendly began the count. 'Nineteen whores and four pimps—'

'They'll be busy,' said Cosca.

'—twenty-two wagon-drivers and porters including the cripple Hedges, who keeps demanding to speak to you—'

'Everyone wants a slice of me! You'd think I was a feast-day currant cake!'

'—thirteen assorted merchants, pedlars and tinkers, six of whom complain of having been robbed by members of the Company—'

'I consort with criminals! I was a Grand Duke, you know. So many disappointments.'

'—two blacksmiths, a horse trader, a fur trader, an undertaker, a barber boasting of surgical qualifications, a pair of laundry women, a vintner with no stock, and seventeen persons of no stated profession.'

'Vagrants and layabouts hoping to grow fat on my crumbs! Is there no honour left, Temple?'

'Precious little,' said Temple. Certainly his own stock was disgracefully meagre.

'And is Superior Pike's . . .' Cosca leaned close to Friendly and after taking another swallow from his flask whispered, entirely audibly, '*secret wagon* in the camp?'

'It is,' said Friendly.

'Place it under guard.'

'What's in it, anyway?' asked Brachio, wiping some damp from his weepy eye with a fingernail.

'Were I to share that information, it would no longer be a secret wagon, merely . . . a wagon. I think we can agree that lacks mystique.'

'Where will all this flotsam find shelter?' Jubair wished to know. 'There is hardly room for the fighting men.'

'What of the barrows?' asked the Old Man.

'Empty,' said Sweet. 'Robbed centuries ago.'

'I daresay they'll warm up something snug. The irony, eh, Temple? Yesterday's heroes kicked from their graves by today's whores!'

'I thrill to the profundity,' muttered Temple, shivering at the thought of sleeping in the dank innards of those ancient tombs, let alone fucking in them.

'Not wanting to spoil your preparations, General,' said Sweet, 'but I'd best be on my way.'

'Of course! Glory is like bread, it stales with time! Was it Farans who said so, or Stolicus? What is your plan?'

'I'm hoping that scout'll run straight back and tell his Dragon friends there's no more'n twenty of us down here.'

'The best opponent is one befuddled and mystified! Was that Farans? Or Bialoveld?' Cosca treated Sworbreck, busy with his notebooks, to a contemptuous glare. 'One *writer* is very much like another. You were saying?'

'Reckon they'll set to wondering whether to stay tucked up at Ashranc and ignore us, or come down and wipe us out.'

'They'll trip over a shock if they try it,' said Brachio, jowls wobbling as he chuckled.

'That's just what we want 'em to do,' said Sweet. 'But they ain't prone to come down without good reason. A little trespass on their ground should hook 'em. Prickly as all hell about their ground. Crying Rock knows the way. She knows secret ways right into Ashranc, but that's a hell of a risk. So all we do is creep up there and leave some sign they won't miss. A burned-out fire, some nice clear tracks across their road—'

'A turd,' said Jubair, pronouncing the word as solemnly as a prophet's name.

Cosca raised his flask. 'Marvellous! Lure them with a turd! I'm reasonably sure Stolicus never recommended *that*, eh, Temple?'

Brachio squeezed his big lower lip thoughtfully between finger and thumb. 'You're sure they'll fall for this turd trap?'

'They've been the big dogs around here for ever,' said Sweet. 'They're used to slaughtering Ghosts and scaring off prospectors. All that winning's made 'em arrogant. Set in old ways. But they're dangerous, still.

You'd best be good and ready. Don't reel 'em in 'til they've swallowed the hook.'

Cosca nodded. 'Believe me when I say I have stood at both ends of an ambush and fully understand the principles. What would be your opinion of this scheme, Master Cantliss?'

The wretched bandit, his clothes splitting at the seams and stuffed with straw against the cold, had until then been sitting in the corner of the room nursing his broken hand and quietly sniffling. He perked up at the sound of his name and nodded vigorously, as though his support might be help to any cause. 'Sounds all right. They think they own these hills, that I can chime with. And that Waerdinur killed my friend Blackpoint. Snuffed him out casual as you please. Can I . . .' licking his scabbed lips and reaching towards Cosca's flask.

'Of course,' said Cosca, draining it, upending it to show it was empty, then shrugging. 'Captain Jubair has picked out eight of his most competent men to accompany you.'

Sweet looked less than reassured as he gave the hulking Kantic a sidelong glance. 'I'd rather stick with folks I know I can count on.'

'So would we all, but are there truly any such in life, eh, Temple?'

'Precious few.' Temple certainly would not have counted himself among their number, nor anyone else currently in the room.

Sweet affected an air of injured innocence. 'You don't trust us?'

'I have been often disappointed by human nature,' said Cosca. 'Ever since Grand Duchess Sefeline turned on me and poisoned my favourite mistress I have tried never to encumber working relationships with the burden of trust.'

Brachio gave vent to a long burp. 'Better to watch each other carefully, stay well armed and mutually suspicious, and keep our various self-interests as the prime motives.'

'Nobly said!' And Cosca slapped his thigh. 'Then, like a knife in the sock, we make trust our secret weapon in the event of emergencies.'

'I tried a knife in the sock,' muttered Brachio, patting the several he had stowed in his bandolier. 'Chafed terribly.'

'Shall we depart?' rumbled Jubair. 'Time is wasting, and there is God's work to be done.'

'There's work, anyway,' said Sweet, pulling the collar of his big fur coat up to his ears as he ducked out into the night.

Cosca tipped up his flask, realised it was empty and held it aloft for a refill. 'Bring me more spirit! And Temple, come, talk to me as you used to! Offer me comfort, Temple, offer me advice.'

Temple took a long breath. 'I'm not sure what advice I can offer. We're far beyond the reach of the law out here.'

'I don't speak of the law, man, but of the righteous path! Thank you.' This as Sergeant Friendly began to decant a freshly opened bottle into Cosca's waving flask with masterful precision. 'I feel I am adrift upon strange seas and my moral compass spins entirely haywire! Find me an ethical star to steer by, Temple! What of God, man, what of God?'

'I fear we may be far beyond the reach of God as well,' muttered Temple as he made for the door. Hedges limped in as he opened it, clutching tight to his ruin of a hat and looking sicker than ever, if that was possible.

'Who's this now?' demanded Cosca, peering into the shadows.

'The name's Hedges, Captain General, sir, one of the drovers from Crease. Injured at Osrung, sir, leading a charge.'

'The very reason charges are best left led by others.'

Hedges sidled past into the room, eyes nervously darting. 'Can't say I disagree, sir. Might I have a moment?' Grateful for the distraction, Temple slipped out into the bitter darkness.

In the camp's one street, secrecy did not seem a prime concern. Men swathed in coats and furs, swaddled in torn-up blankets and mismatched armour stomped cursing about, churning the snow to black slush, holding rustling torches high, dragging reluctant horses, unloading boxes and barrels from listing wagons, breath steaming from wrappings around their faces.

'Might I accompany you?' asked Sworbreck, threading after Temple through the chaos.

'If you're not scared my luck will rub off.'

'It could be no worse than mine,' lamented the biographer.

They passed a group huddled in a hut with one missing wall, playing dice for bedding, a man sharpening blades at a shrieking grindstone, sparks showering into the night, three women arguing over how best to get a cook-fire started. None had the answer.

'Do you ever feel . . .' Sworbreck mused, face squashed down for warmth into the threadbare collar of his coat, 'as though you have somehow blundered into a situation you never intended to be in, but now cannot see your way clear of?'

Temple looked sidelong at the writer. 'Lately, every moment of every day.'

'As if you were being punished, but you were not sure what for.'

'I know what for,' muttered Temple.

'I don't belong here,' said Sworbreck.

'I wish I could say the same. But I fear that I do.'

Snow had been dug away from one of the barrows and torchlight flickered in its moss-caked archway. One of the pimps was busy hanging a worn hide at the entrance of another, a disorderly queue already forming outside. A shivering pedlar had set up shop between the two, offering belts and boot-polish to the heedless night. Commerce never sleeps.

Temple caught Inquisitor Lorsen's grating tones emerging from a cabin's half-open door, '. . . Do you really believe there are rebels in these mountains, Dimbik?'

'Belief is a luxury I have not been able to afford for some time, Inquisitor. I simply do as I'm told.'

'But by whom, Captain, by whom is the question. I, after all, have the ear of Superior Pike, and the Superior has the ear of the Arch Lector himself, and a recommendation from the Arch Lector . . .' His scheming was lost in the babble.

In the darkness at the edge of the camp, Temple's erstwhile fellows were already mounting up. It had begun to snow again, white specks gently settling on the manes of the horses, on Crying Rock's grey hair and the old flag it was bound up with, across Shy's shoulders, hunched as she steadfastly refused to look over, on the packages Lamb was busy stowing on his horse.

'Coming with us?' asked Savian as he watched Temple approach.

'My heart is willing but the rest of me has the good sense to politely decline.'

'Crying Rock!' Sworbreck produced his notebook with a flourish. 'It is a most intriguing name!'

She stared down at him. 'Yes.'

'I daresay an intriguing story lies behind it.'

'Yes.'

'Would you care to share it?'

Crying Rock slowly rode off into the gathering darkness.

'I'd call that a no,' said Shy.

Sworbreck sighed. 'A writer must learn to flourish on scorn. No passage, sentence or even word can be to the taste of *every* reader. Master Lamb, have you ever been interviewed by an author?'

'We've run across just about every other kind of liar,' said Shy.

The biographer persisted. 'I've heard it said that you have more experience of single combat than any man alive.'

Lamb pulled the last of the straps tight. 'You believe everything you hear?'

'Do you deny it, then?'

Lamb did not speak.

'Have you any insights into the deadly business, for my readers?'

'Don't do it.'

Sworbreck stepped closer. 'But is it true what General Cosca tells me?'

'From what I've seen, I wouldn't rate him the yardstick of honesty.'

'He told me you were once a king.'

Temple raised his brows. Sweet cleared his throat. Shy burst out laughing, but then she saw Lamb wasn't, and trailed off.

'He told me you were champion to the King of the Northmen,' continued Sworbreck, 'and that you won ten duels in the Circle in his name, were betrayed by him but survived, and finally killed him and took his place.'

Lamb dragged himself slowly up into his saddle and frowned off into the night. 'Men put a golden chain on me for a while, and knelt, because it suited 'em. In violent times folk like to kneel to violent men. In peaceful times they remember they're happier standing.'

'Do you blame them?'

'I'm long past blaming. That's just the way men are.' Lamb looked over at Temple. 'Can we count on your man Cosca, do you reckon?'

'Absolutely not,' said Temple.

'Had a feeling you'd say that.' And Lamb nudged his horse uphill into the darkness.

'And they say I've got stories,' grumbled Sweet as he followed.

Sworbreck stared after them for a moment, then fumbled out his pencil and began to scratch feverishly away.

Temple met Shy's eye as she turned her mount. 'I hope you find them!' he blurted. 'The children.'

'We will. Hope you find . . . whatever you're looking for.'

'I think I did,' he said softly. 'And I threw it away.'

She sat there a moment as though considering what to say, then clicked her tongue and her horse walked on.

'Good luck!' he called after her. 'Take care of yourself, among the barbarians!'

She glanced over towards the fort, from which the sounds of off-key singing were already beginning to float, and raised one eyebrow. 'Likewise.'

Bait

The first day they rode through towering forest, trees far bigger'n Shy ever saw, branch upon branch upon branch blocking out the sun so she felt they stole through some giant's crypt, sombre and sacred. The snow had found its way in still, drifted a stride deep between the crusted trunks, frozen to a sparkling crust that skinned the horse's legs, so they had to take turns breaking new ground. Here and there a freezing fog had gathered, curling round men and mounts as they passed like spirits jealous of their warmth. Not that there was much of that to be had. Crying Rock gave a warning hiss whenever anyone started in to talk so they just nodded in dumb misery to the crunching of snow and the laboured breaths of the struggling horses, Savian's coughing and a soft mumbling from Jubair which Shy took for prayers. He was a pious bastard, the big Kantic, that you couldn't deny. Whether piety made him a safe man to have at your back she profoundly doubted. Folk she'd known to be big on religion had tended to use it as an excuse for doing wrong rather'n a reason not to.

Only when the light had faded to a twilight glimmer did Sweet lead them to a shallow cave under an overhang and let them stop. By then the mounts and the spare mounts were all blown and shuddering and Shy wasn't in a state much better, her whole body one stiff and aching, numbed and prickling, chafed and stinging competition of complaints.

No fire allowed, they ate cold meat and hard biscuit and passed about a bottle. Savian put a hard face over his coughing like he did over everything else, but Shy could tell he was troubled with it, bent and hacking and his pale hands clawing his coat shut at his neck.

One of the mercenaries, a Styrian with a jutting jaw by the name of Sacri, who struck Shy as the sort whose only comfort in life is others' discomfort, grinned and said, 'You got a cough, old man. You want to go back?'

Shy said, 'Shut your mouth,' with as much fire as she could muster which right then wasn't much.

'What'll you do?' he sneered at her. 'Slap me?'

That struck a hotter spark from her. 'That's right. With a fucking axe. Now shut your mouth.'

This time he did shut it, too, but by the moon's glimmering she gathered he was working out how to even the score, and reckoned she'd better mind her back even closer than before.

They kept watch in pairs, one from the mercenaries, one from the Fellowship that had been, and they watched each other every bit as hard as they watched the night for Dragon People. Shy marked time by Sweet's snoring, and when the moment came she shook Lamb and whispered in his ear.

'Wake up, your Majesty.'

He gave a grunting sigh. 'Wondered how long it'd be 'fore that floated up again.'

'Pardon the foolishness of a witless peasant. I'm just overcome at having the King of the Northmen snoring in my blankets.'

'I spent ten times as long poorer'n a beggar and without a friend to my name. Why does no one want to talk about that?'

'In my case 'cause I know well enough what that feels like. I haven't had occasion to wear a crown that often.'

'Neither have I,' he said, crawling stiffly clear of the bedding. 'I had a chain.'

'A golden one?'

'With a diamond like that.' And he made a shape the size of a hen's egg with his thumb and forefinger and eyed her through it.

She still wasn't sure whether this was all some kind of a joke. 'You.'

'Me.'

'That got through a whole winter in one pair of trousers.'

He shrugged. 'I'd lost the chain by then.'

'Any particular way I should act around royalty?'

'The odd curtsy wouldn't go amiss.'

She snorted. 'Fuck yourself.'

'Fuck yourself, *your Majesty*.'

'King Lamb,' she muttered, crawling into the blankets to make the most of his already fading warmth. 'King Lamb.'

'I had a different name.'

Shy looked sideways at him. 'What name?'

He sat there in the wide mouth of the cave, hunched black against

317

the star-speckled night, and she couldn't guess at what was on his face. 'Don't matter,' he said. 'No good ever came of it.'

Next morning the snow whirled down on a wind that came from every way at once, bitter as a bankrupt. They mounted up with all the joy of folk riding to their own hangings and pressed on, uphill, uphill. The forest thinned out, trees shrinking, withering, twisting like folk in pain. They threaded through bare rocks and the way grew narrow – an old stream bed, maybe, though sometimes it looked more like a man-made stair worn almost smooth by years and weather. Jubair sent one of his men back with the horses and Shy half-wished she was going with him. The rest of them toiled on by foot.

'What the hell are these Dragon bastards doing up here anyhow?' Shy grunted at Sweet. Didn't seem like a place anyone in their right mind would want to visit, let alone live in.

'Can't say I know exactly . . . why they're up here.' The old scout had to talk in rushes between his heaving breaths. 'But they been here a long time.'

'She hasn't told you?' asked Shy, nodding at Crying Rock, striding on hard up ahead.

'I reckon it's on account . . . o' my reluctance to ask those kind o' questions . . . she's stuck with me down the years.'

'Ain't for your good looks, I can tell you that.'

'There's more to life than looks.' He glanced sideways at her. 'Luckily for us both.'

'What would they want with children?'

He stopped to take a swallow of water and offered one to her while the mercenaries laboured past under the considerable burden of their many weapons. 'The way I hear it, no children are born here. Something in the land. They turn barren. All the Dragon People were taken from someone else, one time or another. Used to be that meant Ghosts mostly, maybe Imperials, the odd Northman strayed down from the Sea of Teeth. Looks like since the prospectors drove the Ghosts out they're casting their net wider. Buying children off the likes of Cantliss.'

'Less talk!' hissed Crying Rock from above. 'More walk!'

The snow came down weightier than ever but didn't drift as deep, and when Shy peeled the wrappings off her face she found the wind wasn't half so keen. An hour later the snow was slippery slush on the wet rock, and she pulled her soaked gloves off and could still feel her fingertips. An hour after that the snow still fell but the ground was bare, and Shy was sweating fast enough she had to strip her coat off and wedge it in her pack. The others were doing the same. She bent and pressed her palm to the earth and there was a strange warmth, like it was the wall of a baker's and the oven was stoked on the other side.

'There is fire below,' said Crying Rock.

'There is?' Shy snatched her hand back like flames might pop from the dirt then and there. 'Can't say that notion floods a woman with optimism.'

'Better'n freezing the crap up my arse, ain't it?' said Sweet, pulling his shirt off to reveal another underneath. Shy wondered how many he had on. Or if he'd keep taking them off until he disappeared altogether.

'Is that why the Dragon People live up here?' Savian pressed his own palm to the warm dirt. 'Because of the fire?'

'Or because they live here there is a fire.' Crying Rock stared up the slope, bare rock and scree now, crusted in places with stains of yellow sulphur, overlooked by a towering bastard of a rock face. 'This way may be watched.'

'Certainly it will be,' said Jubair. 'God sees all.'

'Ain't God as'll put an arrow in your arse if we keep on this path,' said Sweet.

Jubair shrugged. 'God puts all things where they must be.'

'What now, then?' asked Savian.

Crying Rock was already uncoiling a rope from her pack. 'Now we climb.'

Shy rubbed at her temples. 'Had a nasty feeling she'd say that.'

Damn it if the climbing wasn't even harder than the walking and a long drop scarier. Crying Rock swarmed up like a spider and Lamb wasn't much slower, seeming well at home among the mountains, the two of them getting ropes ready for the rest. Shy brought up the rear with Savian, cursing and fumbling at the slick rock, arms aching from the effort and her hands burning from the hemp.

'Haven't had the chance to thank you,' she said as she waited on a ledge.

He didn't make a sound but the hissing of the rope through his gnarled hands as he pulled it up behind them.

'For what you did back in Crease.' Silence. 'Ain't had my life saved so often that I overlook it.' Silence. 'Remember?'

She thought he gave the tiniest shrug.

'Get the feeling you've been avoiding mention of it.'

Silence. He avoided mentioning anything wherever possible.

'Probably you ain't much of a one for taking thanks.'

More silence.

'Probably I ain't much of a one for giving 'em.'

'You're taking your time about it, all right.'

'Thanks, then. Reckon I'd be good and dead if it weren't for you.'

Savian pressed his thin lips together even tighter and gave a throaty grunt. 'Reckon you or your father would've done the same for me.'

'He ain't my father.'

'That's between you two. But if you were to ask, I'd say you could do worse.'

Shy snorted. 'I used to think so.'

'This isn't what he wanted, you know. Or the way he wanted it.'

'I used to think that, too. Not so sure any more. Family, eh?'

'Family.'

'Where's Corlin got to?'

'She can look after herself.'

'Oh, no doubt.' Shy dropped her voice. 'Look, Savian, I know what you are.'

He looked up at her hard. 'That so?'

'I know what you got under there,' and she moved her eyes down to his forearms, blue with tattoos, she knew, under his coat.

'Can't fathom your meaning,' but tweaking one of his sleeves down even so.

She leaned closer and whispered, 'Just pretend you can, then. When Cosca got to talking about rebels, well, my big fucking mouth ran away with me, like always. I meant well, like always, trying to help out . . . but I haven't, have I?'

'Not a lot.'

'My fault you're in this fix. If that bastard Lorsen finds out what you got there . . . what I'm saying is, you should go. This ain't your fight. Naught to stop you slipping away, and no shortage of empty to slip into.'

'And you'd say what? Forgot all about my lost boy, did I? It'd just make 'em curious. Might make trouble for you. Might make trouble for me, in the end. Reckon I'll just keep my head down and my sleeves down too and stick with you. Best all round.'

'My big fucking mouth,' she hissed to herself.

Savian grinned. It might have been the first time she'd ever seen him do it and it was like a lantern uncovered, the lines shifting in his weathered face and his eyes suddenly gleaming. 'You know what? Your big fucking mouth ain't to everyone's taste but I've almost got to like it.' And he put his hand down on her shoulder and gave it a squeeze. 'You'd best watch out for that prick Sacri, though. Don't think he sees it that way.'

Nor did she. Not long after that, a rock came clattering down that missed her head by a whisker. She saw Sacri grinning above and was sure he'd kicked it loose on purpose. Soon as she got the chance she told him so and where she'd stick her knife if another rock came along. The other mercenaries were quite tickled by her language.

'I should teach you some manners, girl,' snapped Sacri, sticking his jutting jaw out even further, trying to save what face he could.

'You'd have to fucking know some to teach some.'

He put his hand on his sword, more bluster than meaning to use it, but before he even got the chance Jubair loomed between them.

'There will be weapons drawn, Sacri,' he said, 'but when and against whom I say. These are our allies. We need them to show us the way. Leave the woman be or we will quarrel and a quarrel with me is a heavy weight to carry.'

'Sorry, Captain,' said Sacri, scowling.

Jubair offered him the way with one open hand. 'Regret is the gateway to salvation.'

Lamb scarcely even looked over while they were arguing, and trudged off when they were done like none of it was his concern.

'Thanks for your help back there,' she snapped as she caught him up.

'You'd have had it if you'd needed it. You know that.'

'A word or two wouldn't have hurt.'

He leaned close. 'Way I see it, we've got two choices. Try and use these bastards, or kill 'em all. Hard words have never won a battle yet, but they've lost a few. You mean to kill a man, telling him so don't help.'

Lamb walked on, and left her to think about that.

They camped near a steaming stream that Sweet said not to drink from. Not that anyone was keen to try since it smelled like feast-day farts. All night the water hissing in Shy's ears and she dreamed of falling. Woke sweating with her throat raw from the warm stink to see Sacri on guard and watching her and thought she caught the gleam of metal in his hand. She lay awake after that, her own knife drawn in her fist. The way she had long ago when she was on the run. The way she'd hoped she never would again. She found herself wishing that Temple was there. Surely the man was no hero, but somehow he made her feel braver.

In the morning, grey shadows of crags loomed over them that through the shifting veil of snow looked like the ruins of walls, towers, fortresses. Holes were cut in the rock, too square to be natural, and near them mounds of spoil.

'Prospectors get this far?' one of the mercenaries asked.

Sweet shook his head. 'Nowhere near. These is older diggings.'

'How much older?'

'Much older,' said Crying Rock.

'Seems like the closer we get the more I worry,' Shy muttered at Lamb as they set off, bent and sore.

He nodded. 'Starting to think about all the thousand things could go wrong.'

'Scared we won't find 'em.'

'Or scared we will.'

'Or just plain scared,' she muttered.

'Scared is good,' he said. 'The dead are fearless and I don't want either of us joining 'em.'

They stopped beside a deep gorge, the sound of water moving far below, steam rising and everywhere the reek of brimstone. An arch spanned the canyon, black rock slick with wet and bearded with dripping icicles of lime. From its middle a great chain hung, links a stride high, rust-eaten metal squealing faintly as the wind stirred them. Savian sat with his head back, breathing hard. The mercenaries slouched in a group nearby, passing round a flask.

'And here she is!' Sacri chuckled. 'The child hunter!' Shy looked at him, and at the drop beside him, and thought how dearly she'd like to introduce one to the other. 'What kind of fool would hope to find children alive in a place like this?'

'Why do big mouths and little brains so often go together?' she muttered, but she thought about Lamb's words, realised her question might apply to herself just as easily, and stopped her tongue for once.

'Nothing to say?' Sacri grinned down his nose as he tipped his flask up. 'At least you've learned some—'

Jubair put out a great arm and brushed him off the cliff. The Styrian made a choking whoop, flask tumbling from his hand, and he was gone. A thump and a clatter of stones, then another, and another, fading out of hearing in the gorge below.

The mercenaries stared, one with a piece of dried meat halfway to his open mouth. Shy watched, skin prickling, as Jubair stepped to the brink, lips thoughtfully pursed, and looked down. 'The world is filled with folly and waste,' he said. 'It is enough to shake a man's faith.'

'You killed him,' said one of the mercenaries, with that talent for stating the obvious some men have.

'God killed him. I was but the instrument.'

'God sure can be a thorny bastard, can't He?' croaked Savian.

Jubair solemnly nodded. 'He is a terrible and a merciless God and all things must bend to His design.'

'His design's left us a man short,' said Sweet.

Jubair shrugged his pack over his shoulder. 'Better that than discord. We must be together in this. If we disagree, how can God be for all of us?' He waved Crying Rock forward, and let his surviving men step, more than a little nervously, past him, one swallowing as he peered down into the gorge.

Jubair took Sacri's fallen flask from the brink. 'In the city of Ul-Nahb in Gurkhul, where I was born, thanks be to the Almighty, death is a great thing. All efforts are taken with the body and a family wails and a procession of mourners follows the flower-strewn way to the place of burial. Out here, death is a little thing. A man who expects more than one chance is a fool.' He frowned out at the vast arch and its broken chain, and took a thoughtful swig. 'The further I go into the unmapped extremes of this country, the more I become convinced these are the end times.'

Lamb plucked the flask from Jubair's hand, drained it, then tossed it after its owner. 'All times are end times for someone.'

They squatted among ruined walls, between stones salt-streaked and crystal-crusted, and watched the valley. They'd been watching it for what felt like for ever, squinting into the sticky mist while Crying Rock hissed at them to keep low, stay out of sight, shut their mouths. Shy was getting just a little tired of being hissed at. She was getting a little tired altogether. Tired, and sore, and her nerves worn down to aching stubs with fear, and worry, and hope. Hope worst of all.

Now and again Savian broke out in muffled coughs and Shy could hardly blame him. The very valley seemed to breathe, acrid steam rising from hidden cracks and turning the broken boulders to phantoms, drifting down to make a fog over the pool in the valley's bottom, slowly fading only to gather again.

Jubair sat cross-legged, eyes closed and arms folded, huge and patient, lips silently moving, a sheen of sweat across his forehead.

They all were sweating. Shy's shirt was plastered to her back, hair stuck clammy to her face. She could hardly believe she'd felt close to death from cold a day or two before. She'd have given her teeth to strip and drop into a snowdrift now. She crawled over to Crying Rock, the stones wet and sticky warm under her palms.

'They're close?'

The Ghost shifted her frown up and down a fraction.

'Where?'

'If I knew that, I would not have to watch.'

'We leave this bait soon?'

'Soon.'

'I hope it ain't really a turd you got in mind,' grunted Sweet, surely down to his last shirt now, ''cause I don't fancy dropping my trousers here.'

'Shut up,' hissed Crying Rock, sticking her hand out hard behind her.

A shadow was shifting in the murk on the valley's side, a figure hopping from one boulder to another. Hard to tell for the distance and the mist but it looked like a man, tall and heavy-built, dark-skinned, bald-headed, a staff carried loose in one hand.

'Is he whistling?' Shy muttered.

'Shh,' hissed Crying Rock.

The old man left his staff beside a flat rock at the water's edge, shrugged off his robe and left it folded carefully on top, then did a little dance, spinning naked in and out of some broken pillars at the shoreline.

'He don't look all that fearsome,' whispered Shy.

'Oh, he is fearsome,' said Crying Rock. 'He is Waerdinur. My brother.'

Shy looked at her, pale as new milk, then back to the dark-skinned man, still whistling as he waded out into the pool. 'Ain't much resemblance.'

'We came of different wombs.'

'Good to know.'

'What is?'

'Had a feeling you might've hatched from an egg, you're that painless.'

'I have my pains,' said Crying Rock. 'But they must serve me, not the other way about.' And she stuck the stained stem of her pipe between her jaws and chomped down hard on it.

'What is Lamb doing?' came Jubair's voice.

Shy turned and stared. Lamb was scurrying through the boulders and down towards the water, already twenty strides away.

'Oh, hell,' muttered Sweet.

'Shit!' Shy forced her stiff knees into life and vaulted over the crumbling wall. Sweet made a grab at her but she slapped his hand off and threaded after Lamb, one eye on the old man still splashing happily below them, his whistling floating through the mist. She winced and skidded over the slick rocks, almost on all fours, ankles aching as her feet were jarred this way and that, burning to shout to Lamb but knowing she couldn't make a peep.

He was too far ahead to catch, had made it all the way down to the water's edge. She could only watch as he perched on that flat rock with the folded robe as a cushion, laid his drawn sword across one knee, took out his whetstone and licked it. She flinched as he set it to the blade and gave it a single grating stroke.

Shy caught the surprise in the tightening of Waerdinur's shoulders, but he didn't move right off. Only as the second stroke cut the silence did he slowly turn. A kind face, Shy would've said, but she'd seen kind-looking men do some damned mean things before.

'Here is a surprise.' Though he seemed more puzzled than shocked as his dark eyes shifted from Lamb to Shy and back again. 'Where did you two come from?'

'All the way from the Near Country,' said Lamb.

'The name means nothing to me.' Waerdinur spoke common without much of an accent. More'n likely he spoke it better'n Shy did. 'There is only here and not here. How did you get here?'

'Rode some, walked the rest,' grunted Lamb. 'Or do you mean, how did we get here without you knowing?' He gave his sword another shrieking stroke. 'Maybe you ain't as clever as you think you are.'

Waerdinur shrugged his broad shoulders. 'Only a fool supposes he knows everything.'

Lamb held up the sword, checked one side and the other, blade flashing. 'I've got some friends waiting, down in Beacon.'

'I had heard.'

'They're killers and thieves and men of no character. They've come for your gold.'

'Who says we have any?'

'A man named Cantliss.'

'Ah.' Waerdinur splashed water on his arms and carried on washing.

'That is a man of no substance. A breeze would blow him away. You are not one such, though, I think.' His eyes moved across to Shy, weighing her, no sign of fear at all. 'Neither of you. I do not think you came for gold.'

'We came for my brother and sister,' grated Shy, voice harsh as the stone on the blade.

'Ah.' Waerdinur's smile slowly faded as he considered her, then he hung his head, water trickling down his shaved scalp. 'You are Shy. She said you would come and I did not believe her.'

'Ro said?' Her throat almost closing up around the words. 'She's alive?'

'Healthy and flourishing, safe and valued. Her brother, too.'

Shy's knees went for a moment and she had to lean on the rock beside Lamb.

'You have come a long, hard way,' said Waerdinur. 'I congratulate you on your courage.'

'We didn't come for your fucking congratulations!' she spat at him. 'We came for the children!'

'I know. But they are better off with us.'

'You think I care a fuck?' There was a look on Lamb's face then, vicious as an old fighting dog, made Shy go cold all over. 'This ain't about them. You've stolen from me, fucker. From *me*!' Spit flicked from his bared teeth as he stabbed at his chest with a finger. 'And I'll have back what's mine or I'll have blood.'

Waerdinur narrowed his eyes. 'You, she did not mention.'

'I got one o' those forgettable faces. Bring the children down to Beacon, you can forget it, too.'

'I am sorry but I cannot. They are my children now. They are Dragon People, and I have sworn to protect this sacred ground and those upon it with my last blood and breath. Only death will stop me.'

'He won't stop me.' Lamb gave his sword another grinding lick. 'He's had a thousand chances and never took a one.'

'Do you think death fears you?'

'Death loves me.' Lamb smiled, black-eyed, wet-eyed, and the smile was worse even than the snarl had been. 'All the work I done for him? The crowds I've sent his way? He knows he ain't got no better friends.'

The leader of the Dragon People looked back sad and level. 'If we must fight it would be . . . a shame.'

'Lot o' things are,' said Lamb. 'I gave up trying to change 'em a long time ago.' He stood and slid his sword back into its sheath with a scraping whisper. 'Three days to bring the children down to Beacon. Then I come back to your sacred ground.' He curled his tongue and blew spit into the water. 'And I'll bring death with me.' And he started picking his way back towards the ruins on the valley side.

Shy and Waerdinur looked at each other a moment longer. 'I am sorry,' he said. 'For what has happened, and for what must happen now.'

She turned and hurried to catch up to Lamb. What else could she do?

'You didn't mean that, did you?' she hissed at his back, slipping and sliding on the broken rocks. 'About the children? That this ain't about them? That it's about blood?' She tripped and skinned her shin, cursed and stumbled on. 'Tell me you didn't mean that!'

'He got my meaning,' snapped Lamb over his shoulder. 'Trust me.'

But there was the problem – Shy was finding that harder every day. 'Weren't you just saying that when you mean to kill a man, telling him so don't help?'

Lamb shrugged. 'There's a time for breaking every rule.'

'What the hell did you do?' hissed Sweet when they clambered back into the ruin, scrubbing at his wet hair with his fingernails and no one else looking too happy about their unplanned expedition either.

'I left him some bait he'll have to take,' said Lamb.

Shy glanced back through one of the cracks towards the water. Waerdinur was only now wading to the shore, scraping the wet from his body, putting on his robe, no rush. He picked up his staff, looked towards the ruins for a while, then turned and strode away through the rocks.

'You have made things difficult.' Crying Rock had already stowed her pipe and was tightening her straps for the trip back. 'They will be coming now, and quickly. We must return to Beacon.'

'I ain't going back,' said Lamb.

'What?' asked Shy.

'That was the agreement,' said Jubair. 'That we would draw them out.'

'You draw 'em out. Delay's the parent o' disaster, and I ain't waiting for Cosca to blunder up here drunk and get my children killed.'

'What the hell?' Shy was tiring of not knowing what Lamb would do one moment to the next. 'What's the plan now, then?'

'Plans have a habit o' falling apart when you lean on 'em,' said Lamb. 'We'll just have to think up another.'

The Kantic cracked a bastard of a frown. 'I do not like a man who breaks an agreement.'

'Try and push me off a cliff.' Lamb gave Jubair a flat stare. 'We can find out who God likes best.'

Jubair pressed one fingertip against his lips and considered that for a long, silent moment. Then he shrugged. 'I prefer not to trouble God with every little thing.'

Savages

'**I**'ve finished the spear!' called Pit, doing his best to say the new words just the way Ro had taught him, and he offered it up for his father to see. It was a good spear. Shepat had helped him with the binding and declared it excellent, and everyone said that the only man who knew more about weapons than Shepat was the Maker himself, who knew more about everything than anyone, of course. So Shepat knew a lot about weapons, was the point, and he said it was good, so it must be good.

'Good,' said Pit's father, but he didn't really look. He was walking fast, bare feet slapping against the ancient bronze, and frowning. Pit wasn't sure he'd ever seen him frown before. Pit wondered if he'd done wrong. If his father could tell his new name still sounded strange to him. He felt ungrateful, and guilty, and worried that he'd done something very bad even though he hadn't meant to.

'What have I done?' he asked, having to hurry to keep up, and realised he'd slipped back to his old talk without thinking.

His father frowned down, and it seemed then he did it from a very long way up.

'Who is Lamb?'

Pit blinked. It was about the last thing he'd expected his father to ask.

'Lamb's my father,' he said without thinking, then put it right, '*was* my father, maybe . . . but Shy always said he wasn't.' Maybe neither of them were his father or maybe both, and thinking about Shy made him think about the farm and the bad things, and Gully saying run, run, and the journey across the plains and into the mountains and Cantliss laughing and he didn't know what he'd done wrong and he started to cry and he felt ashamed and so he cried more, and he said, 'Don't send me back.'

'No!' said Pit's father. 'Never!' Because he was Pit's father, you

329

could see it in the pain in his face. 'Only death will part us, do you understand?'

Pit didn't understand the least bit but he nodded anyway, crying now with relief that everything would be all right, and his father smiled, and knelt beside him, and put his hand on Pit's head.

'I am sorry.' And Waerdinur was sorry, truly and completely, and he spoke in the Outsiders' tongue because he knew it was easier on the boy. 'It is a fine spear, and you a fine son.' And he patted his son's shaved scalp. 'We will go hunting, and soon, but there is business I must see to first, for all the Dragon People are my family. Can you play with your sister until I call for you?'

He nodded, blinking back tears. He cried easily, the boy, and that was a fine thing, for the Maker taught that closeness to one's feelings was closeness to the divine.

'Good. And . . . do not speak to her of this.'

Waerdinur strode to the Long House, his frown returning. Six of the Gathering were naked in the hot dimness, hazy in the steam, sitting on the polished stones around the fire-pit, listening to Uto sing the lessons, words of the Maker's father, all-mighty Euz, who split the worlds and spoke the First Law. Her voice faltered as he strode in.

'There were outsiders at the Seeking Pool,' he growled as he stripped off his robe, ignoring the proper forms and not caring.

The others stared upon him, shocked, as well they might be. 'Are you sure?' Ulstal's croaking voice croakier still from breathing the Seeing Steam.

'I spoke to them! Scarlaer?'

The young hunter stood, tall and strong and the eagerness to act hot in his eye. Sometimes he reminded Waerdinur so much of his younger self it was like gazing in Juvens' glass, through which it was said one could look into the past.

'Take your best trackers and follow them. They were in the ruins on the north side of the valley.'

'I will hunt them down,' said Scarlaer.

'They were an old man and a young woman, but they might not be alone. Go armed and take care. They are dangerous.' He thought of the man's dead smile, and his black eye, like gazing into a great depth, and was sore troubled. 'Very dangerous.'

'I will catch them,' said the hunter. 'You can depend on me.'

'I do. Go.'

He bounded from the hall and Waerdinur took his place at the fire-pit, the heat of it close to painful before him, perching on the rounded stone where no position was comfortable, for the Maker said they should never be comfortable who weigh great matters. He took the ladle and poured a little water on the coals, and the hall grew gloomier yet with steam, rich with the scents of mint and pine and all the blessed spices. He was already sweating, and silently asked the Maker that he sweat out his folly and his pride and make pure choices.

'Outsiders at the Seeking Pool?' Hirfac's withered face was slack with disbelief. 'How did they come to the sacred ground?'

'They came to the barrows with the twenty Outsiders,' said Waerdinur. 'How they came further I cannot say.'

'Our decision on those twenty is more pressing.' Akarin's blind eyes were narrowed. They all knew what decision he would favour. Akarin tended bloody, and bloodier with each passing winter. Age sometimes distils a person – rendering the calm more calm, the violent more violent.

'Why have they come?' Uto leaned forward into the light, shadow patching in the hollows of her skull. 'What do they want?'

Waerdinur glanced around the old sweat-beaded faces and licked his lips. If they knew the man and woman had come for his children they might ask him to give them up. A faint chance, but a chance, and he would give them up to no one but death. It was forbidden to lie to the Gathering, but the Maker set down no prohibition on offering half the truth.

'What all outsiders want,' said Waerdinur. 'Gold.'

Hirfac spread her gnarled hands. 'Perhaps we should give it to them? We have enough.'

'They would always want more.' Shebat's voice was low and sad. 'Theirs is a hunger never satisfied.'

A silence while all considered, and the coals shifted and hissed in the pit and sparks whirled and glowed in the dark and the sweet smell of the Seeing Steam washed out among them.

The colours of fire shifted across Akarin's face as he nodded. 'We must send everyone who can hold a blade. Eighty of us are there, fit to go, who did not travel north to fight the Shanka?'

'Eighty swords upon my racks.' Shebat shook his head as if that was a matter for regret.

'It worries me to leave Ashranc guarded only by the old and young,' said Hirfac. 'So few of us now—'

'Soon we will wake the Dragon.' Ulstal smiled at the thought.

'Soon.'

'Soon.'

'Next summer,' said Waerdinur, 'or perhaps the summer after. But for now we must protect ourselves.'

'We must drive them out!' Akarin slapped knobbly fist into palm. 'We must journey to the barrows and drive out the savages.'

'Drive them out?' Uto snorted. 'Call it what it is, since you will not be the one to wield the blade.'

'I wielded blades enough in my time. Kill them, then, if you prefer to call it that. Kill them all.'

'We killed them all, and here are more.'

'What should we do, then?' he asked, mocking her. 'Welcome them to our sacred places with arms wide?'

'Perhaps the time has come to consider it.' Akarin snorted with disgust, Ulstal winced as though at blasphemy, Hirfac shook her head, but Uto went on. 'Were we not all born savage? Did not the Maker teach us to first speak peace?'

'So he did,' said Shebat.

'I will not hear this!' Ulstal struggled to his feet, wheezing with the effort.

'You will.' Waerdinur waved him down. 'You will sit and sweat and listen as all sit and listen here. Uto has earned her right to speak.' And Waerdinur held her eye. 'But she is wrong. Savages at the Seeking Pool? Outsiders' boots upon the sacred ground? Upon the stones where trod the Maker's feet?' The others groaned at each new outrage, and Waerdinur knew he had them. 'What should we do, Uto?'

'I do not like that there are only six to make the choice—'

'Six is enough,' said Akarin.

Uto saw they were all fixed on the steel road and she sighed, and reluctantly nodded. 'We kill them all.'

'Then the Gathering has spoken.' Waerdinur stood, and took the blessed pouch from the altar, knelt and scooped up a handful of dirt from the floor, the sacred dirt of Ashranc, warm and damp with life, and he put it in the pouch and offered it to Uto. 'You spoke against this, you must lead.'

She slipped from her stone and took the pouch. 'I do not rejoice in this,' she said.

'It is not necessary that we rejoice. Only that we do. Prepare the weapons.' And Waerdinur put his hand on Shebat's shoulder.

*

Shebat slowly nodded, slowly rose, slowly put on his robe. He was no young man any more and it took time, especially since, even if he saw the need, there was no eagerness in his heart. Death sat close beside him, he knew, too close for him to revel in bringing it to others.

He shuffled from the steam and to the archway as the horn was sounded, shrill and grating, to arms, to arms, the younger people putting aside their tasks and stepping out into the evening, preparing themselves for the journey, kissing their closest farewell. There would be no more than sixty left behind, and those children and old ones. Old and useless and sitting close to death, as he was.

He passed the Heartwoods, and patted his fondly, and felt the need to work upon it, and so he took out his knife, and considered, and finally stripped the slightest shaving. That would be today's change. Tomorrow might bring another. He wondered how many of the People had worked upon it before his birth. How many would work upon it after his death.

Into the stone darkness he went, the weight of mountains heavy above him, the flickering oil wicks making gleam the Maker's designs, set into the stone of the floor in thrice-blessed metal. Shebat's footsteps echoed in the silence, through the first hall to the place of weapons, his sore leg dragging behind him. Old wound, old wound that never heals. The glory of victory lasts a moment, the wounds are always. Though he loved the weapons, for the Maker taught the love of metal and of the thing well made and fitted for its purpose, he gave them out only with regret.

'For the Maker taught also that each blow struck is its own failure,' he sang softly as one blade at a time he emptied the racks, wood polished smooth by the fingertips of his forebears. 'Victory is only in the hand taken, in the soft word spoken, in the gift freely given.' But he watched the faces of the young ones as they took from him the tools of death, hot and eager, and feared they heard his words but let their meaning slip away. Too often of late the Gathering spoke in steel.

Uto came last, as fitted the leader. Shebat still thought she should have been the Right Hand, but in these hard days soft words rarely found willing ears. Shebat handed her the final blade.

'This one I kept for you. Forged with my own hands, when I was young and strong and had no doubts. My best work. Sometimes the metal . . .' and he rubbed dry fingertips against thumb as he sought the words, 'comes out *right*.'

She sadly smiled as she took the sword. 'Will this come out right, do you think?'

'We can hope.'

'I worry we have lost our way. There was a time I felt so sure of the path I had only to walk forward and I would be upon it. Now I am hemmed in by doubts and know not which way to turn.'

'Waerdinur wants what is best for us.' But Shebat wondered if it was himself he struggled to convince.

'So do we all. But we disagree on what is best and how to get it. Waerdinur is a good man, and strong, and loving, and can be admired for many reasons.'

'You say that as if it is a bad thing.'

'It makes us likely to agree when we had better consider. The soft voices are all lost in the babble. Because Waerdinur is full of fire. He burns to wake the Dragon. To make the world as it was.'

'Would that be such a bad thing?'

'No. But the world does not go back.' She lifted the blade he had given her and looked at it, the flickering reflection of the lights on her face. 'I am afraid.'

'You?' he said. 'Never!'

'Always. Not of our enemies. Of ourselves.'

'The Maker taught us it is not fear, but how we face it that counts. Be well, my old friend.' And he folded Uto in his arms, and wished that he was young again.

They marched through the High Gate swift and sure, for once the Gathering has debated the arguments and spoken its judgement there is no purpose in delay. They marched with swords sharpened and shields slung that had been ancient in the days of Uto's great-grandfather's great-grandfather. They marched over the names of their ancestors, etched in bronze, and Uto asked herself whether those Dragon People of the past would have stood shoulder to shoulder with this cause of theirs. Would the Gatherings of the past have sent them out to kill? Perhaps. Times rarely change as much as we suppose.

They left Ashranc behind, but they carried Ashranc with them, the sacred dirt of their home kept in her pouch. Swift and sure they marched and it was not long before they reached the valley of the Seeking Pool, the mirror of the surface still holding a patch of sky. Scarlaer was waiting in the ruin.

'Have you caught them?' asked Uto.

'No.' The young hunter frowned as if the Outsiders' escape was an insult to him alone. Some men, especially young ones, are fixed on taking offence at everything, from a rain shower to a fallen tree. From that offence they can fashion an excuse for any folly and any outrage. He would need watching. 'But we have their tracks.'

'How many are they?'

Maslingal squatted over the ground, lips pressed tight together. 'The marks are strange. Sometimes it has the feel of two trying to seem a dozen, sometimes of a dozen trying to seem like two. Sometimes it has the feel of carelessness, sometimes the feel of wanting to be followed.'

'They will receive their wish and far more than they wished for, then,' growled Scarlaer.

'It is best never to give your enemy what they most desire.' But Uto knew she was without choice. Who has choice, in the end? 'Let us follow. But let us be watchful.'

Only when snow came and hid the moon did Uto give the sign to stop, lying awake under the burden of leadership as the time slipped by, feeling the warmth of the earth and fearing for what would come.

In the morning they felt the first chill and she waved to the others to put on their furs. They left the sacred ground and passed into the forest, jogging in a rustling crowd. Scarlaer led them fast and merciless after the tracks, always ahead, always beckoning them on, and Uto ached and trembled and breathed hard, wondering how many more years she could run like this.

They stopped to eat near a place where there were no trees, only unsullied snow, a field of white innocence, but Uto knew what lay beneath. A crust of frozen dirt, then the bodies. The rotting remains of the Outsiders who had come to stab at the earth and delve in the streams and cut down the trees and plant their rotting shacks among the barrows of the old and honoured dead, using up the world and using up each other and spreading a plague of greed into the sacred places.

Uto squatted, and looked across that clean whiteness. Once the Gathering has debated the arguments and spoken its judgement there is no place for regrets, and yet she had kept hers, as often checked and polished and as jealously guarded as any miser's hoard. Something of her own, perhaps.

The Dragon People had fought, always. Won, always. They fought to protect the sacred ground. To protect the places where they mined for the Dragon's food. To take children so that the Maker's teaching and the Maker's work might be passed on and not be lost like smoke on the wind of time. The bronze sheets reminded them of those who had fought and those fallen, of what was won and what lost in those battles of the past, and the far past, back into the Old Time and beyond. Uto did not think the Dragon People had ever killed so many to so little purpose as they had here.

There had been a baby in the miners' camp but she had died, and two boys who were with Ashod now, and prospering. Then there had been a girl with curly hair and pleading eyes just on the cusp of womanhood. Uto had offered to take her but she was thirteen, and even at ten winters there were risks. She remembered Waerdinur's sister, taken from the Ghosts too old, who could not change and carried a fury of vengeance in her until she had to be cast out. So Uto had cut the girl's throat instead and laid her gently in the pit and wondered again what she dare not say – could the teachings that led them to this be right?

Evening was settling when they looked down upon Beacon. The snow had stopped but the sky was gloomy with more. A flame twinkled in the top of the broken tower and she counted four more lights at the windows, but otherwise the place was dark. She saw the shapes of wagons, one very large, almost like a house on wheels. A few horses huddled at a rail. What she might have expected for twenty men, all unwary, except . . .

Tracks sparkled faintly with the twilight, filled with fresh snow so they were no more than dimples, but once she saw one set, like seeing one insect then realising the ground crawled with them, she saw more, and more. Criss-crossing the valley from treeline to treeline and back. Around the barrows and in at their fronts, snow dug away from their entrances. Now she saw the street between the huts, rutted and trampled, the ancient road up to the camp no better. The snow on the roofs was dripping from warmth inside. All the roofs.

Too many tracks for twenty men. Far too many, even careless as the Outsiders were. Something was wrong. She held her hand up for a halt, watching, studying.

Then she felt Scarlaer move beside her, looked around to see him already slipping through the brush, without orders.

'Wait!' she hissed at him.

He sneered at her. 'The Gathering made their decision.'

'And they decided I lead! I say wait!'

He snorted his contempt, turned for the camp, and she lunged for his heels.

*

Uto snatched at him but she was weak and slow and Scarlaer brushed off her fumbling hand. Perhaps she had been something in her day, but her day was long past and today was his. He bounded down the slope, swift and silent, scarcely leaving marks in the snow, up to the corner of the nearest hut.

He felt the strength of his body, the strength of his beating heart, the strength of the steel in his hand. He should have been sent north to fight the Shanka. He was ready. He would prove it whatever Uto might say, the withered-up old hag. He would write it in the blood of the Outsiders and make them regret their trespass on the sacred ground. Regret it in the instant before they died.

No sound from within the shack, built so poorly of split pine and cracking clay it almost hurt him to look upon its craftsmanship. He slipped low beside the wall, under the dripping eaves and to the corner, looking into the street. A faint crust of new snow, a few new trails of boot-prints and many, many older tracks. Maker's breath but they were careless and filthy, these Outsiders, leaving dung scattered everywhere. So much dung for so few beasts. He wondered if the men shat in the street as well.

'Savages,' he whispered, wrinkling his nose at the smell of their fires, of their burned food, of their unwashed bodies. No sign of the men, though, no doubt all deep in drunken sleep, unready in their arrogance, shutters and doors all fastened tight, light spilling from cracks and out into the blue dawn.

'You damned fool!' Uto slipped up, breathing hard from the run, breath puffing before her face. But Scarlaer's blood was up too hot to worry at her carping. 'Wait!' This time he dodged her hand and was across the street and into the shadow of another shack. He glanced over his shoulder, saw Uto beckoning and the others following, spreading out through the camp, silent shadows.

Scarlaer smiled, hot all over with excitement. How they would make these Outsiders pay.

'This is no game!' snarled Uto, and he only smiled again, rushed on towards the iron-bound door of the largest building, feeling the folk behind him in a rustling group, strong in numbers and strong in resolve—

The door opened and Scarlaer was left frozen for a moment in the lamplight that spilled forth.

'Morning!' A wispy-haired old man leaned against the frame in a bedraggled fur with a gilded breastplate spotted with rust showing beneath. He had a sword at his side, but in his hand only a bottle. He raised it now to them, spirit sloshing inside. 'Welcome to Beacon!'

Scarlaer lifted his blade and opened his mouth to make a fighting scream, and there was a flash at the top of the tower, a pop in his ears and he was shoved hard in the chest and found himself on his back.

He groaned but could not hear it. He sat up, head buzzing, and stared into oily smoke.

Isarult helped with the cooking at the slab and smiled at him when he brought the kill home blooded, and sometimes, if he was in a generous mood, he smiled back. She had been ripped apart. He could tell it was her corpse by the shield on her arm but her head was gone, and the other arm, and one leg so that it hardly looked like it could ever have been a person but just lumps of stuff, the snow all around specked, spattered, scattered with blood and hair and splinters of wood and metal, other friends and lovers and rivals flung about and torn and smouldering.

Tofric, who was known to be the best skinner anywhere, staggered two stiff-legged steps and dropped to his knees. A dozen wounds in him turned dark the furs he wore and one under his eye dripped a black line. He stared, not looking pained, but sad and puzzled at the way the world had changed so suddenly, all quiet, all in silence, and Scarlaer wondered, *What sorcery is this?*

Uto lay next to him. He put a hand under her head and lifted it. She shuddered, twitched, teeth rattling, red foam on her lips. She tried to pass the blessed pouch to him but it was ripped open and the sacred dust of Ashranc spilled across the bloodied snow.

'Uto? Uto?' He could not hear his own voice.

He saw friends running down the street to their aid, Canto in the lead, a brave man and the best to have beside you in a fix. He thought how foolish he had been. How lucky he was to have such friends. Then as they passed one of the barrows smoke burst from its mouth and Canto was flung away and over the roof of the shack beside. Others tumbled sideways, spun about, reeled blinking in the fog or strained as if into a wind, hands over their faces.

Scarlaer saw shutters open, the glint of metal. Arrows flitted silently across the street, lodged in wooden walls, dropped harmlessly in snow, found tottering targets, brought them to their knees, on their faces, clutching, calling, silently screaming.

He struggled to his feet, the camp tipping wildly. The old man still stood in the doorway, pointing with the bottle, saying something.

338

Scarlaer raised his sword but it felt light, and when he looked at his hand his bloody palm was empty. He tried to search for it and saw there was a short arrow in his leg. It did not hurt, but it came upon him like a shock of cold water that he might fail. And then that he might die. And suddenly there was a fear upon him like a weight.

He tottered for the nearest wall, saw an arrow flicker past and into the snow. He laboured on, chest shuddering, floundering up the slope. He snatched a look over his shoulder. The camp was shrouded in smoke as the Gathering was in the Seeing Steam, giant shadows moving inside. Some of his people were running for the trees, stumbling, falling, desperate. Then shapes came from the whirling fog like great devils – men and horses fused into one awful whole. Scarlaer had heard tales of this obscene union and laughed at its foolishness but now he saw them and was struck with horror. Spears and swords flashed, armour glittered, towering over the runners, cutting them down.

Scarlaer struggled on but his arrow-stuck leg would hardly move, a trail of blood following him up the slope and a horse-man following that, his hooves mashing the snow, a blade in his hand.

Scarlaer should have turned and shown his defiance, at least, proud hunter of the Dragon People that he was. Where had his courage gone? Once there had seemed no end to it. Now there was only the need to run, as desperate as a drowning man's need to breathe. He did not hear the rider behind him but he felt the jarring blow across his back and the snow cold, cold on his face as he fell.

Hooves thumped about him, circling him, showering him with white dust. He fought to get up but he could get no further than his hands and knees, trembling with that much effort. His back would not straighten, agony, all burning, and he whimpered and raged and was helpless, his tears melting tiny holes in the snow beneath his face, and someone seized him by the hair.

Brachio put his knee in the lad's back and forced him down into the snow, pulled a knife out and, taking care not to make a mess of it, which was something of a challenge with the lad still struggling and gurgling, cut his ears off. Then he wiped the knife in the snow and slipped it back into his bandolier, reflecting that a bandolier of knives was a damn useful thing to have in his business and wondering afresh why it hadn't caught on more widely. Might be the lad was alive when Brachio winced and grunted his bulk back up into his saddle, but he wasn't going anywhere. Not with that sword-cut in him.

Brachio chuckled over his trophies and, riding down to the camp, thought they'd be the perfect things to scare his daughters with when Cosca had made him rich and he finally came home to Puranti. Genuine Ghost ears, how about that? He imagined the laughter as he chased them around the parlour, though in his imaginings they were little girls still, and it made him sad to think they would be nearly women grown when he saw them again.

'Where does the time go?' he muttered to himself.

Sworbreck was standing at the edge of the camp, staring, mouth open as the horsemen chased the last few savages up into the woods. He was a funny little fellow but Brachio had warmed to him.

'You're a man of learning,' he called as he rode up, holding high the ears. 'What do you think I should do? Dry them? Pickle them?' Sworbreck did not answer, only stood there looking decidedly bilious. Brachio swung down from his saddle. There was riding to do but damn it if he'd be hurrying anywhere, he was out of breath already. No one was as young as they used to be, he supposed. 'Cheer up,' he said. 'We won, didn't we?' And he clapped the writer on his scrawny back.

Sworbreck stumbled, put out a hand to steady himself, felt a warmth, and realised he had sunk his fingers into a savage's steaming guts, separated by some distance from the ruined body.

Cosca took another deep swallow from his bottle – if Sworbreck had read in print the quantity of spirits the Old Man was currently drinking each day he would have cursed it for an outrageous lie – and rolled the corpse over with his boot, then, wrinkling his pinked nose, wiped the boot on the side of the nearest shed.

'I have fought Northmen, Imperials, Union men, Gurkish, every variety of Styrian and plenty more whose origin I never got to the bottom of.' Cosca gave a sigh. 'And I am forced to consider the Dragon Person vastly overrated as an opponent. You may quote me on that.' Sworbreck only just managed to swallow another rush of nausea while the Old Man burbled on. 'But then courage can often be made to work against a man in a carefully laid ambuscade. Bravery, as Verturio had it, is the dead man's virtue— Ah. You are . . . discomfited. Sometimes I forget that not everyone is familiar with such scenes as this. But you came to witness battle, did you not? Battle is . . . not always glorious. A general must be a realist. Victory first, you understand?'

'Of course,' Sworbreck found he had mumbled. He had reached the point of agreeing with Cosca on instinct, however foul, ridiculous or outrageous his utterances. He wondered if he had ever come close to hating anyone as much as he did the old mercenary. Or relying on anyone so totally for everything. No doubt the two were not unrelated.

'Victory first.'

'The losers are always the villains, Sworbreck. Only winners can be heroes.'

'You are absolutely right, of course. Only winners.'

'The one good way to fight is that which kills your enemy and leaves you with the breath to laugh . . .'

Sworbreck had come to see the face of heroism and instead he had seen evil. Seen it, spoken with it, been pressed up against it. Evil turned out not to be a grand thing. Not sneering Emperors with world-conquering designs. Not cackling demons plotting in the darkness beyond the world. It was small men with their small acts and their small reasons. It was selfishness and carelessness and waste. It was bad luck, incompetence and stupidity. It was violence divorced from conscience or consequence. It was high ideals, even, and low methods.

He watched Inquisitor Lorsen move eagerly among the bodies, turning them to see their faces, waving away the thinning, stinking smoke, tugging up sleeves in search of tattoos. 'I see no sign of rebels!' he rasped at Cosca. 'Only these savages!'

The Old Man managed to disengage lips from bottle for long enough to shout back, 'In the mountains, our friend Cantliss told us! In their so-called sacred places! In this town they call Ashranc! We will begin the pursuit right away!'

Sweet looked up from the bodies to nod. 'Crying Rock and the rest'll be waiting for us.'

'Then it would be rude to delay! Particularly with the enemy so denuded. How many did we kill, Friendly?'

The sergeant wagged his thick index finger as he attempted to number the dead. 'Hard to say which pieces go with which.'

'Impossible. We can at least tell Superior Pike that his new weapon is a great success. The results scarcely compare to when I blew up that mine beneath the fortress of Fontezarmo but then neither does the effort involved, eh? It employs explosive powders, Sworbreck, to propel a hollow ball which shatters upon detonation sending splinters—boom!' And Cosca demonstrated with an outward thrusting of both hands. An entirely unnecessary demonstration, since the proof of its effectiveness was distributed across the street in all directions, bloody and raw and in several cases barely recognisable as human.

'So this is what success looks like,' Sworbreck heard Temple murmur. 'I have often wondered.'

The lawyer saw it. The way he took in the charnel-house scene with his black eyes wide and his jaw set tight and his mouth slightly twisted. It was some small comfort to know there was one man in this gang who, in better company, might have approached decency, but he was just as helpless as Sworbreck. All they could do was watch and, by doing nothing more, participate. But how could it be stopped? Sworbreck cowered as a horse thundered past, showering him with gory snow. He was one man, and that one no fighter. His pen was his only weapon and, however highly the scribes might rate its power, it was no match for axe and armour in a duel. If he had learned nothing else the past few months, he had learned that.

'Dimbik!' shrieked Cosca, and took another swig from his bottle. He had abandoned the flask as inadquate to his needs and would no doubt soon graduate to sucking straight from the cask. 'Dimbik? There you are! I want you to lead off, root out any of these creatures left in the woods. Brachio, get your men ready to ride! Master Sweet will show us the way! Jubair and the others are waiting to open the gates! There's gold to be had, boys, and no time to waste! And rebels!' he added hastily. 'Rebels, too, of course. Temple, with me, I want to be certain on the terms of the contract as regard plunder. Sworbreck, it might be better if you were to remain here. If you haven't the stomach for this, well . . .'

'Of course,' said Sworbreck. He felt so very tired. So very far from home. Adua, and his neat office with the clean walls and the new Rimaldi printing press of which he had been so particularly proud. All so far away, across an immeasurable gulf in time and space and thinking. A place where straightening the collar seemed important and a bad review was a disaster. How could such a fantastical realm occupy the same world as this slaughter-yard? He stared at his hands: calloused, blood-daubed, dirt-scraped. Could they be the same ones that had so carefully set the type, inky at the fingertips? Could they ever do so again?

He let them drop, too tired to ride let alone write. People do not realise the crushing effort of creation. The pain of dragging the words from a tortured mind. Who read books out here, anyway? Perhaps he would lie down. He began to shamble for the fort.

'Take care of yourself, author,' said Temple, looking grimly down from horseback.

'You too, lawyer,' said Sworbreck, and patted him on the leg as he passed.

The Dragon's Den

'When do we go?' whispered Shy.

'When Savian says go,' came Lamb's voice. He was close enough she could almost feel his breath, but all she could see in the darkness of the tunnel was the faintest outline of his stubbled skull. 'Soon as he sees Sweet bring Cosca's men up the valley.'

'Won't these Dragon bastards see 'em, too?'

'I expect so.'

She wiped her forehead for the hundredth time, rubbing the wet out of her eyebrows. Damn, but it was hot, like squatting in an oven, the sweat tickling at her, hand slippery-slick on the wood of her bow, mouth sticky-dry with heat and worry.

'Patience, Shy. You won't cross the mountains in a day.'

'Easily said,' she hissed back. How long had they been there? Might've been an hour, might've been a week. Twice already they'd had to slink back into the deeper blackness of the tunnel when Dragon People had strayed close, all pressed together in a baking panic, her heart beating so hard it made her teeth rattle. So many hundreds of thousands of things that could go wrong she could hardly breathe for their weight.

'What do we do when Savian says go?' she asked.

'Open the gate. Hold the gate.'

'And after?' Providing they were still alive after, which she wouldn't have wanted to bet good money on.

'We find the children,' said Lamb.

A long pause. 'Starting to look like less and less of a plan, ain't it?'

'Do the best you can with what there is, then.'

She puffed her cheeks out at that. 'Story of my life.'

She waited for an answer but none was forthcoming. She guessed danger makes some folk blather and some clamp tight. Sadly, she was in the former camp, and surrounded by the latter. She crept forwards on all fours, stone hot under her hands, up next to Crying Rock, wondering afresh what the Ghost woman's interest in all this was. Didn't seem the type to be interested in gold, or rebels, or children neither. No way of knowing what went on behind that lined mask of a face, though, and she wasn't shining any lights inward.

'What's this Ashranc place like?' asked Shy.

'A city carved from the mountain.'

'How many are in there?'

'Thousands once. Few now. Judging from those who left, very few, and mostly the young and old. Not good fighters.'

'A bad fighter sticks a spear in you, you're just as dead as with a good one.'

'Don't get stuck, then.'

'You're just a mine of good advice, ain't you?'

'Fear not,' came Jubair's voice. Across the passageway she could only see the gleam of his eyes, the gleam of his ready sword, but she could tell he was smiling. 'If God is with us, He will be our shield.'

'If He's against?' asked Shy.

'Then no shield can protect us.'

Before Shy could tell him what a great comfort that was there was scuffling behind, and a moment later Savian's crackling voice. 'It's time. Cosca's boys are in the valley.'

'All of them?' asked Jubair.

'Enough of them.'

'You're sure?' The shudder of nerves up Shy's throat almost choked her. For months now she'd been betting everything she had on finding Pit and Ro. Now the moment might've come she would've given anything to put it off.

'Course I'm bloody sure! Go!'

A hand shoved at her back and she knocked into someone and almost fell, staggered on a few steps, fingers brushing the stone to keep her bearings. The tunnel made a turn and suddenly she felt cooler air on her face and was out blinking into the light.

Ashranc was a vast mouth in the mountainside, a cavern cut in half, its floor scattered with stone buildings, a huge overhang of rock shadowing everything above. Ahead of them, beyond a daunting drop, a grand expanse of sky and mountain opened out. Behind the cliff was riddled with openings – doorways, windows, stairways, bridges, a confusion of wall and walkway on a dozen levels, houses half-built into the rock face, a city sunk in stone.

An old man stared at them, shaved bald, a horn frozen on the way to his mouth. He muttered something, took a shocked step back, then Jubair's sword split his head and he went over in a shower of blood, horn bouncing from his hand.

Crying Rock darted right and Shy followed, someone whispering, 'Shit, shit, shit,' in her ear and she realised it was her. She rushed along low beside a crumbling wall, breath punching hard, every part of her singing with an unbearable fear and panic and rage, so wild and strong she thought she might burst open with it, sick it up, piss it out. Shouting from high above. Shouting from all around. Her boots clanked over metal plates polished smooth and scrawled with writing, grit pinging and rattling from her heels. A tall archway in a cleft in the rocks, bouncing and shuddering as she ran. A heavy double-door, one leaf already closed, two figures straining to haul the other fast, a third on the wall above, pointing at them, bow in hand. Shy went down on one knee and nocked her own arrow. A shaft looped down, missed one of the running mercenaries and clattered away across the bronze. Snap of the bowstring as Shy let fly and she watched her own arrow cover the distance, hanging in the still air. It caught the archer in the side and she gave a yelp – a woman's voice, or maybe a child's – staggered sideways and off the parapet, bounced from the rock and fell crumpled beside the gate.

The two Dragon People who'd been shutting the doors had found weapons. Old men, she saw now, very old. Jubair hacked at one and sent him reeling into the rock face. Two of the mercenaries caught up with the other and cut him down, swearing, chopping, stamping.

Shy stared at the girl she'd shot, lying there. Not much older'n Ro, she reckoned. Part Ghost, maybe, from the whiteness of her skin and the shape of her eyes. Just like Shy. Blame it on your Ghost blood. She stared down and the girl stared up, breathing fast and shallow, saying nothing, eyes so dark and wet and blood across her cheek. Shy's free hand opened and closed, useless.

'Here!' roared Jubair, raising one hand. Shy heard a faint answering call, through the gate saw men struggling up the mountainside. Cosca's men, weapons drawn. Caught a glimpse of Sweet, maybe, struggling along on foot. The other mercenaries started dragging the doors wide to let them through. Doors of metal four fingers thick but swinging as smooth as a box lid.

'God is with us,' said Jubair, his grin spotted with blood.

God might've been, but Lamb was nowhere to be seen. 'Where's Lamb?' she asked, staring about.

'Don't know.' Savian only just managed to force the words out. He was breathing hard, bent over. 'Went the other way.'

She took off again.

'Wait!' Savian wheezed after her, but he weren't running anywhere. Shy dashed to the nearest house, about enough thought in her pounding head to sling her bow over her shoulder and pull her short-sword. Wasn't sure she'd ever swung a sword in anger. When she killed that Ghost that killed Leef, maybe. Wasn't sure why she was thinking about that now. Heaved in a great breath and tore aside the hide that hung in the doorway, leaped in, blade-first.

Maybe she'd been expecting Pit and Ro to look up, weeping grateful tears. Instead a bare room, naught there but strips of light across a dusty floor.

She barrelled into another house, empty as the first.

She dashed up a set of steps and through an archway in the rock face. This room had furniture, polished by time, bowls neatly stacked, no sign of life.

An old man blundered from the next doorway and right into Shy, slipped and fell, a big pot dropping from his hands and shattering across the ground. He scrambled away, holding up a trembling arm, muttering something, cursing Shy, or pleading for his life, or calling on some forgotten god, and Shy lifted the sword, standing over him. Took an effort to stop herself killing him. Her body burned to do it. But she had to find the children. Before Cosca's men boiled into this place and caught the killing fever. Had to find the children. If they were here. She let the old man crawl away through a doorway.

'Pit!' she screamed, voice cracking. Back down the steps and into another dim, hot, empty room, an archway at the back leading to another yet. The place was a maze. A city built for thousands, like Crying Rock had said. How the hell to find two children in this? A roar came from somewhere, strange, echoing.

'Lamb?' She clawed sweaty hair out of her face.

Someone gave a panicked screech. There were people spilling from the doorways now, from the low houses below, some with weapons, others with tools, one grey-haired woman with a baby in her arms. Some stared about, sensing something was wrong but not sure what.

Others were hurrying off, away from the gate, away from Shy, towards a tall archway in the rock at the far end of the open cavern.

A black-skinned man stood beside it, staff in hand, beckoning people through into the darkness. Waerdinur. And close beside him a much smaller figure, thin and pale, shaven-headed. But Shy knew her even so.

'Ro!' she screamed, but her voice was lost. The clatter of fighting echoed from the rocky ceiling, bounced from the buildings, coming from everywhere and nowhere. She vaulted over a parapet, hopped a channel where water flowed, startled as a huge figure loomed over her, realised it was a tree-trunk carved into a twisted man-shape, ran on into an open space beside a long, low building and slid to a stop.

A group of Dragon People had gathered ahead of her. Three old men, two old women and a boy, all shaven-headed, all armed, and none of them looking like they planned to move.

Shy hefted her sword and screamed, 'Get out o' my fucking way!'

She knew she wasn't that imposing a figure, so it was something of a shock when they began to back off. Then a flatbow bolt flitted into the stomach of one of the old men and he clutched at it, dropping his spear. The others turned and ran. Shy heard feet slapping behind her and mercenaries rushed past, whooping, shouting. One of them hacked an old woman across the back as she tried to limp away.

Shy looked towards that archway, flanked by black pillars and full of shadow. Waerdinur had vanished inside now. Ro too, if it had been her. It must have been.

She set off running.

In so far as Cosca had a best, danger brought it out in him. Temple hurried cringing along, sticking so close to the walls that he would occasionally scrape his face upon them, his fingernails so busy with the hem of his shirt he was halfway to unravelling the whole thing. Brachio scuttled bent almost double. Even Friendly prowled with shoulders suspiciously hunched. But the Old Man had no fear. Not of death, at least. He strode through the ancient settlement utterly heedless of the arrows that occasionally looped down, chin high, eyes aglitter, steps only slightly wayward from drink, snapping out orders that actually made sense.

'Bring down that archer!' Pointing with his sword at an old woman on top of a building.

'Clear those tunnels!' Waving towards some shadowy openings beside them.

'Kill no children if possible, a deal is a deal!' Wagging a lecturing finger at a group of Kantics already daubed with blood.

Whether anyone took any notice of him, it was hard to say. The Company of the Gracious Hand were not the most obedient at the best of times, and these times in no way qualified.

Danger brought no best from Temple. He felt very much as he had in Dagoska, during the siege. Sweating in that stinking hospital, and cursing, and fumbling with the bandages, and tearing up the clothes of the dead for more. Passing the buckets, all night long, lit by fires, water slopping, and for nothing. It all burned anyway. Weeping at each death. Weeping with sorrow. Weeping with gratitude that it was not him. Weeping with fear that it would be him next. Months in fear, always in fear. He had been in fear ever since.

A group of mercenaries had gathered around an ancient man, growling unintelligible insults through clenched teeth in a language something like Old Imperial, swinging a spear wildly in both hands. It did not take long to for Temple to realise he was blind. The mercenaries darted in and out. When he turned, one would poke him in the back with a weapon, when he turned again, another would do the honours. The old man's robe was already dark with blood.

'Should we stop them?' muttered Temple.

'Of course,' said Cosca. 'Friendly?'

The sergeant caught the blind man's spear just below the blade in one big fist, whipped a cleaver from his coat with the other and split his head almost in half in one efficient motion, letting his body slump to the ground and tossing the spear clattering away.

'Oh God,' muttered Temple.

'We have work to do!' snapped the Old Man at the disappointed mercenaries. 'Find the gold!'

Temple tore his hands away from his shirt and scratched at his hair instead, scrubbed at it, clawed at it. He had promised himself, after Averstock, that he would never stand by and watch such things again. The same promise he had made in Kadir. And before that in Styria. And here he was, standing uncomplaining by. And watching. But then he had never been much for keeping promises.

Temple's nose kept running, tickling, running. He rubbed it with the heel of his hand until it bled, and it ran again. He tried to look only at the ground, but sounds kept jerking his wet eyes sideways. To crashes and screams and laughs and bellows, to whimpers and gurgles and sobs and screeches. Through the windows and the doorways he caught glimpses, glimpses he knew would be with him as long as he lived and he rooted his running eyes on the ground again and whispered to himself, 'Oh God.'

How often had he whispered it during the siege? Over and over as he hurried through the scorched ruins of the Lower City, the bass rumble of the blasting powder making the earth shake as he rolled over the bodies, seeking for survivors, and when he found them burned and scarred and dying, what could he do? He had learned he was no worker of miracles. Oh God, oh God. No help had come then. No help came now.

'Shall we burn 'em?' asked a bow-legged Styrian, hopping like a child eager to go out and play. He was pointing up at some carvings chiselled from ancient tree-trunks, wood polished to a glow by the years, strange and beautiful.

Cosca shrugged. 'If you must. What's wood for, after all, if not to take a flame?' He watched the mercenary shower oil on the nearest one and pull out his tinderbox. 'The sad fact is I just don't care much any more, either way. It bores me.'

Temple startled as a naked body crashed into the ground next to them. Whether it had been alive or dead on the way down, he could not say. 'Oh God,' he whispered.

'Careful!' bellowed Friendly, frowning up at the buildings on their left.

Cosca watched the blood spread from the corpse's broken skull, scarcely interrupted in his train of thought. 'I look at things such as this and feel only . . . a mild ennui. My mind wanders on to what's for dinner, or the recurrent itch on the sole of my foot, or when and where I might next be able to get my cock sucked.' He started to scratch absently at his codpiece, then gave up. 'What horror, eh, to be bored by such as this?' Flames flickered merrily up the side of the nearest carving, and the Styrian pyromaniac skipped happily over to the next. 'The violence, treachery and waste that I have seen. It's quite squeezed the enthusiasm out of me. I am numbed. That's why I need you, Temple. You must be my conscience. I want to believe in something!'

He slapped a hand down on Temple's shoulder and Temple twitched, heard a squeal and turned just in time to see an old woman kicked from the precipice.

'Oh God.'

'Exactly what I mean!' Cosca slapped him on the shoulder again. 'But if there is a God, why in all these years has He not raised a hand to stop me?'

'Perhaps we are His hand,' rumbled Jubair, who had stepped from a doorway wiping blood from his sword with a cloth. 'His ways are mysterious.'

Cosca snorted. 'A whore with a veil is mysterious. God's ways appear to be . . . insane.'

Temple's nose tickled with perfumed smoke as the wood burned. It had smelled that way in Dagoska when the Gurkish finally broke into the city. The flames spraying the slum buildings, spraying the slum-dwellers, people on fire, flinging themselves from the ruined docks into the sea. The noise of fighting coming closer. Kahdia's face, lit in flickering orange, the low murmur of the others praying and Temple tugging at his sleeve and saying, 'You must go, they will be coming,' and the old priest shaking his head, and smiling as he squeezed at Temple's shoulder, and saying, 'That is why I must stay.'

What could he have done then? What could he do now?

He caught movement at the corner of his eye, saw a small shape flit between two of the low stone buildings. 'Was that a child?' he muttered, already leaving the others behind.

'Why does everyone pout so over children?' Cosca called after him. 'They'll turn out just as old and disappointing as the rest of us!'

Temple was hardly listening. He had failed Sufeen, he had failed Kahdia, he had failed his wife and daughter, he had sworn always to take the easy way, but perhaps this time . . . he rounded the corner of the building.

A boy stood there, shaven-headed. Pale-skinned. Red-brown eye-brows, like Shy's. The right age, perhaps, could it—

Temple saw he had a spear in his hands. A short spear, but held with surprising purpose. In his worry for others, Temple had for once neglected to feel worried for himself. Perhaps that showed some level of personal growth. The self-congratulations would have to wait, however.

'I'm scared,' he said, without needing to dissemble. 'Are you scared?'

No response. Temple gently held out his hands, palms up. 'Are you Pit?'

A twitch of shock across the boy's face. Temple slowly knelt and tried to dig out that old earnestness, not easy with the noises of destruction filtering from all around them. 'My name is Temple. I am a friend of

350

Shy's.' That brought out another twitch. 'A good friend.' A profound exaggeration at that moment, but a forgivable one. The point of the spear wavered. 'And of Lamb's too.' It started to drop. 'They came to find you. And I came with them.'

'They're here?' It was strange to hear the boy speak the common tongue with the accent of the Near Country.

'They're here,' he said. 'They came for you.'

'Your nose is bleeding.'

'I know.' Temple wiped it on his wrist again. 'No need to worry.'

Pit set down his spear, and walked to Temple and hugged him tight. Temple blinked for a moment, then hesitantly put his arms around the boy and held him.

'You are safe now,' he said. 'You are safe.'

It was hardly the first lie he had ever told.

Shy padded down the hallway, desperate to run on and scared to the point of shitting herself at once, clinging to the slippery grip of her sword. The place was lit only by flickering little lamps that struck a gleam from the metal designs on the floor – circles within circles, letters and lines – and from the blood smeared across them. Her eyes flicked between the tricking shadows, jumped from body to body – Dragon People and mercenaries, too, hacked and punctured and still leaking.

'Lamb?' she whispered, but so quietly even she could hardly hear it.

Sounds echoed from the warm rock, spilled from the openings to either side – screams and crashes, whispering steam, weeping and laughter leaching through the walls. The laughter worst of all.

'Lamb?'

She edged to the archway at the end of the hall and pressed herself to the wall beside it, a hot draught sweeping past. She clawed the wet hair from her stinging eyes again, flicked sweat from her fingertips and gathered her tattered courage. For Pit and Ro. No turning back now.

She slipped through and her jaw fell. A vast emptiness opened before her, a great rift, an abyss inside the mountain. A ledge ahead was scattered with benches, anvils, smith's tools. Beyond a black gulf yawned, crossed by a bridge no more than two strides wide, no handrail, arching through darkness to another ledge and another archway, maybe fifty strides distant. The heat was crushing, the bridge lit underneath by fires that growled far out of sight below, streaks of crystal in the rocky walls sparkling, everything metal from the hammers and anvils and ingots to her own sword catching a smelter's glow. Shy swallowed as she edged out towards that empty plunge and the far wall dropped down, down, down. As if this were some upper reach of hell the living never should've broached.

'You'd think they'd give it a fucking rail,' she muttered.

Waerdinur stood on the bridge behind a great square shield, a dragon worked into the face, bright point of a spear-blade showing beside it, blocking the way. One mercenary lay dead in front of him, another was trying to ease back to safety, poking away wildly with a halberd. A third knelt not far from Shy, cranking a flatbow. Waerdinur lunged and smoothly skewered the halberdier with his spear, then stepped forward and brushed him off the bridge. He fell without a sound. Not of his falling. Not of his reaching the bottom.

The Dragon Man set himself again, bottom edge of that big shield clanging against the bridge as he brought it down, and he shouted over his shoulder in words Shy didn't understand. People shuffled through the shadows behind him – old ones, and children, too, and a girl running last of all.

'Ro!' Shy's scream was dead in the throbbing heat and the girl ran on, swallowed in the shadows at the far end of the bridge.

Waerdinur stayed, squatting low behind his shield and watching her over the rim, and she gritted her teeth and gave a hiss of frustrated fury. To come so close, and find no way around.

'Have this, arsehole!' The last mercenary levelled his flatbow and the bolt rattled from Waerdinur's dragon shield and away into the dark, spinning end-over-end, a tiny orange splinter in all that inky emptiness. 'Well, he's going nowhere.' The archer fished a bolt from his quiver and set to cranking back the string again. 'Couple more bows up here and we'll get him. Sooner or later. Don't you fucking worry about—'

Shy saw a flicker at the corner of her eye and the mercenary lurched against the wall, Waerdinur's spear right through him. He said, 'Oh,' and slid to sitting, setting his bow carefully on the ground. Shy was just taking a step towards him when she felt a gentle touch on her shoulder.

Lamb was at her back, but no kind of reassurance. He'd lost his coat and stood in his leather vest all scar and twisted sinew and his sword broken off halfway, splintered blade slathered in blood to his elbow.

'Lamb?' she whispered. He didn't even look at her, just brushed her away with the back of his arm, black eyes picked up a fiery glimmer and fixed across that bridge, muscles starting from his neck, head hanging on one side, pale skin all sweat-beaded, blood-dotted, his bared teeth shining in a skull-grin. Shy shrank out of his way like death itself had come tapping at her shoulder. Maybe it had.

As if it was a meeting long arranged, Waerdinur drew a sword, long and straight and dull, a silver mark glinting near the hilt.

'I used to have one o' those.' Lamb tossed his own broken blade skittering across the floor and over the edge into nothingness.

'The work of the Maker himself,' said Waerdinur. 'You should have kept it.'

'Friend o' mine stole it.' Lamb stepped towards one of the anvils, fingers whitening as he wrapped them around a great iron bar that lay against it, tall as Shy was. 'And everything else.' Metal grated as he dragged it after him towards the bridge. 'And it was better'n I deserved.'

Shy thought about telling him not to go but the words didn't come. Like she couldn't get the air to speak. Wasn't another way through that she could see, and it wasn't as if she was about to turn back. So she sheathed her sword and shrugged her bow into her hand. Waerdinur saw it and took a few cautious steps away, light on the balls of his bare feet, calm as if he trod a dance floor rather'n a strip of stone too narrow for the slimmest of wagons to roll down.

'Told you I'd be back,' said Lamb as he stepped out onto the bridge, the tip of the metal bar clattering after him.

'And so you are,' said Waerdinur.

Lamb nudged the corpse of the dead mercenary out of his way with a boot and it dropped soundless into the abyss. 'Told you I'd bring death with me.'

'And so you have. You must be pleased.'

'I'll be pleased when you're out o' my way.' Lamb stopped a couple of paces short of Waerdinur, a trail of glistening footprints left behind him, the two old men facing each other in the midst of that great void.

'Do you truly think the right is with you?' asked the Dragon Man.

'Who cares about right?' And Lamb sprang, lifting that big length of metal high and bringing it down on Waerdinur's shield with a boom made Shy wince, leaving a great dent in the dragon design and one corner bent right back. The Dragon Man was driven sprawling, legs kicking as he scrambled from the brink. Before the echoes had faded Lamb was roaring as he swung again.

This time Waerdinur was ready, though, angled his shield so the bar glanced clear and swung back. Lamb jerked away snake-quick and the sword missed him by a feather, jerked forward snake-quick and caught Waerdinur under the jaw, sent him tottering, spitting blood. He found his balance quick, though, lashed left and right, sent sparks and splinters flying from the metal bar as Lamb brought it up to block.

Shy drew a bead but even close as she was the two old men were moving too fast – deadly, murderous fast so any step or twitch could be their last – no telling who she'd hit if she let loose the arrow. Her hand jerked about as she eased onto the bridge, trying to find the shot, always a few moments behind, sweat tickling at her flickering eyelids as she looked from the fight ahead to the void under her feet.

Waerdinur saw the next blow coming and slipped clear, nimble for all his size. The bar caught the bridge with a shrieking crash, struck sparks, left Lamb off balance long enough for the Dragon Man to swing. Lamb jerked his head away and rather'n splitting his skull the bright point left a red line down his face, drops of blood flicking into nothingness. He staggered three steps, heel slapping at the very brink on the last, space opening between the two men for just a breath as Waerdinur brought his sword back to thrust.

Shy might not have been much at waiting but when the moment came she'd always had a talent for just diving in. She didn't even think about shooting. Her arrow flitted through the darkness, glanced the edge of the shield and into Waerdinur's sword-arm. He grunted, point of his blade dropping and scraping harmlessly against the bridge as Shy lowered her bow, hardly believing she'd taken the shot, still less hit the target.

Lamb bellowed like a mad bull, swinging that length of metal as if it was no heavier than a willow switch, knocking Waerdinur this way and that, sending him reeling along the bridge, no chance to hit back even if he'd been able with Shy's arrow through his arm, no chance to do anything but fight to keep his footing. Lamb kept after, tireless, merciless, driving him off the bridge and onto the ledge at the far end. One last blow tore the shield from Waerdinur's arm and sent it tumbling away into the darkness. He stumbled against the wall, sword clattering from his limp hand, bloody now from the leaking arrow-wound.

A shape came flying from the shadows in the archway, the flash of a knife as it sprang on Lamb and he staggered back towards the brink, wrestled with it, flung it off and into the wall. A shaven-headed girl crumpled against the floor. Changed, so changed, but Shy knew her.

She flung her bow away and ran, no thought for the drop to either side, no thought for anything but the space between them.

Lamb plucked the knife out of his shoulder along with a string of blood and flicked it away like a spent toothpick, face still locked in that red smile, bloody as a new wound, seeing nothing, caring for nothing. Not the man who'd sat beside her on that wagon so many swaying miles, or patiently ploughed the field or sang to the children or warned her to be realistic. Another man, if he was a man at all. The one who'd murdered those two bandits in Averstock, who'd hacked Sangeed's head off on the plains, who'd killed Glama Golden with his hands in the Circle. Death's best friend indeed.

He arched back with that length of metal in his fists, cuts and notches from the Maker's sword all angrily glinting, and Shy screamed out but it was wasted breath. He'd no more mercy in him now than the winter. All those miles she'd come, all that ground struggled over, and just those few paces left were too many as he brought the bar hissing down.

Waerdinur flung himself on top of Ro and the metal caught his big forearm and snapped it like a twig, crashed on into his shoulder, opened a great gash down his head, knocked him senseless. Lamb raised the bar again, screaming froth on his twisted lips, and Shy caught hold of the other end of it as she hurtled off the bridge, whooped as she was jerked into the air. Wind rushed, the glowing cavern flipped over, and she crashed upside down into stone.

Then all quiet.

Just a faint ringing.

Shuffling boots.

Get up, Shy.

Can't just lie around all day.

Things need doing on a farm.

But breathing was quite the challenge.

She pushed against the wall, or the floor, or the ceiling, and the world spun right over, everything whirling like a leaf on a flood.

Was she standing? No. On her back. One arm dangling. Dangling over the edge of the drop, blackness and fire, tiny in the distant depth. That didn't seem a good idea. She rolled the other way. Managed to find her knees, everything swaying, trying to shake the fog from her skull.

People were shouting, voices vague, muffled. Something knocked against her and she nearly fell again.

A tangle of men, shuffling, wrestling. Lamb was in the midst, face wild as an animal's, red wet from a long cut right across it, squealing and gurgling sounds that weren't even halfway to swearing.

Cosca's big sergeant, Friendly, was behind him with one arm around his neck, sweat standing from his forehead with the effort but his face just faintly frowning like he was teasing out a troubling sum.

Sweet was trying to keep a grip on Lamb's left arm, getting dragged about like a man who'd roped a crazy horse. Savian had Lamb's right and he was croaking, 'Stop! Stop, you mad fucker!' Shy saw he had a knife drawn and didn't think she could stop him using it. Didn't even know if she wanted to.

Lamb had tried to kill Ro. All they'd gone through to find her and he'd tried to kill her. He would've killed Shy, too, whatever he'd promised her mother. He would've killed all of them. She couldn't make sense of it. Didn't want to.

Then Lamb went rigid, near dragging Sweet off the edge of the cliff, whites of his eyes showing under flickering lids. Then he sagged, gasping, whimpering, and he put his bloody three-fingered hand over his face, all the fight suddenly put out.

And Savian patted Lamb on the chest, drawn knife still held behind his back and said, 'Easy, easy.'

Shy tottered up, the world more or less settled but her head throbbing, blood tickling at the back of her skull.

'Easy, easy.'

Right arm hard to move and her ribs aching so it hurt to breathe but she started shuffling for the archway. Behind her she could hear Lamb sobbing.

'Easy . . . easy . . .'

A narrow passageway, hot as a forge, black but for a flaring glow up ahead and glimmering spots across the floor. Waerdinur's blood. Shy limped after, remembered her sword, managed to get it drawn but could hardly grip the thing in her numb right hand, fumbled it across to her left and went on, getting steadier, halfway to jogging now, the tunnel getting brighter, hotter still, and an opening ahead, a golden light spilling across the stones. She burst through and slid to a sudden stop, went over on her arse and lay still, propped on her elbows, gaping.

'Fuck,' she breathed.

They were called Dragon People, that much she knew. But she'd never guessed they actually had a dragon.

It lay there in the centre of a vast domed chamber like the big scene from a storybook – beautiful, terrible, strange, its thousand thousand metal scales dull-glistered with the light of fires.

It was hard to judge its size, coiled about and about as it was, but its tapered head might've been long as a man was tall. Its teeth were dagger-blades. No claws. Each of its many legs ended in a hand, golden rings upon the graceful metal fingers. Beneath its folded paper wings gears gently clicked and clattered, wheels slowly, slowly turned, and the faintest breath of steam issued from its vented nostrils, the tip of a tongue like a forked chain softly rattling, a tiny slit of emerald eye showing under each of its four metal eyelids.

'Fuck,' she whispered again, eyes drifting down to the dragon's bed, no less of a child's daydream than the monster itself. A hill of money. Of ancient gold and silver plate. Of chains and chalices, coins and coronets. Of gilded arms and armour. Of gem-encrusted everythings. The silver standard of some long-lost legion thrust up at a jaunty angle. A throne of rare woods adorned with gold leaf stuck upside down from the mass. There was so much it became absurd. Priceless treasures rendered to gaudy trash by sheer quantity.

'Fuck,' she muttered one last time, waiting for the metal beast to wake and fall in blazing rage upon this tiny trespasser. But it didn't stir, and Shy's eyes crept down to the ground. The dotted tracks of blood became a smear, then a trickle, and now she saw Waerdinur, lying back against the dragon's foreleg, and Ro beside him, staring, face streaked with blood from a cut on her scalp.

Shy struggled up, and crept down the bowl-shaped floor of the chamber, the stone underfoot all etched with writing, gripping tight to her sword, as though that feeble splinter of steel was anything more than a petty reassurance.

She saw other things among the hoard as she came closer. Papers with heavy seals. Miners' claims. Bankers' drafts. Deeds to buildings long ago fallen. Wills to estates long ago divided. Shares in Fellowships, and companies, and enterprises long deceased. Keys to who knew what forgotten locks. Skulls, too. Dozens of them. Hundreds. Coins and gemstones cut and raw spilling from their empty eye sockets. What things more valued than the dead?

Waerdinur's breath came shallow, robe blood-soaked, shattered arm limp beside him and Ro clutching at the other, Shy's broken arrow still lodged near the shoulder.

'It's me,' Shy whispered, scared to raise her voice, edging forward, stretching out her hand. 'Ro. It's me.'

She wouldn't let go of the old man's arm. It took him reaching up and gently peeling her hand away. He nudged her towards Shy, spoke some soft words in his language and pushed again, more firmly. More words and Ro hung her shaved head, tears in her eyes, and started to shuffle away.

Waerdinur looked at Shy with pain-bright eyes. 'We only wanted what was best for them.'

Shy knelt and gathered the girl up in her arms. She felt thin, and stiff, and reluctant, nothinga left of the sister she'd had so long ago. Scarcely the reunion Shy had dreamed of. But it was a reunion.

'Fuck!' Nicomo Cosca stood in the entrance of the chamber, staring at the dragon and its bed.

Sergeant Friendly walked towards it, sliding a heavy cleaver from inside his coat, took one crunching step onto the bed of gold and bones and papers, coins sliding in a little landslip behind his boot-heel and, reaching forward, tapped the dragon on the snout.

His cleaver made a solid clank, as if he'd tapped an anvil.

'It is a machine,' he said, frowning down.

'Most sacred of the Maker's works,' croaked Waerdinur. 'A thing of wonder, of power, of—'

'Doubtless.' Cosca smiled wide as he walked into the chamber, fanning himself with his hat. But it wasn't the dragon that held his eye. It was its bed. 'How great a sum, do you think, Friendly?'

The sergeant raised his brows and took a long breath through his nose. 'Very great. Shall I count it?'

'Perhaps later.'

Friendly looked faintly disappointed.

'Listen to me . . .' Waerdinur tried to prop himself up, blood oozing from around the shaft in his shoulder, smearing the bright gold behind him. 'We are close to waking the dragon. So close! The work of centuries. This year . . . perhaps next. You cannot imagine its power. We could . . . we could share it between us!'

Cosca grimaced. 'Experience has taught me I'm no good at sharing.'

'We will drive the Outsiders from the mountains and the world will be right again, as it was in the Old Time. And you . . . whatever you want is yours!'

Cosca smiled up at the dragon, hands on hips. 'It certainly is a remarkable curiosity. A magnificent relic. But against what is already boiling across the plains? The legion of the dumb? The merchants and farmers and makers of trifles and filers of papers? The infinite tide of greedy little people?' He waved his hat towards the dragon. 'Such things as this are worthless as a cow against a swarm of ants. There will be no place in the world to come for the magical, the mysterious, the strange. They will come to your sacred places and build . . . tailors' shops. And dry-goods emporia. And lawyers' offices. They will make of them bland copies of everywhere else.' The old mercenary scratched thoughtfully at his rashy neck. 'You can wish it were not so. I wish it were not so. But it is so. I tire of lost causes. The time of men like me is passing. The time of men like you?' He wiped a little blood from under his fingernails. 'So long passed it might as well have never been.'

Waerdinur tried to reach out, his hand dangling from the broken forearm, skin stretched around the splintered bones. 'You do not understand what I am offering you!'

'But I do.' And Cosca set one boot upon a gilded helmet wedged into the hoard and smiled down upon the Maker's Right Hand. 'You may be surprised to learn this, but I have been made many outlandish offers. Hidden fortunes, places of honour, lucrative trading rights along the Kadiri coast, an entire city once, would you believe, though admittedly in poor condition. I have come to realise . . .' and he peered discerningly up at the dragon's steaming snout, 'a painful realisation, because I enjoy a fantastic dream just as much as the next man . . .' and he fished up a single golden coin and held it to the light. 'That one mark is worth a great deal more than a thousand promises.'

Waerdinur slowly let his broken arm drop. 'I tried to do . . . what was best.'

'Of course.' Cosca gave him a reassuring nod, and flicked the coin back onto the heap. 'Believe it or not, so do we all. Friendly?'

The sergeant leaned down and neatly split Waerdinur's head with his cleaver.

'No!' shrieked Ro, and Shy could hardly hold on to her, she started thrashing so much.

Cosca looked mildly annoyed at the interruption. 'It might be best if you removed her. This really is no place for a child.'

Greed

They set off in a happy crowd, smiling, laughing, congratulating
one another on their work, comparing the trophies of gold and
flesh they had stolen from the dead. Ro had not thought ever
in her life to look upon a man worse than Grega Cantliss. Now they
were everywhere she turned. One had Akarin's pipe and he tooted a
mindless three-noted jig and some danced and capered down the valley,
their clothes made motley by the blood of Ro's family.

They left Ashranc in ruins, the carvings smashed and the Heartwoods smoking charcoal and the bronze panels gouged up and the
Long House burned with the blessed coals from its fire-pit, all forever
stained with death. They despoiled even the most sacred caves and
tipped the Dragon over so they could steal the coins that made its bed,
then they sealed it in its cavern and brought down the bridge with a
burning powder that made the very earth shake in horror at the heresy.

'Better to be safe,' the murderer Cosca had said, then leaned towards
the old man called Savian and asked, 'Did you find your boy? My
notary salvaged several children. He's discovered quite the talent for it.'

Savian shook his head.

'A shame. Will you keep searching?'

'Told myself I'd go this far. No further.'

'Well. Every man has his limit, eh?' And Cosca gave him a friendly
slap on the arm then chucked Ro under the chin and said, 'Cheer up,
your hair will grow back in no time!'

And Ro watched him go, wishing she had had the courage, or the
presence of mind, or the anger in her to find a knife and stab him, or
rip him with her nails, or bite his face.

They set off briskly but soon slowed, tired and sore and gorged on
destruction. Bent and sweating under the weight of their plunder,
packs and pockets bulging with coins. Soon they were jostling and

cursing each other and arguing over fallen trinkets. One man tore the pipe away and smashed it on a rock and the one who had been playing it struck him and the great black man had to drag the two of them apart and spoke about God, as if He was watching, and Ro thought, if God can see anything, why would He watch this?

Shy talked, talked, different than she had been. Pared down and pale and tired as a candle burned to the stub, bruised as a beaten dog so Ro hardly recognised her. Like a woman she saw in a dream once. A nightmare. She blathered, nervous and foolish with a mask of a smile. She asked the nine children to tell their names and some gave their old names and some their new, hardly knowing who they were any more.

Shy squatted in front of Evin when he told his name, and said, 'Your brother Leef was with us, for a bit.' She put the back of her hand to her mouth and Ro saw it was trembling. 'He died out on the plains. We buried him in a good spot, I reckon. Good as you get out there.' And she put her hand on Ro's shoulder then and said, 'I wanted to bring you a book or something, but . . . didn't work out.' And the world in which there were books was a half-remembered thing, and the faces of the dead so real and new about her, Ro could not understand it. 'I'm sorry . . . we took so long.' Shy looked at her with wet in the corners of her pink rimmed eyes and said, 'Say something, can't you?'

'I hate you,' said Ro, in the language of the Dragon People so she would not understand.

The dark-skinned man called Temple looked sadly at her and said, in the same tongue, 'Your sister came a long way to find you. For months you have been all she has wanted.'

Ro said, 'I have no sister. Tell her that.'

Temple shook his head. 'You tell her.'

All the while the old Northman watched them, eyes wide but looking through her, as if he had seen an awful thing far-off, and Ro thought of him standing over her with that devil smile and her father giving his life for hers and wondered who this silent killer was who looked so much like Lamb. When his cut face started bleeding, Savian knelt near him to stitch it and said, 'Hardly seemed like demons, in the end, these Dragon Folk.'

The man who looked like Lamb didn't flinch as the needle pierced his skin. 'The real demons you bring with you.'

When Ro lay in the darkness, even with fingers stuck in her ears all she could hear was Hirfac screaming and screaming as they burned her on the cooking-slab, the air sweet with the smell of meat. Even with her hands over her eyes, all she could see was Ulstal's face, sad and dignified, as they pushed him off the cliff with their spears and he fell without a cry, the bodies left broken at the foot, good people she had laughed with, each with their own wisdom, made useless meat and she could not understand the waste of it. She felt she should have hated all these Outsiders beyond hating but somehow she was only numb and withered inside, as dead a thing as her family herded off the cliff, as her father with his head split, as Gully swinging from his tree.

The next morning, men were missing and gold and food missing with them. Some said they had deserted and some that they had been lured by spirits in the night and some that the Dragon People were following, vengeful. While they argued, Ro looked back towards Ashranc, a pall of smoke still hanging over the mountainside in the pale blue, and felt she was stolen from her home once again, and she reached inside her robe and clutched the dragon scale her father had given her, cool against her skin. Beside her on a rock, the old Ghost Woman stood frowning.

'Bad luck to look back too long, girl,' said the white-bearded one called Sweet, though Ro reckoned the Ghost fifty years old at the least, only a few yellow hairs left among the grey she had bound up with a rag.

'It does not feel so fine as I thought it would.'

'When you spend half your life dreaming of a thing, its coming to pass rarely measures up.'

Ro saw Shy look at her, then down at the ground, and she curled her lip back and spat through the gap in her teeth. A memory came up then all unbidden of Shy and Gully having a contest at spitting in a pot and Ro laughing, and Pit laughing, and Lamb watching and smiling, and Ro felt a pain in her chest and looked away, not knowing why.

'Maybe the money'll make it feel finer,' Sweet was saying.

The old Ghost woman shook her head. 'A rich fool is still a fool. You will see.'

Sick of waiting for their missing friends, the men went on. Bottles were opened and they got drunk and slowed under the weight of their booty, toiling in the heat over broken rocks, straining and cursing with mighty burdens as though gold was worth more than their own flesh, more than their own breath. Even so they left discarded baubles scattered in their wake, sparkling like a slug's trail, some picked up by those behind only to be dropped a mile further on. More food had gone in the night and more water and they squabbled over what was

362

left, a haunch of bread worth its weight in gold, then ten times its weight, jewels given over for half a flask of spirits. A man killed another for an apple and Cosca ordered him hanged. They left him swinging behind them, still with the silver chains rattling around his neck.

'Discipline must be maintained!' Cosca told everyone, wobbling with drunkenness in the saddle of his unfortunate horse, and up on Lamb's shoulders Pit smiled, and Ro realised she had not seen him smile in a long time.

They left the sacred places behind and passed into the forest, and the snow began to fall, and then to settle, and the Dragon's warmth faded from the earth and it grew bitter chill. Temple and Shy handed out furs to the children as the trees reared taller and taller around. Some of the mercenaries had thrown their coats away so as to carry more gold, and now shivered where they had sweated before, curses smoking on the chill, cold mist catching at their heels.

Two men were found dead in the trees, shot in the back with arrows while they were shitting. Arrows that the mercenaries had themselves abandoned in Ashranc so they could stuff their quivers with loot.

They sent out other men to find and kill whoever had done the shooting but they did not come back and after a while the rest pressed on, but with a panic on them now, weapons drawn, staring into the trees, starting at shadows. Men kept vanishing, one by one, and one man took another who had strayed for an enemy and shot him down, and Cosca spread his hands and said, 'In war, there are no straight lines.' They argued over how they might carry the wounded man or whether they should leave him, but before they decided he died anyway and they picked things from his body and kicked it into a crevasse.

Some of the children gave each other grins because they knew their own family must be following, the bodies left as a message to them, and Evin walked close beside her and said in the Dragon People's tongue, 'Tonight we run,' and Ro nodded.

The darkness settled without stars or moon and the snow falling thick and soft and Ro waited, trembling with the need to run and the fear of being caught, marking the endless time by the sleeping breath of the Outsiders, Shy's quick and even and Savian's crackling loud in his chest and the Ghost Woman prone to mutter as she turned, more to say when she was sleeping than waking. Until the old man Sweet, who she took for the slowest runner among them, was roused for his watch and grumbled to a place on the other side of their camp. Then she tapped Evin's shoulder, and he nodded to her, and prodded the others, and in a silent row they stole away into the darkness.

She shook Pit awake and he sat. 'Time to go.' But he only blinked. 'Time to go!' she hissed, squeezing his arm.

He shook his head. 'No.'

She dragged him up and he struggled and shouted, 'I won't go! Shy!' And someone flung back their blankets, a can clattering, all commotion, and Ro let go Pit's hand and ran, floundering in the snow, away into the trees, caught her boot on a root and tumbled over and over and up and on. Struggling, striving, this time she would get free. Then a terrible weight took her around the knees and she fell.

She screeched and kicked and punched but she might as well have struggled with a stone, with a tree, with the mighty earth itself. The weight was around her hips, then her chest, trapping her helpless. She thought she saw Evin as the snow swirled, looking back, and she strained towards him with one hand and shouted, 'Help me!'

Then he was lost in the darkness. Or she was.

'Damn you!' Ro snarled and wept and twisted but all in vain.

She heard Lamb's voice in her ear. 'I'm already damned. But I ain't letting you go again,' and he held her so tight she could scarcely move, could scarcely breathe.

So that was all.

V
Trouble

'Each land in the world produces its own men individually bad – and, in time, other bad men who kill them for the general good.'

Emerson Hough

The Tally

They smelled Beacon long before they saw it. A waft of cooking meat set the famished column shambling downhill through the trees, men slipping and barging and knocking each other over in their haste, sending snow showering. An enterprising hawker had set sticks of meat to cook high up on the slope above the camp. Alas for her, the mercenaries were in no mood to pay and, brushing her protests aside, plundered every shred of gristle as efficiently as a horde of locusts. Even meat as yet uncooked was fought over and wolfed down. One man had his hand pressed into the glowing brazier in the commotion and knelt moaning in the snow, clutching his black-striped palm as Temple laboured past, hugging himself against the cold.

'What a set o' men,' muttered Shy. 'Richer than Hermon and they'd still rather steal.'

'Doing wrong gets to be a habit,' answered Temple, teeth chattering.

The smell of profit must have drifted all the way to Crease because the camp itself was positively booming. Several more barrows had been dug out and several new shacks thrown up and their chimneys busily smoking. More pedlars had set up shop and more whores set down mattress, all crowding happily out to offer succour to the brave conquerors, price lists surreptitiously amended as salesmen noticed, all avaricious amaze, the weight of gold and silver with which the men were burdened.

Cosca was the only one mounted, leading the procession on an exhausted mule. 'Greetings!' He delved into his saddlebag and with a carefree flick of the wrist sent a shower of ancient coins into the air. 'And a happy birthday to you all!'

A stall was toppled, pots and pans clattering as people dived after the pinging coins, huddling about the hooves of the Old Man's mount and jostling each other like pigeons around a handful of seed. An

367

emaciated fiddler, undeterred by his lack of a full complement of strings, struck up a merry jig and capered among the mercenaries, toothlessly grinning.

Beneath that familiar sign proclaiming *Majud and Curnsbick Metalwork*, to which had been carefully added *Weapons and Armour Manufactured and Repaired*, stood Abram Majud, a couple of hirelings keeping the patent portable forge aglow on a narrow strip of ground behind him.

'You've found a new plot,' said Temple.

'A small one. Would you build me a house upon it?'

'Perhaps later.' Temple clasped the merchant's hand, and thought with some nostalgia of an honest day's work done for a half-honest master. Nostalgia was becoming a favoured hobby of his. Strange, how the best moments of our lives we scarcely notice except in looking back.

'And are these the children?' asked Majud, squatting down before Pit and Ro.

'We found 'em,' said Shy, without displaying much triumph.

'I am glad.' Majud offered the boy his hand. 'You must be Pit.'

'I am,' he said, solemnly shaking.

'And you, Ro.'

The girl frowned away, and did not answer.

'She is,' said Shy. 'Or . . . was.'

Majud slapped his knees. 'And I am sure will be again. People change.'

'You sure?' asked Temple.

The merchant put a hand on his shoulder. 'Does not the proof stand before me?'

He was wondering whether that was a joke or a compliment when Cosca's familiar shriek grated at his ear. 'Temple!'

'Your master's voice,' said Shy.

Where was the purpose in disputing it? Temple nodded his apologies and slunk off towards the fort like the beaten dog he was. He passed a man ripping a cooked chicken apart with his hands, face slick with grease. Two others fought over a flask of ale, accidently pulled the stopper, and a third dived between them, mouth open, in a vain effort to catch the spillings. A cheer rang out as a whore was hoisted up on three men's shoulders, festooned with ancient gold, a coronet clasped lopsided to her head and screeching, 'I'm the Queen of the fucking Union! I'm the fucking Queen of the fucking Union!'

'I am glad to see you well.' Sworbreck clapped him on the arm with what felt like genuine warmth.

'Alive, at least.' It had been some time since Temple last felt well.

'How was it?'

Temple considered that. 'No stories of heroism for you to record, I fear.'

'I have given up hope of finding any.'

'I find hope is best abandoned early,' muttered Temple.

The Old Man was beckoning his three captains into a conspiratorial and faintly unpleasant-smelling huddle in the shadow of Superior Pike's great fortified wagon.

'My trusted friends,' he said, starting, as he would continue, with a lie. 'We stand upon the heady pinnacle of attainment. But, speaking as one who has often done so, there is no more precarious perch and those that lose their footing have far to fall. Success tests a friendship far more keenly than failure. We must be doubly watchful of the men and triply cautious in our dealings with all outsiders.'

'Agreed,' nodded Brachio, jowls trembling.

'Indeed,' sneered Dimbik, sharp nose pinked by the cold.

'God knows it,' rumbled Jubair, eyes rolling to the sky.

'How can I fail with three such pillars to support me? The first order of business must be to collect the booty. If we leave it with the men they will have frittered the majority away to these vultures by first light.'

Men cheered as a great butt of wine was tapped, red spots spattering the snow beneath, and began happily handing over ten times the price of the entire barrel for each mug poured.

'By that time they will probably find themselves in considerable debt,' observed Dimbik, slicking back a loose strand of hair with a dampened fingertip.

'I suggest we gather the valuables without delay, then, observed by us all, counted by Sergeant Friendly, notarised by Master Temple, and stored in this wagon under triple-lock.' And Cosca thumped the solid wood of which the wagon was made as though to advertise the good sense and dependability of his suggestion. 'Dimbik, set your most loyal men to guard it.'

Brachio watched a fellow swing a golden chain around his head, jewels sparkling. 'The men won't hand their prizes over happily.'

'They never do, but if we stand together and provide enough distractions they will succumb. How many do we number now, Friendly?'

'One hundred and forty-three,' said the sergeant.

Jubair shook his heavy head at the faithlessness of mankind. 'The Company dwindles alarmingly.'

'We can afford no further desertions,' said Cosca. 'I suggest all mounts be gathered, corralled and closely watched by trusted guards.'

'Risky.' Brachio scratched worriedly at the crease between his chins. 'There are some skittish ones among 'em—'

'That's horses for you. See it done. Jubair, I want a dozen of your best in position to make sure our little surprise goes to plan.'

'Already awaiting your word.'

'What surprise?' asked Temple. God knew, he was not sure he could endure any further excitement.

The captain general grinned. 'A surprise shared is no surprise at all. Don't worry! I feel sure you'll approve.' Temple was in no way reassured. His idea of a good thing and Cosca's intersected less with every passing day. 'Each to our work, then, while I address the men.'

As he watched his three captains move off, Cosca's smile slowly faded, leaving him with eyes narrowed to slits of suspicion. 'I don't trust those bastards further than I could shit.'

'No,' said Friendly.

'No,' said Temple. Indeed, the only man he trusted less stood beside him now.

'I want the two of you to account for the treasure. Every brass bit properly tallied, noted and stored away.'

'Counted?' said Friendly.

'Absolutely, my old friend. And see to it also that there is food and water in the wagon, and a team of horses hitched and at the ready. If things turn . . . ugly here, we may require a swift exit.'

'Eight horses,' said Friendly. 'Four pairs.'

'Now help me up. I have a speech to make.'

With a great deal of grimacing and grumbling, the Old Man managed to clamber onto the seat and then the roof of the wagon, fists bunched upon its wooden parapet, facing out into the camp. By that stage, those not already thoroughly occupied had begun a chant in his honour, weapons, bottles and half-devoured morsels shaken at the evening sky. Tiring of their burden, they unceremoniously deposed the newly crowned Queen of the Union screeching in the mud and plundered her of her borrowed valuables.

'Cosca! Cosca! Cosca!' they roared as the captain general removed his hat, smoothed the white wisps across his pate and spread his arms

370

wide to receive their adulation. Someone seized the beggar's fiddle and smashed it to pieces, then further ensured his silence with a punch in the mouth.

'My honoured companions!' bellowed the Old Man. Time might have dulled some of his faculties but the volume of his voice was unimpaired. 'We have done well!' A rousing cheer. Someone threw money in the air, provoking an ugly scuffle. 'Tonight we celebrate! Tonight we drink, and sing, and revel, as befits a triumph worthy of the heroes of old!' Further cheers, and brotherly embraces, and slapping of backs. Temple wondered whether the heroes of old would have celebrated the herding of a few dozen ancients from a cliff. More than likely. That's heroes for you.

Cosca held up a gnarled hand for quiet, eventually achieved aside from the soft sucking sounds of a couple who were beginning the celebrations early. 'Before the revelry, however, I regret that there must be an accounting.' An immediate change in mood. 'Each man will surrender his booty—' Angry mutterings now broke out. '*All* his booty!' Angrier yet. 'No swallowed jewels, no coins up arses! No one wants to have to look for them there.' A few distinct boos. 'That our majestic haul may be properly valued, recorded, safely kept under triple-lock in this very wagon, to be dispersed as appropriate when we have reached civilisation!'

The mood now verged on the ugly. Temple noted some of Jubair's men, threading watchfully through the crowd. 'We start out tomorrow morning!' roared Cosca. 'But for tonight each man will receive one hundred marks as a bonus to spend as he sees fit!' Some amelioration of the upset at that. 'Let us not spoil our triumph with sour dissent! Remain united, and we can leave this benighted country rich beyond the dreams of greed. Turn against each other, and failure, shame and death will be our just deserts.' Cosca thumped one fist against his breastplate. 'I think, as ever, only of the safety of our noble brother-hood! The sooner your booty is tallied, the sooner the fun begins!'

'What of the rebels?' rang out a piercing voice. Inquisitor Lorsen was shoving his way through the press towards the wagon, and from the look on his gaunt face the fun would not be starting any time soon. 'Where are the rebels, Cosca?'

'The rebels? Ah, yes. The strangest thing. We scoured Ashranc from top to bottom. Would you use the word "scoured", Temple?'

'I would,' said Temple. They had smashed anything that might hold a coin, let alone a rebel.

'But no sign of them?' growled Lorsen.

'We were deceived!' Cosca thumped the parapet in frustration. 'Damn, but these rebels are a slippery crowd! The alliance between them and the Dragon People was a ruse.'

'Their ruse or yours?'

'Inquisitor, you wrong me! I am as disappointed as you are—'

'I hardly think so!' snapped Lorsen. 'You have lined your own pockets, after all.'

Cosca spread his hands in helpless apology. 'That's mercenaries for you.'

A scattering of laughter from the Company but their employer was in no mood to participate. 'You have made me an accomplice to robbery! To murder! To massacre!'

'I held no dagger to your neck. Superior Pike did ask for chaos, as I recall—'

'To a purpose! You have perpetrated mindless slaughter!'

'Mind*ful* slaughter would surely be even worse?' Cosca burst out in a chuckle but Lorsen's black-masked Practicals, scattered about the shadows, lacked all sense of humour.

The Inquisitor waited for silence. 'Do you believe in anything?'

'Not if I can help it. Belief alone is nothing to be proud of, Inquisitor. Belief without evidence is the very hallmark of the savage.'

Lorsen shook his head in amazement. 'You truly are disgusting.'

'I would be the last to disagree, but you fail to see that you are worse. No man capable of greater evil than the one who thinks himself in the right. No purpose more evil than the higher purpose. I freely admit I am a villain. That's why you hired me. But I am no hypocrite.' Cosca gestured at the ragged remnants of his Company, fallen silent to observe the confrontation. 'I have mouths to feed. You could just go home. If you are set on doing good, make something to be proud of. Open a bakery. Fresh bread every morning, there's a noble cause!'

Inquisitor Lorsen's thin lip curled. 'There truly is nothing in you of what separates man from animal, is there? You are bereft of conscience. An utter absence of morality. You have no principle beyond the selfish.'

Cosca's face hardened as he leaned forwards. 'Perhaps when you have faced as many disappointments and suffered as many betrayals as I, you will see it – there is no principle beyond the selfish, Inquisitor, and men *are* animals. Conscience is a burden we choose to bear. Morality is the lie we tell ourselves to make its bearing easier. There have been many times in my life when I have wished it was not so. But it is so.'

372

Lorsen slowly nodded, bright eyes fixed on Cosca. 'There will be a price for this.'

'I am counting on it. Though it seems an almost ludicrous irrelevance now, Superior Pike promised me fifty thousand marks.'

'For the capture of the rebel leader Conthus!'

'Indeed. And there he is.'

There was a scraping of steel, a clicking of triggers, a rattling of armour as a dozen of Jubair's men stepped forward. A circle of drawn swords, loaded flatbows, levelled polearms all suddenly pointed in towards Lamb, Sweet, Shy and Savian. Gently, Majud drew the wide-eyed children close to him.

'Master Savian!' called Cosca. 'I deeply regret that I must ask you to lay down your weapons. Any and all, if you please!'

Betraying no emotion, Savian slowly reached up to undo the buckle on the strap across his chest, flatbow and bolts clattering to the mud. Lamb watched him do it, and calmly bit into a leg of chicken. No doubt that was the easy way, to stand and watch. God knew, Temple had taken that way often enough. Too often, perhaps . . .

He dragged himself up onto the wagon to hiss in Cosca's ear. 'You don't have to do this!'

'Have to? No.'

'Please! How does it help you?'

'Help *me*?' The Old Man raised one brow at Temple as Savian unbuttoned his coat and one by one shed his other weapons. 'It helps me not at all. That is the very essence of selflessness and charity.'

Temple could only stand blinking.

'Are you not always telling me to do the right thing?' asked Cosca. 'Did we not sign a contract? Did we not accept Inquisitor Lorsen's noble cause as our own? Did we not lead him a merry chase up and down this forsaken gulf of distance? Pray be silent, Temple. I never thought to say this, but you are impeding my moral growth.' He turned away to shout, 'Would you be kind enough to roll up your sleeves, Master Savian?'

Savian cleared his throat, metal rattling as the mercenaries nervously shifted, took the button at his collar and undid it, then the next, then the next, the fighters and pedlars and whores all watching the drama unfold in silence. Hedges too, Temple noticed, for some reason with a smile of feverish delight on his face. Savian shrugged his shirt off and stood stripped to the waist, and his whole body from his pale neck to his pale hands was covered in writing, in letters large and tiny, in slogans in a dozen languages: *Death to the Union, Death to the King. The only good Midderlander is a dead one. Never kneel. Never surrender. No Mercy. No Peace. Freedom. Justice. Blood.* He was blue with them.

'I only asked for the sleeves,' said Cosca, 'but I feel the point is made.'

Savian gave the faintest smile. 'What if I said I'm not Conthus?'

'I doubt we'd believe you.' The Old Man looked over at Lorsen, who was staring at Savian with a hungry intensity. 'In fact, I very much doubt we would. Do you have any objections, Master Sweet?'

Sweet blinked around at all that sharpened metal and opted for the easy way. 'Not me. I'm shocked as anyone at this surprising turn of events.'

'You must be quite discomfited to learn you've been travelling with a mass-murderer all this time.' Cosca grinned. 'Well, two, in fact, eh, Master Lamb?' The Northman still picked at his drumstick as though there was no steel pointed in his direction. 'Anything to say on behalf of your friend?'

'Most o' my friends I've killed,' said Lamb around a mouthful. 'I came for the children. The rest is mud.'

Cosca pressed one sorry hand to his breastplate. 'I have stood where you stand, Master Savian, and entirely sympathise. We all are alone in the end.'

'It's a hard fucking world,' said Savian, looking neither right nor left.

'Seize him,' growled Lorsen, and his Practicals swarmed forwards like dogs off the leash. For a moment it looked as if Shy's hand was creeping towards her knife but Lamb held her arm with his free hand, eyes on the ground as the Practicals marched Savian towards the fort. Inquisitor Lorsen followed them inside, smiled grimly out into the camp and slammed the door with a heavy bang.

Cosca shook his head. 'Not even so much as a thank you. Doing right is a dead end, Temple, as I have often said. Queue up, my boys, it's time for an accounting!'

Brachio and Dimbik began to circulate, ushering the men into a grumbling queue, the excitement of Savian's arrest already fading. Temple stared across at Shy, and she stared back at him, but what could either of them do?

'We will need sacks and boxes!' Cosca was shouting. 'Open the wagon and find a table for the count. A door on trestles, then, good enough! Sworbreck? Fetch pen and ink and ledger. Not the writing you came to do, but no less honourable a task!'

'Deeply honoured,' croaked the writer, looking slightly sick.

'We'd best be heading out.' Dab Sweet had made his way over to the wagon and was looking up. 'Get the children back to Crease, I reckon.'

'Of course, my friend,' said Cosca, grinning down. 'You will be sorely missed. Without your skills – let alone the fearsome talents of Master Lamb – the task would have been nigh impossible. The tall tales don't exaggerate in your cases, eh, Sworbreck?'

'They are legends made flesh, captain general,' mumbled the writer.

'We will have to give them a chapter to themselves. Perhaps two! The very best of luck to you and your companions. I will recommend you wherever I go!' Cosca turned away as though that concluded their business.

Sweet looked to Temple, and Temple could only shrug. There was nothing he could do about this either.

The old scout cleared his throat. 'There's just the matter of our share o' the proceeds. As I recall, we discussed a twentieth—'

'What about my share?' Cantliss elbowed his way past Sweet to stare up. 'It was me told you there'd be rebels up there! Me who found those bastards out!'

'Why, so you did!' said Cosca. 'You are a veritable child-stealing Prophet and we owe you all our success!'

Cantliss' bloodshot eyes lit with a fire of greed. 'So . . . what am I due?'

Friendly stepped up from behind, innocuously slipped a noose over his head, and as Cantliss glanced around, Jubair hauled with all his considerable weight on the rope, which had been looped over a beam projecting from the side of the broken tower. Hemp grated as the bandit was hoisted off his feet. One kicking foot knocked a black spray of ink across Sworbreck's ledger and the writer stumbled up, ashen-faced, as Cantliss pawed feebly at the noose with his broken hand, eyes bulging.

'Paid in full!' shouted Cosca. Some of the mercenaries half-heartedly cheered. A couple laughed. One threw an apple core and missed. Most barely raised an eyebrow.

'Oh God,' whispered Temple, picking at the stitching on his buttons and staring at the tarred planks under his feet. But he could still see Cantliss' squirming shadow there. 'Oh God.'

Friendly wound the rope about a tree-stump and tied it off. Hedges, who'd been shoving his way towards the wagon, cleared his throat and carefully retreated, smiling no longer. Shy spat through the gap in her front teeth, and turned away. Lamb stood watching until Cantliss stopped twisting about, one hand resting slack on the hilt of the sword he had taken from the Dragon People. Then he frowned towards the door through which Savian had been taken, and flicked his stripped chicken bone into the mud.

'Seventeen times,' said Friendly, frowning up.

'Seventeen times what?' asked Cosca.

'He kicked. Not counting that last one.'

'That last one was more of a twitch,' said Jubair.

'Is seventeen a lot?' asked the Old Man.

Friendly shrugged. 'About average.'

Cosca looked down at Sweet, grey brows high. 'You were saying something about a share, I think?'

The old scout watched Cantliss creaking back and forth, with a hooked finger gently loosened his collar and opted for the easy way again. 'Must've misremembered. Reckon I'll just be heading on back to Crease, if that's all the same with you.'

'As you wish.' Below them, the first man in line upended his pack and sent gold and silver sliding across the table in a glittering heap. The captain general plumped his hat back on and flicked the feather. 'Happy journey!'

Going Back

'That fucking old shit-fucker!' snarled Sweet, slashing with a stick at a branch that hung over the road and showering snow all over himself. 'Prickomo fucking Cocksca! That bastard old arsehole-fucker!'

'You said that one already, as I recall,' muttered Shy.

'He said old arsehole bastard-fucker,' said Crying Rock.

'My mistake,' said Shy. 'That's a whole different thing.'

'Ain't fucking disagreeing, are you?' snapped Sweet.

'No I'm not,' said Shy. 'He's a hell of a fucker, all right.'

'Shit . . . fuck . . . shit . . . fuck . . .' And Sweet kicked at his horse and whipped at the tree-trunks in a rage as he passed. 'I'll get even with that maggot-eaten bastard, I can tell you that!'

'Let it be,' grunted Lamb. 'Some things you can't change. You got to be realistic.'

'That was my damn retirement got stole there!'

'Still breathing, ain't you?'

'Easy for you to say! You didn't lose no fortune!'

Lamb gave him a look. 'I lost plenty.'

Sweet worked his mouth for a moment, then shouted, 'Fuck!' one last time and flung his stick away into the trees.

A cold and heavy quiet, then. The iron tyres of Majud's wagon scrape-scraping and some loose part in Cursnbick's apparatus in the back clank-clanking under its canvas cover and the horse's hooves crunch-crunching in the snow on the road, rutted from the business flowing up from Crease. Pit and Ro lay in the back under a blanket, faces pressed up against each other, peaceful now in sleep. Shy watched them rocking gently as the axles shifted.

'I guess we did it,' she said.

'Aye,' said Lamb, but looking a long stretch short of a celebration. 'Guess so.'

They rounded another long bend, road switching back one last time as it dropped down steep off the hills, the stream beside half-frozen, white ice creeping out jagged from each bank to almost meet in the middle.

Shy didn't want to say anything. But once a thought was in her head she'd never been much good at keeping it there, and this thought had been pricking at her ever since they left Beacon. 'They're going to be cutting into him, ain't they? Asking questions.'

'Savian?'

'Who else?'

The scarred side of Lamb's face twitched a little. 'That's a fact.'

'Ain't a pretty one.'

'Facts don't tend to be.'

'He saved me.'

'Aye.'

'He saved you.'

'True.'

'We really going to fucking leave him, then?'

Lamb's face twitched again, jaw-muscles working as he frowned out hard across the country ahead. The trees were thinning as they dropped out of the mountains, the moon fat and full in a clear sky star-dusted, spilling light over the high plateau. A great flat expanse of dry dirt and thorny scrub looked like it could never have held life, all half carpeted now with sparkling snow. Through the midst, straight as a sword-cut, the white strip of the old Imperial Road, a scar through the country angling off towards Crease, wedged somewhere in the black rumour of hills on the horizon.

Lamb's horse slowed to a walk, then stopped.

'Shall we halt?' asked Majud.

'You told me you'd be my friend for life,' said Lamb.

The merchant blinked. 'And I meant it.'

'Then keep on.' Lamb turned in his saddle to look back. Behind them, somewhere high up in the folded, forested ridges there was a glow. The great bonfire the mercenaries had stacked high in the middle of Beacon to light their celebrations. 'Got a good road here and a good moon to steer by. Keep on all night, quick and steady, you might make Crease by dark tomorrow.'

'Why the rush?'

378

Lamb took a long breath, looked to the starry sky and breathed out smoke in a grumbling sigh. 'There's going to be trouble.'

'We going back?' asked Shy.

'You're not.' The shadow of his hat fell across his face as he looked at her so his eyes were just two gleams. 'I am.'

'What?'

'You're taking the children. I'm going back.'

'You always were, weren't you?'

He nodded.

'Just wanted to get us far away.'

'I've only had a few friends, Shy. I've done right by even fewer. Could count 'em on one hand.' He turned his left hand over and looked at the stump of his missing finger. 'Even this one. This is how it has to be.'

'Ain't nothing has to be. I ain't letting you go alone.'

'Yes y'are.' He eased his horse closer, looking her in the eye. 'Do you know what I felt, when we came over that hill and saw the farm all burned out? The first thing I felt, before the sorrow and the fear and the anger caught up?'

She swallowed, her mouth all sticky-dry, not wanting to answer, not wanting to know the answer.

'Joy,' whispered Lamb. 'Joy and relief. 'Cause I knew right off what I'd have to do. What I'd have to be. Knew right off I could put an end on ten years of lying. A man's got to be what he is, Shy.' He looked back at his hand and made a three-fingered fist of it. 'I don't . . . *feel* evil. But the things I done. What else can you call 'em?'

'You ain't evil,' she whispered. 'You're just . . .'

'If it hadn't been for Savian I'd have killed you in them caves. You and Ro.'

Shy swallowed. She knew it well enough. 'If it hadn't been for you, we'd never have got the children back.'

Lamb looked at the pair of 'em, Ro with her arm over Pit. Stubble of hair showing dark now, almost grown over the scratch down her scalp. Both so changed. 'Did we get 'em back?' he asked, and his voice was rough. 'Sometimes I think we just lost us, too.'

'I'm who I was.'

Lamb nodded, and it seemed he had the glimmer of tears in his eyes. 'You are, maybe. But I don't reckon there's any going back for me.' He leaned from his saddle then and hugged her tight. 'I love you. And them. But my love ain't a weight anyone should have to carry. Best of luck, Shy. The very best.' And he let her go, and turned his horse, and he rode away, following their tracks back towards the trees, and the hills, and the reckoning beyond.

'What the hell happened to being realistic?' she called after him.

He stopped just a moment, a lonely figure in all that moonlit white. 'Always sounded like a good idea but, being honest? It never worked for me.'

Slow, and numb, Shy turned her back on him. Turned her back and rode on across the plateau, after the wagon and Majud's hired men, after Sweet and Crying Rock, staring at the white road ahead but seeing nothing, tongue working at the gap between her teeth and the night air cold, cold in her chest with each breath. Cold and empty. Thinking about what Lamb had said to her. What she'd said to Savian. Thinking about all the long miles she'd covered the last few months and the dangers she'd faced to get this far, and not knowing what she could do. This was how it had to be.

Except when folk told Shy how things had to be, she started thinking on how to make 'em otherwise.

The wagon hit a lump and with a clatter Pit got jolted awake. He sat up, and he stared blinking about him, and said, 'Where's Lamb?' And Shy's hands went slack on the reins, and she let her horse slow, then stop, and she sat there solemn.

Majud looked over his shoulder. 'Lamb said keep on!'

'You got to do what he tells you? He ain't your father, is he?'

'I suppose not,' said the merchant, pulling up the horses.

'He's mine,' muttered Shy. And there it was. Maybe he wasn't the father she'd want. But he was still the only one she'd got. The only one all three of 'em had got. She'd enough regrets to live with.

'I've got to go back,' she said.

'Madness!' snapped Sweet, sitting his horse not far off. 'Bloody madness!'

'No doubt. And you're coming with me.'

A silence. 'You know there's more'n a hundred mercenaries up there, don't you? Killers, every man?'

'The Dab Sweet I heard stories of wouldn't take fright at a few mercenaries.'

'Don't know if you noticed, but the Dab Sweet you heard stories of ain't much like the one wearing my coat.'

'I hear you used to be.' She rode up to him and reined in close. 'I hear you used to be quite a man.'

Crying Rock slowly nodded. 'That is true.'

Sweet frowned at the old Ghost woman, and frowned at Shy, and finally frowned at the ground, scratching at his beard and bit by bit slumping down in his saddle. 'Used to be. You're young and got dreams ahead of you still. You don't know how it is. One day you're something, so promising and full o' dares, so big the world's too small a place to hold you. Then, 'fore you know it, you're old, and you realise all them things you had in mind you'll never get to. All them doors you felt too big to fit through have already shut. Only one left open and it leads to nothing but nothing.' He pulled his hat off and scrubbed at his white hair with his dirty nails. 'You lose your nerve. And once it's gone where do you find it? I got scared, Shy South. And once you get scared there ain't no going back, there just ain't no—'

Shy caught a fist of his fur coat and dragged him close. 'I ain't giving up this way, you hear me? I just ain't *fucking* having it! Now I need that bastard who killed a red bear with his hands up at the source of the Sokwaya, whether it bloody well happened or not. You hear me, you old shit?'

He blinked at her for a moment. 'I hear you.'

'Well? You want to get even with Cosca or you just want to swear about it?'

Crying Rock had brought her horse close. 'Maybe do it for Leef,' she said. 'And those others buried on the plains.'

Sweet stared at her weather-beaten face for a long moment, for some reason with the strangest, haunted look in his eye. Then his mouth twitched into a smile. 'How come after all this time you're still so damn beautiful?' he asked.

Crying Rock just shrugged, like facts were facts, and stuck her pipe between her teeth.

Sweet reached up and brushed Shy's hand away. He straightened his fur coat. He leaned from his saddle and spat. He looked with narrowed eyes up towards Beacon and set his jaw. 'If I get killed I'm going to haunt your skinny arse for life.'

'If you get killed I doubt my life'll be too long a stretch.' Shy slipped down from her saddle and crunched stiff-legged to the wagon, stood looking down at her brother and sister. 'Got something to take care of,' she said, putting a gentle hand on each of them. 'You go on with Majud. He's a little on the stingy side but he's one of the good ones.'

'Where you going?' asked Pit.

'Left something behind.'

'Will you be long?'

She managed to smile. 'Not long. I'm sorry, Ro. I'm sorry for everything.'

'So am I,' said Ro. Maybe that was something. For sure it was all she'd get.

She touched Pit's cheek. Just a brush with her fingertips. 'I'll see you two in Crease. You'll hardly notice I'm gone.'

Ro sniffed, sleepy and sullen, and wouldn't meet her eye, and Pit stared at her, face all tracked with tears. She wondered if she really would see them in Crease. Madness, like Sweet said, to come all this way just to let them go. But there was no point to long goodbyes. Sometimes it's better to do a thing than live with the fear of it. That's what Lamb used to say.

'Go!' she shouted at Majud, before she had the chance to change her mind. He nodded to her, and snapped the reins, and the wagon rolled on.

'Better to do it,' she whispered at the night sky, and she clambered back into her saddle, turned her horse about, and gave it her heels.

Answered Prayers

Temple drank. He drank like he had after his wife died. As if there was something at the bottom of the bottle he desperately needed. As if it was a race he had bet his life on. As if drinking was a profession he planned on rising right to the top of. Tried most of the others, hadn't he?

'You should stop,' said Sworbreck, looking worried.

'You should start,' said Temple, and laughed, even if he'd never felt like laughing less. Then he burped and there was some sick in it, and he washed the taste away with another swallow.

'You have to pace yourself,' said Cosca, who was not pacing himself in the least. 'Drinking is an art, not a science. You caress the bottle. You tease it. You romance it. A drink . . . a drink . . . a drink . . .' kissing at the air with each repetition, eyelids flickering. 'Drinking is like . . . *love.*'

'What the fuck do you know about love?'

'More than I'd like,' answered the Old Man, a faraway look in his yellowed eye, and he gave a bitter laugh. 'Despicable men still love, Temple. Still feel pain. Still nurse wounds. Despicable men most of all, maybe.' He slapped Temple on the back, sent a searing swig the wrong way and induced a painful coughing fit. 'But let's not be maudlin! We're rich, boy! All rich. And rich men need make no apologies. To Visserine for me. Take back what I lost. What was stolen.'

'What you threw away,' muttered Temple, quietly enough not to be heard over the racket.

'Yes,' mused Cosca. 'Soon there'll be space for a new captain general.' He took in the noisy, crowded, sweltering room with a sweep of his arm. 'All this will be yours.'

It was quite a scene of debauch to cram into a one-roomed hovel, lit by a single guttering lamp and hazy with chagga smoke, noisy with laughter and conversations in several languages. Two big Northmen were wrestling, possibly in fun, possibly with the intention of killing each other, people occasionally lurching out of their way. Two natives of the Union and an Imperial bitterly complained as their table was jogged in the midst of a card-game, bottles tottering on top. Three Styrians had shared a husk-pipe and were blissfully lounging on a burst mattress in one corner, somewhere between sleep and waking. Friendly was sitting with legs crossed and rolling his dice between them, over and over and over, frowning down with furious concentration as though the answers to everything would soon appear on their dozen faces.

'Hold on,' muttered Temple, his pickled mind only now catching up. 'Mine?'

'Who better qualified? You've learned from the best, my boy! You're a lot like me, Temple, I've always said so. Great men march often in the same direction, did Stolicus say?'

'Like you?' whispered Temple.

Cosca tapped his greasy grey hair. 'Brains, boy, you've got the brains. Your morals can be stiff at times but they'll soon soften up once you have to make the tough choices. You can talk well, know how to spot people's weaknesses, and above all you understand the *law*. The strong-arm stuff's all going out of fashion. I mean, there'll always be a place for it, but the law, Temple, that's where the money's going to be.'

'What about Brachio?'

'Family in Puranti.'

'Really?' Temple blinked across the room at Brachio, who was in a vigorous embrace with a large Kantic woman. 'He never mentioned them.'

'A wife and two daughters. Who talks about their family with scum like us?'

'What about Dimbik?'

'Pah! No sense of humour.'

'Jubair?'

'Mad as a plum jelly.'

'But I'm no soldier. I'm a fucking coward!'

'Admirable thing in a mercenary.' Cosca stretched forward his chin and scratched at his rashy neck with the backs of his yellowed nails. 'I'd have done far better with a healthy respect for danger. It's not as if you'll be swinging the steel yourself. The job's all talk. Blah, blah, blah and big hats. That and knowing when not to keep your word.'

He wagged a knobbly finger. 'I was always too bloody emotional. Too bloody loyal. But you? You're a treacherous bastard, Temple.'

'I am?'

'You abandoned me when it suited and found new friends, then when it suited you abandoned them and sauntered straight back without so much as a by-your-leave!'

Temple blinked at that. 'I rather had the feeling you'd have killed me otherwise.'

Cosca waved it away. 'Details! I've had you marked as my successor for some time.'

'But . . . no one respects me.'

'Because you don't respect yourself. Doubt, Temple. Indecision. You simply worry too much. Sooner or later you have to do something, or you'll never do anything. Overcome that, you could be a wonderful captain general. One of the greats. Better than me. Better than Sazine. Better than Murcatto, even. You might want to cut down on the drinking, though.' Cosca tossed his empty bottle away, pulled the cork from another with his teeth and spat it across the room. 'Filthy habit.'

'I don't want to do this any more,' Temple whispered.

Cosca waved that away, too. 'You say that all the time. Yet here you are.'

Temple lurched up. 'Got to piss.'

The cold air slapped him so hard he nearly fell against one of the guards, sour-faced from having to stay sober. He stumbled along the wooden side of Superior Pike's monstrous wagon, thinking how close his palm was to a fortune, past the stirring horses, breath steaming out of their nosebags, took a few crunching steps into the trees, sounds of revelry muffled behind him, shoved his bottle down in the frozen snow and unlaced with drunken fingers. Bloody hell, it was cold still. He leaned back, blinking at the sky, bright stars spinning and dancing beyond the black branches.

Captain General Temple. He wondered what Haddish Kahdia would have thought of that. He wondered what God thought of it. How had it come to this? He'd always had good intentions, hadn't he? He'd always tried to do his best.

It's just that his best had always been shit.

'God?' he brayed at the sky. 'You up there, you bastard?' Perhaps He was the mean bully Jubair made Him out to be, after all. 'Just . . . give me a sign, will you? Just a little one. Just steer me the right way. Just . . . just give me a nudge.'

385

'I'll give you a nudge.'

He froze for a moment, still dripping. 'God? Is that you?'

'No, fool.' There was a crunch as someone pulled his bottle out of the snow.

He turned. 'I thought you left.'

'Came back.' Shy tipped the bottle up and took a swig, one side of her face all dark, the other lit by the flickering bonfire in the camp. 'Thought you'd never come out o' there,' she said, wiping her mouth.

'Been waiting?'

'Little while. Are you drunk?'

'Little bit.'

'That works for us.'

'It works for me.'

'I see that,' she said, glancing down.

He realised he hadn't laced-up yet and started fumbling away. 'If you wanted to see my cock that badly, you could just have asked.'

'No doubt a thing o' haunting beauty but I came for something else.'

'Got a window needs jumping through?'

'No. I might need your help.'

'Might?'

'Things run smooth you can just creep back to drowning your sorrows.'

'How often do things run smooth for you?'

'Not often.'

'Is it likely to be dangerous?'

'Little bit.'

'Really a little bit?'

She drank again. 'No. A lot.'

'This about Savian?'

'Little bit.'

'Oh God,' he muttered, rubbing at the bridge of his nose and willing the dark world to be still. Doubt, that was his problem. Indecision. Worrying too much. He wished he was less drunk. Then he wished he was more. He'd asked for a sign, hadn't he? Why had he asked for a sign? He'd never expected to get one.

'What do you need?' he muttered, his voice very small.

Sharp Ends

Practical Wile slid a finger under his mask to rub at the little chafe marks. Not the worst part of the job, but close.

'There it is, though,' he said, rearranging his cards, as if that made his hand any less rotten, 'I daresay she's found someone else by now.'

'If she's got any sense,' grunted Pauth.

Wile nearly thumped the table, then worried that he might hurt his hand and stopped short. 'This is what I mean by undermining! We're supposed to look out for each other but you're always talking me down!'

'Weren't nothing in the oaths I swore about not talking you down,' said Pauth, tossing a couple of cards and sliding a couple more off the deck.

'Loyalty to his Majesty,' threw out Bolder, 'and obedience to his Eminence and the ruthless rooting out of treasons, but nothing about looking out for no one.'

'Doesn't mean it's a bad idea,' grumbled Wile, re-rearranging his rotten hand.

'You're confusing how you'd like the world to be with how it is,' said Bolder. 'Again.'

'A little solidarity is all I'm asking. We're all stuck in the same leaky boat.'

'Start baling and stop bloody moaning, then.' Pauth had a good scratch under his own mask. 'All the way out here you've done nothing but moan. The food. The cold. Your mask sores. Your sweetheart. My snoring. Bolder's habits. Lorsen's temper. It's enough to make a man quite aggravated.'

'Even if life weren't aggravating enough to begin with,' said Ferring, who was out of the game and had been sitting with his boots up on the table for the best part of an hour. Ferring had the most unnatural patience with doing nothing.

Pauth eyed him. 'Your boots are pretty damn aggravating.'

Ferring eyed him back. Those sharp blue eyes of his. 'Boots is boots.'

'Boots is boots? What does that even mean? Boot is boots?'

'If you've nothing worth saying, you two might consider not saying it.' Bolder nodded his lump of a head towards the prisoner. 'Take a page out of his book.' The old man hadn't said a word to Lorsen's questions. Hadn't done much more than grunt even when they burned him. He just watched, eyes narrowed, raw flesh glistening in the midst of his tattoos.

Ferring's eyes shifted over to Wile's. 'You think you'd take a burning that well?'

Wile didn't reply. He didn't like thinking about taking a burning. He didn't like giving one to someone else, whatever oaths he'd sworn, whatever treasons, murders or massacres the man was meant to have masterminded. One thing holding forth about justice at a thousand miles removed. Another having to press metal into flesh. He just didn't like thinking about it at all.

It's a steady living, the Inquisition, his father had told him. *Better asking the questions than giving the answers anyway, eh?* And they'd laughed together at that, though Wile hadn't found it funny. He used to laugh a lot at unfunny things his father said. He wouldn't have laughed now. Or maybe that was giving himself too much credit. He'd a bad habit of doing that.

Sometimes Wile wondered whether a cause could be right that needed folk burned, cut and otherwise mutilated. Hardly the tactics of the just, was it, when you took a step back? Rarely seemed to produce any truly useful results either. Unless pain, fear, hate and mutilation were what you were after. Maybe it *was* what they were after.

Sometimes Wile wondered whether the torture might cause the very disloyalty the Inquisition was there to stop, but he kept that notion very much to himself. Takes courage to lead a charge, but you've got people behind you there. Takes a different and rarer kind to stand up all alone and say, 'I don't like the way we do things.' Especially to a set of torturers. Wile didn't have either kind of courage. So he just did as he was told and tried not to think about it, and wondered what it would be like to have a job you believed in.

Ferring didn't have that same problem. He liked the work. You could see it in those blue, blue eyes of his. He grinned over at the tattooed old man now and said, 'Doubt he'll be taking a burning that well by the time he gets back to Starikland.' The prisoner just sat and watched, blue-painted ribs shifting with his crackly breathing. 'Lot of nights between here and there. Lot of burnings, maybe. Yes, indeedy. Reckon he'll be good and talkative by—'

'I already suggested you shut up,' said Bolder. 'Now I'm thinking o' making it an instruction. What do you—'

There was a knock at the door. Three quick knocks, in fact. The Practicals looked at each other, eyebrows up. Lorsen back with more questions. Once Lorsen had a question in mind, he wasn't a man to wait for an answer.

'You going to get that?' Pauth asked Ferring.

'Why would I?'

'You're closest.'

'You're shortest.'

'What's that got to fucking do with anything?'

'It amuses me.'

'Maybe my knife up your arse will amuse me!' And Pauth slipped his knife out of his sleeve, blade appearing as if by magic. He loved to do that. Bloody show-off.

'Will you two infants *please* shut up?' Bolder chucked down his cards, levered his bulk from his chair and slapped Pauth's knife aside. 'I came out here to get a break from my bloody children, not to mind three more.'

Wile rearranged his cards again, wondering if there was some way he could win. One win, was that too much to ask? But such a rotten hand. His father had always said *there are no rotten hands, only rotten players*, but Wile believed otherwise.

Another insistent knocking. 'All right, I'm coming!' snapped Bolder, dragging back the bolts. 'It's not as if—'

There was a clatter, and Wile looked up to see Bolder lurching against the wall looking quite put out and someone barging past. Seemed a bit strong even if they'd taken a while to answer the door. Bolder obviously agreed, because he opened his mouth to complain, then looked surprised when he gurgled blood everywhere instead. That was when Wile noticed there was a knife-handle sticking from his fat throat.

He dropped his cards.

'Eh?' said Ferring, trying to get up, but his boots were tangled with the table. It wasn't Lorsen who'd been knocking, it was the big

Northman, the one with all the scars. He took a stride into the room, teeth bared, and crunch! Left a knife buried in Ferring's face to the cross-piece, his nose flattened under it and blood welling and Ferring wheezed and arched back and kicked the table over, cards and coins flying.

Wile stumbled up, the Northman turning to look at him, blood dotting his face and pulling another knife from inside his coat, and—

'Stop!' hissed Pauth. 'Or I kill him!' Somehow he'd got to the prisoner, kneeling behind the chair he was roped to, knife blade pressed against his neck. Always been a quick thinker, Pauth. Good thing someone was.

Bolder had slid to the floor, was making a honking sound and drooling blood into a widening pool.

Wile realised he was holding his breath and took a great gasp.

The scarred Northman looked from Wile, to Pauth, and back, lifted his chin slightly, then gently lowered his blade.

'Get help!' snapped Pauth, and he tangled his fingers in the prisoner's grey hair and pulled his head back, tickling his stubbled neck with the point of his knife. 'I'll see to this.'

Wile circled the Northman, his knees all shaky, pushing aside one of the leather curtains that divided up the fort's downstairs, trying to keep as safe a distance as possible. He slithered in Bolder's blood and nearly went right over, then dived out of the open door and was running.

'Help!' he screeched. 'Help!'

One of the mercenaries lowered a bottle and stared at him, cross-eyed. 'Wha?' The celebrations were still half-heartedly dragging on, women laughing and men singing and shouting and rolling in a stupor, none of them enjoying it but going through the motions anyway like a corpse that can't stop twitching, all garishly lit by the sizzling bonfire. Wile slid over in the mud, staggered up, dragging down his mask so he could shout louder.

'Help! The Northman! The prisoner!'

Someone was pointing at him and laughing, and someone shouted at him to shut up, and someone was sick all over the side of a tent, and Wile stared about for anyone who might exert some control over this shambles and suddenly felt somebody clutch at his arm.

'What are you jabbering about?' None other than General Cosca, dewy eyes gleaming with the firelight, lady's white powder smeared across one hollow, rash-speckled cheek.

'That Northman!' squealed Wile, grabbing the captain general by his stained shirt. 'Lamb! He killed Bolder! And Ferring!' He pointed a trembling finger towards the fort. 'In there!'

To give him his due, Cosca needed no convincing. 'Enemies in the camp!' he roared, flinging his empty bottle away. 'Surround the fort! You, cover the door, make sure no one leaves! Dimbik, get men around the back! You, put that woman down! Arm yourselves, you wretches!'

Some snapped to obey. Two found bows and pointed them uncertainly towards the door. One accidently shot an arrow into the fire. Others stared baffled, or continued with their revelry, or stood grinning, imagining that this was some elaborate joke.

'What the hell happened?' Lorsen, black coat flapping open over his nightshirt, hair wild about his head.

'It would appear our friend Lamb attempted a rescue of your prisoner,' said Cosca. 'Get away from that door, you idiots – do you think this is a joke?'

'Rescue?' muttered Sworbreck, eyebrows raised and eyeglasses skewed, evidently having recently crawled from his bed.

'Rescue?' snapped Lorsen, grabbing Wile by the collar.

'Pauth took the prisoner . . . prisoner. He's seeing to it—'

A figure lurched from the fort's open door, took a few lazy steps, eyes wide above his mask, hands clasped to his chest. Pauth. He pitched on his face, blood turning the snow around him pink.

'You were saying?' snapped Cosca. A woman shrieked, stumbled back with a hand over her mouth. Men started to drag themselves from tents and shacks, bleary-eyed, pulling on clothes and bits of armour, fumbling with weapons, breath smoking in the cold.

'Get more bows up here!' roared Cosca, clawing at his blistered neck with his fingernails. 'I want a pincushion of anything that shows itself! Clear the bloody civilians away!'

Lorsen was hissing in Wile's face. 'Is Conthus still alive?'

'I think so . . . he was when I . . . when I—'

'Cravenly fled? Pull your mask up, damn it, you're a disgrace!'

Probably the Inquisitor was right, and Wile was a disgraceful Practical. He felt strangely proud of that possibility.

'Can you hear me, Master Lamb?' called Cosca, as Sergeant Friendly helped him into his gilded, rusted breastplate, a combination of pomp and decay that rather summed up the man.

'Aye,' came the Northman's voice from the black doorway of the fort. The closest thing to silence had settled over the camp since the mercenaries returned in triumph the previous day.

'I am so pleased you have graced us with your presence again!' The captain general waved half-dressed bowmen into the shadows around the shacks. 'I wish you'd sent word of your coming, though, we could have prepared a more suitable reception!'

'Thought I'd surprise you.'

'We appreciate the gesture! But I should say I have some hundred and fifty fighting men out here!' Cosca took in the wobbling bows, dewy eyes and bilious faces of his Company. 'Several of them are very drunk, but still. Long established admirer though I am of lost causes, I really don't see the happy ending for you!'

'I've never been much for happy endings,' came Lamb's growl. Wile didn't know how a man could sound so steady under these circumstances.

'Nor me, but perhaps we can engineer one between us!' With a couple of gestures Cosca sent more men scurrying down either side of the fort and ordered a fresh bottle. 'Now why don't you two put your weapons down and come out, and we can all discuss this like civilised men!'

'Never been much for civilisation either,' called Lamb. 'Reckon you'll have to come to me.'

'Bloody Northmen,' muttered Cosca, ripping the cork from his latest bottle and flinging it away. 'Dimbik, are any of your men not drunk?'

'You wanted them as drunk as possible,' said the captain, who had got himself tangled with his bedraggled sash as he tried to pull it on.

'Now I need them sober.'

'A few who were on guard, perhaps—'

'Send them in.'

'And we want Conthus alive!' barked Lorsen.

Dimbik bowed. 'We will do our best, Inquisitor.'

'But there can be no promises.' Cosca took a long swallow from his bottle without taking his eyes from the house. 'We'll make that Northern bastard regret coming back.'

'You shouldn't have come back,' grunted Savian as he loaded the flatbow.

Lamb edged the door open to peer through. 'Regretting it already.' A thud, splinters, and the bright point of a bolt showed between the planks. Lamb jerked his head back and kicked the door wobbling shut. 'Hasn't quite gone the way I'd hoped.'

'You could say that about most things in life.'

'In my life, no doubt.' Lamb took hold of the knife in the Practical's neck and ripped it free, wiped it on the front of the dead man's black jacket and tossed it to Savian. He snatched it out of the air and slid it into his belt.

'You can never have too many knives,' said Lamb.

'It's a rule to live by.'

'Or die by,' said Lamb as he tossed over another. 'You need a shirt?'

Savian stretched out his arms and watched the tattoos move. The words he'd tried to live his life by. 'What's the point in getting 'em if you don't show 'em off? I've been covering up too long.'

'Man's got to be what he is, I reckon.'

Savian nodded. 'Wish we'd met thirty years ago.'

'No you don't. I was a mad fucker then.'

'And now?'

Lamb stuck a dagger into the tabletop. 'Thought I'd learned something.' He thumped another into the doorframe. 'But here I am, handing out knives.'

'You pick a path, don't you?' Savian started drawing the string on the other flatbow. 'And you think it's just for tomorrow. Then thirty years on you look back and see you picked your path for life. If you'd known it then, you'd maybe have thought more carefully.'

'Maybe. Being honest, I've never been much for thinking carefully.'

Savian finally fumbled the string back, glancing at the word *freedom* tattooed around his wrist like a bracelet. 'Always thought I'd die fighting for the cause.'

'You will,' said Lamb, still busy scattering weapons around the room. 'The cause of saving my fat old arse.'

'It's a noble calling.' Savian slipped a bolt into place. 'Reckon I'll get upstairs.'

'Reckon you'd better.' Lamb drew the sword he'd taken from Waerdinur, long and dull with that silver letter glinting. 'We ain't got all night.'

'You'll be all right down here?'

'Might be best if you just stay up there. That mad fucker from thirty years ago – sometimes he comes visiting.'

'Then I'll leave the two of you to it. You shouldn't have come back.' Savian held out his hand. 'But I'm glad you did.'

'Wouldn't have missed it.' Lamb took a grip on Savian's hand and gave it a squeeze, and they looked each other in the eye. Seemed in that moment they had as good an understanding between them as if they had met thirty years ago. But the time for friendship was over. Savian had always put more effort into his enemies, and there was no shortage outside. He turned and took the stairs three at a time, up into the garret, a flatbow in each hand and the bolts over his shoulder.

Four windows, two to the front, two to the back. Straw pallets around the walls and a low table with a lit lamp, and in its flickering pool of light a hunting bow and a quiver of arrows, and a spiked mace, too, metal gleaming. One handy thing about mercenaries, they leave weapons lying about wherever they go. He slipped in a crouch to the front, propped one of the flatbows carefully under the left-hand window and then scurried over to the right with the other, hooking the shutters open and peering out.

There was a fair bit of chaos underway outside, lit by the great bonfire, sparks whirling, folk hurrying this way and that on the far side. Seemed some of those who'd come to get rich on the Company's scraps hadn't reckoned on getting stuck in the middle of a fight. The corpse of one of the Practicals was stretched out near the door but Savian shed no tears for him. He'd cried easily as a child, but his eyes had good and dried up down the years. They'd had to. With what he'd seen, and what he'd done, too, there wouldn't have been enough salt water in the world.

He saw archers, squatting near the shacks, bows trained towards the fort, made a quick note of the positions, of the angles, of the distances. Then he saw men hurrying forward, axes at the ready. He snatched the lamp off the table and tossed it spinning through the dark, saw it shatter on the thatch roof of one of the shacks, streaks of fire shooting hungrily out.

'They're coming for the door!' he shouted.

'How many?' came Lamb's voice from downstairs.

'Five, maybe!' His eyes flickered across the shadows down there around the bonfire. 'Six!' He worked the stock of the flatbow into his shoulder, settling down still and steady around it, warm and familiar as curling around a lover's back. He wished he'd spent more of his time curled around a lover and less around a flatbow, but he'd picked his path and here was the next step along it. He twitched the trigger and felt the bow jolt and one of the axemen took a tottering step sideways and sat down.

'Five!' shouted Savian as he slipped away from the window and over to another, setting down the first bow and hefting the second. Heard arrows clatter against the frame behind, one spinning into the darkness of the room. He levelled the bow, caught a black shape against the fire and felt the shot, a mercenary staggered back and tripped into the flames and even over the racket Savian could hear him screaming as he burned.

He slid down, back against the wall under the window. Saw an arrow flit through above him and shudder into a rafter. He was caught for a moment with a coughing fit, managed to settle it, breath rasping, the burns around his ribs all stinging fresh. Axes at the door, now, he could hear them thudding. Had to leave that to Lamb. Only man alive he'd have trusted alone with that task. He heard voices at the back, quiet, but he heard them. Up onto his feet and he scuttled to the back wall, taking up the hunting bow, no time to buckle the quiver, just wedging it through his belt.

He dragged in a long, crackling breath, stifled a cough and held it, nocked an arrow, drew the string, in one movement poked the limb of the bow behind the shutters and flicked them open, stood, leaned out and pushed the air slow through his pursed lips.

Men crouched in the shadows against the foot of the back wall. One looked up, eyes wide in his round face, and Savian shot him in his open mouth no more than a stride or two away. He nocked another shaft. An arrow whipped past him, flicking his hair. He drew the bow, calm and steady. He could see light gleam on the archer's arrowhead as he did the same. Shot him in the chest. Drew another arrow. Saw a man running past. Shot him too and saw him crumple in the snow. Crunching of footsteps as the last of them ran away. Savian took a bead and shot him in the back, and he crawled and whimpered and coughed, and Savian nocked an arrow and shot him a second time, elbowed the shutters closed and breathed in again.

He was caught with a coughing fit and stood shuddering against the wall. He heard a roar downstairs, clash of steel, swearing, crashing, ripping, fighting.

He stumbled to the front window again, nocking an arrow, saw two men rushing for the door, shot one in the face and his legs went from under him. The other skidded to a stop, scuttled off sideways. Arrows were frozen in the firelight, clattering against the front of the building as Savian twisted away.

A crack and the shutters in the back window swung open showing a square of night sky. Savian saw a hand on the sill, let fall the bow and snatched up the mace as he went, swinging it low and fast to miss the rafters and smashing it into a helmeted head as it showed itself at the window, knocking someone tumbling out into the night.

He spun, black shape in the window as a man slipped into the attic, knife in his teeth. Savian lunged at him but the haft of the mace glanced off his shoulder and they grappled and struggled, growling at each other. Savian felt a burning in his gut, fell back against the wall with the man on top of him, reached for the knife at his belt. He saw one half of the mercenary's snarling face lit by firelight and Savian stabbed at it, ripped it open, black pulp hanging from his head as he stumbled, thrashing blindly around the attic. Savian clawed his way up and fell on him, dragged him down and stabbed and coughed and stabbed until he stopped moving, knelt on top of him, each cough ripping at the wound in his guts.

A bubbling scream had started downstairs, and Savian heard someone squealing, 'No! No! No!' slobbering, desperate, and he heard Lamb growl, 'Yes, you fucker!' Two heavy thuds, then a long silence.

Lamb gave a kind of groan downstairs, another crash like he was kicking something over.

'You all right?' he called, his own voice sounding tight and strange.

'Still breathing!' came Lamb's, even stranger. 'You?'

'Picked up a scratch.' Savian peeled his palm away from his tattooed stomach, blood there gleaming black. Lot of blood.

He wished he could talk to Corlin one last time. Tell her all those things you think but never say because they're hard to say and there'll be time later. How proud he was of what she'd become. How proud her mother would've been. To carry on the fight. He winced. Or maybe to give up the fight, because you only get one life and do you want to look back on it and see just blood on your hands?

But it was too late to tell her anything. He'd picked his path and here was where it ended. Hadn't been too poor a showing, all told. Some good and some bad, some pride and some shame, like most men. He crawled coughing to the front, took up one of the flatbows and started wrestling at the string with sticky hands. Damn hands. Didn't have the strength they used to.

He stood up beside the window, men still moving down there, and the shack he threw the lamp on sending up a roaring blaze now, and he bellowed out into the night. 'That the best you can do?'

'Sadly for you,' came Cosca's voice. 'No!'

Something sparked and fizzled in the darkness, and there was a flash like daylight.

It was a noise like to the voice of God, as the scriptures say, which levelled the city of the presumptuous Nemai with but a whisper. Jubair peeled his hands from his ears, all things still ringing even so, and squinted towards the fort as the choking smoke began to clear.

Much violence had been done to the building. There were holes finger-sized, and fist-sized, and head-sized rent through the walls of the bottom floor. Half of the top floor had departed the world, splintered planks smouldering in places, three split beams still clinging together at one corner as a reminder of the shape of what had been. There was a creaking and half the roof fell in, broken shingles clattering to the ground below.

'Impressive,' said Brachio.

'The lightning harnessed,' murmured Jubair, frowning at the pipe of brass. It had nearly leaped from its carriage with the force of the blast and now sat skewed upon it, smoke still issuing gently from its blackened mouth. 'Such a power should belong only to God.'

He felt Cosca's hand upon his shoulder. 'And yet He lends it to us to do His work. Take some men in there and find those two old bastards.'

'I want Conthus alive!' snapped Lorsen.

'If possible.' The Old Man leaned close to whisper. 'But dead is just as good.'

Jubair nodded. He had come to a conclusion long years before that God sometimes spoke through the person of Nicomo Cosca. An unlikely prophet, some might say – a treacherous, lawless pink drunkard who had never uttered a word of prayer in all his long life – but from the first moment Jubair had seen him in battle, and known he had no fear, he had sensed in him some splinter of the divine. Surely he walked in God's shadow, as the Prophet Khalul had walked naked through a rain of arrows with only his faith to protect him and emerged untouched, and so forced the Emperor of the Gurkish to honour his promise and abase himself before the Almighty.

'You three,' he said, picking out some of his men with a finger, 'on my signal go in by the door. You three, come with me.'

One of them, a Northman, shook his head with starting eyes round as full moons. 'It's . . . *him*,' he whispered.

'Him?'

'The . . . the . . .' And in dumbstruck silence he folded the middle finger on his left hand back to leave a gap.

Jubair snorted. 'Stay then, fool.' He trotted around the side of the fort, through shadow and deeper shadow, all the same to him for he carried the light of God within. His men peered up at the building, breathing hard, afraid. They supposed the world was a complicated place, full of dangers. Jubair pitied them. The world was simple. The only danger was in resisting God's purpose.

Fragments of timber, rubbish and dust were scattered across the snow behind the building. That and several arrow-shot men, one sitting against the wall and softly gurgling, hand around a shaft through his mouth. Jubair ignored them and quietly scaled the back wall of the fort. He peered into the ruined loft, furniture ripped apart, a mattress spilling straw, no signs of life. He brushed some embers away and pulled himself up, slid out his sword, metal glinting in the night, fearless, righteous, godly. He eased forward, watching the stairwell, black with shadows. He heard a sound from down there, a regular thump, thump, thump.

He leaned out at the front of the building and saw his three men clustered below. He hissed at them, and the foremost kicked the door wide and plunged inside. Jubair pointed the other two to the stairwell. He felt something give beneath the sole of his boot as he turned. A hand. He bent and dragged a timber aside.

'Conthus is here!' he shouted.

'Alive?' came Lorsen's shrill bleat.

'Dead.'

'Damn it!'

Jubair gathered up what was left of the rebel and rolled it over the ragged remnant of the wall, tumbling down the snow drifted against the side of the building to lie broken and bloody, tattoos ripped with a score of wounds. Jubair thought of the parable of the proud man. God's judgement comes to great and small alike, all equally powerless before the Almighty, inevitable and irreversible, and so it was, so it was. Now there was only the Northman, and however fearsome he might be, God had a sentence already in mind—

A scream split the night, a crashing below, roars and groans and a metal scraping, then a strange hacking laugh, another scream. Jubair strode to the stairs. A wailing below, now, as horrible as the sinful dead consigned to hell, blubbering off into silence. The point of Jubair's sword showed the way. Fearless, righteous . . . He hesitated, licking at his lips. To feel fear was to be without faith. It is not given to man to understand God's design. Only to accept his place in it.

And so he clenched his jaw tight, and padded down the steps.

Black as hell below, light shining in rays of flickering red, orange, yellow, through the holes in the front wall, casting strange shadows. Black as hell and like hell it reeked of death, so strong the stench it seemed a solid thing. Jubair half-held his breath as he descended, step by creaking step, eyes adjusting to the darkness by degrees.

What revelation?

The leather curtains that had divided up the space hung torn, showered and spotted with black, stirred a little as if by wind though the space was still. His boot caught something on the bottom step and he looked down. A severed arm. Frowning, he followed its glistening trail to a black slick, flesh humped and mounded and inhumanly abused, hacked apart and tangled together in unholy configurations, innards dragged out and rearranged and unwound in glistening coils.

In the midst stood a table and upon the table a pile of heads, and as the light shifted from the flames outside they looked upon Jubair with expressions awfully vacant, madly leering, oddly questioning, angrily accusatory.

'God . . .' he said. Jubair had done butchery in the name of the Almighty and yet he had seen nothing like this. This was written in no scripture, except perhaps in the forbidden seventh of the seven books, sealed within the tabernacle of the Great Temple in Shaffa, in which were recorded those things that Glustrod brought from hell.

'God . . .' he muttered. And jagged laughter bubbled from the shadows, and the skins flapped, and rattled the rings they hung upon. Jubair darted forward, stabbed, cut, slashed at darkness, caught nothing but dangling skin, blade tangled with leather and he slipped in gore, and fell, and rose, turning, turning, the laugher all around him.

'God?' mumbled Jubair, and he could hardly speak the holy word for a strange feeling, beginning in his guts and creeping up and down his spine to set his scalp to tingle and his knees to shake. All the more terrible for being only dimly remembered. A childish recollection, lost in darkness. For as the Prophet said, the man who knows fear every day becomes easy in its company. The man who knows not fear, how shall he face this awful stranger?

'God . . .' whimpered Jubair, stumbling back towards the steps, and suddenly there were arms around him.

'Gone,' came a whisper. 'But I am here.'

'Damn it!' snarled Lorsen again. His long-cherished dream of presenting the infamous Conthus to the Open Council, chained and humbled and plastered with tattoos that might as well have read *give Inquisitor Lorsen the promotion he has so long deserved*, had gone up in smoke. Or down in blood. Thirteen years minding a penal colony in Angland, for this. All the riding, all the sacrifice, all the indignity. In spite of his best efforts the entire expedition had devolved into a farce, and he had no doubt upon which undeserving head would be heaped the blame. He slapped at his leg in a fury. 'I wanted him alive!'

'So did he, I daresay.' Cosca stared narrow-eyed through the haze of smoke towards the ruined fort. 'Fate is not always kind to us.'

'Easy for you to say,' snapped Lorsen. To make matters worse – if that were possible – he had lost half his Practicals in one night, and that the better half. He frowned over at Wile, still fussing with his mask. How was it possible for a Practical to look so pitiably unthreatening? The man positively radiated doubt. Enough to plant the seeds of doubt in everyone around him. Lorsen had entertained doubts enough over the years but he did what one was supposed to, and kept them crushed into a tight little packet deep inside where they could not leak out and poison his purpose.

The door slowly creaked open and Dimbik's archers shifted nervously, flatbows all levelled towards that square of darkness.

'Jubair?' barked Cosca. 'Jubair, did you get him? Answer me, damn it!'

Something flew out, bounced once with a hollow clonk and rolled across the snow to rest near the fire.

'What is that?' asked Lorsen.

Cosca worked his mouth. 'Jubair's head.'

'Fate is not always kind,' murmured Brachio.

Another head arced from the doorway and bounced into the fire. A third landed on the roof of one of the shacks, rolled down it and lodged in the gutter. A fourth fell among the archers and one of them let his bow off as he stumbled away from it, the bolt thudding into a barrel nearby. More heads, and more, hair flapping, tongues lolling, spinning, and dancing, and scattering spots of blood.

The last head bounced high and rolled an elliptical course around the fire to stop just next to Cosca. Lorsen was not a man to be put off by a little gore, but even he had to admit to being a little unnerved by this display of mute brutality.

Less squeamish, the captain general stepped forward and angrily kicked the head into the flames. 'How many men have those two old bastards killed between them?' Though the Old Man was no doubt a good deal older than either.

'About twenty, now,' said Brachio.

'We'll fucking run out at this rate!' Cosca turned angrily upon Sworbreck, who was frantically scratching away in his notebook. 'What the hell are you writing for?'

The author looked up, reflected flames dancing in his eyeglasses. 'Well, this is . . . rather dramatic.'

'Do you find?'

Sworbreck gestured weakly towards the ruined fort. 'He came to the rescue of his friend against impossible odds—'

'And got him killed. Is not a man who takes on impossible odds generally considered an incorrigible idiot rather than a hero?'

'The line between the two has always been blurry . . .' murmured Brachio.

Sworbreck raised his palms. 'I came for a tale to stir the blood—'

'And I've been unable to oblige you,' snapped Cosca, 'is that it? Even my bloody biographer is deserting me! No doubt I'll end up the villain in the book I commissioned while yonder decapitating madman is celebrated to the rafters! What do you make of this, Temple? Temple? Where's that bloody lawyer got to? What about you, Brachio?'

The Styrian wiped fresh tears from his weepy eye. 'I think the time has come to put an end to the ballad of the nine-fingered Northman.'

'Finally some sense! Bring up the other tube. I want that excuse for a fort levelled to a stump. I want that meddling fool made mush, do you hear? Someone bring me another bottle. I am sick of being taken fucking lightly!' Cosca slapped Sworbreck's notebook from his hands. 'A little respect, is that too much to ask?' He slapped the biographer to boot and the man sat down sharply in the snow, one hand to his cheek in surprise.

'What's that noise?' said Lorsen, holding up a palm for silence. A thumping and rumbling spilled from the darkness, rapidly growing louder, and he took a nervous step towards the nearest shack.

'Bloody hell,' said Dimbik.

A horse came thundering from the night, eyes wild, and a moment later dozens more, surging down the slope towards the camp, snow flying, a boiling mass of animals, a flood of horseflesh coming at the gallop.

Men flung their weapons down and ran, dived, rolled for any cover. Lorsen tripped over his flapping coat-tail and sprawled in the mud. He heard a whooping and caught a glimpse of Dab Sweet, mounted at the rear of the herd, grinning wildly, lifting his hat in salute as he skirted the camp. Then the horses were among the buildings and all was a hell of milling, kicking, battering hooves, of screaming, thrashing, rearing beasts, and Lorsen flattened himself helplessly against the nearest hovel, clinging with his fingernails to the rough-sawn wood.

Something knocked his head, almost sent him down, but he clung on, clung on, while a noise like the end of the world broke around him, the very earth trembling under the force of all those maddened animals. He gasped and grunted and squeezed his teeth and eyes together so hard they hurt, splinters and dirt and stones stinging his cheek.

Then suddenly there was silence. A throbbing, ringing silence. Lorsen unpeeled himself from the side of the shack and took a wobbling step or two through the hoof-hammered mud, blinking into the haze of smoke and settling dirt.

'They stampeded the horses,' he muttered.

'Do you fucking think so?' shrieked Cosca, tottering from the nearest doorway.

The camp was devastated. Several of the tents had ceased to be, the canvas and their contents – both human and material – trampled into the snow. The ruined fort continued to smoulder. Two of the shacks were thoroughly aflame, burning straw fluttering down and leaving small fires everywhere. Bodies were humped between the buildings, trampled men and women in various states of dress. The injured howled or wandered dazed and bloodied. Here and there a wounded horse lay, kicking weakly.

Lorsen touched one hand to his head. His hair was sticky with blood. A trickle tickling his eyebrow.

'Dab fucking Sweet!' snarled Cosca.

'I did say he had quite a reputation,' muttered Sworbreck, fishing his tattered notebook from the dirt.

'Perhaps we should have paid him his share,' mused Friendly.

'You can take it to him now if you please!' Cosca pointed with a clawing finger. 'It's in . . . *the wagon*.' He trailed off into a disbelieving croak.

The fortified wagon that had been Superior Pike's gift, the wagon in which the fire tubes had been carried, the wagon in which the Dragon People's vast treasure had been safely stowed . . .

The wagon was gone. Beside the fort there was only a conspicuously empty patch of darkness.

'Where is it?' Cosca shoved Sworbreck out of the way and ran to where the wagon had stood. Clearly visible in the snowy mud among the trampled hoof-prints were two deep wheel-ruts, angling down the slope towards the Imperial Road.

'Brachio,' Cosca's voice rose higher and higher until it was a demented shriek, 'find some fucking horses and *get after them!*'

The Styrian stared. 'You wanted all the horses corralled together. They're stampeded!'

'Some must have broken from the herd! Find half a dozen and get after those bastards! Now! Now! Now!' And he kicked snow at Brachio in a fury and nearly fell over. 'Where the hell is Temple?'

Friendly looked up from the wagon-tracks and raised an eyebrow.

Cosca closed his hands to trembling fists. 'Everyone who can, get ready to *move!*'

Dimbik exchanged a worried look with Lorsen. 'On foot? All the way to Crease?'

'We'll gather mounts on the way!'

'What about the injured?'

'Those who can walk are welcome. Any who cannot mean greater shares for the rest of us. Now get them moving, you damned idiot!'

'Yes, sir,' muttered Dimbik, pulling off and sourly flinging away his sash which, already a ruin, had become thoroughly besmirched with dung when he dived for cover.

Friendly nodded towards the fort. 'And the Northman?'

'Fuck the Northman,' hissed Cosca. 'Soak the building with oil and burn it. They've stolen our gold! They've stolen my dreams, do you understand?' He frowned off down the Imperial Road, the wagon-tracks vanishing into the darkness. 'I will *not* be disappointed again.'

Lorsen resisted the temptation to echo Cosca's sentiments that fate is not always kind. Instead, as the mercenaries scrambled over each other in their preparations to leave, he stood looking down at Conthus' forgotten body, lying broken beside the fort.

'What a waste,' he muttered. In every conceivable sense. But Inquisitor Lorsen had always been a practical man. A man who did not balk at hardship and hard work. He took his disappointment and crushed it down into that little packet along with his doubts, and turned his thoughts to what could be salvaged.

'There will be a price for this, Cosca,' he muttered at the captain general's back. 'There will be a price.'

Nowhere Fast

Every bolt, bearing, plank and fixing in that monster of a wagon banged, clattered or screeched in an insane cacophony so deafening that Temple could scarcely hear his own squeals of horror. The seat hammered at his arse, bounced him around like a heap of cheap rags, threatening to rattle the teeth right out of his head. Tree-limbs came slicing from the darkness, clawing at the wagon's sides, slashing at his face. One had snatched Shy's hat off and now her hair whipped around her staring eyes, fixed on the rushing road, lips peeled back from her teeth as she yelled the most blood-curdling abuse at the horses.

Temple dreaded to imagine the weight of wood, metal and above all gold they were currently hurtling down a mountainside on top of. Any moment now, the whole, surely tested beyond the limits of human engineering, would rip itself apart and the pair of them into the bargain. But dread was a fixture of Temple's life, and what else could he do now but cling to this bouncing engine of death, muscles burning from fingertips to armpits, stomach churning with drink and terror. He hardly knew whether eyes closed or eyes open was the more horrifying.

'Hold on!' Shy screamed at him.

'What the fuck do you think I'm—'

She dragged back on the brake lever, boots braced against the foot-board and her shoulders against the back of the seat, fibres starting from her neck with effort. The tyres shrieked like the dead in hell, sparks showering up on both sides like fireworks at the Emperor's birthday. Shy hauled on the reins with her other hand and the whole world began to turn, then to tip, two of the great wheels parting company with the flying ground.

Time slowed. Temple screamed. Shy screamed. The wagon screamed.

Trees off the side of the bend hurtled madly towards them, death in their midst. Then the wheels jolted down again and Temple was almost flung over the footboard and among the horses' milling hooves, biting his tongue and choking on his own screech as he was tossed back into the seat.

Shy let the brake off and snapped the reins. 'Might've taken that one a little too fast!' she shouted in his ear.

The line between terror and exultation was ever a fine one and Temple found, all of a sudden, he had broken through. He punched at the air and howled, 'Fuck you, Coscaaaaaaaa!' into the night until his breath ran out and left him gasping.

'Feel better?' asked Shy.

'I'm alive! I'm free! I'm rich!' Surely there was a God. A benevolent, understanding, kindly grandfather of a God and smiling down indulgently upon him even now. "Sooner or later you have to do something, or you'll never do anything," Cosca had said. Temple wondered if this was what the Old Man had in mind. It did not seem likely. He grabbed hold of Shy and half-hugged her and shouted in her ear, 'We did it!'

'You sure?' she grunted, snapping the reins again.

'Didn't we do it?'

'The easy part.'

'Eh?'

'They won't just be letting this go, will they?' she called over the rushing wind as they picked up pace. 'Not the money! Not the insult!'

'They'll be coming after us,' he muttered.

'That was the whole point o' the exercise!'

Temple cautiously stood to look behind them, wishing he was less drunk. Nothing but snow and dirt spraying up from the clattering back wheels and the trees to either side vanishing into the darkness.

'They've got no horses, though?' His voice turning into a hopeful little whine at the end.

'Sweet slowed 'em down, but they'll still be coming! And this contraption ain't the fastest!'

Temple took another look back, wishing he was more drunk. The line between exultation and terror was ever a fine one and he was rapidly crossing back over. 'Maybe we should stop the wagon! Take two of the horses! Leave the money! Most of the money, anyway—'

'We need to give Lamb and Savian time, remember?'

'Oh, yes. That.' The problem with courageous self-sacrifice was the self-sacrifice part. It had just never come naturally to him. The next jolt brought a wash of choking vomit to the back of Temple's mouth and he tried to swallow it, choked, spluttered and felt it burning all the way up his nose with a shiver. He looked up at the sky, stars vanished now and shifting from black to iron-grey as the dawn came on.

'Woah!' Another bend came blundering from the gloom and Shy dragged the shrieking breaks on again. Temple could hear the cargo sliding and jingling behind them as the wagon bounded around the corner, the earnest desire of all that weight to plunge on straight and send them tumbling down the mountainside in ruin.

As they clattered back onto the straight there was an almighty cracking and Shy reeled in her seat, one leg kicking, yelling out as she started to tumble off the wagon. Temple's hand snapped closed around her belt and hauled her back, the limb of the bow over her shoulder nearly taking his eye out as she fell against him, reins flapping.

She held something up. The brake lever. And decidedly no longer attached. 'That's the end of that, then!'

'What do we do?'

She tossed the length of wood over her shoulder and it bounced away up the road behind them. 'Not stop?'

The wagon shot from the trees and onto the plateau. The first glimmer of dawn was spilling from the east, a bright shaving of sun showing over the hills, starting to turn the muddy sky a washed-out blue, the streaked clouds a washed-up pink, setting the frozen snow that blanketed the flat country to glitter.

Shy worked the reins hard and insulted the horses again, which felt a little unfair to Temple until he remembered how much better insults had worked on him than encouragement. Their heads dipped and manes flew and the wagon picked up still more speed, wheels spinning faster on the flat, and faster yet, the snowy scrub whipping past and the wind blasting at Temple's face and plucking at his cheeks and rushing in his cold nose.

Far ahead he could see horses scattering across the plateau, Sweet and Crying Rock no doubt further off with most of the herd. No dragon's hoard to retire on, but they'd cash in a decent profit on a couple of hundred mounts. When it came to stock, people out here were more concerned with price than origin.

'Anyone following?' called Shy, without taking her eyes off the road.

Temple managed to pry his hand from the seat long enough to stand and look behind them. Just the jagged blackness of the trees, and a rapidly growing stretch of flat whiteness between them and the wagon

'No!' he shouted, confidence starting to leak back. 'No one . . . wait!' He saw movement. A rider. 'Oh God,' he muttered, confidence instantly draining. More of them. 'Oh God!'

'How many?'

'Three! No! Five! No! Seven!' They were still a few hundred strides behind, but they were gaining. 'Oh God,' he said again as he dropped back down into the shuddering seat. 'Now what's the plan?'

'We're already off the end of the plan!'

'I had a nasty feeling you'd say that.'

'Take the reins!' she shouted, thrusting them at him.

He jerked his hands away. 'And do what?'

'Can't you drive?'

'Badly!'

'I thought you'd done everything?'

'Badly!'

'Shall I stop and give you a fucking lesson? Drive!' She pulled her knife from her belt and offered that to him as well. 'Or you could fight.'

Temple swallowed. Then he took the reins. 'I'll drive.' Surely there was a God. A mean little trickster laughing His divine arse off at Temple's expense. And hardly for the first time.

Shy wondered how much of her life she'd spent regretting her last decision. Too much, that was sure. Looked like today was going to plough the same old furrow.

She dragged herself over the wooden parapet and onto the wagon's tar-painted roof, bucking under her feet like a mean bull trying to toss a rider. She lurched to the back, shrugged her bow off into her hand, clawed away her whipping hair and squinted across the plateau.

'Oh, shit,' she muttered.

Seven riders, just like Temple said, and gaining ground. All they had to do was get ahead of the wagon, bring down a horse or two in the team and that'd be that. They were out of range still, specially shooting from what might as well have been a raft in rapids. She wasn't bad with a bow but she was no miracle-worker either. Her eyes went to the hatch on the roof, and she tossed the bow down and slithered over to it on her hands and knees, drew her sword and jammed it into the hasp the padlock was on. Way too strong and heavy. The tar around the hinges was carelessly painted, though, the wood more'n halfway rotten. She jammed the point of the sword into it, twisted, gouged, working out the fixings, digging at the other hinge.

'Are they still following?' she heard Temple shriek.

'No!' she forced through her gritted teeth as she wedged her sword under the hatch and hauled back on it. 'I've killed them all!'

'Really?'

'No, not fucking really!' And she went skittering over on her arse as the hatch ripped from its hinges and flopped free. She flung the sword away, thoroughly bent, dragged the hatch open with her fingertips, started clambering down into the darkness. The wagon hit something and gave a crashing jolt, snatched the ladder from her hands and flung her on her face.

Light spilled in from above, through cracks around the shutters of the narrow windows. Heavy gratings down both sides, padlocked and stacked with chests and boxes and saddlebags bouncing and thumping and jingling, treasure spilling free, gold gleaming, gems twinkling, coins sliding across the plank floor, five king's ransoms and change left over for a palace or two. There were a couple of sacks under her, too, crunchy with money. She stood, bouncing from the gratings to either side as the wagon twitched left and right on its groaning springs, started dragging the nearest sack towards the bright line between the back doors. Heavy as all hell but she'd hauled a lot of sacks in her time and she wasn't about to let this one beat her. Shy had taken beatings enough but she'd never enjoyed them.

She fumbled the bolts free, cursing, sweat prickling her forehead, then, holding tight to the grate beside her, booted the doors wide. The wind whipped in, the bright, white emptiness of the plateau opening up, the clattering blur of the wheels and the snow showering from them, the black shapes of the riders following, closer now. Much closer.

She whipped her knife out and hacked the sack gaping open, dug her fist in and threw a handful of coins out the back, and another, and the other hand, and then both, flinging gold like she was sowing the seed on the farm. It came to her then how hard she'd fought as a bandit and slaved as a farmer and haggled as a trader for a fraction of what she was flinging away with every movement. She jammed the next fistful down into her pocket 'cause – well, why not die rich? Then she scooped more out with both hands, threw the empty bag away and went back for seconds.

The wagon hit a rut and tossed her in the air, smashed her head into the low ceiling and sent her sprawling. Everything reeled for a moment, then she staggered up and clawed the next sack towards the swinging, banging doors, growling curses at the wagon, and the ceiling, and her bleeding head. She braced herself against the grate and shoved the sack out with her boot, bursting open in the snow and showering gold across the empty plain.

A couple of the riders had stopped, one already off his horse and on his hands and knees after the coins, dwindling quickly into the distance. But the others came on regardless, more determined than she'd hoped. That's hopes for you. She could almost see the face of the nearest mercenary, bent low over his horse's dipping head. She left the doors banging and scrambled back up the ladder, dragged herself out onto the roof.

'They still following?' shrieked Temple.

'Yes!'

'What are you doing?'

'Having a fucking lie down before they get here!'

The wagon was hurtling into broken land, the plateau folded with little streams, scattered with boulders and pillars of twisted rock. The road dropped down into a shallow valley, steep sides blurring past, wheels rattling harder than ever. Shy wiped blood from her forehead with the back of her hand, slithered across the shuddering roof to the back, scooping up the bow and drawing an arrow. She squatted there for a moment, breathing hard.

Better to do it than live with the fear of it. Better to do it.

She came up. The nearest rider wasn't five strides back from the swinging doors. He saw her, eyes going wide, yellow hair and a broad chin and cheeks pinked from the wind. She thought she'd seen him writing a letter back in Beacon. He'd cried while he did it. She shot his horse in the chest. Its head went back, it caught one hoof with the other and horse and rider went down together, tumbling over and over, straps and tackle flapping in a tangle, the others swerving around the wreckage as she ducked back down to get another arrow, thought she could hear Temple muttering something.

'You praying?'

'No!'

'Better start!' She came up again and an arrow shuddered into the wood just beside her. A rider, black against the sky on the valley's edge, drawing level with them, horse's hooves a blur, standing in his stirrups with masterful skill and already pulling back his string again.

'Shit!' She dropped down and the shaft flitted over her head and clicked into the parapet on the other side. A moment later another joined it. She could hear the rest of the riders now, shouting to each other just at the back of the wagon. She put her head up to peer over and a shaft twitched into the wood, point showing between two planks not a hand's width from her face, made her duck again. She'd seen some Ghosts damn good at shooting from horseback, but never as good as this. It was bloody unfair, that's what it was. But fair has never been an enforceable principle in a fight to the death.

She nocked her shaft, took a breath and stuck her bow up above the parapet. Right away an arrow flitted between the limb and the string, and up she came. She knew she was nowhere near as good with a bow as he was, but she didn't have to be. A horse is a pretty big target.

Her shaft stuck to the flights in its ribs and it lost its footing right off, fell sideways, rider flying from his saddle with a howl, his bow spinning up in the air and the pair of them tumbling down the side of the valley behind.

Shy shouted, 'Ha!' and turned just in time to see a man jump over the parapet behind her.

She got a glimpse of him. Kantic, with eyes narrowed and his teeth showing in a black beard, a hooked blade in each hand he must've used for climbing the side of the speeding wagon, an endeavour she'd have greatly admired if he hadn't been fixed on killing her. The threat of murder surely can cramp your admiration for a body.

She threw her bow at him and he knocked it away with one arm while he swung at her overhand with the other. She twisted to the side and the blade thudded into the parapet. She caught his other arm as it came at her and punched him in the ribs as she slipped around him. The wagon jolted and ditched her on her side. He twisted his curved blade but couldn't get it free of the wood, jerked his hand out of the thong around his wrist. By then she was up in a crouch and had her knife out, drawing little circles in the air with the point of the blade, circles, circles, and they watched each other, both with boots planted wide and knees bent low and the juddering wagon threatening to shake them off their feet and the wind threatening to buffet them right over.

'Hell of a spot for a knife-fight,' she muttered.

The wagon bumped and he stumbled a little, took his eye off her just long enough. She sprang at him, raising the knife like she'd stab him overhand, then whipped down low and past, slashing at his leg as she went, turning to stab him in the back, but the wagon jumped and spun her all the way round and grunting into the parapet.

When she turned he was coming at her roaring, cutting at the wind and her jerking back from the first slash and weaving away from the second, roof of the wagon treacherous as quicksand under her boot-heels and her eyes crossed on that blur of metal. She caught the third cut on her own blade, steel scraping on steel and off and leaving a cut down her left forearm, ripped sleeve flapping.

They faced each other again, both breathing hard, both a little bit knifed but nothing too much changed. Her arm sang as she squeezed her bloody fingers but they still worked. She feinted, and a second, trying to draw him into a mistake, but he kept watching, swishing that hooked knife in front of him as if he was trying to snag a fish, the broken valley still thundering past on both sides.

The wagon bounced hard and Shy was off her feet a moment, yelping as she toppled sideways. He slashed at her and missed, she stabbed at him and the blade just grazed his cheek. Another jolt flung them together and he caught her wrist with his free hand, tried to stab at her but got his knife tangled in her coat and she grabbed his wrist, twisted it up, not that she wanted the fucking thing but there was no letting go of it now, their knives both waggling hopelessly at the sky, streaked with each other's blood as they staggered around the bucking roof.

She kicked at his knee and made it buckle but he had the strength, and step by wobbling step he wrestled her to the parapet and started to bend her over it, his weight on top of her. He twisted his knife, twisting her grip loose, getting it free, both of them snarling spit at each other, wood grinding into her back and the wagon's wheels battering the ground not so far behind her head, specks of dirt stinging her cheek, his snarling face coming closer and closer and closer—

She darted forwards and sank her teeth into his nose, biting, biting, her mouth salty with blood and him roaring and twisting and pulling away and suddenly she was right over backwards, breath whooping in as she tumbled over the parapet, plummeted down and smashed against the side of the wagon, breath groaning out, her fallen knife pinging from the road and somehow holding on by one clutching hand, all the fibres in her shoulder strained right to the point of tearing.

She swung wriggling around, road rushing underneath her, honking mad sounds through gritted teeth, legs milling at the air as she tried to get her other hand onto the parapet. Made a grab and missed and swung away and the whirling wheel clipped her boot and near snatched her off. Made another grab and got her fingertips over, worked her hand, groaning and whimpering and almost out of effort, everything numb, but she wouldn't be beaten and she growled as she dragged herself back over.

The mercenary was staggering about with an arm around his neck, Temple's face next to his, both of them grunting through bared teeth. She lunged at him, half-falling, grabbed hold of his knife-arm in both hands and twisted it, twisted it down, both arms straining, and his jowls were trembling, torn nose oozing blood, eyes rolling towards the point of his knife as she forced it down towards him. He said something in Kantic, shaking his head, the same word over and over, but she wasn't in a mood to listen even if she'd understood. He wheezed as the point cut through his shirt and into his chest, mouth going wide open as the blade slid further, right to the cross-piece, and she fell on top of him, blood slicking the roof of the wagon.

There was something in her mouth. The tip of his nose. She spat it out and mumbled at Temple, 'Who'th driving?'

The wagon tipped, there was a grinding jolt, and Shy was flying.

Temple groaned as he rolled over to lie staring at the sky, arms out wide, the snow pleasantly cool against his bare neck—

'Uh!' He sat up, wincing at a range of stabbing pains, and stared wildly about.

A shallow canyon with walls of streaked stone and earth and patched snow, the road down the centre, the rest strewn with boulders and choked with thorny scrub. The wagon lay on its side a dozen strides away, one door ripped off and the other hanging wide, one of the uppermost wheels gone and the other still gently turning. The tongue had sheared through and the horses were still going, no doubt delighted by their sudden liberation, already a good way down the road and dwindling into the distance.

The sun was just finding its way into the bottom of the canyon, making gold glitter, a trail of treasure spilled from the back of the stricken wagon and for thirty strides or so behind. Shy sat in the midst of it.

He started running, immediately fell and took a mouthful of snow, spat out a tiny golden coin and floundered over. She was trying to stand, torn coat tangled in a thorn bush, and sank back down as he got there.

'My leg's fucked,' she forced through gritted teeth, hair matted and face streaked with blood.

'Can you use it?'

'No. Hence *fucked*.'

He hooked an arm around her, managed with an effort to get them both to standing, her on one good leg, him on two shaky ones. 'Got a plan yet?'

'Kill you and hide in your body?'

'Better than anything I've got.' He looked about the canyon sides for some means of escape, started tottering over to the most promising place with Shy hopping beside him, both of them wheezing with pain and effort. It might almost have been comical had he not known his erstwhile colleagues must be near. But he did know. So it wasn't.

'Sorry I got you into this,' she said.

'I got myself into this. A long time ago.' He grabbed at a trailing bush but it came free and tumbled hopelessly down in a shower of earth, most of which went straight into his mouth.

'Leave me and run,' said Shy.

'Tempting . . .' He cast about for another way up. 'But I already tried that and it didn't work out too well.' He picked at some roots, brought down some gravel, the slope as unreliable as he'd been down the years. 'I'm trying not to make the same mistakes over and over these days . . .'

'How's that going for you?' she grunted.

'Right now it could be better.' The lip was only a couple of strides above his hand but it might as well have been a mile distant, there was no—

'Hey, hey, Temple!'

A single horseman came up the road at an easy walk, between the two ruts the wagon-wheels had left. Everyone else was thinner than when they left Starikland, but somehow not Brachio. He stopped not far away, leaning his bulk over his saddle horn and speaking in Styrian. 'That was quite a chase. Didn't think you had it in you.'

'Captain Brachio! What a pleasure!' Temple twisted around to put himself between Shy and the mercenary. A pathetic effort at gallantry, he was almost embarrassed to have made it. He felt her take his hand, though, fingers sticky with blood, and was grateful, even if it was just to keep her balance.

Some more earth slid down behind and, looking around, he saw another rider above them, loaded flatbow loose in his hands. Temple realised his knees were shaking. God, he wished he was a brave man. If only for these last few moments.

Brachio nudged his horse lazily forward. 'I told the Old Man you couldn't be trusted, but he always had a blind spot for you.'

'Well, good lawyers are hard to find.' Temple stared around as though the means of their salvation might suddenly present themselves. They did not. He struggled to put some confidence in his creaking voice. 'Take us back to Cosca and maybe I can tidy this up—'

'Not this time.' Brachio drew his heavy sword, steel scraping, and Shy's fingers tightened around Temple's. She might not have understood the words but a naked blade never needs translating. 'Cosca's on his way, and I think he'll want everything tidy when he gets here. That means you dead, in case you were wondering.'

'Yes, I'd gathered,' croaked Temple. 'When you drew the sword. But thanks for the explanation.'

'Least I could do. I like you, Temple. I always have. You're easy to like.'

'But you're going to kill me anyway.'

'You say it like there's a choice.'

'I blame myself. As always. Just . . .' Temple licked his lips, and twisted his hand free of Shy's, and looked Brachio in his tired eyes, and tried to conjure up that earnestness. 'Maybe you could let the girl go? You could do that.'

Brachio frowned at Shy for a moment, who'd sunk back against the bank and was sitting silent. 'I'd like to. Believe it or not, I get no pleasure from killing women.'

'Of course not. You wouldn't want to take a thing like that back to your daughters.' Brachio worked his shoulders uncomfortably, knives shifting across his belly, and Temple felt a crack there that he could work at. He dropped on his knees in the snow, and he clasped his hands, and he sent up a silent prayer. Not for him, but for Shy. She actually deserved saving. 'It was all my idea. All me. I talked her into it. You know I'm awful that way, and she's gullible as a child, poor thing. Let her go. You'll feel better about it in the long run. Let her go. I'm begging you.'

Brachio raised his brows. 'That is quite moving, in fact. I was expecting you to blame her for the whole thing.'

'I'm somewhat moved,' agreed the man with the flatbow.

'We're none of us monsters.' And Brachio reached up and dabbed some tears from his leaky eye. The other one stayed dry, however. 'But she tried to rob us, whoever's idea it was, and the trouble her father caused . . . No. Cosca wouldn't understand. And it isn't as if you'll be repaying the favour, is it?'

'No,' muttered Temple. 'No, I wouldn't have thought so.' He floundered for something to say that might at least delay the inevitable. That might borrow him a few more moments. Just an extra breath. Strange. It was hardly as though he was enjoying himself all that much. 'Would it help if I said I was very drunk?'

Brachio shook his head. 'We all were.'

'Shitty childhood?'

'Mummy used to leave me in a cupboard.'

'Shitty adulthood?'

'Whose isn't?' Brachio nudged his horse forward again, its great shadow falling over Temple. 'Stand up, then, eh? I'd rather get it done quick.' He worked the shoulder of his sword-arm. 'Neither one of us wants me hacking away at you.'

Temple looked back at Shy, sitting there bloody and exhausted. 'What did he say?' she asked.

He gave a tired shrug. She gave a tired nod. It looked like even she had run out of fight. He blinked up at the sky as he got to his feet. An unremarkable, greyish sky. If there was a God, He was a humourless banker. A bloodless pedant, crossing off His debts in some cosmic ledger. All take their loan and, in the end, all must repay.

'Nothing personal,' said Brachio.

Temple closed his eyes, the sun shining pink through the lids. 'Hard not to take it personally.'

'I guess so.'

There was a rattling sound. Temple winced. He'd always dreamed of facing death with some dignity, the way Kahdia had. But dignity requires practice and Temple had none. He couldn't stop himself cringing. He wondered how much it would hurt, having your head cut off. Did you feel it? He heard a couple of clicks, and a grunt, and he cringed even more. How could you not feel it? Brachio's horse snuffled, pawing the ground, then the metallic clatter of a sword falling.

Temple prised one eye open. Brachio was looking down, surprised. There was an arrow through his neck and two others in his chest. He opened his mouth and blathered blood down his shirt, then slowly tipped from the saddle and crumpled face down on the ground next to Temple's boots, one foot still tangled in its stirrup.

Temple looked around. The man with the flatbow had vanished. His mount stood peacefully riderless at the top of the canyon wall.

'Here's a surprise,' croaked Shy.

A horse was approaching. In the saddle, hands crossed over the horn and the breeze stirring her short hair about her sharp-boned frown, sat Corlin. 'A pleasant one, I hope.'

'Little late.' Shy took hold of Temple's limp hand and used it to drag herself wincing up. 'But I guess we'll live with the timing.'

Horses appeared at the valley sides, and riders on the horses, perhaps three dozen of them, all well armed and some armoured. There were men and women, old and young, some faces Temple recognised from Crease, others strange to him. Three or four held half-drawn bows. They weren't pointed right at Temple. But they weren't pointed far away either. Some had forearms showing, and on the forearms were tattoos. *Doom to the Union. Death to the King. Rise up!*

'Rebels,' whispered Temple.

'You always did have a talent for stating the obvious.' Corlin slid from the saddle, kicked Brachio's boot from his stirrup and rolled his corpse over with her foot, leaving him goggling at the sky, fat face caked with dirt. 'That arm all right?'

Shy pulled her ripped sleeve back with her teeth to show a long cut, still seeping, blood streaked down to her fingertips. The sight of it made Temple's knees weak. Or even weaker. It was a surprise he was still standing, all in all. 'Bit sore,' she said.

Corlin pulled a roll of bandage from her pocket. 'Feels as if we've been here before, doesn't it?' She turned her blue, blue eyes on Temple as she started to unroll it around Shy's arm. She never seemed to blink. Temple would have found that unnerving if he'd had any nerves left. 'Where's my uncle?'

'In Beacon,' he croaked, as the rebels dismounted and began to lead their horses down the steep sides of the canyon, scattering dirt.

'Alive?'

'We don't know,' said Shy. 'They found out he was Conthus.'

'That so?' Corlin took Temple's limp hand and clamped it around Shy's wrist. 'Hold that.' She started to unbutton her coat.

'Lamb went back for him but they ran into some trouble. That's when we took the wagon. Sweet stampeded the horses, to give them some . . . time . . .'

Corlin shrugged off her coat and tossed it over her horse's neck, her sinewy arms blue with letters, words, slogans from shoulder to wrist.

'I'm Conthus,' she said, pulling a knife from her belt.

There was a pause.

'Oh,' said Temple.

'Ah,' said Shy.

Corlin, or Conthus, cut the bandage with one quick movement then pushed a pin through it. Her narrowed eyes moved towards the wreckage of the wagon, calmly taking in the gold twinkling in the snow. 'Looks like you came into some money.'

Temple cleared his throat. 'Little bit. Lawyers' fees have been shooting up lately—'

'We could use a couple of horses.' Shy twisted her bandaged forearm free of Temple's grip and worked the fingers. 'Nicomo Cosca won't be far behind us.'

'You just can't stay clear of trouble, can you?' Corlin patted Brachio's mount on the neck. 'We have two spare, as it goes. But it'll cost.'

'Don't suppose you feel like haggling?'

'With you? I don't think so. Let's just call it a generous contribution to the liberation of Starikland.' She jerked her head at her fellows and they hurried forward, sacks and saddlebags at the ready. One big lad nearly knocked Temple over with a shoulder in his hurry. Some started rooting on hands and knees, scooping up the gold scattered about the wreck. Others wriggled inside and soon could be heard smashing the gratings and breaking open the boxes to steal the dragon's hoard for a third time that week.

A few moments ago, Temple had been rich beyond the hopes of avarice, but since a few moments later he had been on the point of losing his head, it felt rude to complain about this outcome.

'A noble cause,' he whispered. 'Do help yourselves.'

Times Change

The Mayor stood in her accustomed position at her balcony, hands at their familiar, polished places on the rail, and watched Curnsbick's men hard at work on his new manufactory. The huge frame already towered over the amphitheatre, the new over the ancient, cobwebbed with scaffolding on the site Papa Ring's White-house had once occupied. That had been a repugnant building in every sense. A building towards which for years she had directed all her hatred, cunning and fury. And how she missed it.

Never mind Mayor, she had been Queen of the Far Country when Ring stopped swinging, but no sooner had she clutched the garland of triumph than it had withered to wretched stalks. The violence and the fires drove off half the population. Whispers mounted that the gold was running dry. Then word came of a strike to the south near Hope and suddenly people were pouring out of Crease by the hundred. With no one left to fight she had dismissed most of her men. Disgruntled, they had dabbled in arson on their way out of town and burned down a good part of what remained. Even so there were buildings empty, and no rents coming in. Lots in town and claims in the hills that men had killed for lost all value overnight. The gaming halls and the bawdy houses were mostly boarded up, only a trickle of passing custom below her in the Church of Dice, where once she had coined money as though she ran a mint.

Crease was her sole dominion. And it was next to worthless.

Sometimes the Mayor felt she had spent her life building things, with painstaking sweat and blood and effort, only to watch them destroyed. Through her own hubris, and others' vindictiveness, and the fickle thrashings of that blind thug fate. Fleeing one debacle after another. Abandoning even her name, in the end. Even now, she always kept a bag packed. She drained her glass and poured herself another.

That's what courage is. Taking your disappointments and your failures, your guilt and your shame, all the wounds received and inflicted, and sinking them in the past. Starting again. Damning yesterday and facing tomorrow with your head held high. Times change. It's those that see it coming, and plan for it, and change themselves to suit that prosper. And so she had struck her deal with Curnsbick, and split her hard-won little empire again without so much as a harsh word spoken.

By that time his small manufactory, which had looked pretty damn big when he converted it from an empty brothel, was already belching black smoke from its two tin chimneys, then from three brick ones, which smogged the whole valley on a still day and chased the few whores still plying a threadbare trade off their balconies and back indoors.

By the looks of it, his new manufactory would have chimneys twice the size. The biggest building within a hundred miles. She hardly even knew what the place was for, except that it had something to do with coal. The hills had hidden little gold in the end but they were surrendering the black stuff in prodigious quantities. As the shadows of the manufactory lengthened, the Mayor had started to wonder whether she might have been better off with Ring across the street. Him, at least, she had understood. But Ring was gone, and the world they had fought over was gone with him, drifted away like smoke on the breeze. Curnsbick was bringing men in to build, and dig, and stoke his furnaces. Cleaner, calmer, more sober men than Crease was used to, but they still needed to be entertained.

'Times change, eh?' She held her drink up in salute to no one. To Papa Ring, maybe. Or to herself, when she still had a name. She caught something through the distorting window of her glass, and lowered it. Two riders were coming down the main street, looking as if they'd been going hard, one cradling an injured arm. It was that girl Shy South. Her and Temple, the lawyer.

The Mayor frowned. After twenty years dodging catastrophes she could smell danger at a thousand paces, and her nose was tickling something fierce as those two riders reigned in at her front door. Temple slithered from his horse, fell in the mud, stumbled up and helped down Shy, who was limping badly.

The Mayor drained her glass and sucked the liquor from her teeth. As she crossed her rooms, buttoning her collar tight, she glanced at the cupboard where she kept that packed bag, wondering if today would be its day.

Some people are trouble. Nicomo Cosca was one. Lamb was another. Then there are people who, without being troublesome in themselves, always manage to let trouble in when they open your door. Temple, she had always suspected, was one of those. Looking at him now as she swept down the stairs, leaning against the counter in her sadly deserted gaming hall, she was sure of it. His clothes were torn and bloodied and caked in dust, his expression wild, his chest heaving.

'You look as if you've come in a hurry,' she said.

He looked up, the slightest trace of guilt in his eye. 'You might say that.'

'And ran into some trouble on the way.'

'You might say that, too. Might I ask you for a drink?'

'Can you pay for it?'

'No.'

'I'm no charity. What are you doing here?'

He took a moment to prepare and then produced, like a magician's trick, an expression of intense earnestness. It put her instantly on her guard. 'I have nowhere else to go.'

'Are you sure you've tried hard enough?' She narrowed her eyes. 'Where's Cosca?'

He swallowed. 'Funny you should ask.'

'I'm not laughing.'

'No.'

'So it's not funny?'

'No.' He visibly abandoned earnestness and settled for simple fear. 'I would guess he's no more than a few hours behind us.'

'He's coming here?'

'I expect so.'

'With all his men?'

'Those that remain.'

'Which is how many?'

'Some died in the mountains, a lot deserted—'

'How many?'

'I would guess at least a hundred still.'

The Mayor's nails dug at her palms as she clenched her fists. 'And the Inquisitor?'

'Very much present, as far as I am aware.'

'What do they want?'

'The Inquisitor wants to torture his way to a brighter tomorrow.'

'And Cosca?'

420

'Cosca wants a fortune in ancient gold that he stole from the Dragon People, and that . . .' Temple picked nervously at his frayed collar. 'I stole from him.'

'And where is this twice-stolen fortune now?'

Temple grimaced. 'Stolen. The woman Corlin took it. She turns out to be the rebel leader Conthus. It's been a day of surprises,' he finished, lamely.

'So . . . it . . . appears,' whispered the Mayor. 'Where is Corlin?'

Temple gave that helpless shrug of which he was so fond. 'In the wind.'

The Mayor was less fond of that shrug. 'I have not the men to fight them,' she said. 'I have not the money to pay them off. I have no ancient hoard for Nicomo *bloody* Cosca and for damn sure no brighter tomorrow for Inquisitor *fucking* Lorsen! Is there any chance your *head* will pacify them?'

Temple swallowed. 'I fear not.'

'So do I. But in the absence of a better suggestion I may have to make the offer.'

'As it happens . . .' Temple licked his lips. 'I have a suggestion.'

The Mayor took a fistful of Temple's shirt and dragged him close. 'Is it a good one? Is it the best suggestion I ever heard?'

'I profoundly doubt it, but, circumstances being what they are . . . do you have that treaty?'

'I'm tired,' said Corporal Bright, glancing unimpressed at the piled-up hovels of Crease.

'Aye,' grunted Old Cog in reply. He kept having to force his eyelids up, they were that heavy from last night's revelry, then the terror o' the stampede, then a healthy trek on foot and a hard ride to follow.

'And dirty,' said Bright.

'Aye.' The smoke of last night's fires, and the rolling through the brush running from stomping horses, then the steady showering of dirt from the hooves of the galloping mounts in front.

'And sore,' said Bright.

'No doubt.' Last night's revelry again, and the riding again, and Cog's arm still sore from the fall in the mountains and the old wound in his arse always aching. You wouldn't think an arrow in the arse would curse you all your days but there it is. Arse armour. That was the key to the mercenary life.

'It's been a testing campaign,' said Cog.

'If you can apply the word to half a year's hard riding, hard drinking, killing and theft.'

'What else would y'apply it to?'

Bright considered that a moment. 'True. Have you seen a worse, though? You been with Cosca for years.'

'The North was colder. Kadir was dustier. That last Styrian mess was bloodier. Full-on revolt in the Company at one point.' He shifted the manacles at his belt. 'Gave up on using chains and had to go with hangings for every infraction. But all considered, no. I ain't seen a worse.' Cog sniffed up some snot, worked it thoughtfully about his mouth, gathering a good sense of its consistency, then leaned back and spat it arcing through a hovel's open window.

'Never saw a man could spit like you,' said Bright.

'It's all about putting the practice in,' said Cog. 'Like anything else.'

'Keep moving!' roared Cosca over his shoulder, up at the head of the column. If you could call eighteen men a column. Still, they were the lucky ones. The rest of the Company were most likely still slogging across the plateau on foot. The ones that were still alive, anyway.

Bright's thoughts were evidently marching in the same direction. 'Lost a lot o' good men these last few weeks.'

'Good might be stretching it.'

'You know what I mean. Can't believe Brachio's gone.'

'He's a loss.'

'And Jubair.'

'Can't say I'm sorry that black bastard's head ain't attached no more.'

'He was a strange one, right enough, but a good ally in a tough corner.'

'I'd rather stay out o' the tough corners.'

Bright looked sideways at him, then dropped his horse back a stretch so the others up front wouldn't mark him. 'Couldn't agree more. I want to go home, is what I'm saying.'

'Where's home to men like us?'

'I want to go anywhere but here, then.'

Cog glanced about at the tangled mass of wood and ruins that was Crease, never a place to delight a cultured fellow and less so than ever now by the looks of things, parts of it burned out and a lot of the rest near deserted. Those left looked like the ones who couldn't find a way to leave, or were too far gone to try. A beggar of truly surpassing wretchedness hobbled after them for a few strides with his hand out before falling in the gutter. On the other side of the street a toothless old woman laughed, and laughed, and laughed. Mad. Or heard something real funny. Mad seemed likelier.

'I take your point,' said Cog. 'But we've got that money to find.' Even though he weren't entirely sure he wanted to find it. All his life he'd been clutching at every copper he could get his warty fingers around. Then suddenly he had so much gold none of it seemed worth anything any more. So much the world seemed to make no sense in the light of it.

'Didn't you keep a little back?'

'O' course. A little.' More than a little, in fact, the pouch under his armpit was heavy with coins. Not so much it made him sweat, but a tidy haul.

'We all did,' muttered Bright. 'So it's Cosca's money we're after really, ain't it?'

Cog frowned. 'There's the principle 'n all.'

'Principle? Really?'

'Can't let folks just up and rob you.'

'We robbed it ourselves, didn't we?' said Bright, an assertion Cog could by no means deny. 'I'm telling you, it's cursed. From the moment we laid our hands on it things have gone from shit to shitter.'

'No such thing as curses.'

'Tell it to Brachio and Jubair. How many of us set off from Starikland?'

'More'n four hundred, according to Friendly, and Friendly don't get a count wrong.'

'How many now?'

Cog opened his mouth, then closed it. The point was obvious to all.

'Exactly,' said Bright. 'Hang around out here much longer we'll be down to none.'

Cog sniffed, and grunted, and spat again, right into a first-floor window this time around. An artist has to challenge himself, after all. 'Been with Cosca a long time.'

'Times change. Look at this place.' Bright nodded towards the vacant hovels that a month or two before had boiled over with humanity. 'What's that stink, anyway?'

Cog wrinkled his nose. The place had always stunk, o' course, but that healthy, heartening stench of shit and low living that had always smelled like home to him. There was an acrid sort of a flavour on the air now, a pall of brownish smoke hanging over everything. 'Don't know. Can't say I care for it one bit.'

'I want to go home,' said Bright, miserably.

The column was coming to the centre of town now, in so far as the place had one. They were building something on one side of the muddy street, teetering scaffold and lumber stacked high. On the other side the Church of Dice still stood, where Cog had spent several very pleasant evenings a month or two before. Cosca held up his fist for a halt in front of it and with the help of Sergeant Friendly disentangled himself from the saddle and clambered stiffly down.

The Mayor stood waiting on the steps in a black dress buttoned to the neck. What a woman that was. A lady, Cog would almost have said, dusting the word off in the deepest recesses of his memory.

'General Cosca,' she said, smiling warmly. 'I did not think—'

'Don't pretend you're surprised!' he snapped.

'But I am. You come at a rather inopportune time, we are expecting—'

'Where is my gold?'

'I'm sorry?'

'By all means play the wide-eyed innocent. But we both know better. Where is my damned notary, then?'

'Inside, but—'

The Old Man shouldered past her and limped grumbling up the steps, Friendly, Sworbreck, and Captain Dimbik following.

The Mayor caught Lorsen's arm with a gentle hand. 'Inquisitor Lorsen, I must protest.'

He frowned back. 'My dear Lady Mayor, I've been protesting for months. Much good it has done me.'

Cosca had seemed heedless of the half dozen frowning thugs lounging on either side of the door. But Cog noted them well enough as he climbed the steps after the others, and from the worried look on Bright's face he did too. Might be that the Company had the numbers, and more coming across the plateau as fast as they could walk, but Cog didn't fancy fighting right then and there.

He didn't fancy fighting one bit.

Captain Dimbik straightened his uniform. Even if the front was crusted with dirt. Even if it was coming apart at the seams. Even if he no longer even belonged to any army, had no nation, fought for no cause or principle a sane man could believe in. Even if he was utterly lost and desperately concealing a bottomless hatred and pity for himself, even then.

Better straight than crooked.

The place had changed since last he visited. The gaming hall had been largely cleared to leave an expanse of creaking boards, the dice- and card-tables shifted against the walls, the women ushered away, the clients vanished. Only ten or so of the Mayor's thugs remained, noticeably armed and scattered watchfully about under the empty alcoves in the walls, a man wiping glasses behind the long counter, and in the centre of the floor a single table, recently polished but still showing the stains of hard use. Temple sat there before a sheaf of papers, peculiarly unconcerned as he watched Dimbik's men tramp in to surround him.

Could you even call them men? Ragged and haggard beyond belief and their morale, never the highest, ebbed to a sucking nadir. Not that they had ever been such very promising examples of human- ity. Dimbik had tried, once upon a time, to impose some discipline upon them. After his discharge from the army. After his disgrace. He remembered, dimly, as if seen through a room full of steam, that first day in uniform, so handsome in the mirror, puffed up on stories of derring-do, a bright career at his fingertips. He miserably straightened the greasy remnants again. How could he have sunk so low? Not even scum. Lackey to scum.

He watched the infamous Nicomo Cosca pace across the empty floor, bent spurs jingling, his eyes fixed upon Temple and his rat-like face locked in an expression of vengeful hatred. To the counter, he went, of course, where else? He took up a bottle, spat out its cork and swallowed a good quarter of the contents in one draught.

'So here he is!' grated the Old Man. 'The cuckoo in the nest! The serpent in the bosom! The . . . the . . .'

'Maggot in the shit?' suggested Temple.

'Why not, since you mention it? What did Verturio say? Never fear your enemies, but your friends, *always*. A wiser man than I, no doubt! I forgave you! *Forgave* you and how am I repaid? I hope you're taking notes, Sworbreck! You can prepare a little parable, perhaps, on the myth of redemption and the price of betrayal.' The author scrambled to produce his pencil as Cosca's grim smile faded to leave him simply grim. 'Where is my gold, Temple?'

'I don't have it.' The notary held up his sheaf of papers. 'But I do have this.'

'It better be valuable,' snapped Cosca, taking another swallow. Ser- geant Friendly had wandered to one of the dice-tables and was sorting dice into piles, apparently oblivious to the escalating tension. Inquisitor Lorsen gave Dimbik a curt nod as he entered. Dimbik respectfully returned it, licked a finger and slicked his front hairs into position, wondering if the Inquisitor had been serious about securing him a new commission in the King's Own when they returned to Adua. Most likely not, but *we all need pretty dreams to cling to. The hope of a second chance, if not the chance itself . . .*

'It is a treaty.' Temple spoke loudly enough for the whole room to hear. 'Bringing Crease and the surrounding country into the Empire. I suspect his Radiance the Emperor will be less than delighted to find an armed party sponsored by the Union has encroached upon his territory.'

'I'll give you an encroachment you won't soon forget.' Cosca let his left hand rest on the hilt of his sword. 'Where the hell is my *gold?*'

With a draining inevitability, the atmosphere ratcheted towards bloodshed. Coats were flicked open, itchy fingers crept to ready grips, blades were loosened in sheaths, eyes were narrowed. Two of Dimbik's men eased the wedges from the triggers of their loaded flatbows. The glass-wiper had put a surreptitious hand on something beneath the counter, and Dimbik did not doubt it would have a point on the end. He watched all this with a helpless sense of mounting horror. He hated violence. *It was the uniforms he'd become a soldier for. The epaulettes, and the marching, and the bands—*

'Wait!' snapped Lorsen, striding across the room. Dimbik was relieved to see that someone in authority still had a grip on their reason. 'Superior Pike said most clearly there were to be no Imperial entanglements!' He snatched the treaty from Temple's hand. 'This expedition has been enough of a disaster without our starting a war!'

'You cannot mean to dignify this charade,' sneered Cosca. 'He lies for a living!'

'Not this time.' The Mayor glided into the room with another pair of her men, one of whom had lost an eye but in so doing gained considerably in menace. 'That document is endorsed by elected representatives of the townspeople of Crease and is fully binding.'

'I consider it my best work.' If he was lying, Temple was even more smug about it than usual. 'It makes use of the principle of inviolate ownership enshrined at the formation of the Union, refers back to the earliest Imperial claim on the territory, and is even fully binding under mining law. I feel confident you will find it incontestable in any court.'

'Alas, my lawyer departed my service under something of a cloud,' forced Cosca through gritted teeth. 'If we contest your treaty it will have to be in the court of sharp edges.'

Lorsen snorted. 'It's not even signed.' And he tossed the document flapping onto the table.

Cosca narrowed his bloodshot eyes. 'What if it were? You of all people should know, Temple, that the only laws that matter are those backed by force. The nearest Imperial troops are weeks away.'

Temple's smile only widened. 'Oh, they're a little closer than that.'

The doors were suddenly flung wide and, under the disbelieving eyes of the heavily armed assembly, soldiers tramped into the Church of Dice. Imperial troops, in gilded greaves and breastplates, with broad-bladed spears in their fists and short-bladed swords at their hips, with round shields marked with the hand of Juvens, and the five thunderbolts, and the sheaf of wheat, and all looking as if they had marched straight from antiquity itself.

'What the *shit* . . .' muttered Cosca.

In the centre of this bizarre honour guard strode an old man, his short beard white as snow, his gilded helm adorned with a tall plume. He walked slowly, deliberately, as though it caused him pain, yet perfectly erect. He looked neither to the left nor to the right, as if Cosca and his men, the Mayor and her men, Temple and Lorsen and everyone else were all insects utterly beneath his notice. As if he were a god obliged for this moment to walk among the filth of humanity. The mercenaries edged nervously away, repelled not so much by fear of the Emperor's legions as by this old man's aura of untouchable command.

The Mayor prostrated herself at his feet in a rustling of skirts. 'Legate Sarmis,' she breathed. 'Your Excellency, we are inexpressibly honoured by your presence . . .'

Dimbik's jaw dropped. Legate Sarmis, who had crushed the Emperor's enemies at the Third Battle of Darmium and ordered every prisoner put to death. Who across the Circle of the World was famous for his military brilliance and infamous for his ruthlessness. Who they had all supposed was many hundreds of miles away to the south. Standing before them now, in the flesh. Dimbik somehow felt he had seen that magnificent face before, somewhere. On a coin, perhaps.

'You *are* honoured,' pronounced the old man, 'for my presence is the presence of his Radiance, the Emperor, Goltus the First.' The Legate's body might have been withered by age but his voice, seasoned with the slightest Imperial accent, was that of a colossus, booming from the lofty rafters, as awe-inspiring as deep thunder close at hand. Dimbik's knees, always weakened by authority, positively itched to bend.

'Where is the instrument?' intoned the Legate.

The Mayor rose and abjectly indicated the table, on which Temple had arranged pen and document. Sarmis grunted as he stiffly leaned over it.

'I sign with the name Goltus, for this hand is the hand of the Emperor.' With a flourish that would have been outrageous under any other circumstances, he signed. 'And so it is done. You stand now upon Imperial soil, and are Imperial subjects under the protection of his Radiance! Warmed by his bounty. Humbled beneath his law.' The ringing echoes faded and he frowned, as though he had only just become aware of the mercenaries. His merciless gaze swept over them and Dimbik felt a chill to his very core.

Sarmis formed his words with fearsome precision. 'Who are these . . . people?'

Even Cosca had been silenced by the theatre of the moment, but now, much to everyone's dismay, he found his voice again. It sounded cracked, weak, almost ridiculous after the Legate's, but he found it nonetheless, waving his half-emptied bottle for added emphasis. 'I am Nicomo Cosca, Captain General of the Company of the Gracious Hand, and—'

'And we were just leaving!' snapped Lorsen, seizing Cosca's elbow.

The Old Man refused to be moved. 'Without my gold? I hardly think so!'

Dimbik did not care in the least for the way things were going. Probably no one did. There was a gentle rattle as Friendly threw his dice. The Mayor's one-eyed thug suddenly had a knife in his hand. That did not strike him as a positive development.

'Enough!' hissed Lorsen, halfway now to wrestling the Old Man by his armpit. 'When we reach Starikland every man will get a bonus! Every man!'

Sworbreck was crouching against the counter, apparently trying to vanish into the floor while madly scribbling in his notebook. Sergeant Cog was edging towards the doorway, and he had good instincts. The odds had changed, and not for the better. Dimbik had begged Cosca to wait for more men, the old fool, but he might as well have argued with the tide. And now all it would take was a loose trigger and there would be a bloodbath.

Dimbik held one hand up to the flatbowmen as to a skittish horse. 'Easy . . .'

'I shit on your bonus!' snarled Cosca, struggling with scant dignity to shake Lorsen off. 'Where's my fucking gold?'

The Mayor was backing away, one pale hand against her chest, but Sarmis only appeared to grow in stature, his white brows drawing inwards. 'What is this impertinence?'

'I can only apologise,' blathered Temple, 'we—'

Sarmis struck him across the face with the back of his hand and knocked him to the floor. 'Kneel when you address me!'

Dimbik's mouth was dry, the pulse pounding in his head. That he would have to die for Cosca's absurd ambitions seemed horribly unfair. His sash had already given its life for the dubious cause and that seemed more than sacrifice enough. Dimbik had once been told that the best soldiers are rarely courageous. That was when he had been sure it was the career for him. He started to slide one hand towards his sword, far from sure what he would do with it once it reached the hilt.

'I will not be disappointed again!' shrieked the Old Man, struggling to reach his own hilt with Lorsen restraining him and a half-full bottle still clutched in his other fist. 'Men of the Gracious Hand! Draw your—'

'No!' Lorsen's voice barked out like a slamming door. 'Captain General Dimbik, take the traitor Nicomo Cosca under arrest!'

There was the very slightest pause.

Probably no more than a breath, for all it felt far longer. While everyone assessed the odds and the outcomes. While everyone judged just where the shifting power sat. While everything dropped into place in Dimbik's mind and, no doubt, the minds of every other person present. Just a breath, and everything was rearranged.

'Of course, Inquisitor,' said Dimbik. The two flatbowmen raised their weapons to point them at Cosca. They looked slightly surprised that they were doing it, but they did it nonetheless.

Friendly looked up from his dice and frowned slightly. 'Two,' he said.

Cosca gazed slack-jawed at Dimbik. 'So that's how it is?' The bottle dropped from his nerveless fingers, clattered to the floor and rolled away, dribbling liquor. 'That's how it is, is it?'

'How else would it be?' said Dimbik. 'Sergeant Cog?'

That venerable soldier stepped forward, for once, with an impressive degree of military snap. 'Sir?'

'Please disarm Master Cosca, Master Friendly, and Master Swor-breck.'

'Place them in irons for the trip,' said Lorsen. 'They will face trial on our return.'

'Why me?' squeaked Sworbreck, eyes wide as saucers.

'Why not you?' Corporal Bright looked the author over and, finding no weapon, he jerked the pencil from his hand, tossed it on the floor and made great show of grinding it under his heel.

'Prisoner?' muttered Friendly. For some reason he had the faintest smile on his face as the manacles were snapped around his wrists.

'I'll be back!' snarled the Old Man, spraying spit over his shoulder as Cog dragged him wriggling away, empty scabbard flapping. 'Laugh while you can, because Nicomo Cosca always laughs last! I'll be revenged on the whole pack of you! I will not be disappointed again! I will—' The door swung shut upon him.

'Who was that drunkard?' asked Sarmis.

'Nicomo Cosca, your Excellency,' muttered Temple, still on his knees and with one hand pressed to his bloody mouth. 'Infamous soldier of fortune.'

The Legate grunted. 'Never heard of him.'

Lorsen placed one hand upon his breast and bowed low. 'Your Excellency, I pray that you accept my apologies for any and all incon-veniences, trespasses and—'

'You have eight weeks to leave Imperial territory,' said Sarmis. 'Any of you found within our borders after that time will be buried alive.' He slapped dust from his breastplate. 'Have you such a thing as a bath?'

'Of course, your Excellency,' murmured the Mayor, virtually grovel-ling. 'We will do the very best we can.' She turned her eyes to Dimbik as she ushered the Legate towards the stairs. 'Get out,' she hissed.

The brand-new captain general was by no means reluctant to oblige. With the greatest of relief, he and his men spilled into the street and prepared their tired mounts for the trip out of town. Cosca had been manhandled into his saddle, sparse hair in disarray, gazing down at Dimbik with a look of stunned upset.

'I remember when I took you on,' he muttered. 'Drunk, and spurned, and worthless. I graciously offering my hand.' He attempted to mime the offering of his hand but was prevented by his manacles.

Dimbik smoothed down his hair. 'Times change.'

'Here is justice, eh, Sworbreck? Here is loyalty! Take a good look,

430

all of you, this is where charity gets you! The fruits of polite behaviour and thought for your fellow man!'

'For pity's sake, someone shut him up,' snapped Lorsen, and Cog leaned from his saddle and stuffed a pair of socks in Cosca's mouth.

Dimbik leaned closer to the Inquisitor. 'It might be best if we were to kill them. Cosca still has friends among the rest of the Company, and—'

'A point well made and well taken, but no. Look at him.' The infamous mercenary did indeed present a most miserable picture, sitting hunched on horseback with hands manacled behind him, his torn and muddied cloak all askew, the gilt on his breastplate all peeling and rust showing beneath, his wrinkled skin blotchy with rash, one of Cog's socks dangling from his mouth. 'Yesterday's man if ever there was one. And in any case, my dear Captain General . . .' Dimbik stood tall and straightened his uniform at the title. He very much enjoyed the ring of it. 'We need someone to blame.'

In spite of the profound pain in his stomach, the ache in his legs, the sweat spreading steadily under his armour, he remained resplendently erect upon the balcony, rigid as a mighty oak, until long after the mercenaries had filed away into the haze. Would the great Legate Sarmis, ruthless commander, undefeated general, right hand of the Emperor, feared throughout the Circle of the World, have allowed himself to display the least trace of weakness, after all?

It felt an age of agony before the Mayor stepped out onto the balcony with Temple behind her, and spoke the longed for words, 'They're gone.'

Every part of him sagged and he gave a groan from the very bottom of his being. He removed that ridiculous helmet, wiping the sweat from his forehead with a trembling hand. He could scarcely recall having donned a more absurd costume in all his many years in the theatre. No garlands of flowers flung by an adoring audience, perhaps, as had littered the broad stage of Adua's House of Drama after his every appearance as the First of the Magi, but his satisfaction was no less complete.

'I told you I had one more great performance in me!' said Lestek.

'And so you did,' said the Mayor.

'You both provided able support, though, for amateurs. I daresay you have a future in the theatre.'

'Did you have to hit me?' asked Temple, probing at his split lip.

'Someone had to,' muttered the Mayor.

'Ask yourself rather, would the terrible Legate Sarmis have struck you, and blame him for your pains,' said Lestek. 'A performance is all in the details, my boy, all in the details! One must inhabit the role entirely. Which occurs to me, do thank my little legion before they disperse, it was an ensemble effort.'

'For five carpenters, three bankrupt prospectors, a barber and a drunk, they made quite an honour guard,' said Temple.

'That drunk scrubbed up surprisingly well,' said Lestek.

'A good find,' added the Mayor.

'It really worked?' Shy South had limped up to lean against the door frame.

'I told you it would,' said Temple.

'But you obviously didn't believe it.'

'No,' he admitted, peering up at the skies. 'There really must be a God.'

'Are you sure they'll believe it?' asked the Mayor. 'Once they've joined up with the rest of their Company and had time to think it over?'

'Men believe what they want to,' said Temple. 'Cosca's done. And those bastards want to go home.'

'A victory for culture over barbarity!' said Lestek, flicking the plume on the helmet.

'A victory for law over chaos,' said Temple, fanning himself with his worthless treaty.

'A victory for lying,' said the Mayor, 'and only by the narrowest of margins.'

Shy South shrugged and said, with her talent for simplicity, 'A win's a win.'

'All too true!' Lestek took a long breath through his nose and, even with the pain, even though he knew he did not have long left, perhaps because he knew it, he breathed out with the deepest fulfillment. 'As a young man I found happy endings cloying but, call me soppy, with age, I have come to appreciate them more and more.'

The Cost

Shy scooped up water and splashed it on her face, and groaned at the cold of it, just this side of ice. She worked her fingertips into her sore eyelids, and her aching cheeks, and her battered mouth. Stayed there, bent over the basin, her faint reflection sent scattering by the drops from her face. The water was pink with blood. Hard to say where from exactly. The last few months had left her beaten as a prizefighter. Just without the prize.

There was the long rope-burn coiling around one forearm and the new cut down the other, blood spotted through the bandage. Her hands were ripped up front and back, crack-nailed and scab-knuckled. She picked at the scar under her ear, a keepsake from that Ghost out on the plains. He'd almost got the whole ear to remember her by. She felt the lumps and scabs on her scalp, the nicks on her face, some of them she couldn't even remember getting. She hunched her shoulders and wriggled her spine and all the countless sores and grazes and bruises niggled at her like a choir of ugly little voices.

She looked down into the street and watched the children for a moment. Majud had found them some new clothes – dark suit and shirt for Pit, green dress with lace at the sleeves for Ro. Better than Shy had ever been able to buy them. They might've passed for some rich man's children if it hadn't been for their shaved heads, the dark fuzz just starting to grow back. Curnsbick was pointing to his vast new building, talking with big, enthusiastic gestures, Ro watching and listening solemnly, taking it all in, Pit kicking a stone about the mud.

Shy sniffed, and swallowed, and splashed more water on her face. Couldn't be crying if her eyes were wet already, could she? She should've been leaping with joy. In spite of the odds, the hardships, the dangers, she'd got them back.

But all she could think of was the cost.

The people killed. A few she'd miss and a lot she wouldn't. Some she'd even have called evil, but no one's evil to themselves, are they? They were still people dead, could do no good now, could make no amends and right no wrongs, people who'd taken a lifetime to make, plucked out from the world and turned to mud. Sangeed and his Ghosts. Papa Ring and his crooks. Waerdinur and his Dragon People. Leef left under the dirt out on the plains, and Grega Cantliss doing the hanged man's dance, and Brachio with the arrows in him, and—

She stuck her face in the cloth and rubbed, hard, like she could rub them all away, but they were stuck tight to her. Tattooed into her sure as the rebel slogans into Corlin's arms.

Was it her fault? Had she set it all rolling when she came out here like the kicked pebble that starts the landslide? Or was it Cantliss' fault, or Waerdinur's, or Lamb's? Was it everyone's? Her head hurt from trying to pull apart the tapestry of everything happened and follow her own nasty little thread through it, sifting for blame like a fevered miner dredging at a stream-bed. No point picking at it any more than at a scab. But still, now it was behind her, she couldn't stop looking back.

She limped to the bed and sat with a groaning of old springs, arms around herself, wincing and twitching at flashes of things happened like they were happening now.

Cantliss smashing her head against a table leg. Her knife sliding into flesh. Grunting in her face. Things she'd had to do. Wrestling with a crazy Ghost. Leef without his ears. Sangeed's head coming off, thud. It had been them or her. Looking down at that girl she'd shot, not much older'n Ro. Arrow in a horse and the rider tumbling. No choice, she'd had no choice. Lamb flinging her against the wall, Waerdinur's skull split, click, and she was flying from the wagon, and over, and over, and over—

She jerked her head up at a knock, wiped her eyes on her bandage. 'Who's there?' Doing her best to sound like it was any other morning.

'Your lawyer.' Temple swung the door open, that earnest look on his face which she could never quite be sure was genuine. 'Are you all right?'

'I've had easier years.'

'Anything I can do?'

'Guess it's a little late to ask you to keep that wagon on the road.'

'A little.' He came and sat down on the bed next to her. Didn't feel uncomfortable. You go through what they'd been through together, maybe uncomfortable goes off the menu. 'The Mayor wants us gone. She says we're bad luck.'

'Hard to argue with her. I'm surprised she hasn't killed you.'

'I suppose she still might.'

'Just need to wait a little longer.' Shy grunted as she wormed her foot into her boot, trying to work out how bad the ankle hurt. Bad enough she stopped trying. 'Just 'til Lamb comes back.'

There was a silence then. A silence in which Temple didn't say, 'Do you really think he's coming back?' Instead he just nodded, as if Lamb coming was as sure as tomorrow, and she was grateful for that much. 'Then where are you heading?'

'That's a question.' New lives out west didn't look much different to the old ones. No short cuts to riches, leastways, or none a sane woman might want to take. And it was no place for children neither. She'd never thought farming would look like the comfortable option, but now she shrugged. 'The Near Country for me, I reckon. It's no easy life but I've spotted nothing easier.'

'I hear Dab Sweet and Crying Rock are putting together a Fellowship for the trip back. Majud's going along, aiming to make some deals in Adua. Lord Ingelstad too.'

'Any Ghosts turn up his wife can frown 'em to death.'

'She's staying. I hear she bought Camling's Hostelry for a song.'

'Good for her.'

'The rest will be heading east within the week.'

'Now? 'Fore the weather breaks?'

'Sweet says now's the time, before the meltwater swells the rivers and the Ghosts get tetchy again.'

She took a long breath. Could've done with a year or two in bed but life hadn't often served her what she ordered. 'Might be I'll sign up.'

Temple looked across from under his brows. Nervous, almost. 'Maybe . . . I'll tag on?'

'Can't stop you, can I?'

'Would you want to?'

She thought about that. 'No. Might need someone to ride drag. Or jump out of a window. Or drive a wagon full of gold off a road.'

He puffed himself up. 'As it happens, I am expert in all three. I'll talk to Sweet and let him know we'll be joining up. I suppose it's possible he won't value my skills as highly as you do, though . . . I might have to buy my way in.'

435

They looked at each other for a moment. 'You coming up a little short?'

'You didn't exactly give me time to pack. I've nothing but the clothes I'm wearing.'

'Lucky for you I'm always willing to help out.' She reached into her pocket and drew out a few of the ancient coins she'd taken while the wagon sped across the plateau. 'Will that cover it?'

'I'd say so.' He took them between finger and thumb but she didn't let go.

'Reckon that's about two hundred marks you owe.'

He stared at her. 'Are you trying to upset me?'

'I can do that without trying.' And she let go the coins.

'I suppose a person should stick to what they're good at.' He smiled, and flicked one of the coins spinning up and snatched it from the air. 'Seems I'm at my best in debt.'

'Tell you what.' She grabbed a bottle from the table by her bed and wedged it in her shirt pocket. 'I'll pay you a mark to help me downstairs.'

Outside a sleety drizzle had set in, falling brown around Curnsbick's belching chimneys, his workmen struggling in the mush on the far side of the street. Temple helped her to the rail and she leaned against it, watching. Funny thing. She didn't want to let go of him.

'I'm bored,' said Pit.

'One day, young man, you will learn what a luxury it is to be bored.' Temple offered him his hand. 'Why not help me seek out that noted scout and frontiersman, Dab Sweet? There may even be gingerbread in it for you. I have recently come into some money.'

'All right.' Temple lifted the boy onto his shoulders and they set off down the rattling porches at half a jog, Pit laughing as he bounced.

He had a touch with the children, had Temple. More than she had, now, it seemed. Shy hopped to the bench against the front of the house and dropped onto it, stretched her hurt leg out in front of her and eased back. She grunted as she let her muscles go soft by slow degrees, and finally pulled the cork from her bottle with that echoing *thwop* that sets your mouth watering. Oh, the simple joy of doing nothing. Thinking nothing. She reckoned she could allow herself a rest.

It had been hard work, the last few months.

She lowered that bottle, looking up the street, liquor burning at the cuts in her mouth in a way that wasn't entirely unpleasant. There was a rider coming through the murk of smoke and drizzle. A particularly slouching rider coming at a slow walk, taking shape as he came closer – big, and old, and battered. His coat was torn, and dirtied, and ash-smeared. He'd lost his hat, short scrub of grey hair matted with blood and rain, face streaked with dirt, mottled with bruise, scabbed and grazed and swollen.

She took another sip from her bottle. 'I was wondering when you'd turn up.'

'You can stop,' grunted Lamb, stopping himself, his old horse looking like it didn't have another stride in it. 'The children all right?'

'They're as well as they were.'

'How about you?'

'Don't know when I was last all right, but I'm still just about alive. You?'

'Just about.' He clambered down from his horse, teeth gritted, not even bothering to tie it up. 'Say one thing for me . . . say I'm a survivor.' He held his ribs as he limped up the steps and onto the porch. He looked at the bench, then his sword, realised he wouldn't be able to sit with it on, started struggling with the buckle on the belt, his knuckles scabbed raw and two of the fingers he still had bandaged together and held stiff.

'By . . . the . . . fucking—'

'Here.' She leaned and flicked the buckle open and he pulled the sword off, belt dangling, cast about for somewhere to put it, then gave up and dropped it on the boards, sank down beside her and slowly, slowly stretched his legs out next to hers.

'Savian?' she asked.

Lamb shook his head a little. Like shaking it a lot would hurt him. 'Where's Cosca?'

'Gone.' She passed him the bottle. 'Temple lawyered him off.'

'Lawyered him?'

'With a little help from the Mayor and a final performance of remarkable quality.'

'Well, I never did.' Lamb took a long swig and wiped his scabbed lips, looking across the street at Curnsbick's manufactory. A couple of doors down, above an old card-hall, they were hauling up a sign reading *Valint and Balk, Bankers*. Lamb took another swallow. 'Times sure are changing.'

'Feel left out?'

He rolled one eye to her, half-swollen shut and all blown and bloodshot, and offered the bottle back. 'For a while now.'

They sat there, looking at each other, like two survivors of an avalanche. 'What happened, Lamb?'

He opened his mouth, as if he was thinking about where to start, then just shrugged, looking even more tired and hurt than she did. 'Does it matter?'

If there's nothing needs saying, why bother? She lifted the bottle. 'No. I guess not.'

Last Words

'Just like old times, eh?' said Sweet, grinning at the snow-patched landscape.

'Colder,' said Shy, wriggling into her new coat.

'Few more scars,' said Lamb, wincing as he rubbed gently at the pinked flesh around one of his face's recent additions.

'Even bigger debts,' said Temple, patting his empty pockets.

Sweet chuckled. 'Bunch o' bloody gripers. Still alive, ain't you, and found your children, and got the Far Country spread out ahead? I'd call that a fair result.'

Lamb frowned off towards the horizon. Shy grumbled her grudging agreement. Temple smiled to himself, and closed his eyes, and tipped his face back to let the sun shine pink through his lids. He was alive. He was free. His debts were deeper than ever, but still, a fair result. If there was a God, He was an indulgent father, who always forgave no matter how far His children strayed.

'Reckon our old friend Buckhorm's prospered,' said Lamb, as they crested a rise and looked down on his farmstead.

It had been carefully sited beside a stream, a set of solid-looking cabins arranged in a square, narrow windows facing outwards, a fence of sharpened logs closing up the gaps and a wooden tower twice a man's height beside the gate. A safe, and civilised, and comfortable-looking place, smoke slipping gently up from a chimney and smudging the sky. The valley around it, as far as Temple could see, was carpeted with tall green grass, patched white with snow in the hollows, dotted brown with cattle.

'Looks like he's got stock to trade,' said Shy.

Sweet stood in his stirrups to study the nearest cow. 'Good stock, too. I look forward to eating 'em.' The cow peered suspiciously back, apparently less enamoured of that idea.

'Maybe we should pick up some extra,' said Shy, 'get a herd together and drive 'em back to the Near Country.'

'Always got your eyes open for a profit, don't you?' asked Sweet.

'Why close your eyes to one? Specially when we've got one of the world's foremost drag riders sitting idle.'

'Oh God,' muttered Temple.

'Buckhorm?' bellowed Sweet as the four of them rode up. 'You about?' But there was no reply. The gate stood ajar, a stiff hinge faintly creaking as the breeze moved it. Otherwise, except for the cattle lowing in the distance, all was quiet.

Then the soft scrape as Lamb drew his sword. 'Something ain't right.'

'Aye,' said Sweet, laying his flatbow calmly across his knees and slipping a bolt into place.

'No doubt.' Shy shrugged her own bow off her shoulder and jerked an arrow from the quiver by her knee.

'Oh God,' said Temple, making sure he came last as they eased through the gateway, hooves of their horses squelching and crunching in the half-frozen mud. Was there no end to it? He peered at the doors and into the windows, grimacing with anticipation, expecting any and every horror from a welter of bandits, to a horde of Ghosts, to Waerdinur's vengeful dragon erupting from the earth to demand its money back.

'Where's my gold, Temple?'

The dragon would have been preferable to the awful phantom that now stooped beneath the low lintel of Buckhorm's house and into the light. Who else but that infamous soldier of fortune, Nicomo Cosca?

His once-fine clothes were reduced to muddy rags, corroded breast-plate lost and his filthy shirt hanging by two buttons, one trouser-leg torn gaping and a length of scrawny, trembling white calf exposed. His magnificent hat was a memory, the few strands of grey hair he had so carefully cultivated to cross his liver-spotted pate now float-ing about his skull in a grease-stiffened nimbus. His rash had turned crimson, scabbed with nail marks and, like mould up a cellar wall, spread flaking up the side of his head to speckle his waxy face. His hand quivered on the door, his gait was uncertain, he looked like nothing so much as a corpse exhumed, brought to a mockery of life by sorcerous intervention.

He turned his mad, bright, feverish eyes on Temple and slapped the hilt of his sword. One trapping of glory he had managed to retain. 'Like the ending of a cheap storybook, eh, Sworbreck?' The writer crept from the darkness behind Cosca, equally filthy and with bare feet to add to his wretchedness, one lens of his eyeglasses cracked, his empty hands fussing with each other. 'One final appearance for the villains!'

Sworbreck licked his lips, and remained silently loitering. Perhaps he could not tell who were the villains in this particular metaphor.

'Where's Buckhorm?' snapped Shy, training her drawn bow on Cosca and prompting his biographer to cower behind him for cover.

The Old Man was less easily rattled. 'Driving some cattle down to Hope with his three eldest sons, I understand. The lady of the house is within but, alas, cannot see visitors just at present. Ever so slightly tied up.' He licked at his chapped lips. 'I don't suppose any of you have a drink to hand?'

'Left mine over the rise with the rest of the Fellowship.' Shy jerked her head towards the west. 'I find if I have it, I drink it.'

'I've always had the very same problem,' said Cosca. 'I would ask one of my men to pour me a glass, but thanks to Master Lamb's fearsome talents and Master Temple's underhanded machinations, my Company is somewhat reduced.'

'You played your own hand in that,' said Temple.

'Doubtless. Live long enough, you see everything ruined. But I still hold a few cards.' Cosca gave a high whistle.

The doorway of the barn banged open and several of Buckhorm's younger children shuffled through into the courtyard, wide-eyed and fearful, some of their faces streaked with tears. Sergeant Friendly was their shepherd, an empty manacle swinging by the chain, the other still locked around his thick wrist. The blade of his cleaver glimmered briefly in the sun.

'Hello, Temple,' he said, showing as little emotion as if they'd been reunited at a tavern counter.

'Hello,' croaked Temple.

'And Master Hedges was good enough to join us.' Cosca pointed past them, finger shaking so badly it was hard at first to tell at what. Looking around, Temple saw a black outline appear at the top of the little turret by the gate. The self-professed hero of the Battle of Osrung, and pointing a flatbow down into the yard.

'Real sorry about this!' he shouted.

'You're that sorry, you can drop the bow,' growled Shy.

'I just want what I'm owed!' he called back.

'I'll give you what you're fucking owed, you treacherous—'

'Perhaps we can establish exactly what everyone is owed once the money is returned?' suggested Cosca. 'As a first step, I believe throwing down your weapons would be traditional?'

Shy spat through the gap in her front teeth. 'Fuck yourself.' The point of her arrow did not deviate by a hair.

Lamb stretched his neck out one way, then the other. 'We don't hold much with tradition.'

Cosca frowned. 'Sergeant Friendly? If they do not lay down their arms within the count of five, kill one of the children.'

Friendly shifted his fingers around the grip of his cleaver. 'Which one?'

'What do I care? You pick.'

'I'd rather not.'

Cosca rolled his eyes. 'The biggest one, then, and work your way down. Must I manage every detail?'

'I mean I'd rather not—'

'One!' snapped the Old Man.

Nobody gave the slightest impression of lowering their weapons. Quite the reverse. Shy stood slightly in her stirrups, scowling down her arrow. 'One o' those children dies, you're next.'

'Two!'

'Then you!' For that of a war hero, Hedges' voice had risen to a decidedly unheroic register.

'Then the fucking lot of you,' growled Lamb, hefting his heavy sword.

Sworbreck stared at Temple around Cosca's shoulder, palms open, as though to say, *What can reasonable men do under such circumstances?*

'Three!'

'Wait!' shouted Temple. 'Just . . . wait, damn it!' And he scrambled down from his horse.

'What the hell are you doing?' Shy snarled around the flights of her arrow.

'Taking the hard way.'

Temple began to walk slowly across the courtyard, mud and straw squelching under his boots, the breeze stirring his hair, the breath cold in his chest. He did not go with a smile, as Kahdia had gone to the Eaters when they padded into the Great Temple, black figures in the darkness, giving his life for the lives of his students. It took a mighty effort, wincing as if he was walking into a gale. But he went.

The sun found a chink in the clouds and glinted on the drawn steel, each edge and point picked out with painful brightness. He was scared.

He wondered if he might piss himself with each step. This was not the easy way. Not the easy way at all. But it was the right way. If there is a God, He is a solemn judge, and sees to it that each man receives his rightful deservings. So Temple knelt in the dung before Nicomo Cosca, and looked up into his bloodshot eyes, wondering how many men he had killed during that long career of his.

'What do you want?' he asked.

The ex-captain general frowned. 'My gold, of course.'

'I'm sorry,' said Temple. He even was a little. 'But it's gone. Conthus has it.'

'Conthus is dead.'

'No. You got the wrong man. Conthus took the money and it isn't coming back.' He did not try to be earnest. He simply gazed into Cosca's worn-out face and told the truth. In spite of the fear, and the high odds on his imminent death, and the freezing water leaking through the knees of his trousers, it felt good.

There was a pause pregnant with doom. Cosca stared at Temple, and Shy at Cosca, and Hedges at Shy, and Sweet at Hedges, and Friendly at Sweet, and Lamb at Friendly, and Sworbreck at everyone. All poised, all ready, all holding their breath.

'You betrayed me,' said Cosca.

'Yes.'

'After all I did for you.'

'Yes.'

The Old Man's wriggling fingers drifted towards his sword hilt. 'I should kill you.'

'Probably,' Temple was forced to admit.

'I want my money,' said Cosca, but the slightest plaintive note had crept into his voice.

'It isn't your money. It never was. Why do you even want it?'

Cosca blinked, hand hovering uncertainly. 'Well . . . I can use it to take back my dukedom—'

'You didn't want the dukedom when you had it.'

'It's . . . money.'

'You don't even like money. When you get it you throw it away.'

Cosca opened his mouth to refute that statement, then had to accept its obvious truth. He stood there, rashy, quivering, hunched, aged even beyond his considerable years, and looked down at Temple as though he was seeing him for the first time. 'Sometimes,' he muttered, 'I think you're hardly like me at all.'

'I'm trying not to be. What do you want?'

'I want . . .' Cosca blinked over at the children, Friendly with one hand on the shoulder of the eldest and his cleaver in the other. Then at Lamb, grim as a gravedigger with his sword drawn. Then at Shy, bow trained on him, and at Hedges, bow trained on her. His bony shoulders sagged.

'I want a chance to do it all again. To do it . . . *right.*' Tears showed in the Old Man's eyes. 'How ever did it go so wrong, Temple? I had so many advantages. So many opportunities. All squandered. All slipped away like sand through a glass. So many disappointments . . .'

'Most of them you brought on yourself.'

'Of course.' He gave a ragged sigh. 'But they're the ones that hurt the worst.' And he reached for his sword.

It was not there. He frowned down, puzzled. 'Where's my— uh?'

The blade slid out of his chest. He and Temple both stared at it, equally shocked, sun glinting on the point, blood spreading quickly out into his filthy shirt. Sworbreck let go of the hilt and stepped back, mouth hanging open.

'Oh,' said Cosca, dropping to his knees. 'There it is.'

Behind him Temple heard a flatbow go off and, almost simultaneously, another. He spun clumsily about, falling in the muck on one elbow.

Hedges gave a cry, bow tumbling from his hand. There was a bolt through the palm of the other. Sweet lowered his own bow, at first looking shocked, then rather pleased with himself.

'I stabbed him,' muttered Sworbreck.

'Am I shot?' asked Shy.

'You'll live,' said Lamb, flicking at the flights of Hedges' bolt. It was stuck through her saddle horn.

'My last words . . .' With a faint groan, Cosca toppled onto his side in the mud next to Temple. 'I had some wonderful ones . . . worked out. What were they now?' And he broke out into that luminous smile of which only he was capable, good humour and good intentions radiating from his deep-lined face. 'Ah! I remember . . .'

Nothing more. He was still.

'He's dead,' said Temple, voice flat. 'No more disappointments.'

'You were the last,' said Friendly. 'I told him we'd be better off in prison.' He tossed his cleaver in the muck and patted Buckhorn's eldest son on the shoulder. 'You four can go inside to your mother.'

'You shot me!' shrieked Hedges, clutching at his skewered hand.

Sworbreck adjusted his broken eyeglasses as though he could scarcely credit the evidence of his senses. 'Astonishing skill!'

'I was aiming for his chest,' said the scout, under his breath.

The author stepped gingerly around Cosca's corpse. 'Master Sweet, I wonder whether I might speak to you about a book I have in mind.'

'Now? I really don't see—'

'A generous share of the profits would be forthcoming.'

'—any way I could turn you down.'

Cold water was leaking through the seat of Temple's trousers, gripping his arse in its icy embrace, but he found he could not move. Facing death certainly can take it out of you. Especially if you've spent most of your life doing your best to avoid facing anything.

He realised Friendly was standing next to him, frowning down at Cosca's body. 'What do I do now?' he asked.

'I don't know,' said Temple. 'What does anyone do?'

'I plan an authentic portrait of the taming and settlement of the Far Country,' Sworbreck was blathering. 'A tale for the ages! One in which you have played a pivotal role.'

'I'm pivotal, all right,' said Sweet. 'What's pivotal?'

'My hand!' shrieked Hedges.

'You're lucky it's not through your face,' said Lamb.

Somewhere inside, Temple could hear the tearful sounds of the Buckhorm children being reunited with their mother. Good news, he supposed. A fair result.

'My readers will thrill to your heroic exploits!'

'I've certainly thrilled to 'em,' snorted Shy. 'The heroic scale of your digestive gases would never be believed back east.'

Temple looked up, and watched the clouds moving. If there was a God, the world seemed exactly the way it would be if there wasn't one.

'I must insist on absolute honesty. I will entertain no more exaggeration! Truth, Master Sweet, is at the heart of all great works of art.'

'No doubt at all. Which makes me wonder – have you heard of the time I killed a great red bear with naught but these two hands . . .'

Some Kind of Coward

Nothing was quite the way she remembered it. All small. All drab. All changed.

Some new folks had happened by and built a house where theirs had stood, and a new barn, too. Couple of fields tilled and coming up nice, by all appearances. Flowers blooming around the tree they'd hanged Gully from. The tree Ro's mother was buried under.

They sat there, on horseback, frowning down, and Shy said, 'Somehow I thought it'd be the way we left it.'

'Times move on,' said Lamb.

'It's a nice spot,' said Temple.

'No it's not,' said Shy.

'Shall we go down?'

Shy turned her horse away. 'Why?'

Ro's hair was grown back to a shapeless mop. She'd taken Lamb's razor one morning meaning to shave it off again, and sat there by still water, holding her dragon scale and thinking of Waerdinur. Couldn't picture his face no more. Couldn't remember his voice or the Maker's lessons he'd so carefully taught her. How could it all have washed away so fast? In the end she just put the razor back and let her hair grow.

Times move on, don't they?

They'd moved on in Squaredeal, all right, lots of land about cleared and drained and put under the plough, and new buildings sprung up all over and new faces everywhere passing through or stopping off or settling down to all sorts of business.

Not everything had prospered. Clay was gone and there was a drunk idiot running his store and it had no stock and half the roof had fallen in. Shy argued him down to one Imperial gold piece and a dozen bottles of cheap spirit and bought the place as a going concern. Nearly going, at least. They all set to work next morning like it was the last day of creation, Shy haggling merciless as a hangman for stock, Pit and Ro laughing as they swept dust over each other, Temple and Lamb hammering away at the carpentry, and it weren't long before things got to feel a bit like they used to. More than Ro had ever thought they would.

Except sometimes she'd think of the mountains and cry. And Lamb still wore a sword. The one he'd taken from her father.

Temple took a room over the road and put a sign above the door saying *Temple and Kahdia: Contracts, Clerking and Carpentry.*

Ro said to him, 'This Kahdia ain't around much, is he?'

'Nor will he be,' said Temple. 'But a man should have someone to blame.'

He started doing law work, which might as well have been magic far as most folk around there were concerned, children peering in at his window to watch him write by candlelight. Sometimes Ro went over there and listened to him talk about the stars, and God, and wood, and the law, and all kinds of faraway places he'd been on his travels, and in languages she'd never even heard before.

'Who needs a teacher?' Shy asked. 'I was taught with a belt.'

'Look how that turned out,' said Ro. 'He knows a lot.'

Shy snorted. 'For a wise man he's a hell of a fool.'

But once Ro woke in the night and came down, restless, and saw them out the back together, kissing. There was something in the way Shy touched him made it seem she didn't think he was quite the fool she said he was.

Sometimes they went out around the farmsteads, more buildings springing up each week that passed, buying and selling. Pit and Ro swaying on the seat of the wagon next to Shy, Lamb riding along beside, always frowning hard at the horizon, hand on that sword.

Shy said to him, 'There's naught to worry about.'

And without looking at her he said, 'That's when you'd better worry.'

They got in one day at closing time, the long clouds pinking over-head as the sun sank in the west and the lonely wind sighing up and sweeping dust down the street and setting that rusty weathervane to squeak. No Fellowships coming through and the town quiet and still, some children laughing somewhere and a grandmother creaking in her rocker on her porch and just one horse Ro didn't know tied up at the warped rail.

'Some days work out,' said Shy, looking at the back of the wagon, just about empty.

'Some don't,' Ro finished for her.

Calm inside the store, just Wist soft snoring in his chair with his boots up on the counter. Shy slapped 'em off and woke him with a jolt. 'Everything good?'

'Slow day,' said the old man, rubbing his eyes.

'All your days are slow,' said Lamb.

'Like you're so bloody quick. Oh, and there's someone been waiting for you. Says you and him got business.'

'Waiting for me?' asked Shy, and Ro heard footsteps in the back of the store.

'No, for Lamb. What did you say your name was?'

A man pushed a hanging coil of rope aside and came into the light. A great, tall man, his head brushing the low rafters, a sword at his hip with a grip of scored grey metal, just like Lamb's. Just like her father's. He had a great scar angled across his face and the guttering candle-flame twinkled in his eye. A silver eye, like a mirror.

'My name's Caul Shivers,' he said, voice quiet and all croaky soft and every hair Ro had stretched up.

'What's your business?' muttered Shy.

Shivers looked down at Lamb's hand, and the stump of the missing finger there, and he said, 'You know my business, don't you?'

Lamb just nodded, grim and level.

'You're after trouble, you can fucking ride on!' Shy's voice, harsh as a crow's. 'You hear me, bastard? We've had all the trouble we—'

Lamb put his hand on her forearm. The one with the scar coiling around it. 'It's all right.'

'It's all right if he wants my knife up his—'

'Stay out of it, Shy. It's an old debt we got. Past time it was paid.' Then he spoke to Shivers in Northern. 'Whatever's between me and you, it don't concern these.'

Shivers looked at Shy, and at Ro, and it seemed to her there was no more feeling in his living eye than in his dead. 'It don't concern these. Shall we head outside?'

They walked down the steps in front of the store, not slow and not fast, keeping a space between them, eyes on each other all the way. Ro, and Shy, and Pit, and Wist edged after them onto the porch, watching in a silent group.

'Lamb, eh?' said Shivers.

'One name's good as another.'

'Oh, not so, not so. Threetrees, and Bethod, and Whirrun of Bligh,

448

and all them others forgotten. But men still sing your songs. Why's that, d'you reckon?'

''Cause men are fools,' said Lamb.

The wind caught a loose board somewhere and made it rattle. The two Northmen faced each other, Lamb's hand dangling loose at his side, stump of the missing finger brushing the grip of his sword, and Shivers gently swept his coat clear of his own hilt and held it back out of the way.

'That my old sword you got there?' asked Lamb.

Shivers shrugged. 'Took it off Black Dow. Guess it all comes around, eh?'

'Always.' Lamb stretched his neck out one way, then the other. 'It always comes around.'

Time dragged, dragged. Those children were still laughing somewhere, and maybe the echoing shout of their mother calling them in. That old woman's rocker softly creak, creaking on the porch. That weathervane squeak, squeaking. A breeze blew up then and stirred the dust in the street and flapped the coats of the two men, no more than four or five strides of dirt between them.

'What's happening?' whispered Pit, and no one answered.

Shivers bared his teeth. Lamb narrowed his eyes. Shy's hand gripped almost painful hard at Ro's shoulder, the blood pounding now in her head, the breath crawling in her throat, slow, slow, the rocker creaking and that loose board rattling and a dog barking somewhere.

'So?' growled Lamb.

Shivers tipped his head back, and his good eye flickered over to Ro. Stayed on her for a long moment. And she bunched her fists, and clenched her teeth, and she found herself wishing he'd kill Lamb. Wishing it with all her being. The wind came again and stirred his hair, flicked it around his face.

Squeak. Creak. Rattle.

Shivers shrugged. 'So I'd best be going.'

'Eh?'

'Long way home for me. Got to tell 'em that nine-fingered bastard is back to the mud. Don't you think, Master Lamb?'

Lamb curled his left hand into a fist so the stump didn't show, and swallowed. 'Long dead and gone.'

'All for the best, I reckon. Who wants to run into him again?' And just like that Shivers walked to his horse and mounted up. 'I'd say I'll be seeing you but . . . I think I'd best not.'

449

Lamb still stood there, watching. 'No.'

'Some men just ain't stamped out for doing good.' Shivers took a deep breath, and smiled. A strange thing to see on that ruined face. 'But it feels all right, even so. To let go o' something.' And he turned his horse and headed east out of town.

They all stood stock still a while longer, with the wind, and the creaking rocker, and the sinking sun, then Wist gave a great rattling sigh and said, 'Bloody hell I near shit myself!'

It was like they could all breathe again, and Shy and Pit hugged each other, but Ro didn't smile. She was watching Lamb. He didn't smile either. Just frowned at the dust Shivers left behind him. Then he strode back to the store, and up the steps, and inside without a word. Shy headed after. He was pulling things down from the shelves like he was in a hurry. Dried meat, and feed, and water, and a bedroll. All the things you'd need for a trip.

'What're you doing, Lamb?' asked Shy.

He looked up for a moment, guilty, and back to his packing. 'I always tried to do the best I could for you,' he said. 'That was the promise I made your mother. The best I can do now is go.'

'Go where?'

'I don't know.' He stopped for a moment, staring at the stump of his middle finger. 'Someone'll come, Shy. Sooner or later. Got to be realistic. You can't do the things I've done and walk away smiling. There'll always be trouble at my back. All I can do is take it with me.'

'Don't pretend this is for us,' said Shy.

Lamb winced. 'A man's got to be what he is. Got to be. Say my goodbyes to Temple. Reckon you'll do all right with him.'

He scooped up those few things and back out into the street, wedged them into his saddlebags and like that he was ready.

'I don't understand,' said Pit, tears on his face.

'I know.' Lamb knelt in front of him, and it seemed his eye was wet too. 'And I'm sorry. Sorry for everything.' He leaned forward and gathered the three of them in an awkward embrace.

'The dead know I've made mistakes,' said Lamb. 'Reckon a man could steer a perfect course through life by taking all the choices I didn't. But I never regretted helping raise you three. And I don't regret that I brought you back. Whatever it cost.'

'We need you,' said Shy.

Lamb shook his head. 'No you don't. I ain't proud o' much but I'm proud o' you. For what that's worth.' And he turned away, and wiped his face, and hauled himself up onto his horse.

'I always said you were some kind of coward,' said Shy.

He sat looking at them for a moment, and nodded. 'I never denied it.'

Then he took a breath, and headed off at a trot towards the sunset. Ro stood there on the porch, Pit's hand in her hand, and Shy's on her shoulder, and they watched him.

Until he was gone.

Acknowledgments

As always, four people without whom:

Bren Abercrombie, whose eyes are sore from reading it.
Nick Abercrombie, whose ears are sore from hearing about it.
Rob Abercrombie, whose fingers are sore from turning the pages.
Lou Abercrombie, whose arms are sore from holding me up.

Then, my heartfelt thanks:

To all the lovely and talented folks at my UK Publisher, Gollancz, and their parent Orion, particularly Simon Spanton, Jon Weir, Jen McMenemy, Mark Stay and Jon Wood.

Then, of course, all those who've helped make, publish, publicise, translate and above all *sell* my books wherever they may be around the world.

To the artists responsible for somehow continuing to make me look classy: Didier Graffet, Dave Senior and Laura Brett.

To editors across the Pond: Devi Pillai and Lou Anders.

For keeping the wolf on the right side of the door: Robert Kirby.

To all the writers whose paths have crossed mine on the internet, at the bar, or in some cases on the D&D table and the shooting range, and who've provided help, support, laughs and plenty of ideas worth the stealing. You know who you are.

And lastly, yet firstly:

My partner in crimes against fantasy fiction—Gillian Redfearn. I mean, Butch Cassidy wasn't gloriously slaughtered on his own, now, was he?